THE
MAGMA
CUP

SORT OF SUPER

THE MAGMA CUP

by Eric Gapstur

COLOR BY
DEARBHLA KELLY

ALADDIN
NEW YORK LONDON TORONTO SYDNEY NEW DELHI

This book is a work of fiction. Any references to historical events, real people, or real places are used fictitiously. Other names, characters, places, and events are products of the author's imagination, and any resemblance to actual events or places or persons, living or dead, is entirely coincidental.

ALADDIN

An imprint of Simon & Schuster Children's Publishing Division

1230 Avenue of the Americas, New York, New York 10020

First Aladdin edition July 2023

Copyright © 2023 by Eric Gapstur

For information about special discounts for bulk purchases, please contact Simon & Schuster Special Sales at 1-866-506-1949 or business@simonandschuster.com.

The Simon & Schuster Speakers Bureau can bring authors to your live event. For more information or to book an event contact the Simon & Schuster Speakers Bureau at 1-866-248-3049 or visit our website at www.simonspeakers.com.

Color by Dearbhla Kelly

Book designed by Laura Lyn DiSiena and Eric Gapstur

The illustrations for this book were rendered in ink and colored digitally.

The text of this book was set in Gapstur and Gapstur Shouting.

Manufactured in China 0723 SCP

2 4 6 8 10 9 7 5 3

Library of Congress Cataloging-in-Publication Data

Names: Gapstur, Eric, author, illustrator.

Title: The magma cup / by Eric Gapstur.

Description: First Aladdin paperback edition. | New York : Aladdin, 2023. | Series: Sort of super ; book 2 | Audience: Ages 8 to 12 | Summary: Eleven-year-old superhero Wyatt Flynn and his little sister, Adeline, go to Camp Igneous, where they secretly explore a mysterious volcano which may be a key piece in the puzzle of what happened to their missing mother.

Identifiers: LCCN 2021057131 (print) | LCCN 2021057132 (ebook) | ISBN 9781534480322 (hardcover) | ISBN 9781534480315 (paperback) | ISBN 9781534480339 (ebook)

Subjects: CYAC: Graphic novels. | Ability—Fiction. | Brothers and sisters—Fiction. | Camps—Fiction. | Volcanoes—Fiction. | LCGFT: Superhero comics. | Detective and mystery comics. | Graphic novels.

Classification: LCC PZ7.7.G365 Mag 2023(print) | LCC PZ7.7.G365(ebook) | DDC 741.5/973—dc23/eng/20220105

LC record available at https://lccn.loc.gov/2021057131

LC ebook record available at https://lccn.loc.gov/2021057132

TO MOM, DAD,
CORY AND LINDSEY

CHAPTER ONE

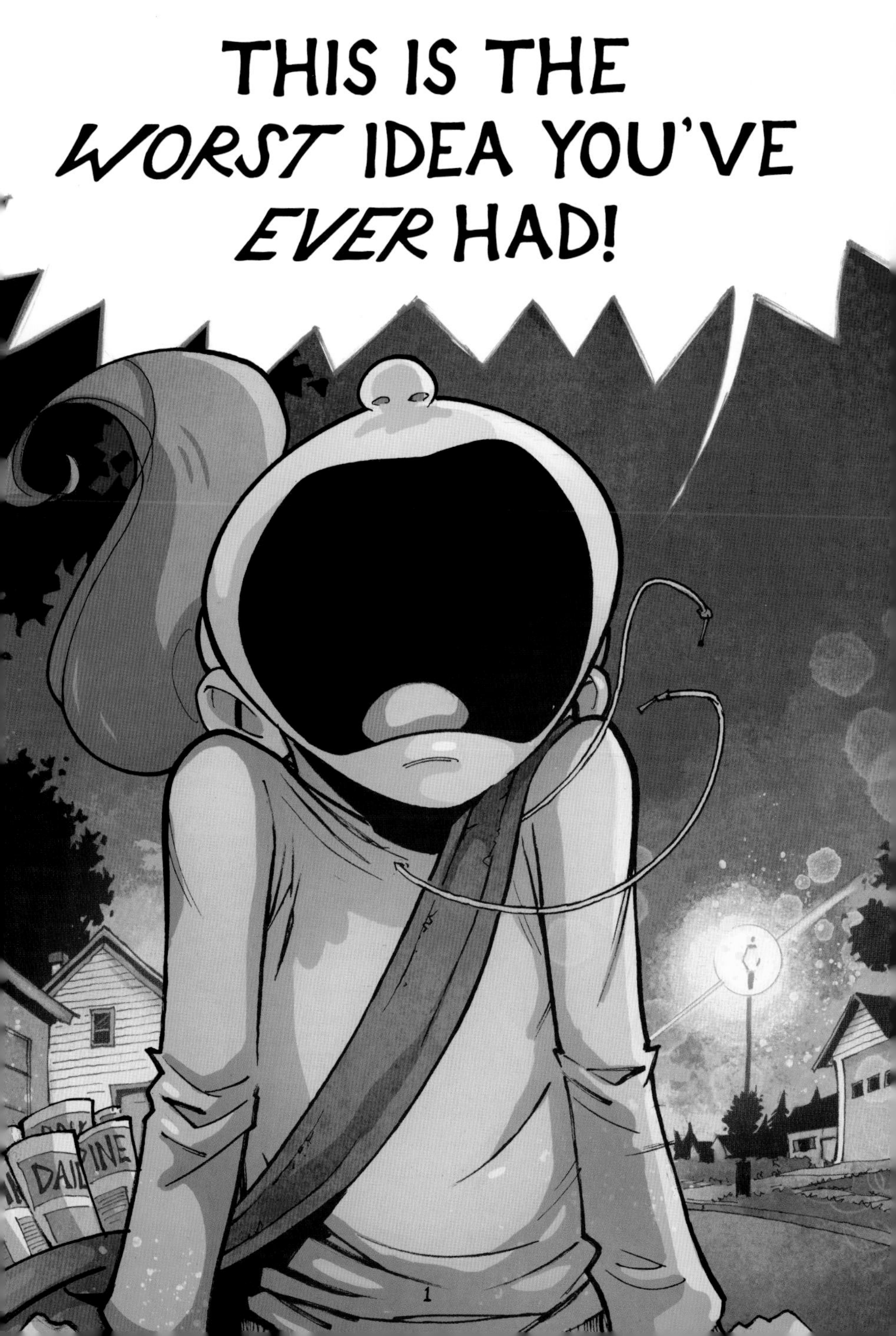
THIS IS THE WORST IDEA YOU'VE EVER HAD!

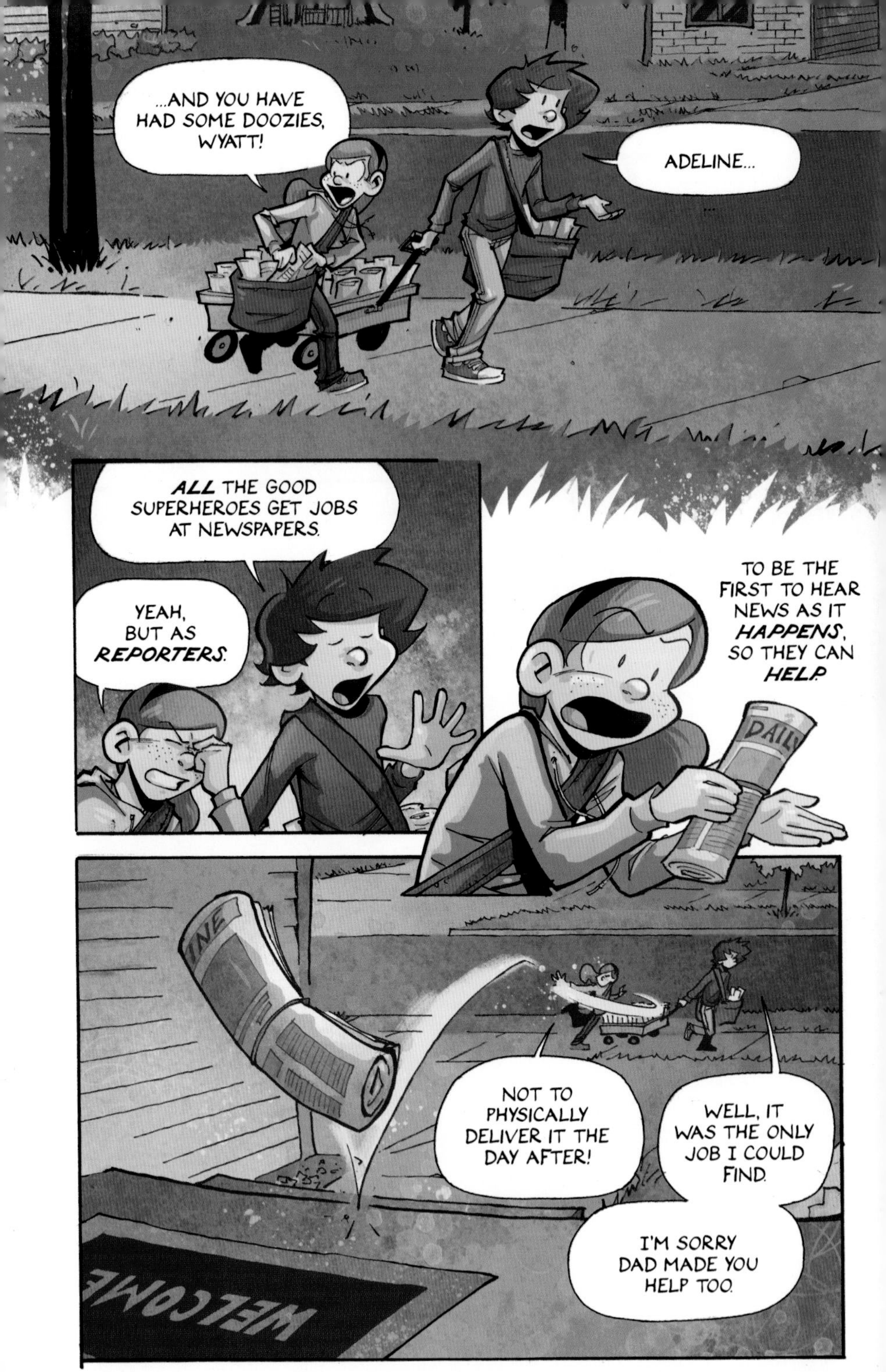
...AND YOU HAVE HAD SOME DOOZIES, WYATT!
ADELINE...
ALL THE GOOD SUPERHEROES GET JOBS AT NEWSPAPERS.
YEAH, BUT AS *REPORTERS*.
TO BE THE FIRST TO HEAR NEWS AS IT *HAPPENS*, SO THEY CAN *HELP*.
NOT TO PHYSICALLY DELIVER IT THE DAY AFTER!
WELL, IT WAS THE ONLY JOB I COULD FIND.
I'M SORRY DAD MADE YOU HELP TOO.
WELCOME

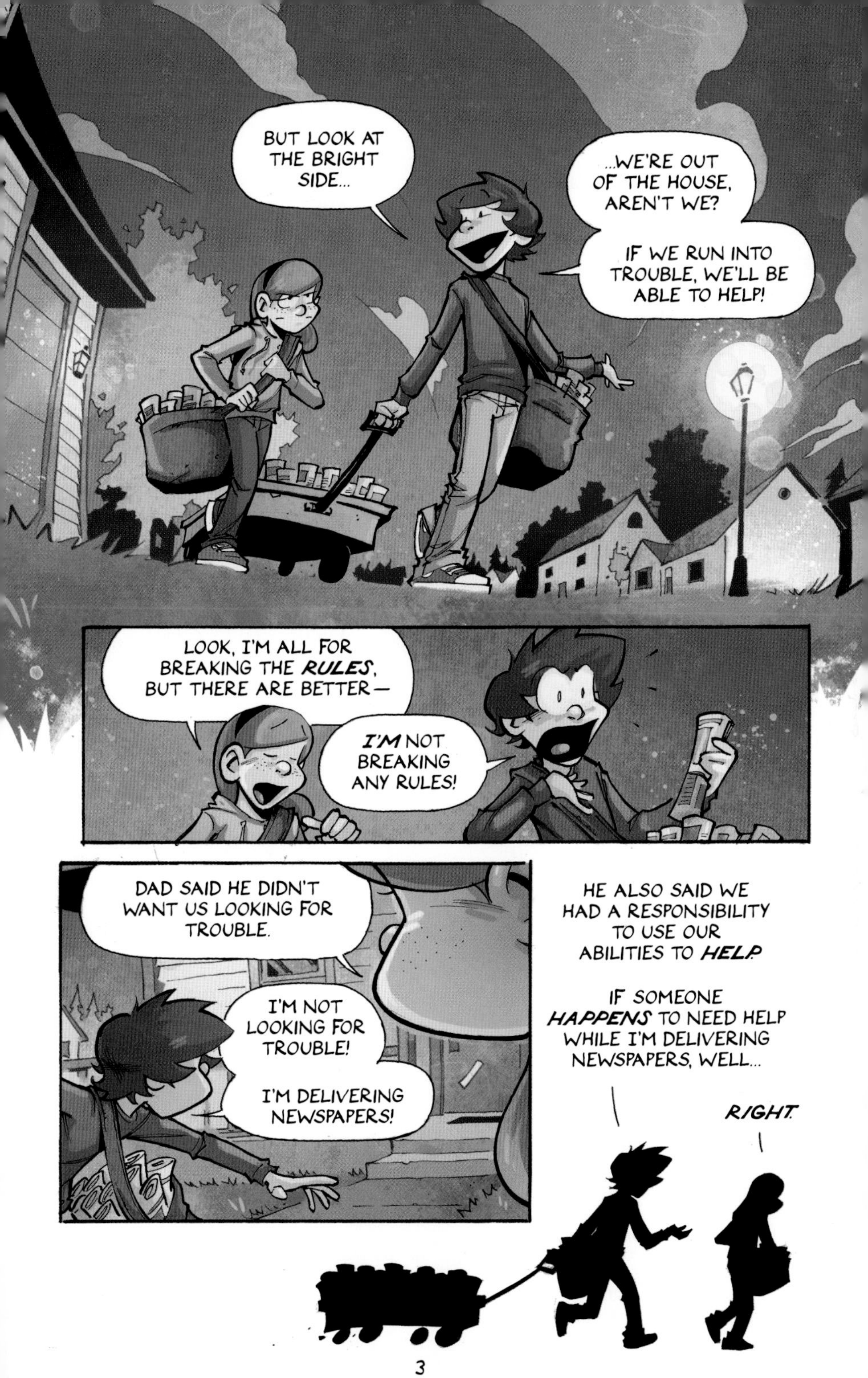
BUT LOOK AT THE BRIGHT SIDE...
...WE'RE OUT OF THE HOUSE, AREN'T WE?
IF WE RUN INTO TROUBLE, WE'LL BE ABLE TO HELP!
LOOK, I'M ALL FOR BREAKING THE *RULES*, BUT THERE ARE BETTER—
I'M NOT BREAKING ANY RULES!
DAD SAID HE DIDN'T WANT US LOOKING FOR TROUBLE.
I'M NOT LOOKING FOR TROUBLE!
I'M DELIVERING NEWSPAPERS!
HE ALSO SAID WE HAD A RESPONSIBILITY TO USE OUR ABILITIES TO *HELP*.
IF SOMEONE *HAPPENS* TO NEED HELP WHILE I'M DELIVERING NEWSPAPERS, WELL...
RIGHT.

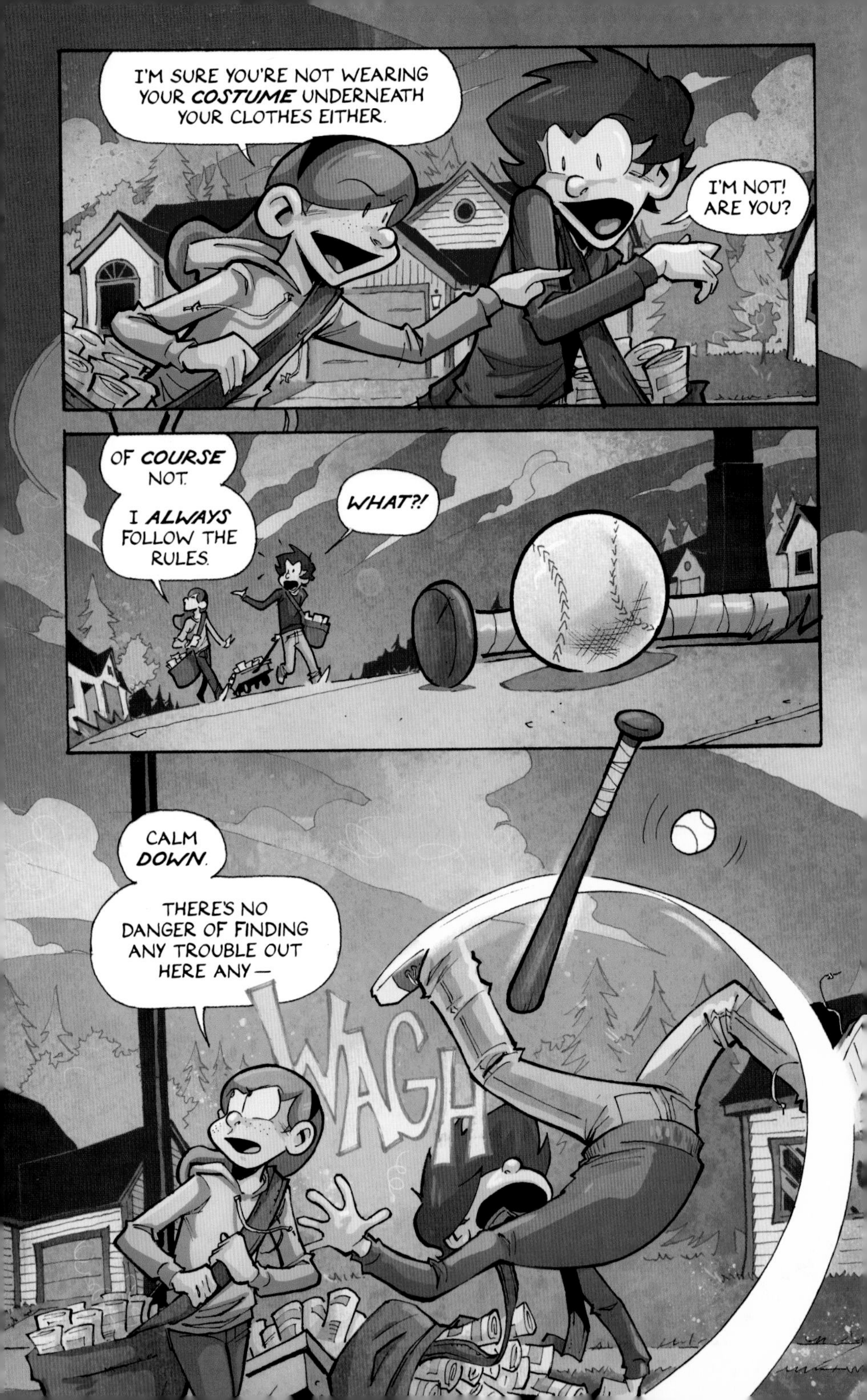
I'M SURE YOU'RE NOT WEARING YOUR COSTUME UNDERNEATH YOUR CLOTHES EITHER.
I'M NOT! ARE YOU?
OF COURSE NOT.
I ALWAYS FOLLOW THE RULES.
WHAT?!
CALM DOWN.
THERE'S NO DANGER OF FINDING ANY TROUBLE OUT HERE ANY—
WAGH

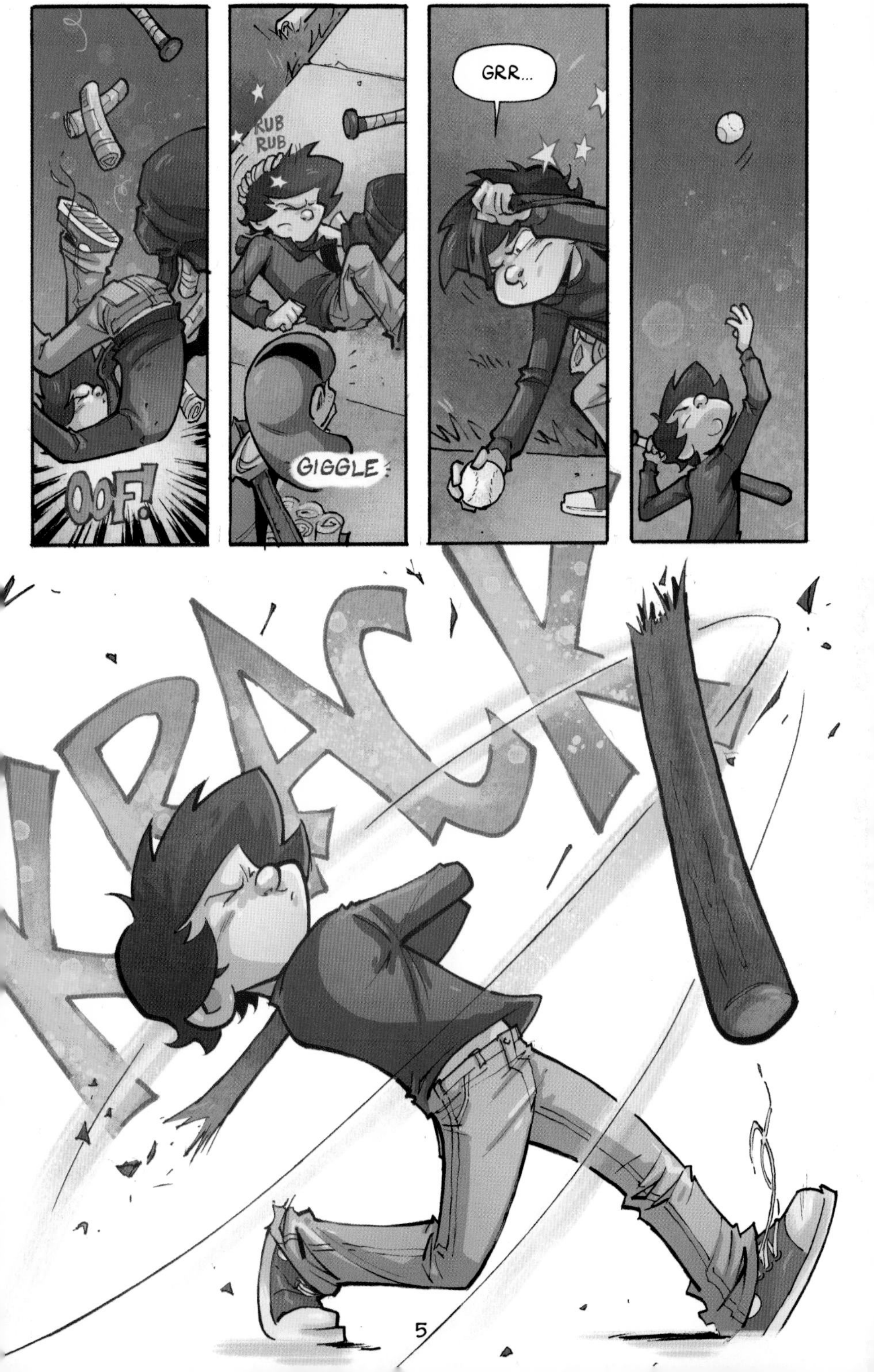
OOF!
RUB
RUB
GIGGLE
GRR...
KRACK!

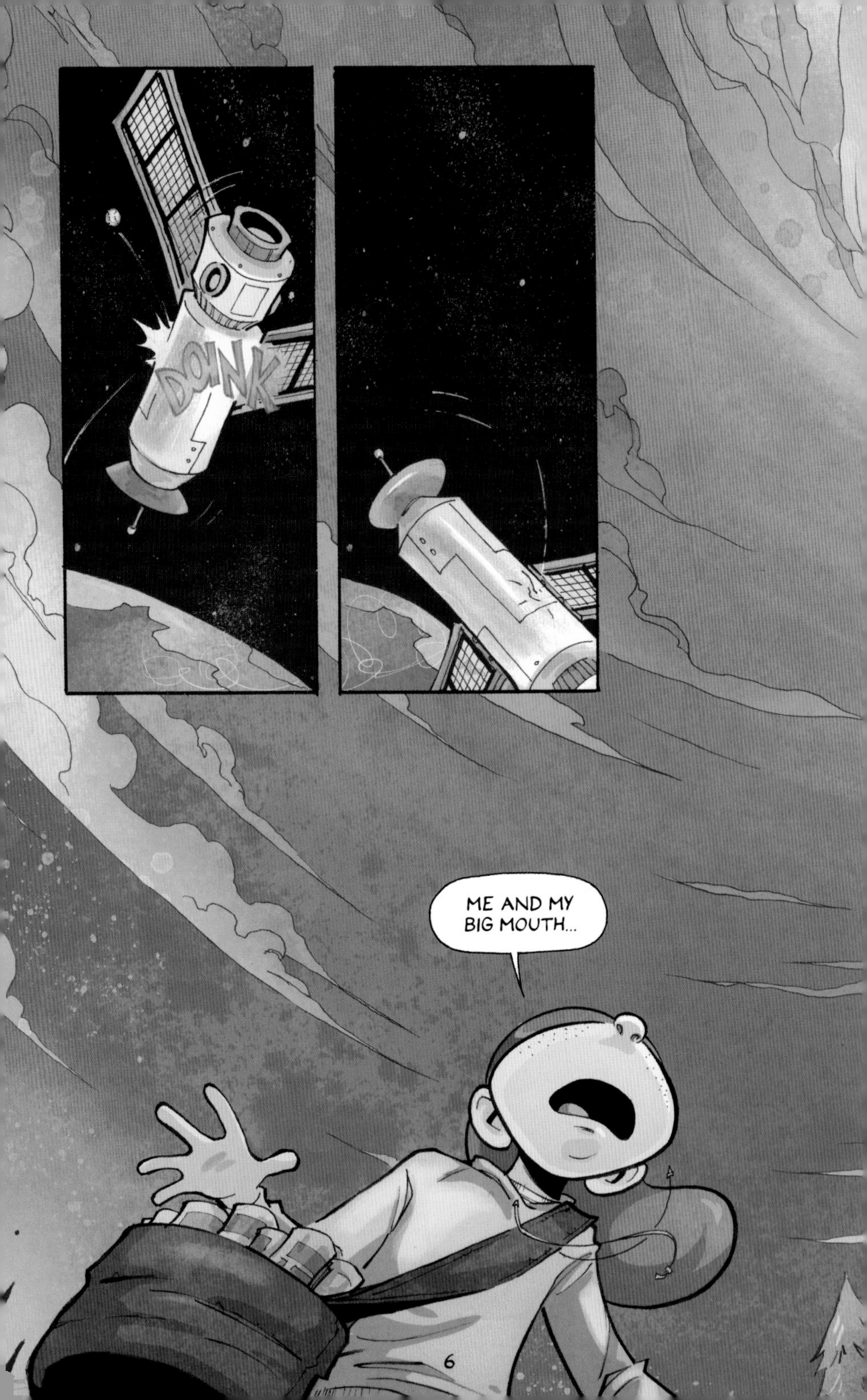
DOINK
ME AND MY BIG MOUTH...

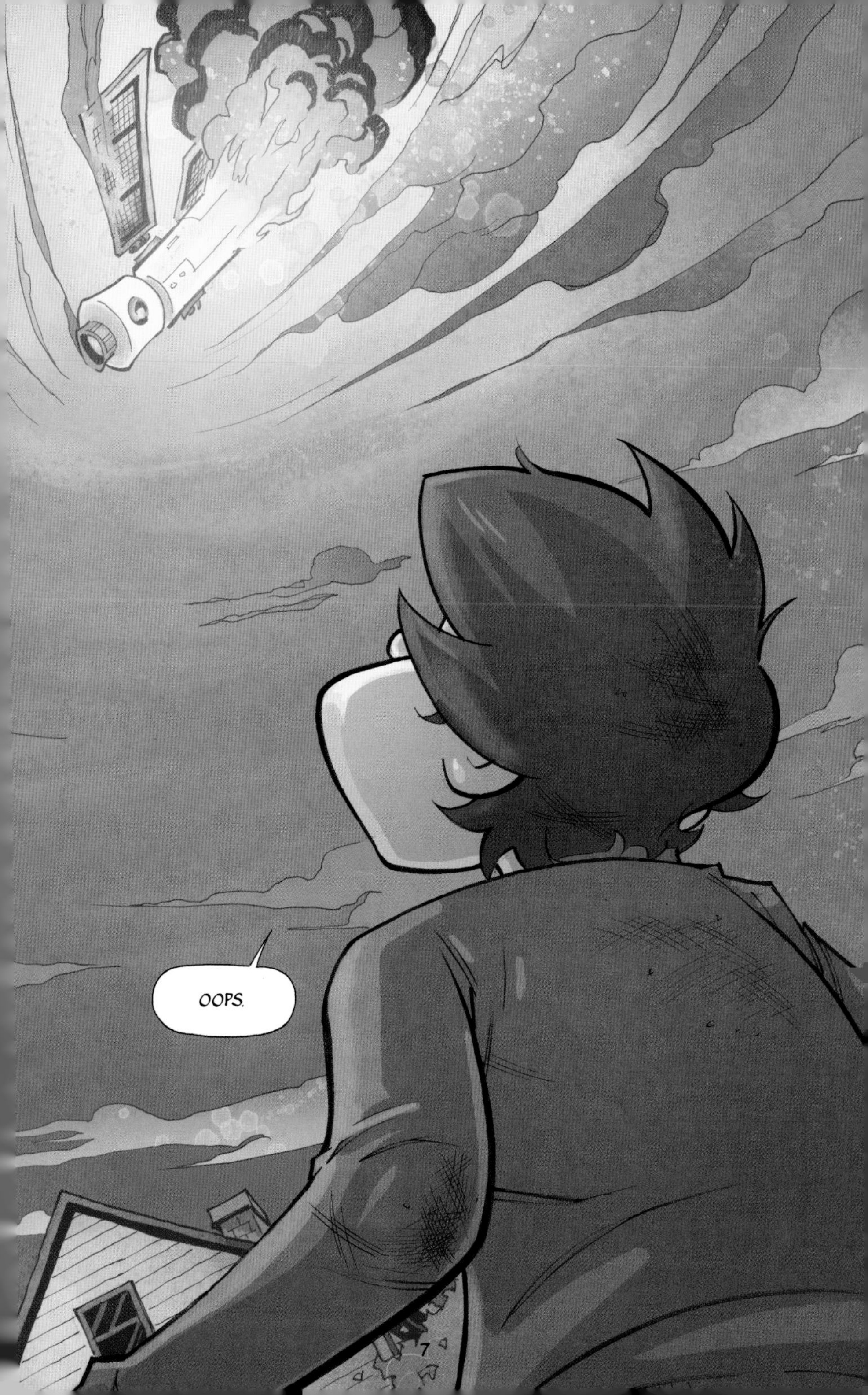
OOPS.

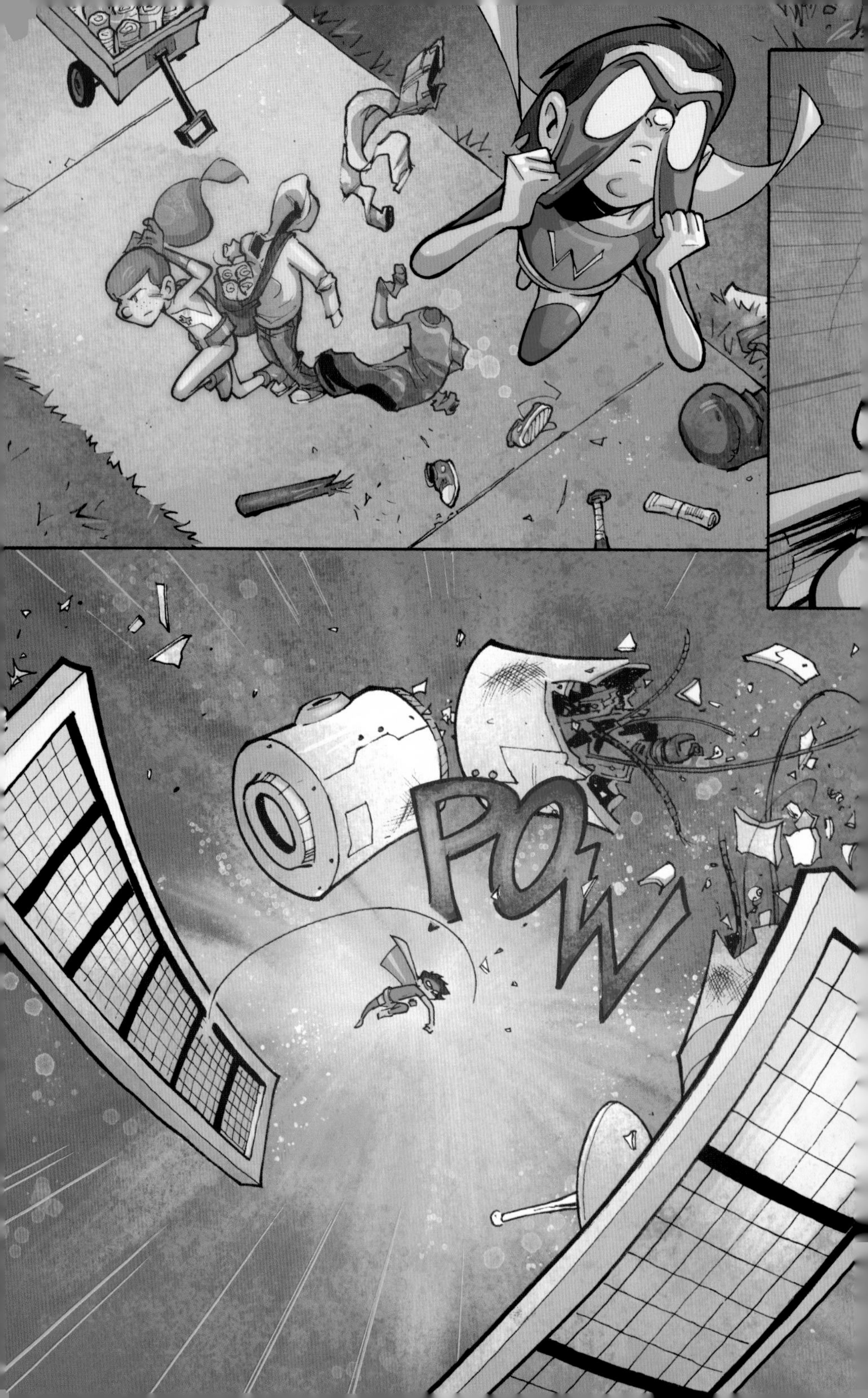
POW

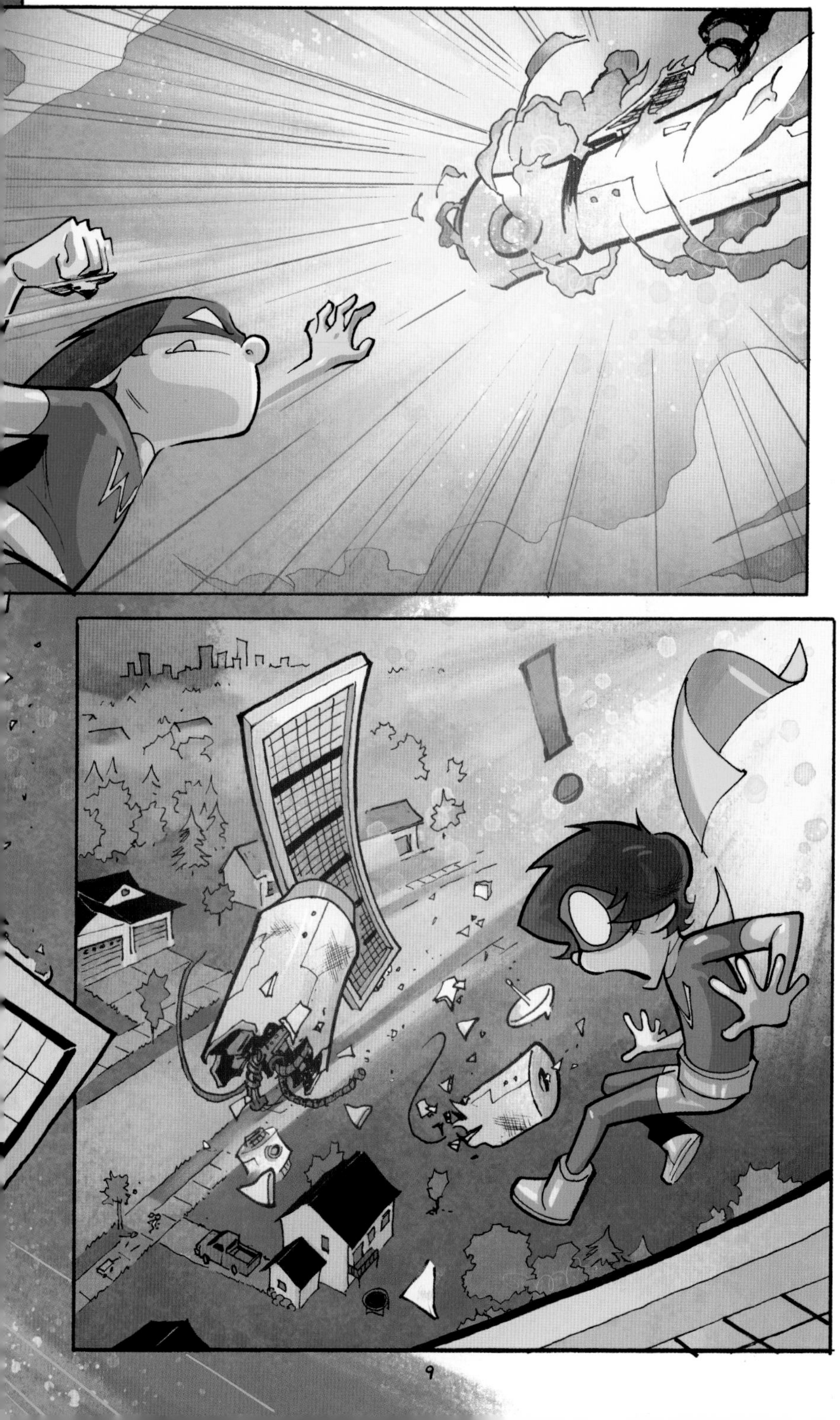
!

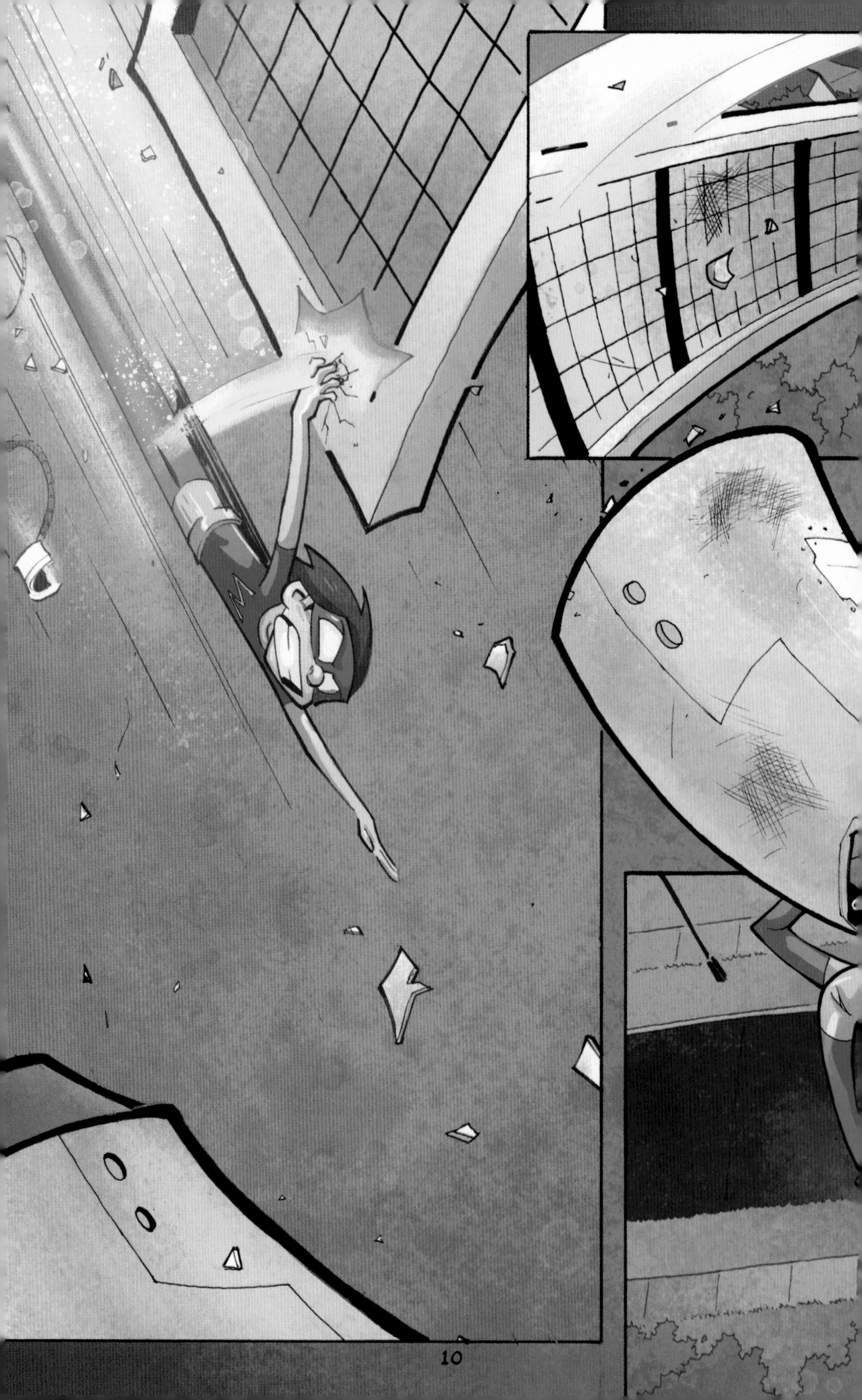

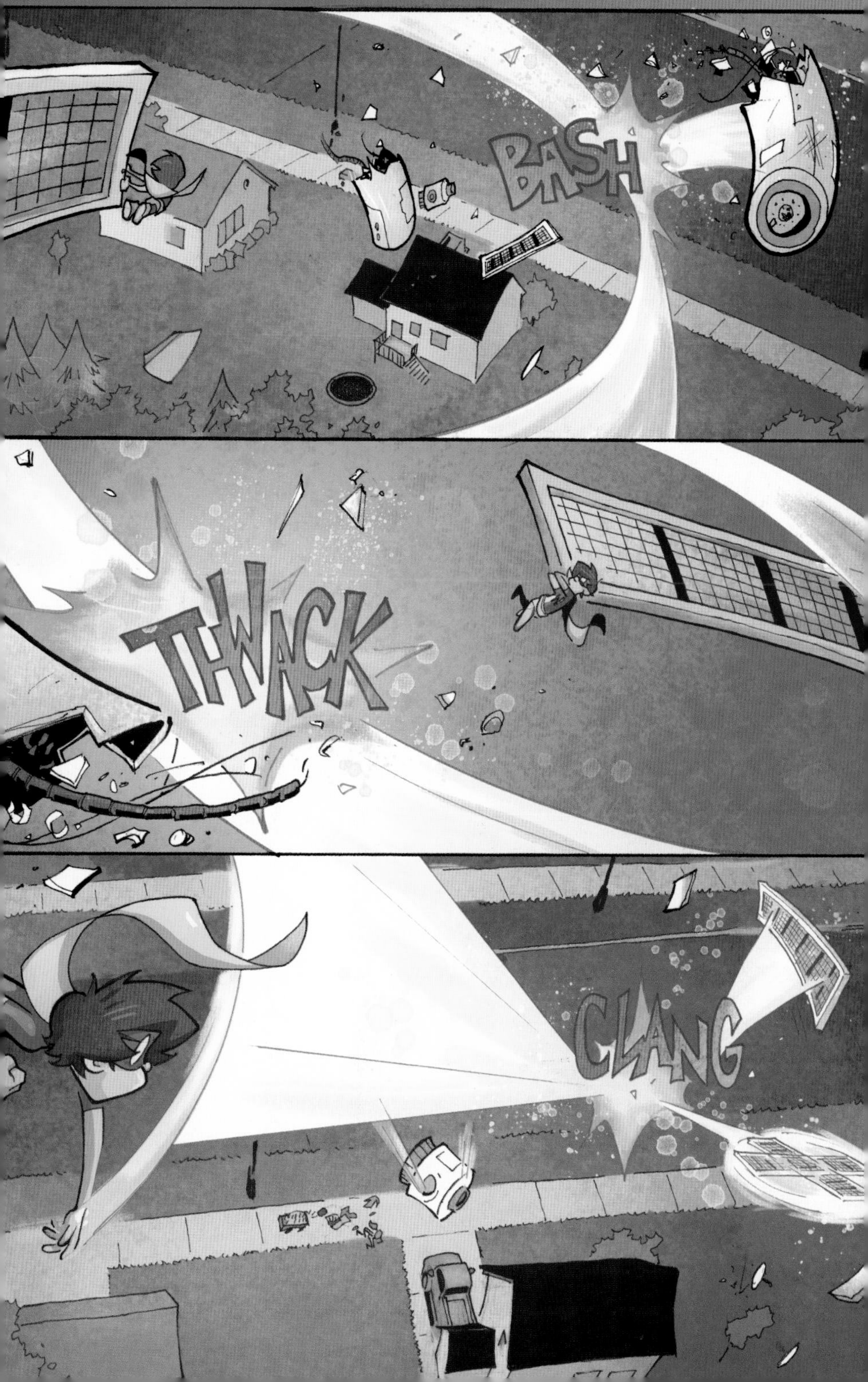
BASH
THWACK
CLANG

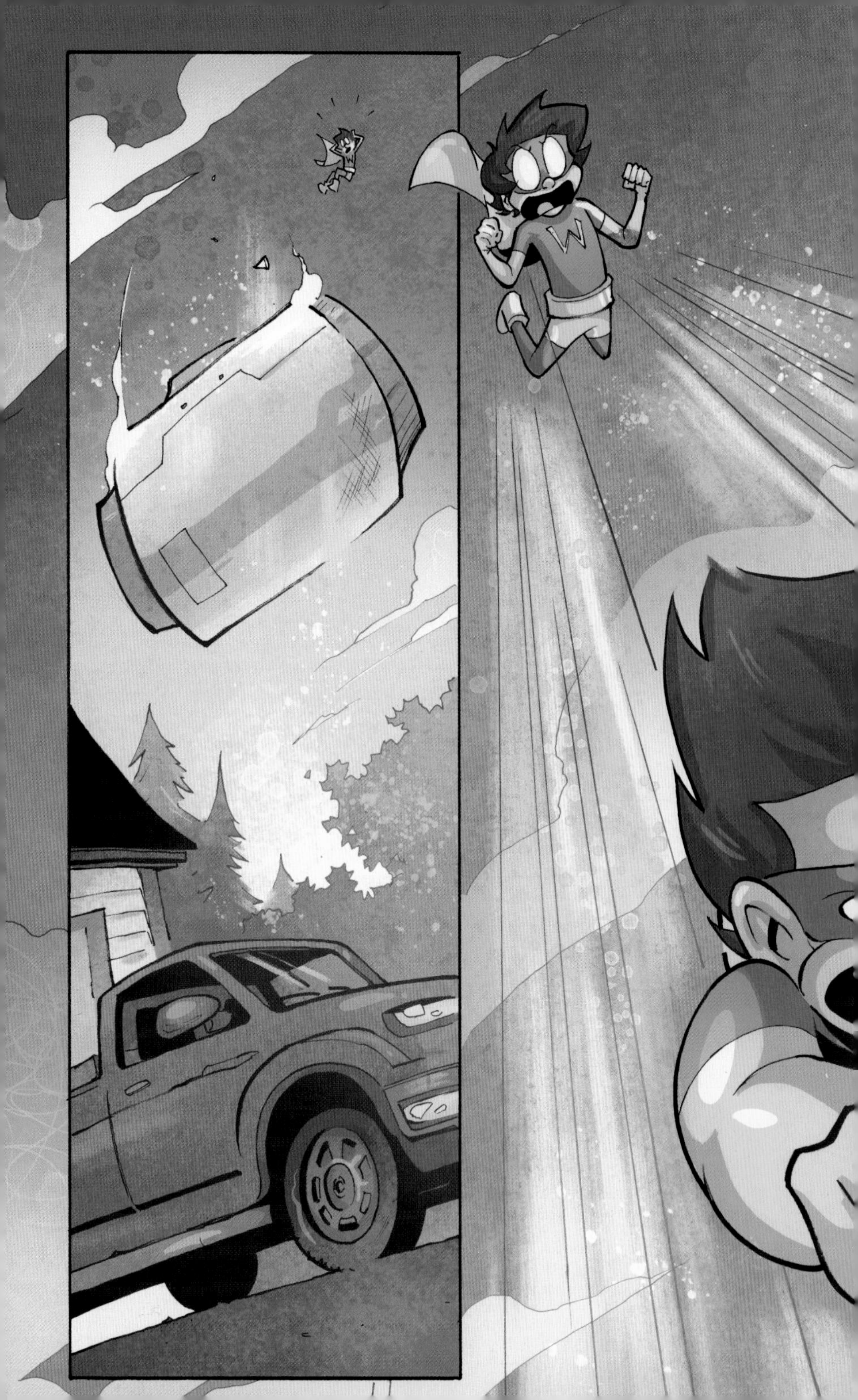

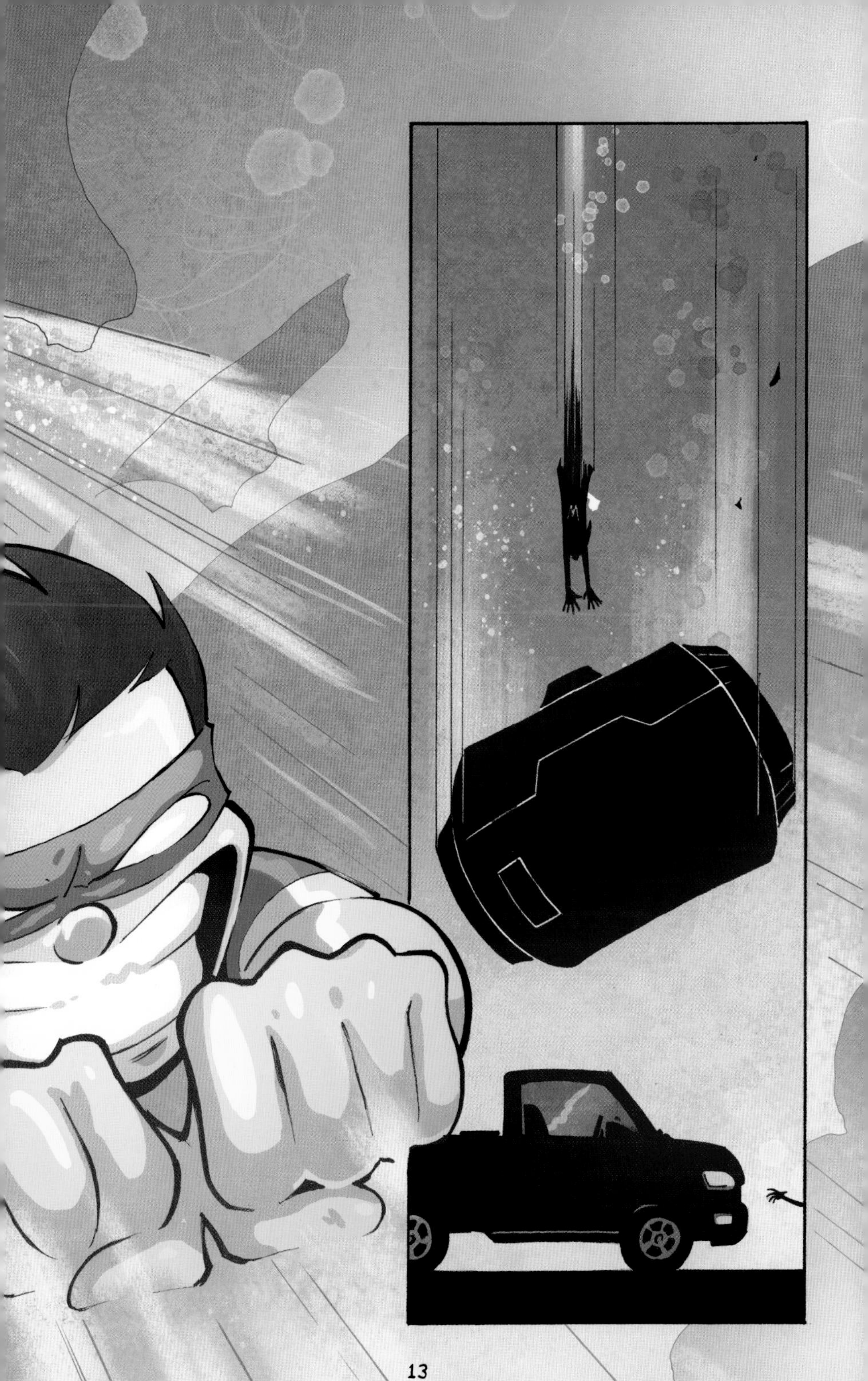

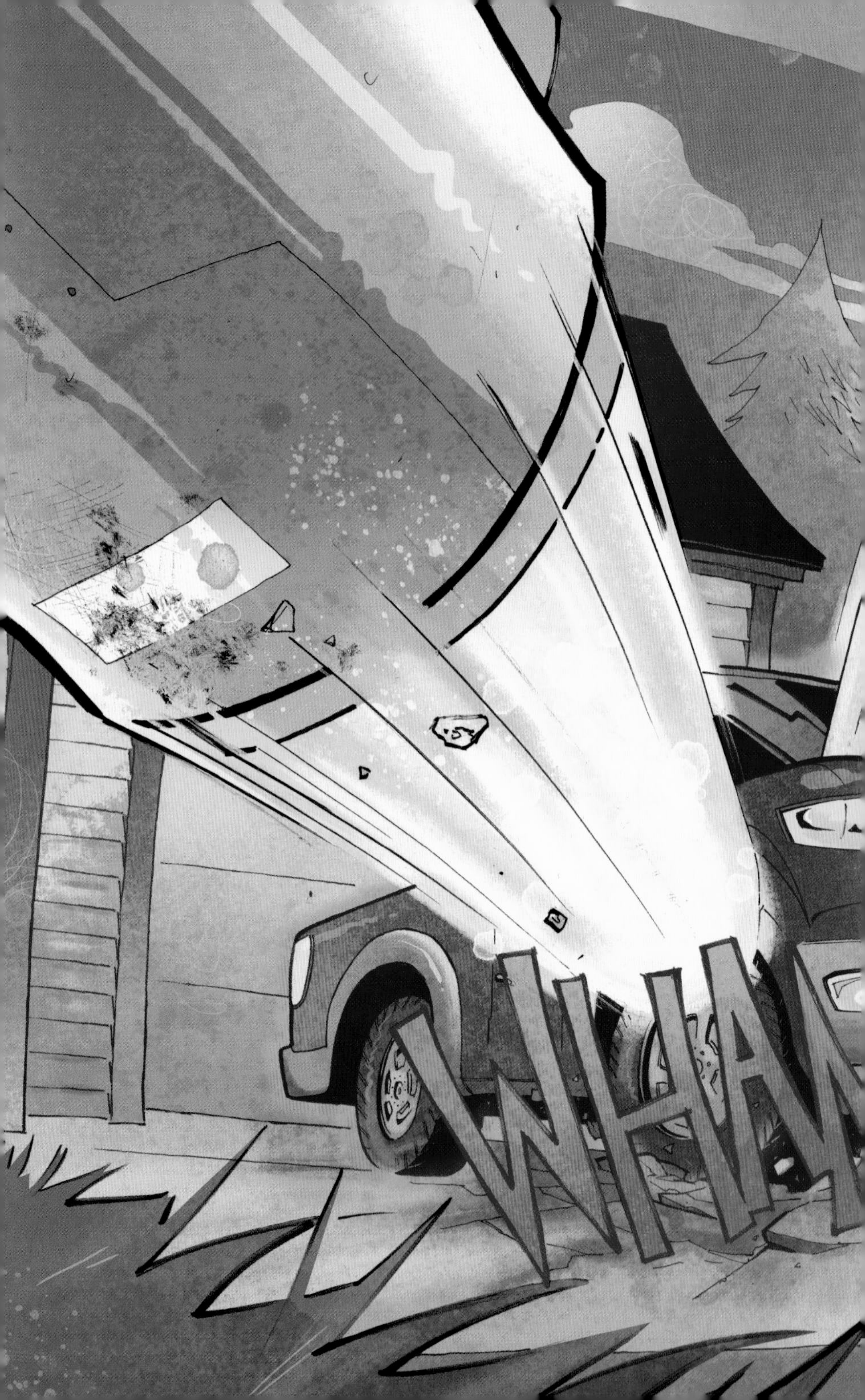
WHA

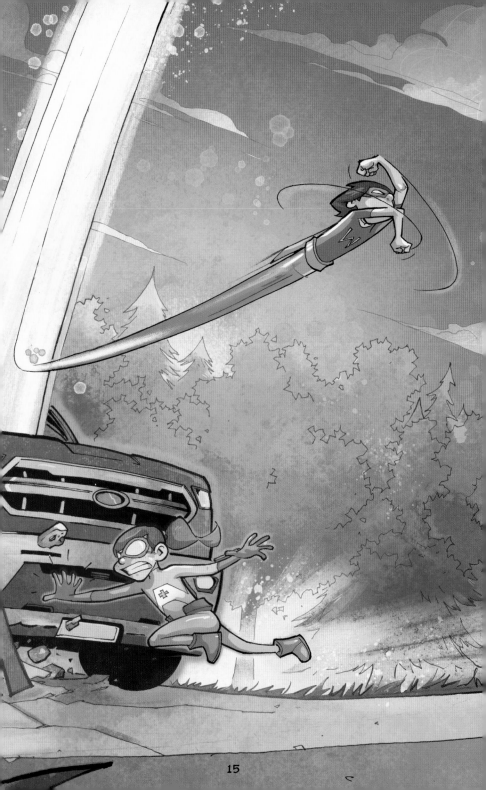

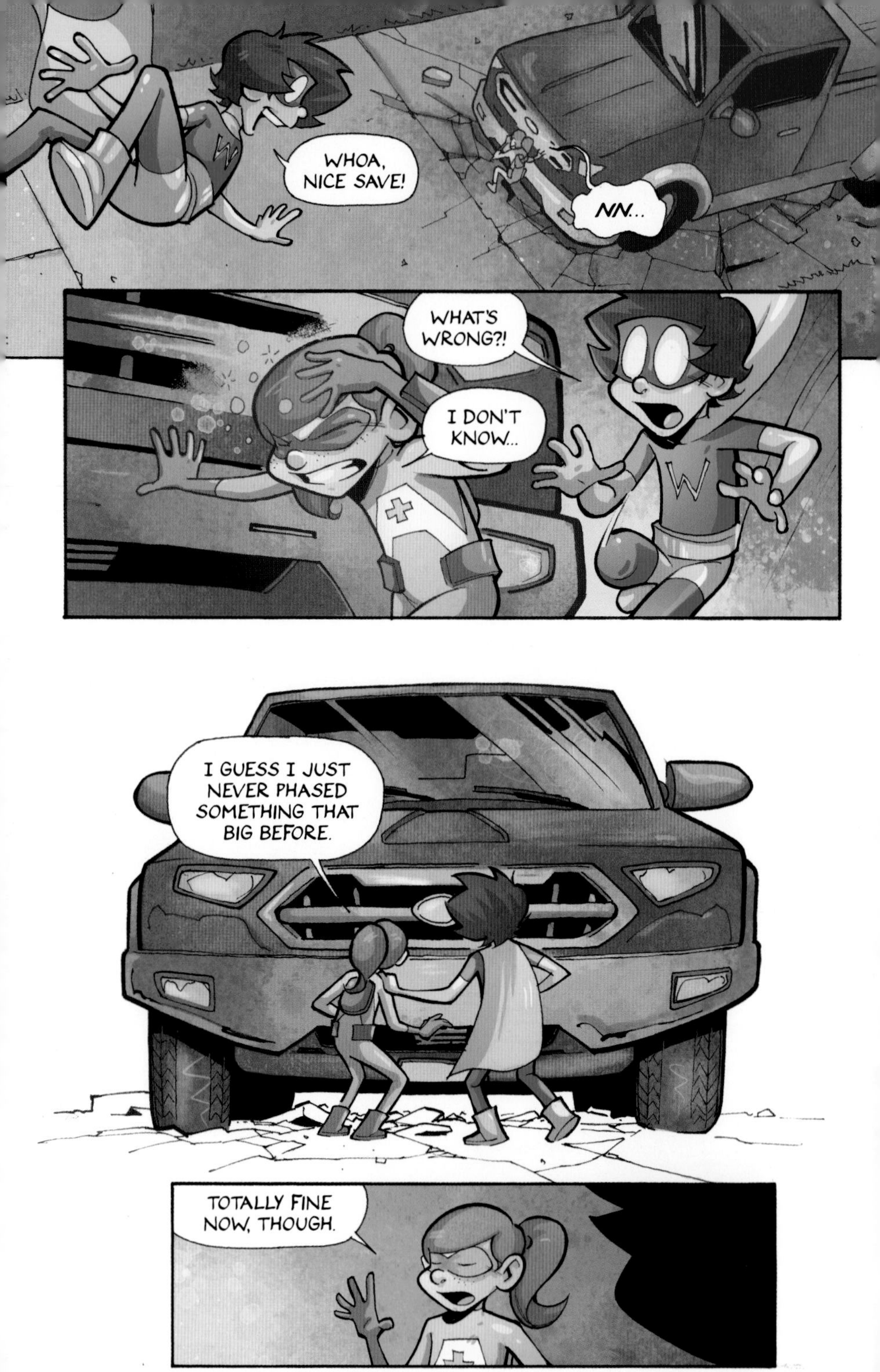
WHOA, NICE SAVE!
NN...
WHAT'S WRONG?!
I DON'T KNOW...
I GUESS I JUST NEVER PHASED SOMETHING THAT BIG BEFORE.
TOTALLY FINE NOW, THOUGH.

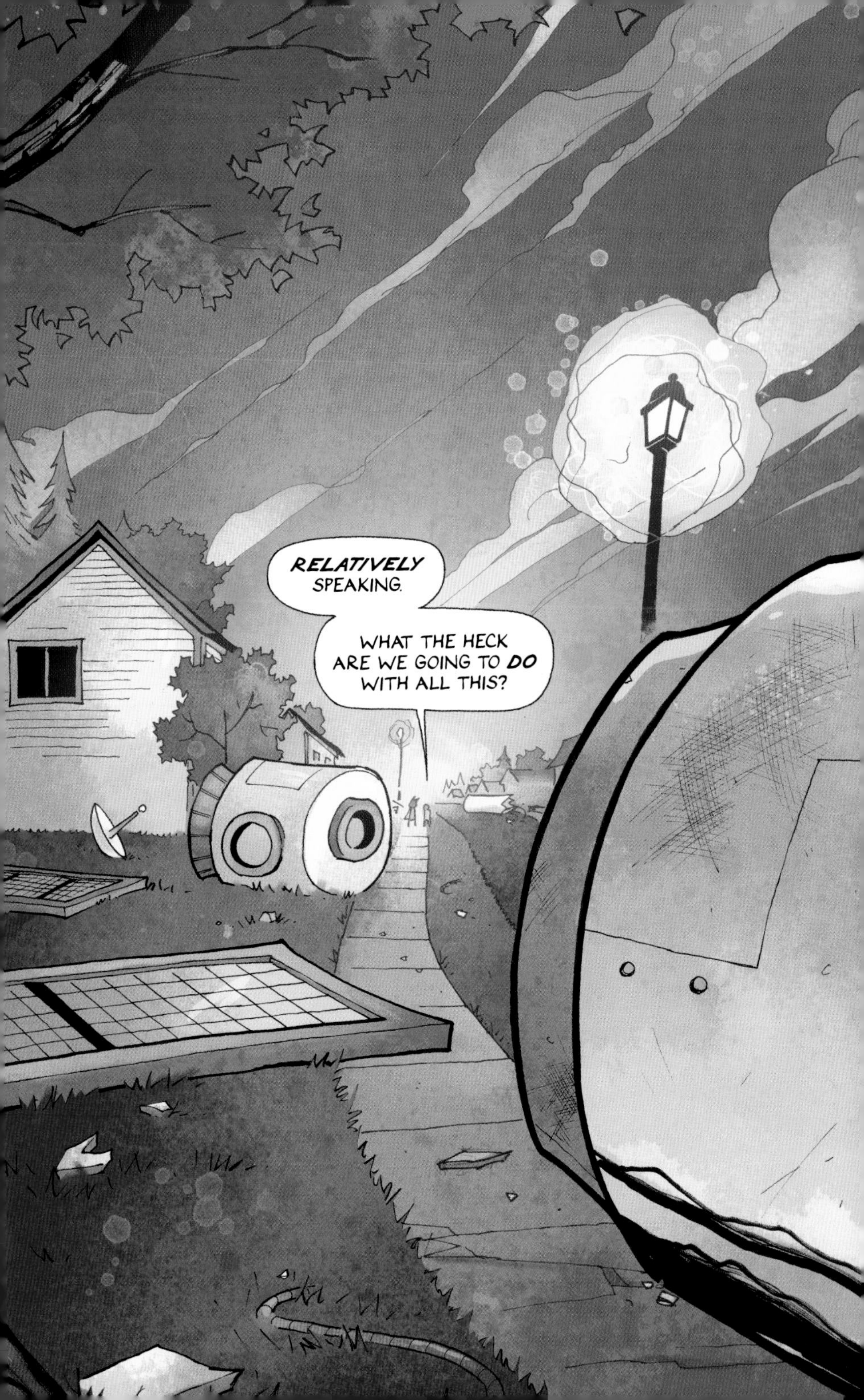
RELATIVELY SPEAKING.
WHAT THE HECK ARE WE GOING TO *DO* WITH ALL THIS?

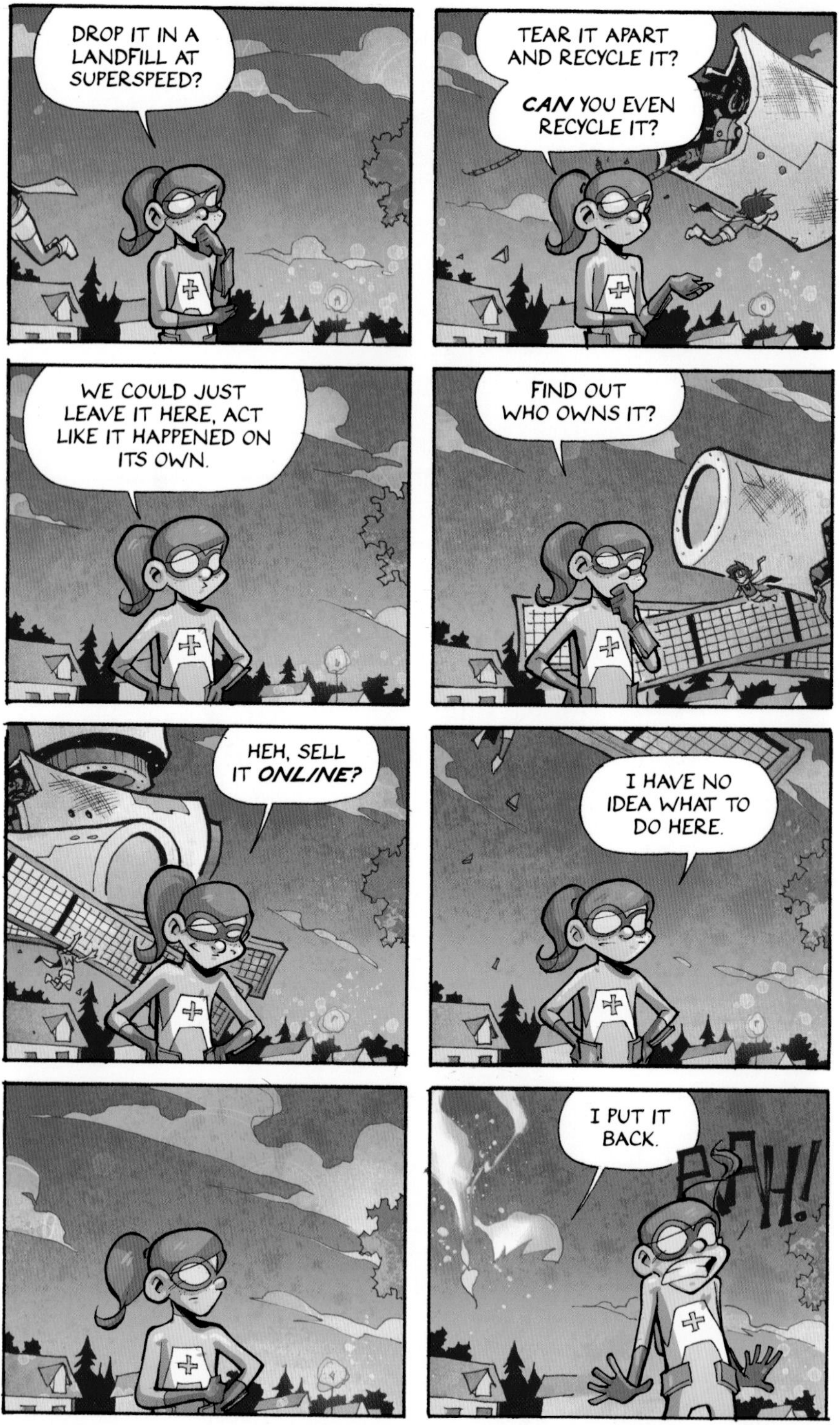
DROP IT IN A LANDFILL AT SUPERSPEED?
TEAR IT APART AND RECYCLE IT?
CAN YOU EVEN RECYCLE IT?
WE COULD JUST LEAVE IT HERE, ACT LIKE IT HAPPENED ON ITS OWN.
FIND OUT WHO OWNS IT?
HEH, SELL IT ONLINE?
I HAVE NO IDEA WHAT TO DO HERE.
I PUT IT BACK.

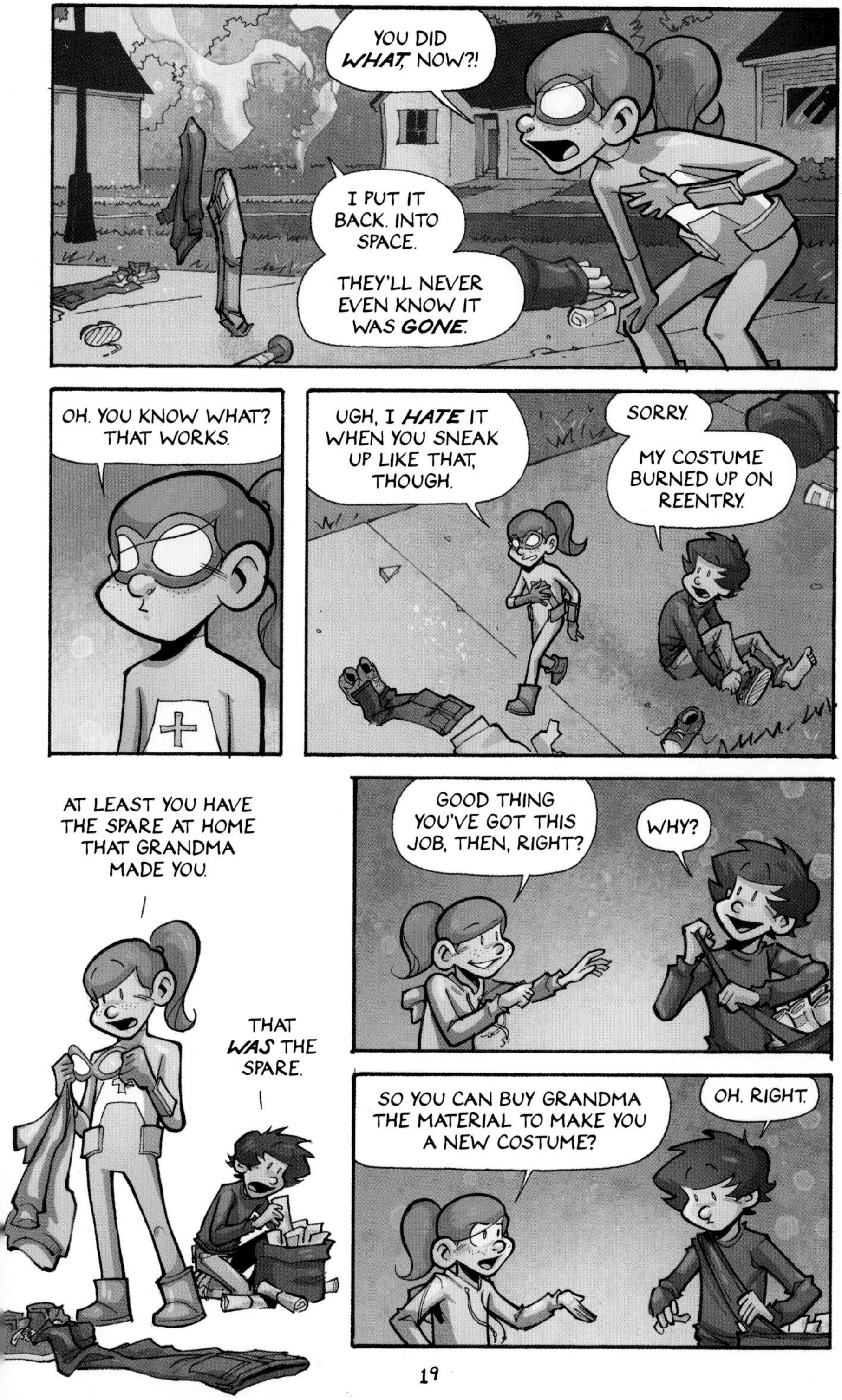
YOU DID *WHAT,* NOW?!
I PUT IT BACK. INTO SPACE.
THEY'LL NEVER EVEN KNOW IT WAS *GONE.*
OH. YOU KNOW WHAT? THAT WORKS.
UGH, I *HATE* IT WHEN YOU SNEAK UP LIKE THAT, THOUGH.
SORRY.
MY COSTUME BURNED UP ON REENTRY.
AT LEAST YOU HAVE THE SPARE AT HOME THAT GRANDMA MADE YOU.
THAT *WAS* THE SPARE.
GOOD THING YOU'VE GOT THIS JOB, THEN, RIGHT?
WHY?
SO YOU CAN BUY GRANDMA THE MATERIAL TO MAKE YOU A NEW COSTUME?
OH. RIGHT.

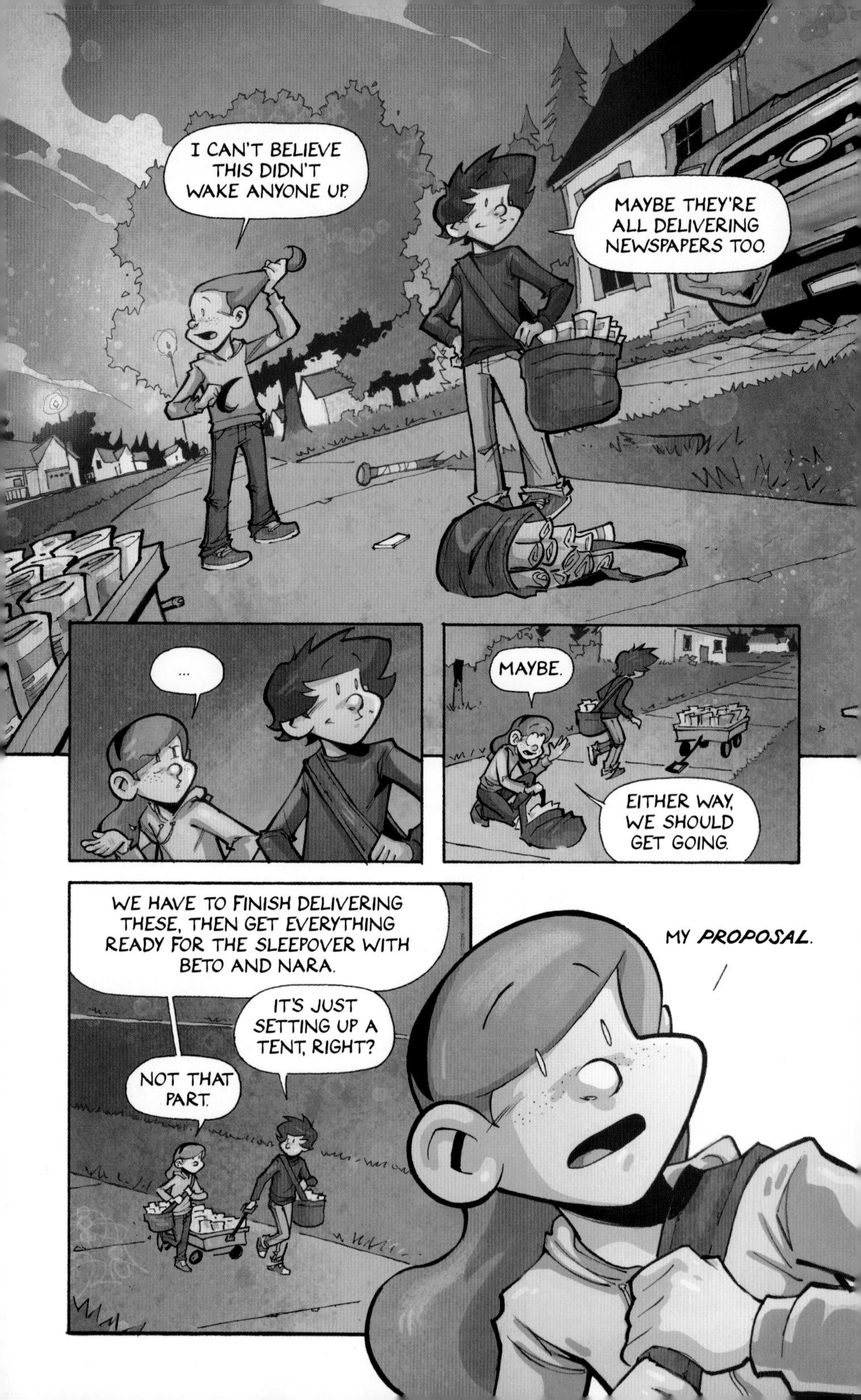
I CAN'T BELIEVE THIS DIDN'T WAKE ANYONE UP.
MAYBE THEY'RE ALL DELIVERING NEWSPAPERS TOO.
...
MAYBE.
EITHER WAY, WE SHOULD GET GOING.
WE HAVE TO FINISH DELIVERING THESE, THEN GET EVERYTHING READY FOR THE SLEEPOVER WITH BETO AND NARA.
IT'S JUST SETTING UP A TENT, RIGHT?
NOT THAT PART.
MY *PROPOSAL*.

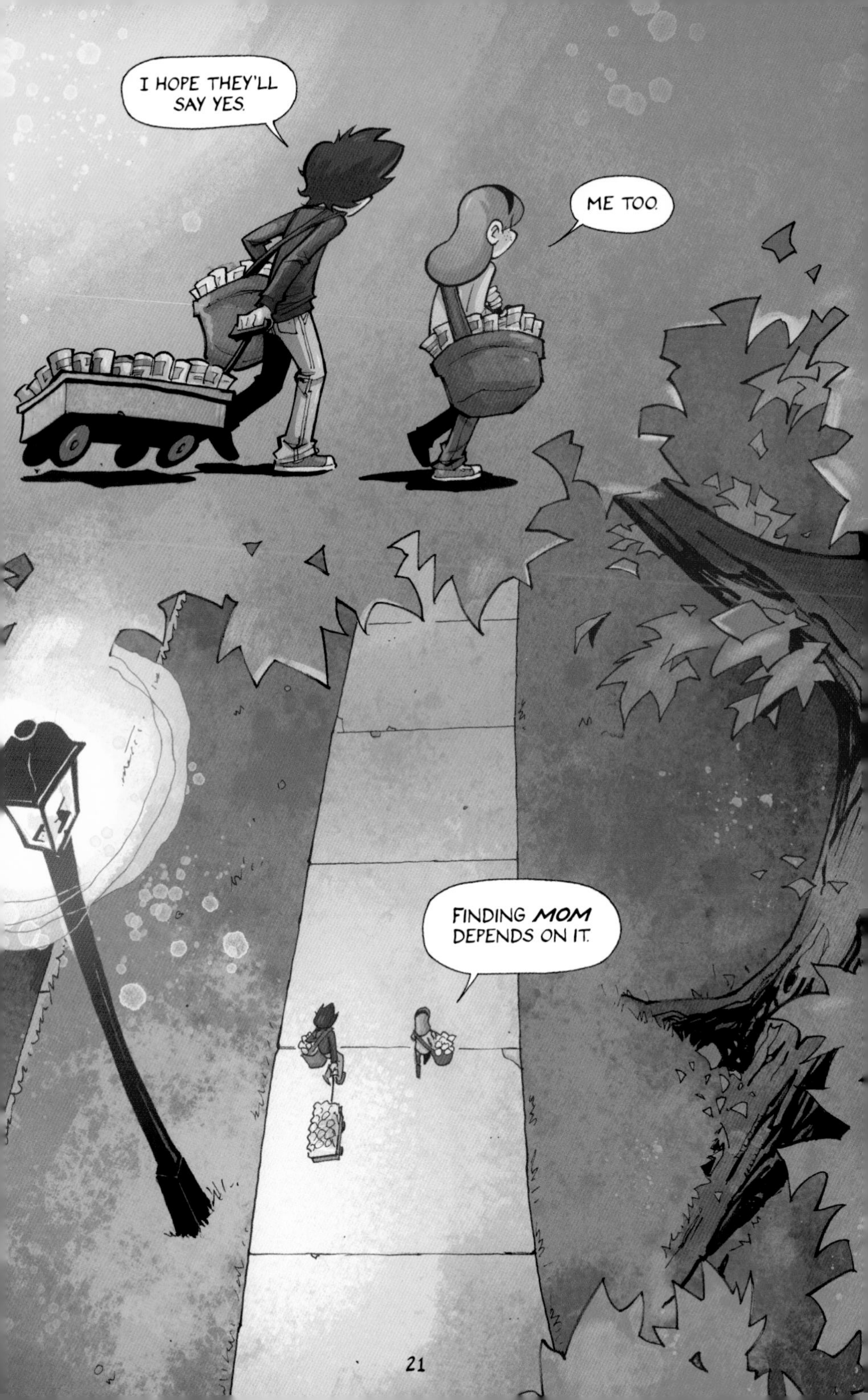
I HOPE THEY'LL SAY YES.
ME TOO.
FINDING ***MOM*** DEPENDS ON IT.

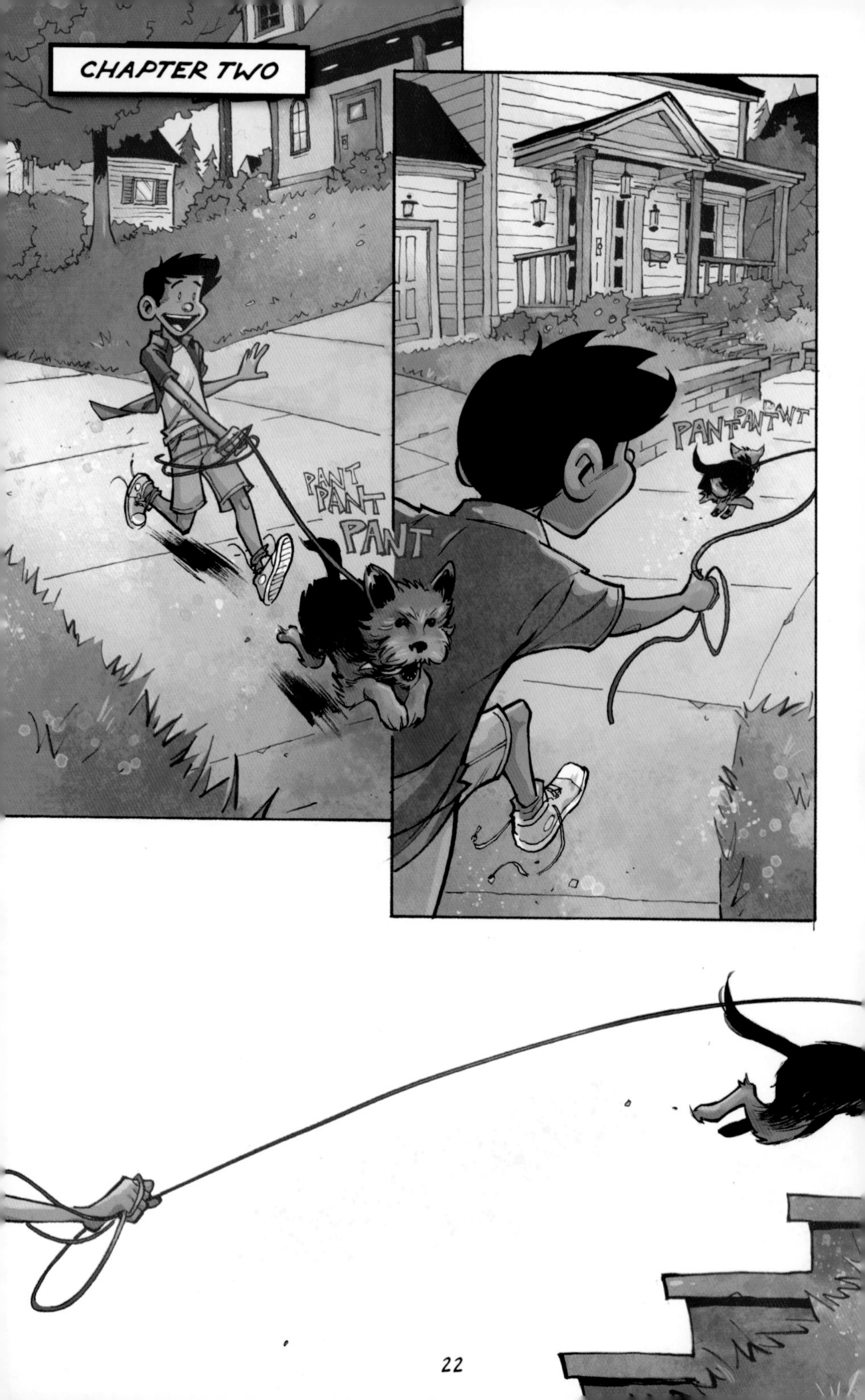
CHAPTER TWO
PANT PANT PANT
PANT PANT PANT PANT

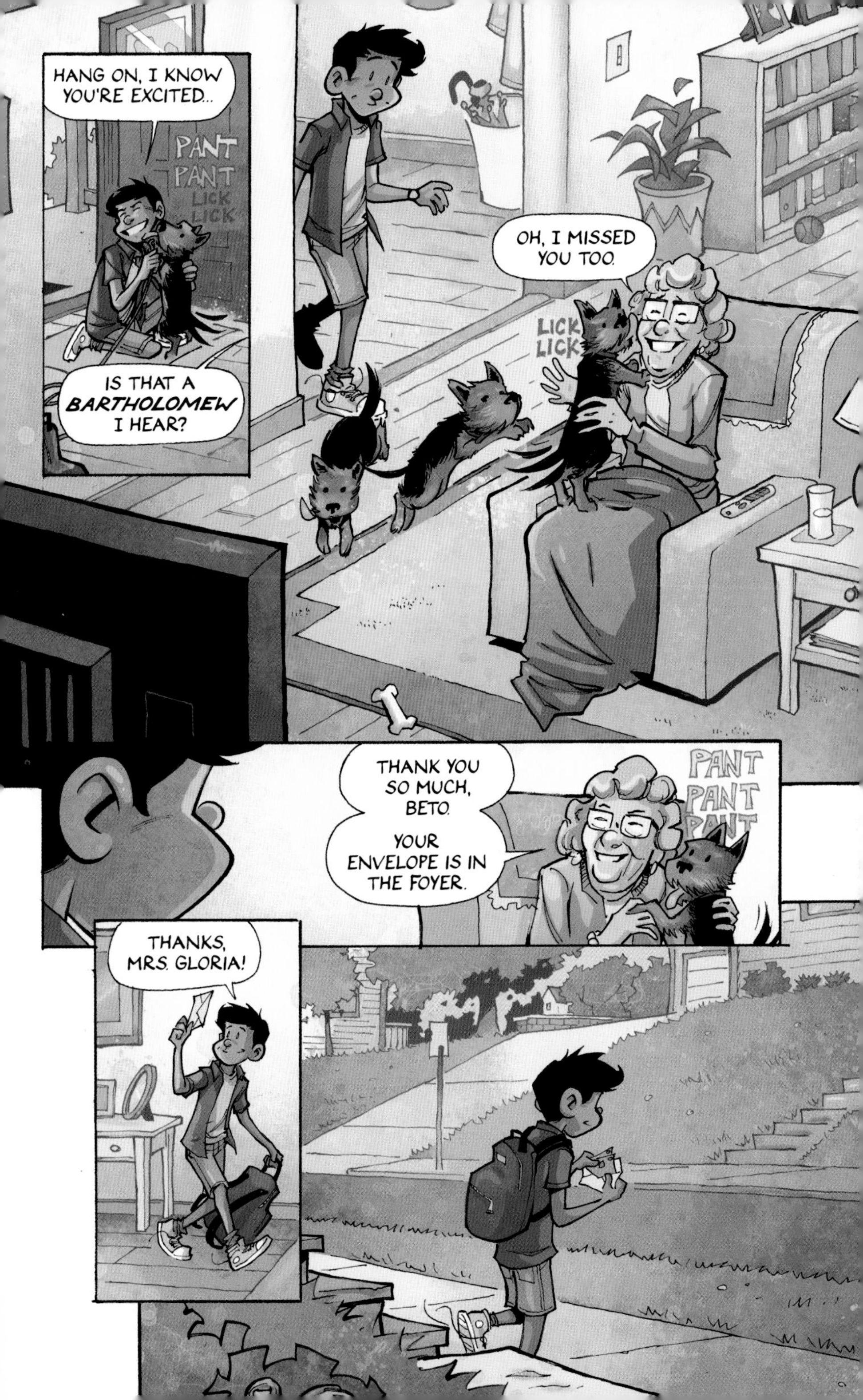

HANG ON, I KNOW YOU'RE EXCITED...
PANT PANT
LICK LICK
IS THAT A *BARTHOLOMEW* I HEAR?
OH, I MISSED YOU TOO.
LICK LICK
THANK YOU SO MUCH, BETO.
YOUR ENVELOPE IS IN THE FOYER.
PANT PANT PANT
THANKS, MRS. GLORIA!

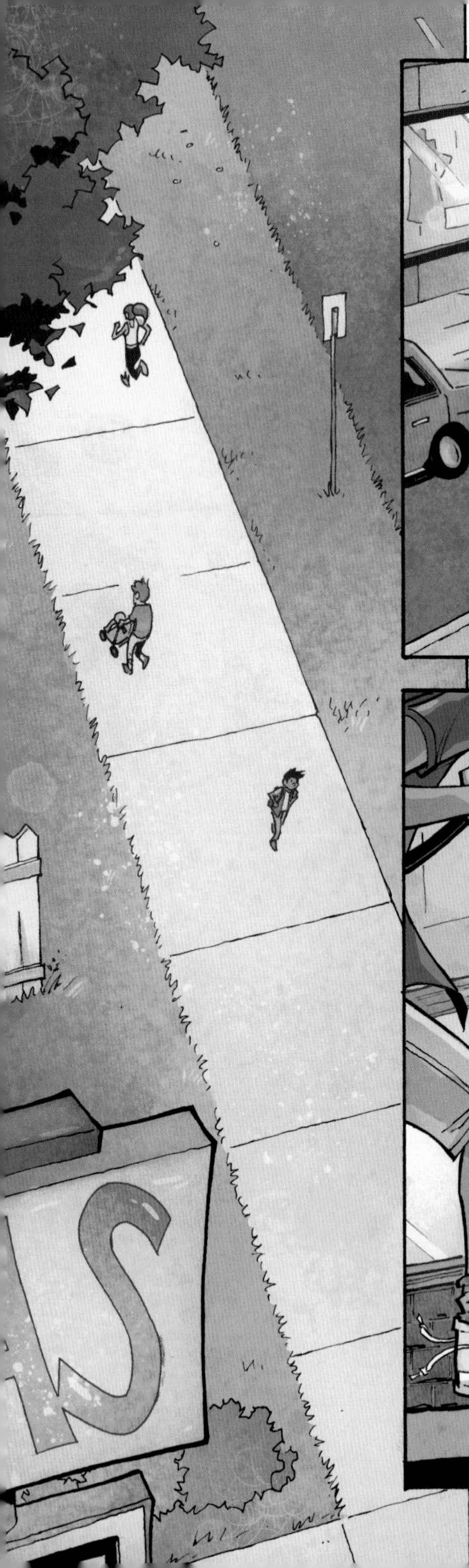

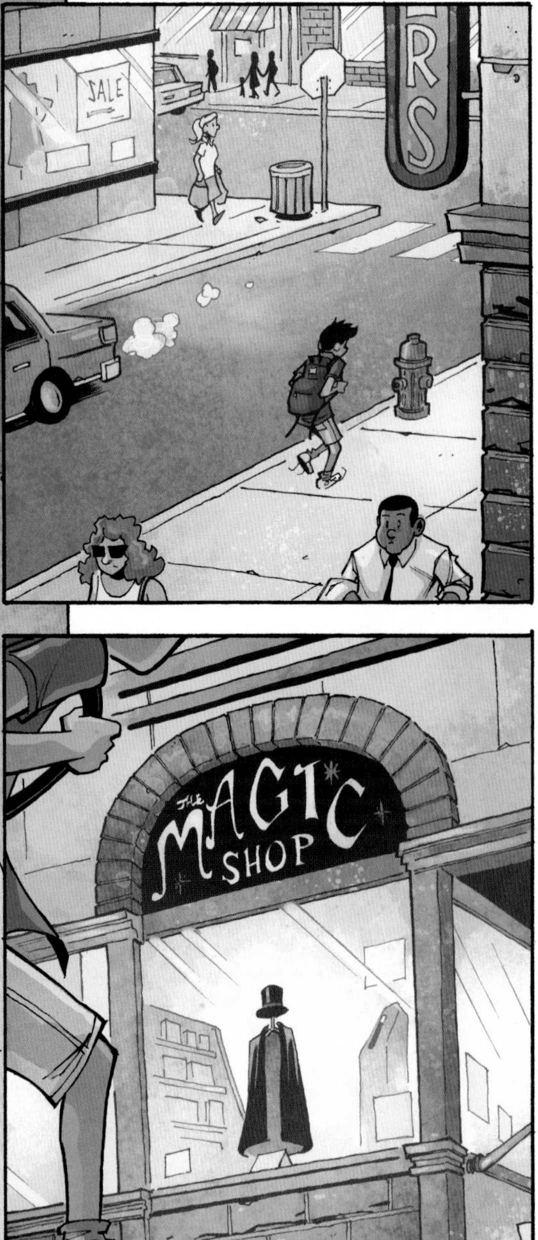
SALE
THE MAGIC SHOP

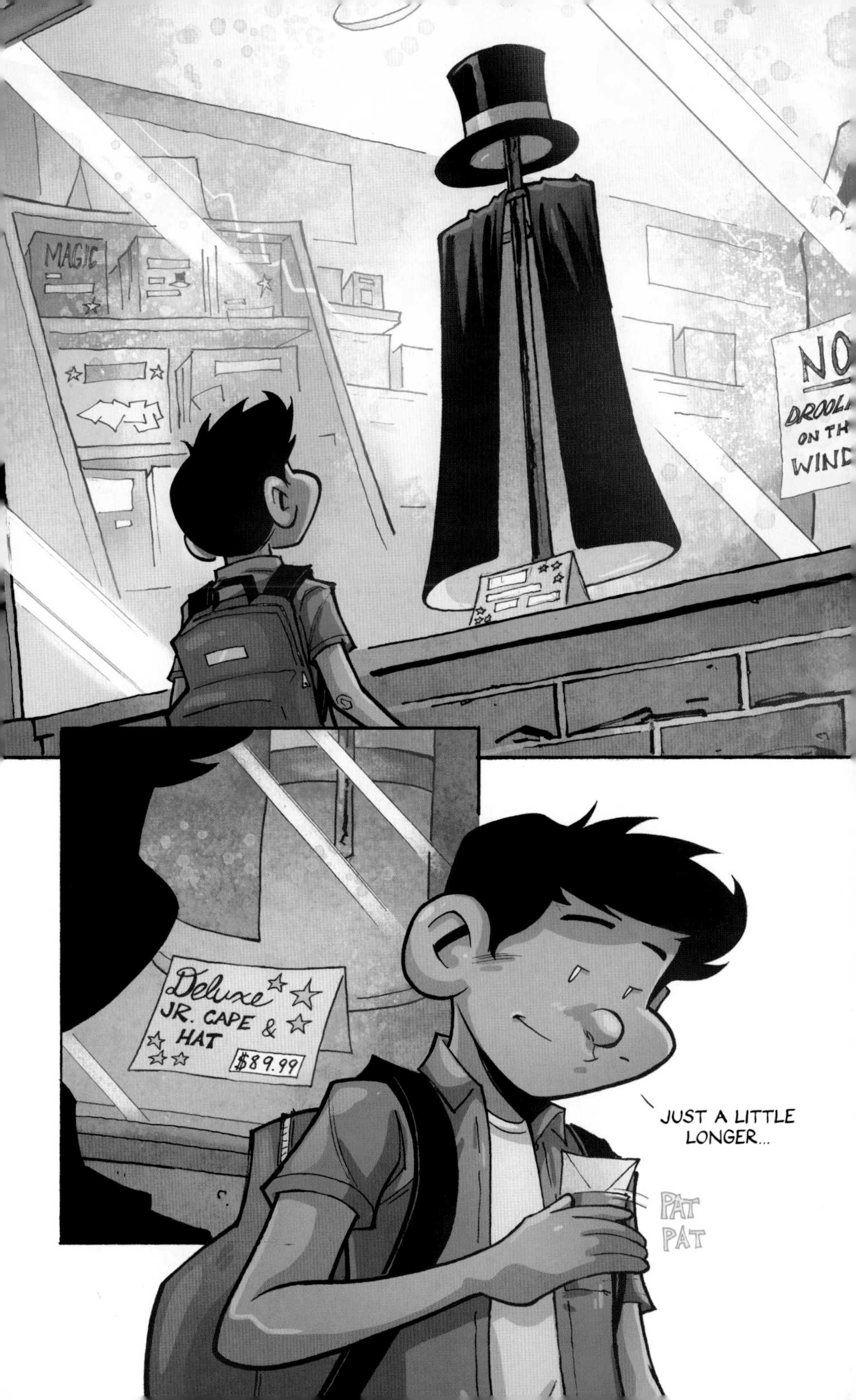
MAGIC
NO
DROOL
ON TH
WIND
Deluxe
JR. CAPE &
HAT
$89.99
JUST A LITTLE LONGER...
PAT
PAT

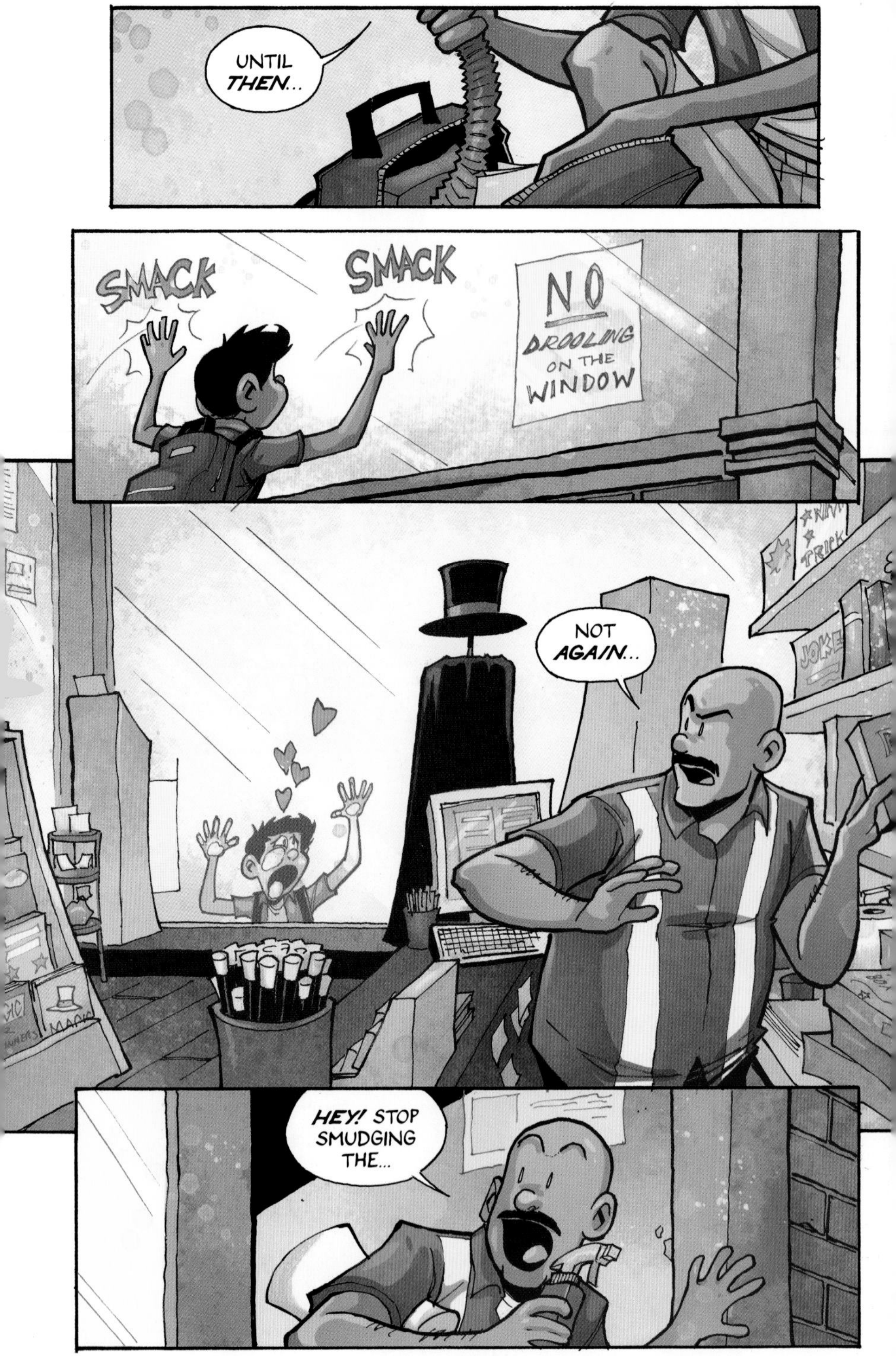
UNTIL *THEN*...
SMACK
SMACK
NO
DROOLING ON THE WINDOW
NOT *AGAIN*...
HEY! STOP SMUDGING THE...

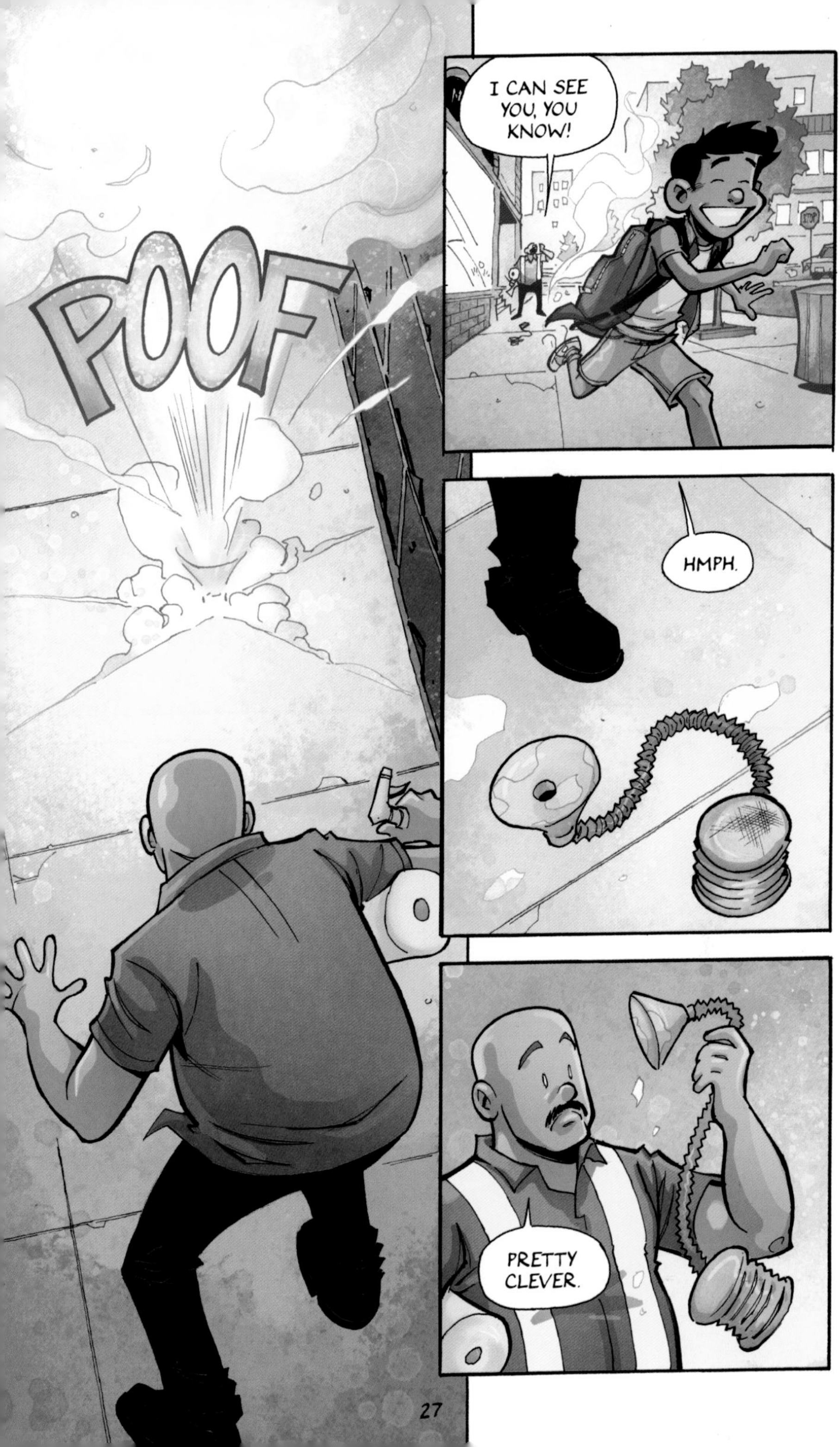
POOF
I CAN SEE YOU, YOU KNOW!
HMPH.
PRETTY CLEVER.

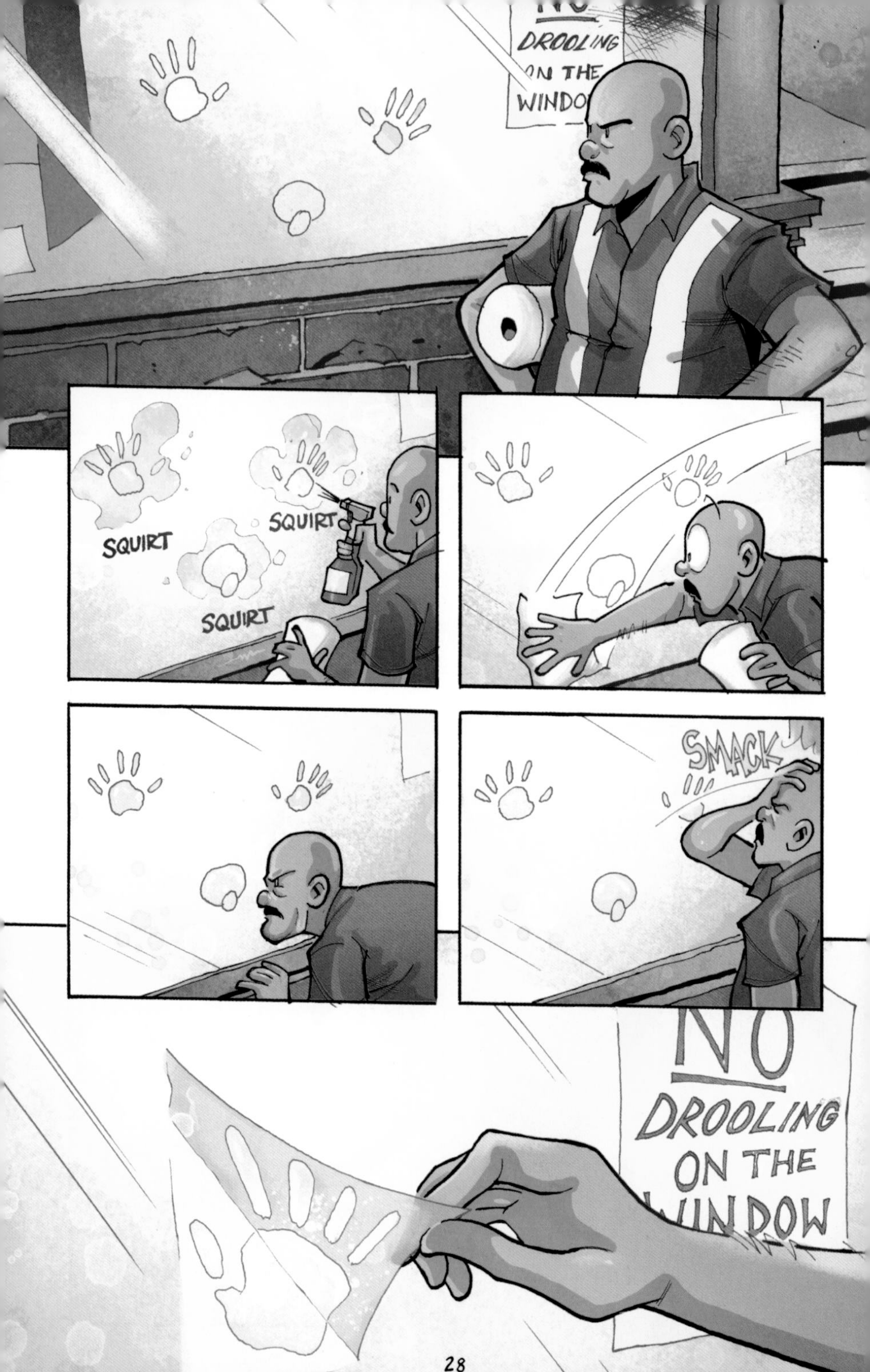
NO DROOLING ON THE WINDOW
SQUIRT
SQUIRT
SQUIRT
SMACK
NO
DROOLING
ON THE
WINDOW

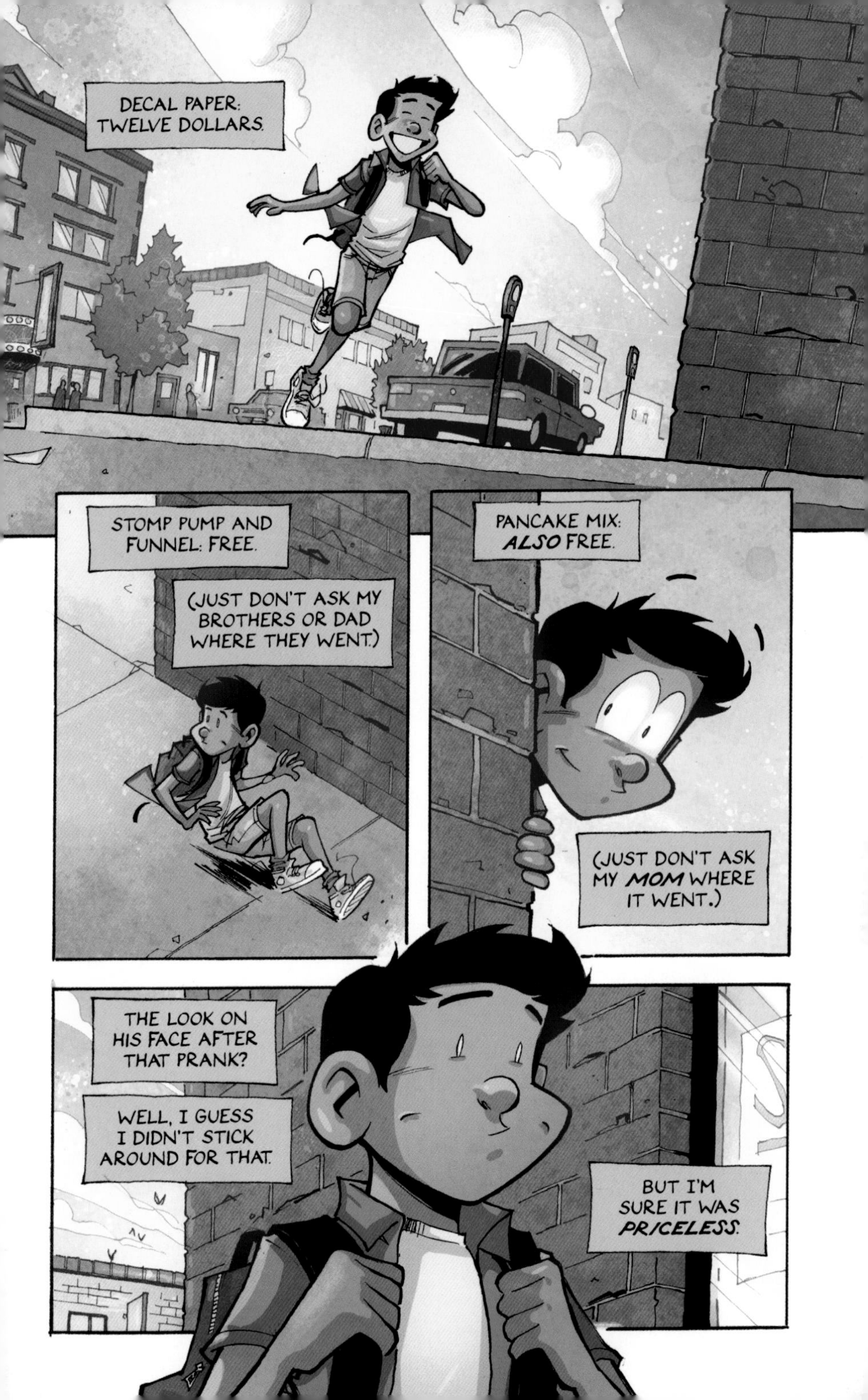
DECAL PAPER:
TWELVE DOLLARS.
STOMP PUMP AND
FUNNEL: FREE.
(JUST DON'T ASK MY
BROTHERS OR DAD
WHERE THEY WENT.)
PANCAKE MIX:
ALSO FREE.
(JUST DON'T ASK
MY MOM WHERE
IT WENT.)
THE LOOK ON
HIS FACE AFTER
THAT PRANK?
WELL, I GUESS
I DIDN'T STICK
AROUND FOR THAT.
BUT I'M
SURE IT WAS
PRICELESS.

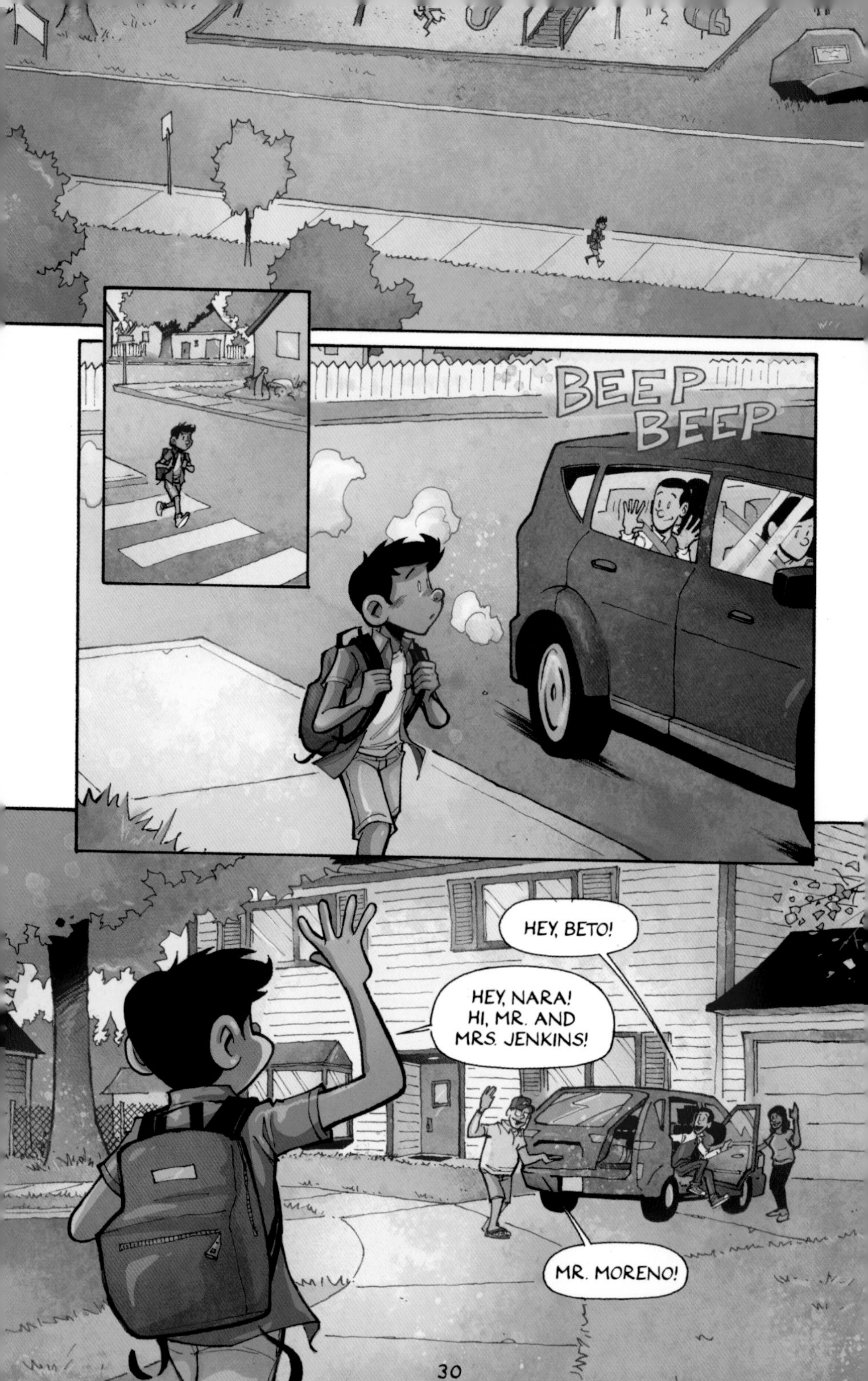
BEEP BEEP
HEY, BETO!
HEY, NARA! HI, MR. AND MRS. JENKINS!
MR. MORENO!

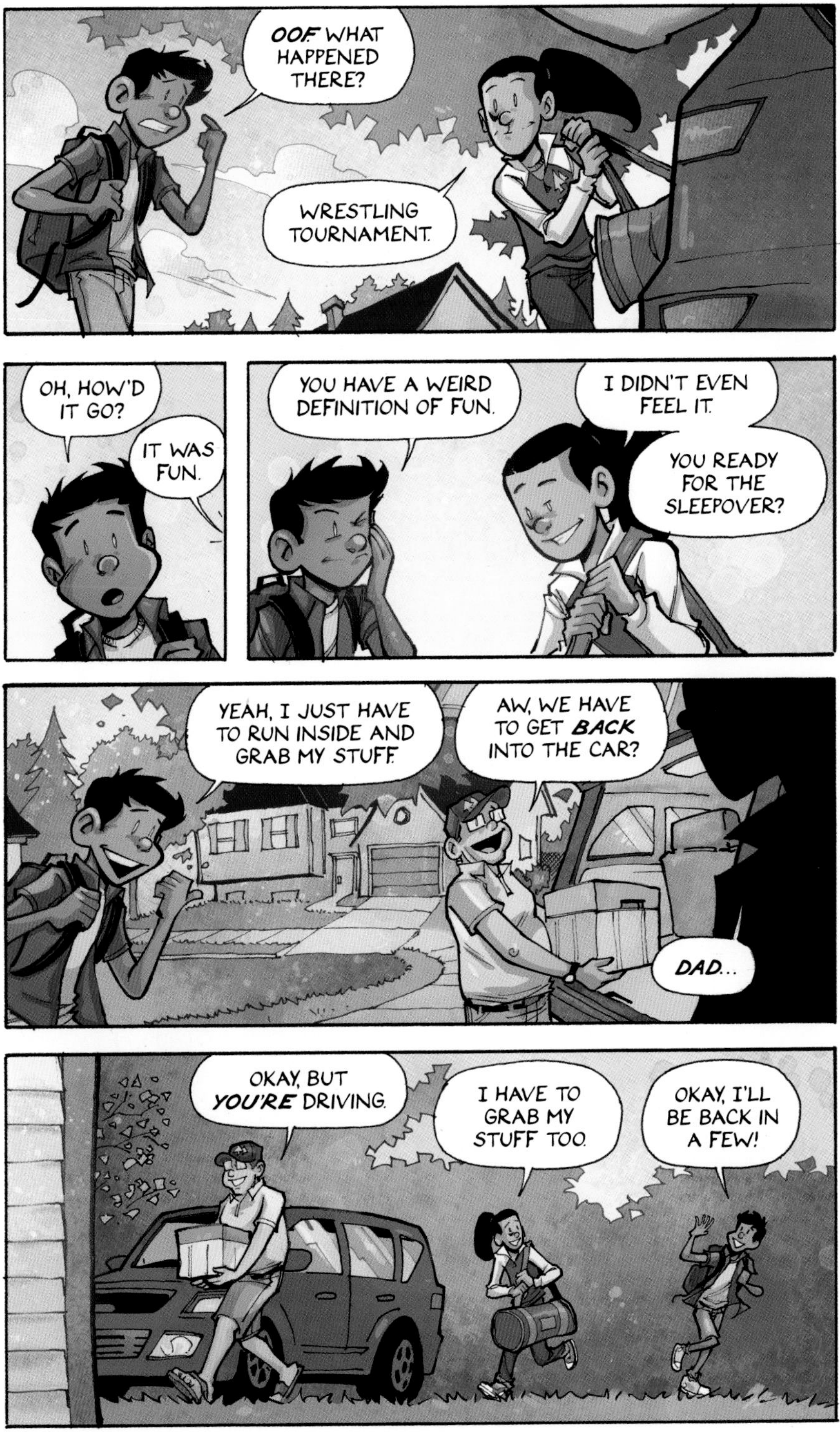
OOF WHAT HAPPENED THERE?
WRESTLING TOURNAMENT.
OH, HOW'D IT GO?
IT WAS FUN.
YOU HAVE A WEIRD DEFINITION OF FUN.
I DIDN'T EVEN FEEL IT.
YOU READY FOR THE SLEEPOVER?
YEAH, I JUST HAVE TO RUN INSIDE AND GRAB MY STUFF.
AW, WE HAVE TO GET BACK INTO THE CAR?
DAD...
OKAY, BUT YOU'RE DRIVING.
I HAVE TO GRAB MY STUFF TOO.
OKAY, I'LL BE BACK IN A FEW!

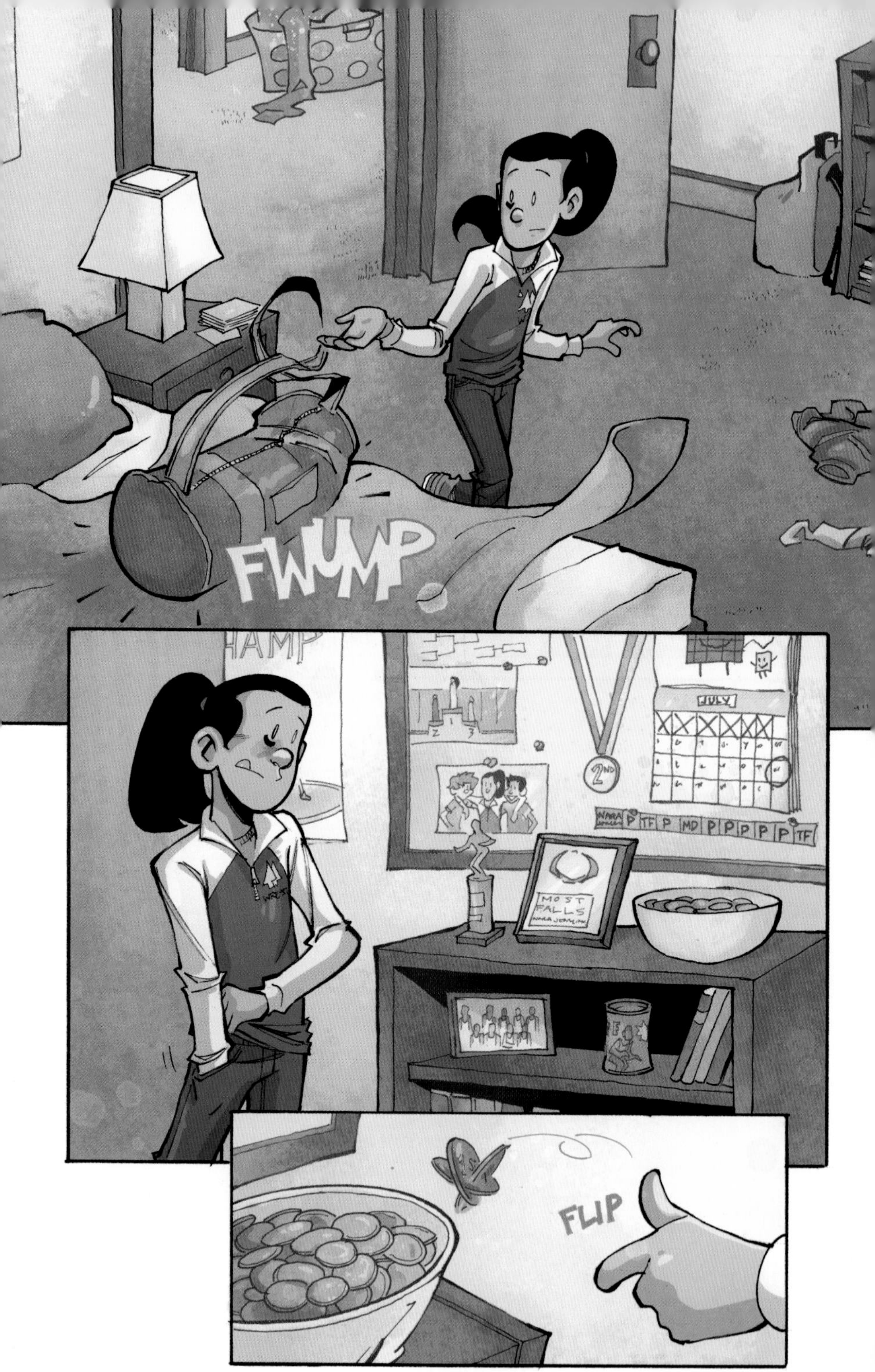
FWUMP
JULY
MOST FALLS
FLIP

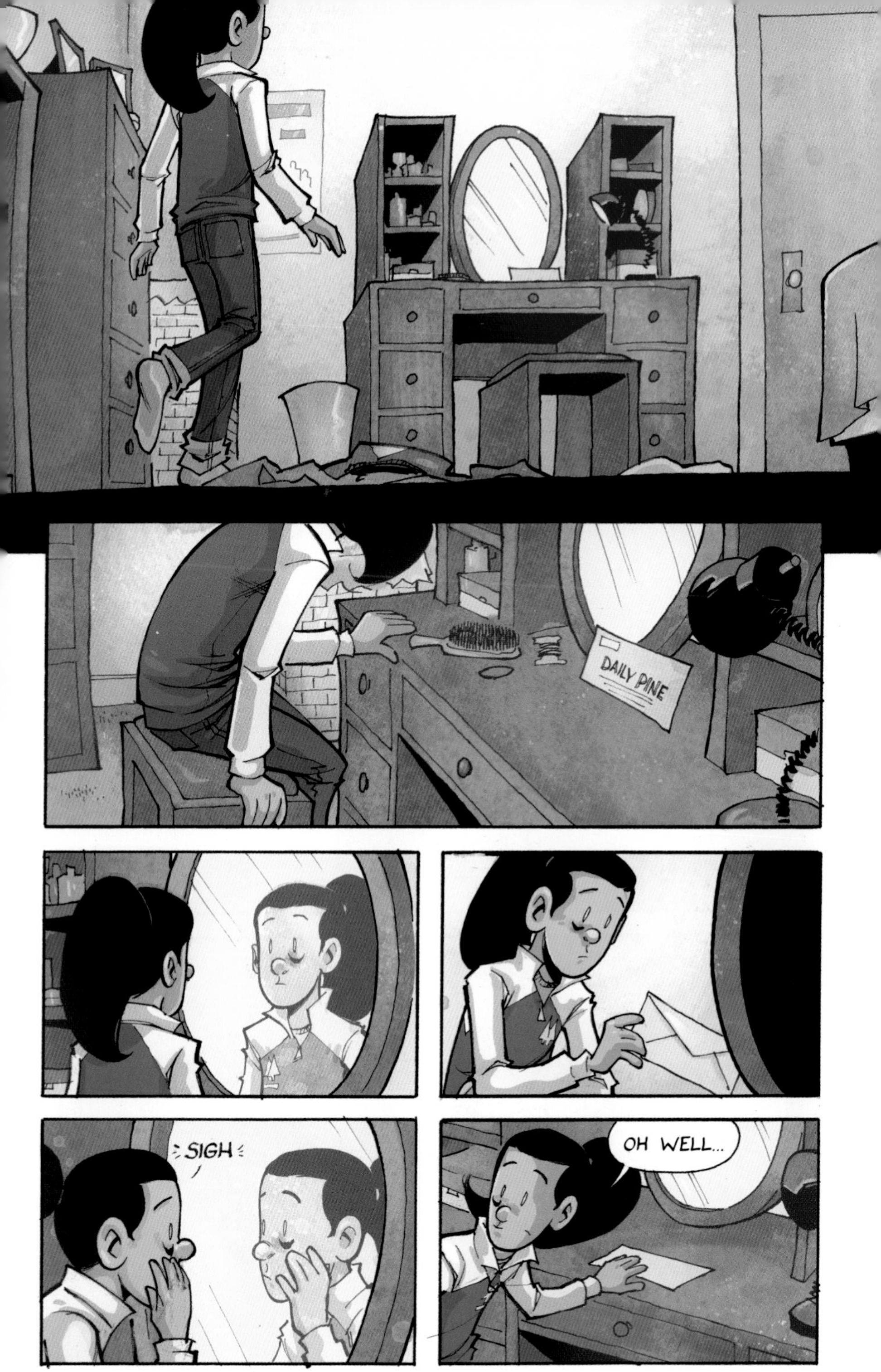
DAILY PINE
SIGH
OH WELL...

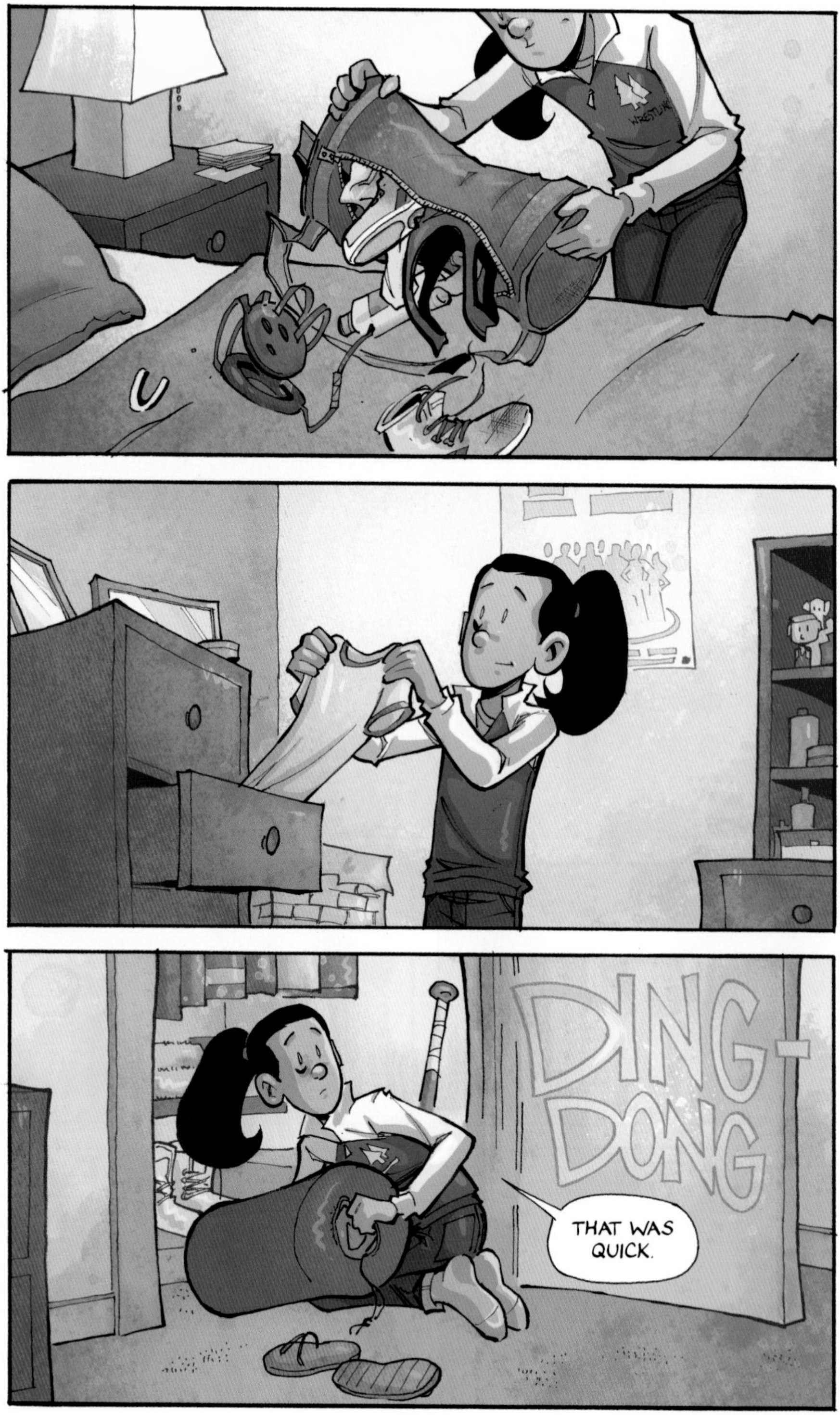
WRESTLING
DING-DONG
THAT WAS QUICK.

NARA, ARE YOU READY?

JUST A SECOND!

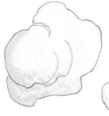

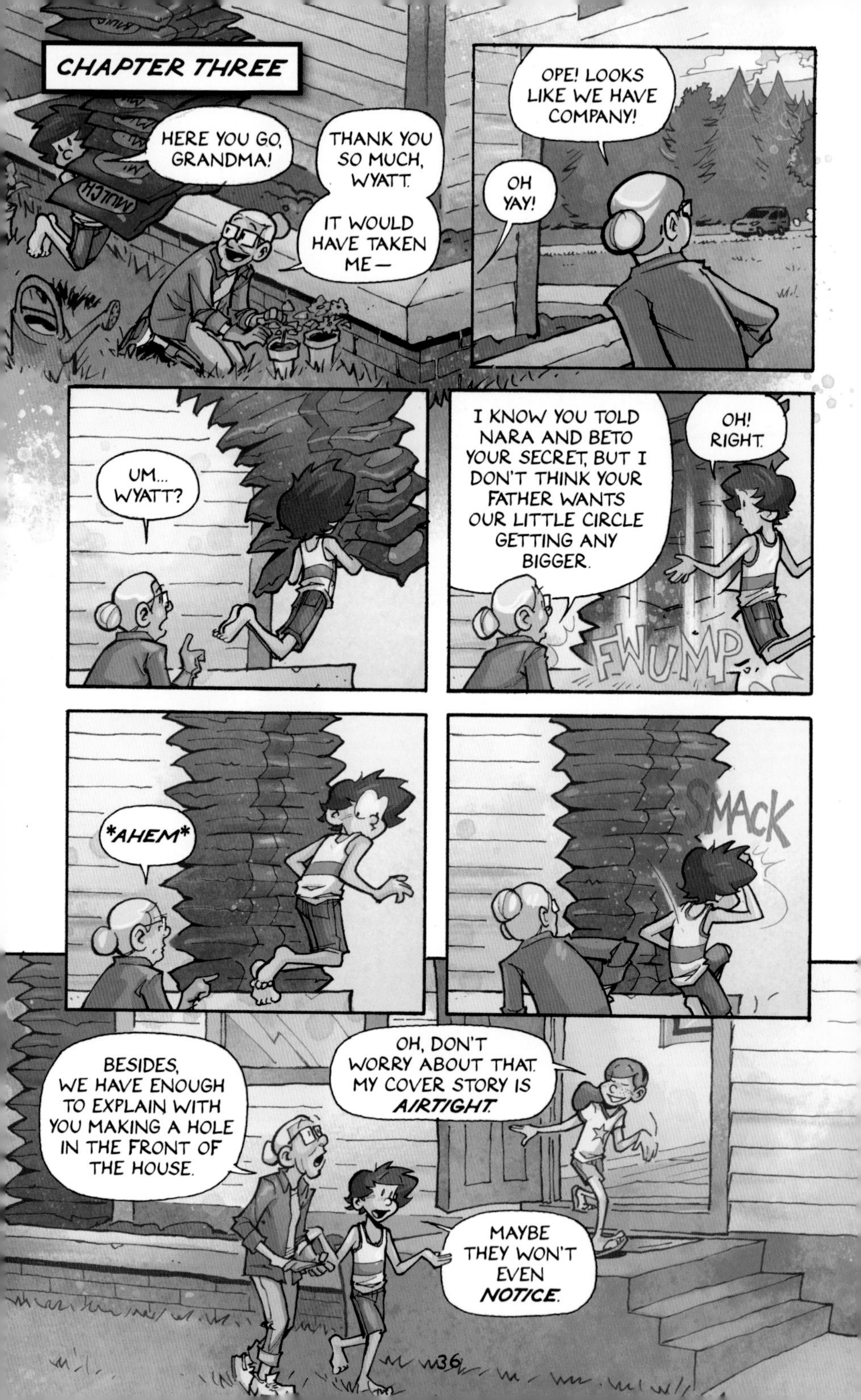
CHAPTER THREE
HERE YOU GO, GRANDMA!
THANK YOU SO MUCH, WYATT.
IT WOULD HAVE TAKEN ME—
OPE! LOOKS LIKE WE HAVE COMPANY!
OH YAY!
UM... WYATT?
I KNOW YOU TOLD NARA AND BETO YOUR SECRET, BUT I DON'T THINK YOUR FATHER WANTS OUR LITTLE CIRCLE GETTING ANY BIGGER.
OH! RIGHT.
FWUMP
AHEM
SMACK
BESIDES, WE HAVE ENOUGH TO EXPLAIN WITH YOU MAKING A HOLE IN THE FRONT OF THE HOUSE.
OH, DON'T WORRY ABOUT THAT. MY COVER STORY IS AIRTIGHT.
MAYBE THEY WON'T EVEN NOTICE.

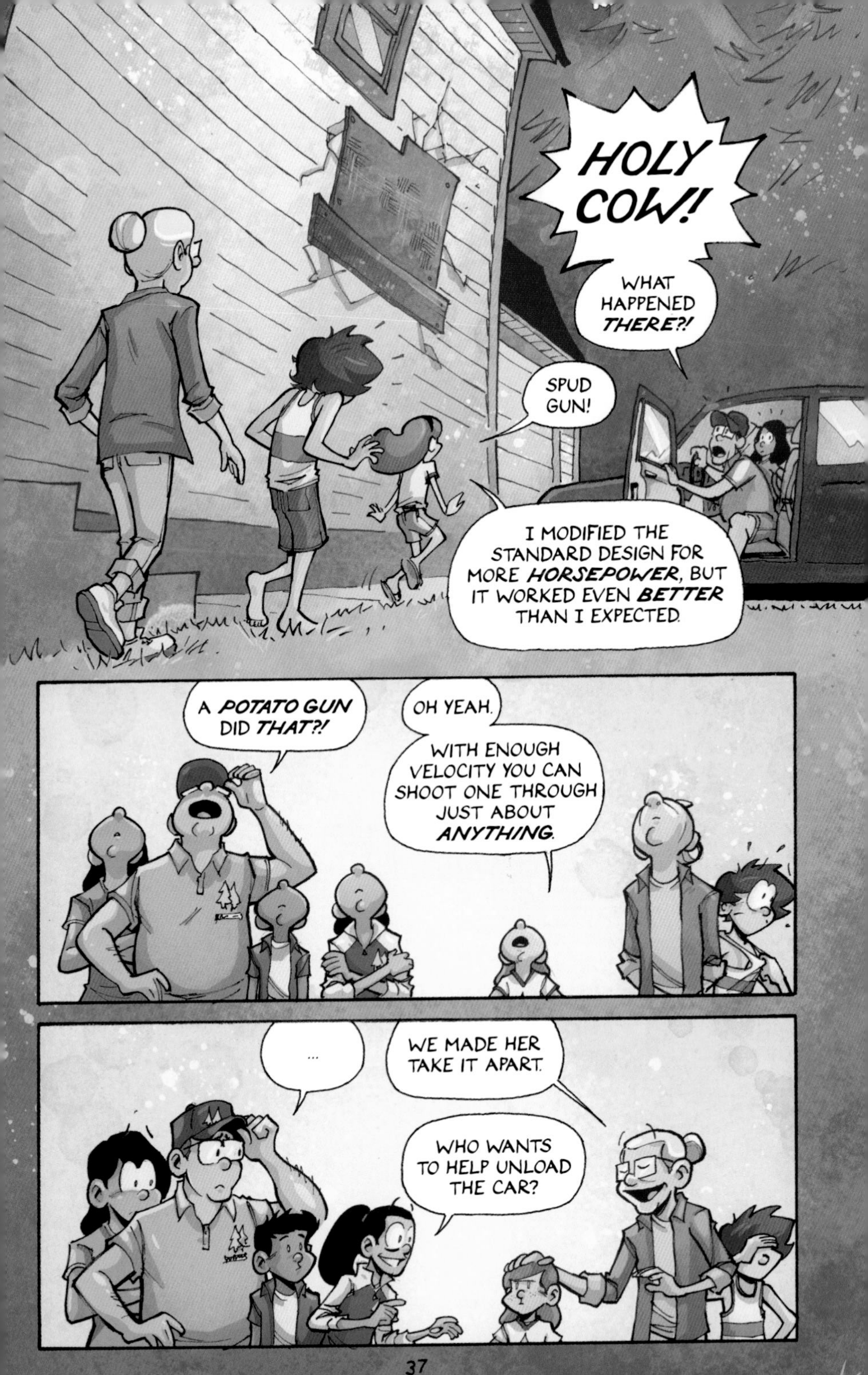
HOLY COW!
WHAT HAPPENED *THERE?!*
SPUD GUN!
I MODIFIED THE STANDARD DESIGN FOR MORE *HORSEPOWER*, BUT IT WORKED EVEN *BETTER* THAN I EXPECTED.
A *POTATO GUN* DID *THAT?!*
OH YEAH.
WITH ENOUGH VELOCITY YOU CAN SHOOT ONE THROUGH JUST ABOUT *ANYTHING*.
...
WE MADE HER TAKE IT APART.
WHO WANTS TO HELP UNLOAD THE CAR?

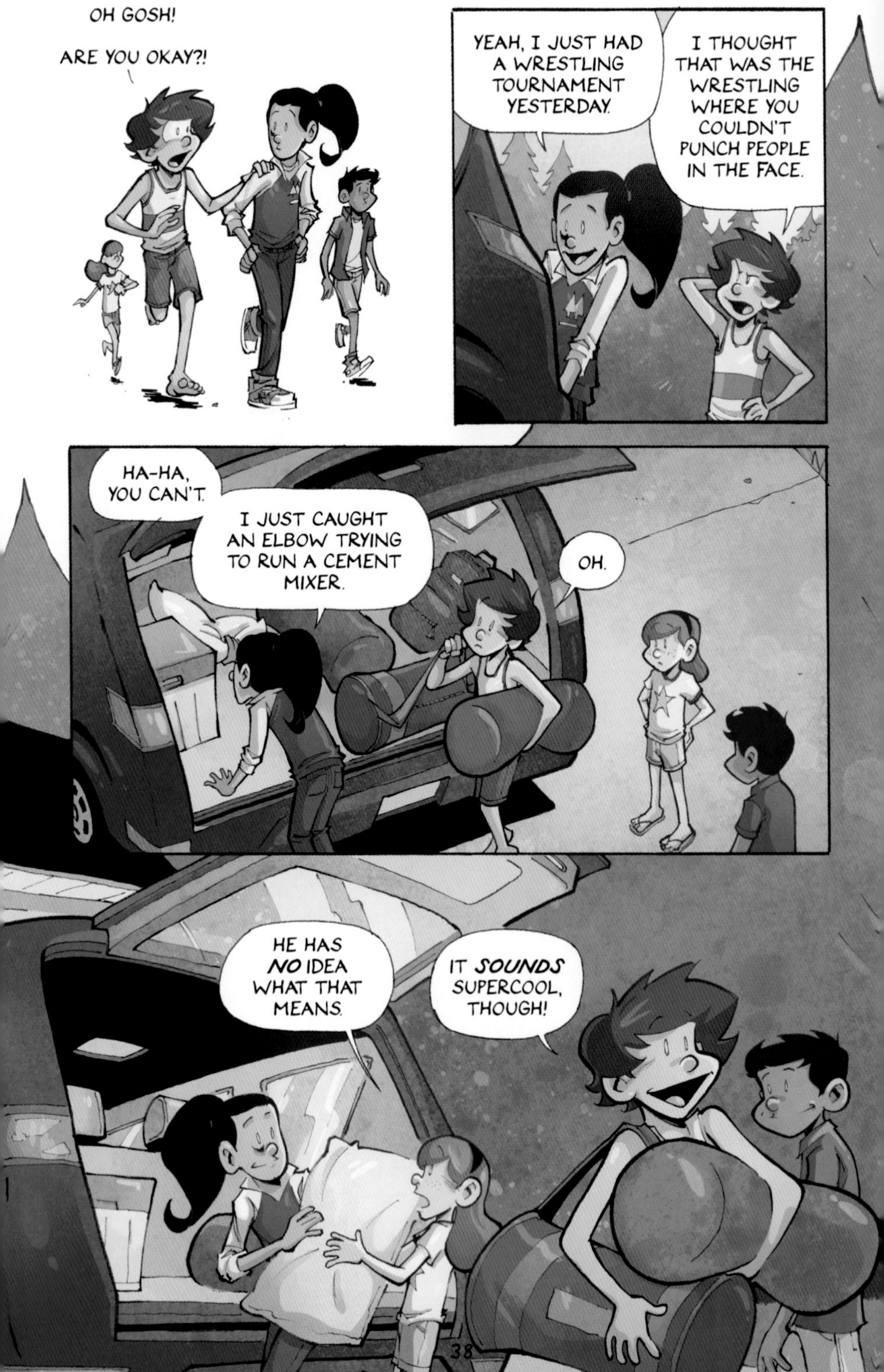
OH GOSH!
ARE YOU OKAY?!
YEAH, I JUST HAD A WRESTLING TOURNAMENT YESTERDAY.
I THOUGHT THAT WAS THE WRESTLING WHERE YOU COULDN'T PUNCH PEOPLE IN THE FACE.
HA-HA, YOU CAN'T.
I JUST CAUGHT AN ELBOW TRYING TO RUN A CEMENT MIXER.
OH.
HE HAS ***NO*** IDEA WHAT THAT MEANS.
IT ***SOUNDS*** SUPERCOOL, THOUGH!

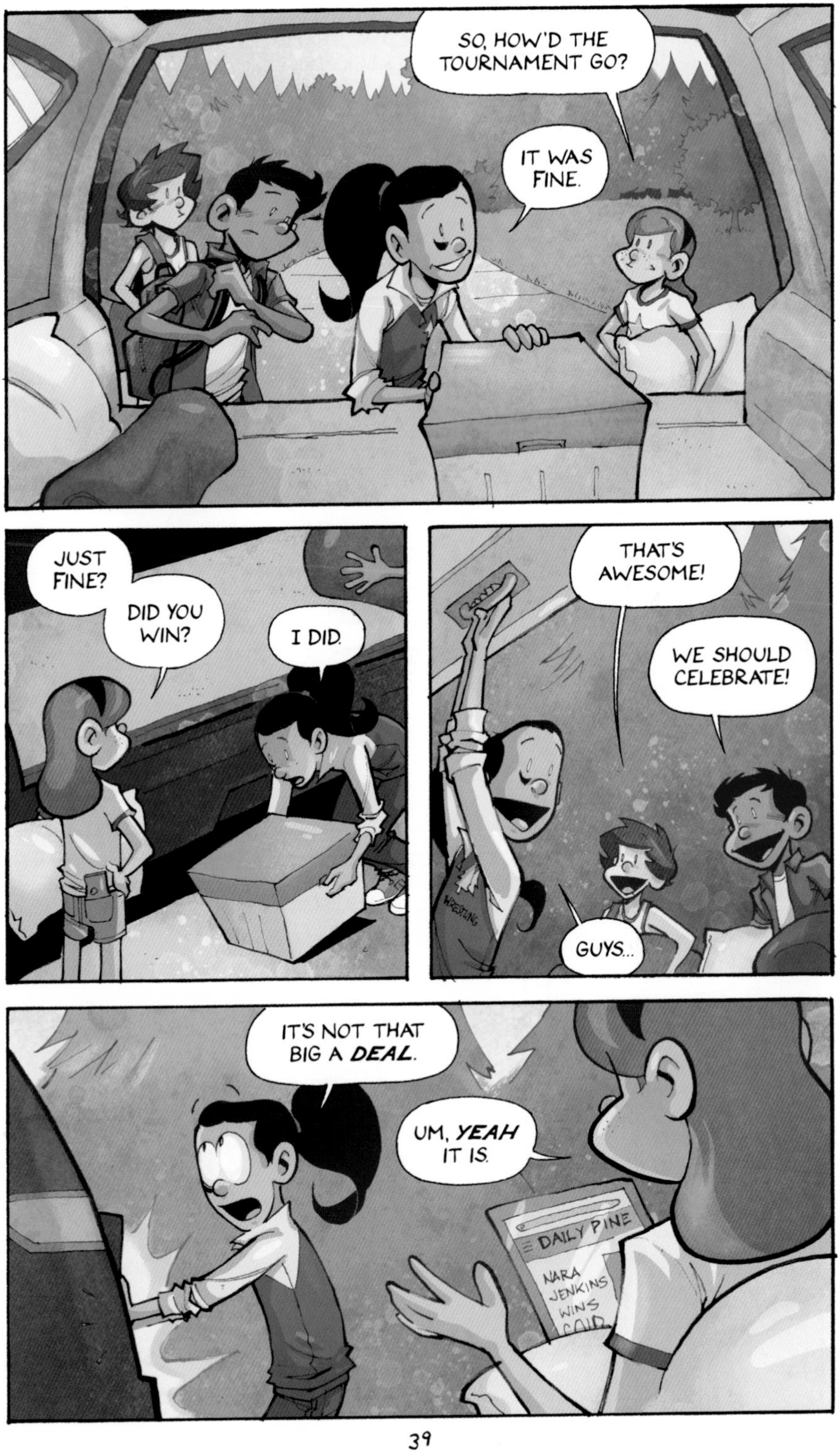
SO, HOW'D THE TOURNAMENT GO?
IT WAS FINE.
JUST FINE?
DID YOU WIN?
I DID.
THAT'S AWESOME!
WE SHOULD CELEBRATE!
GUYS...
IT'S NOT THAT BIG A *DEAL*.
UM, *YEAH* IT IS.
DAILY PINE
NARA JENKINS WINS

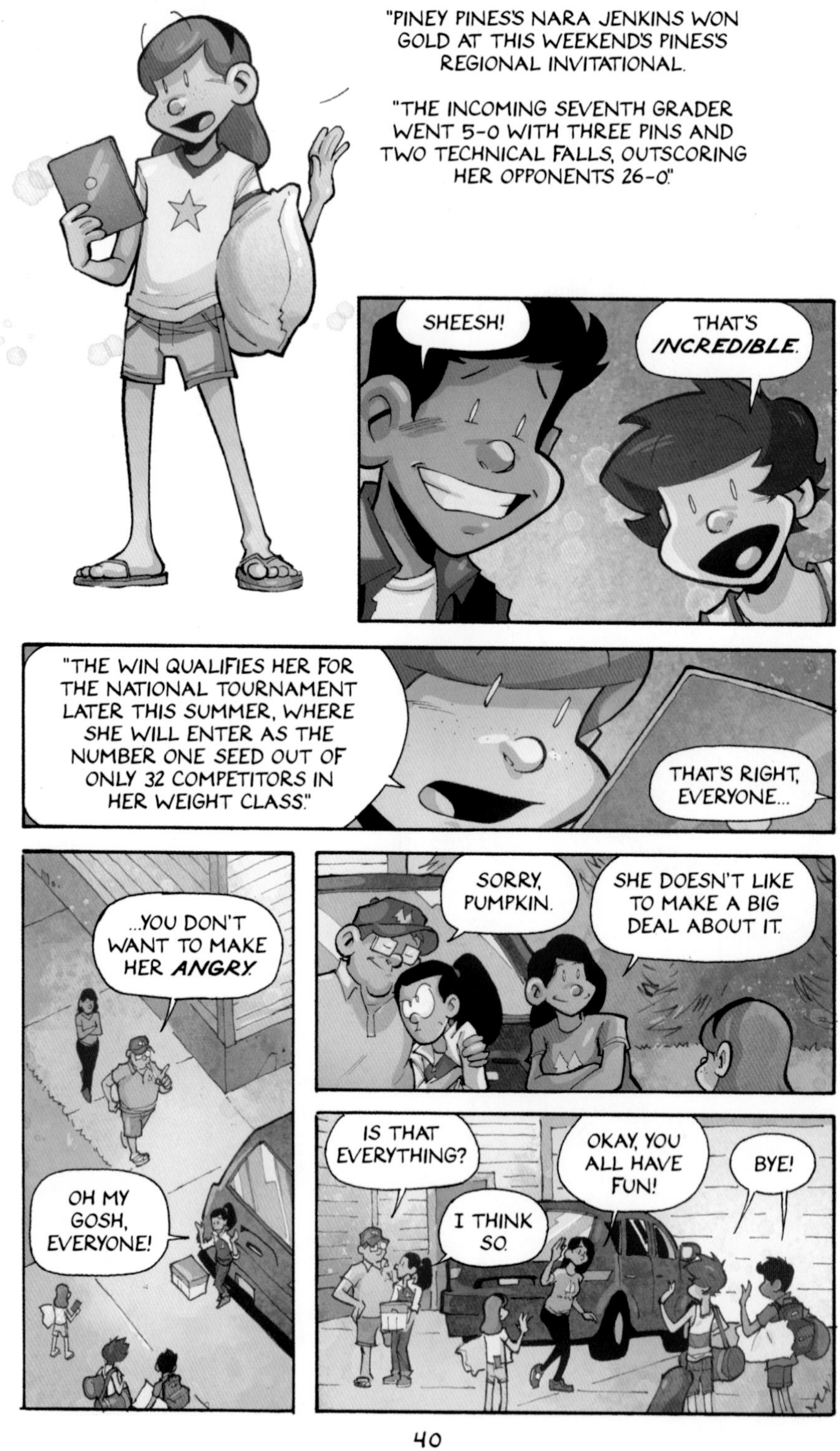
"PINEY PINES'S NARA JENKINS WON GOLD AT THIS WEEKEND'S PINES'S REGIONAL INVITATIONAL.
"THE INCOMING SEVENTH GRADER WENT 5-0 WITH THREE PINS AND TWO TECHNICAL FALLS, OUTSCORING HER OPPONENTS 26-0."
SHEESH!
THAT'S *INCREDIBLE*.
"THE WIN QUALIFIES HER FOR THE NATIONAL TOURNAMENT LATER THIS SUMMER, WHERE SHE WILL ENTER AS THE NUMBER ONE SEED OUT OF ONLY 32 COMPETITORS IN HER WEIGHT CLASS."
THAT'S RIGHT, EVERYONE...
...YOU DON'T WANT TO MAKE HER **ANGRY**.
OH MY GOSH, EVERYONE!
SORRY, PUMPKIN.
SHE DOESN'T LIKE TO MAKE A BIG DEAL ABOUT IT.
IS THAT EVERYTHING?
I THINK SO.
OKAY, YOU ALL HAVE FUN!
BYE!

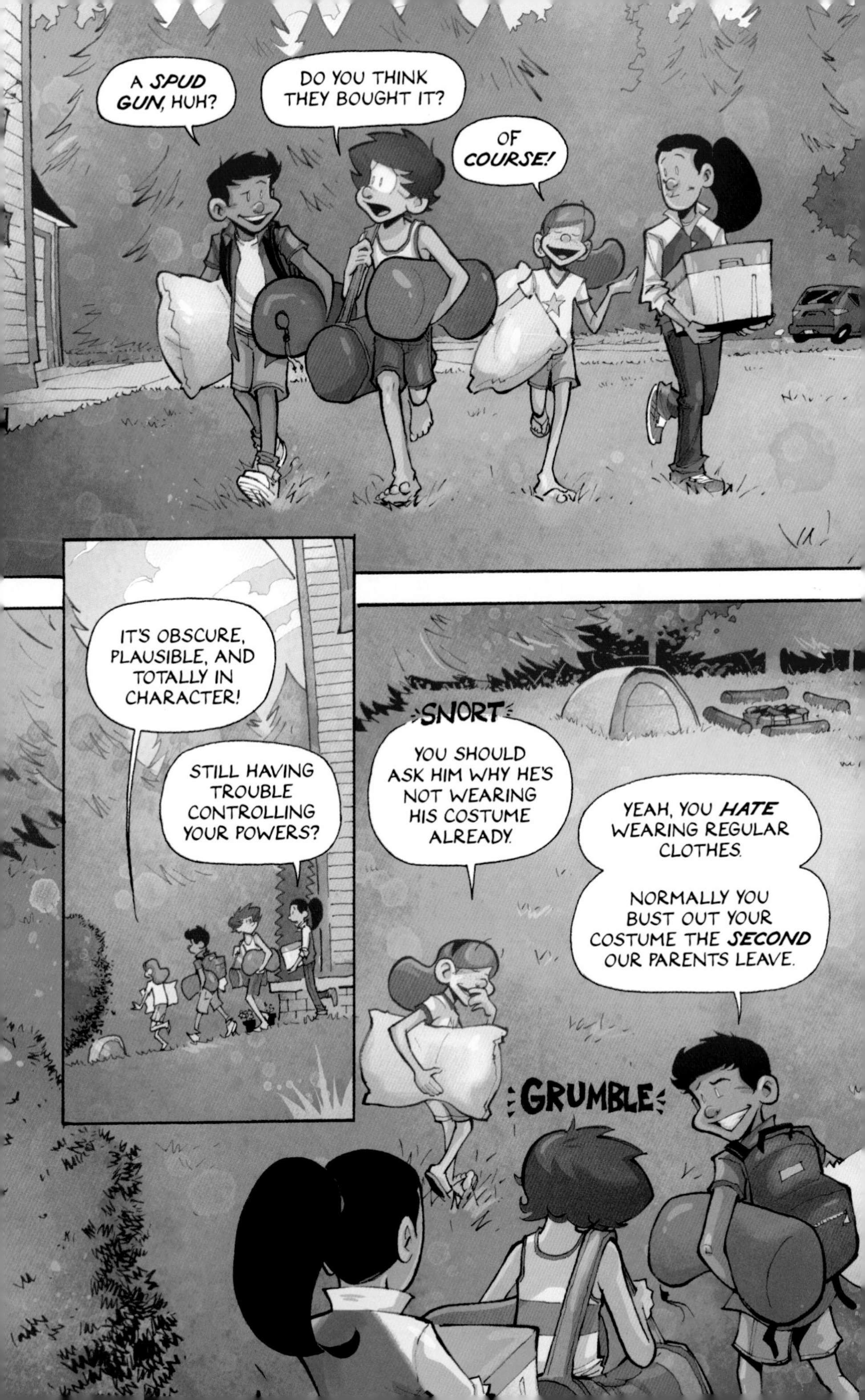
A SPUD GUN, HUH?
DO YOU THINK THEY BOUGHT IT?
OF COURSE!
IT'S OBSCURE, PLAUSIBLE, AND TOTALLY IN CHARACTER!
STILL HAVING TROUBLE CONTROLLING YOUR POWERS?
SNORT
YOU SHOULD ASK HIM WHY HE'S NOT WEARING HIS COSTUME ALREADY.
YEAH, YOU HATE WEARING REGULAR CLOTHES.
NORMALLY YOU BUST OUT YOUR COSTUME THE SECOND OUR PARENTS LEAVE.
GRUMBLE

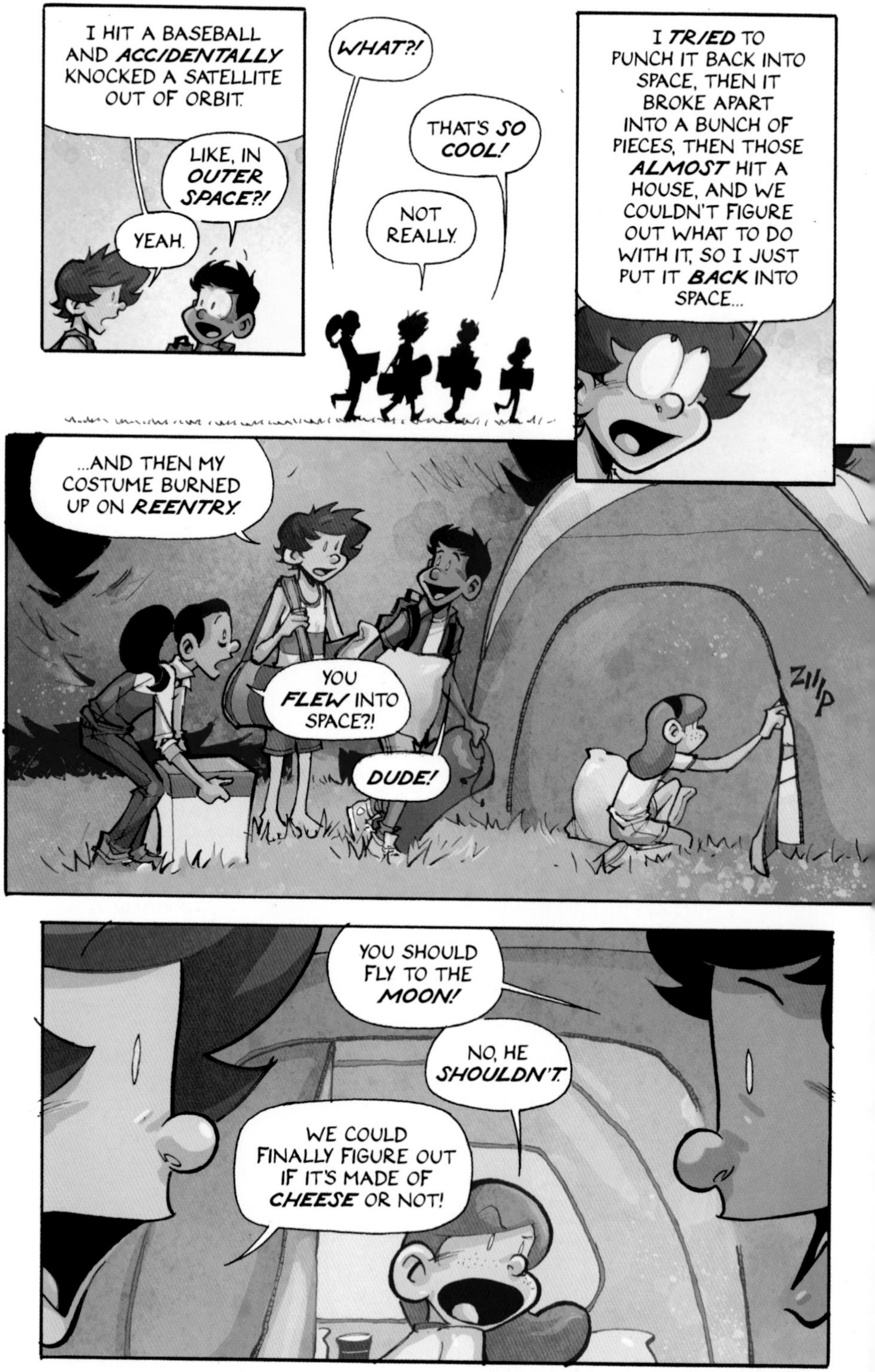

I HIT A BASEBALL AND ACCIDENTALLY KNOCKED A SATELLITE OUT OF ORBIT.
LIKE, IN OUTER SPACE?!
YEAH.
WHAT?!
THAT'S SO COOL!
NOT REALLY.
I TRIED TO PUNCH IT BACK INTO SPACE, THEN IT BROKE APART INTO A BUNCH OF PIECES, THEN THOSE ALMOST HIT A HOUSE, AND WE COULDN'T FIGURE OUT WHAT TO DO WITH IT, SO I JUST PUT IT BACK INTO SPACE...
...AND THEN MY COSTUME BURNED UP ON REENTRY.
YOU FLEW INTO SPACE?!
DUDE!
ZIIIP
YOU SHOULD FLY TO THE MOON!
NO, HE SHOULDN'T.
WE COULD FINALLY FIGURE OUT IF IT'S MADE OF CHEESE OR NOT!

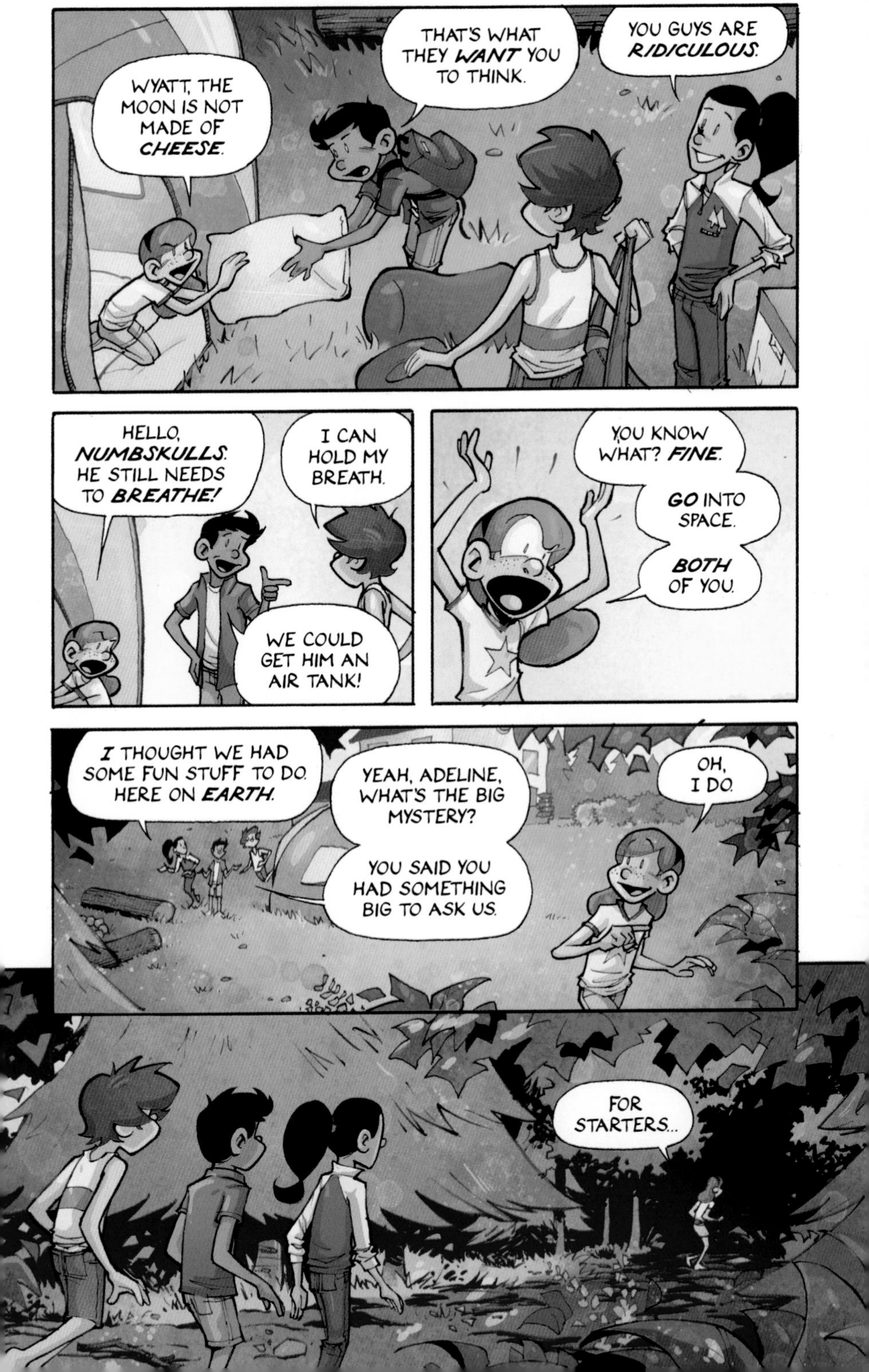
WYATT, THE MOON IS NOT MADE OF CHEESE.
THAT'S WHAT THEY WANT YOU TO THINK.
YOU GUYS ARE RIDICULOUS.
HELLO, NUMBSKULLS. HE STILL NEEDS TO BREATHE!
I CAN HOLD MY BREATH.
WE COULD GET HIM AN AIR TANK!
YOU KNOW WHAT? FINE.
GO INTO SPACE.
BOTH OF YOU.
I THOUGHT WE HAD SOME FUN STUFF TO DO. HERE ON EARTH.
YEAH, ADELINE, WHAT'S THE BIG MYSTERY?
YOU SAID YOU HAD SOMETHING BIG TO ASK US.
OH, I DO.
FOR STARTERS...

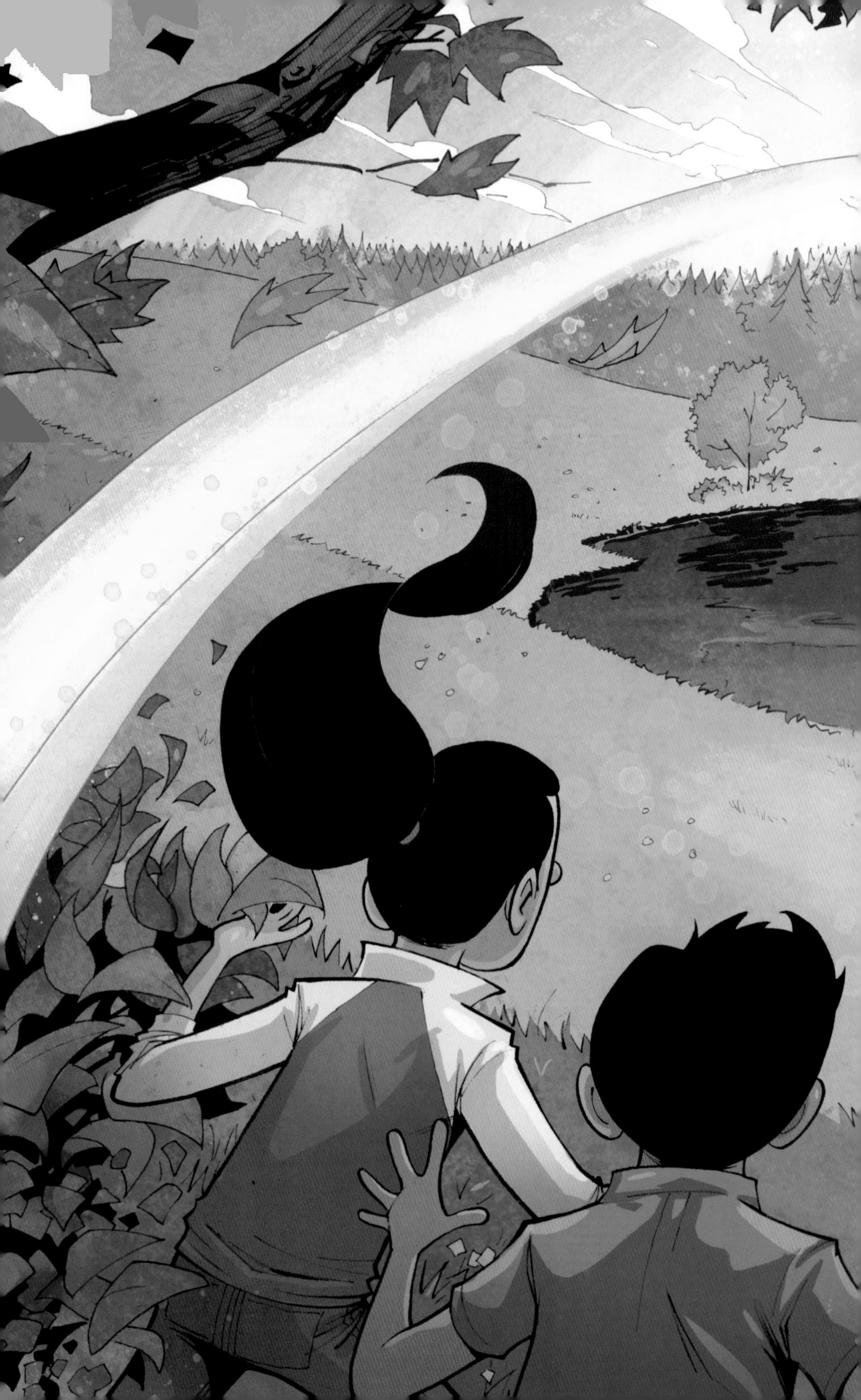

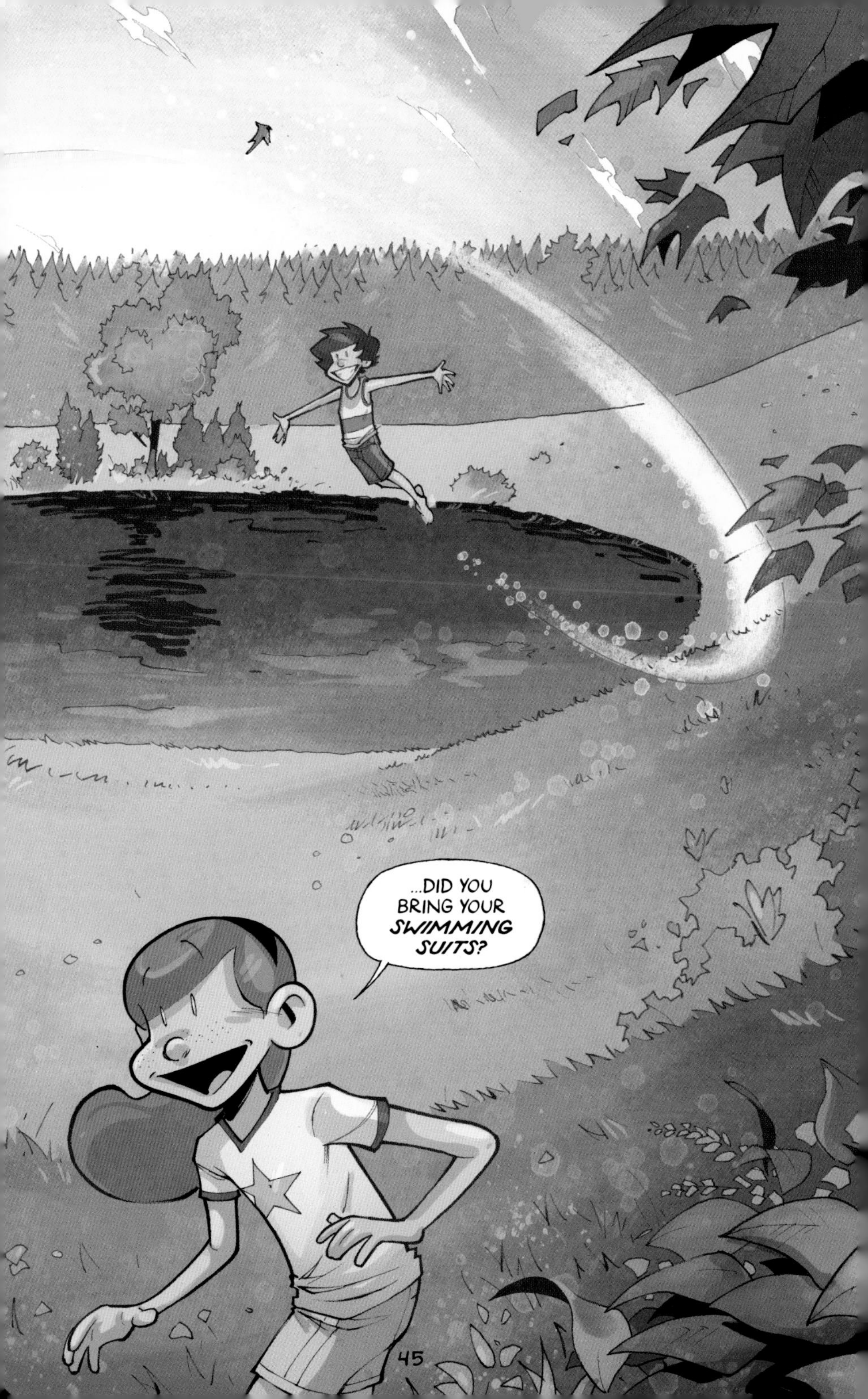
...DID YOU BRING YOUR *SWIMMING SUITS?*

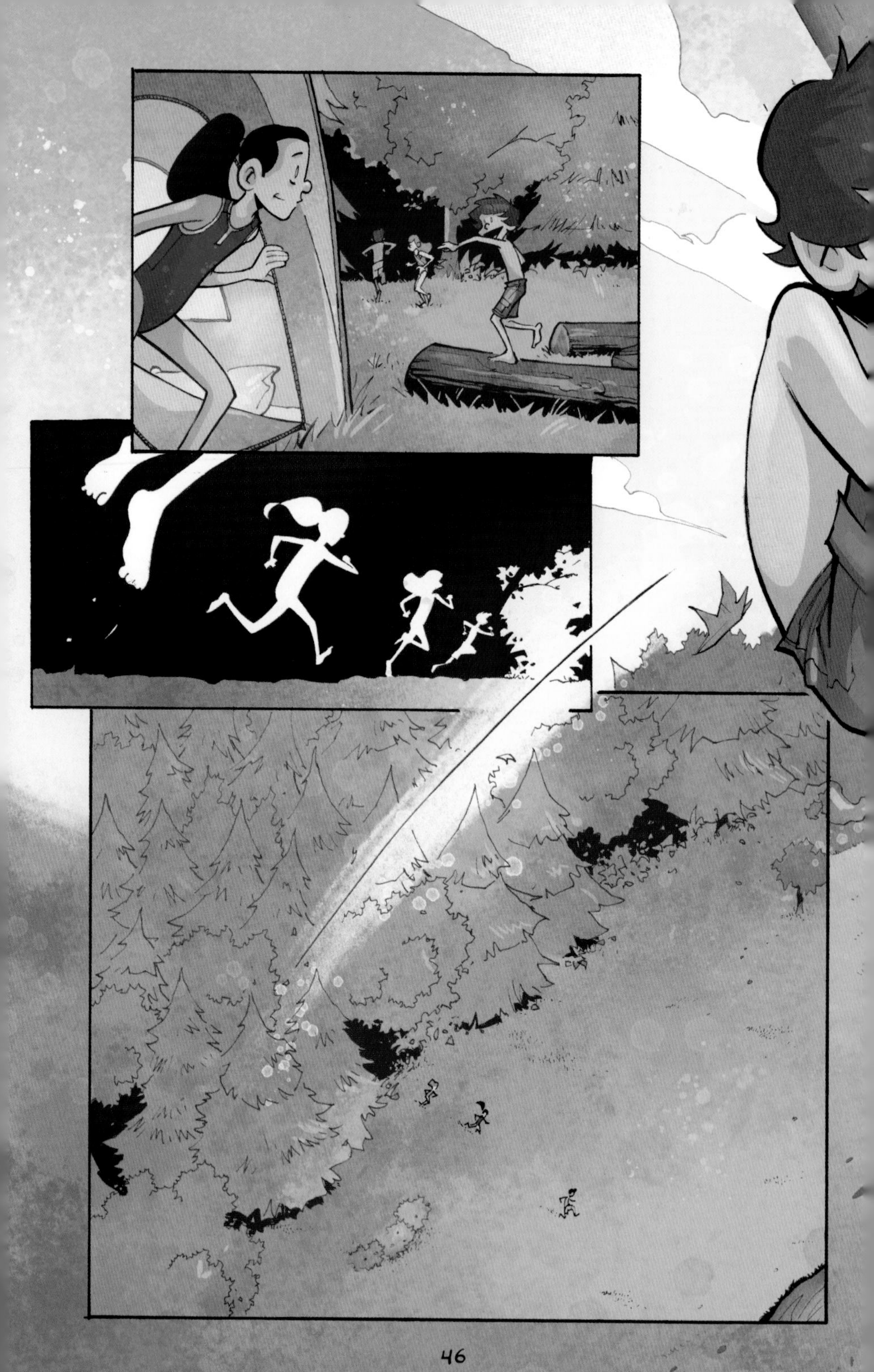

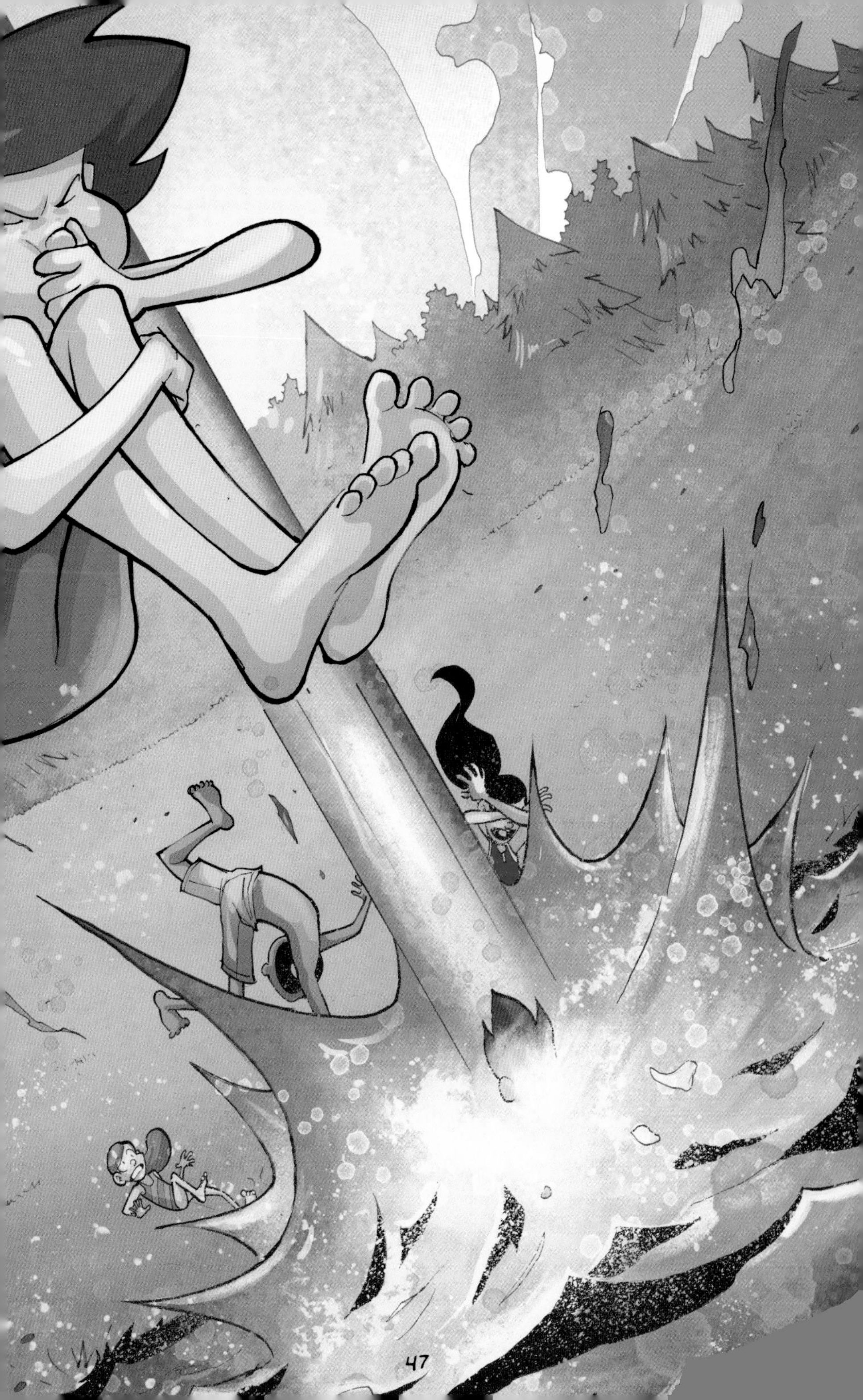

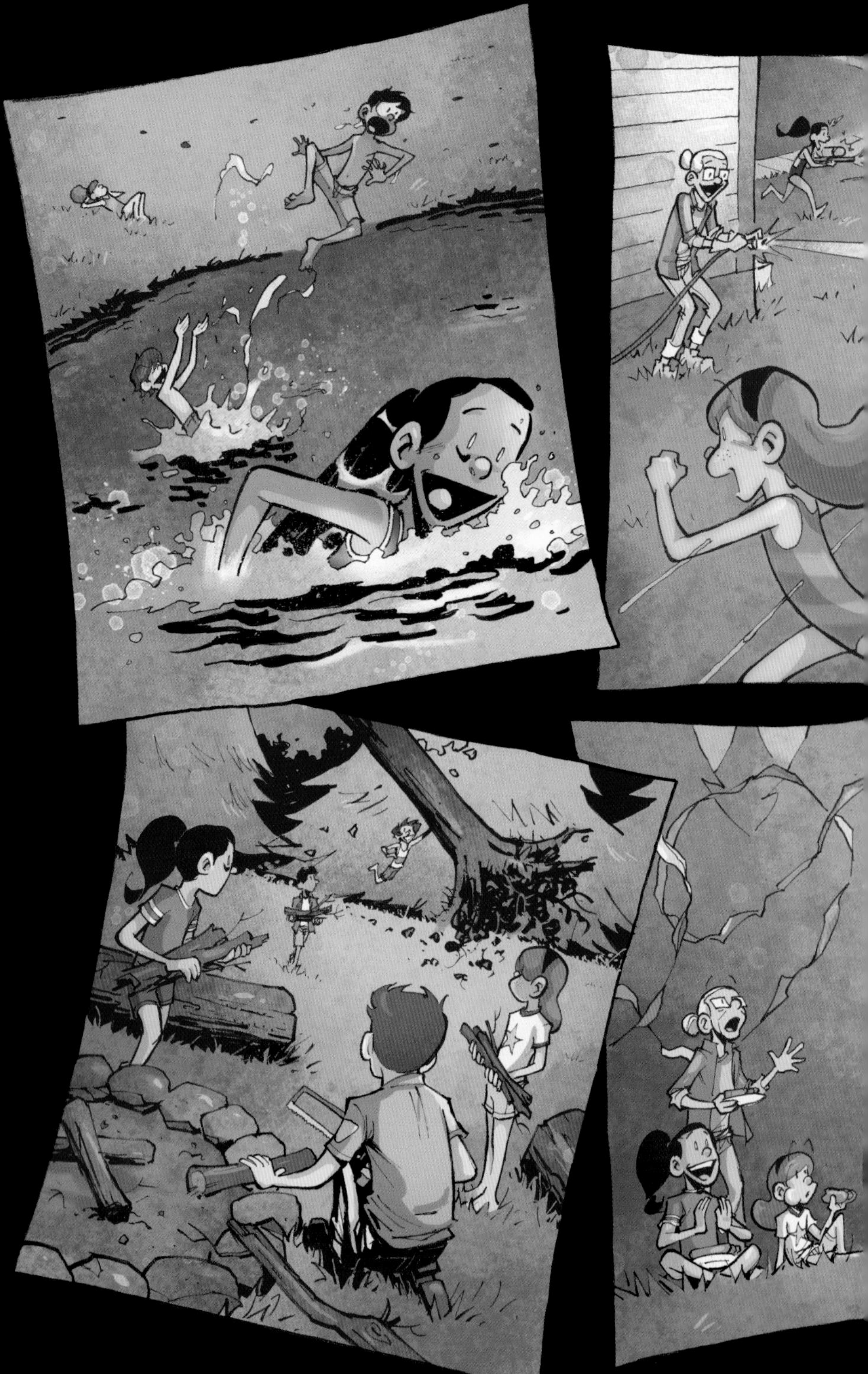

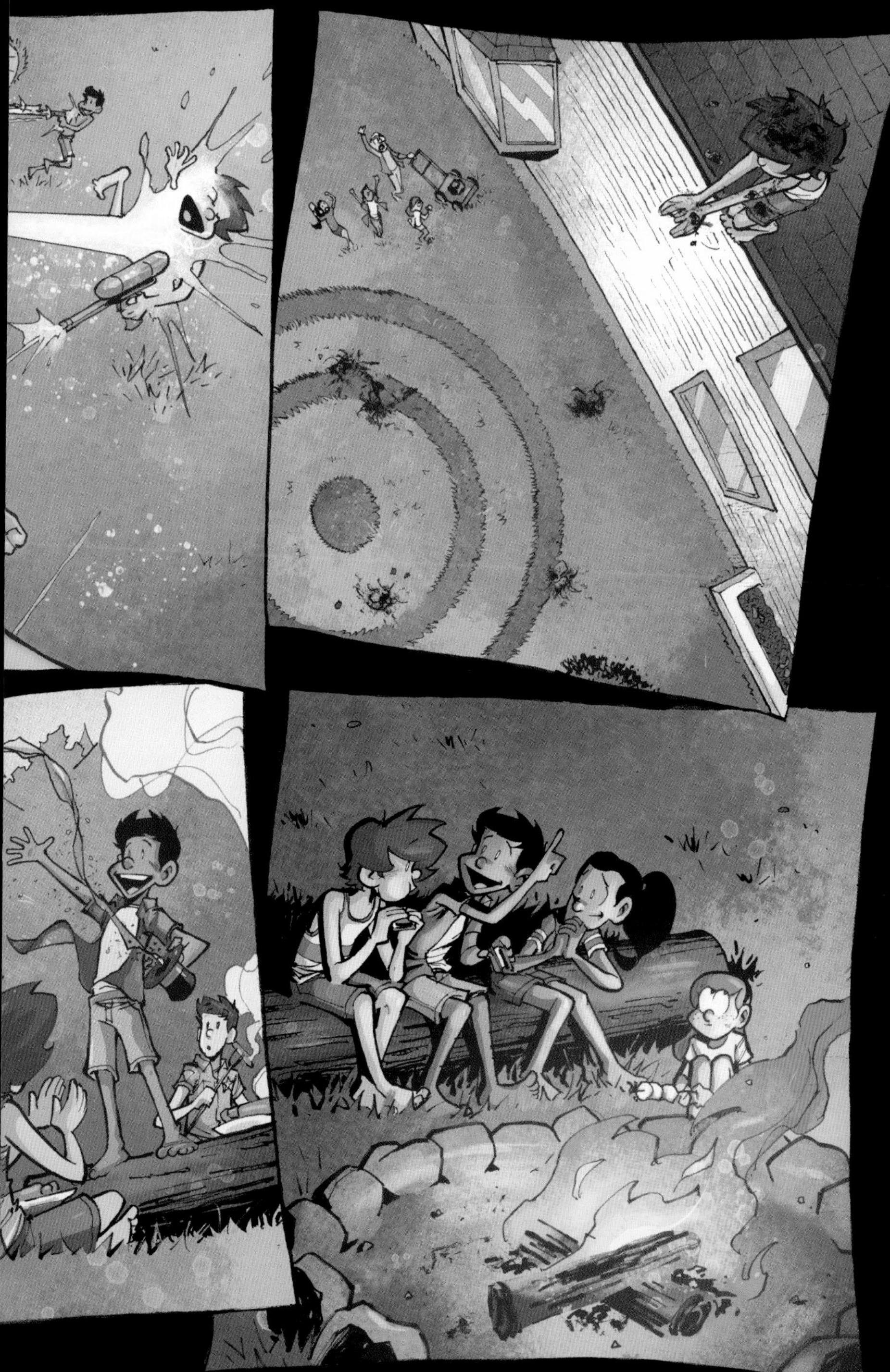

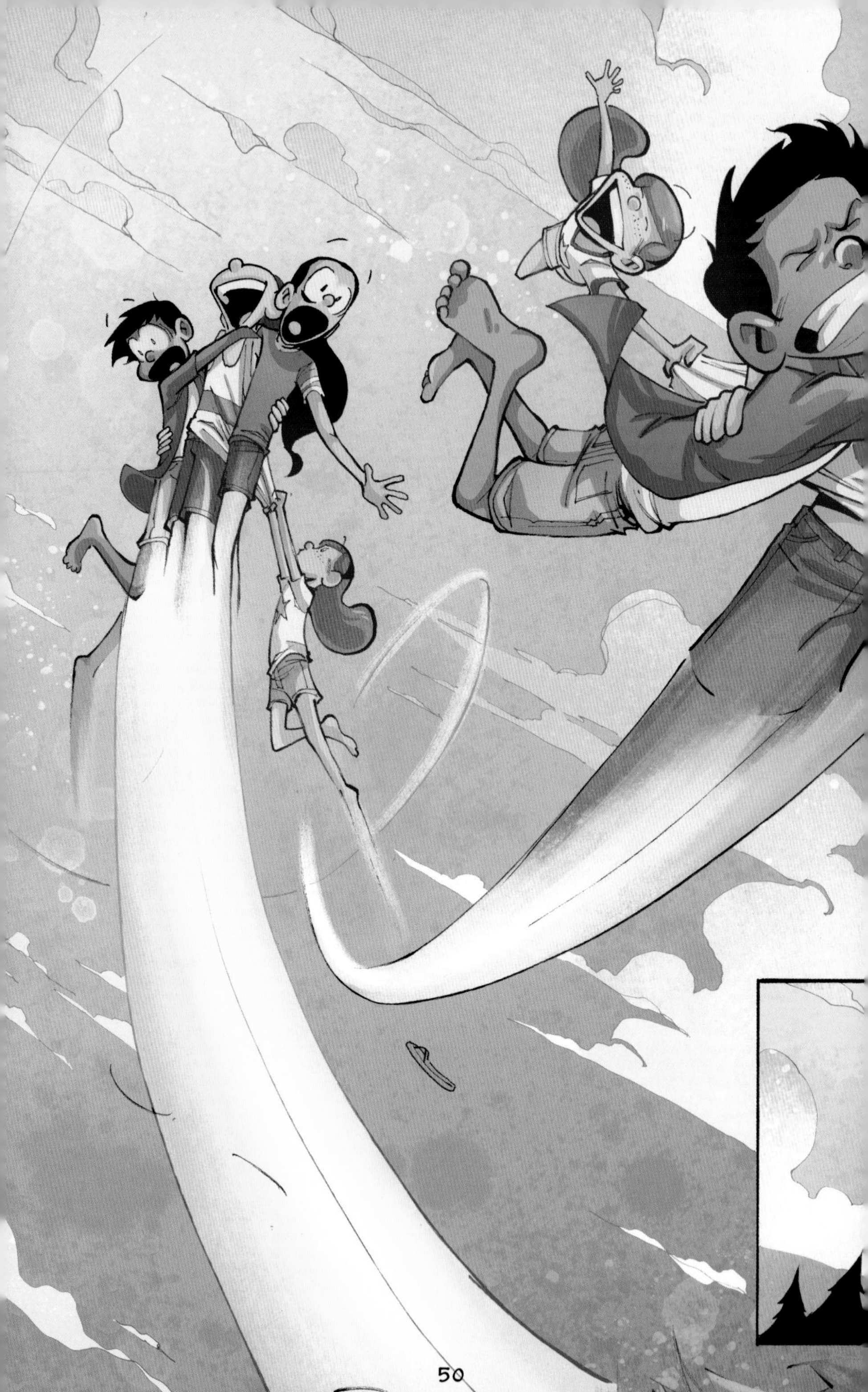

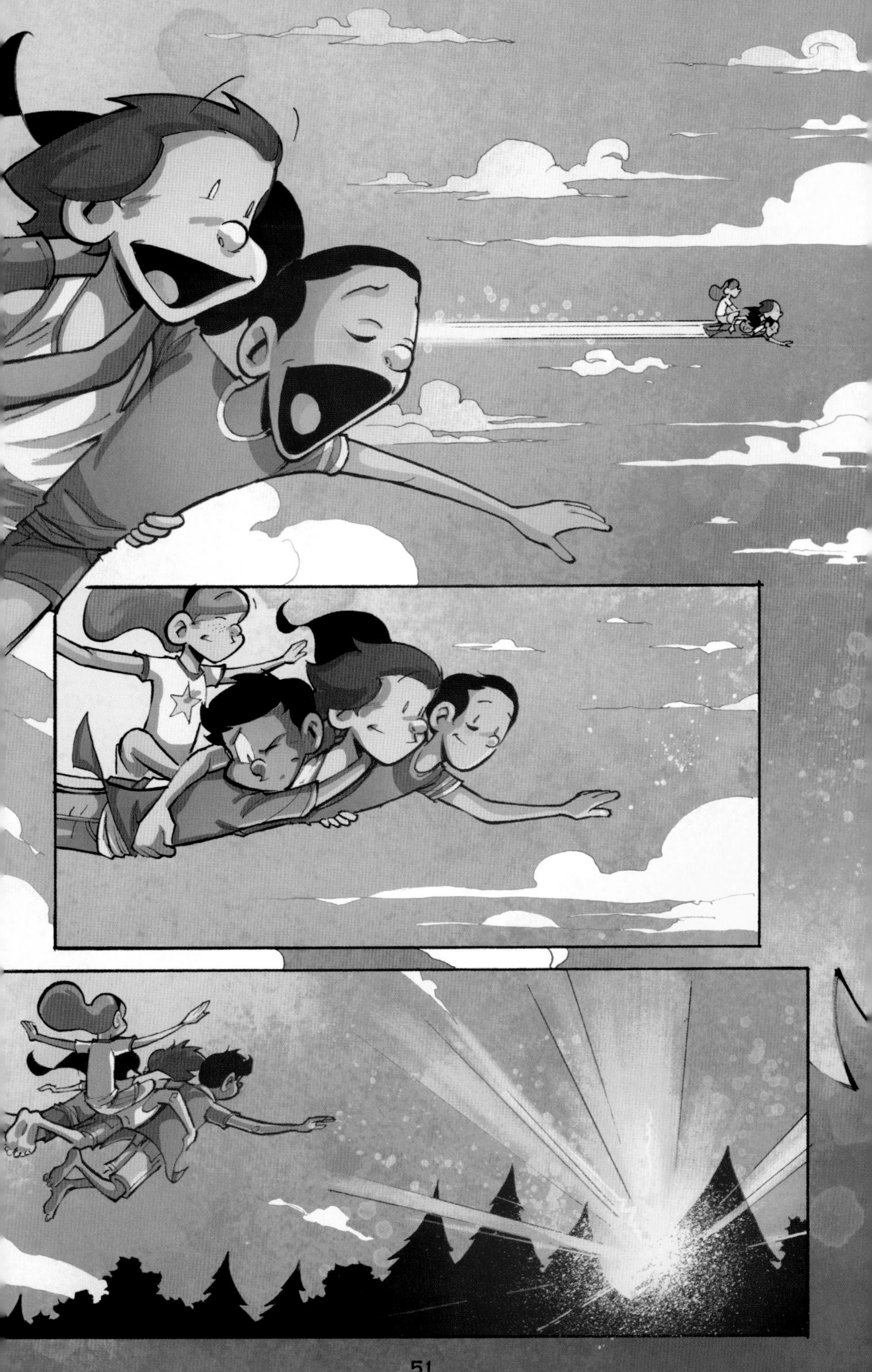

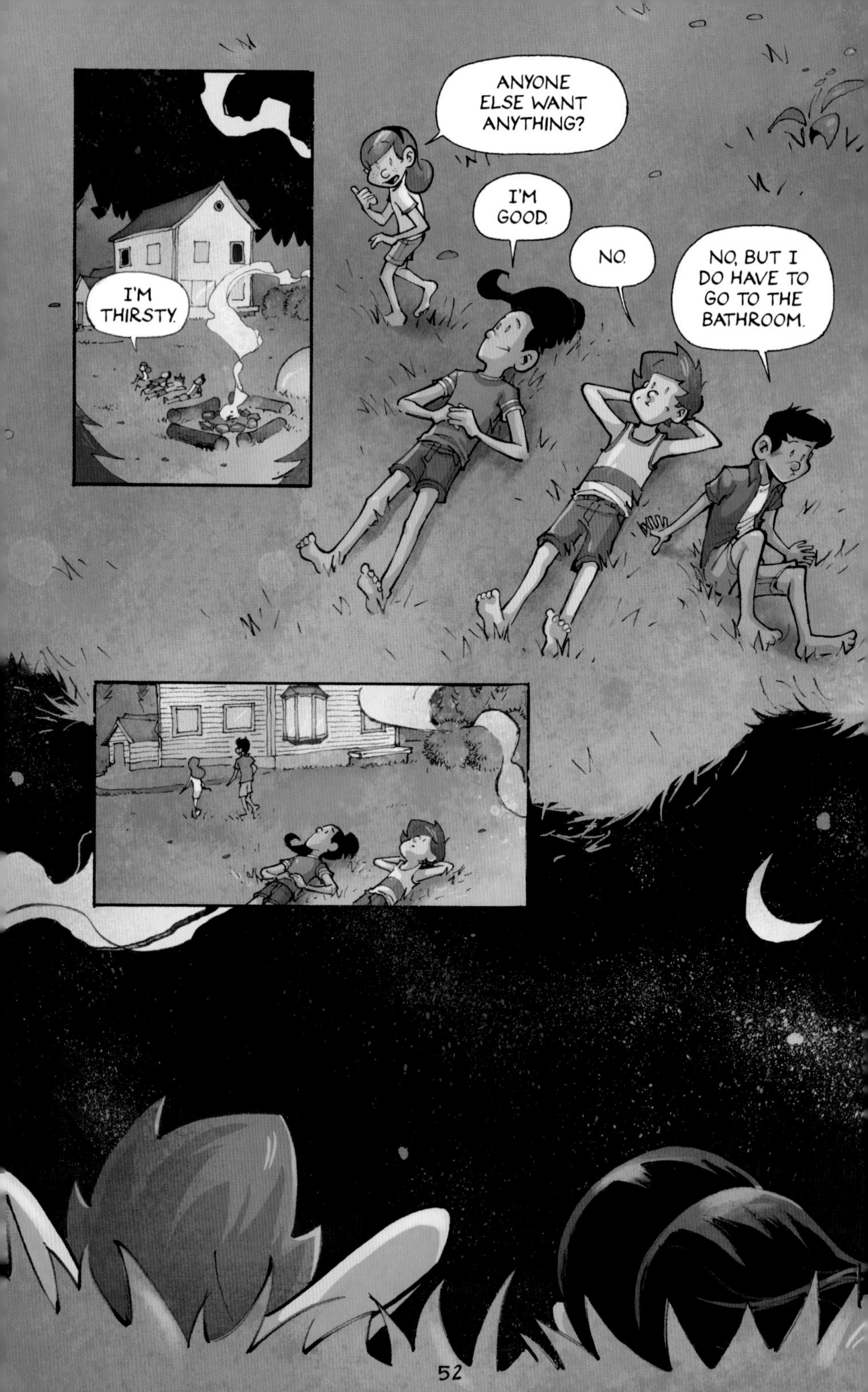
I'M THIRSTY.
ANYONE ELSE WANT ANYTHING?
I'M GOOD.
NO.
NO, BUT I DO HAVE TO GO TO THE BATHROOM.

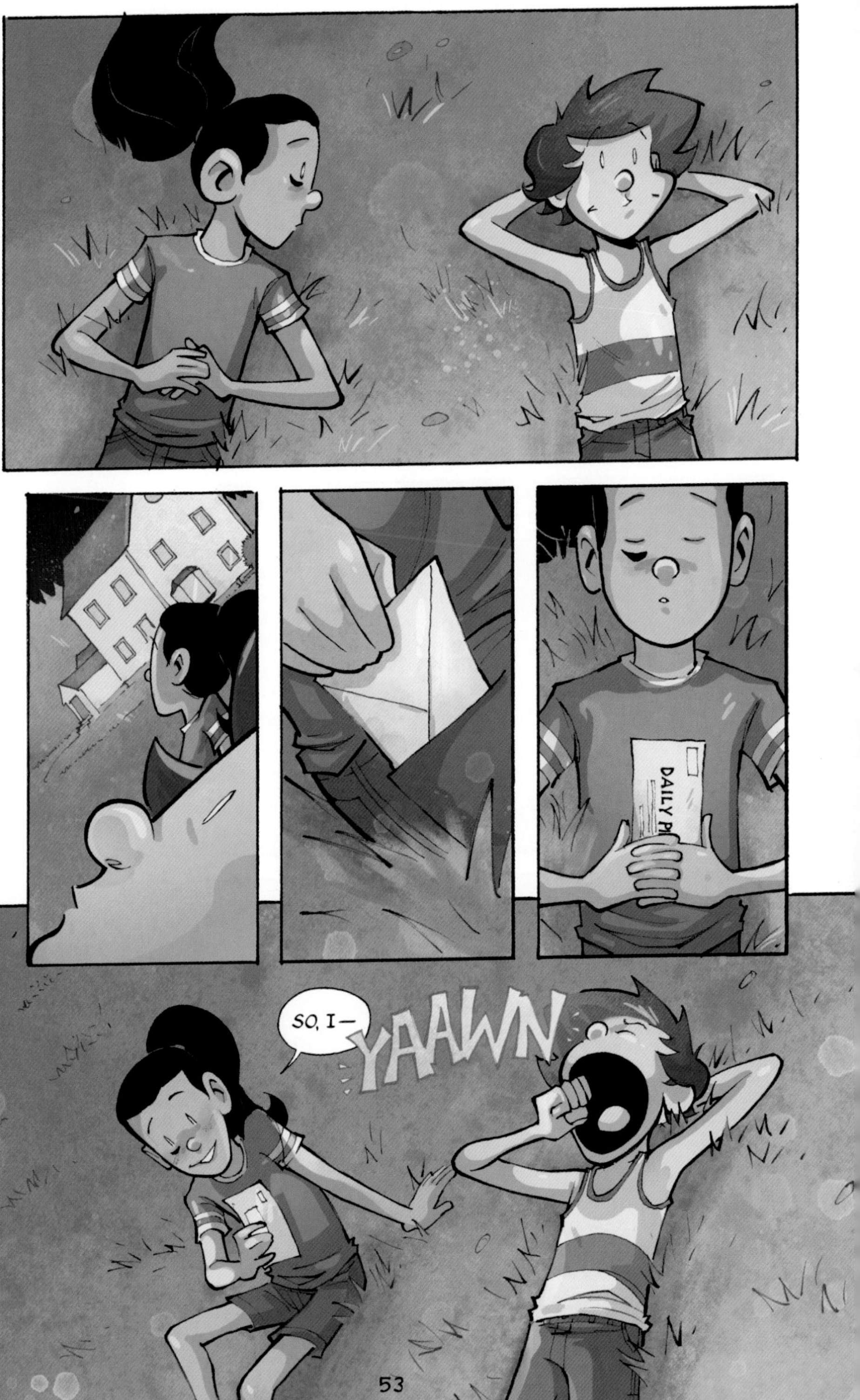
DAILY P
SO, I—
YAAWN

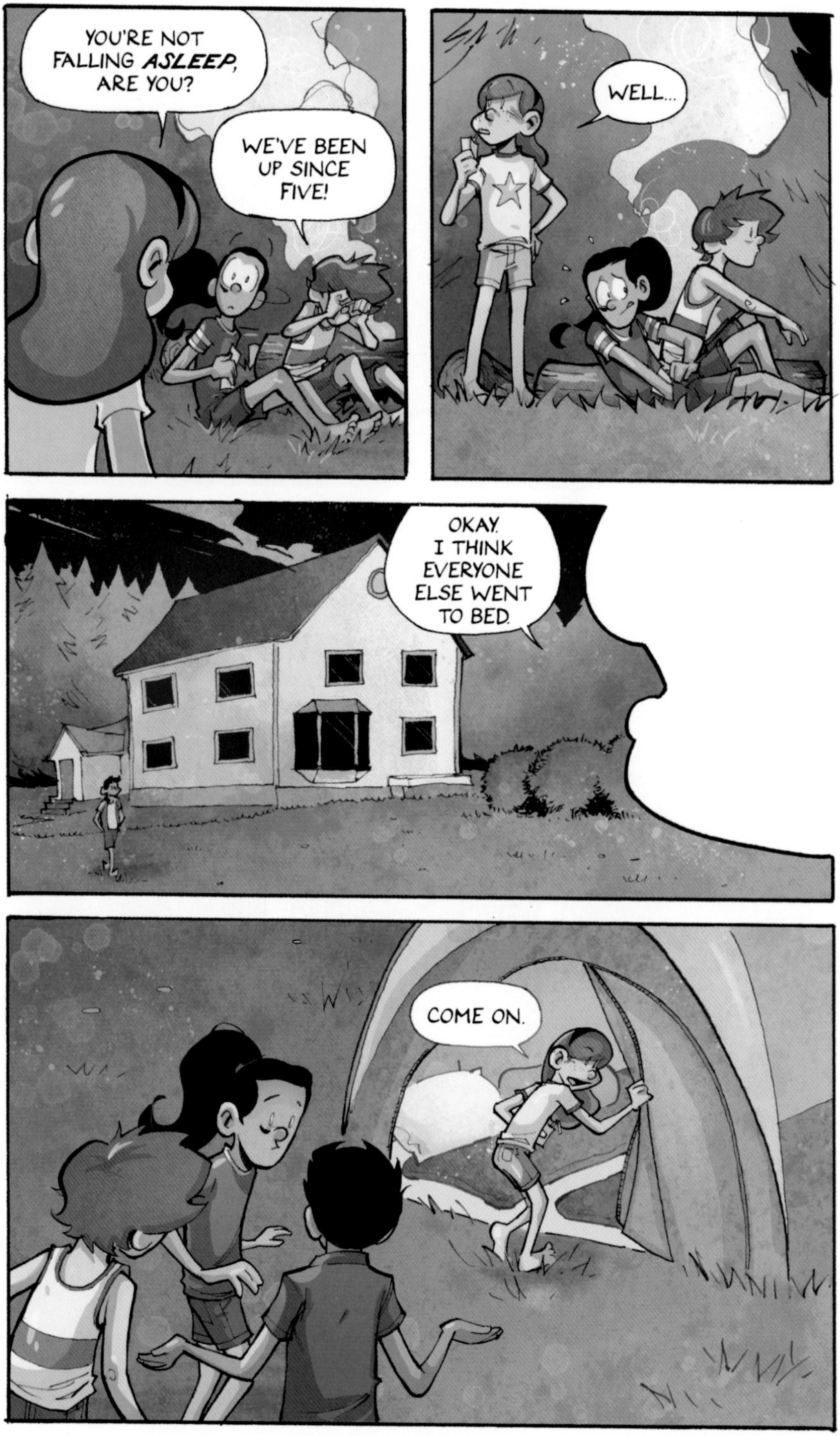
YOU'RE NOT FALLING ASLEEP, ARE YOU?
WE'VE BEEN UP SINCE FIVE!
WELL...
OKAY. I THINK EVERYONE ELSE WENT TO BED.
COME ON.

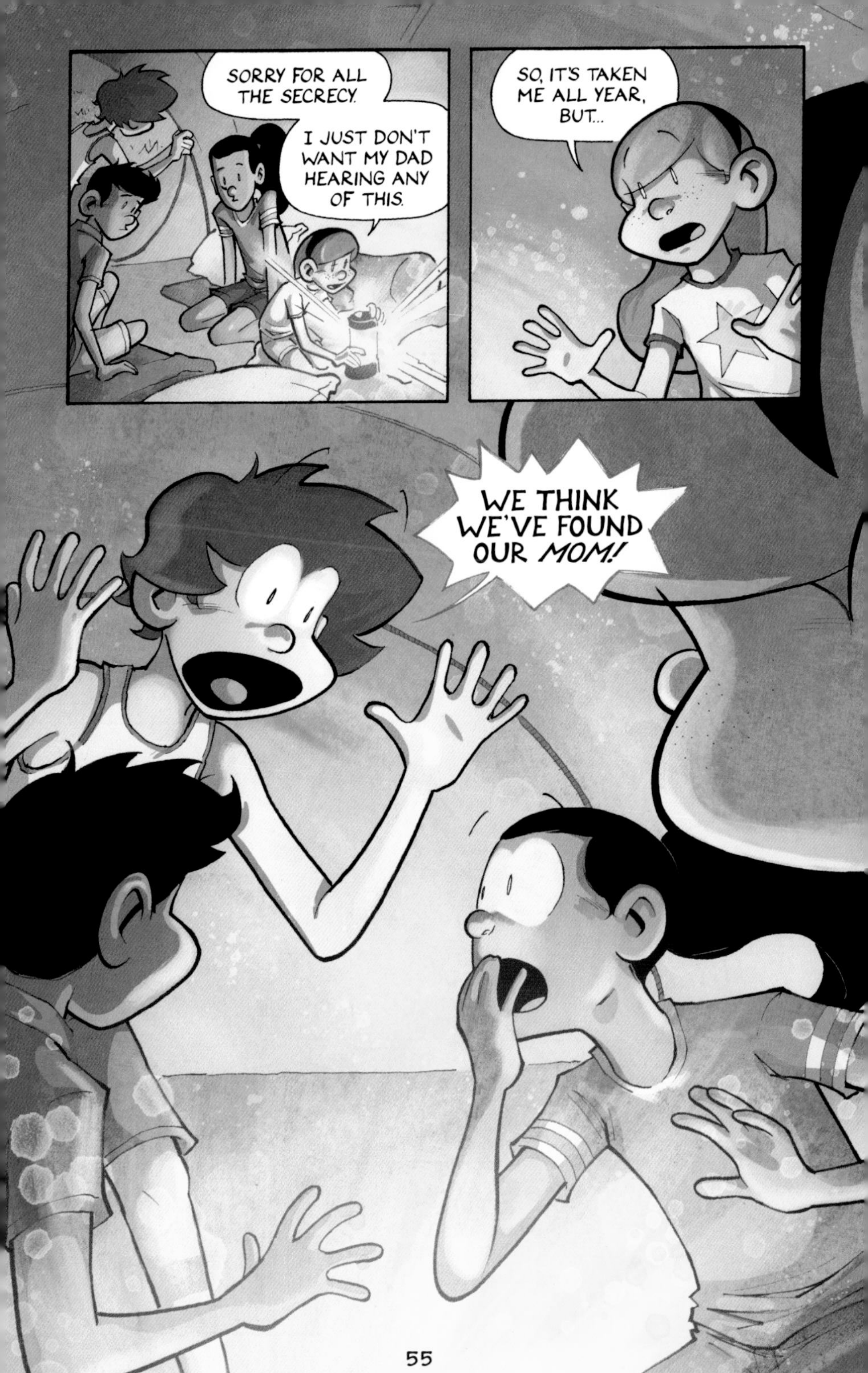
SORRY FOR ALL THE SECRECY.
I JUST DON'T WANT MY DAD HEARING ANY OF THIS.
SO, IT'S TAKEN ME ALL YEAR, BUT...
WE THINK WE'VE FOUND OUR *MOM!*

CHAPTER FOUR

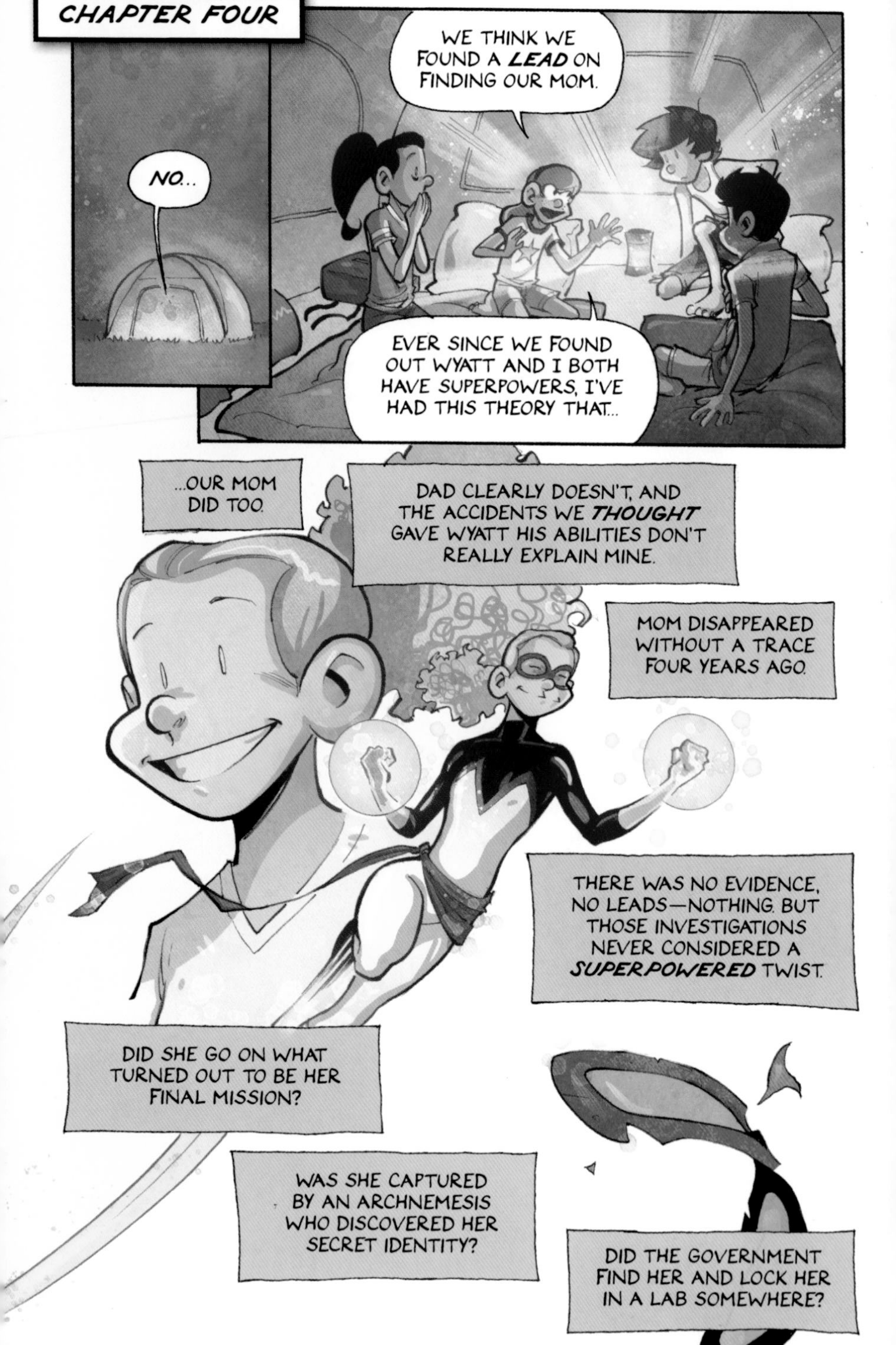
NO...
WE THINK WE FOUND A *LEAD* ON FINDING OUR MOM.
EVER SINCE WE FOUND OUT WYATT AND I BOTH HAVE SUPERPOWERS, I'VE HAD THIS THEORY THAT...
...OUR MOM DID TOO.
DAD CLEARLY DOESN'T, AND THE ACCIDENTS WE *THOUGHT* GAVE WYATT HIS ABILITIES DON'T REALLY EXPLAIN MINE.
MOM DISAPPEARED WITHOUT A TRACE FOUR YEARS AGO.
THERE WAS NO EVIDENCE, NO LEADS—NOTHING. BUT THOSE INVESTIGATIONS NEVER CONSIDERED A *SUPERPOWERED* TWIST.
DID SHE GO ON WHAT TURNED OUT TO BE HER FINAL MISSION?
WAS SHE CAPTURED BY AN ARCHNEMESIS WHO DISCOVERED HER SECRET IDENTITY?
DID THE GOVERNMENT FIND HER AND LOCK HER IN A LAB SOMEWHERE?

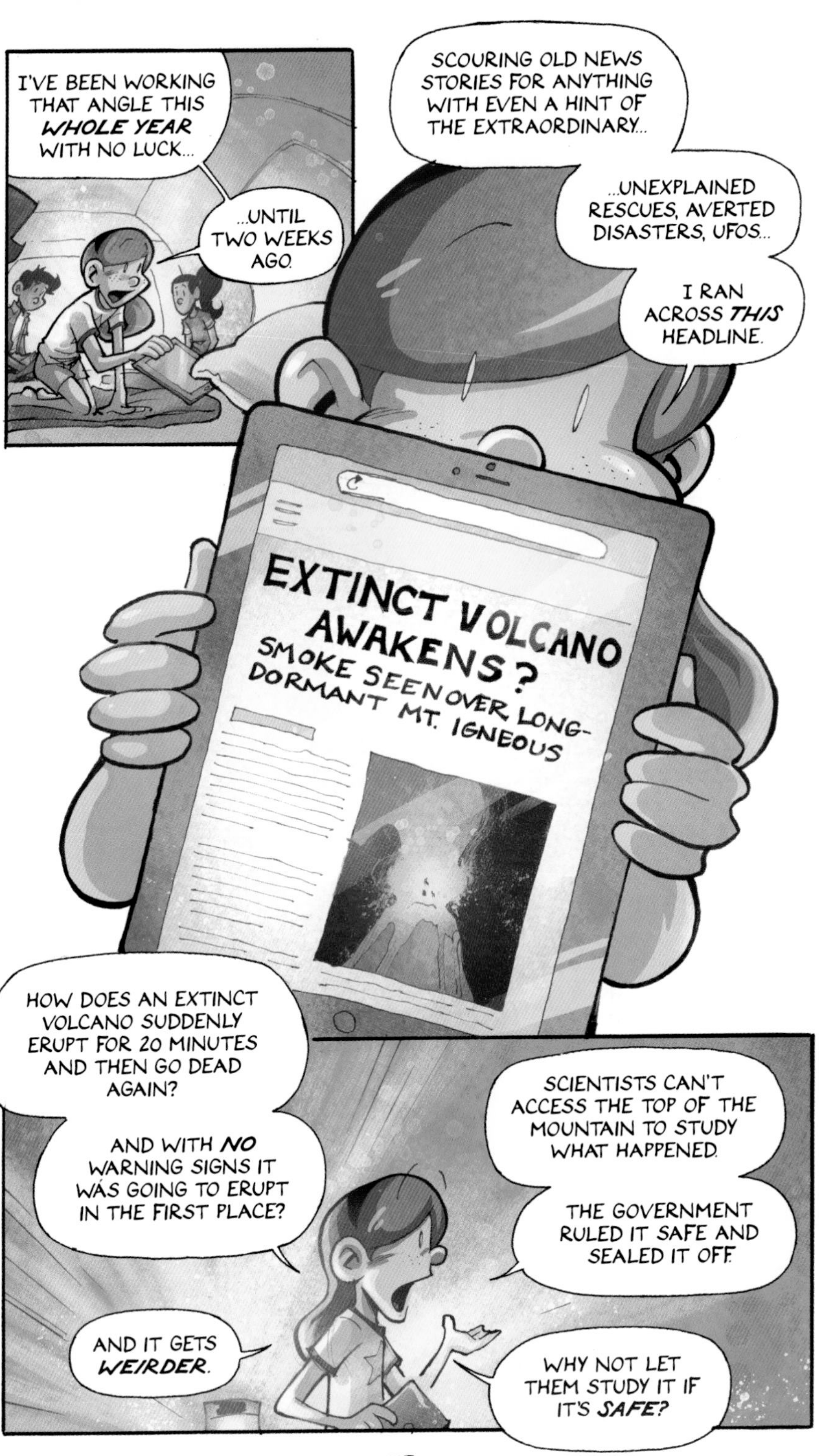
I'VE BEEN WORKING THAT ANGLE THIS WHOLE YEAR WITH NO LUCK...
...UNTIL TWO WEEKS AGO.
SCOURING OLD NEWS STORIES FOR ANYTHING WITH EVEN A HINT OF THE EXTRAORDINARY...
...UNEXPLAINED RESCUES, AVERTED DISASTERS, UFOS...
I RAN ACROSS THIS HEADLINE.
EXTINCT VOLCANO AWAKENS?
SMOKE SEEN OVER LONG-DORMANT MT. IGNEOUS
HOW DOES AN EXTINCT VOLCANO SUDDENLY ERUPT FOR 20 MINUTES AND THEN GO DEAD AGAIN?
AND WITH NO WARNING SIGNS IT WAS GOING TO ERUPT IN THE FIRST PLACE?
SCIENTISTS CAN'T ACCESS THE TOP OF THE MOUNTAIN TO STUDY WHAT HAPPENED.
THE GOVERNMENT RULED IT SAFE AND SEALED IT OFF.
AND IT GETS WEIRDER.
WHY NOT LET THEM STUDY IT IF IT'S SAFE?

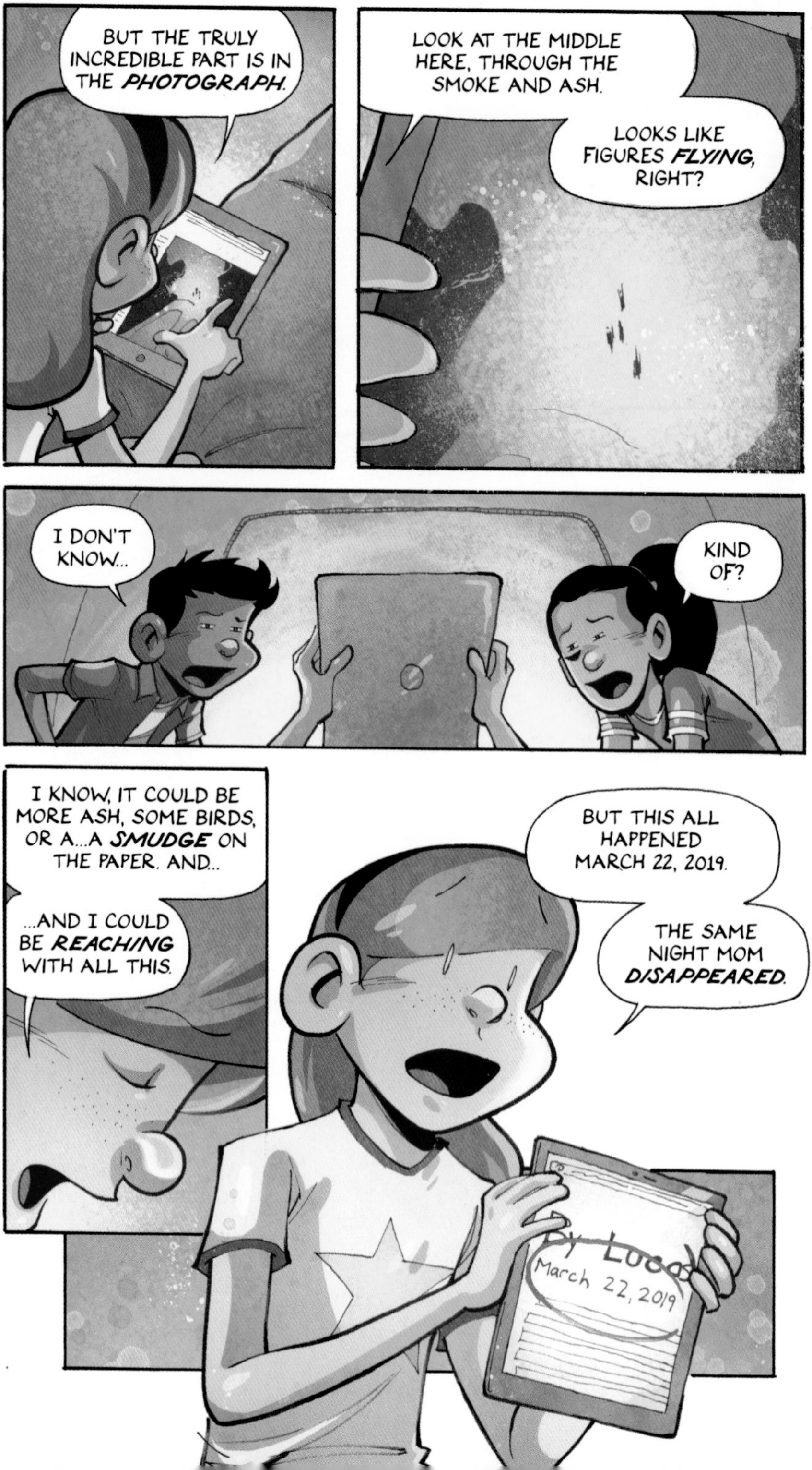
BUT THE TRULY INCREDIBLE PART IS IN THE PHOTOGRAPH.
LOOK AT THE MIDDLE HERE, THROUGH THE SMOKE AND ASH.
LOOKS LIKE FIGURES FLYING, RIGHT?
I DON'T KNOW...
KIND OF?
I KNOW, IT COULD BE MORE ASH, SOME BIRDS, OR A...A SMUDGE ON THE PAPER. AND...
...AND I COULD BE REACHING WITH ALL THIS.
BUT THIS ALL HAPPENED MARCH 22, 2019.
THE SAME NIGHT MOM DISAPPEARED.
By Lucas
March 22, 2019

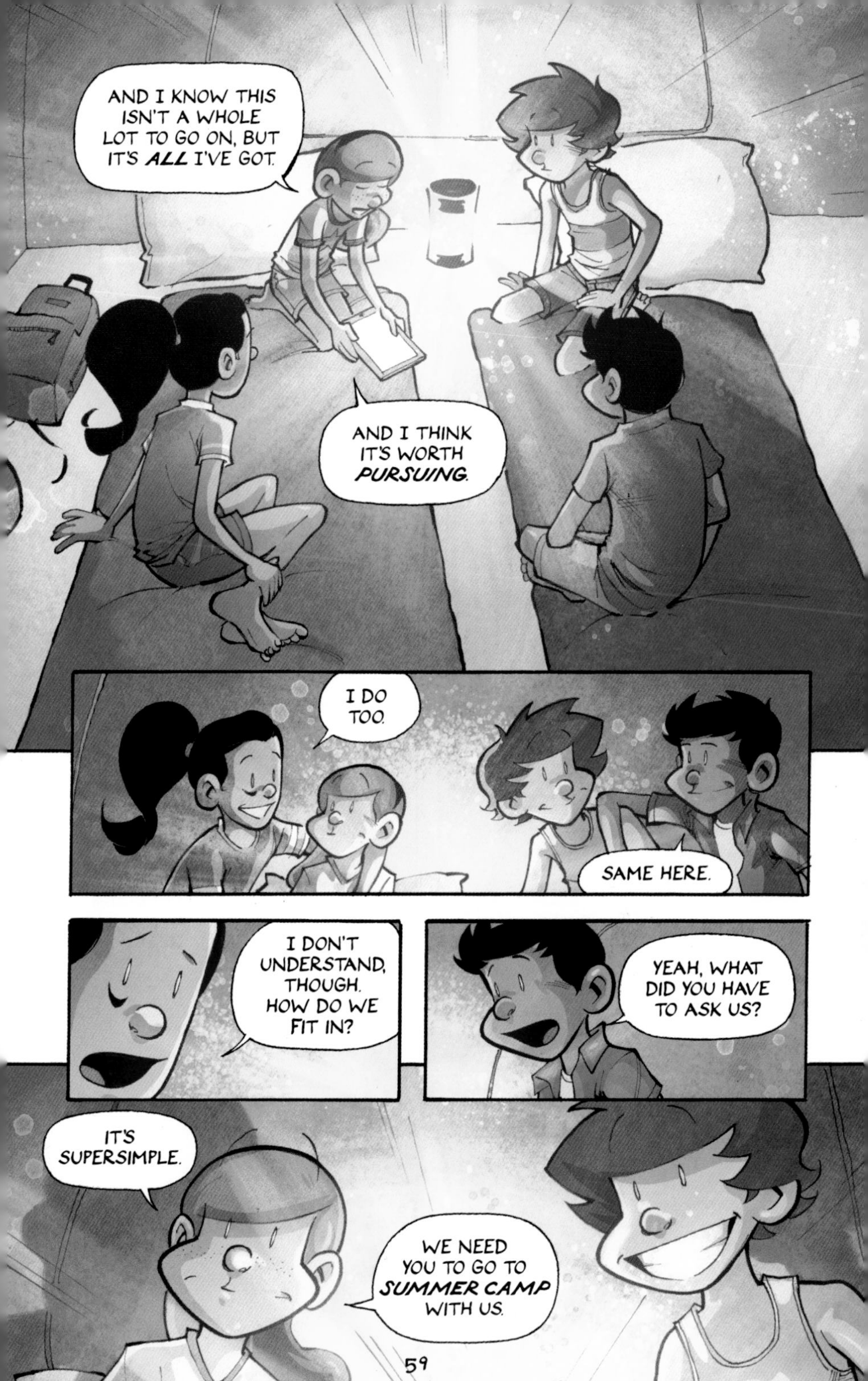
AND I KNOW THIS ISN'T A WHOLE LOT TO GO ON, BUT IT'S ALL I'VE GOT.
AND I THINK IT'S WORTH PURSUING.
I DO TOO.
SAME HERE.
I DON'T UNDERSTAND, THOUGH. HOW DO WE FIT IN?
YEAH, WHAT DID YOU HAVE TO ASK US?
IT'S SUPERSIMPLE.
WE NEED YOU TO GO TO SUMMER CAMP WITH US.

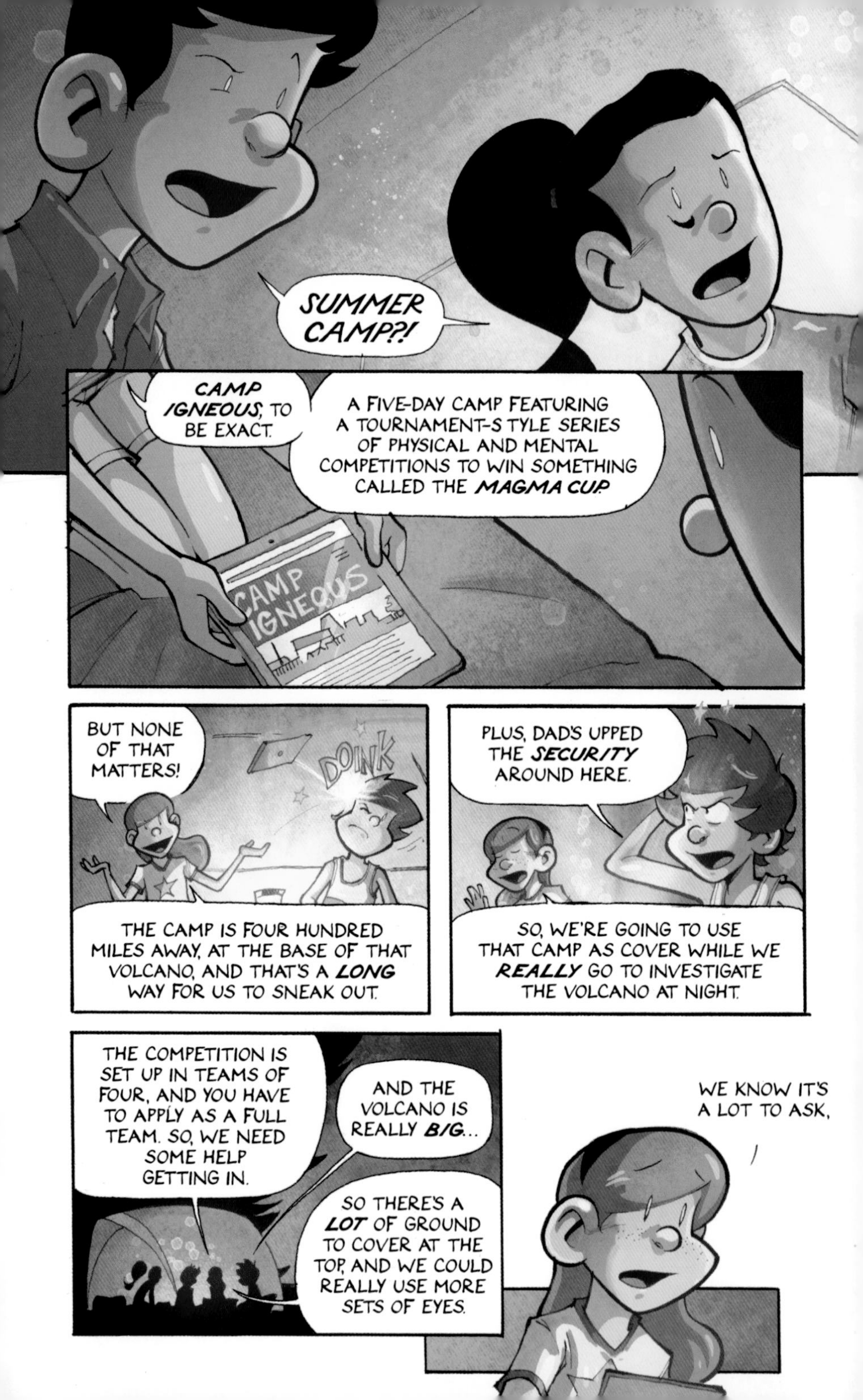
SUMMER CAMP?!
CAMP IGNEOUS, TO BE EXACT.
A FIVE-DAY CAMP FEATURING A TOURNAMENT-STYLE SERIES OF PHYSICAL AND MENTAL COMPETITIONS TO WIN SOMETHING CALLED THE MAGMA CUP.
CAMP IGNEOUS
BUT NONE OF THAT MATTERS!
DOINK
THE CAMP IS FOUR HUNDRED MILES AWAY, AT THE BASE OF THAT VOLCANO, AND THAT'S A LONG WAY FOR US TO SNEAK OUT.
PLUS, DAD'S UPPED THE SECURITY AROUND HERE.
SO, WE'RE GOING TO USE THAT CAMP AS COVER WHILE WE REALLY GO TO INVESTIGATE THE VOLCANO AT NIGHT.
THE COMPETITION IS SET UP IN TEAMS OF FOUR, AND YOU HAVE TO APPLY AS A FULL TEAM. SO, WE NEED SOME HELP GETTING IN.
AND THE VOLCANO IS REALLY BIG...
SO THERE'S A LOT OF GROUND TO COVER AT THE TOP, AND WE COULD REALLY USE MORE SETS OF EYES.
WE KNOW IT'S A LOT TO ASK,

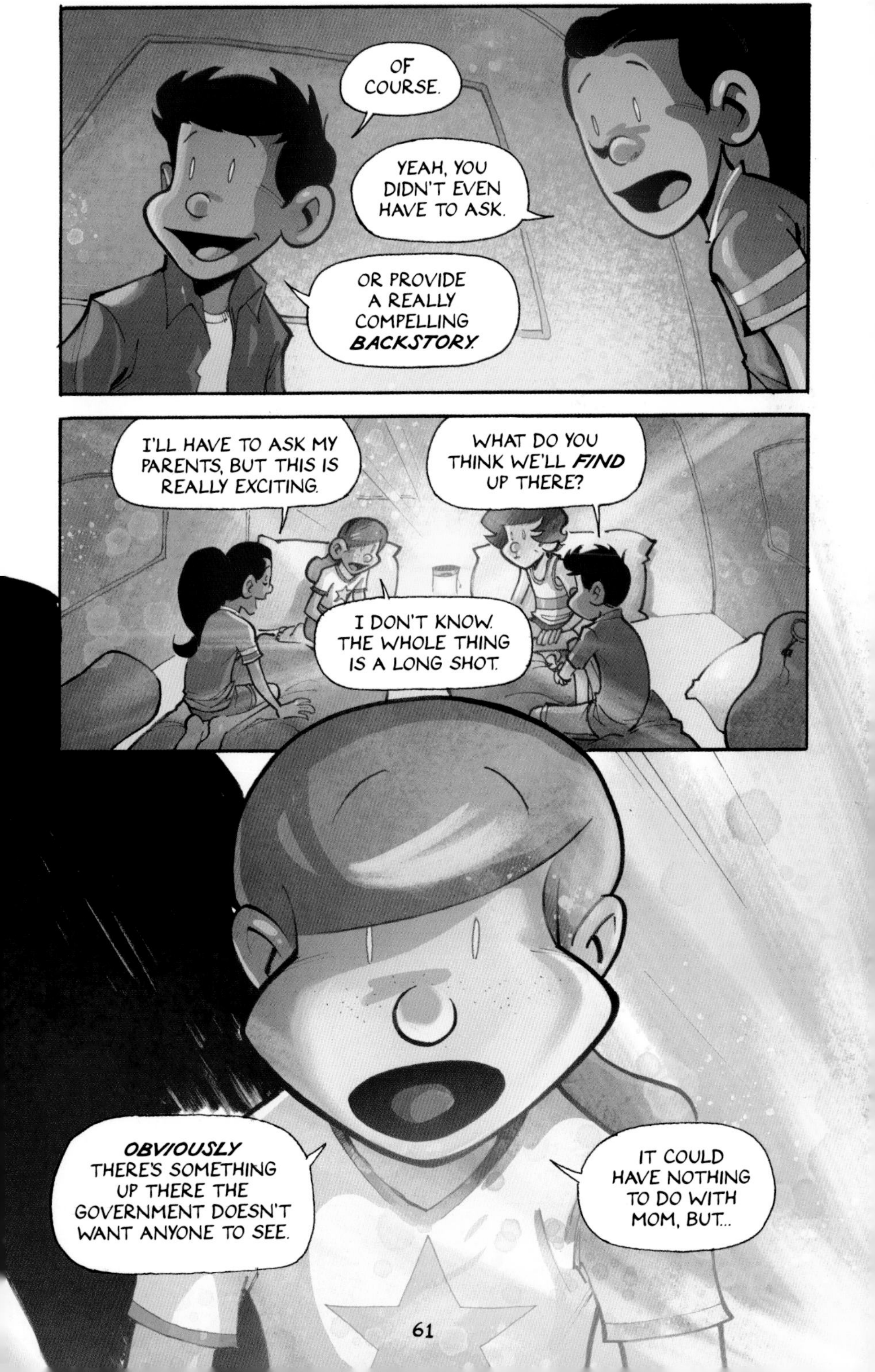
OF COURSE.
YEAH, YOU DIDN'T EVEN HAVE TO ASK.
OR PROVIDE A REALLY COMPELLING BACKSTORY.
I'LL HAVE TO ASK MY PARENTS, BUT THIS IS REALLY EXCITING.
WHAT DO YOU THINK WE'LL FIND UP THERE?
I DON'T KNOW. THE WHOLE THING IS A LONG SHOT.
OBVIOUSLY THERE'S SOMETHING UP THERE THE GOVERNMENT DOESN'T WANT ANYONE TO SEE.
IT COULD HAVE NOTHING TO DO WITH MOM, BUT...

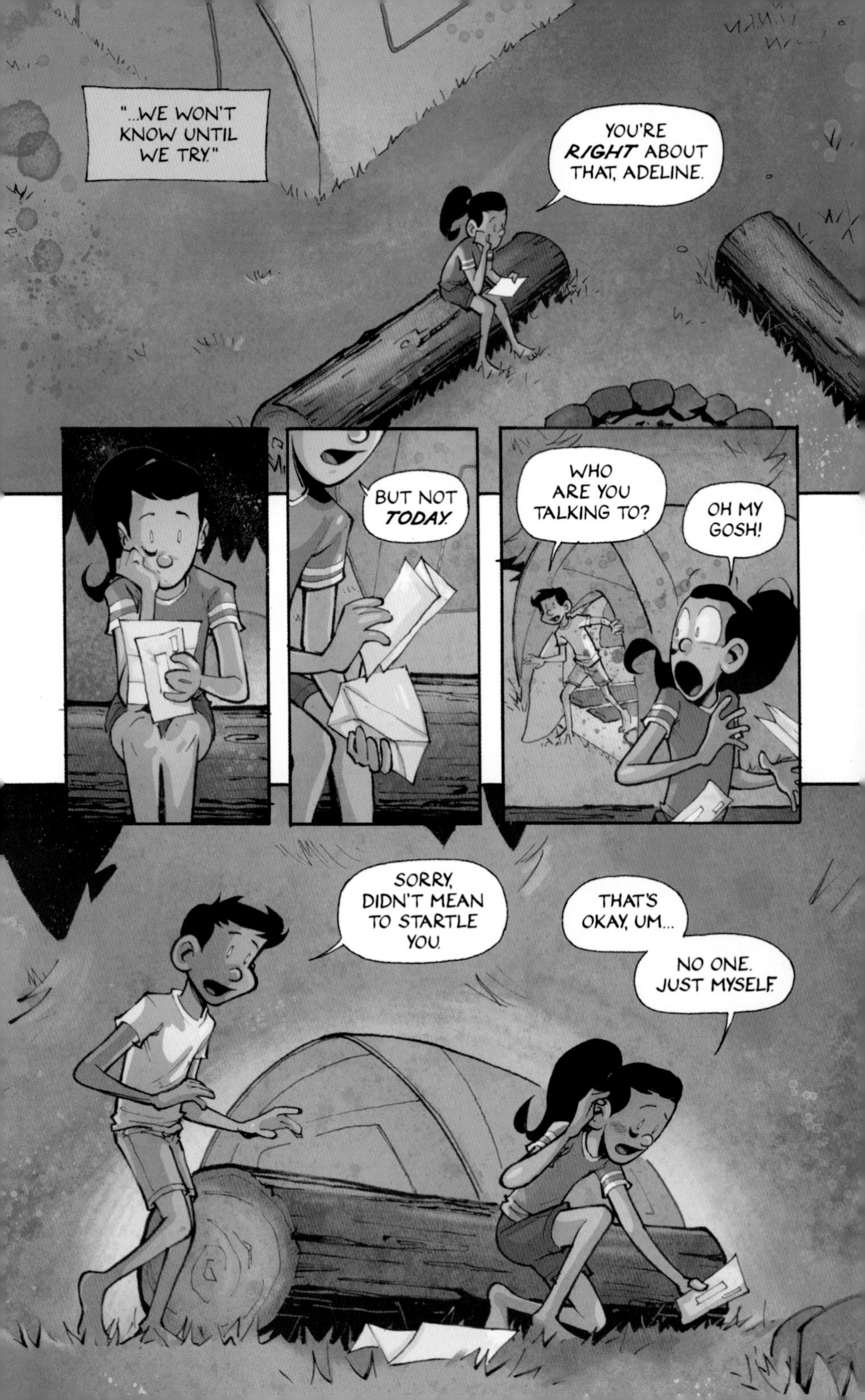
"...WE WON'T KNOW UNTIL WE TRY."
YOU'RE *RIGHT* ABOUT THAT, ADELINE.
BUT NOT *TODAY*.
WHO ARE YOU TALKING TO?
OH MY GOSH!
SORRY, DIDN'T MEAN TO STARTLE YOU.
THAT'S OKAY, UM...
NO ONE. JUST MYSELF.

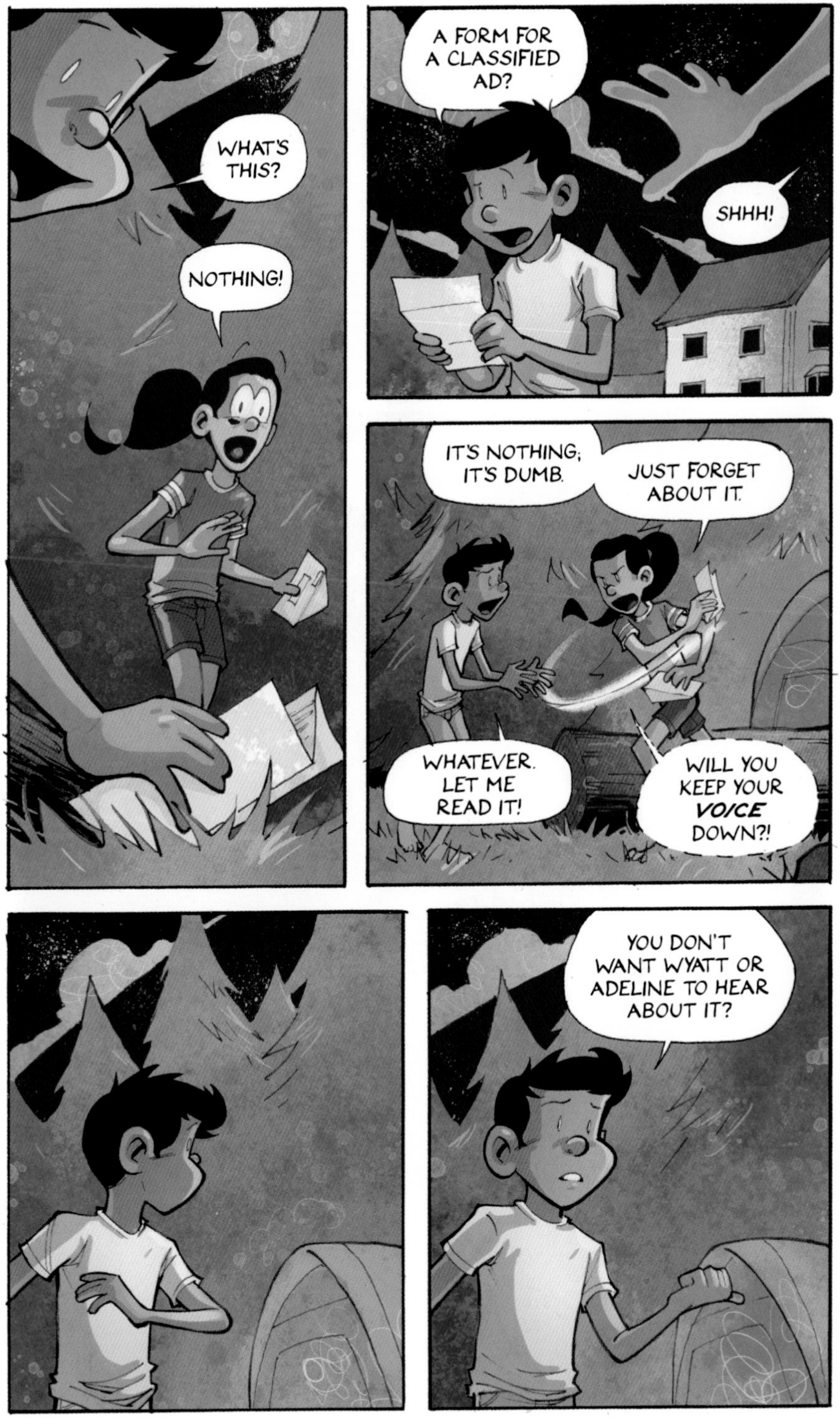
WHAT'S THIS?
NOTHING!
A FORM FOR A CLASSIFIED AD?
SHHH!
IT'S NOTHING; IT'S DUMB.
JUST FORGET ABOUT IT.
WHATEVER. LET ME READ IT!
WILL YOU KEEP YOUR *VOICE* DOWN?!
YOU DON'T WANT WYATT OR ADELINE TO HEAR ABOUT IT?

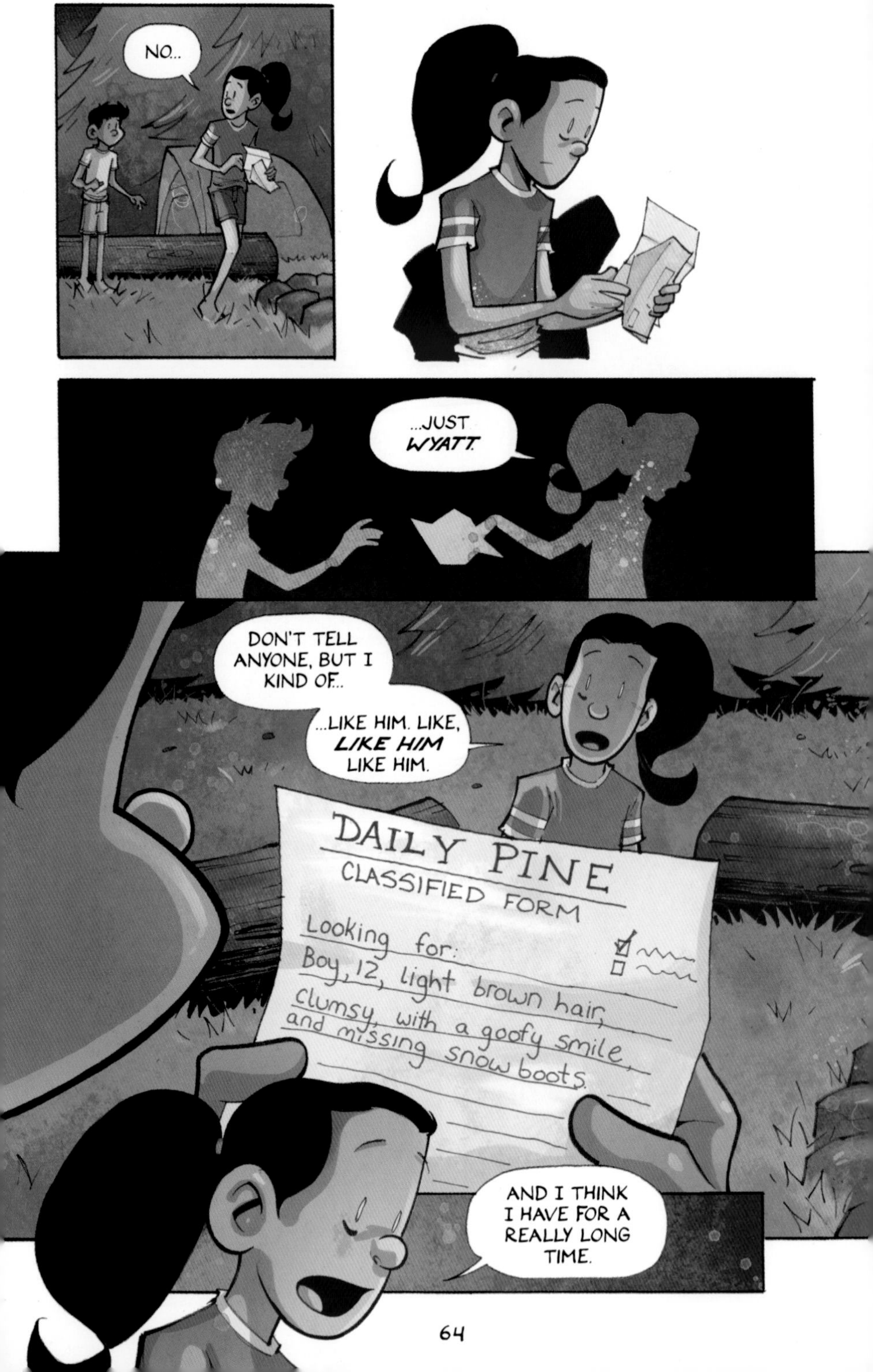
NO...
...JUST WYATT.
DON'T TELL ANYONE, BUT I KIND OF...
...LIKE HIM. LIKE, LIKE HIM LIKE HIM.
DAILY PINE
CLASSIFIED FORM
Looking for:
Boy, 12, light brown hair, clumsy, with a goofy smile, and missing snow boots.
AND I THINK I HAVE FOR A REALLY LONG TIME.

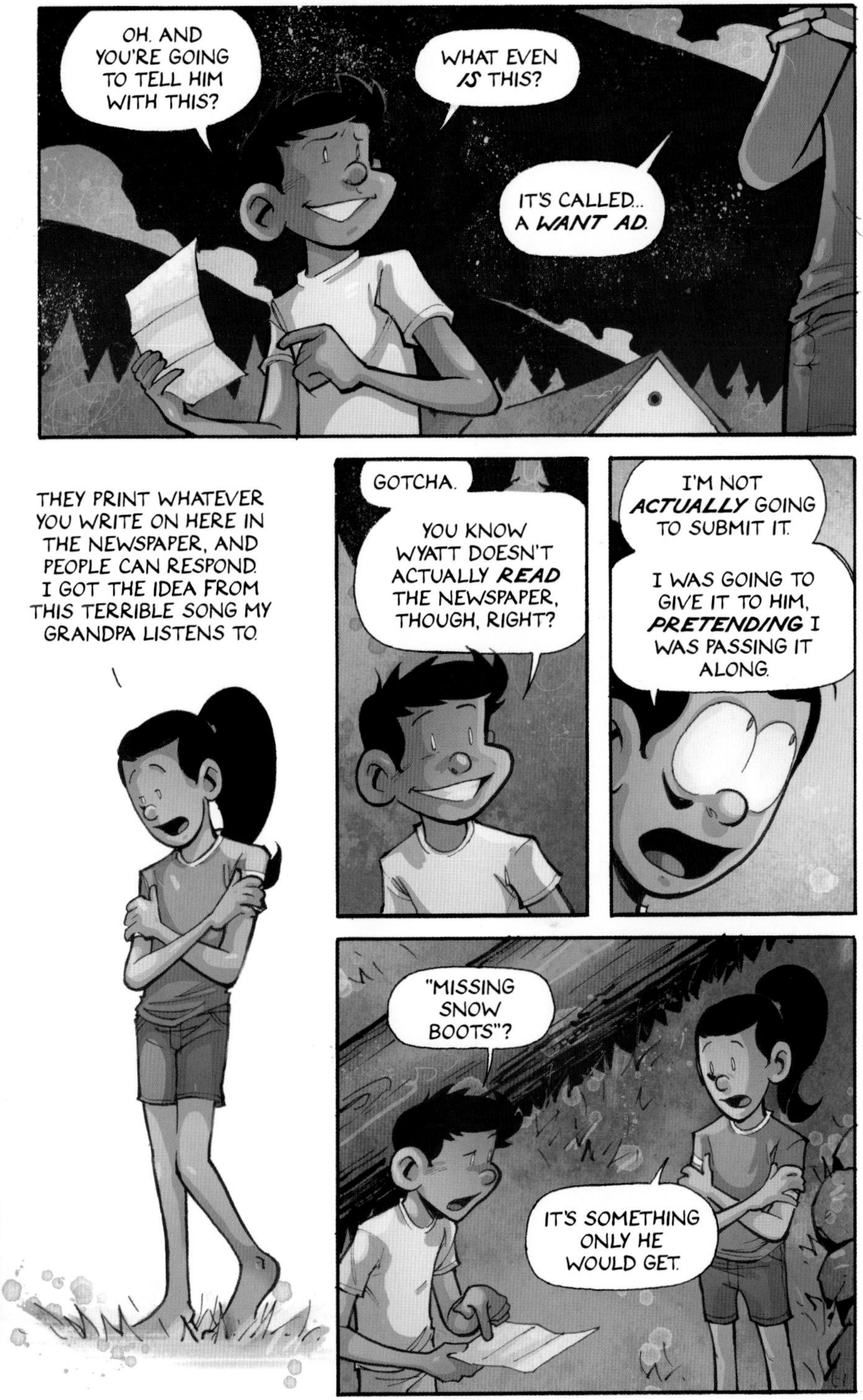
OH. AND YOU'RE GOING TO TELL HIM WITH THIS?
WHAT EVEN *IS* THIS?
IT'S CALLED... A *WANT AD.*
THEY PRINT WHATEVER YOU WRITE ON HERE IN THE NEWSPAPER, AND PEOPLE CAN RESPOND. I GOT THE IDEA FROM THIS TERRIBLE SONG MY GRANDPA LISTENS TO.
GOTCHA.
YOU KNOW WYATT DOESN'T ACTUALLY *READ* THE NEWSPAPER, THOUGH, RIGHT?
I'M NOT *ACTUALLY* GOING TO SUBMIT IT.
I WAS GOING TO GIVE IT TO HIM, *PRETENDING* I WAS PASSING IT ALONG.
"MISSING SNOW BOOTS"?
IT'S SOMETHING ONLY HE WOULD GET.

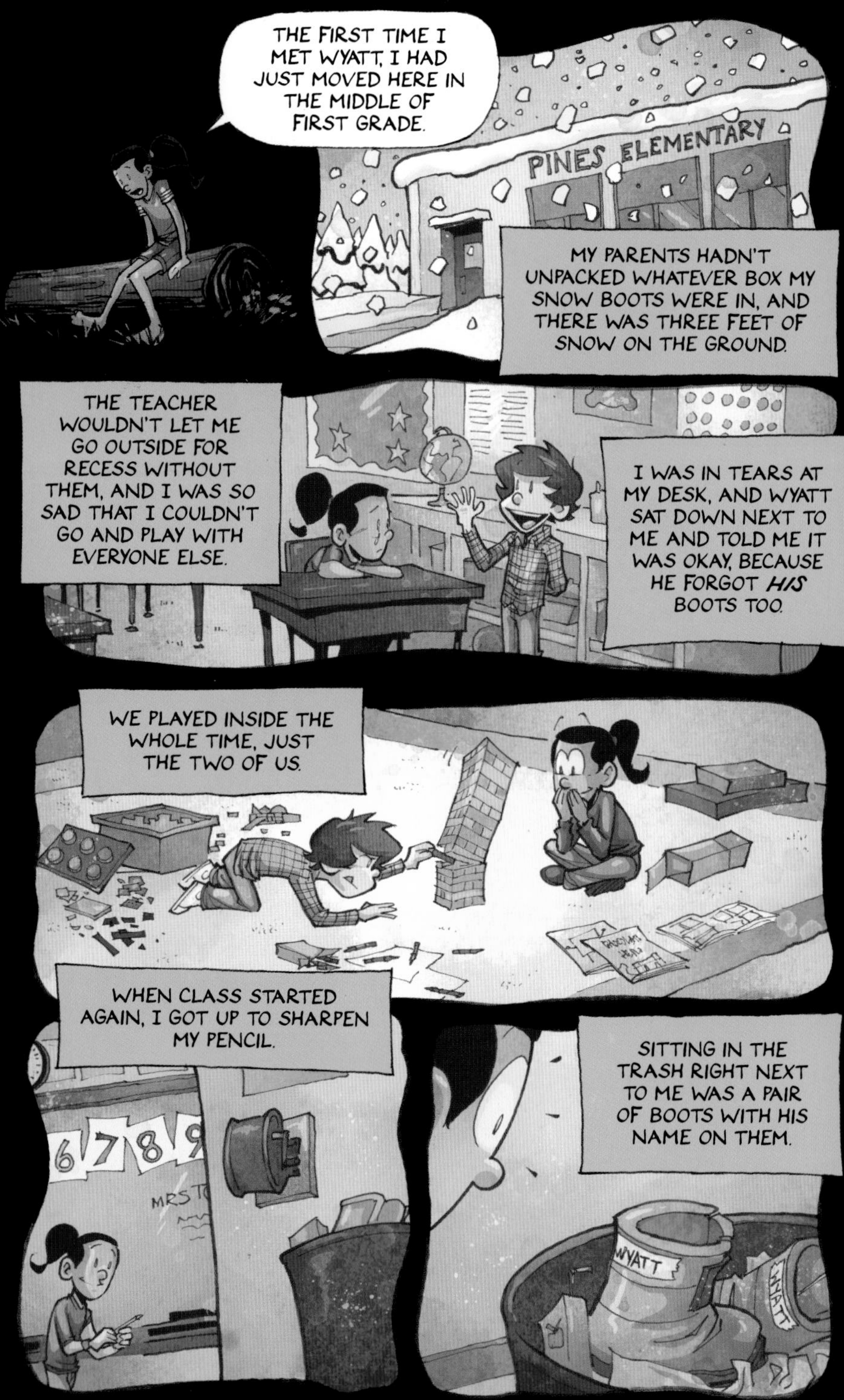
THE FIRST TIME I MET WYATT, I HAD JUST MOVED HERE IN THE MIDDLE OF FIRST GRADE.
PINES ELEMENTARY
MY PARENTS HADN'T UNPACKED WHATEVER BOX MY SNOW BOOTS WERE IN, AND THERE WAS THREE FEET OF SNOW ON THE GROUND.
THE TEACHER WOULDN'T LET ME GO OUTSIDE FOR RECESS WITHOUT THEM, AND I WAS SO SAD THAT I COULDN'T GO AND PLAY WITH EVERYONE ELSE.
I WAS IN TEARS AT MY DESK, AND WYATT SAT DOWN NEXT TO ME AND TOLD ME IT WAS OKAY, BECAUSE HE FORGOT *HIS* BOOTS TOO.
WE PLAYED INSIDE THE WHOLE TIME, JUST THE TWO OF US.
WHEN CLASS STARTED AGAIN, I GOT UP TO SHARPEN MY PENCIL.
6 7 8 9
SITTING IN THE TRASH RIGHT NEXT TO ME WAS A PAIR OF BOOTS WITH HIS NAME ON THEM.
WYATT
WYATT

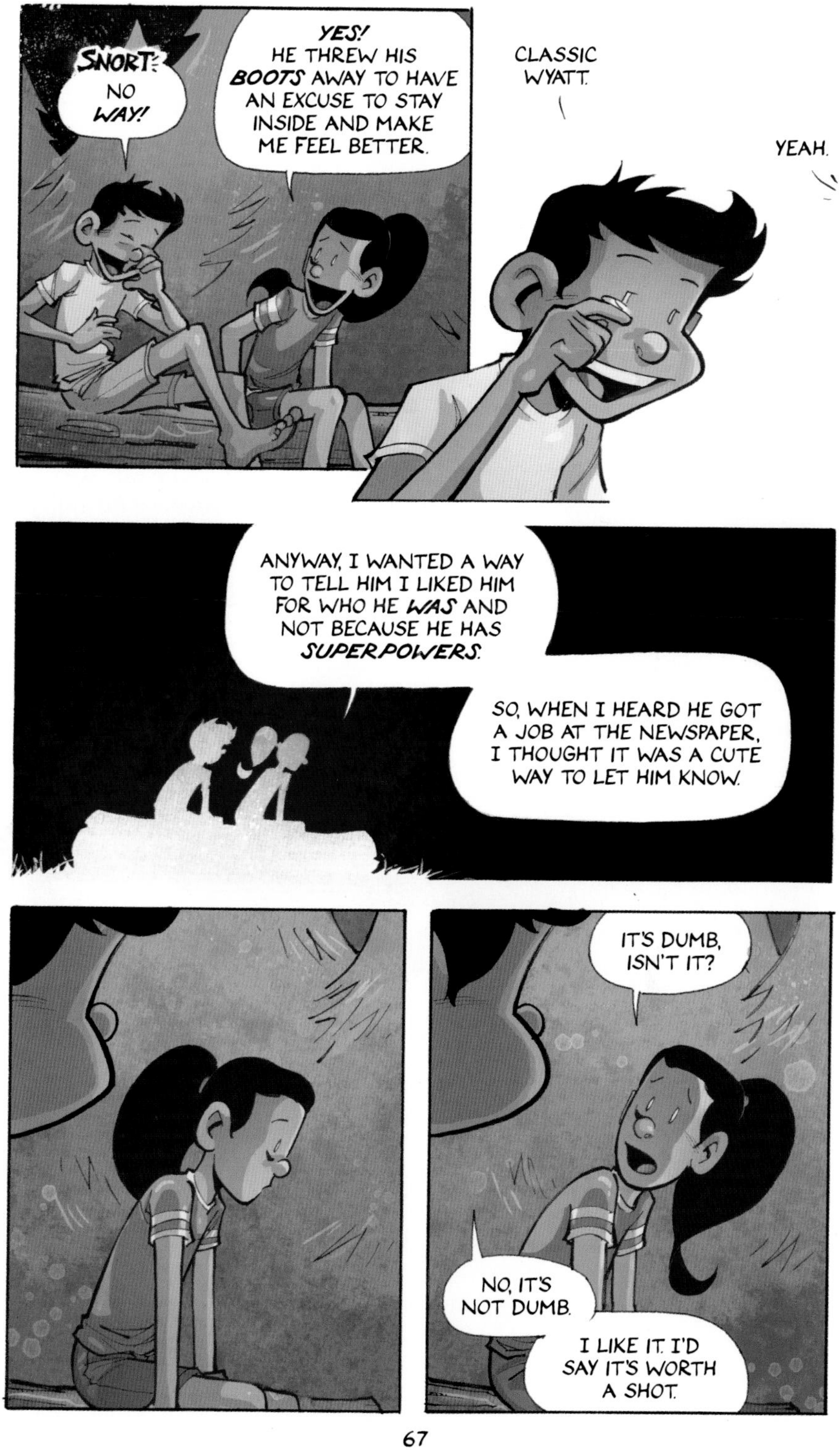
SNORT
NO WAY!
YES! HE THREW HIS BOOTS AWAY TO HAVE AN EXCUSE TO STAY INSIDE AND MAKE ME FEEL BETTER.
CLASSIC WYATT.
YEAH.
ANYWAY, I WANTED A WAY TO TELL HIM I LIKED HIM FOR WHO HE WAS AND NOT BECAUSE HE HAS SUPERPOWERS.
SO, WHEN I HEARD HE GOT A JOB AT THE NEWSPAPER, I THOUGHT IT WAS A CUTE WAY TO LET HIM KNOW.
IT'S DUMB, ISN'T IT?
NO, IT'S NOT DUMB.
I LIKE IT. I'D SAY IT'S WORTH A SHOT.

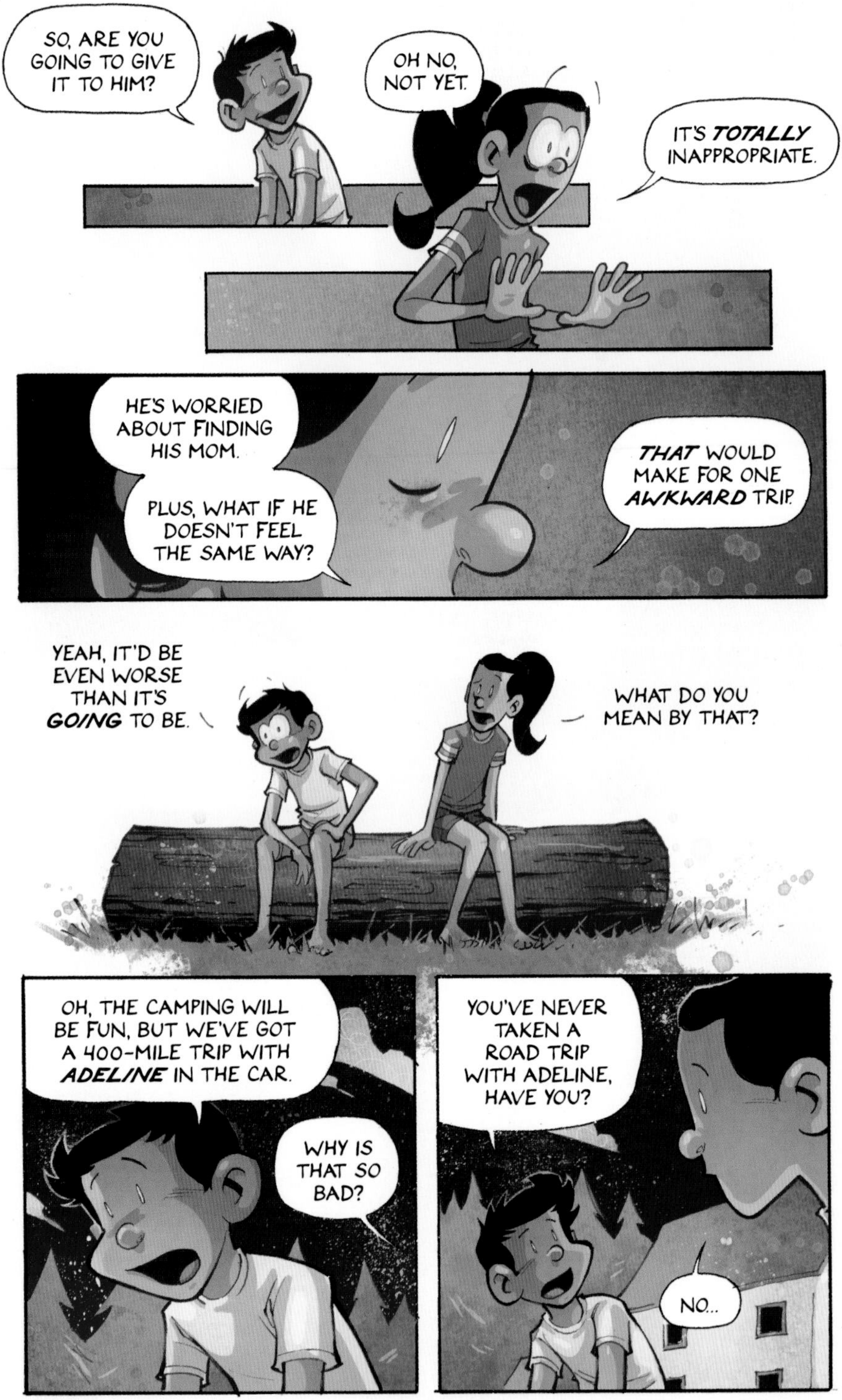
SO, ARE YOU GOING TO GIVE IT TO HIM?
OH NO, NOT YET.
IT'S TOTALLY INAPPROPRIATE.
HE'S WORRIED ABOUT FINDING HIS MOM.
PLUS, WHAT IF HE DOESN'T FEEL THE SAME WAY?
THAT WOULD MAKE FOR ONE AWKWARD TRIP.
YEAH, IT'D BE EVEN WORSE THAN IT'S GOING TO BE.
WHAT DO YOU MEAN BY THAT?
OH, THE CAMPING WILL BE FUN, BUT WE'VE GOT A 400-MILE TRIP WITH ADELINE IN THE CAR.
WHY IS THAT SO BAD?
YOU'VE NEVER TAKEN A ROAD TRIP WITH ADELINE, HAVE YOU?
NO...

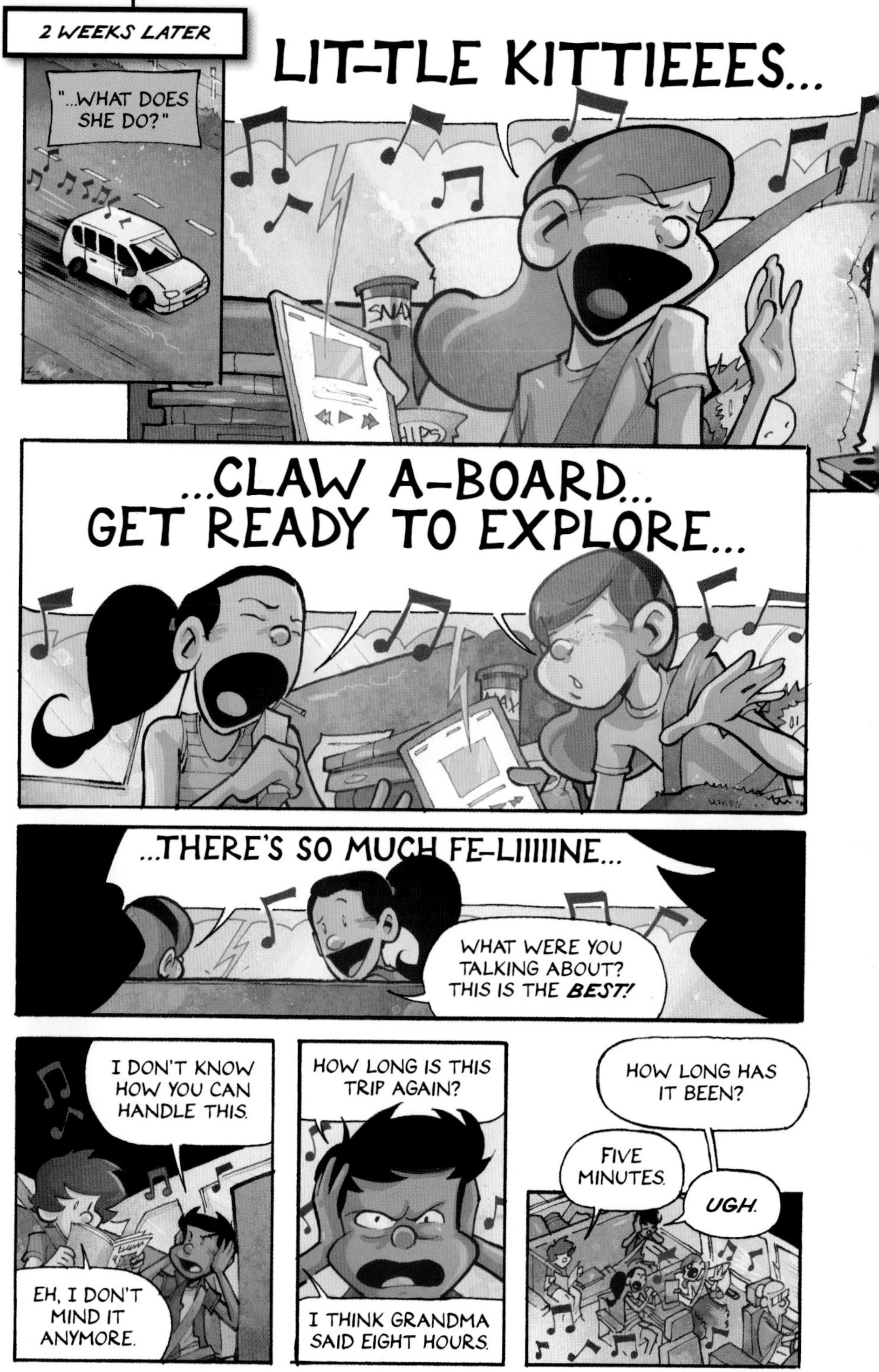
2 WEEKS LATER
"...WHAT DOES SHE DO?"
LIT-TLE KITTIEEES...
SNAX
...CLAW A-BOARD...
GET READY TO EXPLORE...
...THERE'S SO MUCH FE-LIIIIINE...
WHAT WERE YOU TALKING ABOUT? THIS IS THE *BEST!*
I DON'T KNOW HOW YOU CAN HANDLE THIS.
EH, I DON'T MIND IT ANYMORE.
HOW LONG IS THIS TRIP AGAIN?
I THINK GRANDMA SAID EIGHT HOURS.
HOW LONG HAS IT BEEN?
FIVE MINUTES.
UGH.

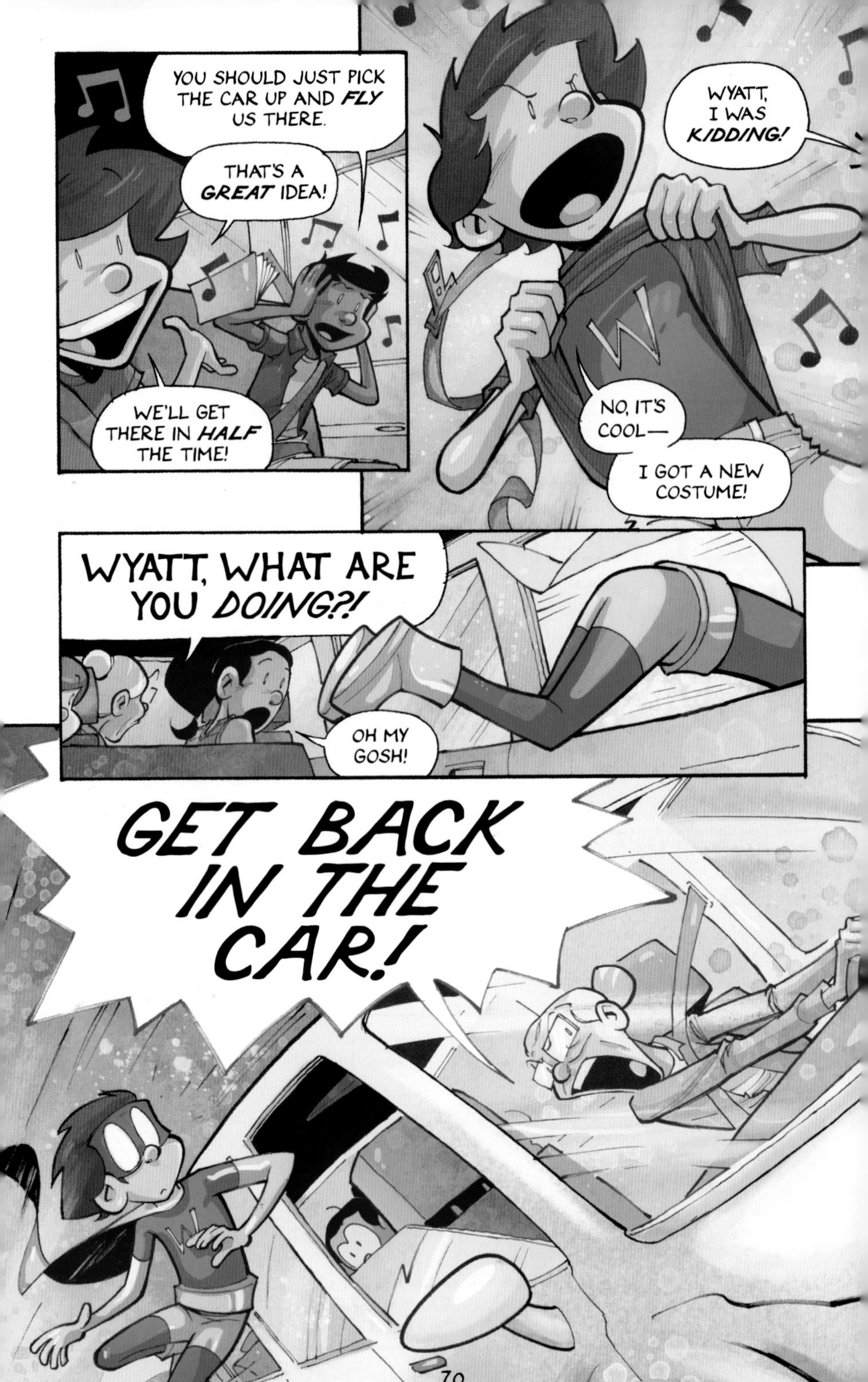
YOU SHOULD JUST PICK THE CAR UP AND FLY US THERE.
THAT'S A GREAT IDEA!
WE'LL GET THERE IN HALF THE TIME!
WYATT, I WAS KIDDING!
NO, IT'S COOL—
I GOT A NEW COSTUME!
WYATT, WHAT ARE YOU DOING?!
OH MY GOSH!
GET BACK IN THE CAR!

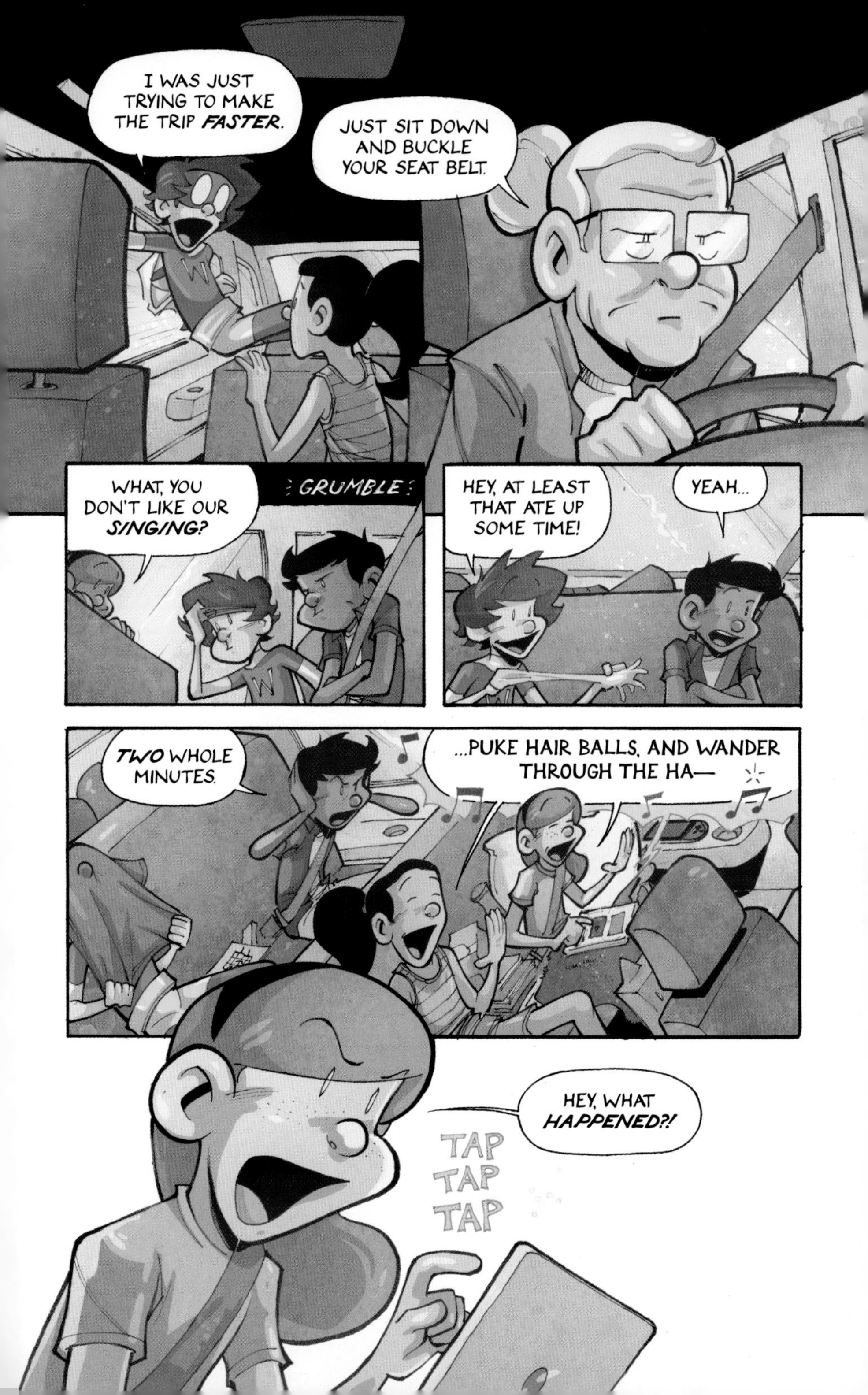
I WAS JUST TRYING TO MAKE THE TRIP FASTER.
JUST SIT DOWN AND BUCKLE YOUR SEAT BELT.
WHAT, YOU DON'T LIKE OUR SINGING?
GRUMBLE
HEY, AT LEAST THAT ATE UP SOME TIME!
YEAH...
TWO WHOLE MINUTES.
...PUKE HAIR BALLS, AND WANDER THROUGH THE HA—
HEY, WHAT HAPPENED?!
TAP TAP TAP

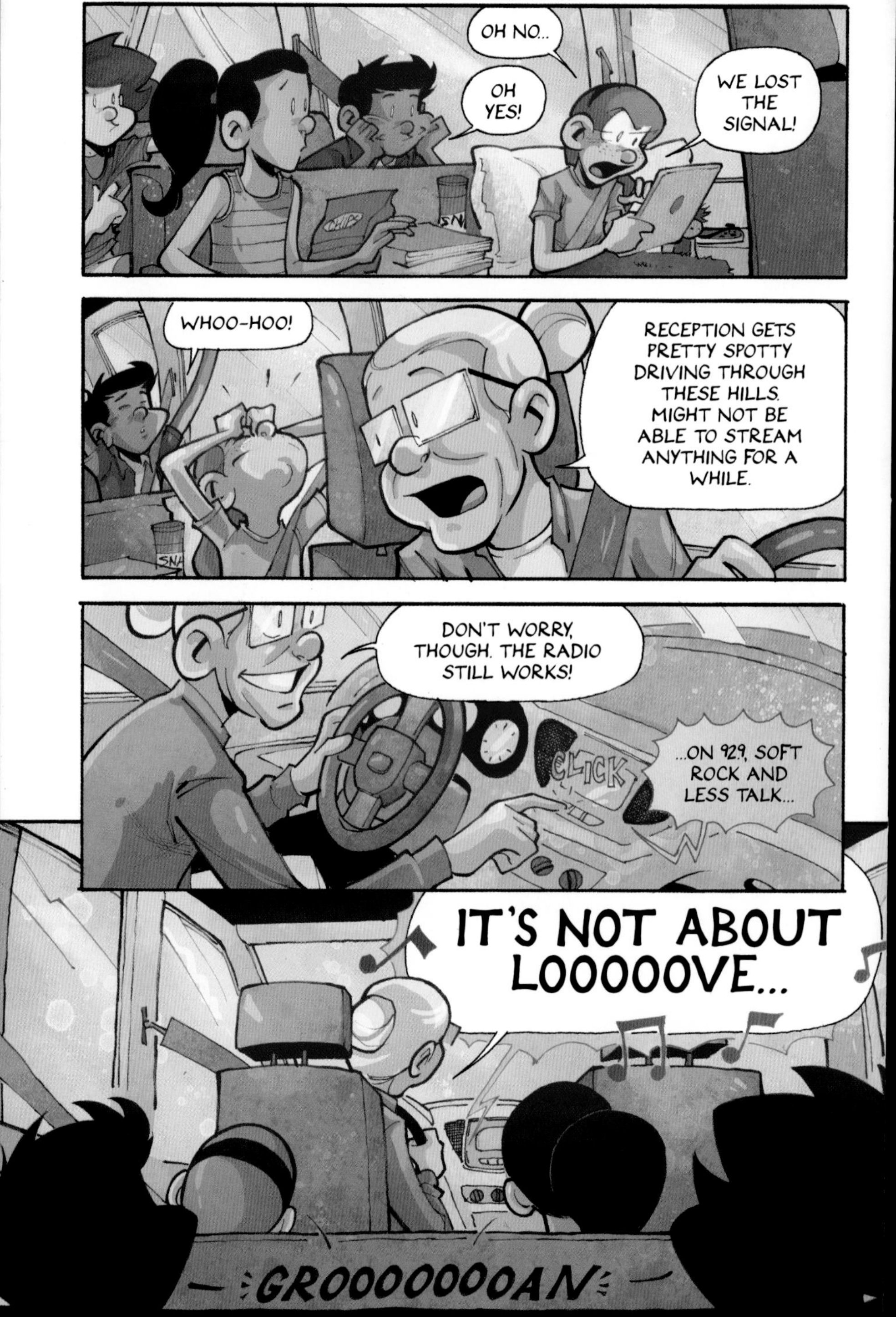
OH NO...
OH YES!
WE LOST THE SIGNAL!
WHOO-HOO!
RECEPTION GETS PRETTY SPOTTY DRIVING THROUGH THESE HILLS. MIGHT NOT BE ABLE TO STREAM ANYTHING FOR A WHILE.
DON'T WORRY, THOUGH. THE RADIO STILL WORKS!
CLICK
...ON 92.9, SOFT ROCK AND LESS TALK...
IT'S NOT ABOUT LOOOOOVE...
GROOOOOOOAN

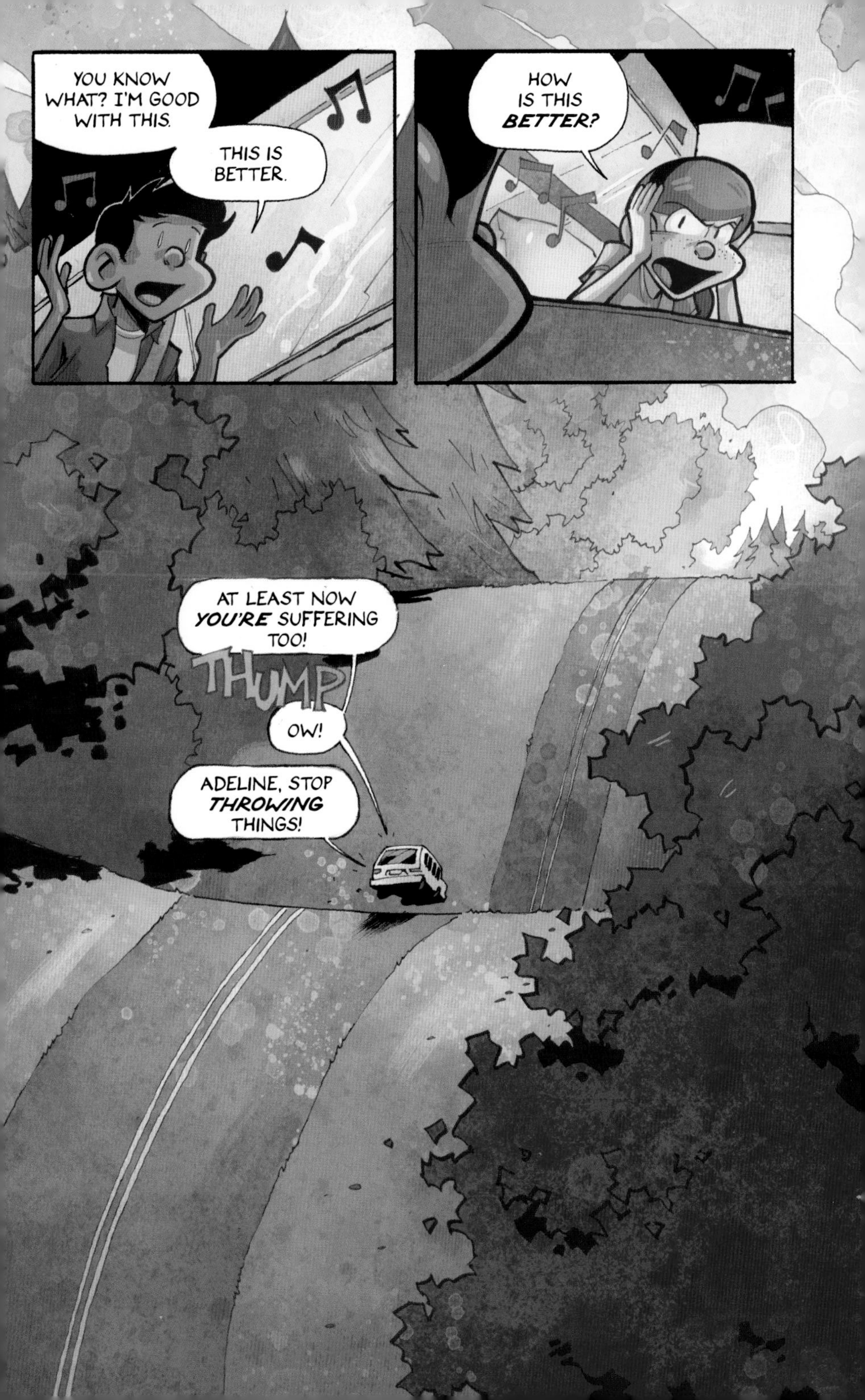
YOU KNOW WHAT? I'M GOOD WITH THIS.
THIS IS BETTER.
HOW IS THIS *BETTER?*
AT LEAST NOW *YOU'RE* SUFFERING TOO!
THUMP
OW!
ADELINE, STOP *THROWING* THINGS!

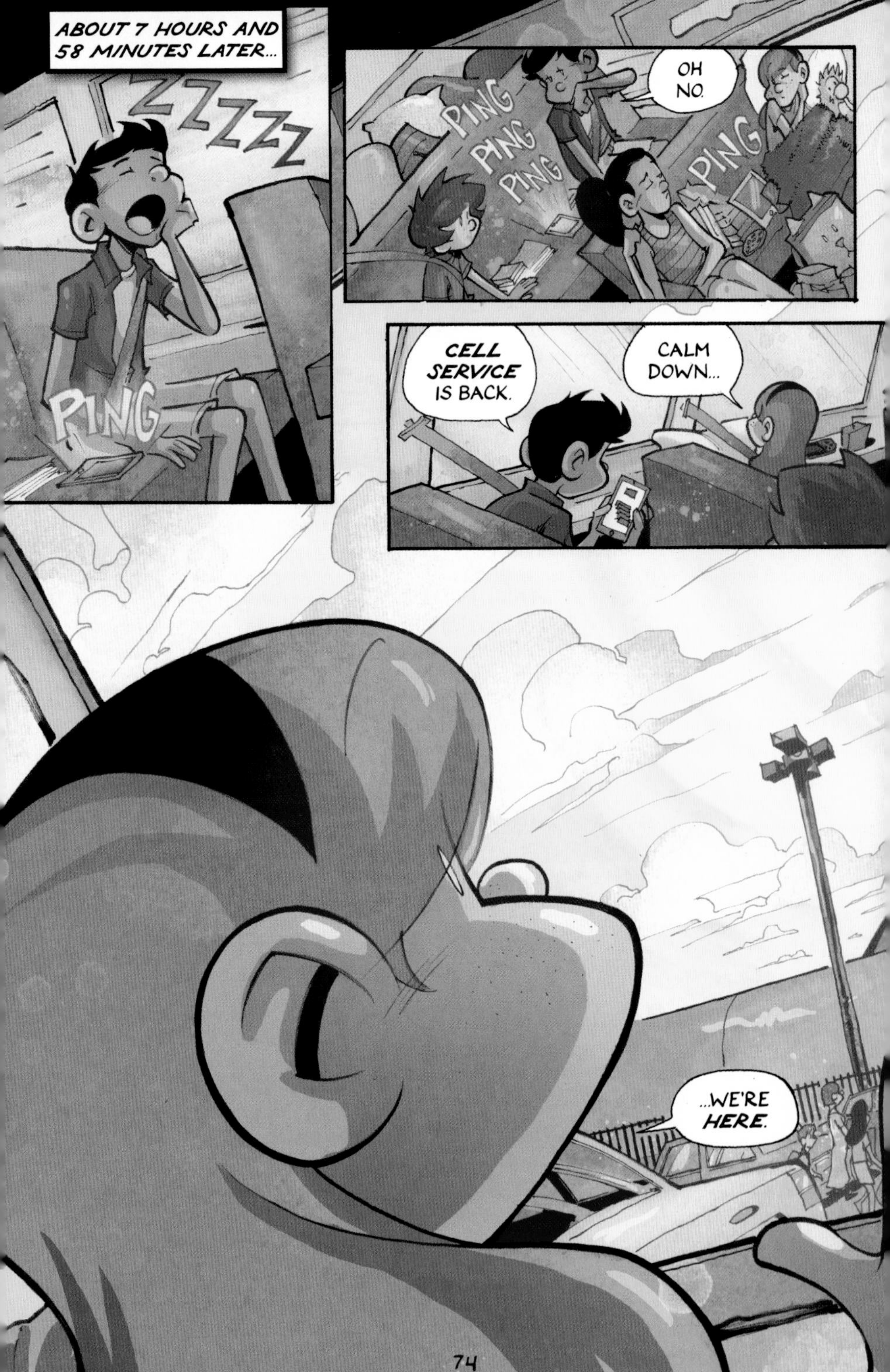
ABOUT 7 HOURS AND 58 MINUTES LATER...
ZZZZZZ
PING
PING PING PING
OH NO.
PING
CELL SERVICE IS BACK.
CALM DOWN...
...WE'RE HERE.

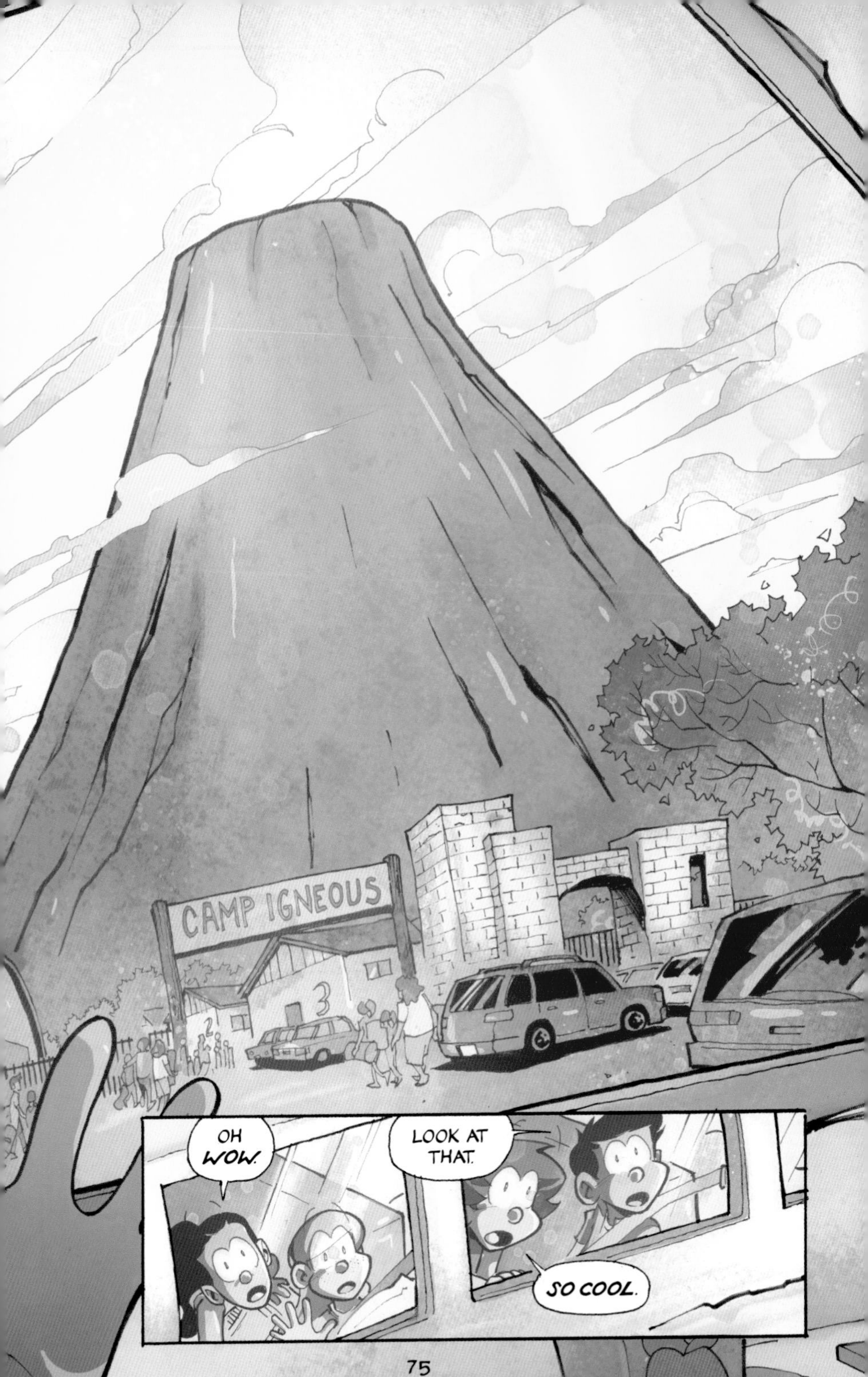
CAMP IGNEOUS
OH WOW.
LOOK AT THAT.
SO COOL.

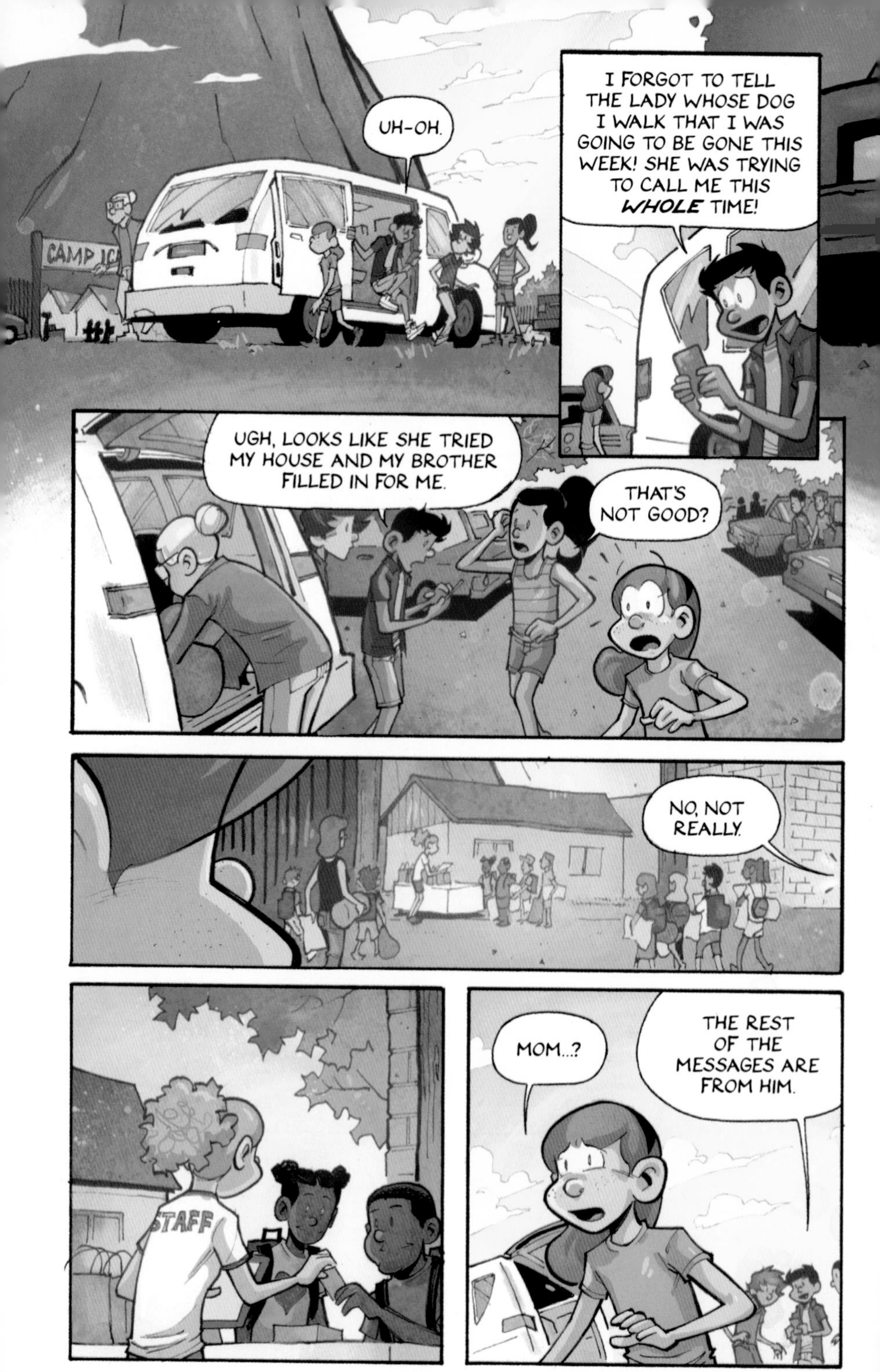
CAMP IC
UH-OH.
I FORGOT TO TELL THE LADY WHOSE DOG I WALK THAT I WAS GOING TO BE GONE THIS WEEK! SHE WAS TRYING TO CALL ME THIS *WHOLE* TIME!
UGH, LOOKS LIKE SHE TRIED MY HOUSE AND MY BROTHER FILLED IN FOR ME.
THAT'S NOT GOOD?
NO, NOT REALLY.
STAFF
MOM...?
THE REST OF THE MESSAGES ARE FROM HIM.

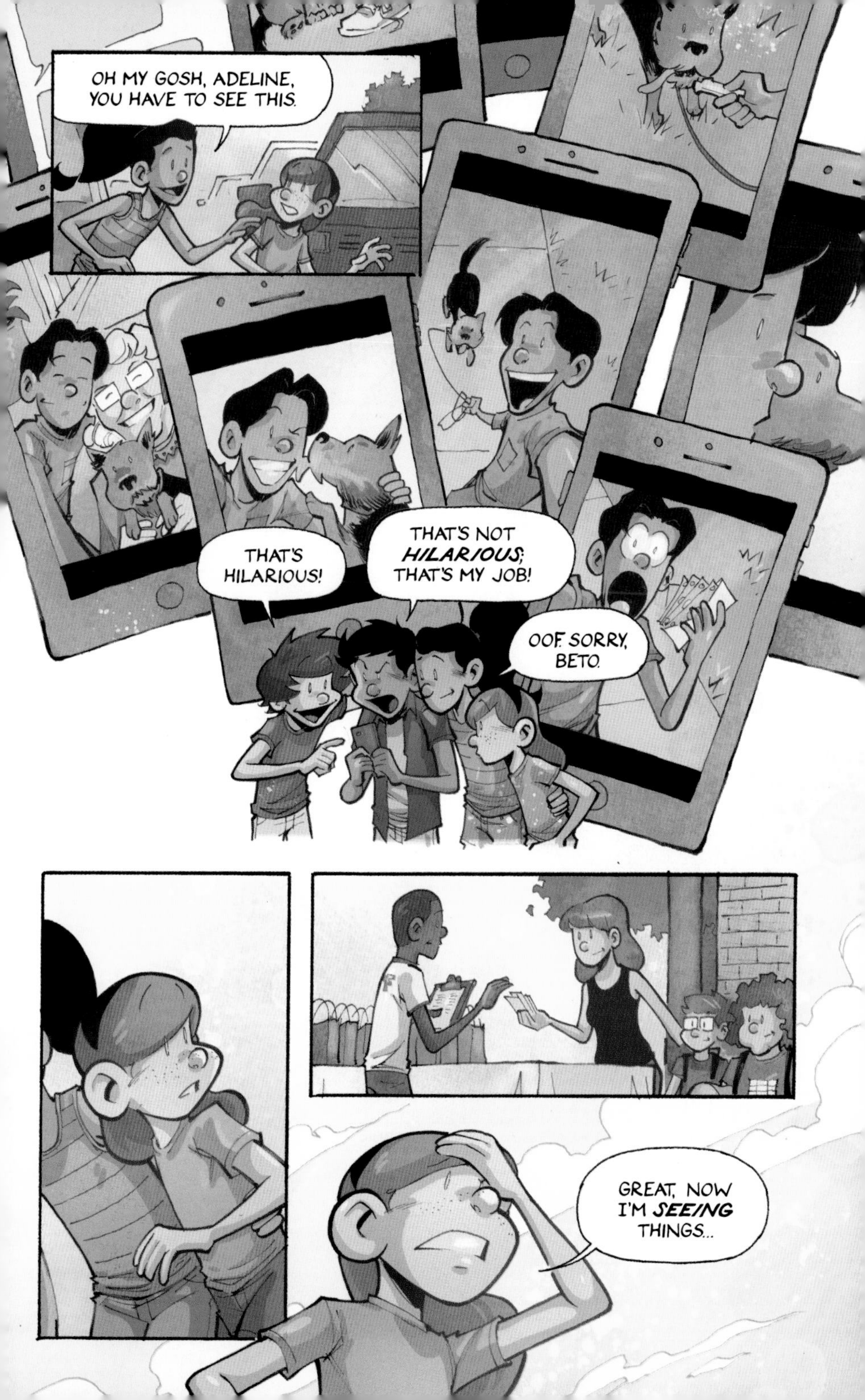
OH MY GOSH, ADELINE, YOU HAVE TO SEE THIS.
THAT'S HILARIOUS!
THAT'S NOT *HILARIOUS*; THAT'S MY JOB!
OOF. SORRY, BETO.
GREAT, NOW I'M *SEEING* THINGS...

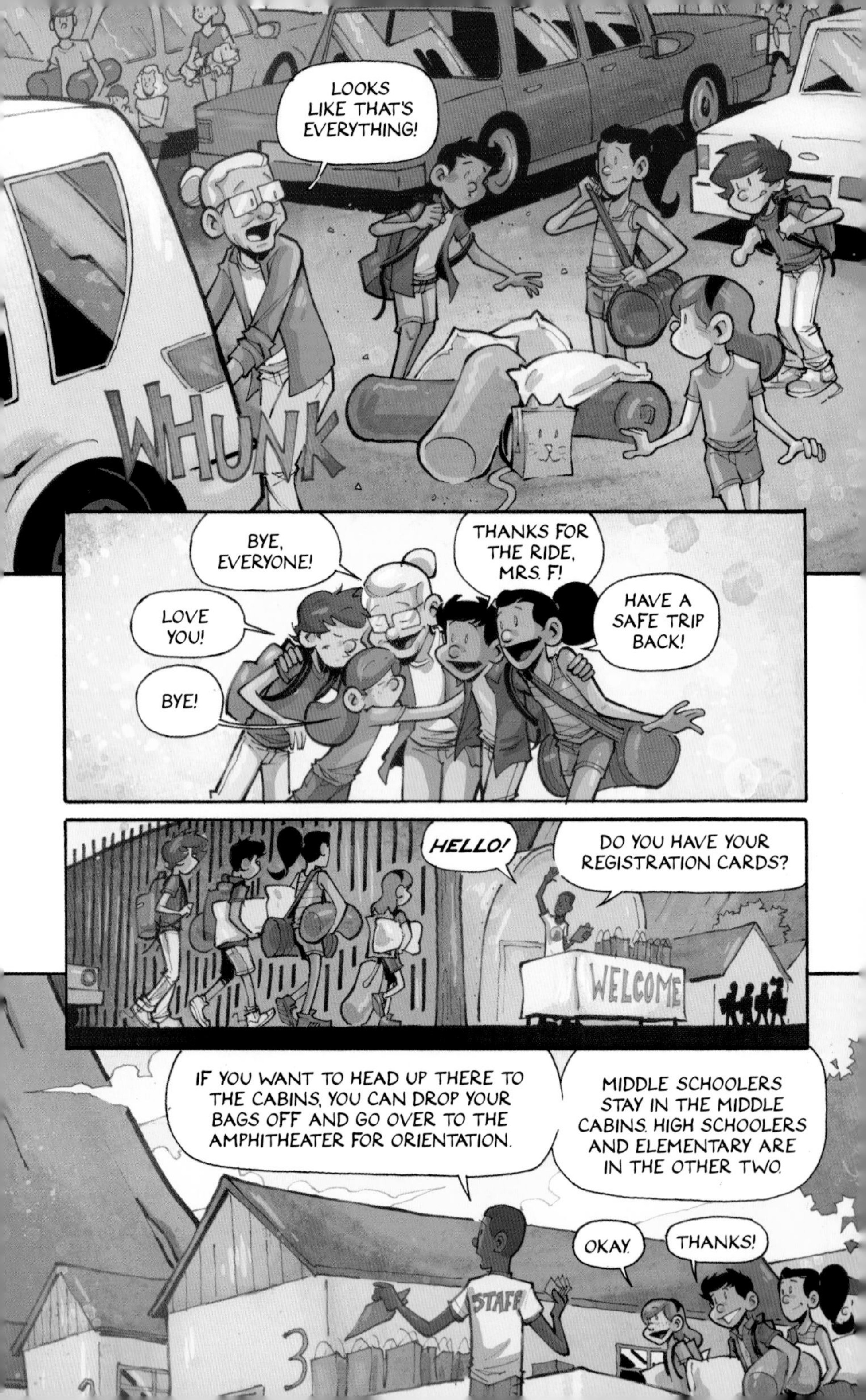
LOOKS LIKE THAT'S EVERYTHING!
WHUNK
BYE, EVERYONE!
THANKS FOR THE RIDE, MRS. F!
LOVE YOU!
HAVE A SAFE TRIP BACK!
BYE!
HELLO!
DO YOU HAVE YOUR REGISTRATION CARDS?
WELCOME
IF YOU WANT TO HEAD UP THERE TO THE CABINS, YOU CAN DROP YOUR BAGS OFF AND GO OVER TO THE AMPHITHEATER FOR ORIENTATION.
MIDDLE SCHOOLERS STAY IN THE MIDDLE CABINS. HIGH SCHOOLERS AND ELEMENTARY ARE IN THE OTHER TWO.
OKAY.
THANKS!
STAFF
3

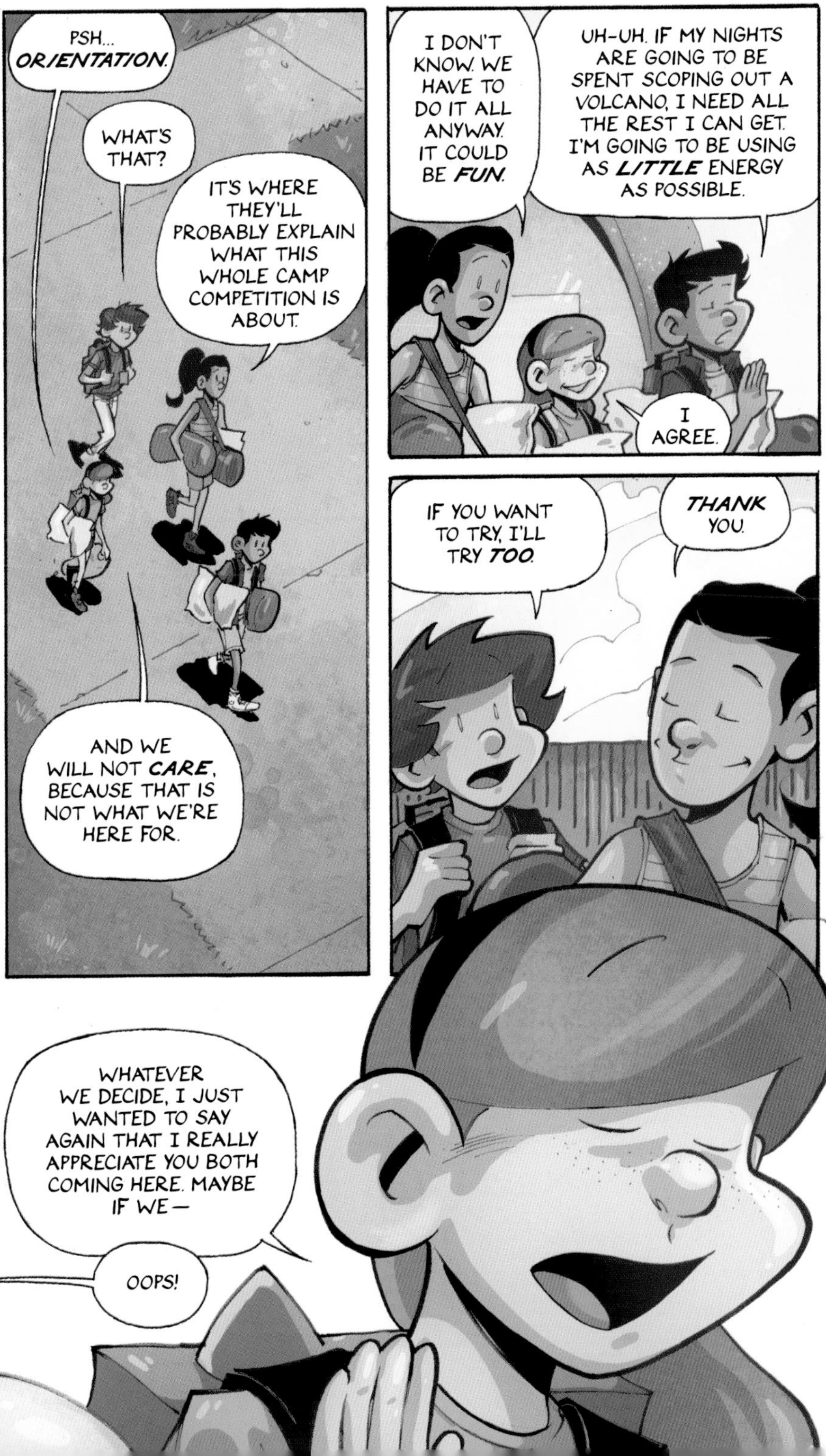
PSH... ORIENTATION.
WHAT'S THAT?
IT'S WHERE THEY'LL PROBABLY EXPLAIN WHAT THIS WHOLE CAMP COMPETITION IS ABOUT.
AND WE WILL NOT CARE, BECAUSE THAT IS NOT WHAT WE'RE HERE FOR.
I DON'T KNOW. WE HAVE TO DO IT ALL ANYWAY. IT COULD BE FUN.
UH-UH. IF MY NIGHTS ARE GOING TO BE SPENT SCOPING OUT A VOLCANO, I NEED ALL THE REST I CAN GET. I'M GOING TO BE USING AS LITTLE ENERGY AS POSSIBLE.
I AGREE.
IF YOU WANT TO TRY, I'LL TRY TOO.
THANK YOU.
WHATEVER WE DECIDE, I JUST WANTED TO SAY AGAIN THAT I REALLY APPRECIATE YOU BOTH COMING HERE. MAYBE IF WE—
OOPS!

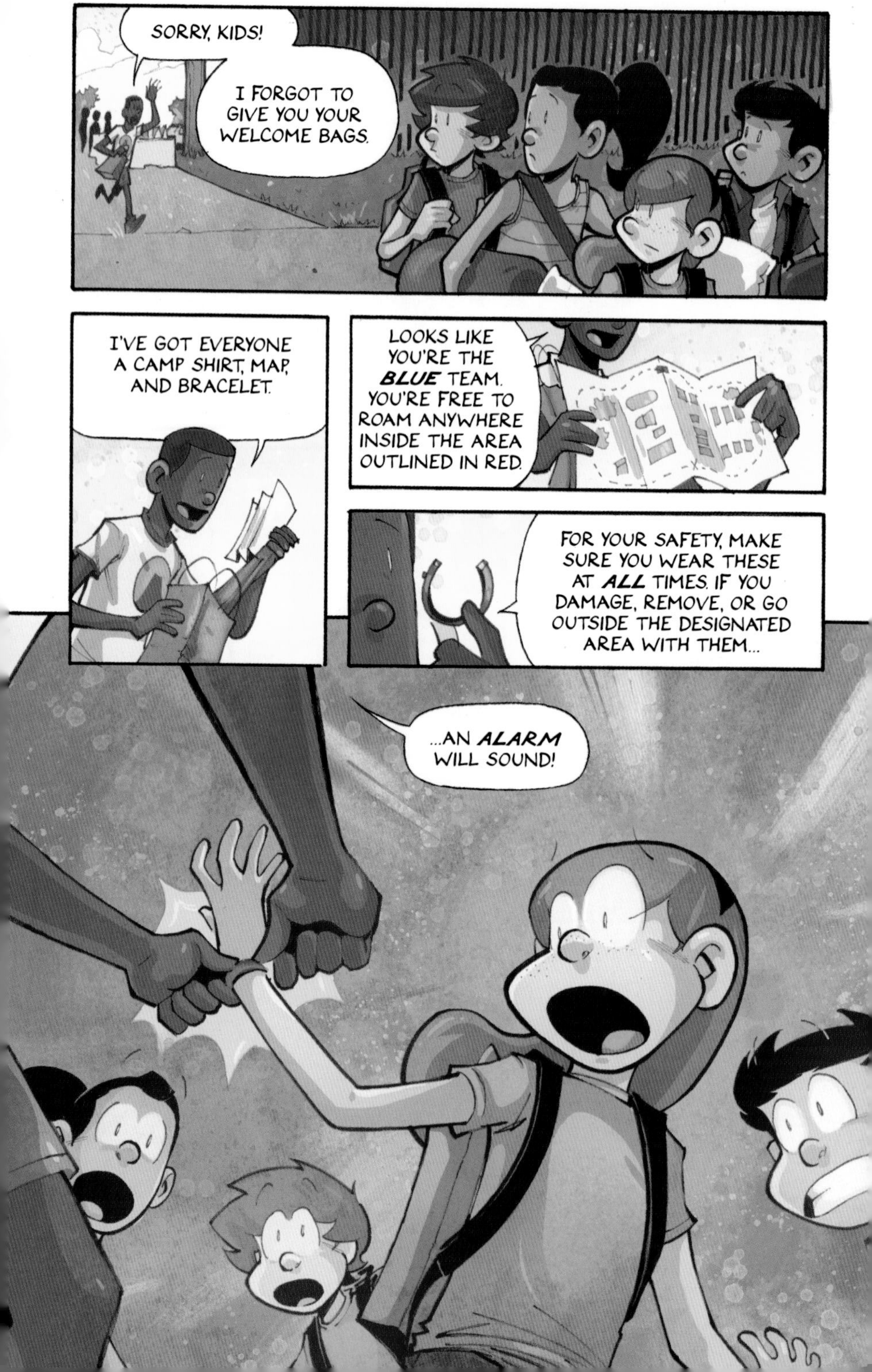
SORRY, KIDS!
I FORGOT TO GIVE YOU YOUR WELCOME BAGS.
I'VE GOT EVERYONE A CAMP SHIRT, MAP, AND BRACELET.
LOOKS LIKE YOU'RE THE BLUE TEAM. YOU'RE FREE TO ROAM ANYWHERE INSIDE THE AREA OUTLINED IN RED.
FOR YOUR SAFETY, MAKE SURE YOU WEAR THESE AT ALL TIMES. IF YOU DAMAGE, REMOVE, OR GO OUTSIDE THE DESIGNATED AREA WITH THEM...
...AN ALARM WILL SOUND!

CHAPTER FIVE

IT DIDN'T SAY *ANYTHING* ABOUT *PERIMETER ALARMS* ON THEIR WEBSITE!

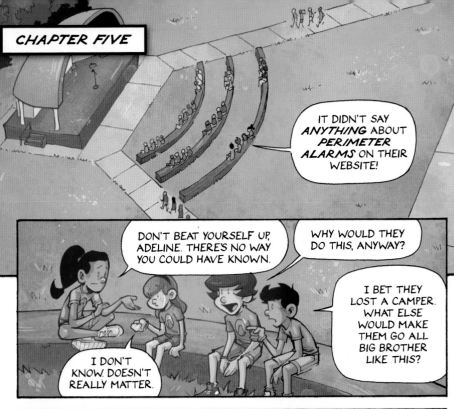

DON'T BEAT YOURSELF UP, ADELINE. THERE'S NO WAY YOU COULD HAVE KNOWN.

WHY WOULD THEY DO THIS, ANYWAY?

I BET THEY LOST A CAMPER. WHAT ELSE WOULD MAKE THEM GO ALL BIG BROTHER LIKE THIS?

I DON'T KNOW. DOESN'T REALLY MATTER.

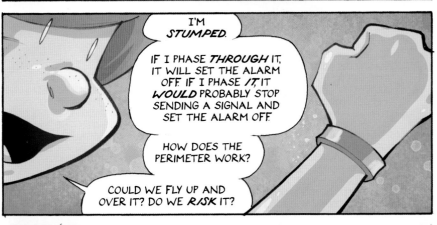

I'M *STUMPED.*

IF I PHASE *THROUGH* IT, IT WILL SET THE ALARM OFF. IF I PHASE *IT,* IT *WOULD* PROBABLY STOP SENDING A SIGNAL AND SET THE ALARM OFF.

HOW DOES THE PERIMETER WORK?

COULD WE FLY UP AND OVER IT? DO WE *RISK* IT?

YOU'LL FIGURE IT OUT.

YOU'RE THE SMARTEST PERSON I *KNOW.*

HELLO, MIDDLE SCHOOLERS!

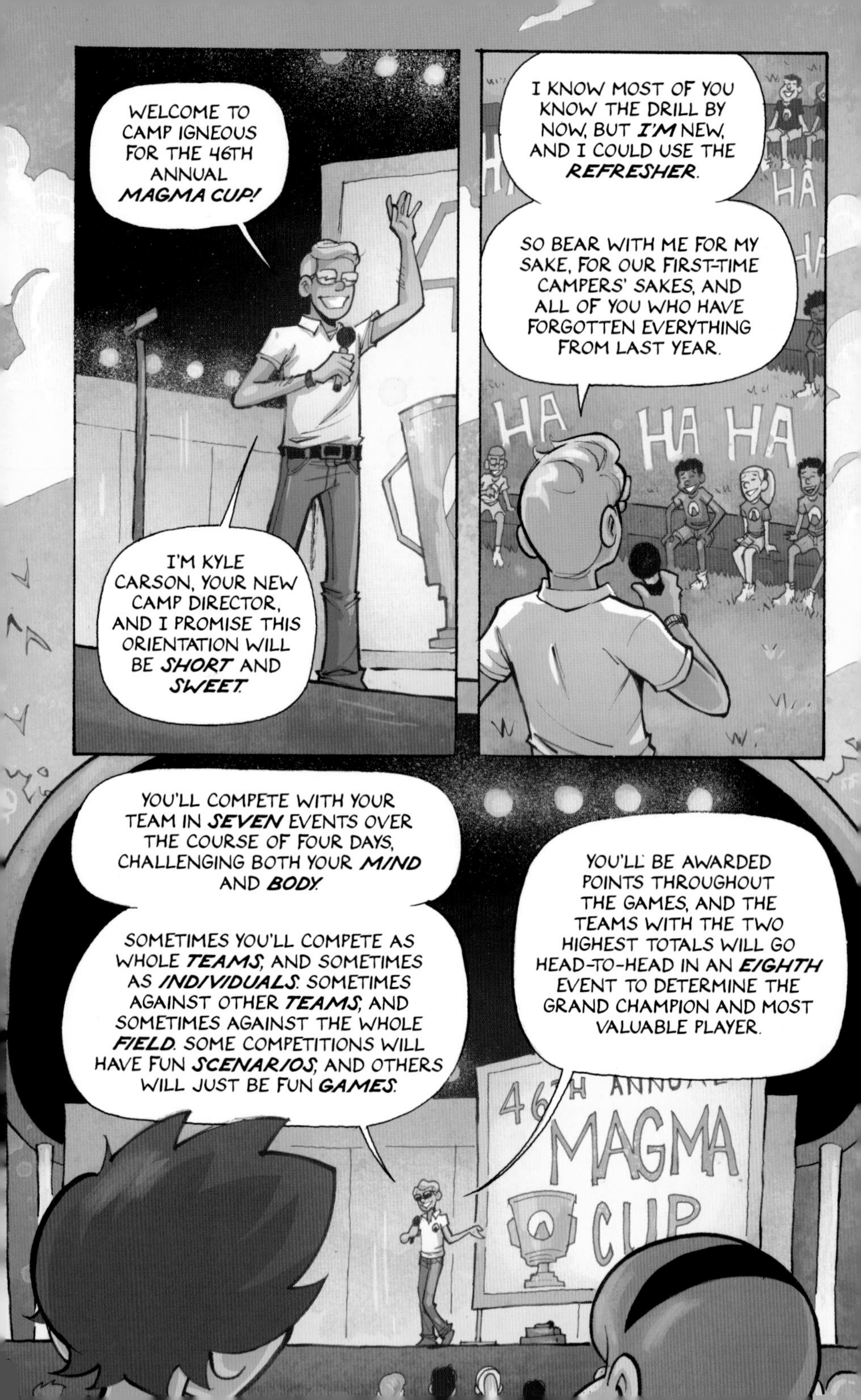
WELCOME TO CAMP IGNEOUS FOR THE 46TH ANNUAL *MAGMA CUP!*
I'M KYLE CARSON, YOUR NEW CAMP DIRECTOR, AND I PROMISE THIS ORIENTATION WILL BE *SHORT* AND *SWEET*.
I KNOW MOST OF YOU KNOW THE DRILL BY NOW, BUT *I'M* NEW, AND I COULD USE THE *REFRESHER*.
SO BEAR WITH ME FOR MY SAKE, FOR OUR FIRST-TIME CAMPERS' SAKES, AND ALL OF YOU WHO HAVE FORGOTTEN EVERYTHING FROM LAST YEAR.
HA HA HA HA HA HA
YOU'LL COMPETE WITH YOUR TEAM IN *SEVEN* EVENTS OVER THE COURSE OF FOUR DAYS, CHALLENGING BOTH YOUR *MIND* AND *BODY*.
SOMETIMES YOU'LL COMPETE AS WHOLE *TEAMS*, AND SOMETIMES AS *INDIVIDUALS*. SOMETIMES AGAINST OTHER *TEAMS*, AND SOMETIMES AGAINST THE WHOLE *FIELD*. SOME COMPETITIONS WILL HAVE FUN *SCENARIOS*, AND OTHERS WILL JUST BE FUN *GAMES*.
YOU'LL BE AWARDED POINTS THROUGHOUT THE GAMES, AND THE TEAMS WITH THE TWO HIGHEST TOTALS WILL GO HEAD-TO-HEAD IN AN *EIGHTH* EVENT TO DETERMINE THE GRAND CHAMPION AND MOST VALUABLE PLAYER.
MAGMA CUP

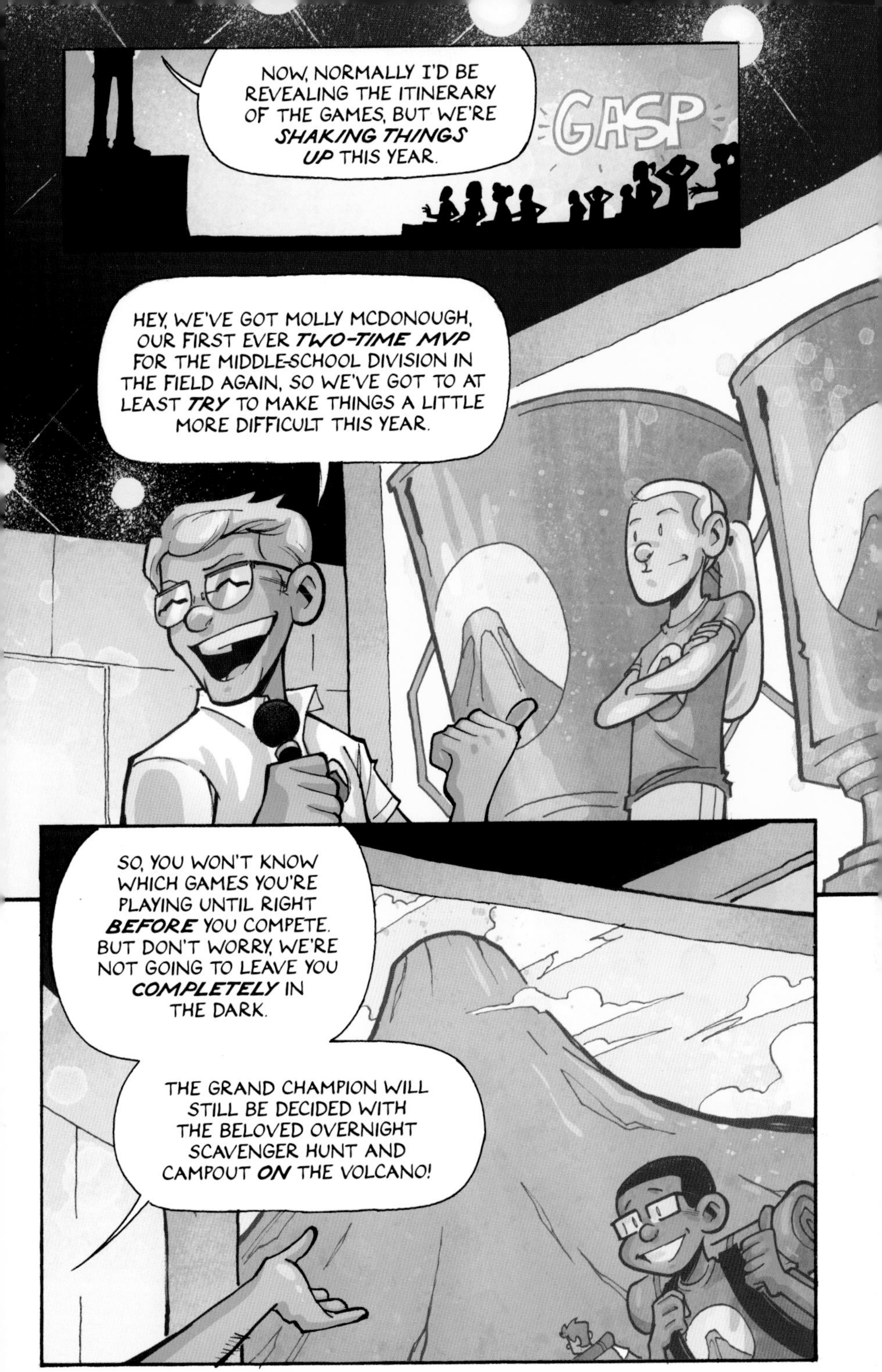
NOW, NORMALLY I'D BE REVEALING THE ITINERARY OF THE GAMES, BUT WE'RE SHAKING THINGS UP THIS YEAR.
GASP
HEY, WE'VE GOT MOLLY MCDONOUGH, OUR FIRST EVER TWO-TIME MVP FOR THE MIDDLE-SCHOOL DIVISION IN THE FIELD AGAIN, SO WE'VE GOT TO AT LEAST TRY TO MAKE THINGS A LITTLE MORE DIFFICULT THIS YEAR.
SO, YOU WON'T KNOW WHICH GAMES YOU'RE PLAYING UNTIL RIGHT BEFORE YOU COMPETE. BUT DON'T WORRY, WE'RE NOT GOING TO LEAVE YOU COMPLETELY IN THE DARK.
THE GRAND CHAMPION WILL STILL BE DECIDED WITH THE BELOVED OVERNIGHT SCAVENGER HUNT AND CAMPOUT ON THE VOLCANO!

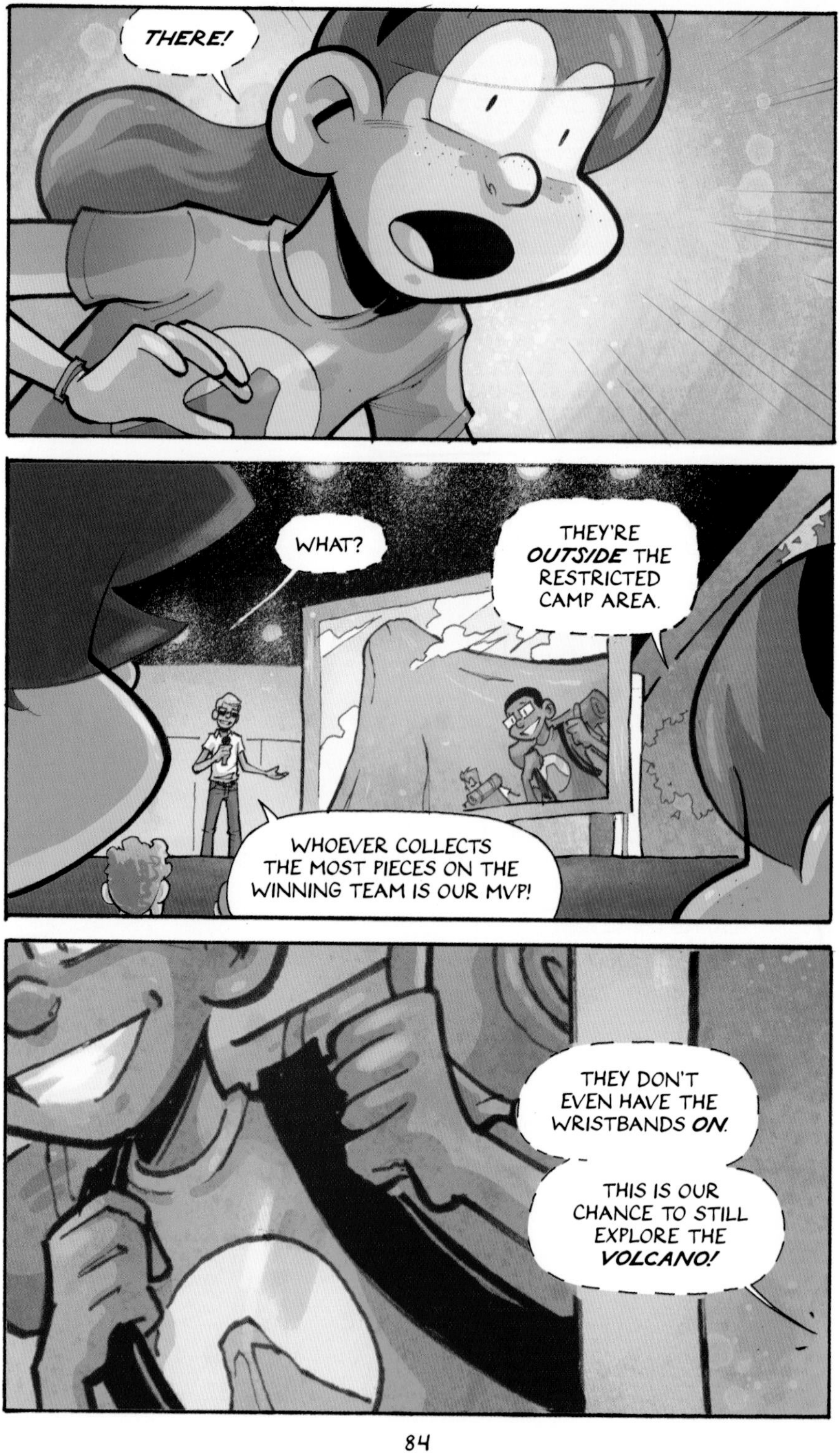
THERE!
WHAT?
THEY'RE *OUTSIDE* THE RESTRICTED CAMP AREA.
WHOEVER COLLECTS THE MOST PIECES ON THE WINNING TEAM IS OUR MVP!
THEY DON'T EVEN HAVE THE WRISTBANDS *ON*.
THIS IS OUR CHANCE TO STILL EXPLORE THE *VOLCANO!*

YEAH, BUT THERE'S STILL A *COUNSELOR* WITH THEM.

PLEASE...

...I THINK WE CAN DITCH *ONE* COUNSELOR.

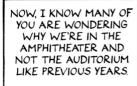

NOW, I KNOW MANY OF YOU ARE WONDERING WHY WE'RE IN THE AMPHITHEATER AND NOT THE AUDITORIUM LIKE PREVIOUS YEARS.

WELL, I'VE GOT *ONE* MORE CHANGE FOR YOU.

YOU SEE, WE NEEDED A CLEAR PATH FROM HERE TO THE *STARTING LINE*, BECAUSE THE FIRST CHALLENGE STARTS IN, SAY...

...*30 SECONDS*.

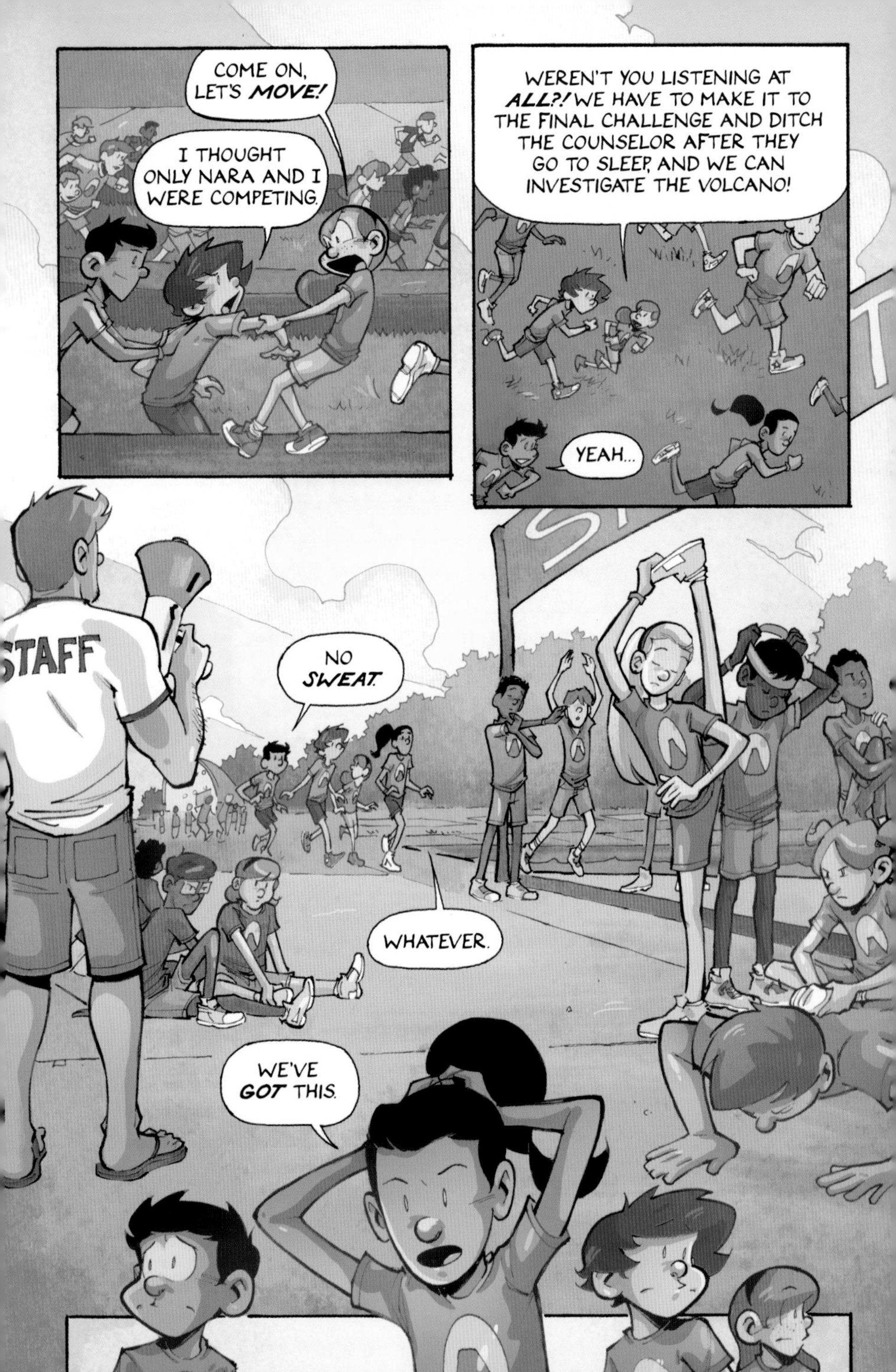
COME ON, LET'S MOVE!
I THOUGHT ONLY NARA AND I WERE COMPETING.
WEREN'T YOU LISTENING AT ALL?! WE HAVE TO MAKE IT TO THE FINAL CHALLENGE AND DITCH THE COUNSELOR AFTER THEY GO TO SLEEP, AND WE CAN INVESTIGATE THE VOLCANO!
YEAH...
STAFF
NO SWEAT.
WHATEVER.
WE'VE GOT THIS.

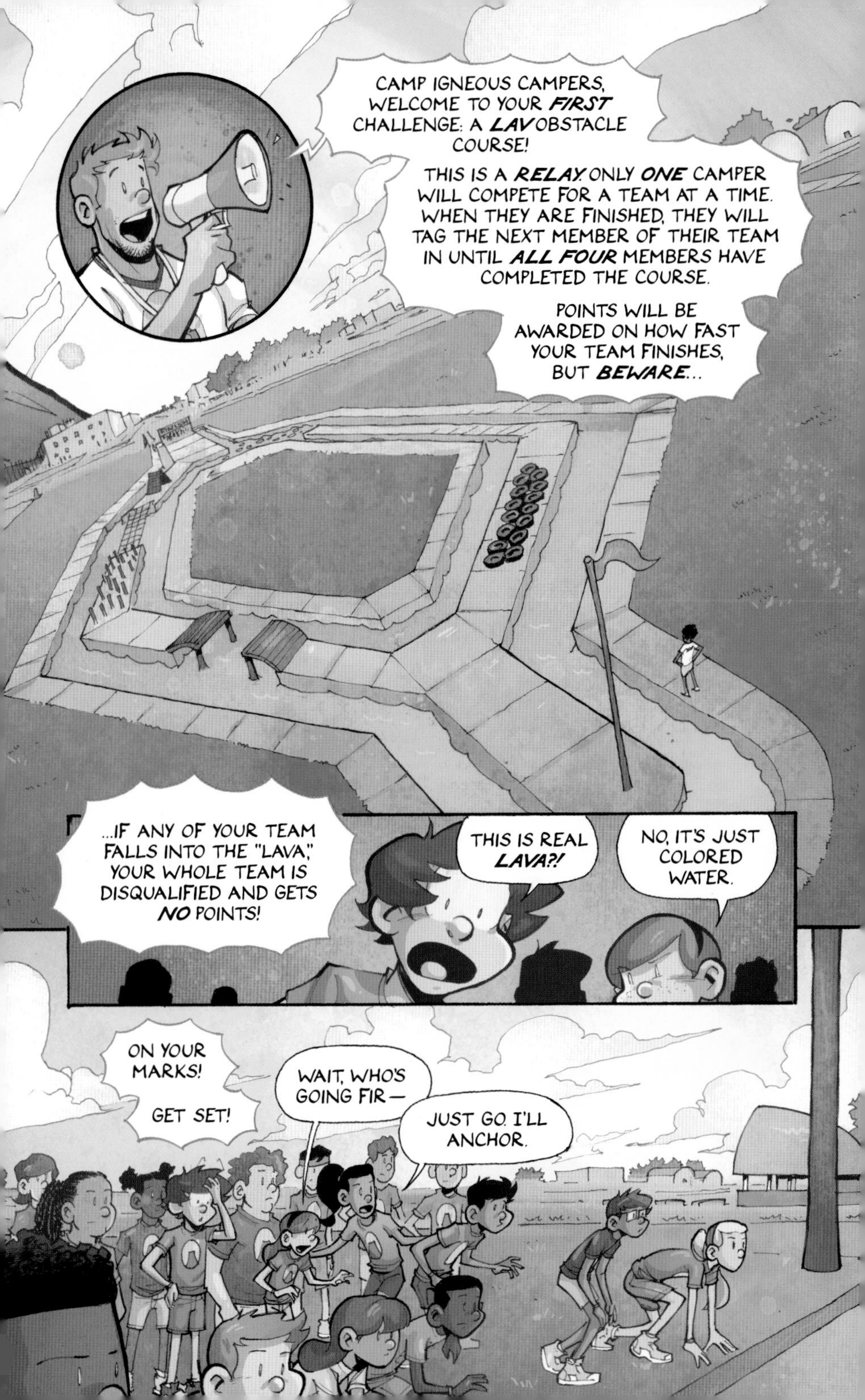
CAMP IGNEOUS CAMPERS, WELCOME TO YOUR FIRST CHALLENGE: A LAVOBSTACLE COURSE!
THIS IS A RELAY. ONLY ONE CAMPER WILL COMPETE FOR A TEAM AT A TIME. WHEN THEY ARE FINISHED, THEY WILL TAG THE NEXT MEMBER OF THEIR TEAM IN UNTIL ALL FOUR MEMBERS HAVE COMPLETED THE COURSE.
POINTS WILL BE AWARDED ON HOW FAST YOUR TEAM FINISHES, BUT BEWARE...
...IF ANY OF YOUR TEAM FALLS INTO THE "LAVA," YOUR WHOLE TEAM IS DISQUALIFIED AND GETS NO POINTS!
THIS IS REAL LAVA?!
NO, IT'S JUST COLORED WATER.
ON YOUR MARKS!
GET SET!
WAIT, WHO'S GOING FIR—
JUST GO. I'LL ANCHOR.

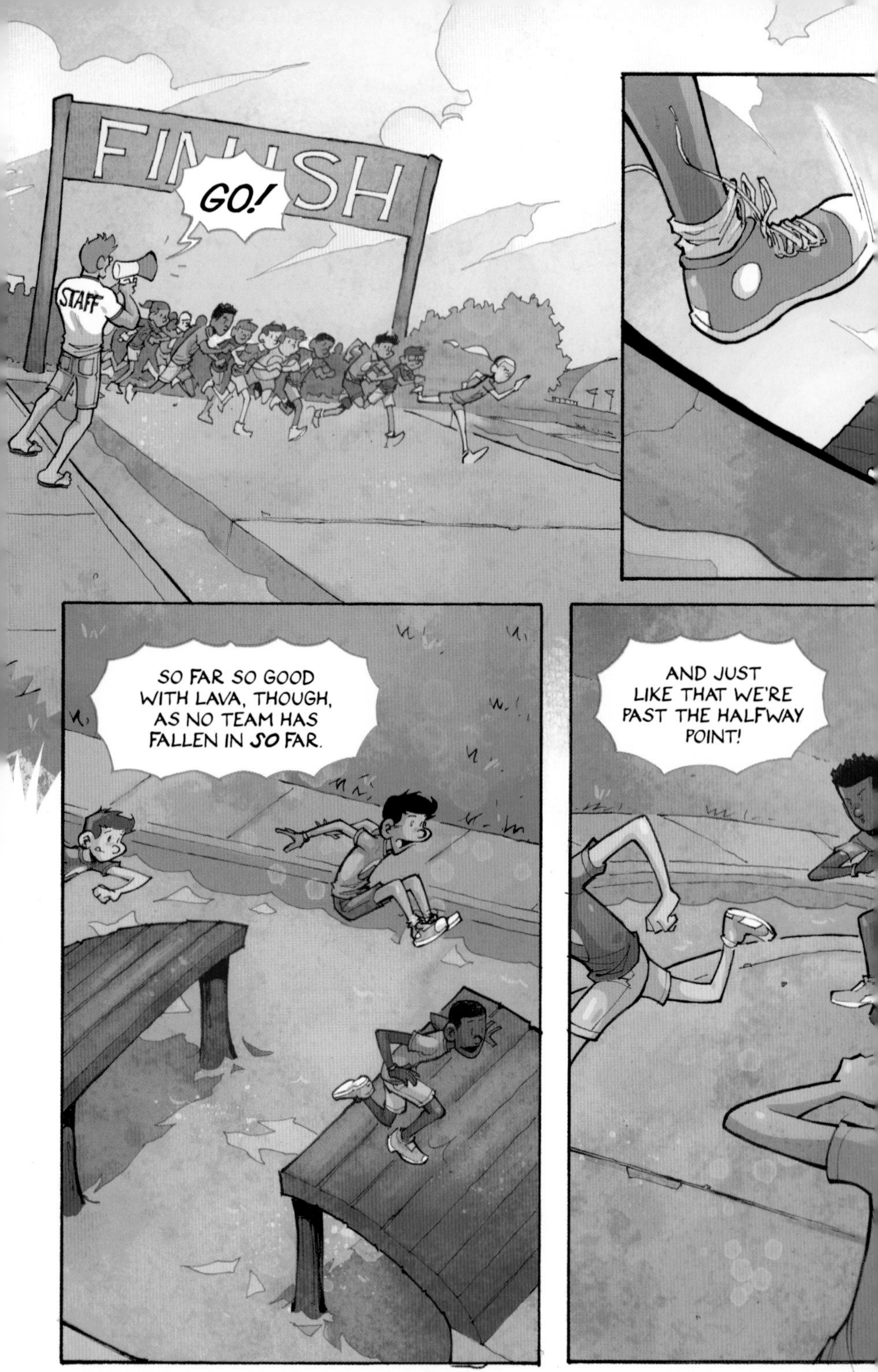
FINISH
GO!
STAFF
SO FAR SO GOOD WITH LAVA, THOUGH, AS NO TEAM HAS FALLEN IN SO FAR.
AND JUST LIKE THAT WE'RE PAST THE HALFWAY POINT!

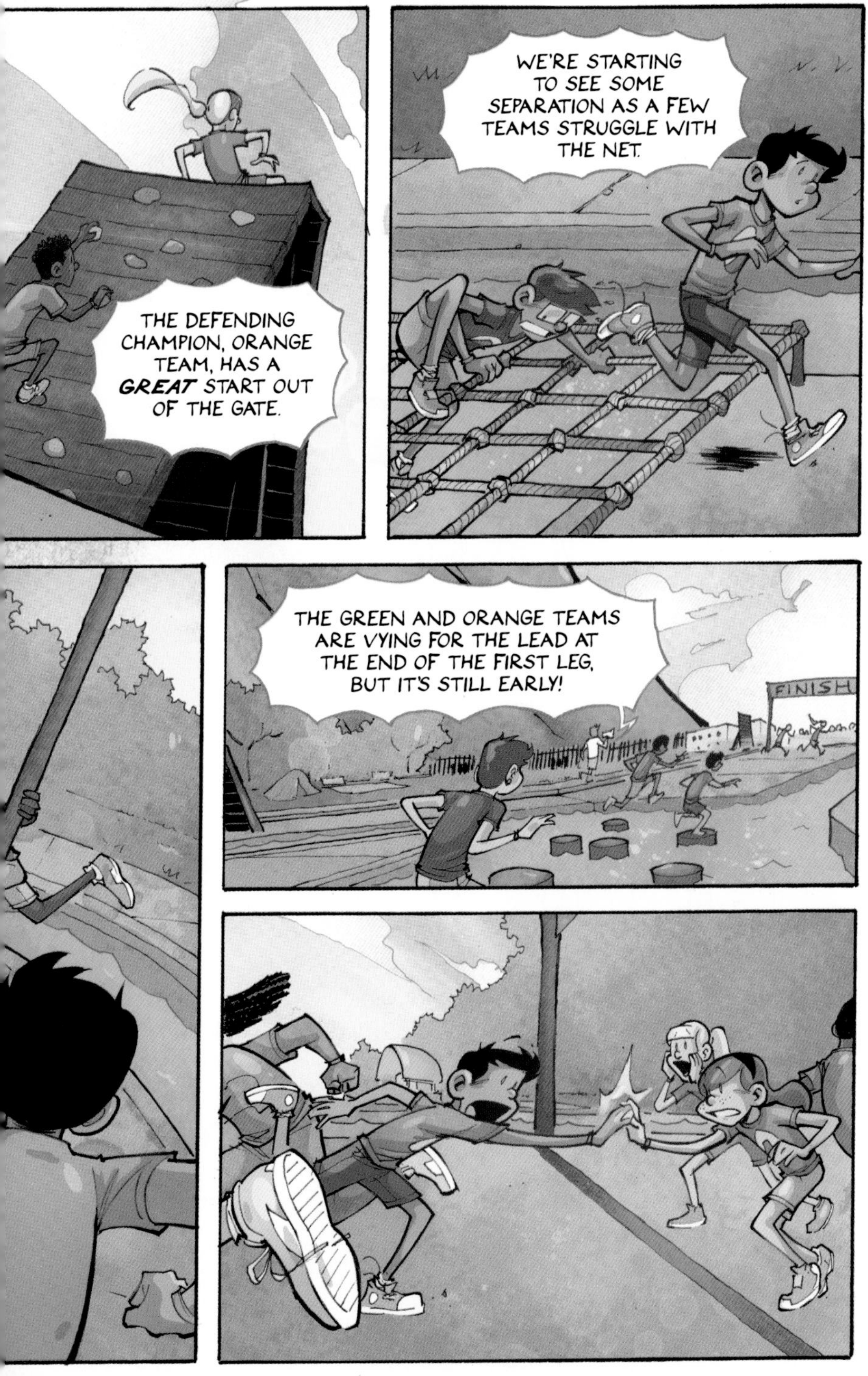
THE DEFENDING CHAMPION, ORANGE TEAM, HAS A GREAT START OUT OF THE GATE.
WE'RE STARTING TO SEE SOME SEPARATION AS A FEW TEAMS STRUGGLE WITH THE NET.
THE GREEN AND ORANGE TEAMS ARE VYING FOR THE LEAD AT THE END OF THE FIRST LEG, BUT IT'S STILL EARLY!
FINISH

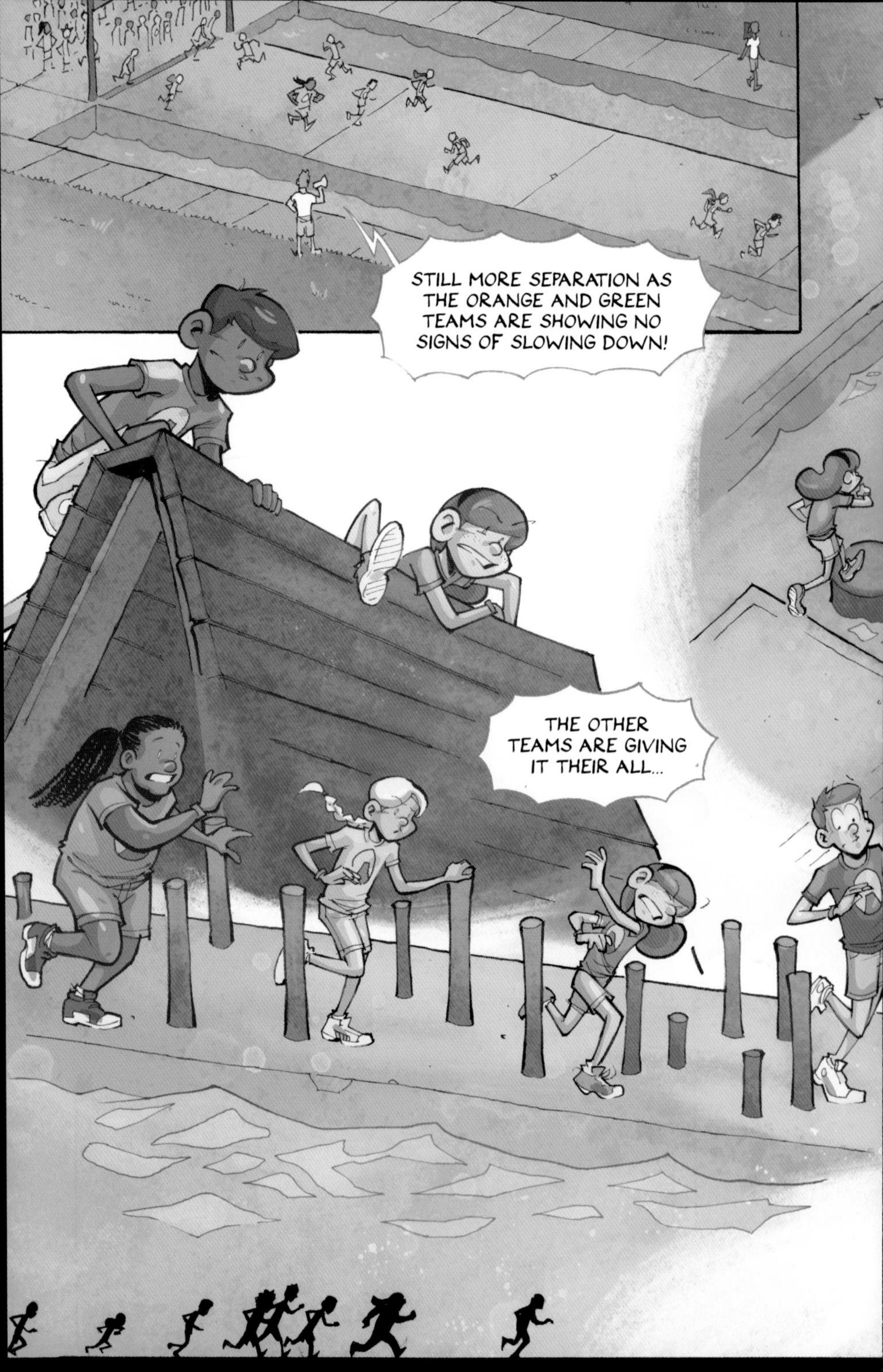
STILL MORE SEPARATION AS THE ORANGE AND GREEN TEAMS ARE SHOWING NO SIGNS OF SLOWING DOWN!
THE OTHER TEAMS ARE GIVING IT THEIR ALL...

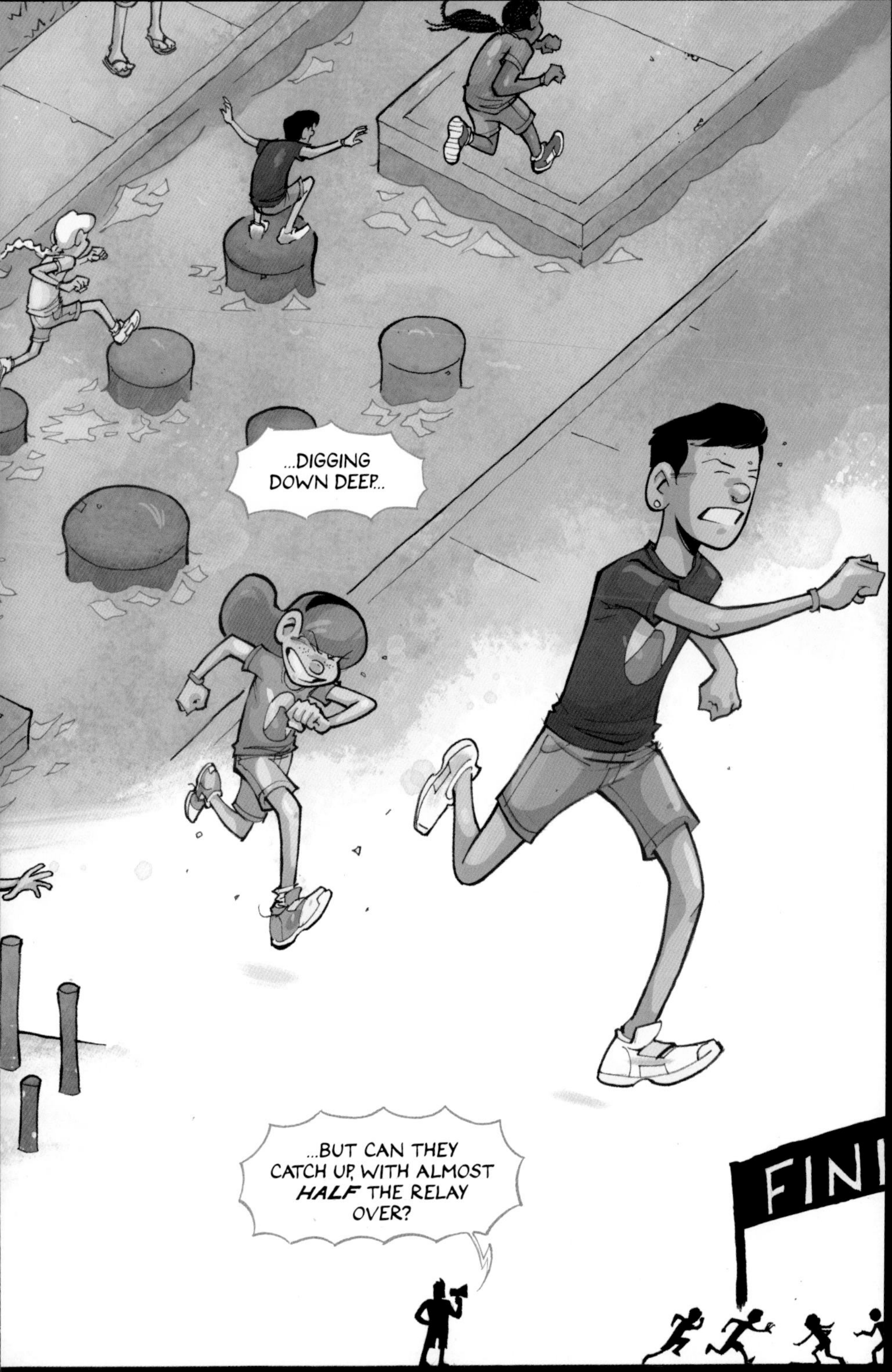
...DIGGING DOWN DEEP...
...BUT CAN THEY CATCH UP, WITH ALMOST *HALF* THE RELAY OVER?
FINI

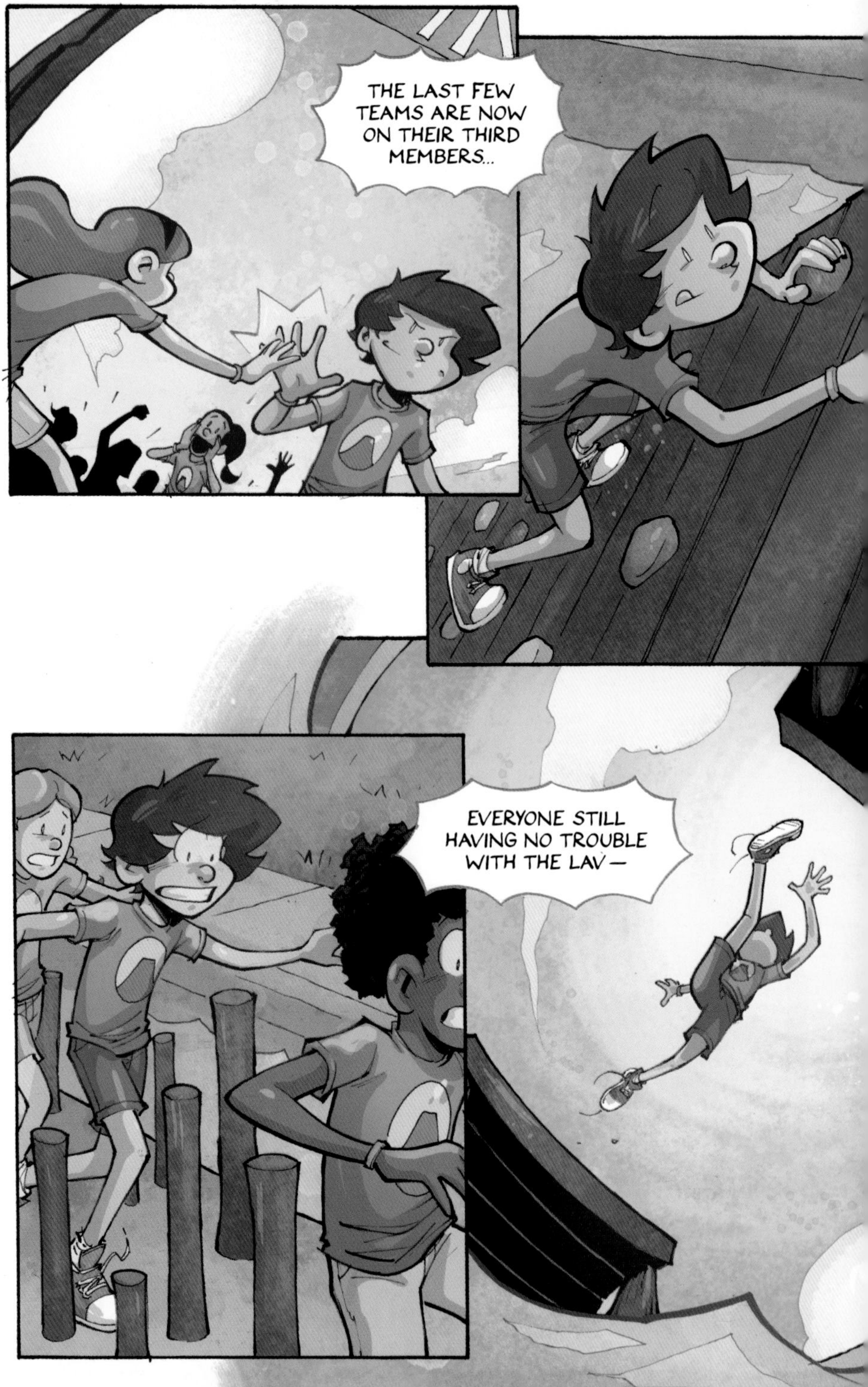
THE LAST FEW TEAMS ARE NOW ON THEIR THIRD MEMBERS...
EVERYONE STILL HAVING NO TROUBLE WITH THE LAV—

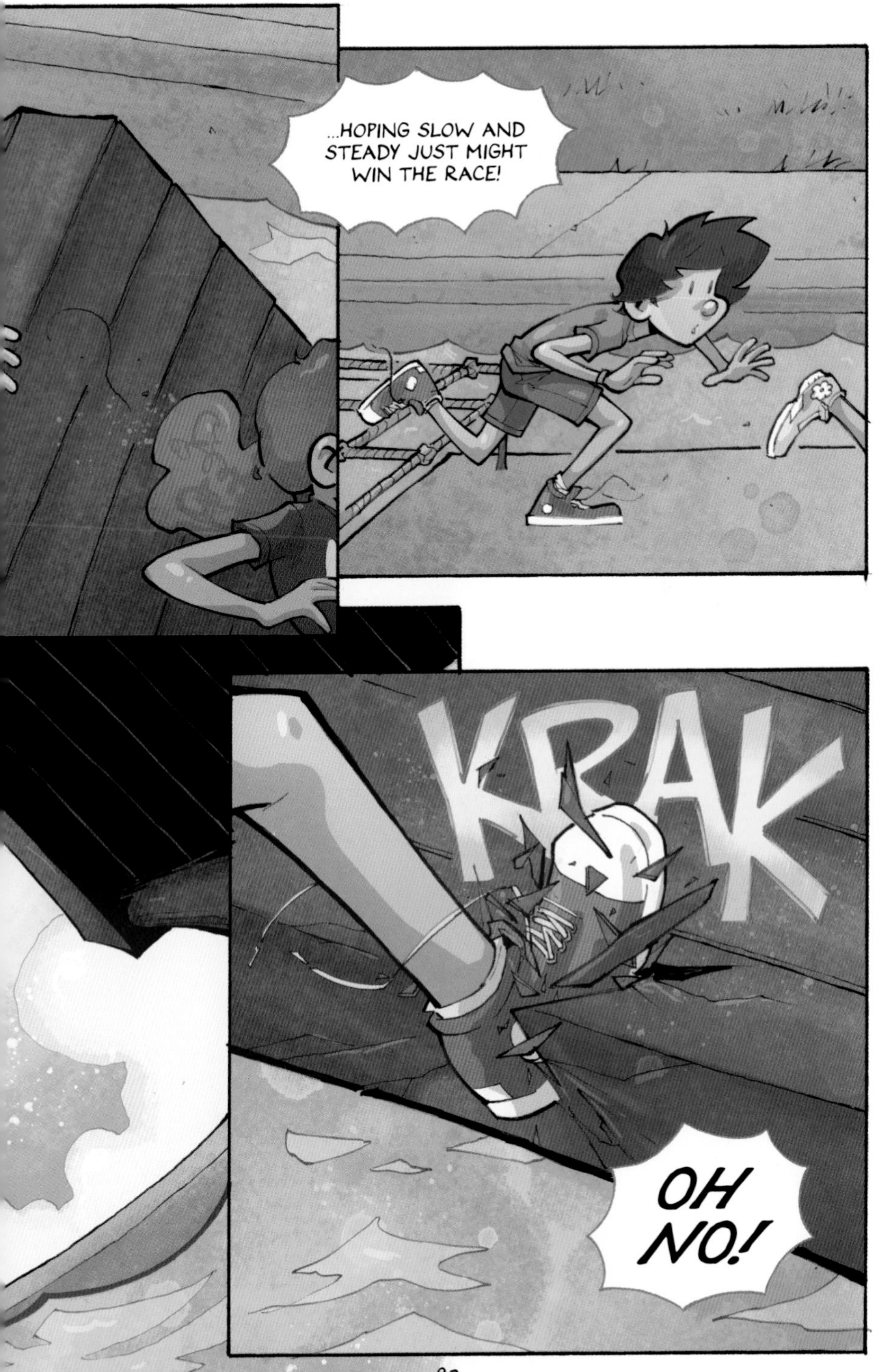
...HOPING SLOW AND STEADY JUST MIGHT WIN THE RACE!
KRAK
OH NO!

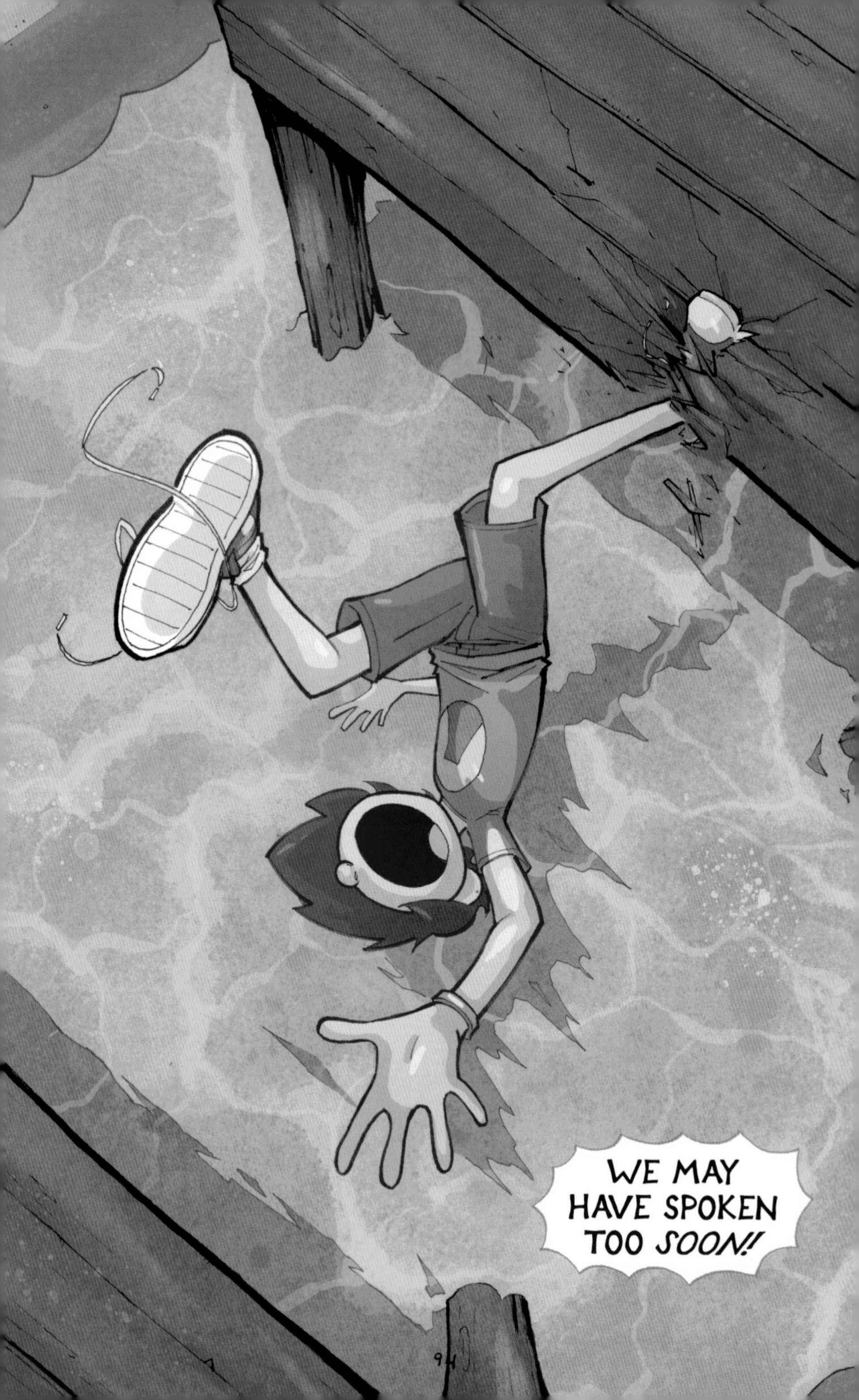
WE MAY HAVE SPOKEN TOO SOON!

CHAPTER SIX

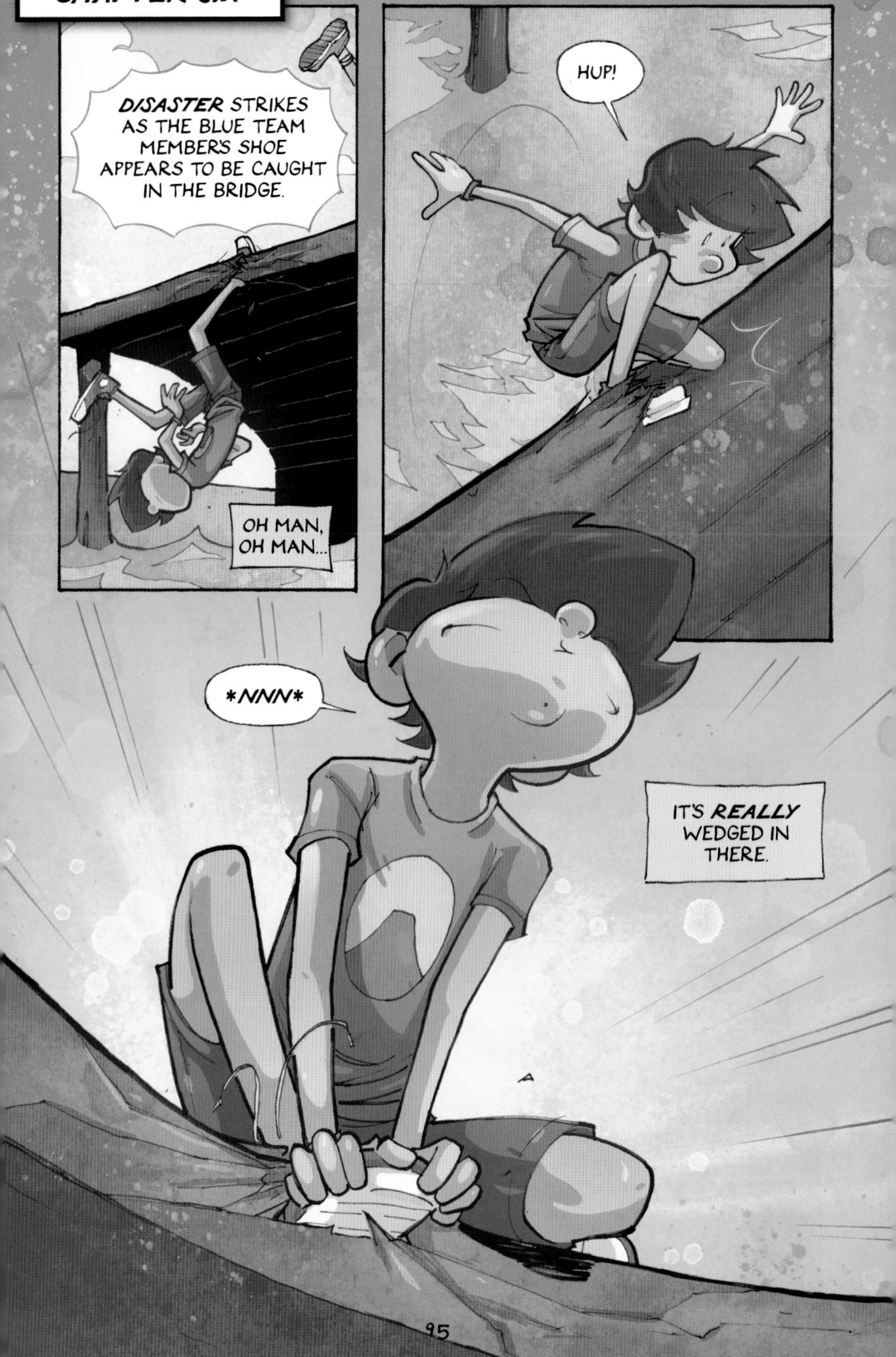
DISASTER STRIKES AS THE BLUE TEAM MEMBER'S SHOE APPEARS TO BE CAUGHT IN THE BRIDGE.
OH MAN, OH MAN...
HUP!
NNN
IT'S REALLY WEDGED IN THERE.

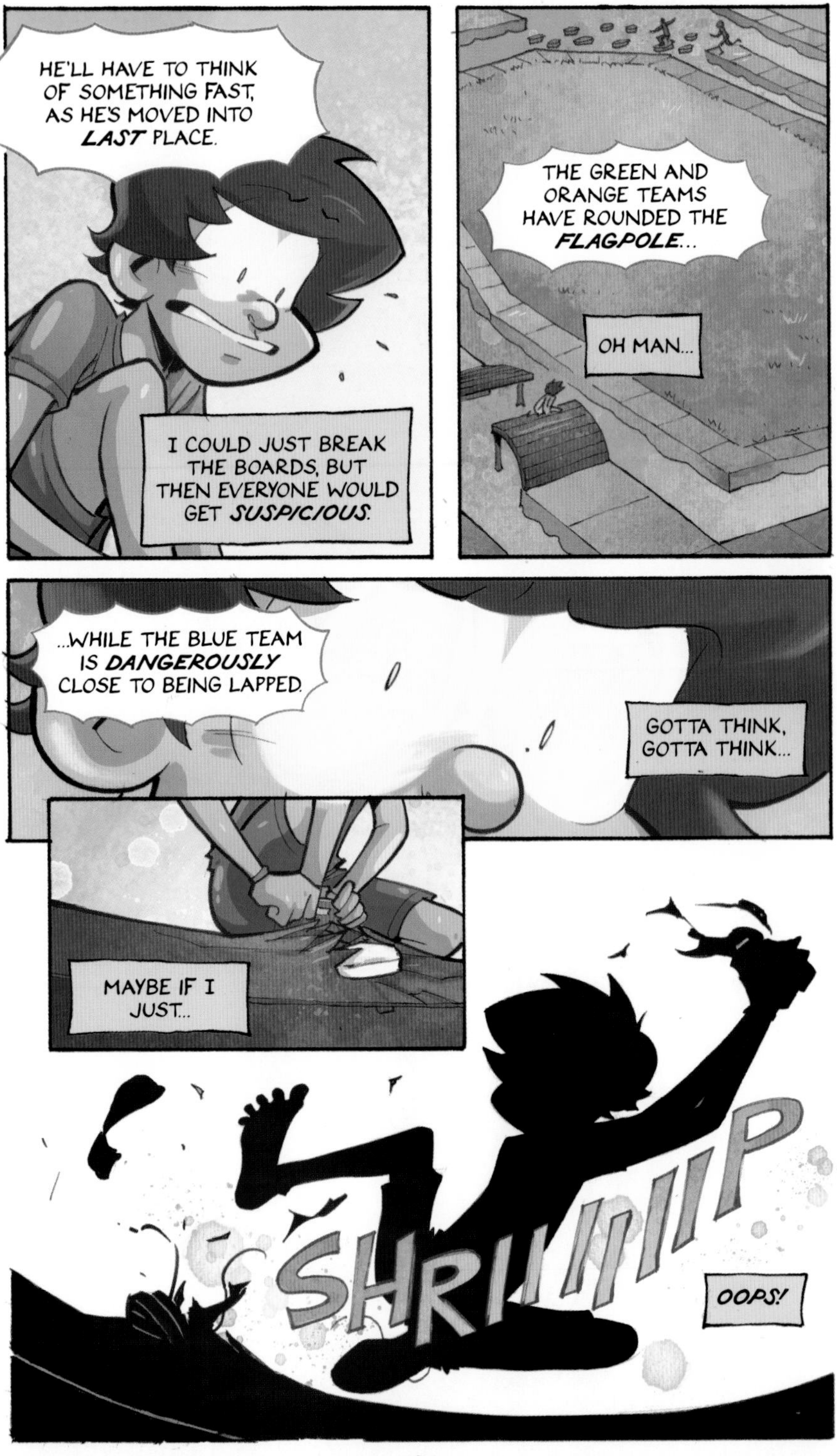
HE'LL HAVE TO THINK OF SOMETHING FAST, AS HE'S MOVED INTO LAST PLACE.
I COULD JUST BREAK THE BOARDS, BUT THEN EVERYONE WOULD GET SUSPICIOUS.
THE GREEN AND ORANGE TEAMS HAVE ROUNDED THE FLAGPOLE...
OH MAN...
...WHILE THE BLUE TEAM IS DANGEROUSLY CLOSE TO BEING LAPPED.
GOTTA THINK, GOTTA THINK...
MAYBE IF I JUST...
SHRIIIIIIP
OOPS!

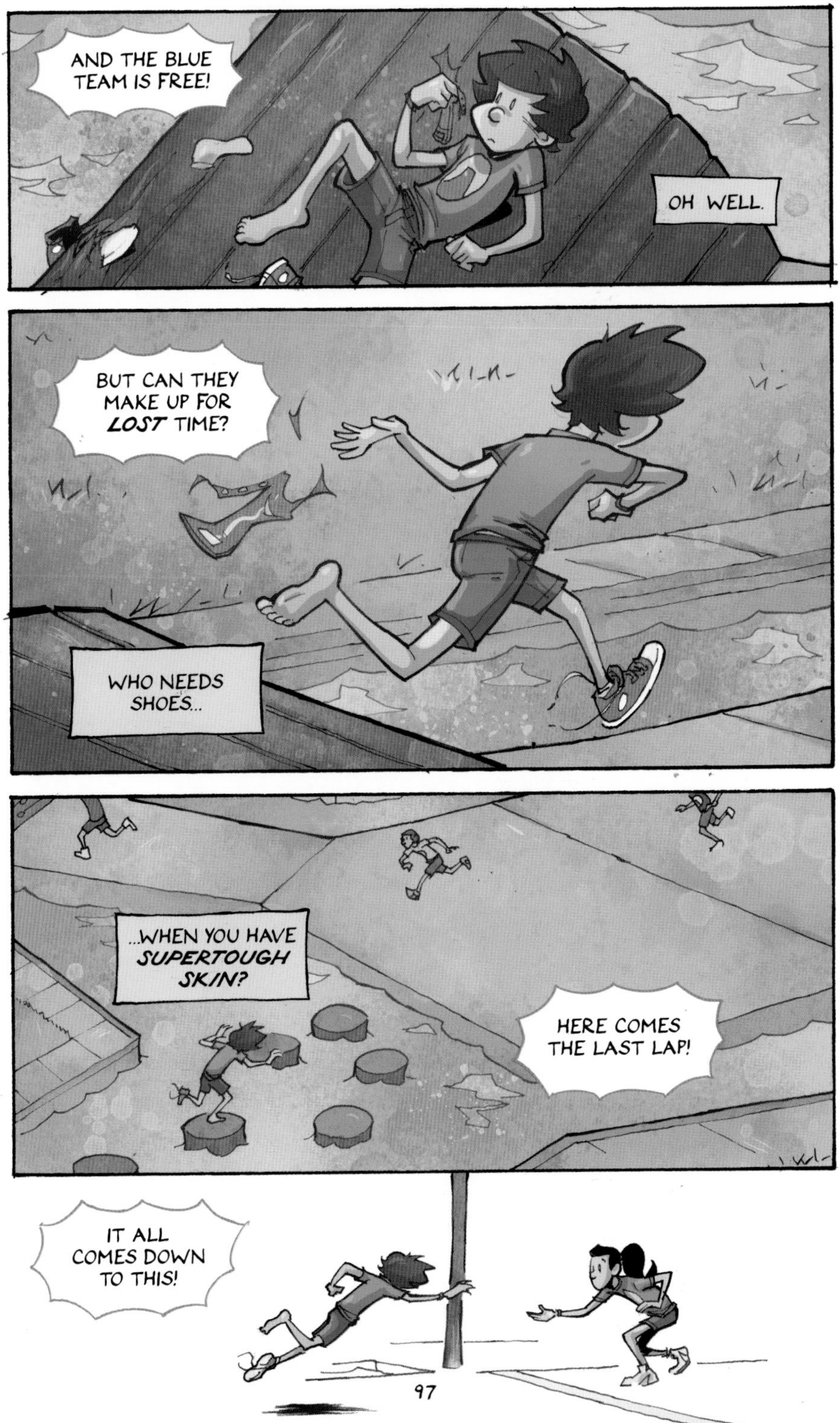
AND THE BLUE TEAM IS FREE!
OH WELL.
BUT CAN THEY MAKE UP FOR LOST TIME?
WHO NEEDS SHOES...
...WHEN YOU HAVE SUPERTOUGH SKIN?
HERE COMES THE LAST LAP!
IT ALL COMES DOWN TO THIS!

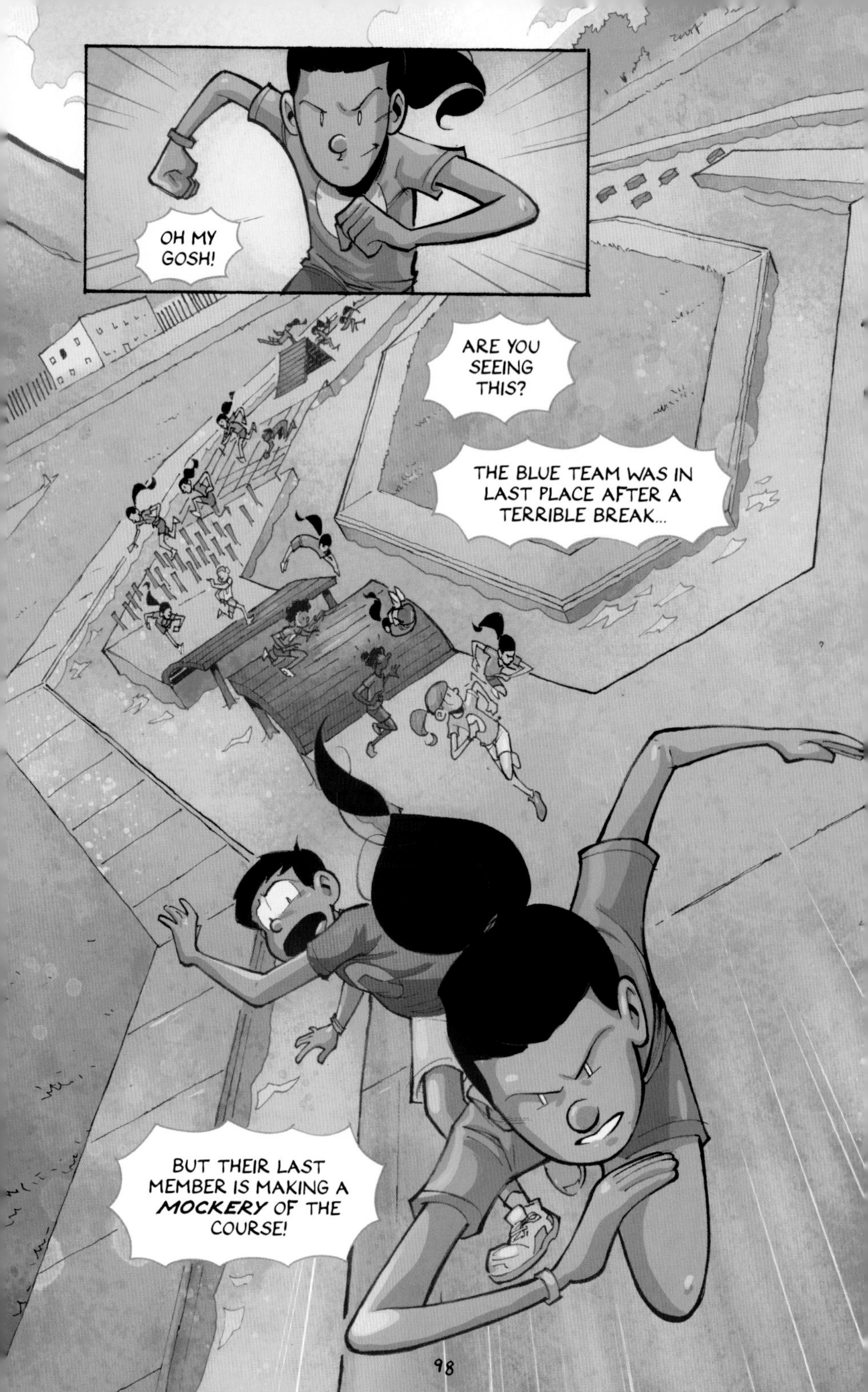
OH MY GOSH!
ARE YOU SEEING THIS?
THE BLUE TEAM WAS IN LAST PLACE AFTER A TERRIBLE BREAK...
BUT THEIR LAST MEMBER IS MAKING A *MOCKERY* OF THE COURSE!

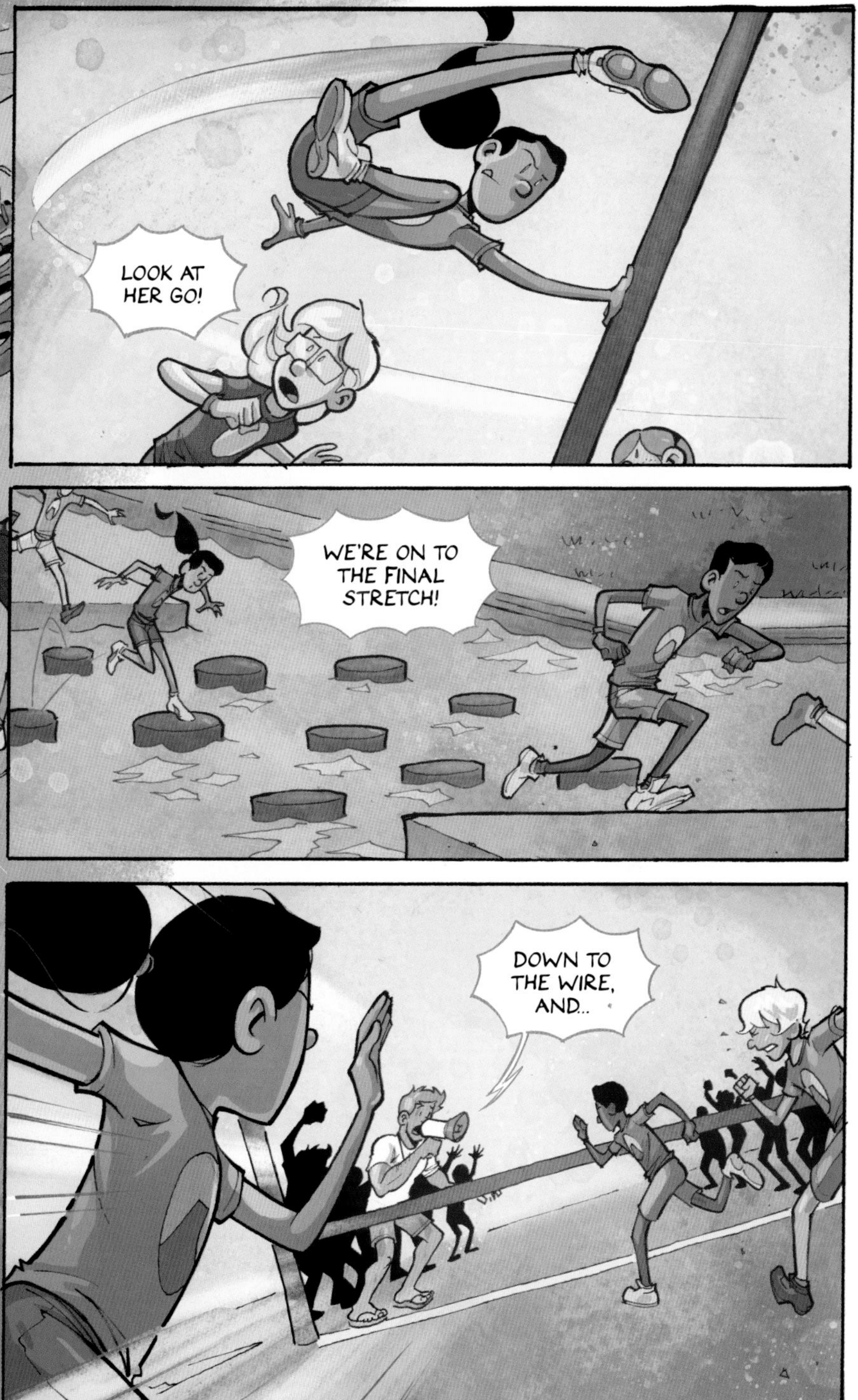
LOOK AT HER GO!
WE'RE ON TO THE FINAL STRETCH!
DOWN TO THE WIRE, AND...

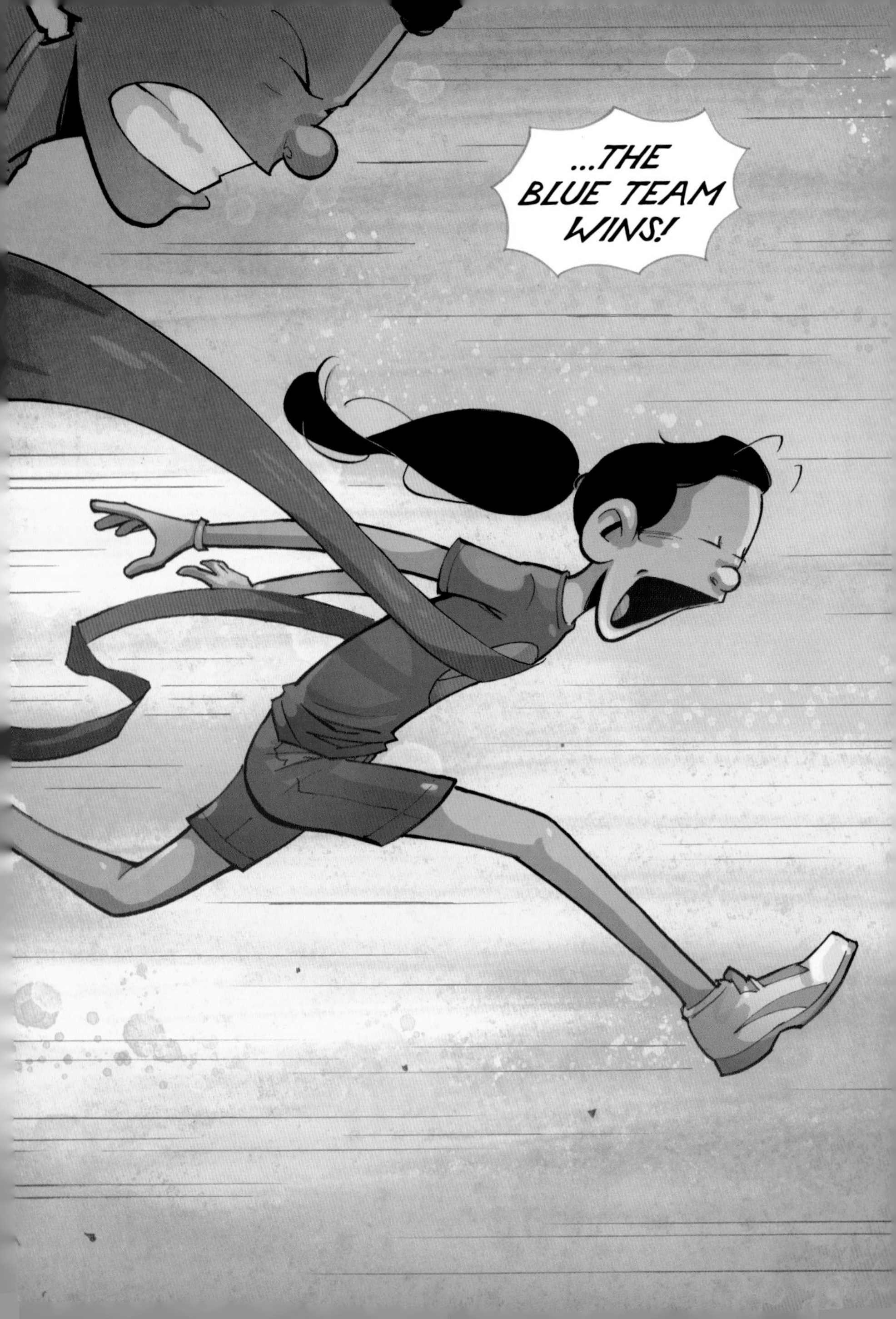
...THE BLUE TEAM WINS!

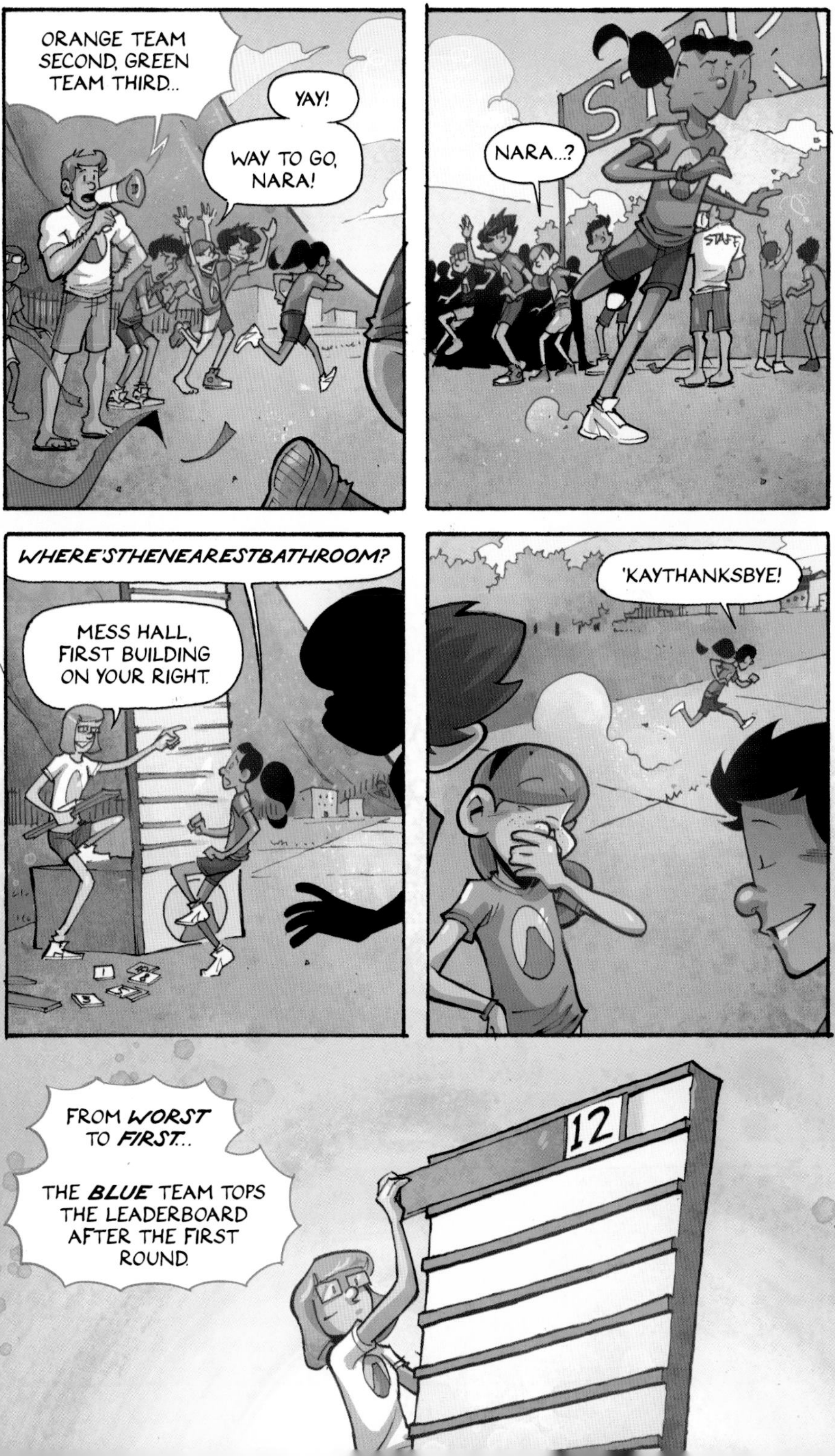

ORANGE TEAM SECOND, GREEN TEAM THIRD...
YAY!
WAY TO GO, NARA!
NARA...?
STAFF
WHERE'STHENEARESTBATHROOM?
MESS HALL, FIRST BUILDING ON YOUR RIGHT.
'KAYTHANKSBYE!
FROM *WORST* TO *FIRST*...
THE *BLUE* TEAM TOPS THE LEADERBOARD AFTER THE FIRST ROUND.
12

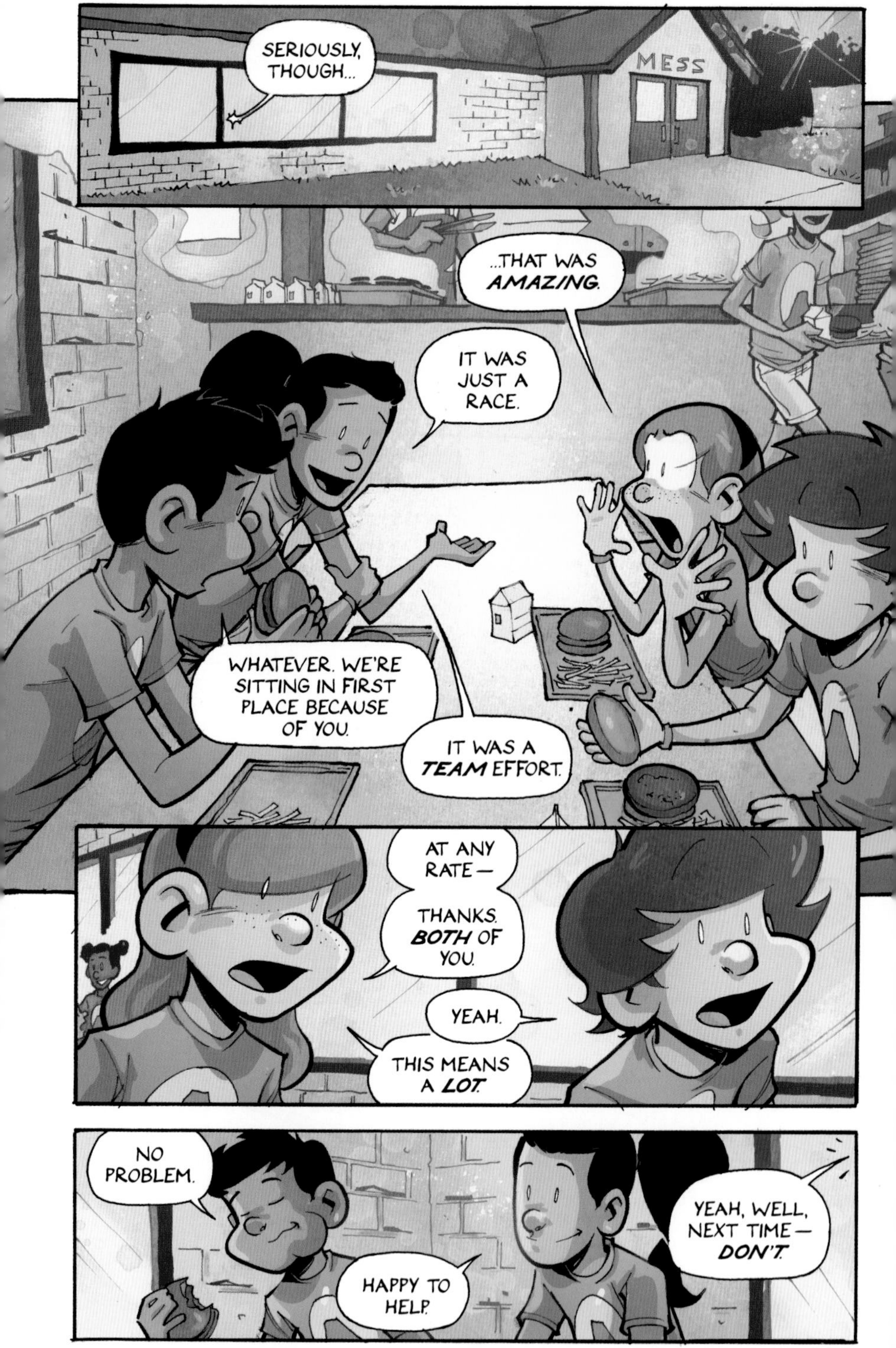
SERIOUSLY, THOUGH...
MESS
...THAT WAS AMAZING.
IT WAS JUST A RACE.
WHATEVER. WE'RE SITTING IN FIRST PLACE BECAUSE OF YOU.
IT WAS A TEAM EFFORT.
AT ANY RATE—
THANKS. BOTH OF YOU.
YEAH.
THIS MEANS A LOT.
NO PROBLEM.
HAPPY TO HELP.
YEAH, WELL, NEXT TIME— DON'T.

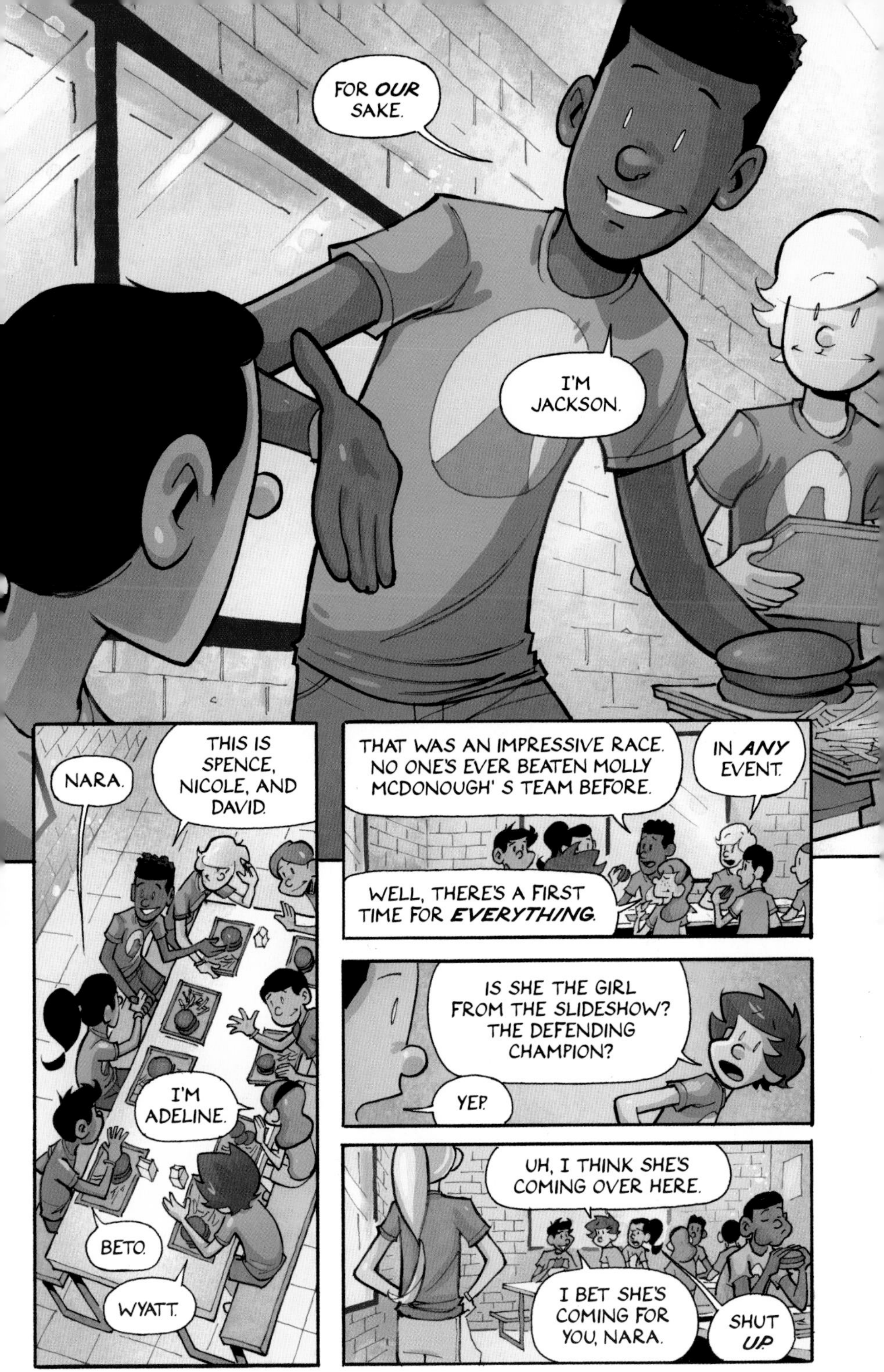
FOR *OUR* SAKE.
I'M JACKSON.
NARA.
THIS IS SPENCE, NICOLE, AND DAVID.
I'M ADELINE.
BETO.
WYATT.
THAT WAS AN IMPRESSIVE RACE. NO ONE'S EVER BEATEN MOLLY MCDONOUGH' S TEAM BEFORE.
IN *ANY* EVENT.
WELL, THERE'S A FIRST TIME FOR ***EVERYTHING***.
IS SHE THE GIRL FROM THE SLIDESHOW? THE DEFENDING CHAMPION?
YEP.
UH, I THINK SHE'S COMING OVER HERE.
I BET SHE'S COMING FOR YOU, NARA.
SHUT *UP*.

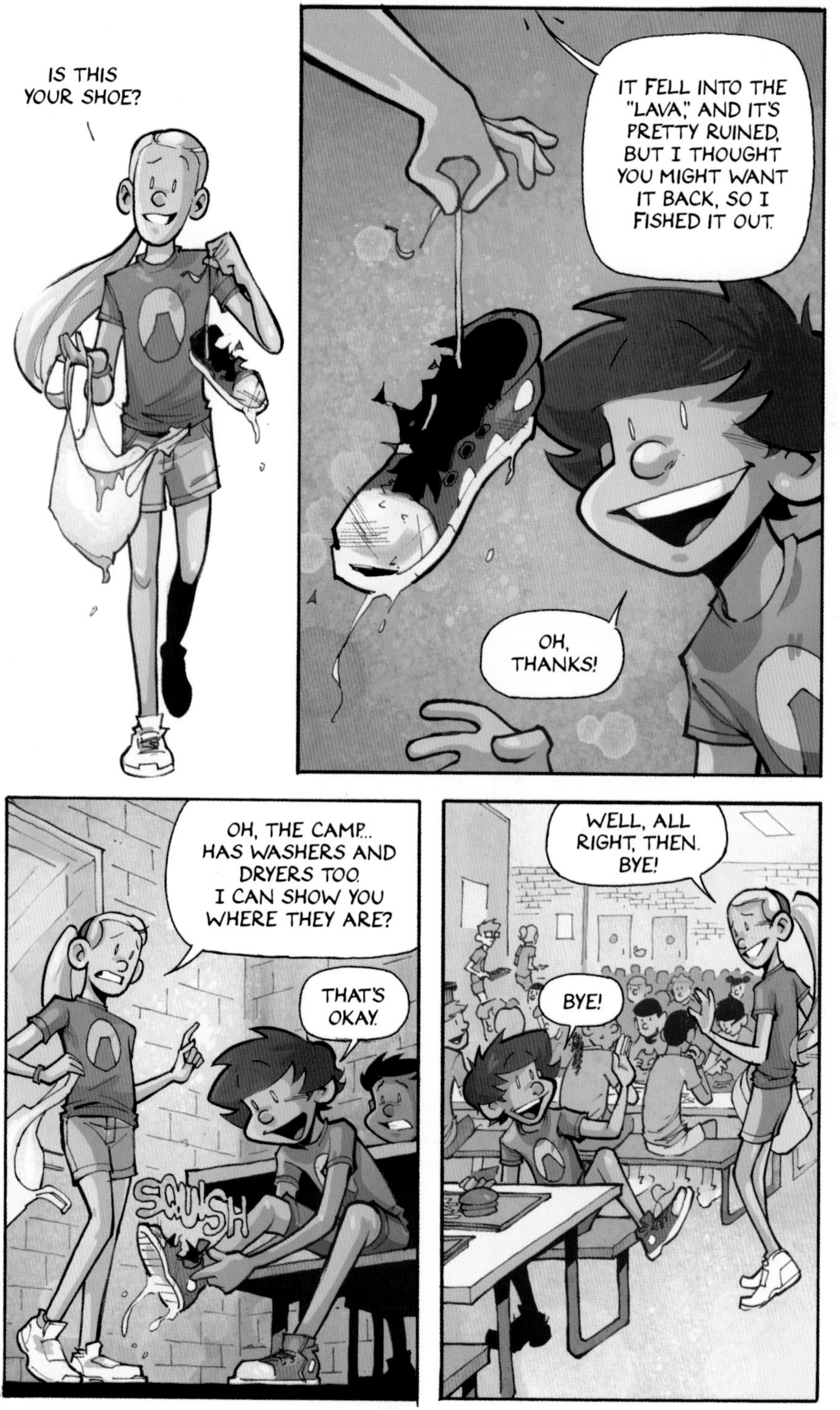
IS THIS YOUR SHOE?
IT FELL INTO THE "LAVA," AND IT'S PRETTY RUINED, BUT I THOUGHT YOU MIGHT WANT IT BACK, SO I FISHED IT OUT.
OH, THANKS!
OH, THE CAMP... HAS WASHERS AND DRYERS TOO. I CAN SHOW YOU WHERE THEY ARE?
THAT'S OKAY.
SQUISH
WELL, ALL RIGHT, THEN. BYE!
BYE!

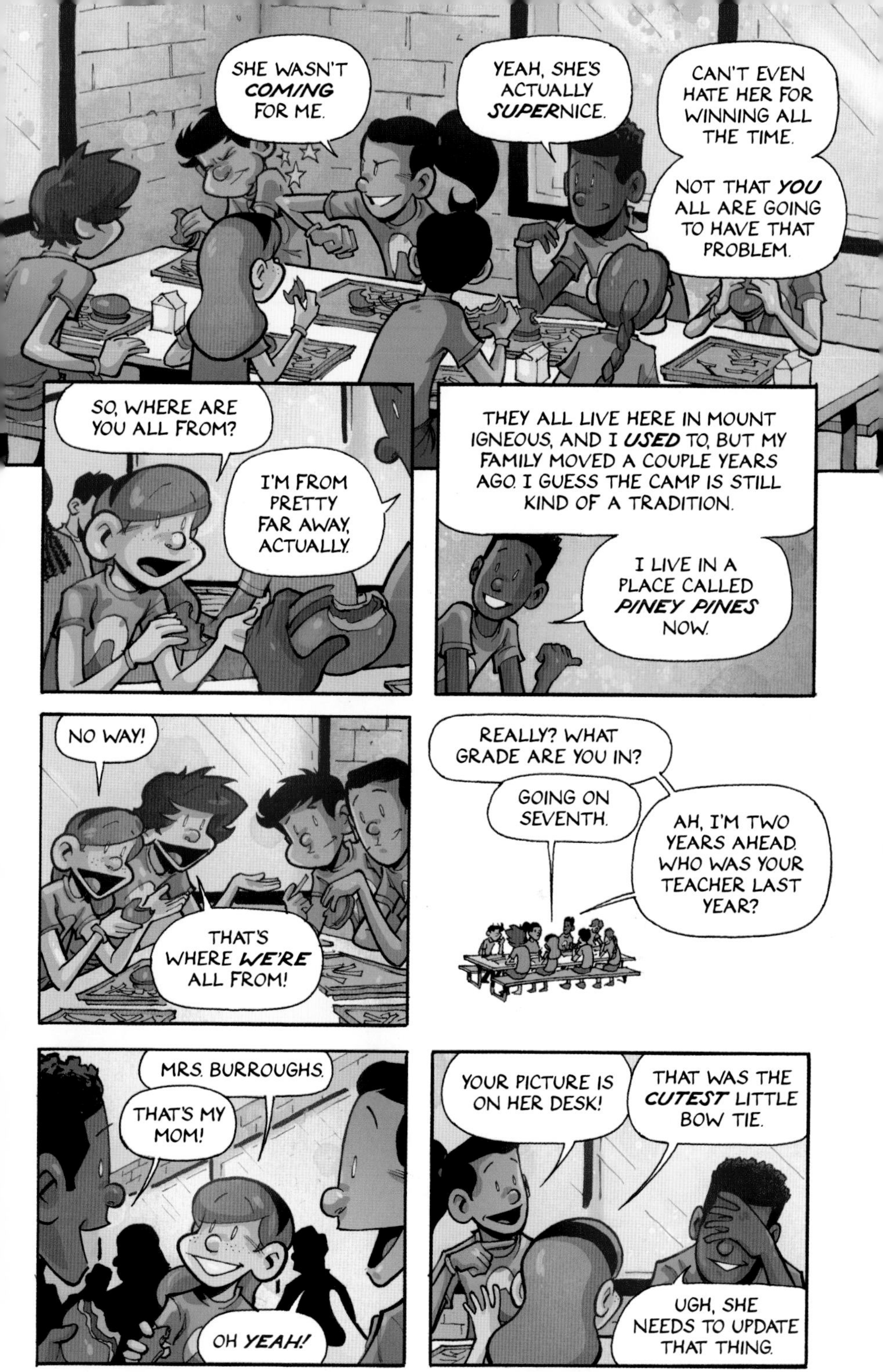
SHE WASN'T COMING FOR ME.
YEAH, SHE'S ACTUALLY SUPERNICE.
CAN'T EVEN HATE HER FOR WINNING ALL THE TIME.
NOT THAT YOU ALL ARE GOING TO HAVE THAT PROBLEM.
SO, WHERE ARE YOU ALL FROM?
I'M FROM PRETTY FAR AWAY, ACTUALLY.
THEY ALL LIVE HERE IN MOUNT IGNEOUS, AND I USED TO, BUT MY FAMILY MOVED A COUPLE YEARS AGO. I GUESS THE CAMP IS STILL KIND OF A TRADITION.
I LIVE IN A PLACE CALLED PINEY PINES NOW.
NO WAY!
THAT'S WHERE WE'RE ALL FROM!
REALLY? WHAT GRADE ARE YOU IN?
GOING ON SEVENTH.
AH, I'M TWO YEARS AHEAD. WHO WAS YOUR TEACHER LAST YEAR?
MRS. BURROUGHS.
THAT'S MY MOM!
OH YEAH!
YOUR PICTURE IS ON HER DESK!
THAT WAS THE CUTEST LITTLE BOW TIE.
UGH, SHE NEEDS TO UPDATE THAT THING.

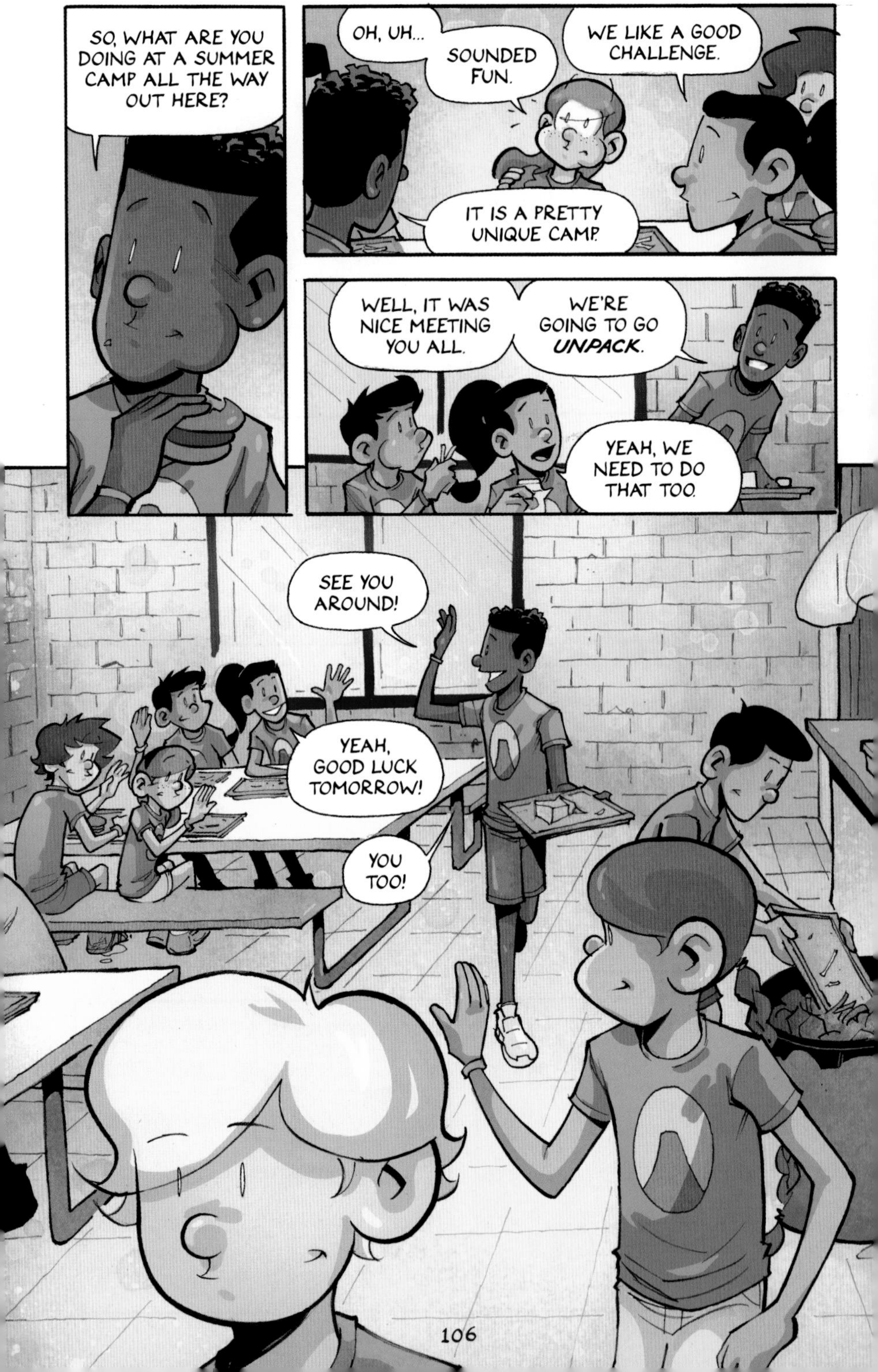
SO, WHAT ARE YOU DOING AT A SUMMER CAMP ALL THE WAY OUT HERE?
OH, UH...
SOUNDED FUN.
WE LIKE A GOOD CHALLENGE.
IT IS A PRETTY UNIQUE CAMP.
WELL, IT WAS NICE MEETING YOU ALL.
WE'RE GOING TO GO UNPACK.
YEAH, WE NEED TO DO THAT TOO.
SEE YOU AROUND!
YEAH, GOOD LUCK TOMORROW!
YOU TOO!

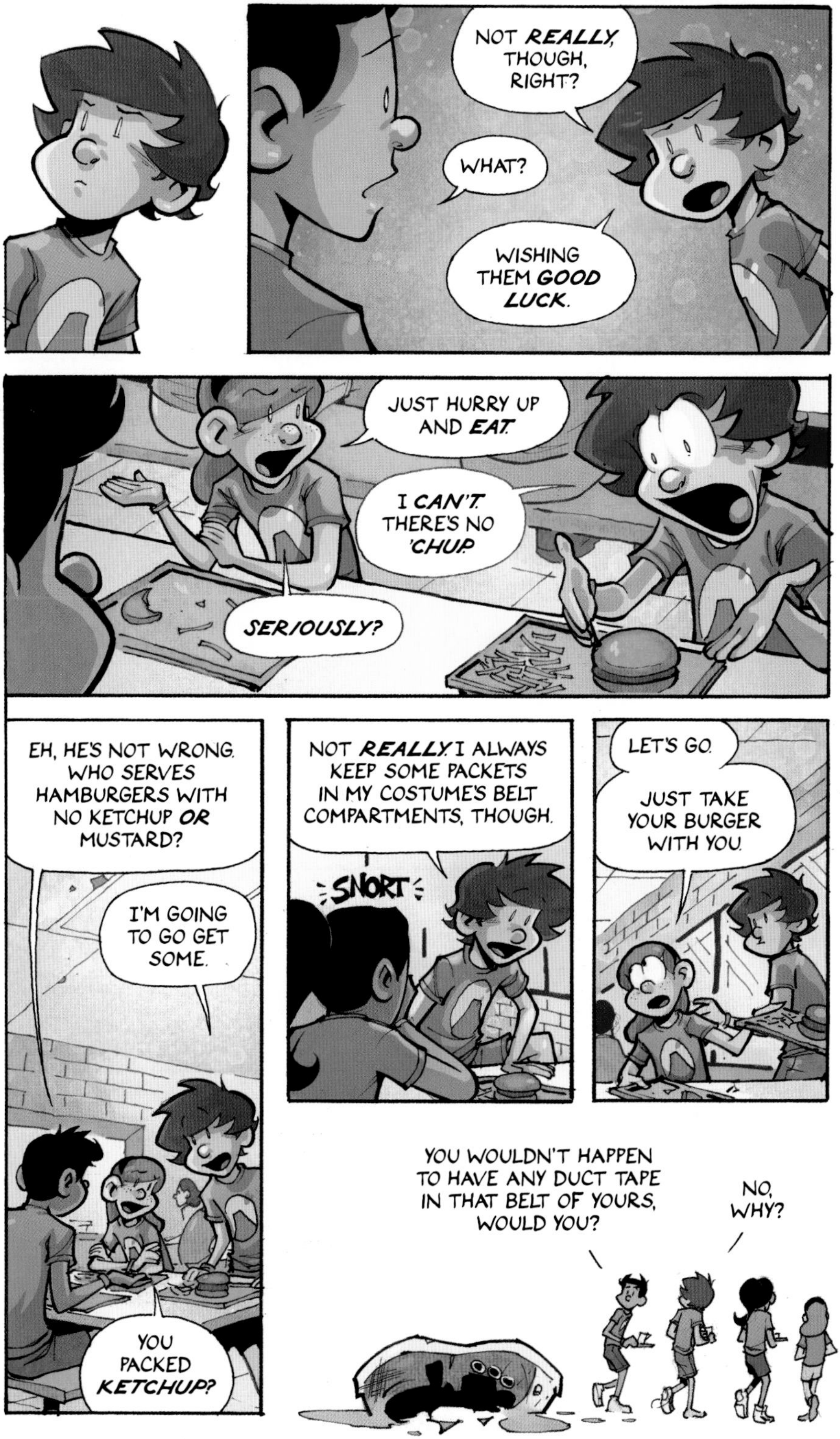
NOT *REALLY*, THOUGH, RIGHT?
WHAT?
WISHING THEM *GOOD LUCK*.
JUST HURRY UP AND *EAT*.
I *CAN'T*. THERE'S NO *'CHUP*.
SERIOUSLY?
EH, HE'S NOT WRONG. WHO SERVES HAMBURGERS WITH NO KETCHUP *OR* MUSTARD?
I'M GOING TO GO GET SOME.
YOU PACKED *KETCHUP?*
NOT *REALLY*. I ALWAYS KEEP SOME PACKETS IN MY COSTUME'S BELT COMPARTMENTS, THOUGH.
SNORT
LET'S GO.
JUST TAKE YOUR BURGER WITH YOU.
YOU WOULDN'T HAPPEN TO HAVE ANY DUCT TAPE IN THAT BELT OF YOURS, WOULD YOU?
NO, WHY?

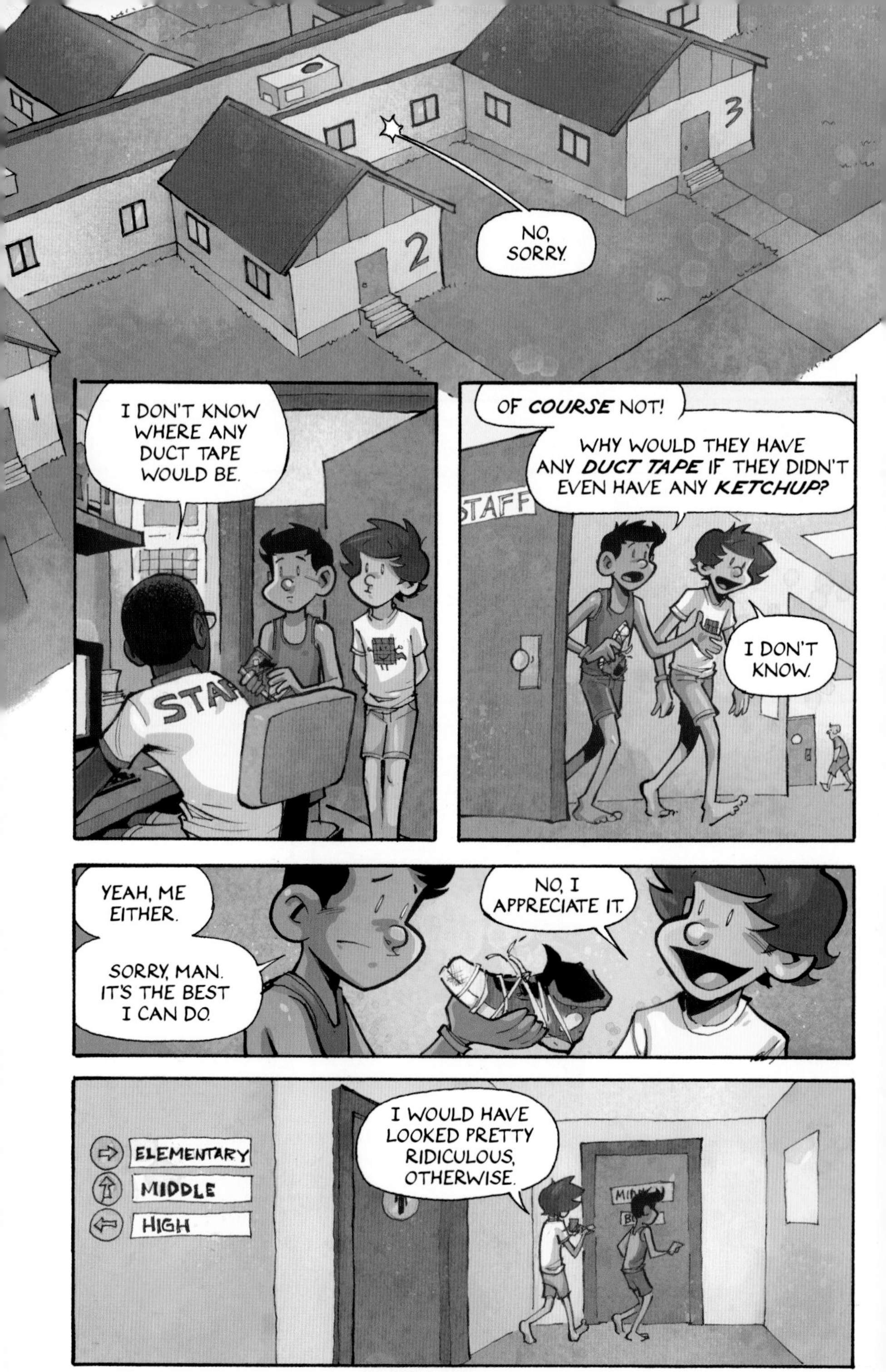
3
NO, SORRY.
2
1
I DON'T KNOW WHERE ANY DUCT TAPE WOULD BE.
STAFF
OF COURSE NOT!
WHY WOULD THEY HAVE ANY DUCT TAPE IF THEY DIDN'T EVEN HAVE ANY KETCHUP?
I DON'T KNOW.
YEAH, ME EITHER.
SORRY, MAN. IT'S THE BEST I CAN DO.
NO, I APPRECIATE IT.
ELEMENTARY
MIDDLE
HIGH
I WOULD HAVE LOOKED PRETTY RIDICULOUS, OTHERWISE.

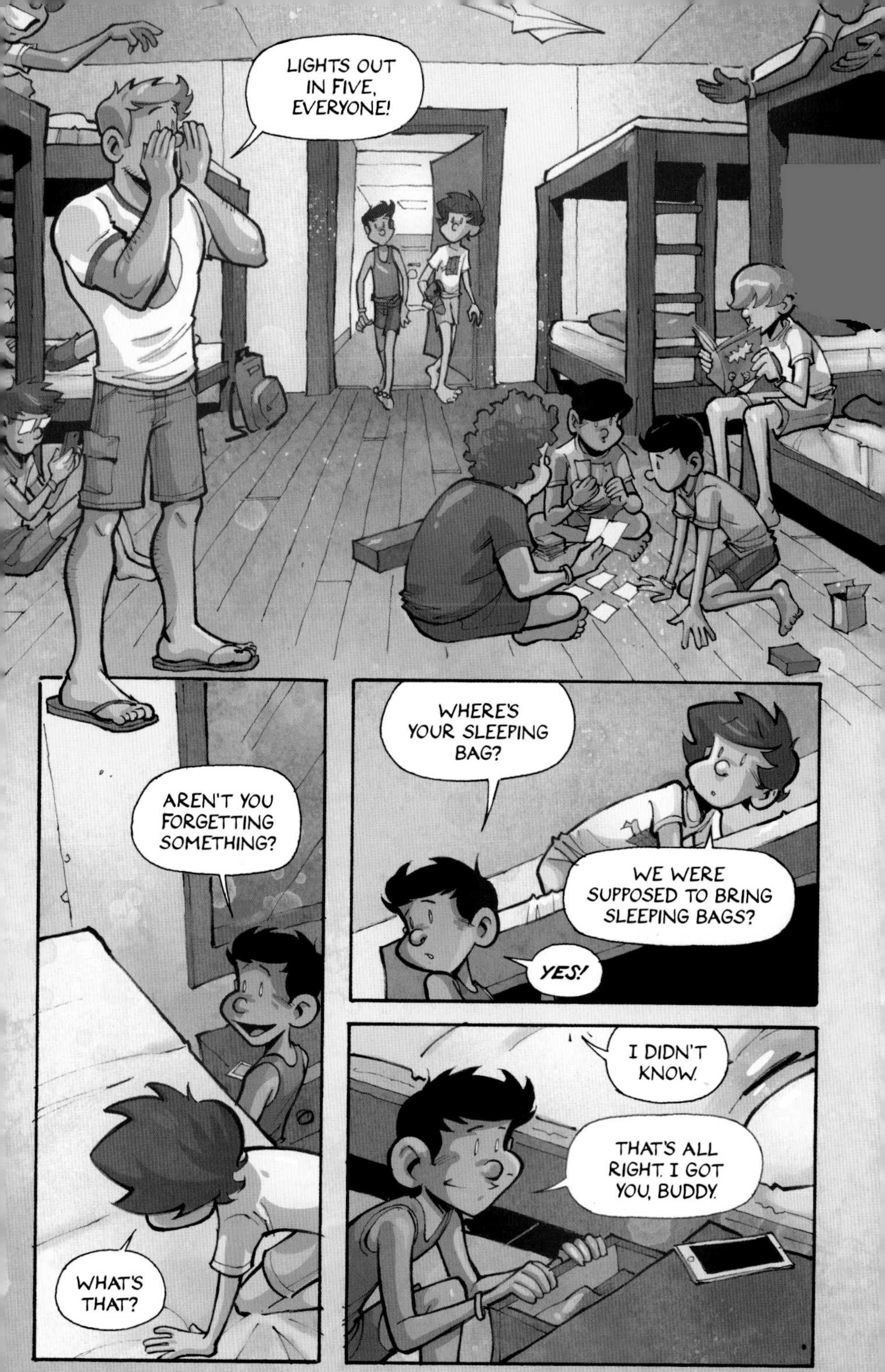
LIGHTS OUT IN FIVE, EVERYONE!
AREN'T YOU FORGETTING SOMETHING?
WHAT'S THAT?
WHERE'S YOUR SLEEPING BAG?
WE WERE SUPPOSED TO BRING SLEEPING BAGS?
YES!
I DIDN'T KNOW.
THAT'S ALL RIGHT. I GOT YOU, BUDDY.

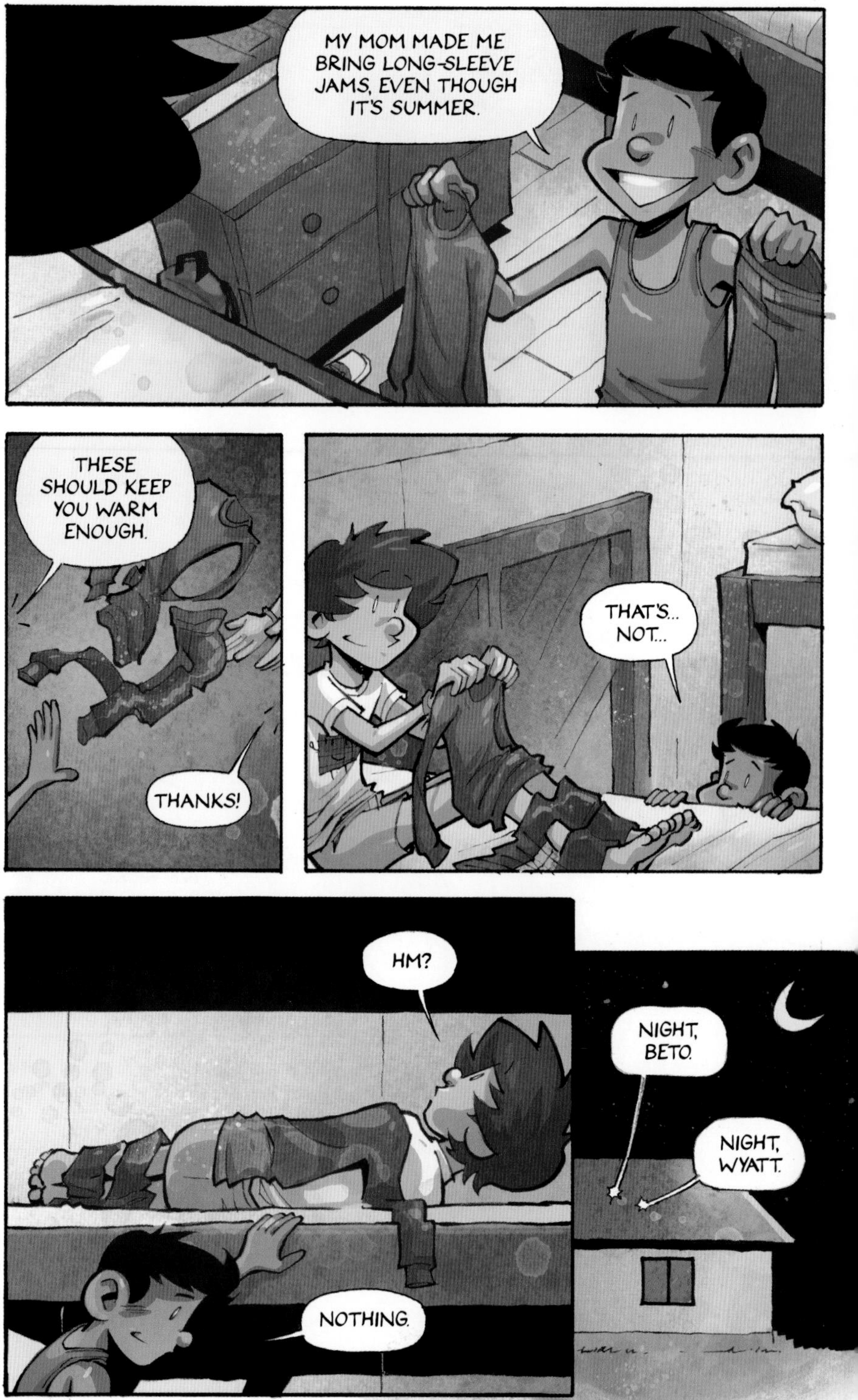
MY MOM MADE ME BRING LONG-SLEEVE JAMS, EVEN THOUGH IT'S SUMMER.
THESE SHOULD KEEP YOU WARM ENOUGH.
THANKS!
THAT'S... NOT...
HM?
NOTHING.
NIGHT, BETO.
NIGHT, WYATT.

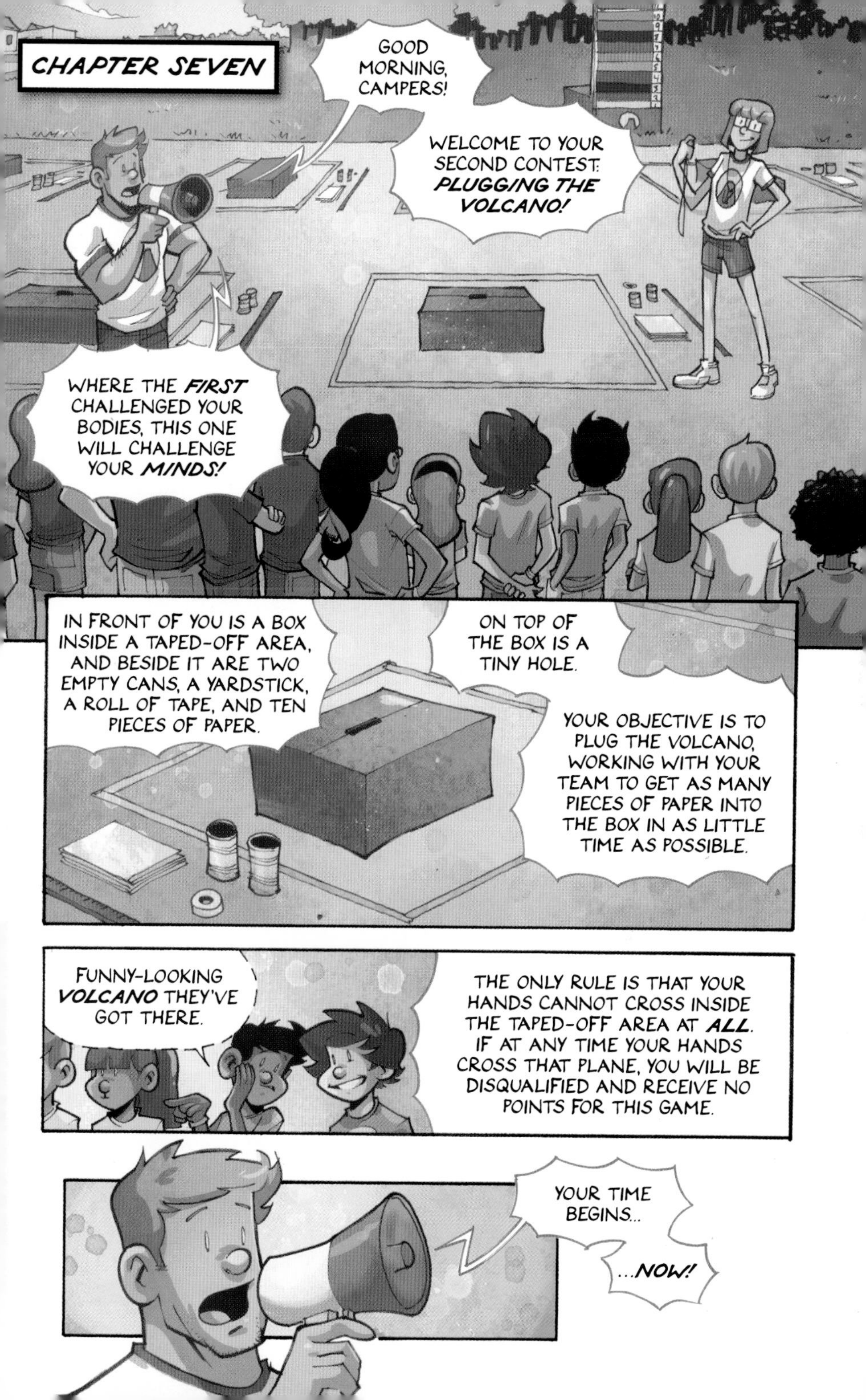
CHAPTER SEVEN
GOOD MORNING, CAMPERS!
WELCOME TO YOUR SECOND CONTEST: PLUGGING THE VOLCANO!
WHERE THE FIRST CHALLENGED YOUR BODIES, THIS ONE WILL CHALLENGE YOUR MINDS!
IN FRONT OF YOU IS A BOX INSIDE A TAPED-OFF AREA, AND BESIDE IT ARE TWO EMPTY CANS, A YARDSTICK, A ROLL OF TAPE, AND TEN PIECES OF PAPER.
ON TOP OF THE BOX IS A TINY HOLE.
YOUR OBJECTIVE IS TO PLUG THE VOLCANO, WORKING WITH YOUR TEAM TO GET AS MANY PIECES OF PAPER INTO THE BOX IN AS LITTLE TIME AS POSSIBLE.
FUNNY-LOOKING VOLCANO THEY'VE GOT THERE.
THE ONLY RULE IS THAT YOUR HANDS CANNOT CROSS INSIDE THE TAPED-OFF AREA AT ALL. IF AT ANY TIME YOUR HANDS CROSS THAT PLANE, YOU WILL BE DISQUALIFIED AND RECEIVE NO POINTS FOR THIS GAME.
YOUR TIME BEGINS...
...NOW!

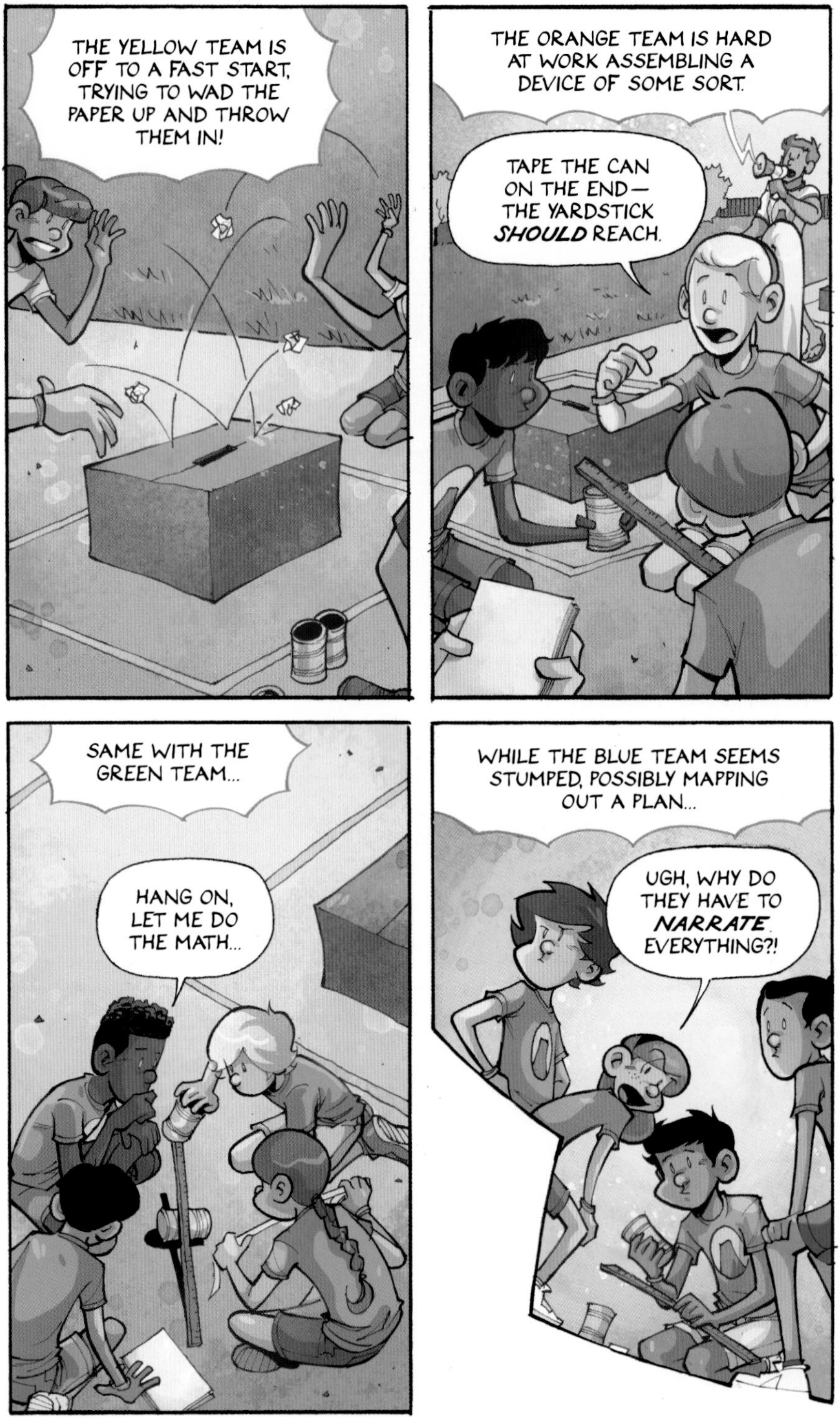
THE YELLOW TEAM IS OFF TO A FAST START, TRYING TO WAD THE PAPER UP AND THROW THEM IN!
THE ORANGE TEAM IS HARD AT WORK ASSEMBLING A DEVICE OF SOME SORT.
TAPE THE CAN ON THE END— THE YARDSTICK *SHOULD* REACH.
SAME WITH THE GREEN TEAM...
HANG ON, LET ME DO THE MATH...
WHILE THE BLUE TEAM SEEMS STUMPED, POSSIBLY MAPPING OUT A PLAN...
UGH, WHY DO THEY HAVE TO *NARRATE* EVERYTHING?!

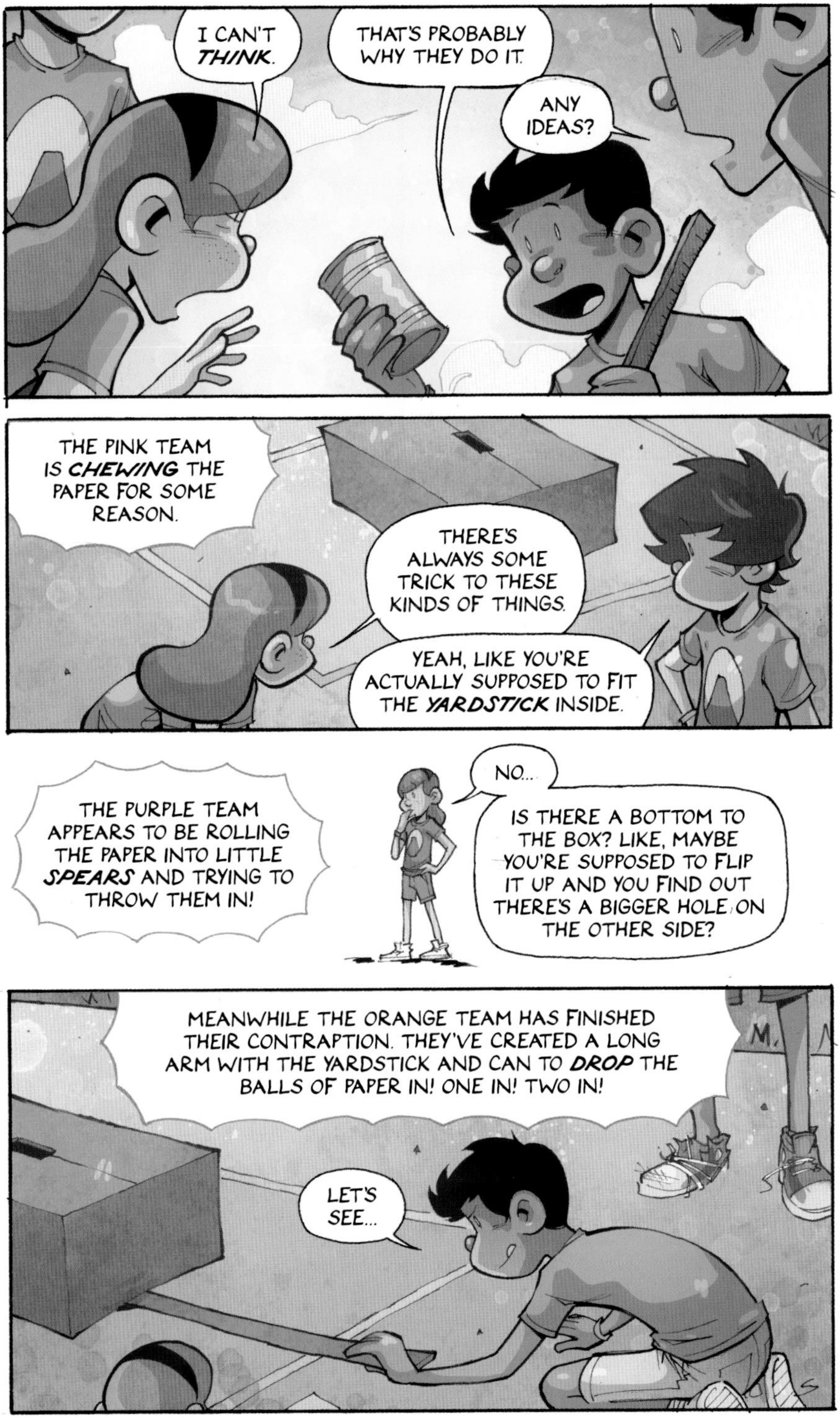
I CAN'T *THINK*.
THAT'S PROBABLY WHY THEY DO IT.
ANY IDEAS?
THE PINK TEAM IS *CHEWING* THE PAPER FOR SOME REASON.
THERE'S ALWAYS SOME TRICK TO THESE KINDS OF THINGS.
YEAH, LIKE YOU'RE ACTUALLY SUPPOSED TO FIT THE *YARDSTICK* INSIDE.
THE PURPLE TEAM APPEARS TO BE ROLLING THE PAPER INTO LITTLE *SPEARS* AND TRYING TO THROW THEM IN!
NO...
IS THERE A BOTTOM TO THE BOX? LIKE, MAYBE YOU'RE SUPPOSED TO FLIP IT UP AND YOU FIND OUT THERE'S A BIGGER HOLE ON THE OTHER SIDE?
MEANWHILE THE ORANGE TEAM HAS FINISHED THEIR CONTRAPTION. THEY'VE CREATED A LONG ARM WITH THE YARDSTICK AND CAN TO *DROP* THE BALLS OF PAPER IN! ONE IN! TWO IN!
LET'S SEE...

AND THE GREEN TEAM HAS FINISHED THEIR DEVICE — AN ASTONISHINGLY ACCURATE *CATAPULT!* THEY CAN'T MAKE THE PAPER BALLS *FAST* ENOUGH!

FLIP

OH!

DUH!

AND IT LOOKS LIKE THE BLUE TEAM'S PLANNING MAY HAVE PAID OFF!

ALWAYS...

BUT THE GREEN TEAM IS ALMOST OUT OF *PAPER!*

REMEMBER...

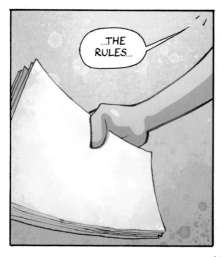

...THE RULES...

...OF *TEST TAKING!*

FWEET

THE BLUE TEAM FINISHES *FIRST!*

WHOO-HOO!

NICE WORK!

YES!

THE ORANGE TEAM *SECOND!*

THE GREEN TEAM *THIRD!*

THE RULES OF *TEST TAKING?*

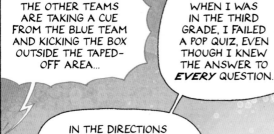

THE OTHER TEAMS ARE TAKING A CUE FROM THE BLUE TEAM AND KICKING THE BOX OUTSIDE THE TAPED-OFF AREA...

WHEN I WAS IN THE THIRD GRADE, I FAILED A POP QUIZ, EVEN THOUGH I KNEW THE ANSWER TO *EVERY* QUESTION.

SO, I LEARNED TWO RULES THAT DAY.

ONE, ALWAYS READ THE DIRECTIONS. AND *TWO...*

IN THE DIRECTIONS WRITTEN AT THE TOP, WHICH I *TOTALLY* DIDN'T READ, IT SAID TO GET UP AND WALK AROUND THE ROOM SILENTLY, AND YOU WOULD PASS THE QUIZ.

...ADULTS THINK THEY'RE *SO* CLEVER.

THEY SAID YOUR *HANDS* COULDN'T CROSS. THEY DIDN'T SAY *ANYTHING* ABOUT ANYTHING *ELSE.*

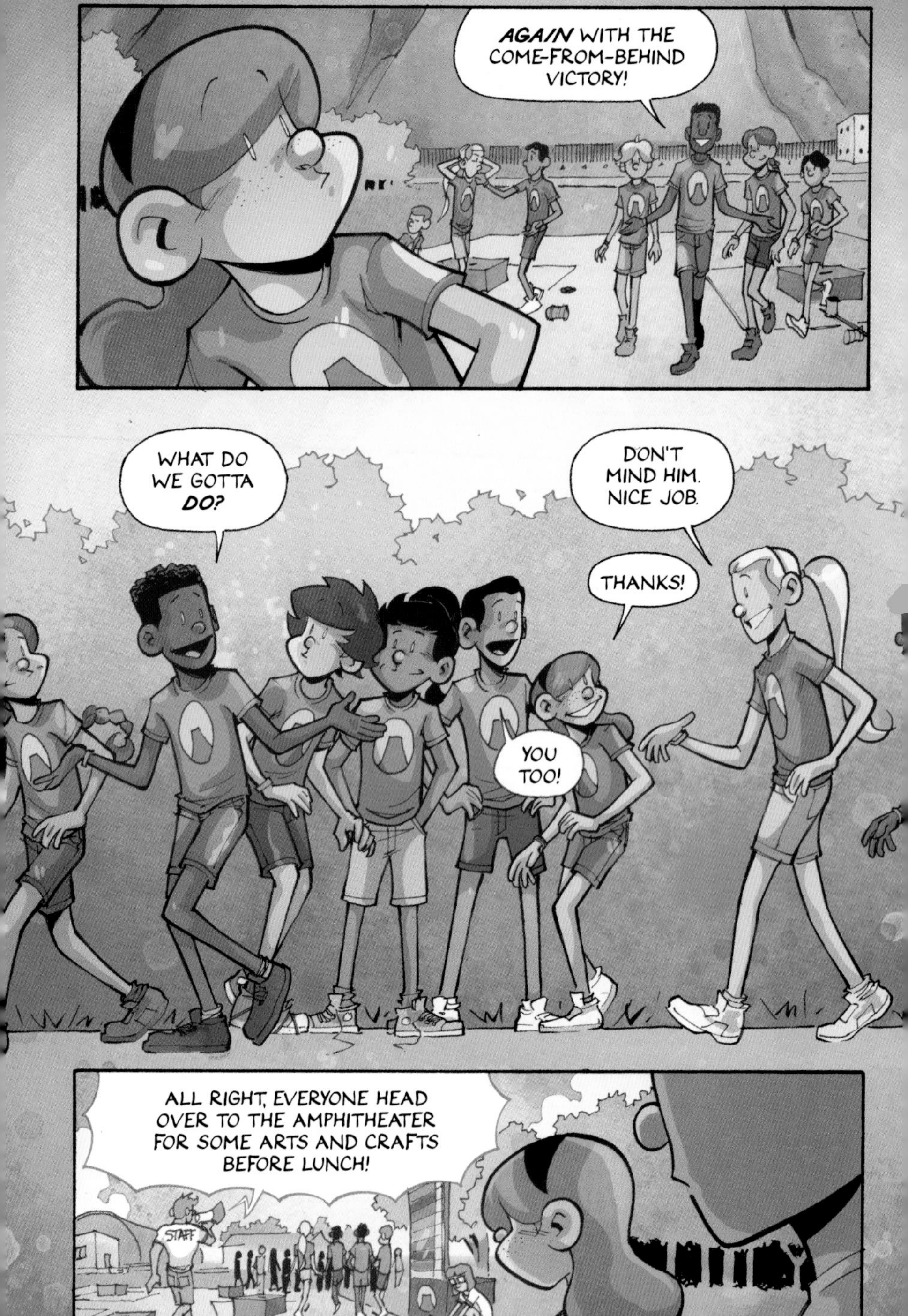
AGAIN WITH THE COME-FROM-BEHIND VICTORY!
WHAT DO WE GOTTA DO?
DON'T MIND HIM. NICE JOB.
THANKS!
YOU TOO!
ALL RIGHT, EVERYONE HEAD OVER TO THE AMPHITHEATER FOR SOME ARTS AND CRAFTS BEFORE LUNCH!
STAFF

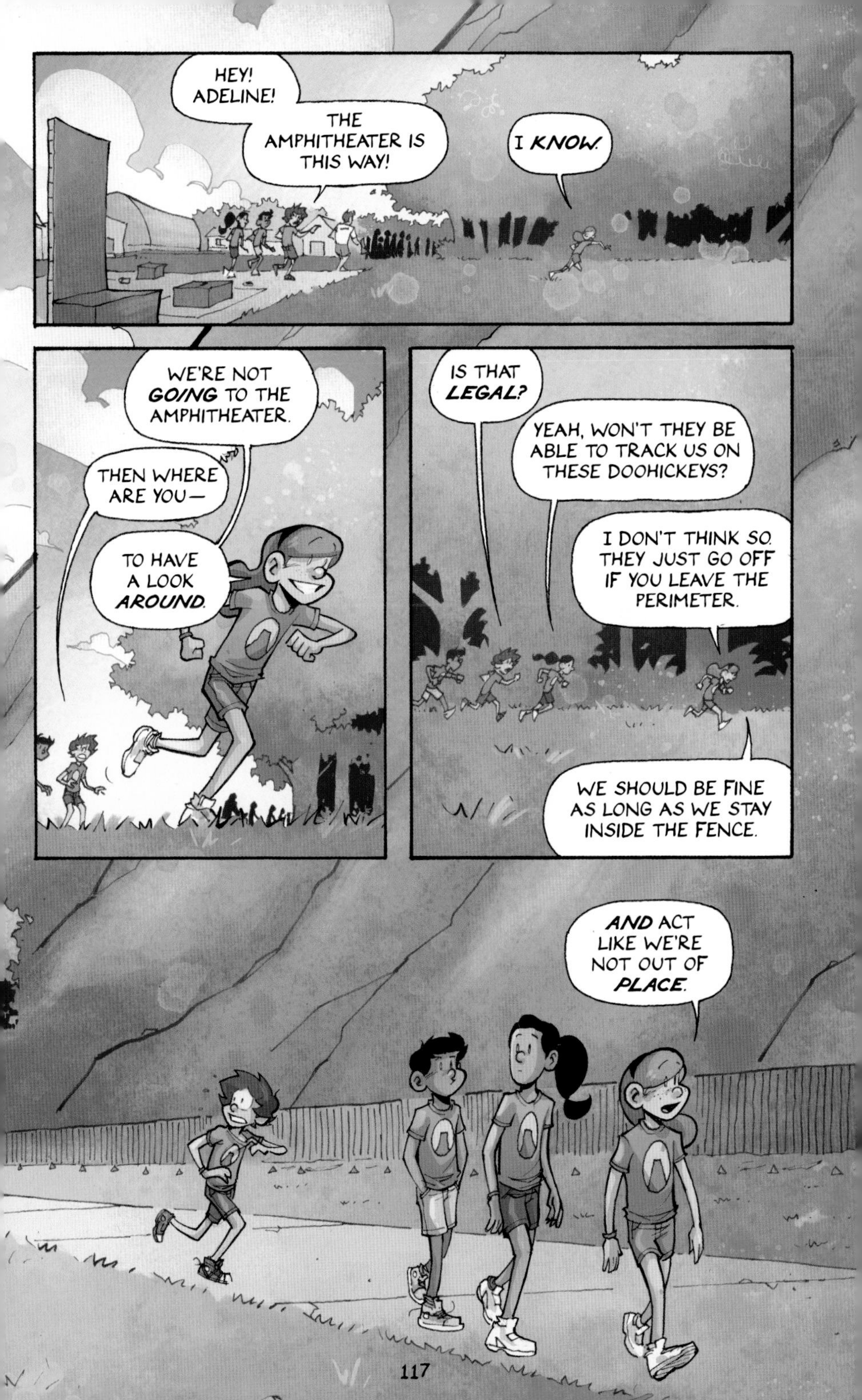
HEY! ADELINE!
THE AMPHITHEATER IS THIS WAY!
I KNOW.
WE'RE NOT GOING TO THE AMPHITHEATER.
THEN WHERE ARE YOU—
TO HAVE A LOOK AROUND.
IS THAT LEGAL?
YEAH, WON'T THEY BE ABLE TO TRACK US ON THESE DOOHICKEYS?
I DON'T THINK SO. THEY JUST GO OFF IF YOU LEAVE THE PERIMETER.
WE SHOULD BE FINE AS LONG AS WE STAY INSIDE THE FENCE.
AND ACT LIKE WE'RE NOT OUT OF PLACE.

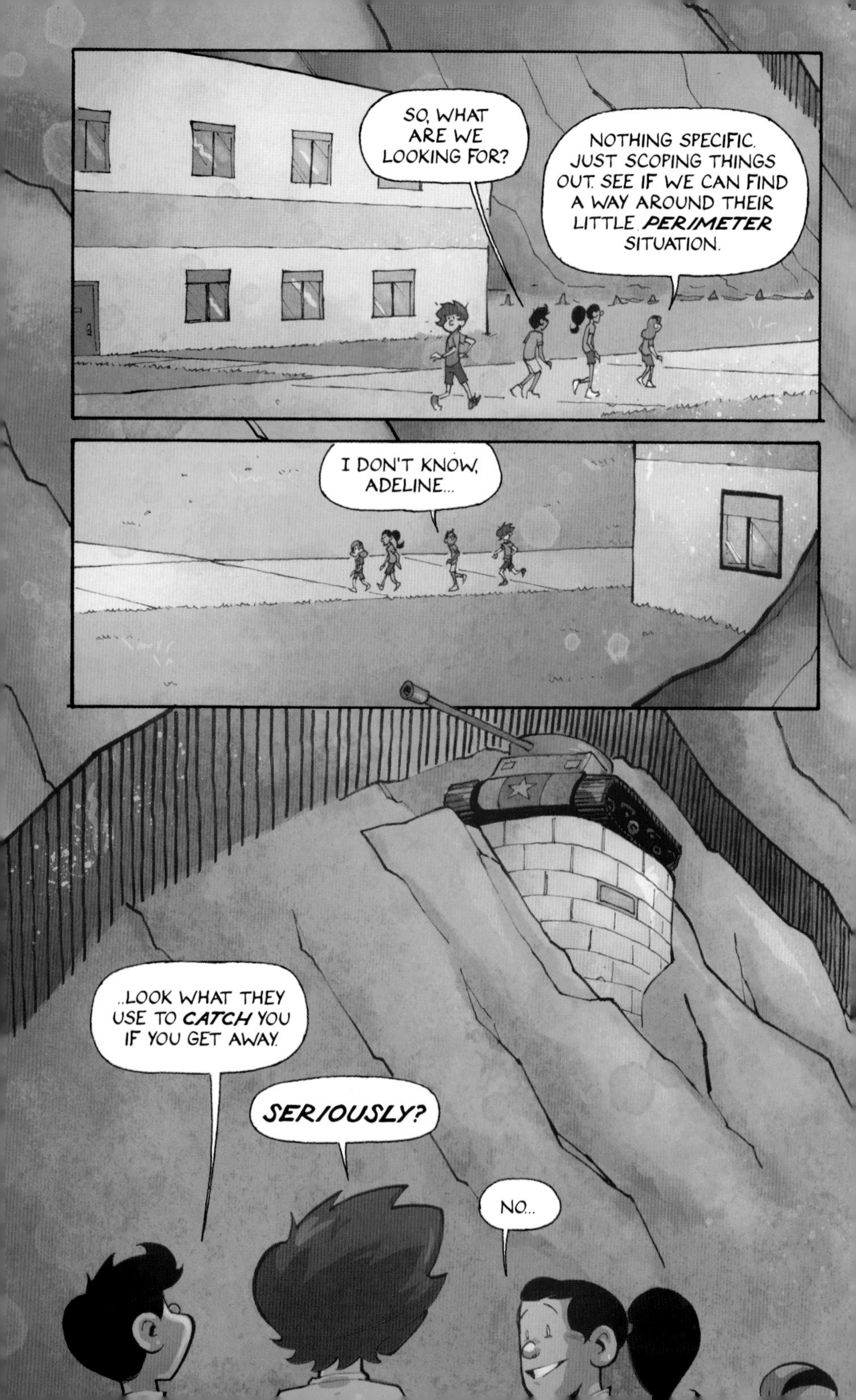
SO, WHAT ARE WE LOOKING FOR?
NOTHING SPECIFIC. JUST SCOPING THINGS OUT. SEE IF WE CAN FIND A WAY AROUND THEIR LITTLE *PERIMETER* SITUATION.
I DON'T KNOW, ADELINE...
...LOOK WHAT THEY USE TO *CATCH* YOU IF YOU GET AWAY.
SERIOUSLY?
NO...

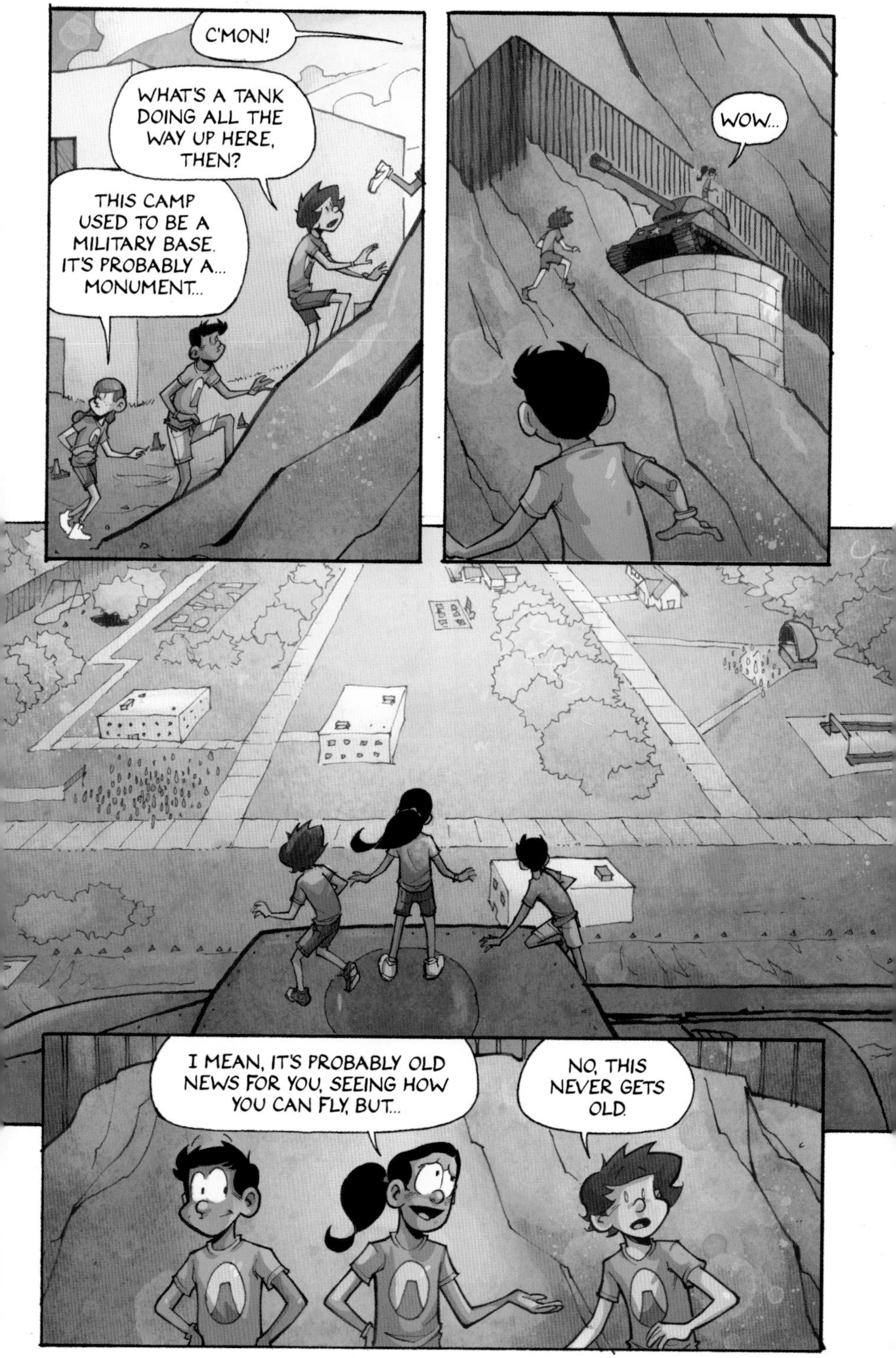
C'MON!
WHAT'S A TANK DOING ALL THE WAY UP HERE, THEN?
THIS CAMP USED TO BE A MILITARY BASE. IT'S PROBABLY A... MONUMENT...
WOW...
I MEAN, IT'S PROBABLY OLD NEWS FOR YOU, SEEING HOW YOU CAN FLY, BUT...
NO, THIS NEVER GETS OLD.

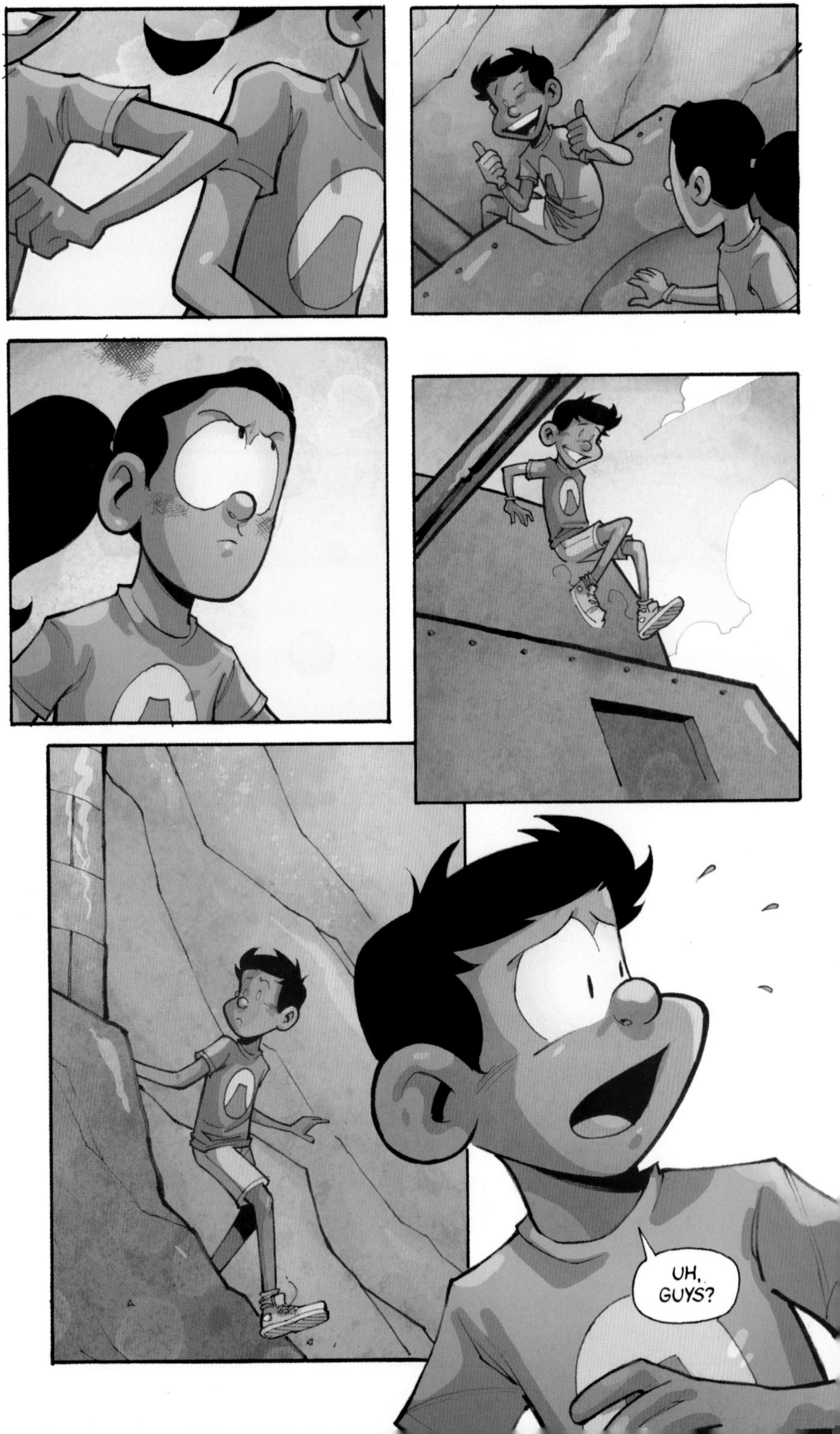
UH, GUYS?

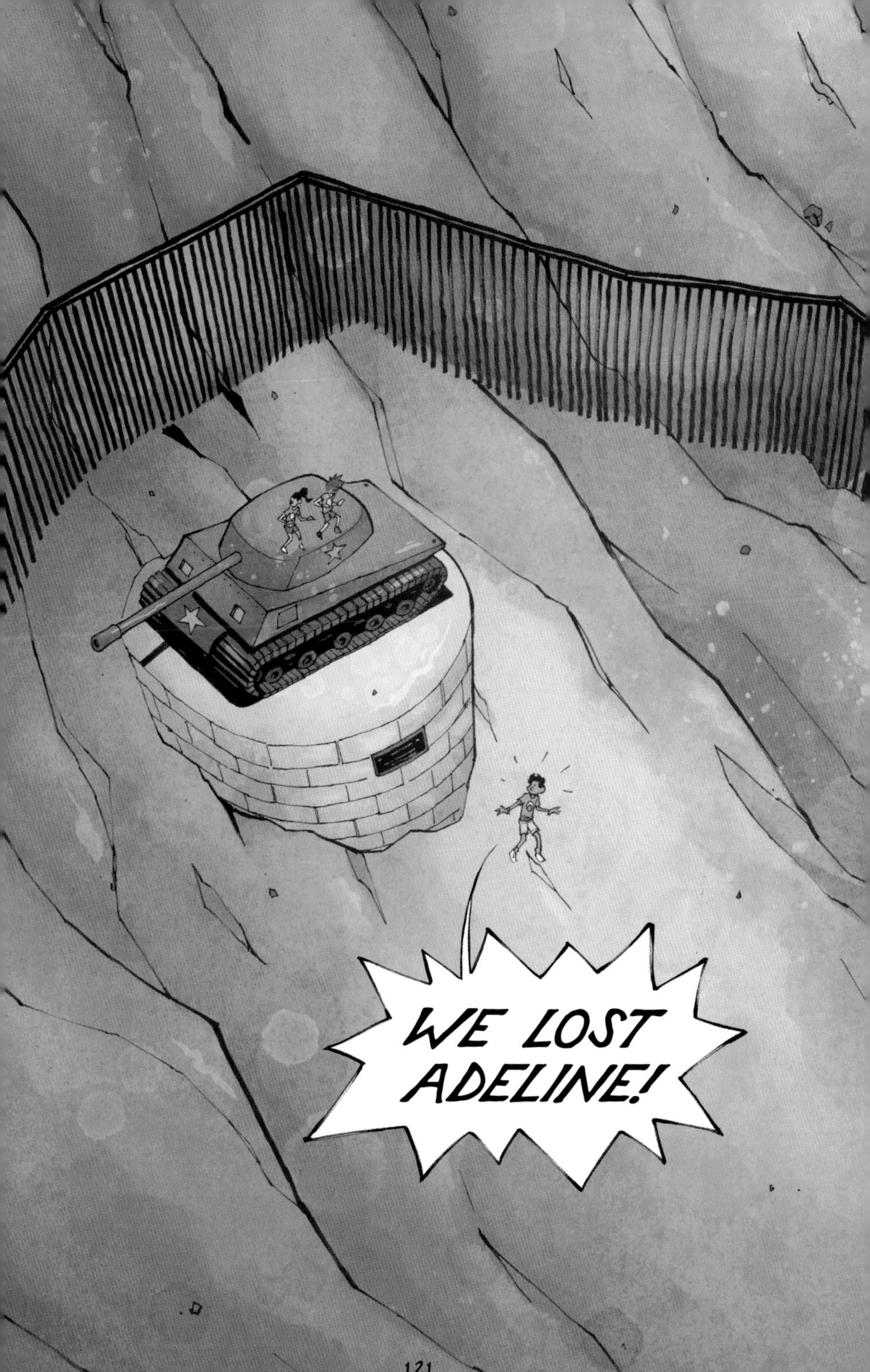
WE LOST ADELINE!

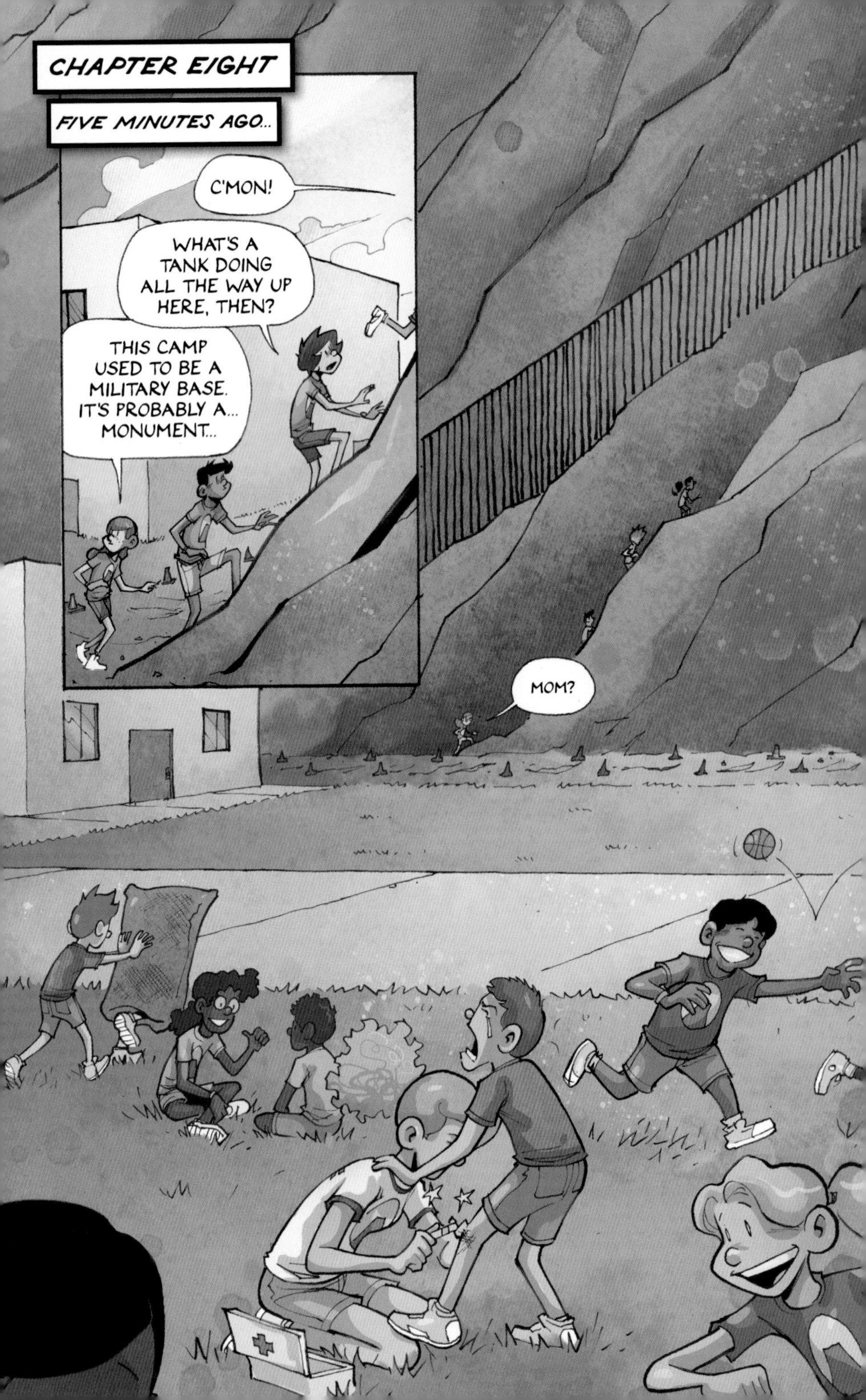
CHAPTER EIGHT
FIVE MINUTES AGO...
C'MON!
WHAT'S A TANK DOING ALL THE WAY UP HERE, THEN?
THIS CAMP USED TO BE A MILITARY BASE. IT'S PROBABLY A... MONUMENT...
MOM?

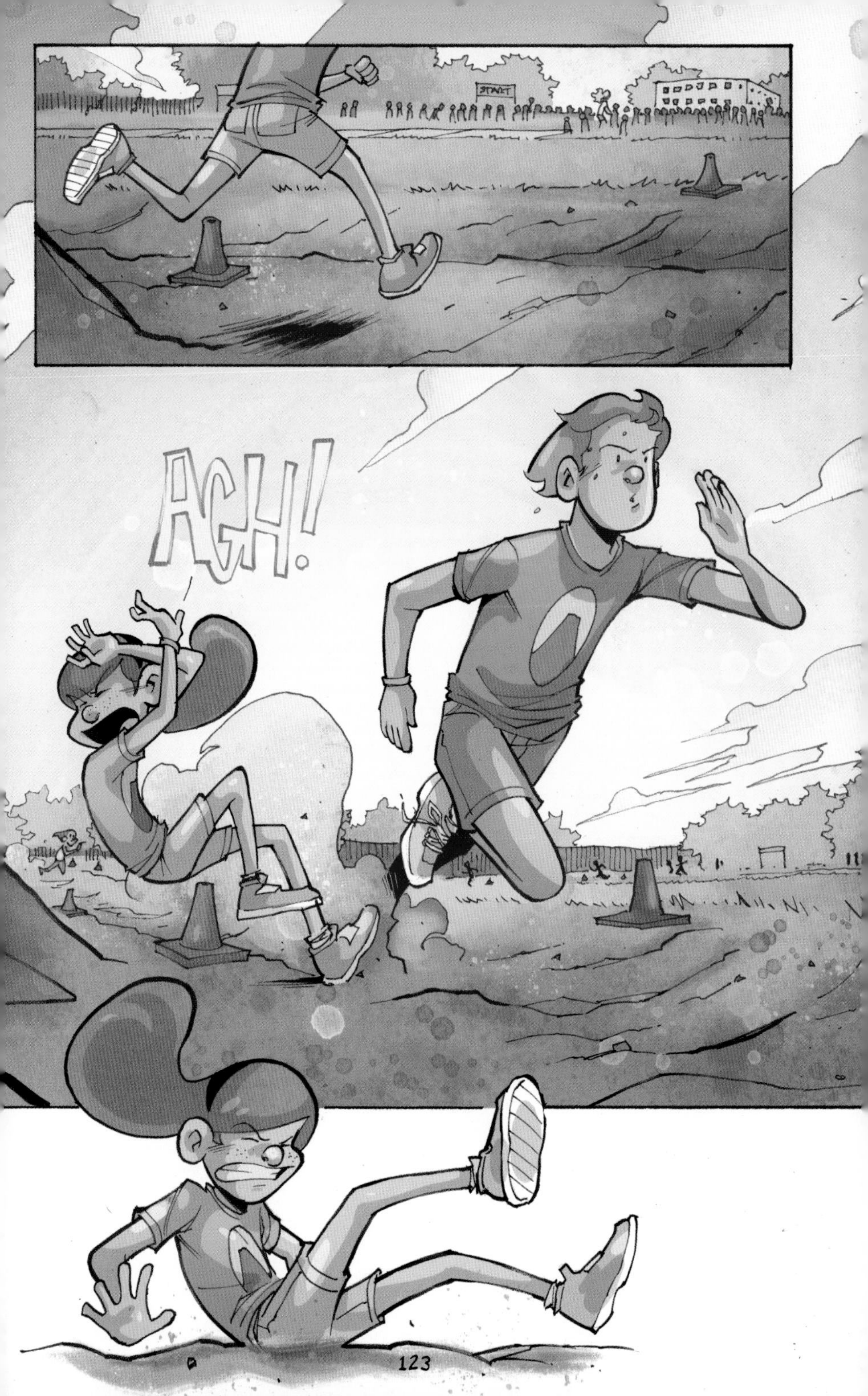
START
AGH!

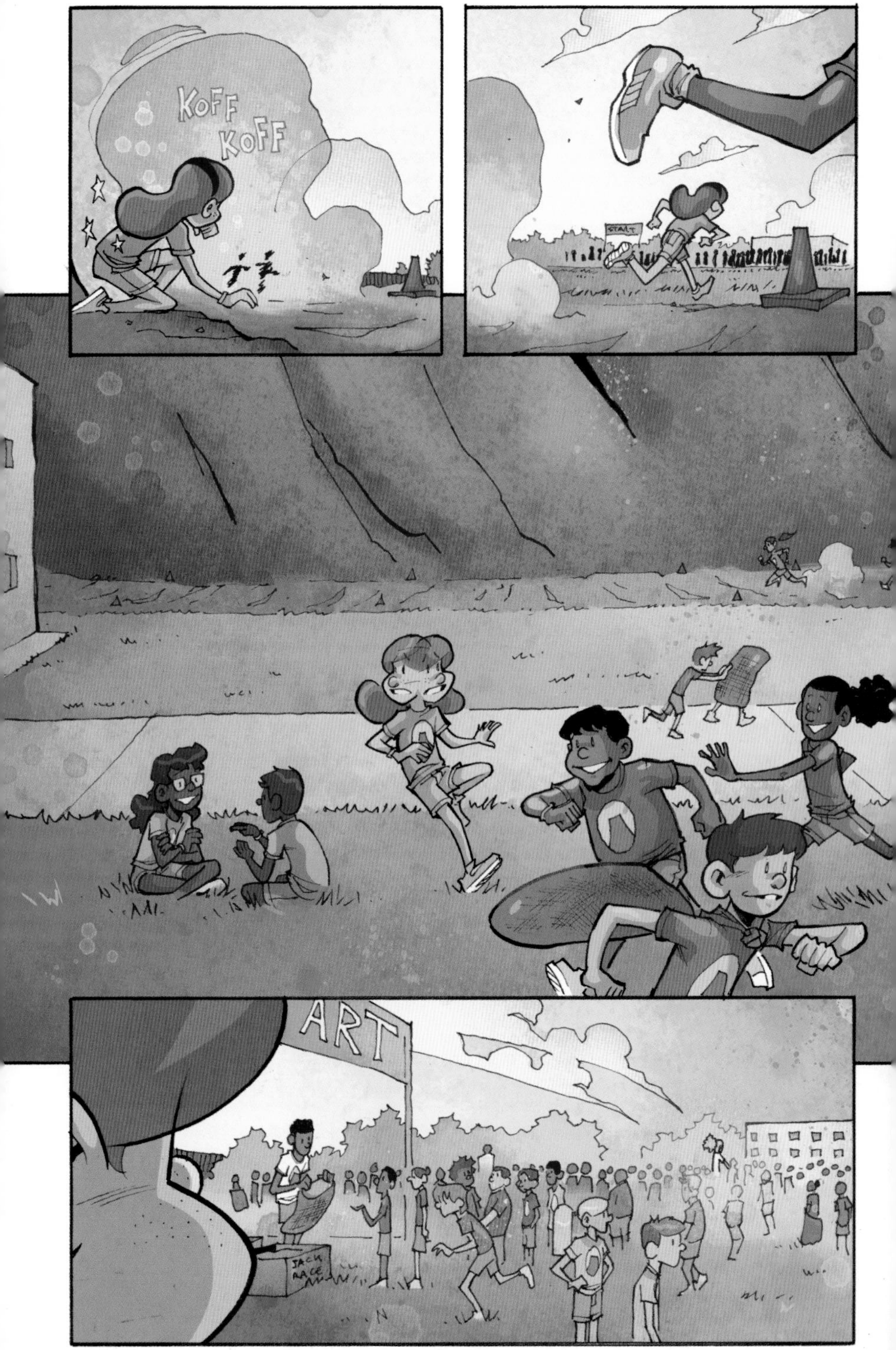
KOFF
KOFF
START
ART
JACK RACE

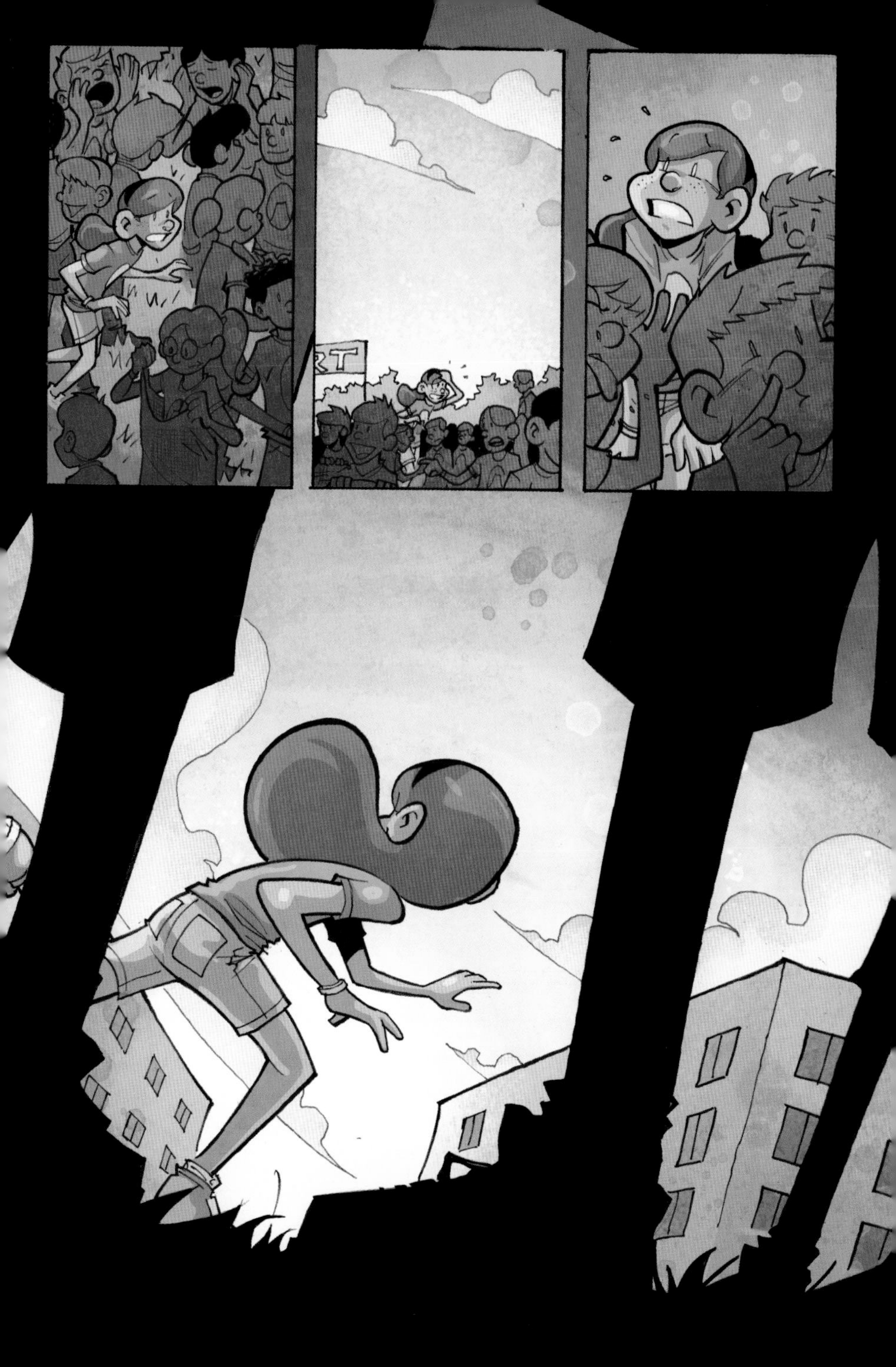

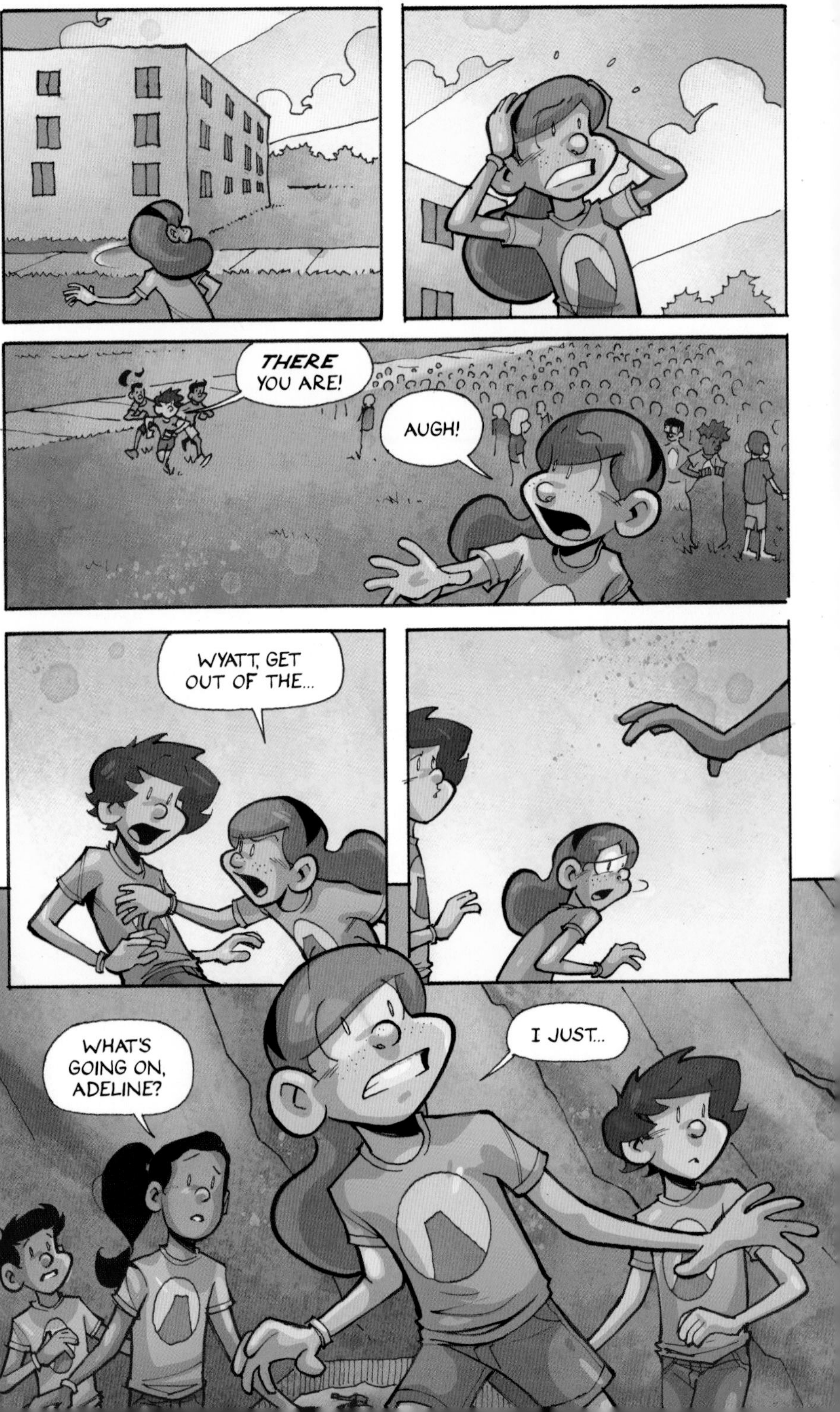
THERE YOU ARE!
AUGH!
WYATT, GET OUT OF THE...
WHAT'S GOING ON, ADELINE?
I JUST...

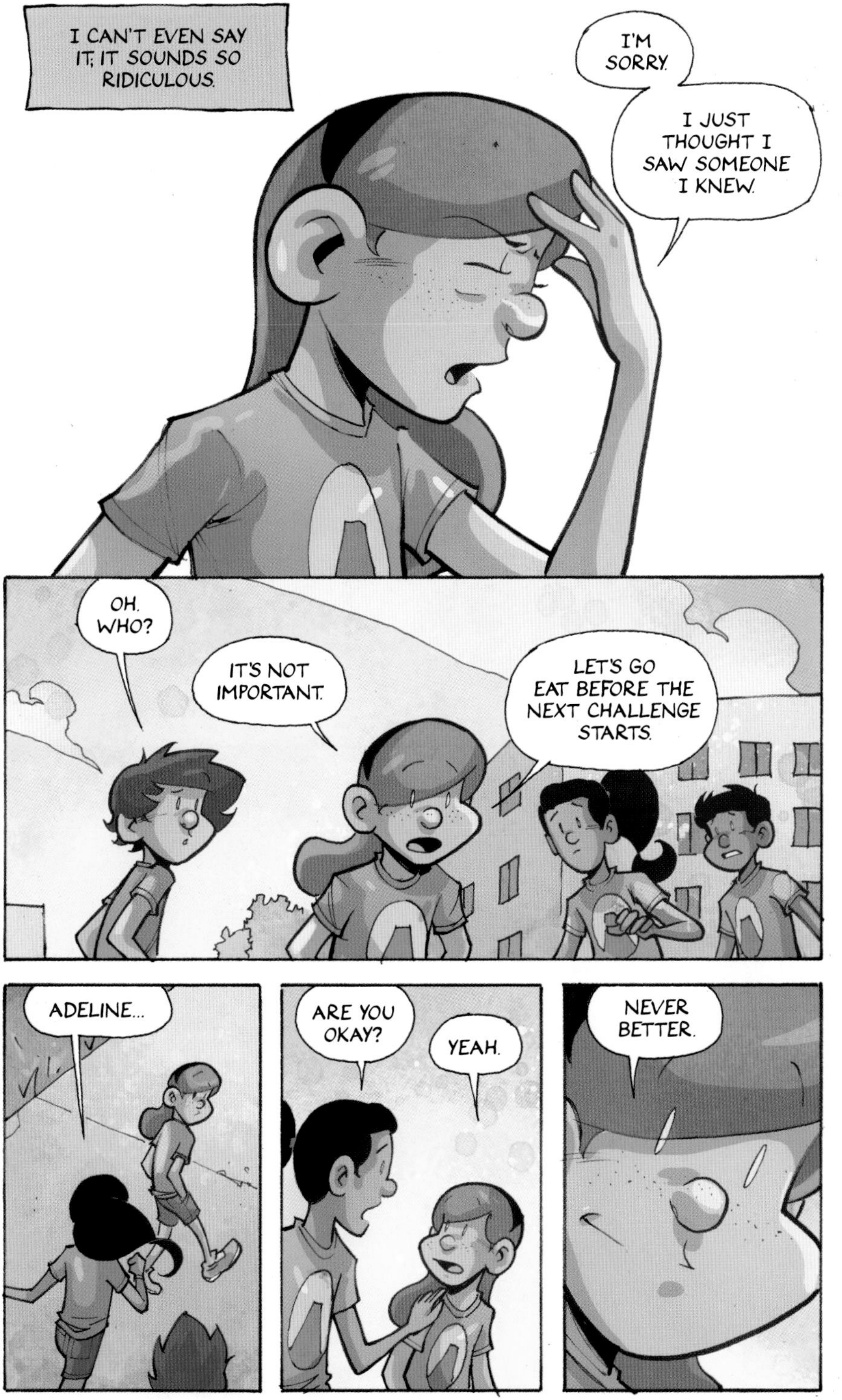

I CAN'T EVEN SAY IT; IT SOUNDS SO RIDICULOUS.
I'M SORRY.
I JUST THOUGHT I SAW SOMEONE I KNEW.
OH. WHO?
IT'S NOT IMPORTANT.
LET'S GO EAT BEFORE THE NEXT CHALLENGE STARTS.
ADELINE...
ARE YOU OKAY?
YEAH.
NEVER BETTER.

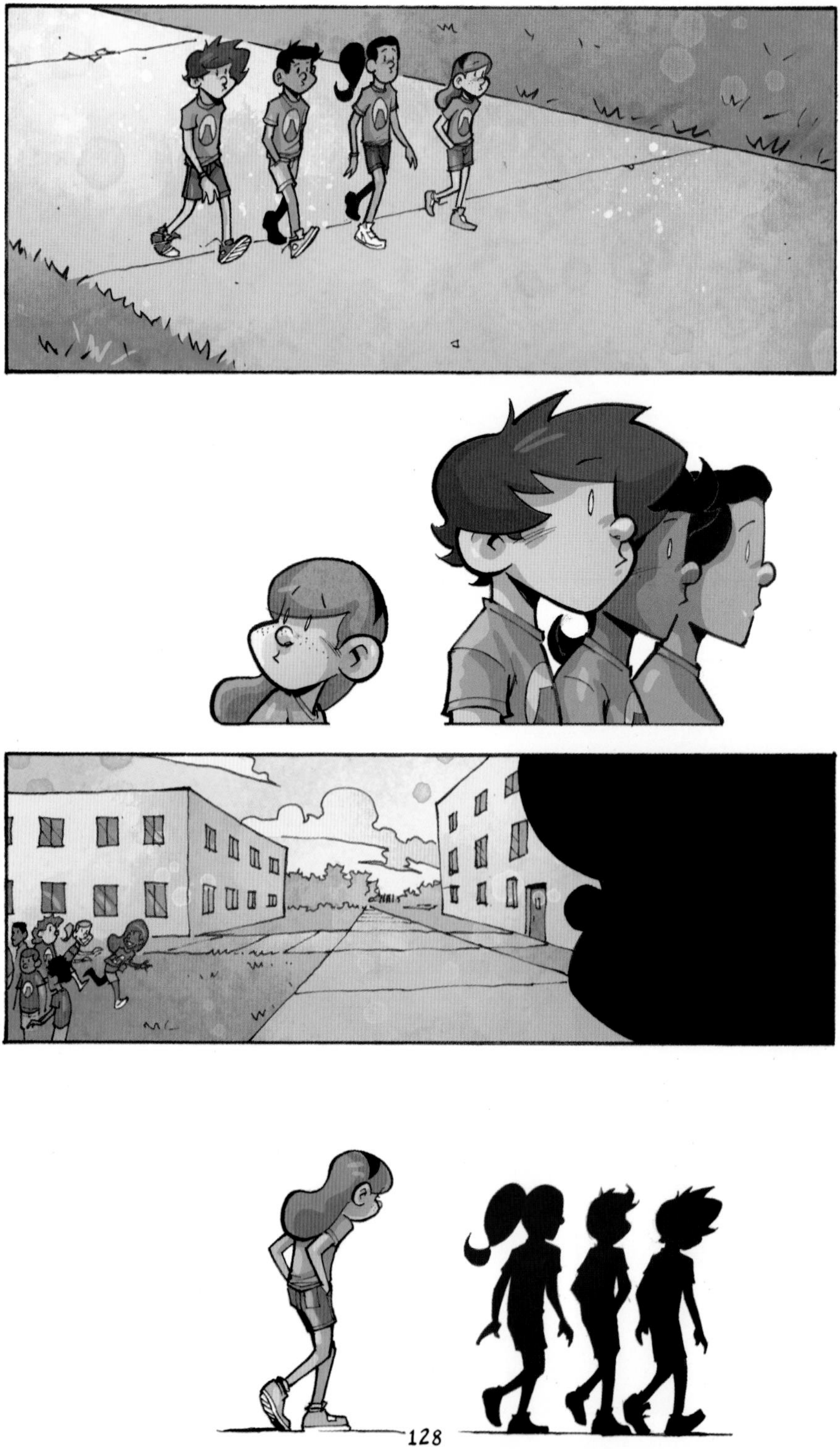

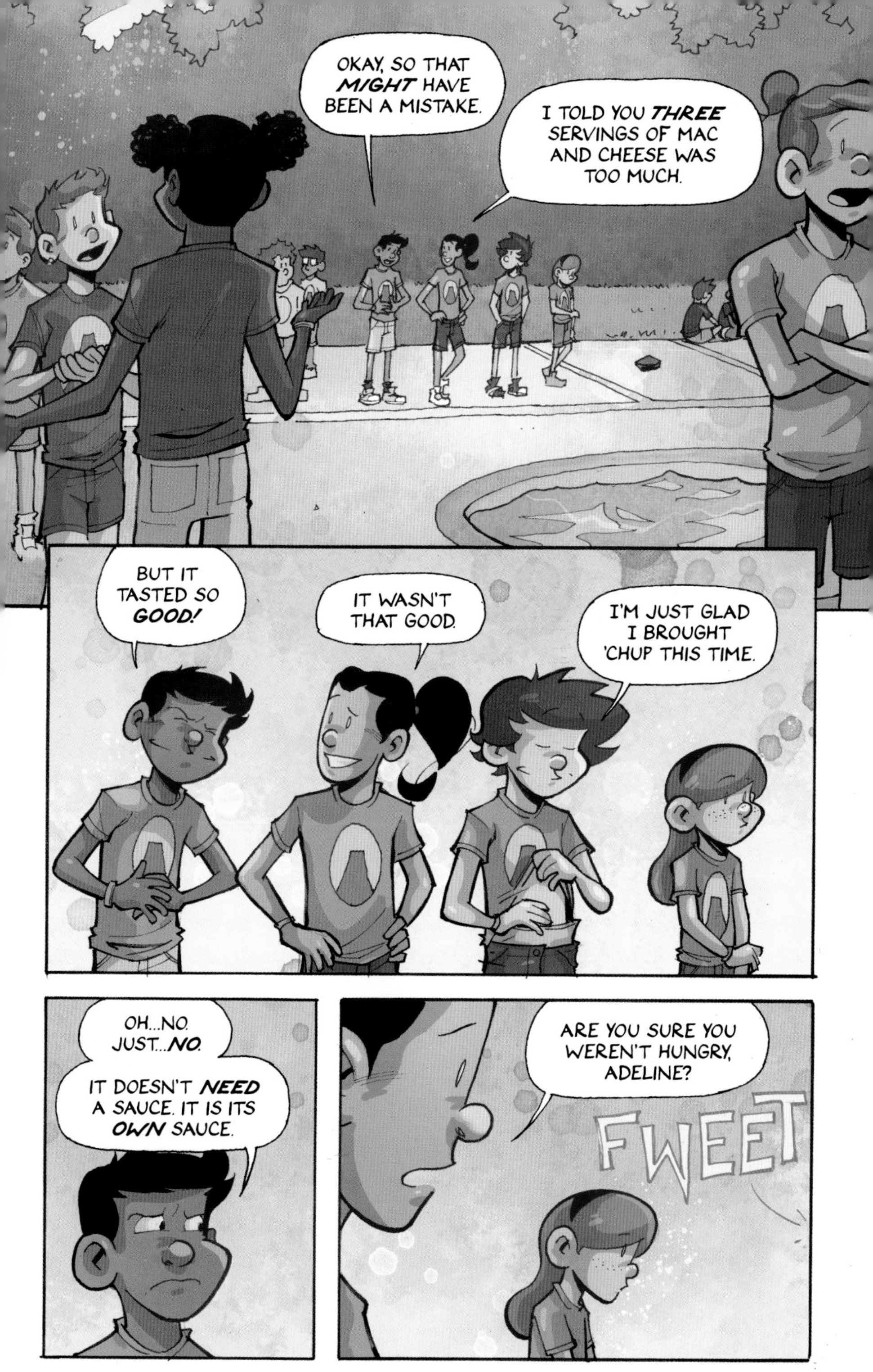
OKAY, SO THAT *MIGHT* HAVE BEEN A MISTAKE.
I TOLD YOU *THREE* SERVINGS OF MAC AND CHEESE WAS TOO MUCH.
BUT IT TASTED SO *GOOD!*
IT WASN'T THAT GOOD.
I'M JUST GLAD I BROUGHT 'CHUP THIS TIME.
OH...NO. JUST...*NO.*
IT DOESN'T *NEED* A SAUCE. IT IS ITS *OWN* SAUCE.
ARE YOU SURE YOU WEREN'T HUNGRY, ADELINE?
FWEET

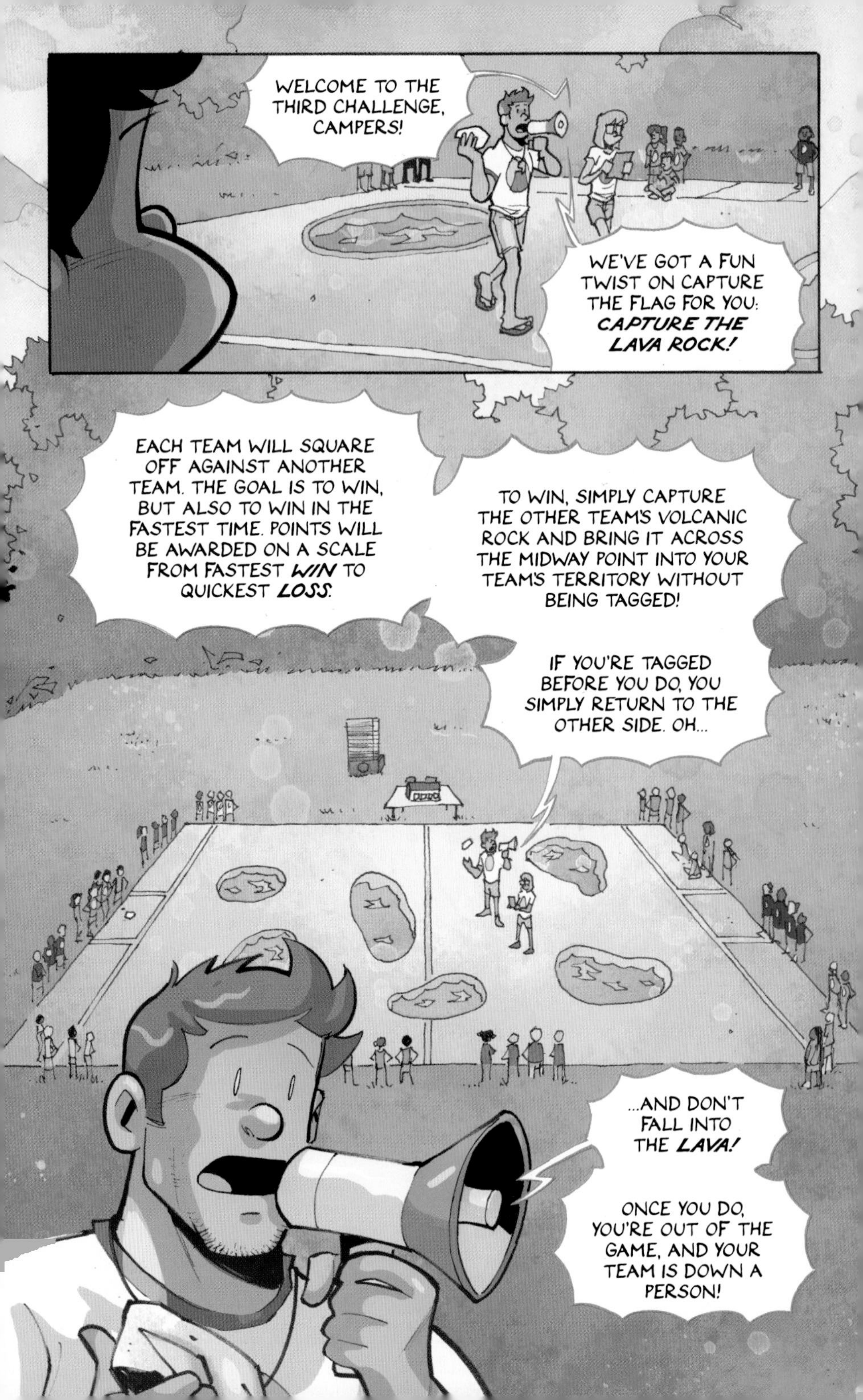
WELCOME TO THE THIRD CHALLENGE, CAMPERS!
WE'VE GOT A FUN TWIST ON CAPTURE THE FLAG FOR YOU: ***CAPTURE THE LAVA ROCK!***
EACH TEAM WILL SQUARE OFF AGAINST ANOTHER TEAM. THE GOAL IS TO WIN, BUT ALSO TO WIN IN THE FASTEST TIME. POINTS WILL BE AWARDED ON A SCALE FROM FASTEST ***WIN*** TO QUICKEST ***LOSS***.
TO WIN, SIMPLY CAPTURE THE OTHER TEAM'S VOLCANIC ROCK AND BRING IT ACROSS THE MIDWAY POINT INTO YOUR TEAM'S TERRITORY WITHOUT BEING TAGGED!
IF YOU'RE TAGGED BEFORE YOU DO, YOU SIMPLY RETURN TO THE OTHER SIDE. OH...
...AND DON'T FALL INTO THE ***LAVA!***
ONCE YOU DO, YOU'RE OUT OF THE GAME, AND YOUR TEAM IS DOWN A PERSON!

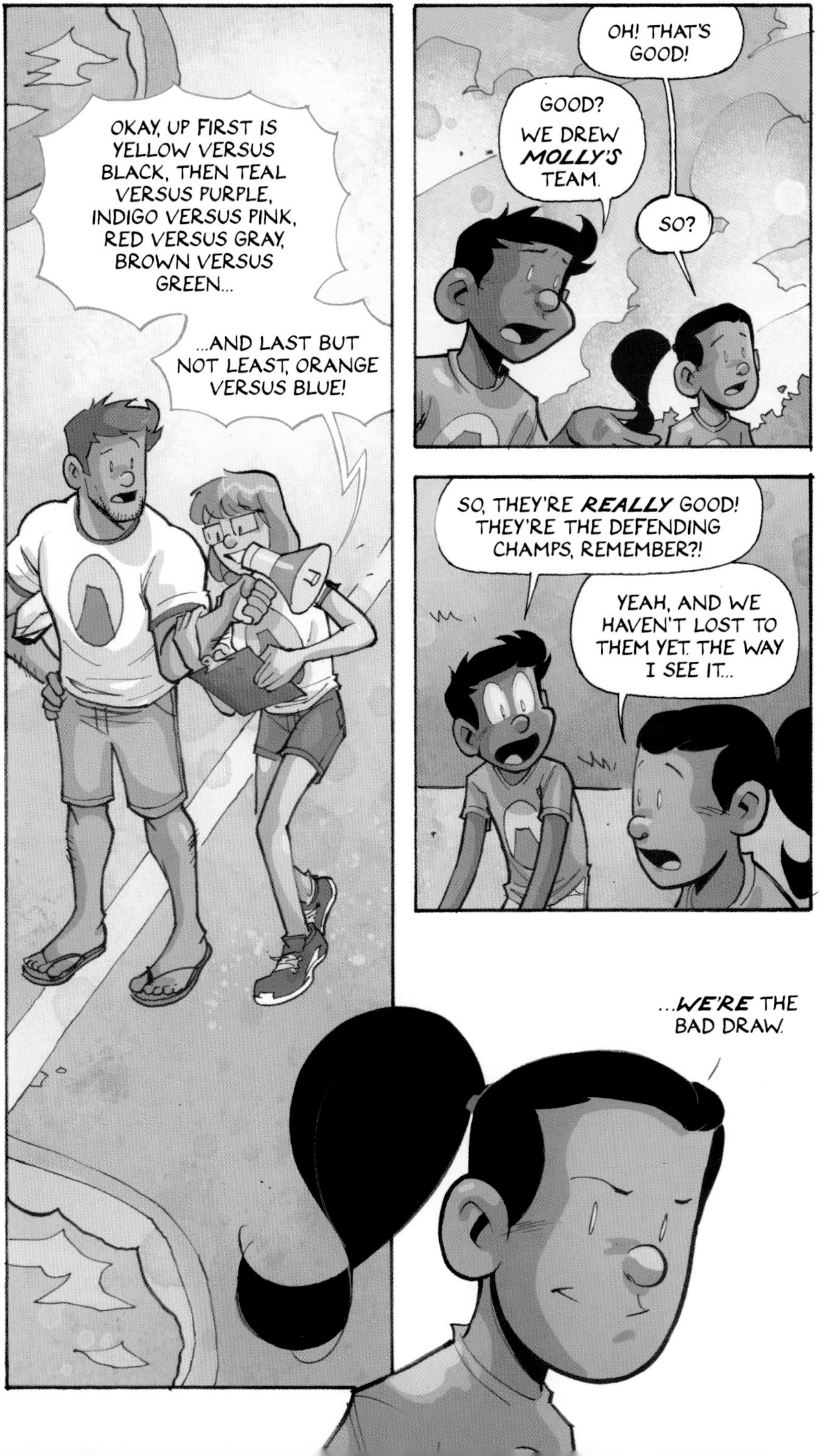
OKAY, UP FIRST IS YELLOW VERSUS BLACK, THEN TEAL VERSUS PURPLE, INDIGO VERSUS PINK, RED VERSUS GRAY, BROWN VERSUS GREEN...
...AND LAST BUT NOT LEAST, ORANGE VERSUS BLUE!
OH! THAT'S GOOD!
GOOD? WE DREW *MOLLY'S* TEAM.
SO?
SO, THEY'RE *REALLY* GOOD! THEY'RE THE DEFENDING CHAMPS, REMEMBER?!
YEAH, AND WE HAVEN'T LOST TO THEM YET. THE WAY I SEE IT...
...*WE'RE* THE BAD DRAW.

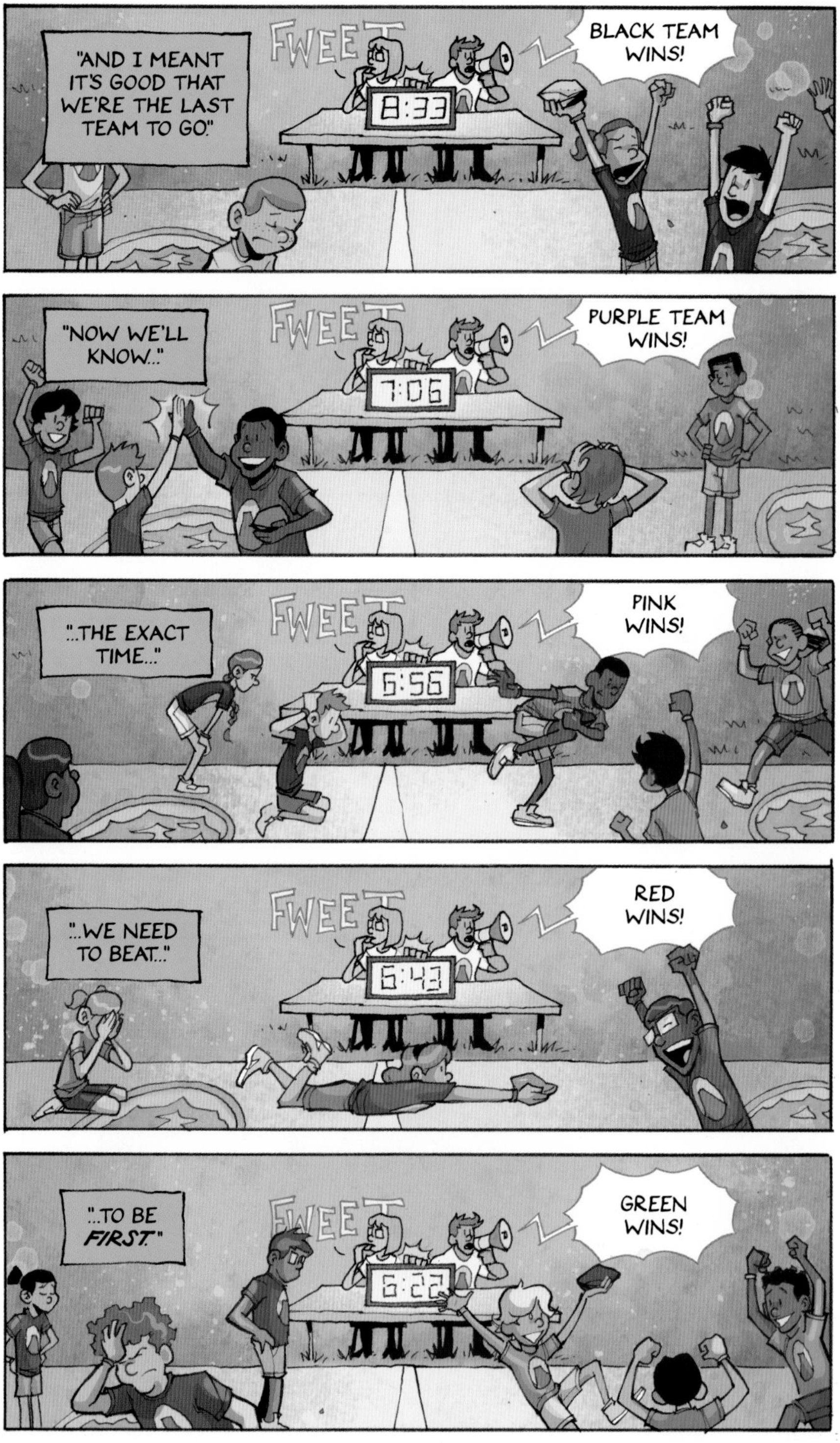
"AND I MEANT IT'S GOOD THAT WE'RE THE LAST TEAM TO GO."
FWEET
8:33
BLACK TEAM WINS!
"NOW WE'LL KNOW..."
FWEET
7:06
PURPLE TEAM WINS!
"...THE EXACT TIME..."
FWEET
6:56
PINK WINS!
"...WE NEED TO BEAT..."
FWEET
6:43
RED WINS!
"...TO BE *FIRST.*"
FWEET
6:22
GREEN WINS!

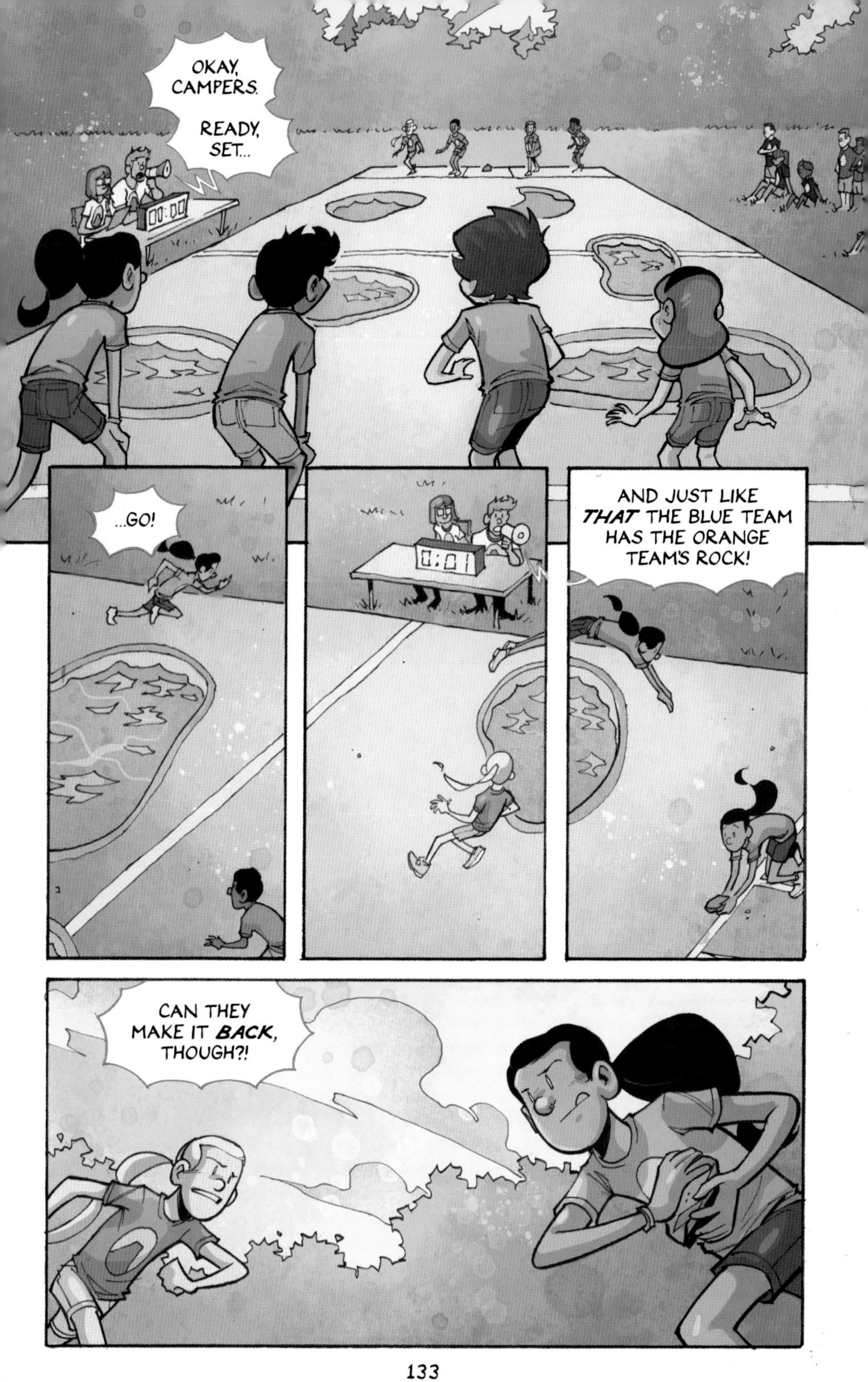
OKAY, CAMPERS.
READY, SET...
00:00
...GO!
0:01
AND JUST LIKE *THAT* THE BLUE TEAM HAS THE ORANGE TEAM'S ROCK!
CAN THEY MAKE IT *BACK*, THOUGH?!

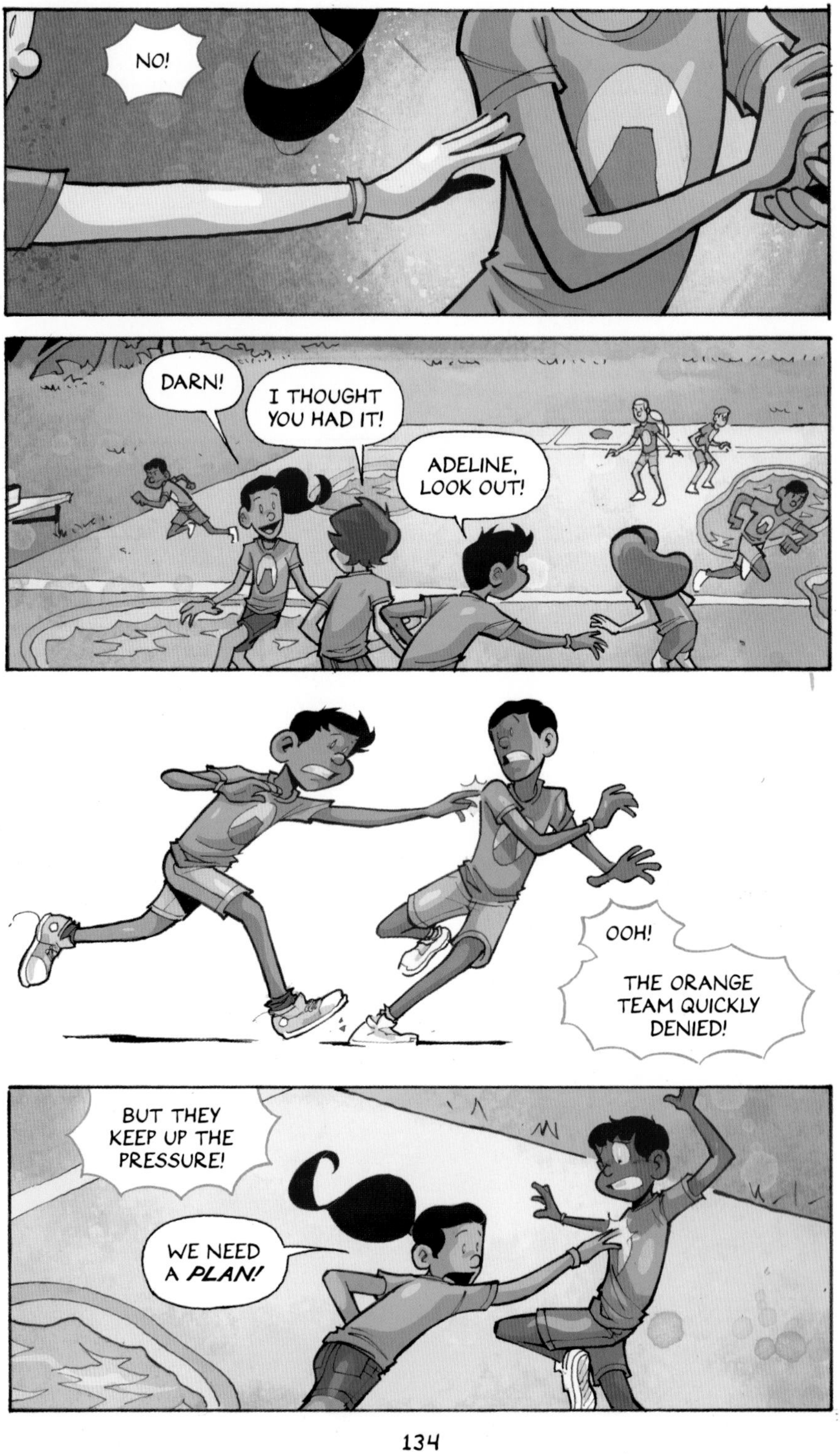
NO!
DARN!
I THOUGHT YOU HAD IT!
ADELINE, LOOK OUT!
OOH!
THE ORANGE TEAM QUICKLY DENIED!
BUT THEY KEEP UP THE PRESSURE!
WE NEED A *PLAN!*

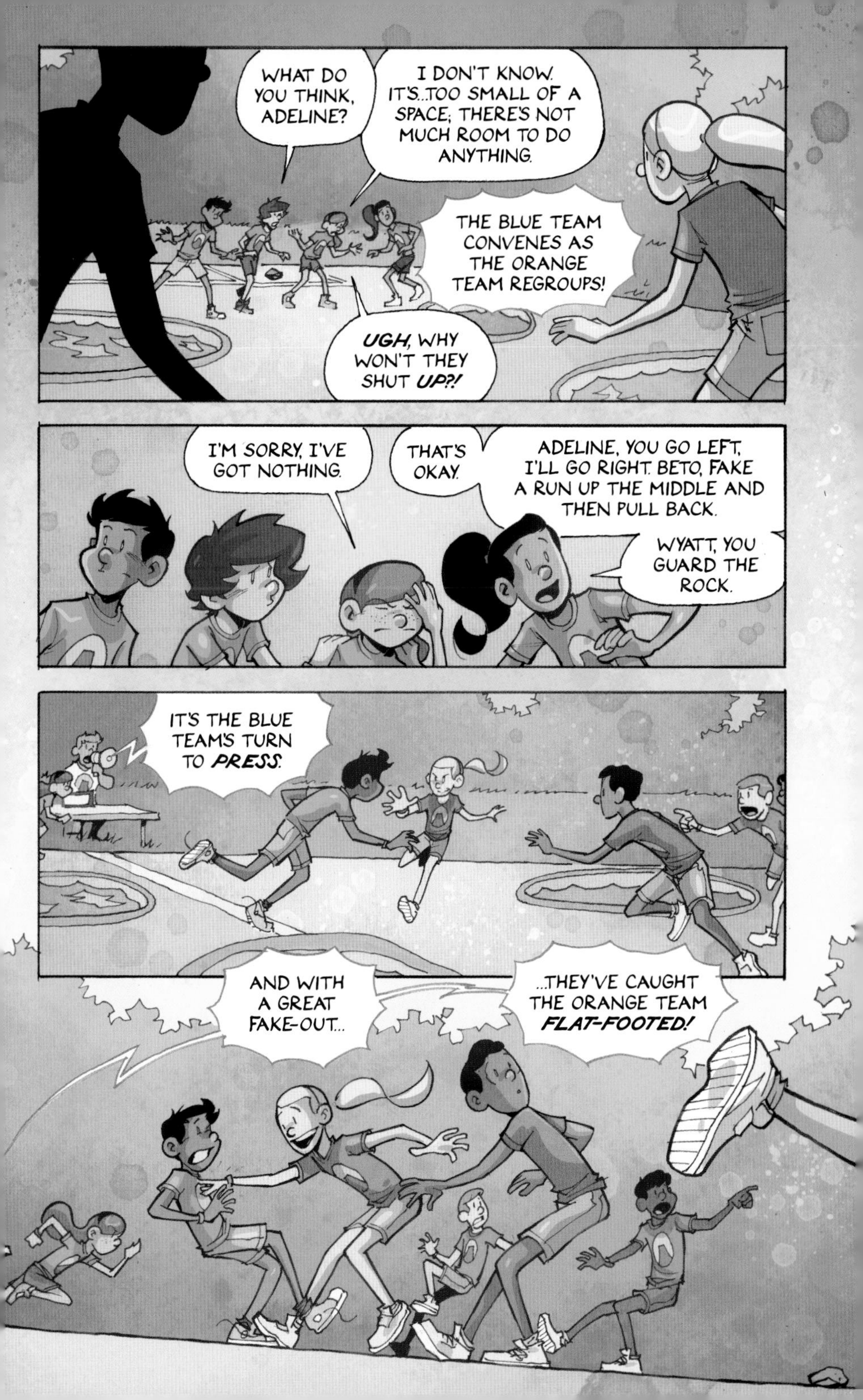
WHAT DO YOU THINK, ADELINE?
I DON'T KNOW. IT'S...TOO SMALL OF A SPACE; THERE'S NOT MUCH ROOM TO DO ANYTHING.
THE BLUE TEAM CONVENES AS THE ORANGE TEAM REGROUPS!
UGH, WHY WON'T THEY SHUT UP?!
I'M SORRY, I'VE GOT NOTHING.
THAT'S OKAY.
ADELINE, YOU GO LEFT, I'LL GO RIGHT. BETO, FAKE A RUN UP THE MIDDLE AND THEN PULL BACK.
WYATT, YOU GUARD THE ROCK.
IT'S THE BLUE TEAM'S TURN TO PRESS.
AND WITH A GREAT FAKE-OUT...
...THEY'VE CAUGHT THE ORANGE TEAM FLAT-FOOTED!

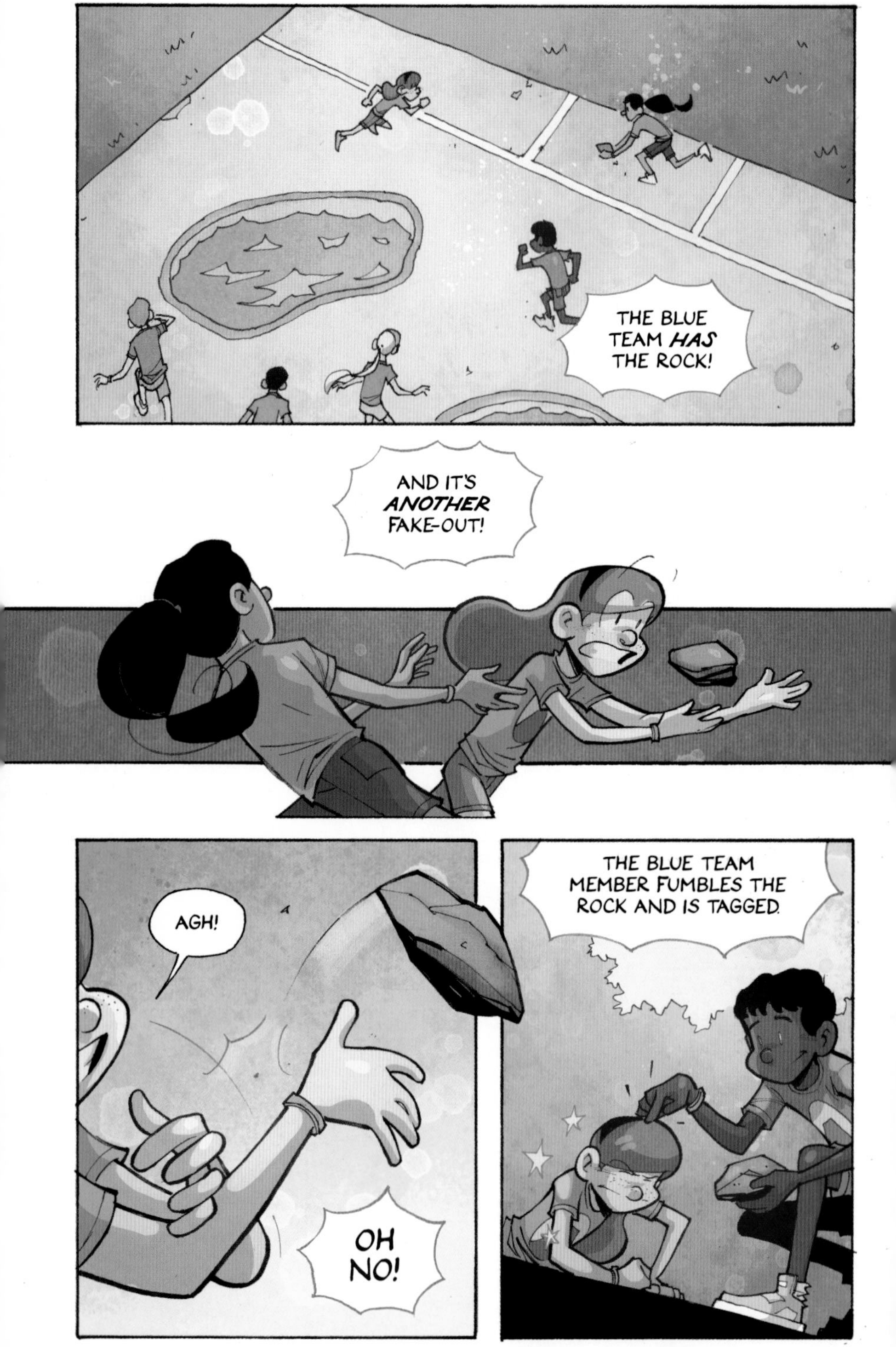
THE BLUE TEAM *HAS* THE ROCK!
AND IT'S *ANOTHER* FAKE-OUT!
AGH!
OH NO!
THE BLUE TEAM MEMBER FUMBLES THE ROCK AND IS TAGGED.

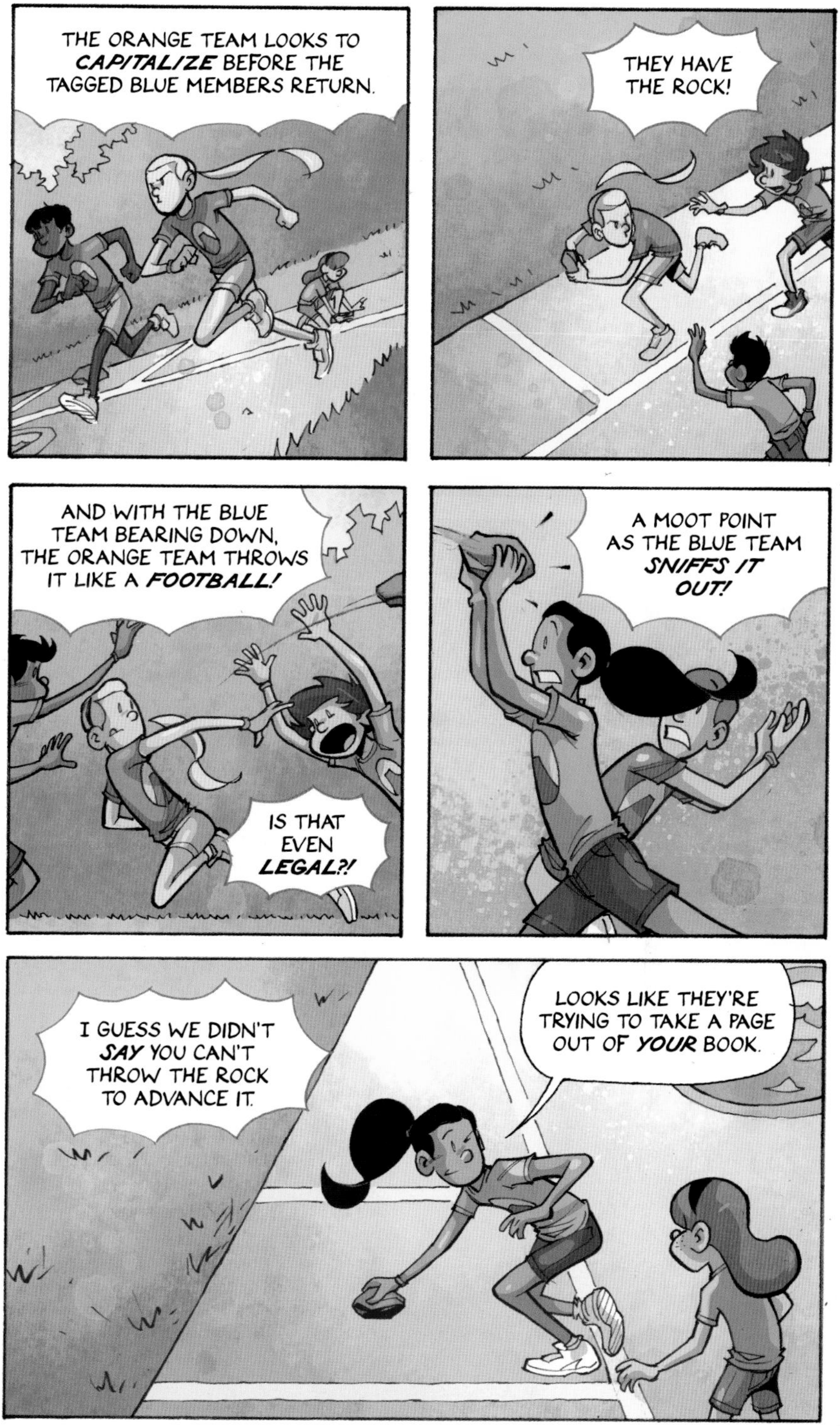
THE ORANGE TEAM LOOKS TO CAPITALIZE BEFORE THE TAGGED BLUE MEMBERS RETURN.
THEY HAVE THE ROCK!
AND WITH THE BLUE TEAM BEARING DOWN, THE ORANGE TEAM THROWS IT LIKE A FOOTBALL!
IS THAT EVEN LEGAL?!
A MOOT POINT AS THE BLUE TEAM SNIFFS IT OUT!
I GUESS WE DIDN'T SAY YOU CAN'T THROW THE ROCK TO ADVANCE IT.
LOOKS LIKE THEY'RE TRYING TO TAKE A PAGE OUT OF YOUR BOOK.

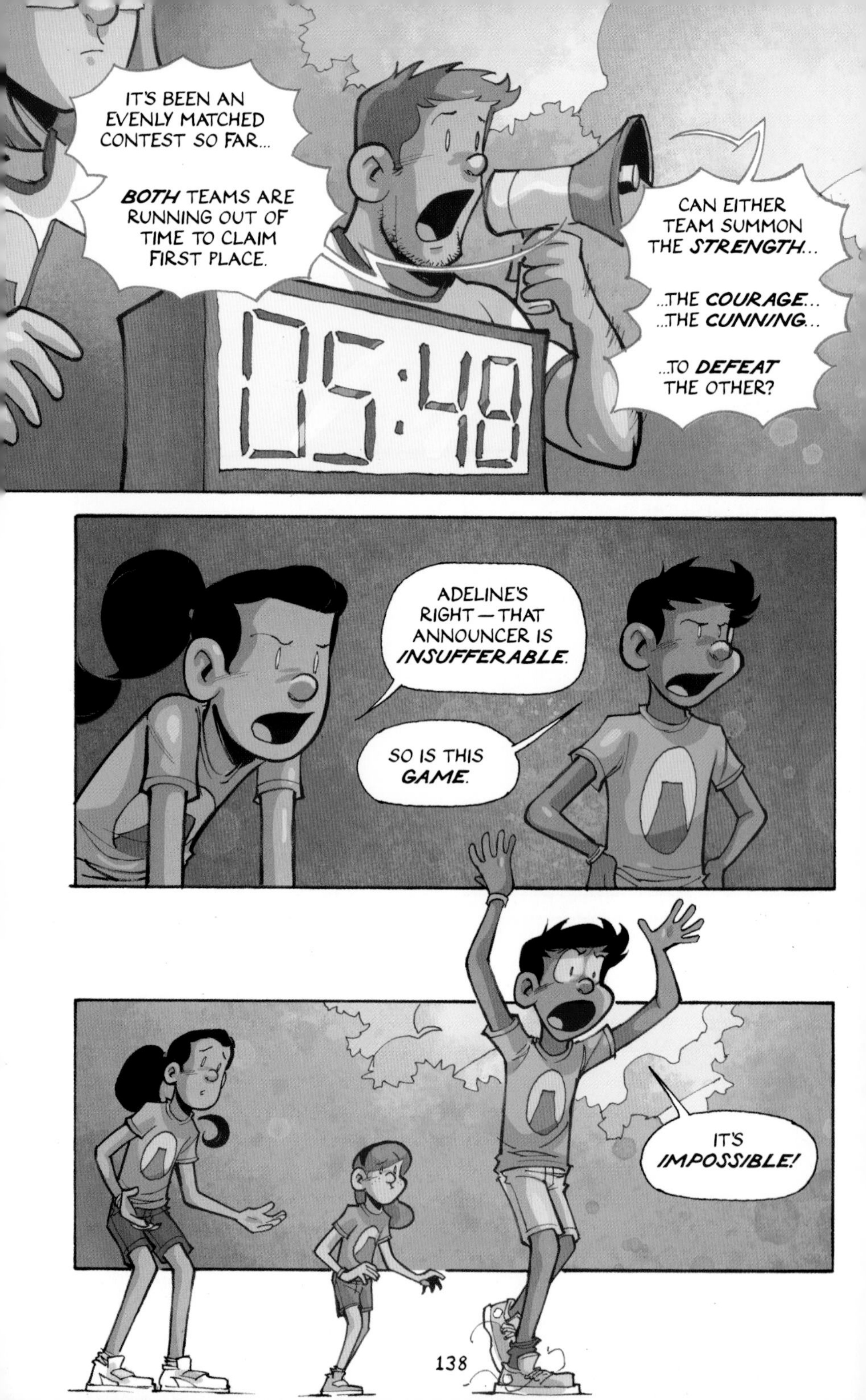
IT'S BEEN AN EVENLY MATCHED CONTEST SO FAR...
BOTH TEAMS ARE RUNNING OUT OF TIME TO CLAIM FIRST PLACE.
CAN EITHER TEAM SUMMON THE STRENGTH...
...THE COURAGE... ...THE CUNNING...
...TO DEFEAT THE OTHER?
05:48
ADELINE'S RIGHT—THAT ANNOUNCER IS INSUFFERABLE.
SO IS THIS GAME.
IT'S IMPOSSIBLE!

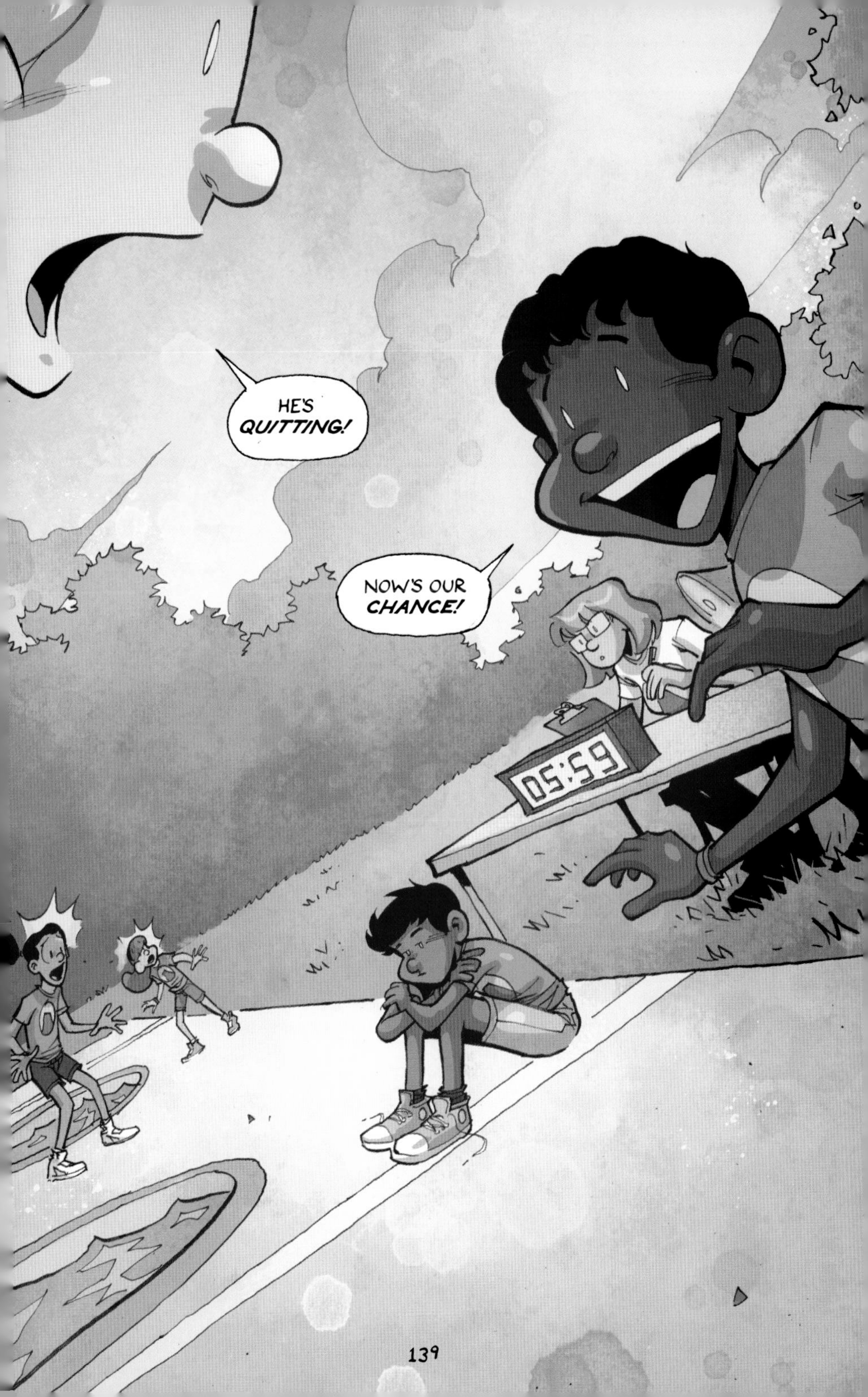
HE'S *QUITTING!*
NOW'S OUR *CHANCE!*
05:59

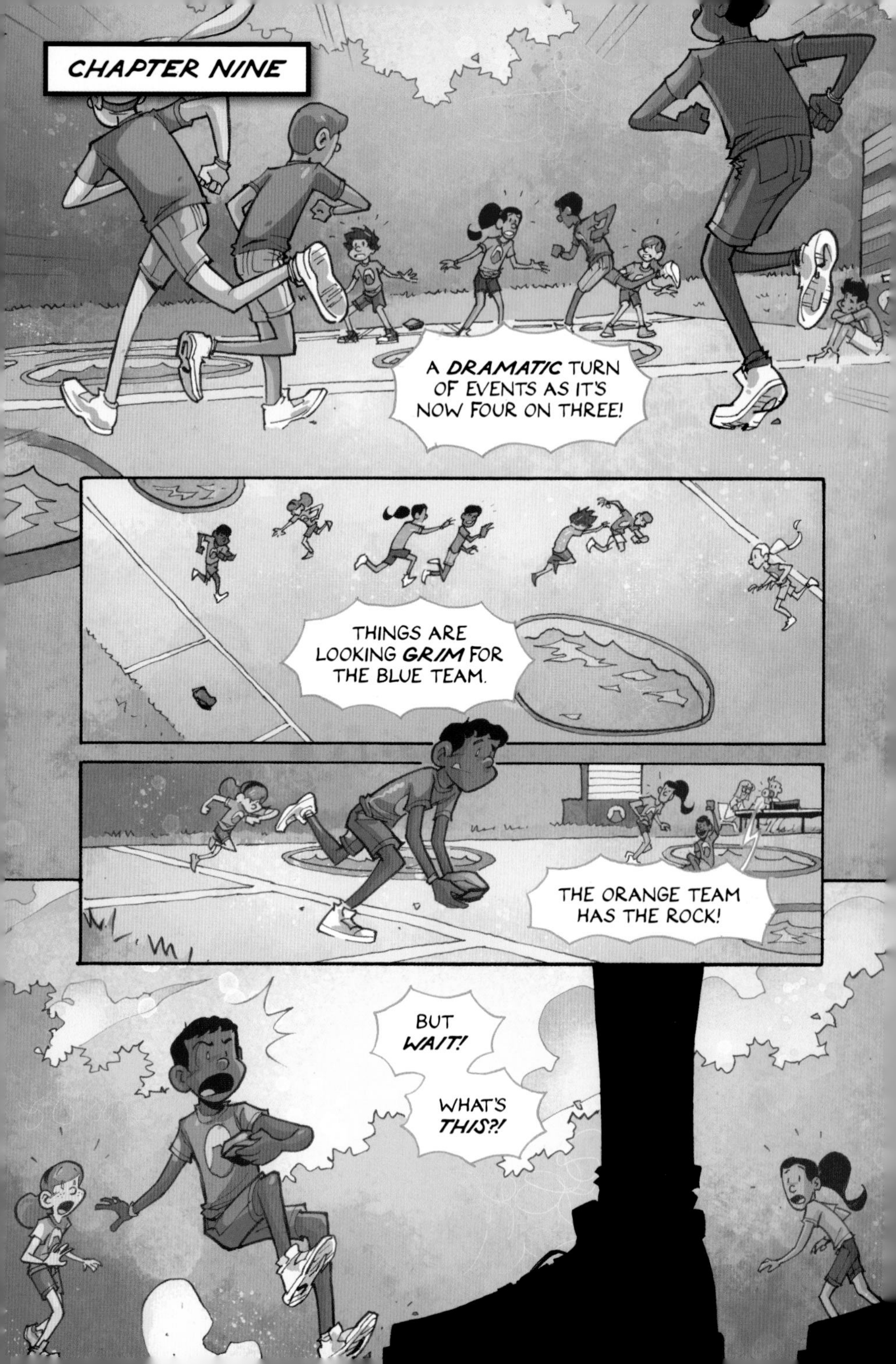
CHAPTER NINE
A DRAMATIC TURN OF EVENTS AS IT'S NOW FOUR ON THREE!
THINGS ARE LOOKING GRIM FOR THE BLUE TEAM.
THE ORANGE TEAM HAS THE ROCK!
BUT WAIT!
WHAT'S THIS?!

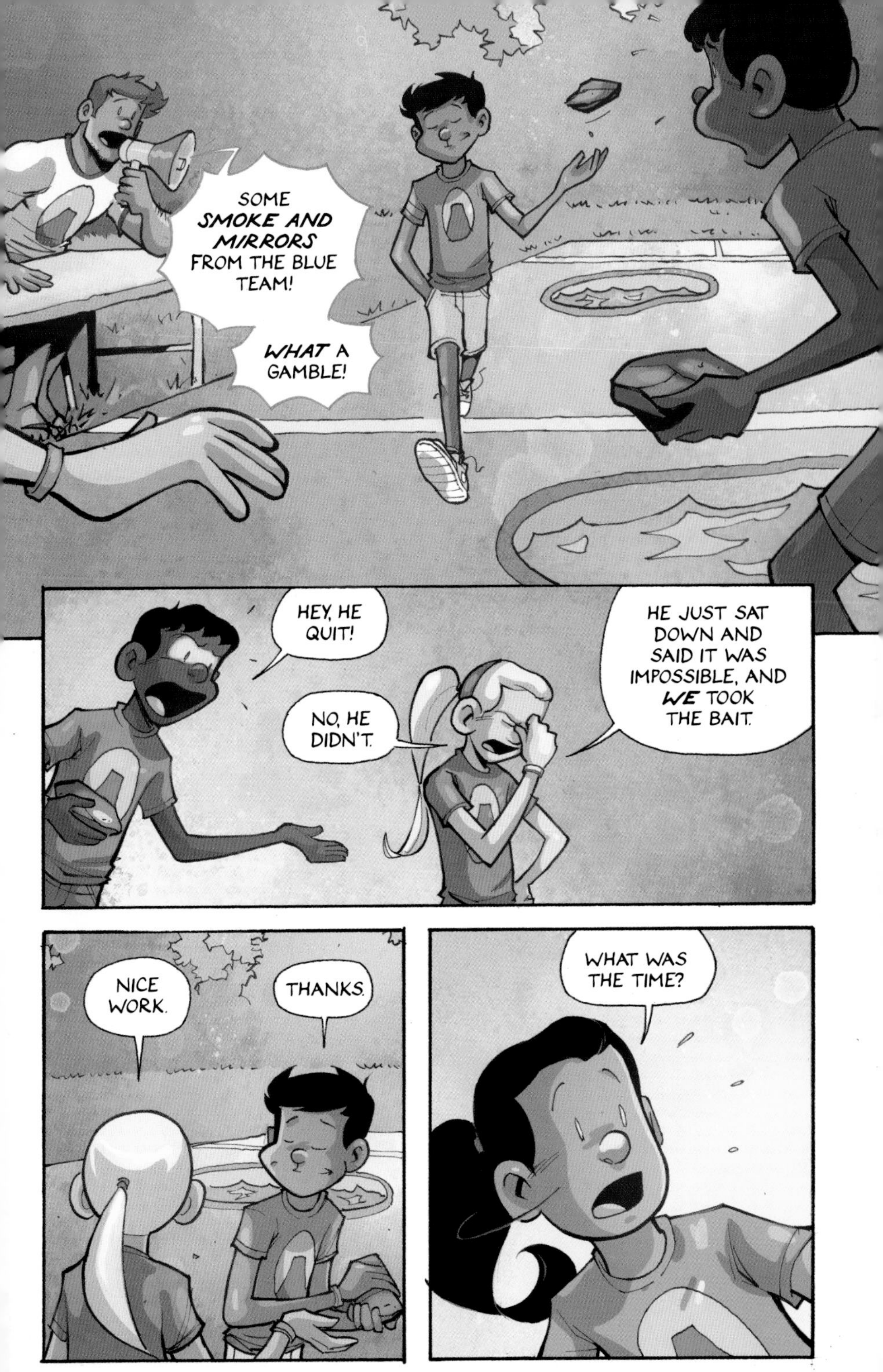
SOME *SMOKE AND MIRRORS* FROM THE BLUE TEAM!
WHAT A GAMBLE!
HEY, HE QUIT!
HE JUST SAT DOWN AND SAID IT WAS IMPOSSIBLE, AND *WE* TOOK THE BAIT.
NO, HE DIDN'T.
NICE WORK.
THANKS.
WHAT WAS THE TIME?

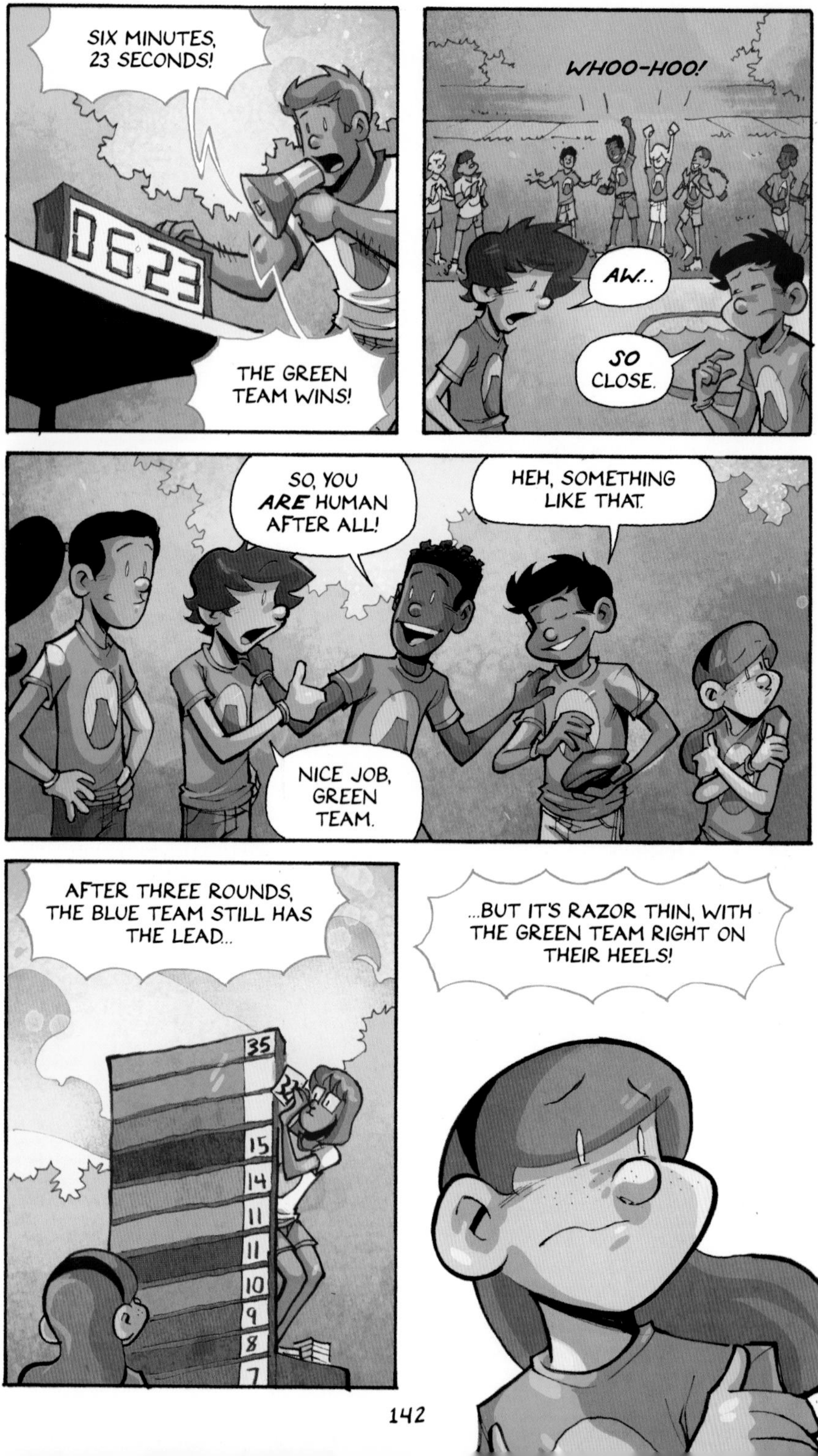
SIX MINUTES, 23 SECONDS!
THE GREEN TEAM WINS!
WHOO-HOO!
AW...
SO CLOSE.
SO, YOU ARE HUMAN AFTER ALL!
NICE JOB, GREEN TEAM.
HEH, SOMETHING LIKE THAT.
AFTER THREE ROUNDS, THE BLUE TEAM STILL HAS THE LEAD...
...BUT IT'S RAZOR THIN, WITH THE GREEN TEAM RIGHT ON THEIR HEELS!

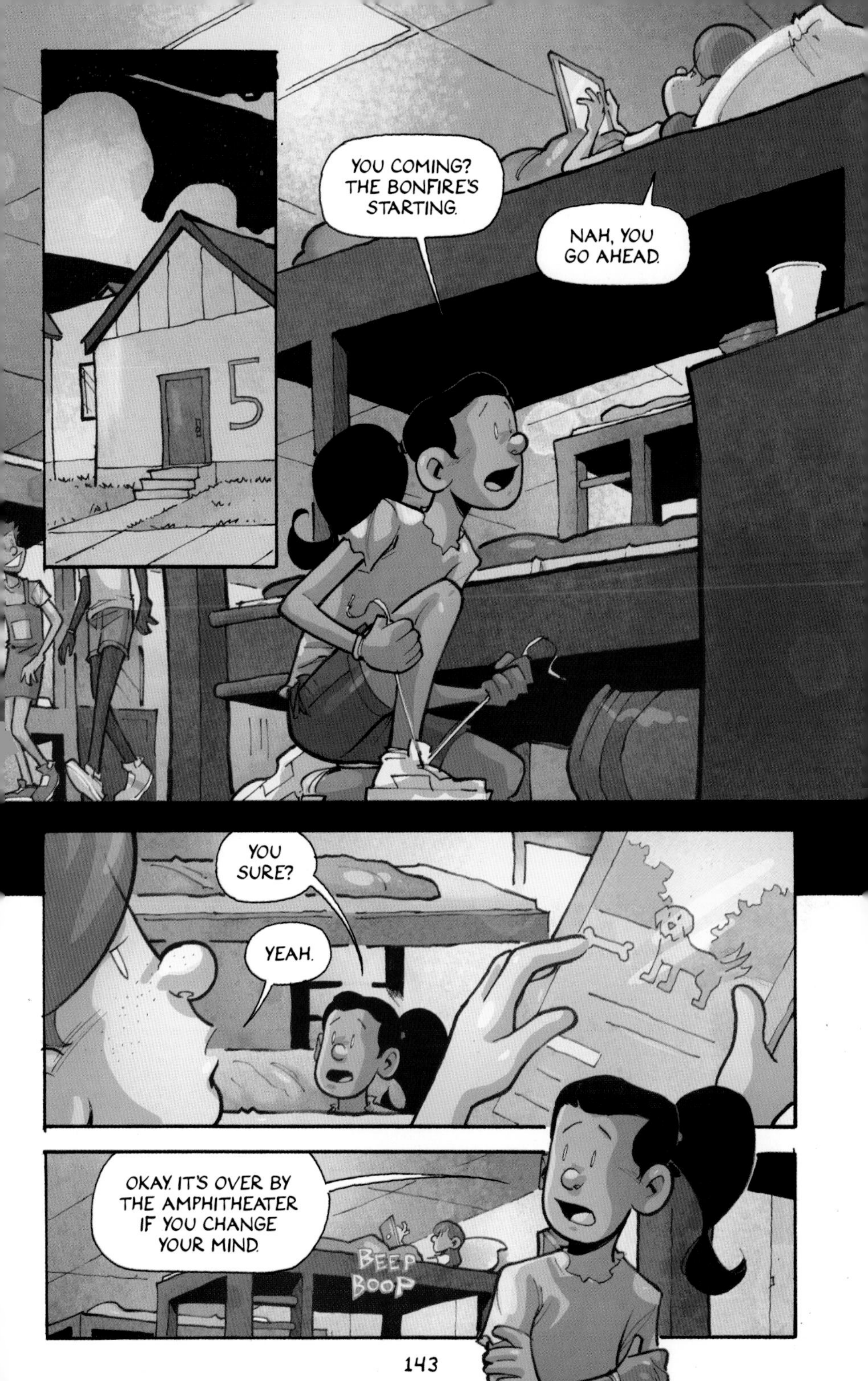
YOU COMING? THE BONFIRE'S STARTING.
NAH, YOU GO AHEAD.
YOU SURE?
YEAH.
OKAY. IT'S OVER BY THE AMPHITHEATER IF YOU CHANGE YOUR MIND.
BEEP BOOP

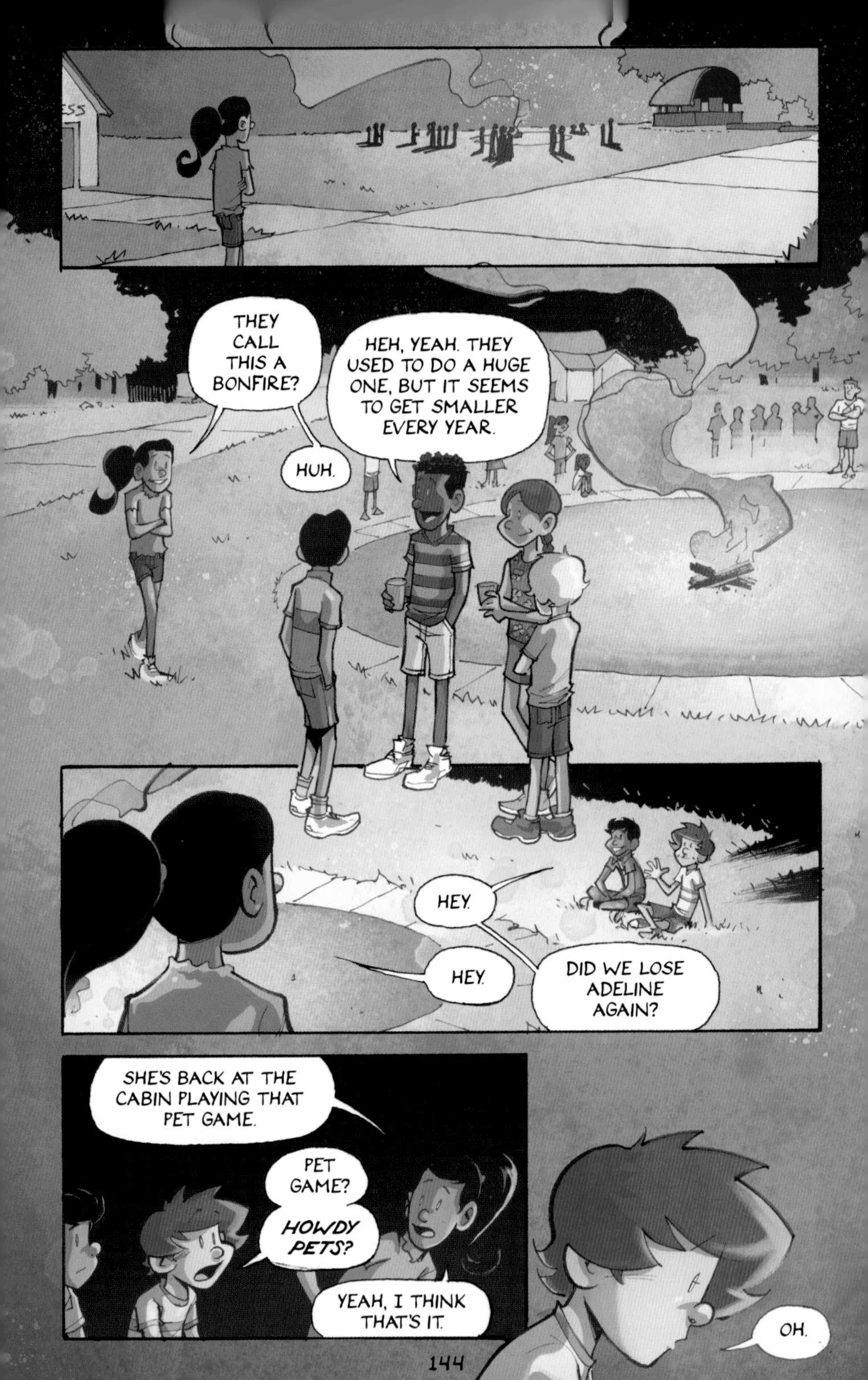
THEY CALL THIS A BONFIRE?
HEH, YEAH. THEY USED TO DO A HUGE ONE, BUT IT SEEMS TO GET SMALLER EVERY YEAR.
HUH.
HEY.
HEY.
DID WE LOSE ADELINE AGAIN?
SHE'S BACK AT THE CABIN PLAYING THAT PET GAME.
PET GAME?
HOWDY PETS?
YEAH, I THINK THAT'S IT.
OH.

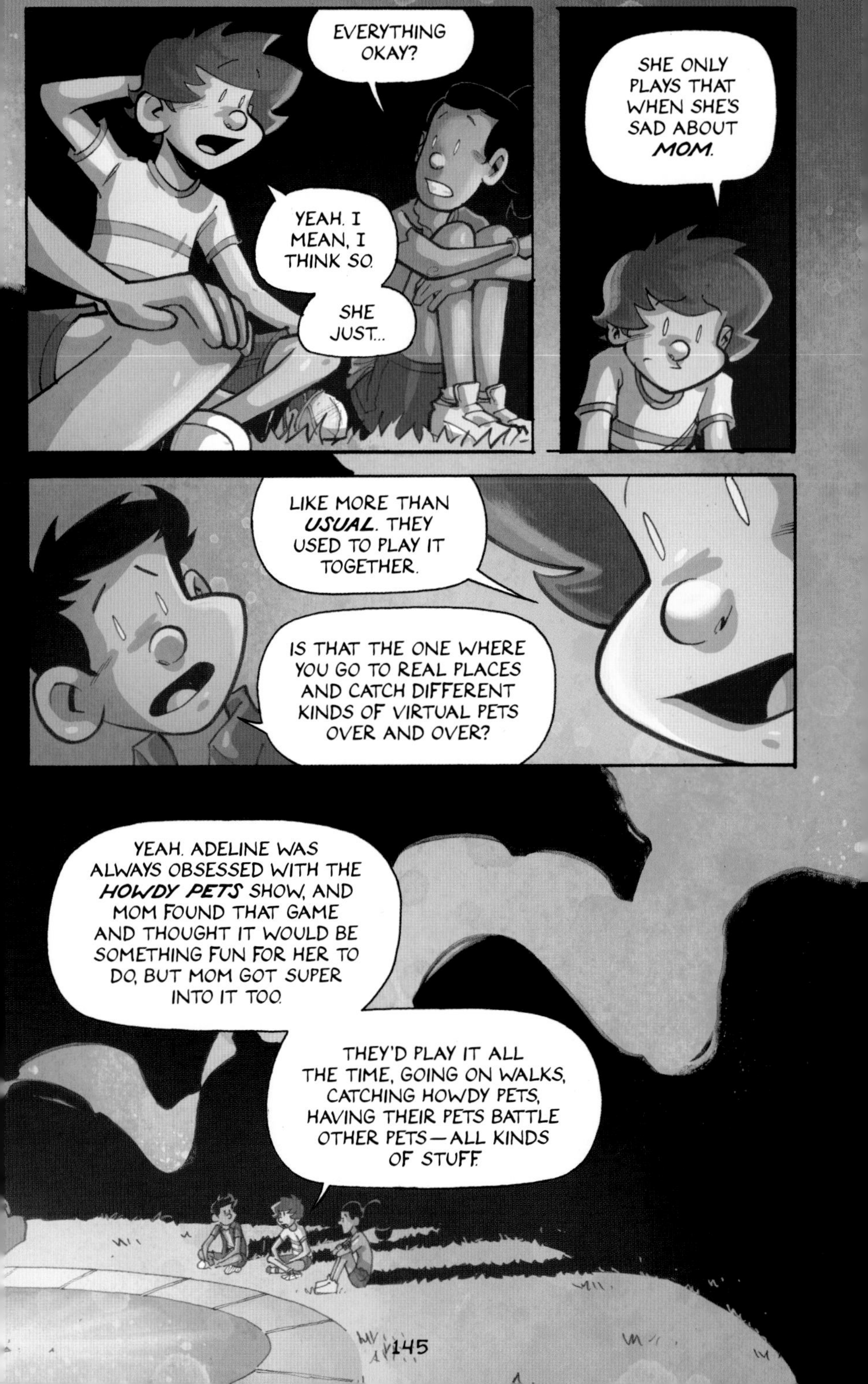
EVERYTHING OKAY?
YEAH. I MEAN, I THINK SO.
SHE JUST...
SHE ONLY PLAYS THAT WHEN SHE'S SAD ABOUT *MOM*.
LIKE MORE THAN *USUAL*. THEY USED TO PLAY IT TOGETHER.
IS THAT THE ONE WHERE YOU GO TO REAL PLACES AND CATCH DIFFERENT KINDS OF VIRTUAL PETS OVER AND OVER?
YEAH. ADELINE WAS ALWAYS OBSESSED WITH THE *HOWDY PETS* SHOW, AND MOM FOUND THAT GAME AND THOUGHT IT WOULD BE SOMETHING FUN FOR HER TO DO, BUT MOM GOT SUPER INTO IT TOO.
THEY'D PLAY IT ALL THE TIME, GOING ON WALKS, CATCHING HOWDY PETS, HAVING THEIR PETS BATTLE OTHER PETS—ALL KINDS OF STUFF.

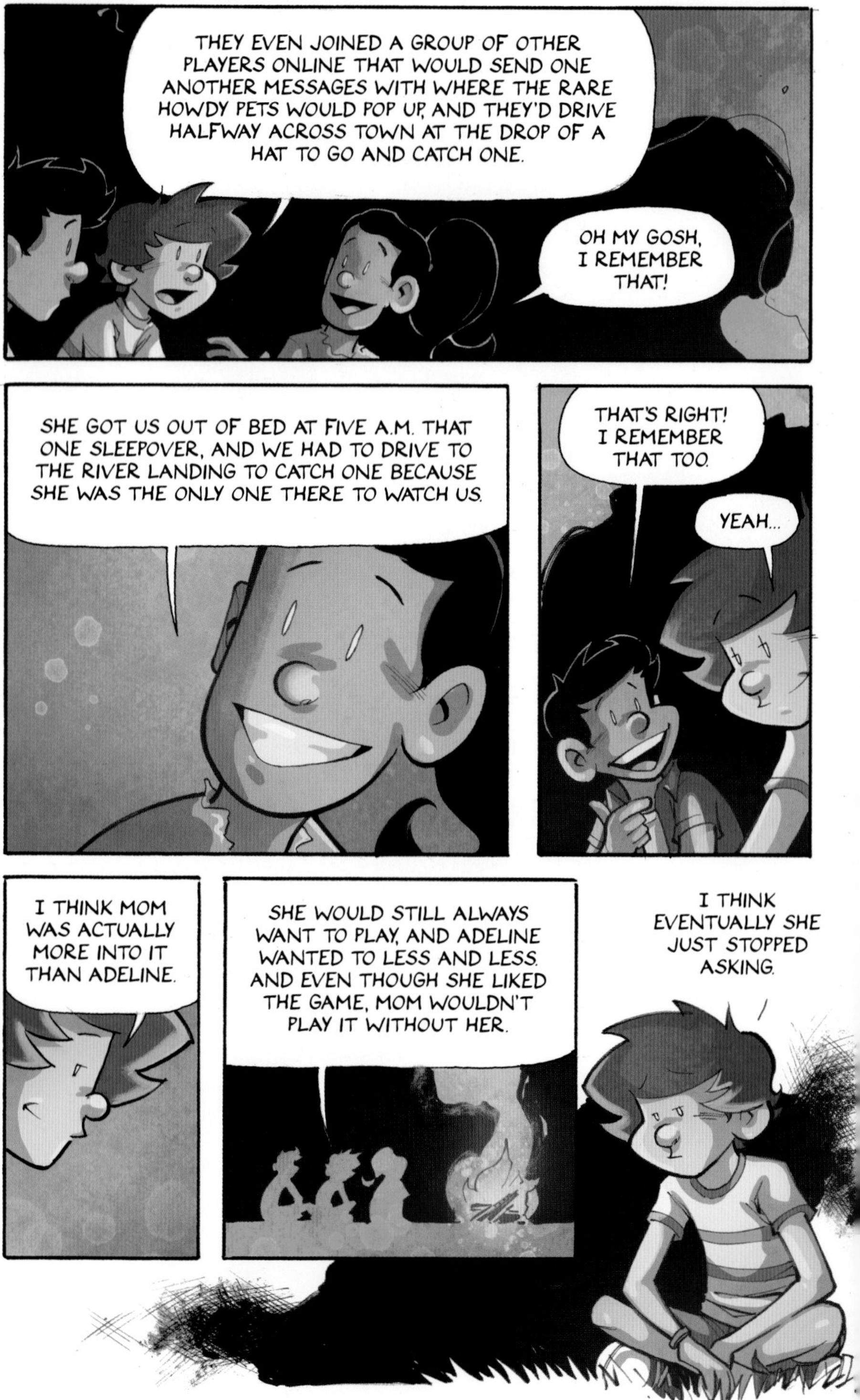
THEY EVEN JOINED A GROUP OF OTHER PLAYERS ONLINE THAT WOULD SEND ONE ANOTHER MESSAGES WITH WHERE THE RARE HOWDY PETS WOULD POP UP, AND THEY'D DRIVE HALFWAY ACROSS TOWN AT THE DROP OF A HAT TO GO AND CATCH ONE.
OH MY GOSH, I REMEMBER THAT!
SHE GOT US OUT OF BED AT FIVE A.M. THAT ONE SLEEPOVER, AND WE HAD TO DRIVE TO THE RIVER LANDING TO CATCH ONE BECAUSE SHE WAS THE ONLY ONE THERE TO WATCH US.
THAT'S RIGHT! I REMEMBER THAT TOO.
YEAH...
I THINK MOM WAS ACTUALLY MORE INTO IT THAN ADELINE.
SHE WOULD STILL ALWAYS WANT TO PLAY, AND ADELINE WANTED TO LESS AND LESS. AND EVEN THOUGH SHE LIKED THE GAME, MOM WOULDN'T PLAY IT WITHOUT HER.
I THINK EVENTUALLY SHE JUST STOPPED ASKING.

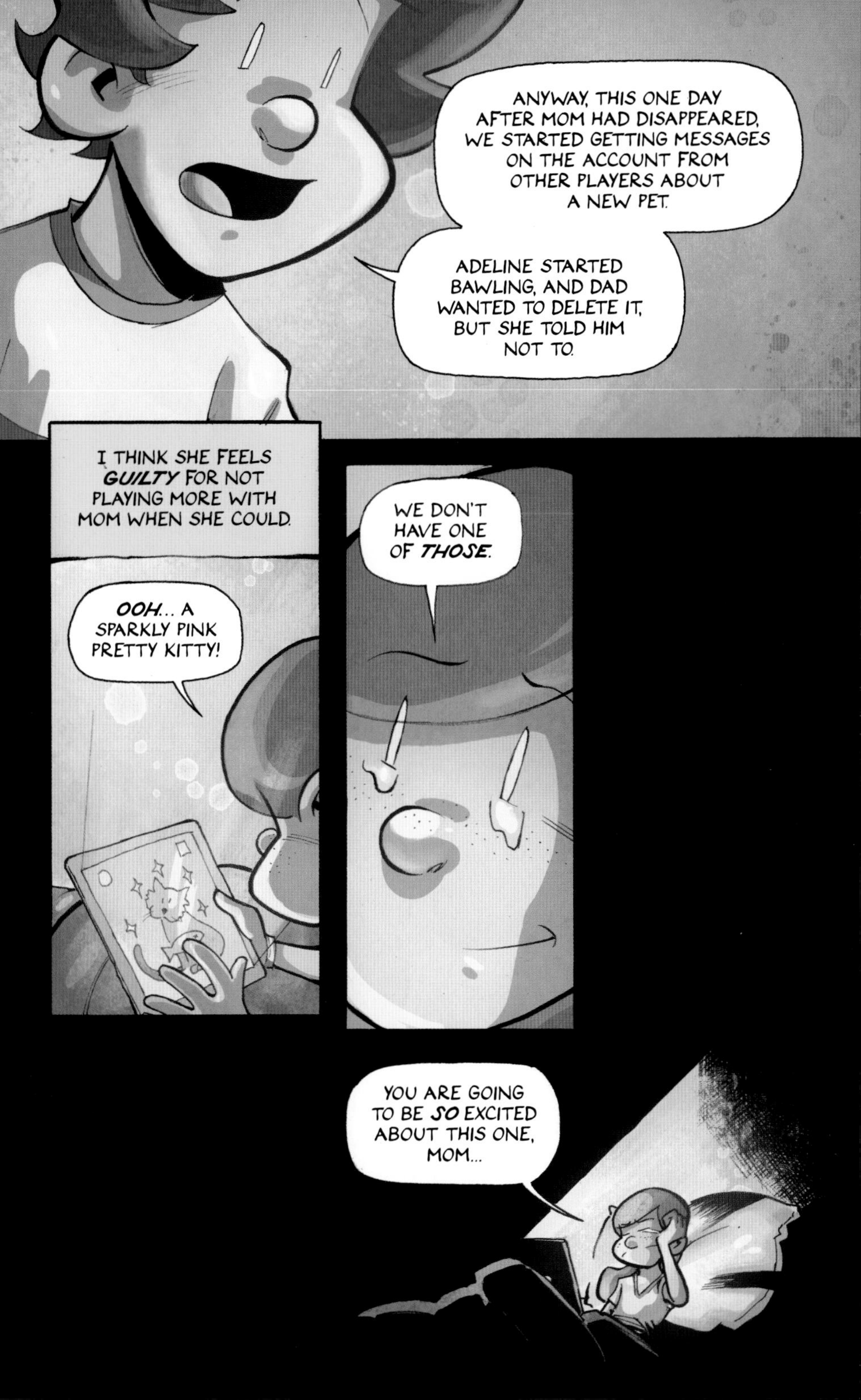
ANYWAY, THIS ONE DAY AFTER MOM HAD DISAPPEARED, WE STARTED GETTING MESSAGES ON THE ACCOUNT FROM OTHER PLAYERS ABOUT A NEW PET.
ADELINE STARTED BAWLING, AND DAD WANTED TO DELETE IT, BUT SHE TOLD HIM NOT TO.
I THINK SHE FEELS *GUILTY* FOR NOT PLAYING MORE WITH MOM WHEN SHE COULD.
OOH... A SPARKLY PINK PRETTY KITTY!
WE DON'T HAVE ONE OF *THOSE*.
YOU ARE GOING TO BE *SO* EXCITED ABOUT THIS ONE, MOM...

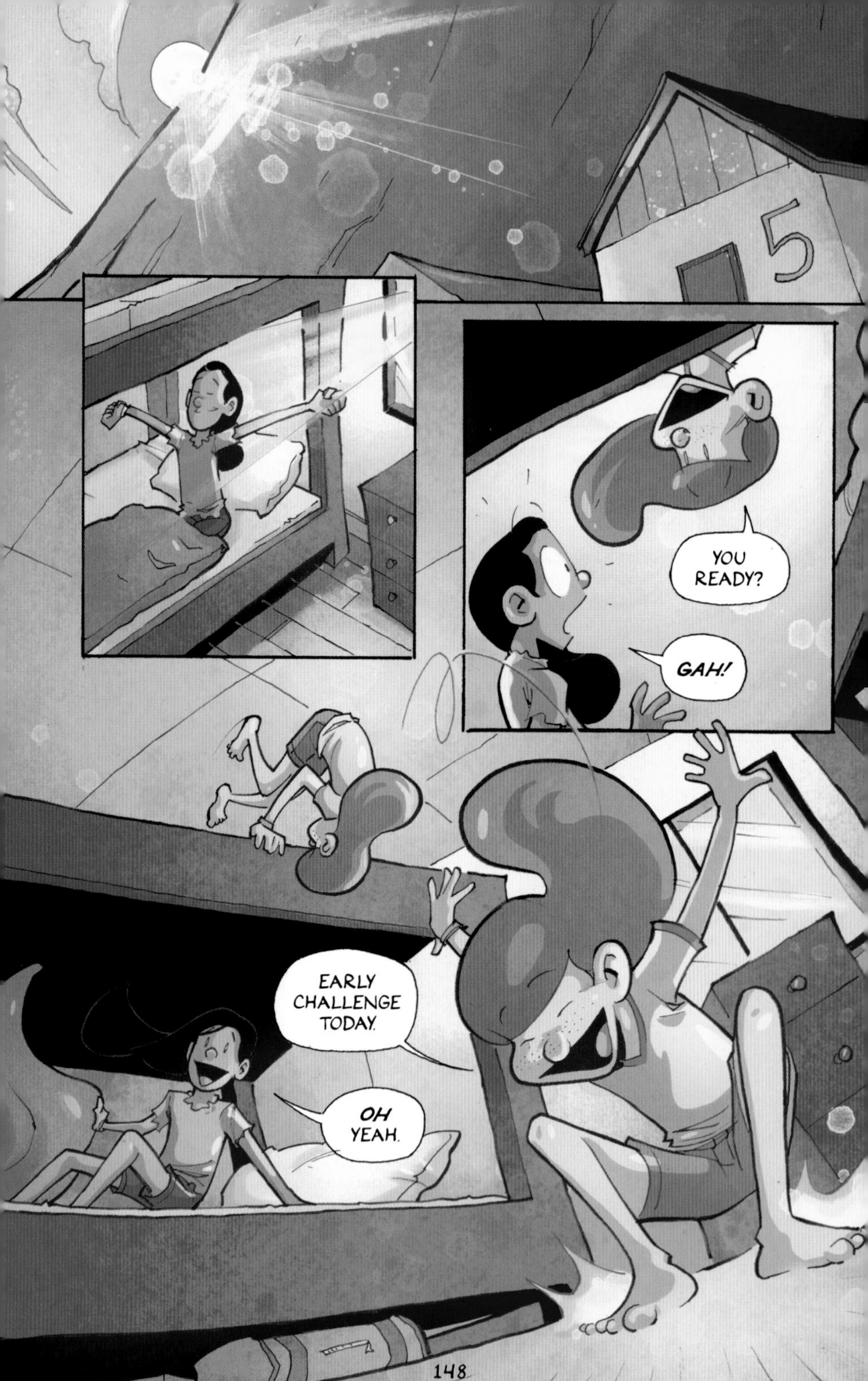
YOU READY?
GAH!
EARLY CHALLENGE TODAY.
OH YEAH.

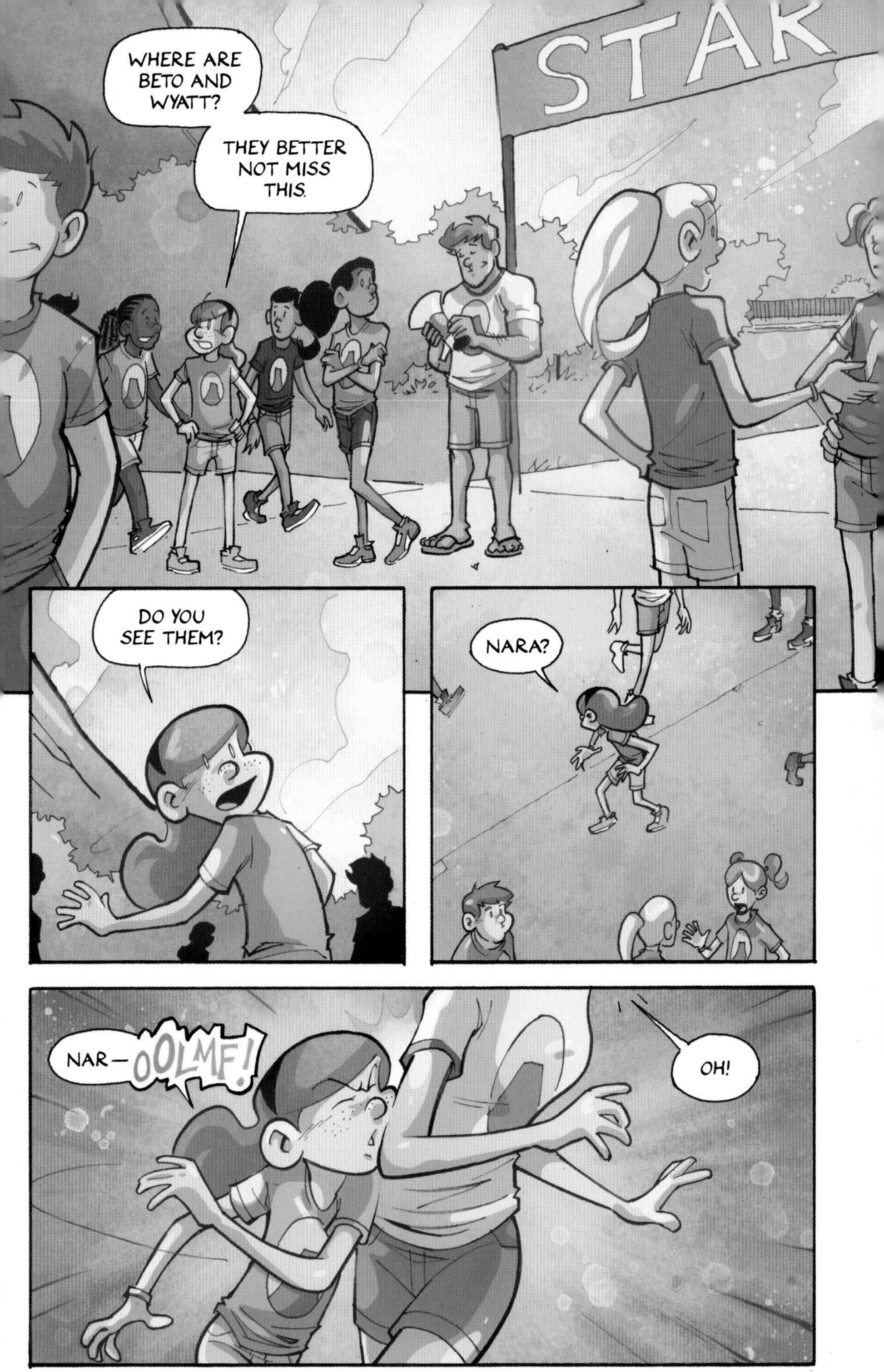
STAR
WHERE ARE BETO AND WYATT?
THEY BETTER NOT MISS THIS.
DO YOU SEE THEM?
NARA?
NAR—OOLMF!
OH!

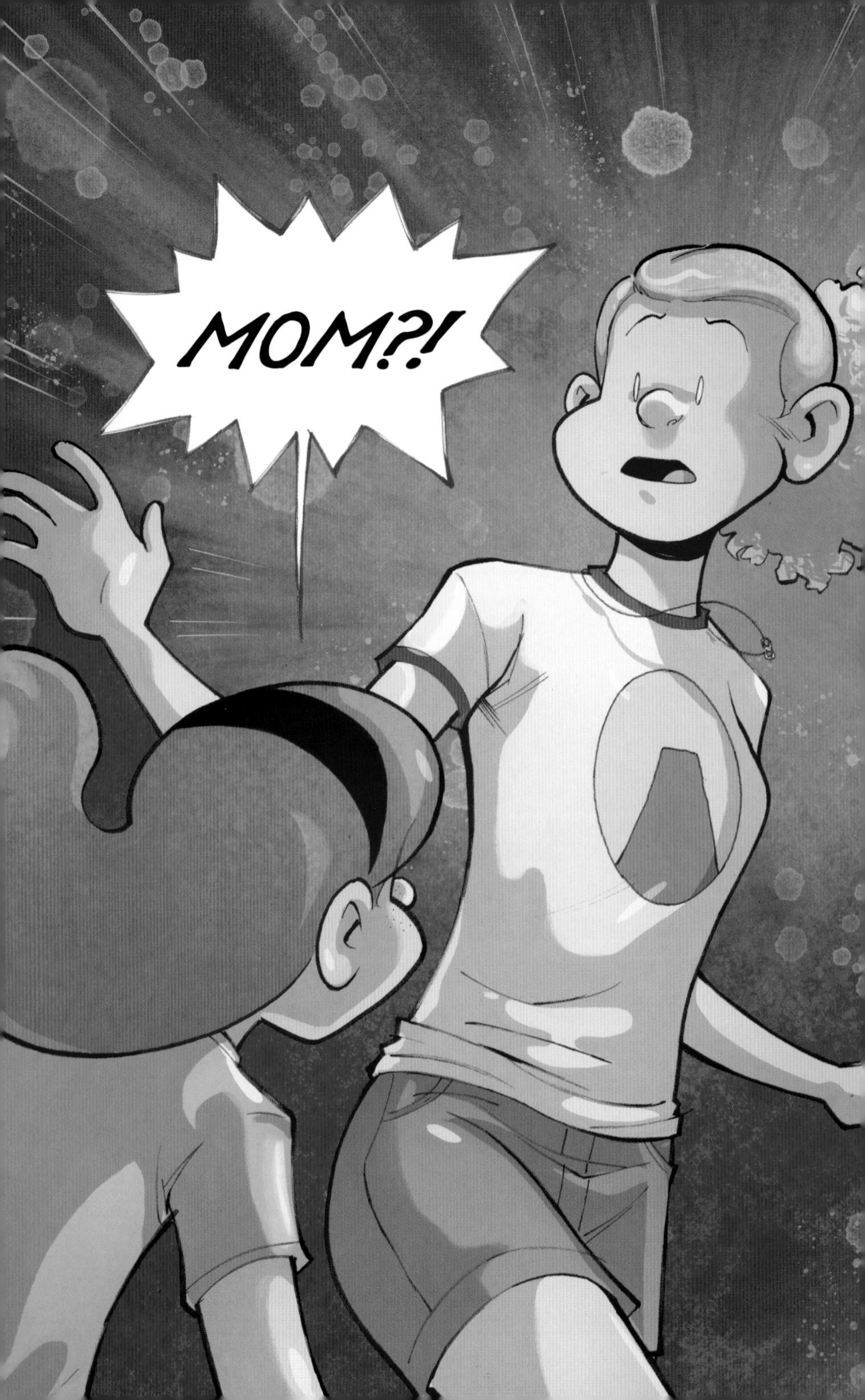
MOM?!

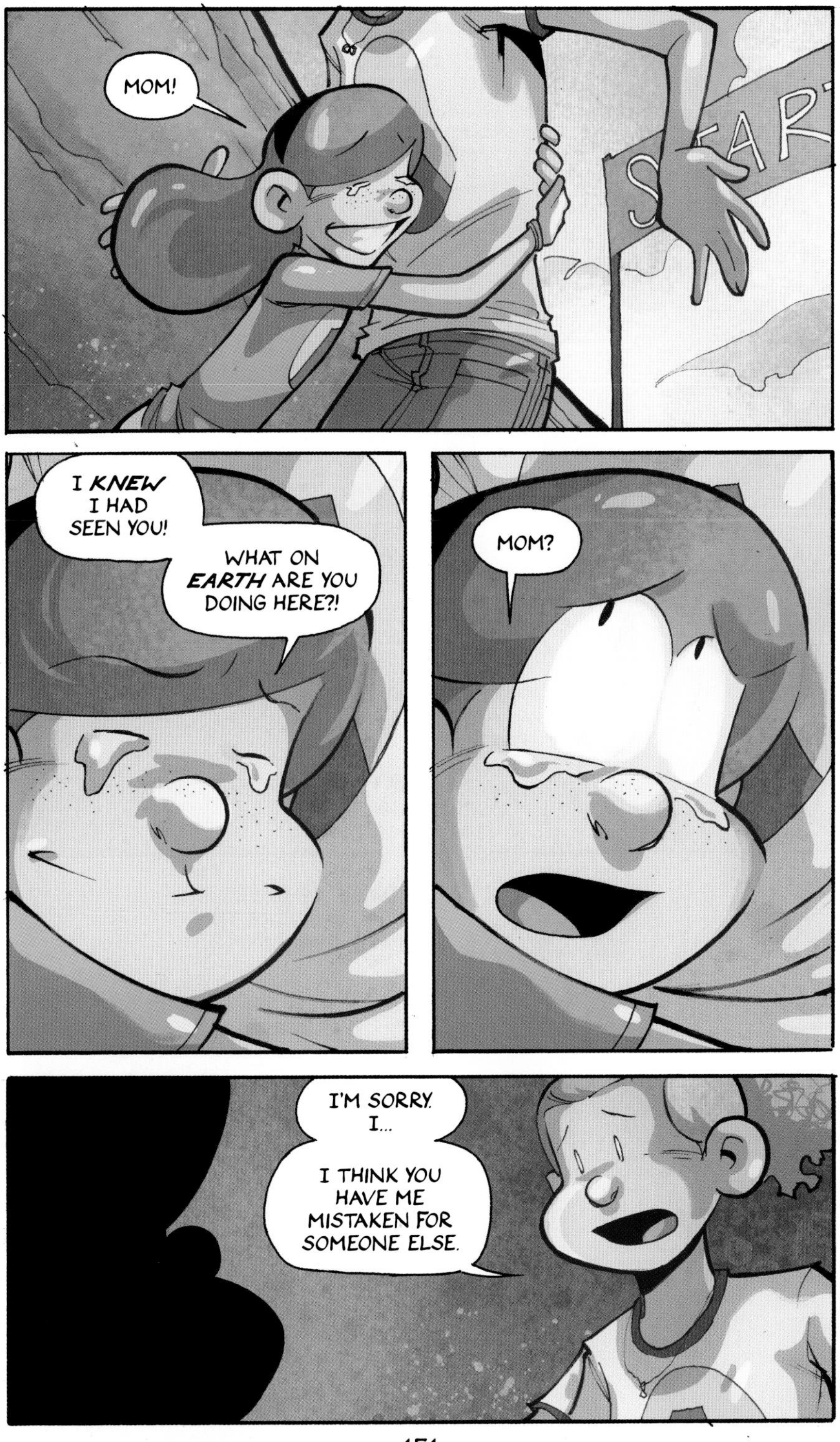
MOM!
I *KNEW* I HAD SEEN YOU!
WHAT ON *EARTH* ARE YOU DOING HERE?!
MOM?
I'M SORRY. I...
I THINK YOU HAVE ME MISTAKEN FOR SOMEONE ELSE.

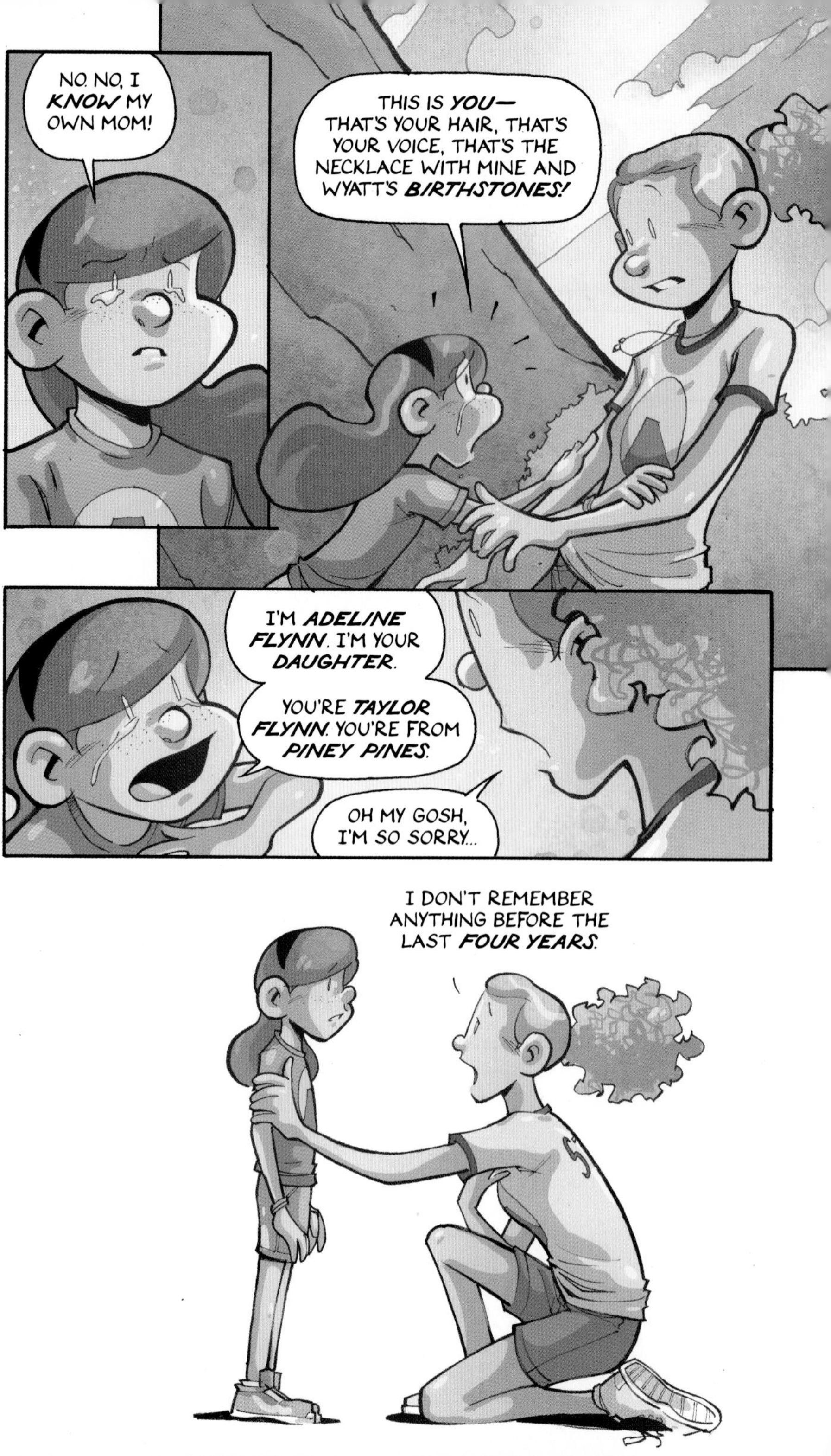
NO. NO, I KNOW MY OWN MOM!
THIS IS YOU— THAT'S YOUR HAIR, THAT'S YOUR VOICE, THAT'S THE NECKLACE WITH MINE AND WYATT'S BIRTHSTONES!
I'M ADELINE FLYNN. I'M YOUR DAUGHTER.
YOU'RE TAYLOR FLYNN. YOU'RE FROM PINEY PINES.
OH MY GOSH, I'M SO SORRY...
I DON'T REMEMBER ANYTHING BEFORE THE LAST FOUR YEARS.

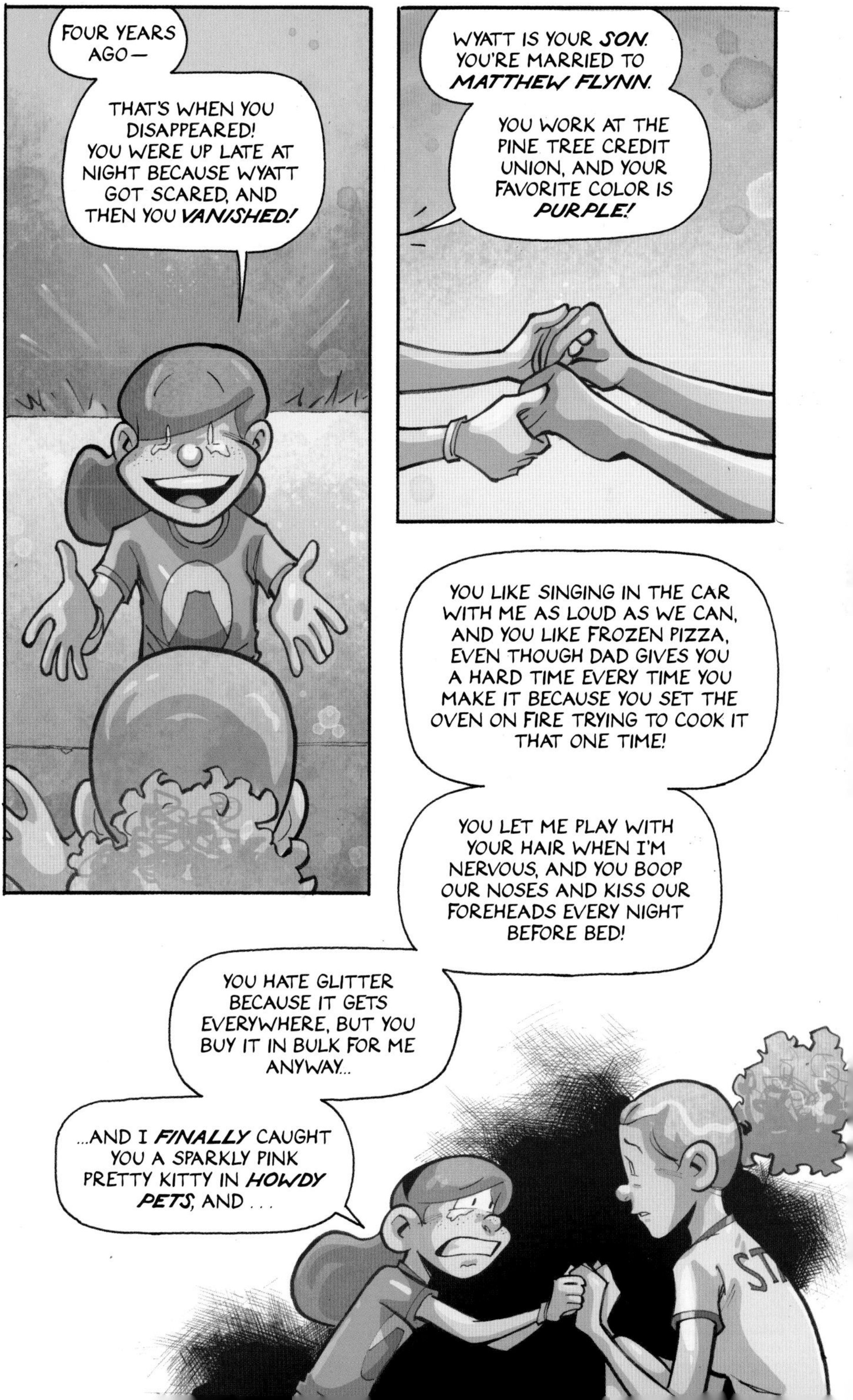
FOUR YEARS AGO—
THAT'S WHEN YOU DISAPPEARED! YOU WERE UP LATE AT NIGHT BECAUSE WYATT GOT SCARED, AND THEN YOU VANISHED!
WYATT IS YOUR SON. YOU'RE MARRIED TO MATTHEW FLYNN.
YOU WORK AT THE PINE TREE CREDIT UNION, AND YOUR FAVORITE COLOR IS PURPLE!
YOU LIKE SINGING IN THE CAR WITH ME AS LOUD AS WE CAN, AND YOU LIKE FROZEN PIZZA, EVEN THOUGH DAD GIVES YOU A HARD TIME EVERY TIME YOU MAKE IT BECAUSE YOU SET THE OVEN ON FIRE TRYING TO COOK IT THAT ONE TIME!
YOU LET ME PLAY WITH YOUR HAIR WHEN I'M NERVOUS, AND YOU BOOP OUR NOSES AND KISS OUR FOREHEADS EVERY NIGHT BEFORE BED!
YOU HATE GLITTER BECAUSE IT GETS EVERYWHERE, BUT YOU BUY IT IN BULK FOR ME ANYWAY...
...AND I FINALLY CAUGHT YOU A SPARKLY PINK PRETTY KITTY IN HOWDY PETS, AND . . .

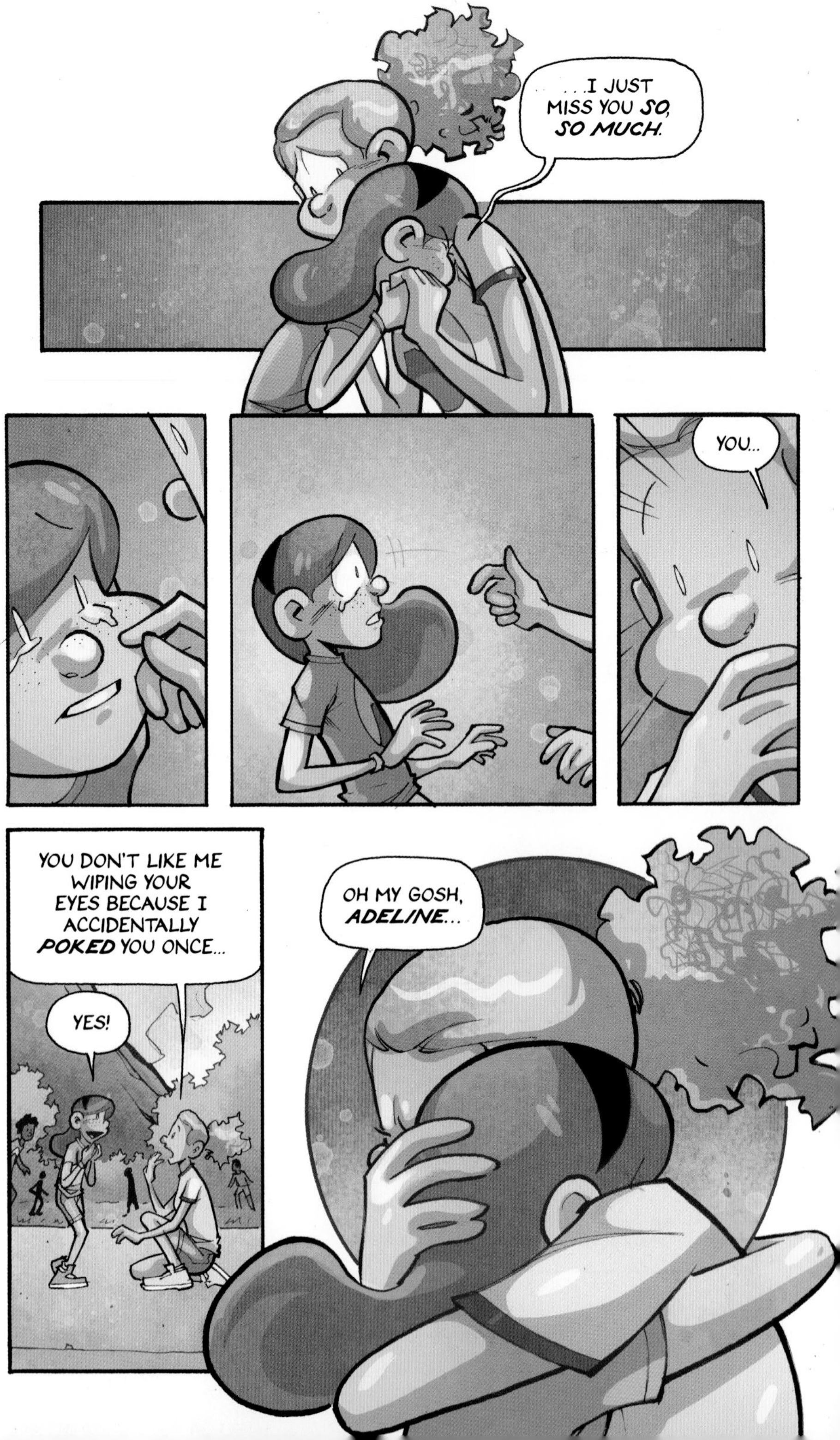
. . .I JUST MISS YOU SO, SO MUCH.
YOU...
YOU DON'T LIKE ME WIPING YOUR EYES BECAUSE I ACCIDENTALLY POKED YOU ONCE...
YES!
OH MY GOSH, ADELINE...

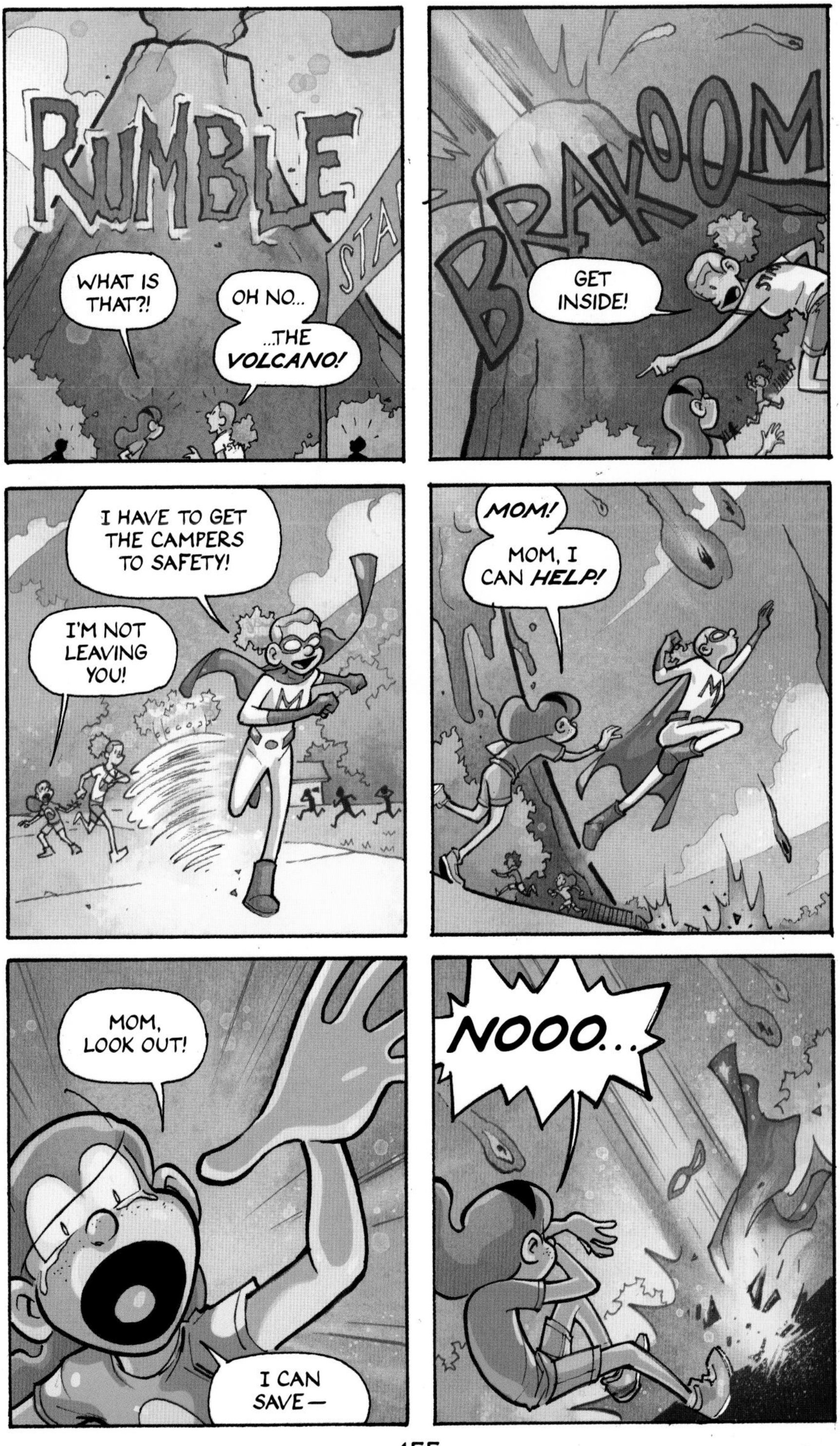
RUMBLE
WHAT IS THAT?!
OH NO...
...THE *VOLCANO!*
BRAKOOM
GET INSIDE!
I HAVE TO GET THE CAMPERS TO SAFETY!
I'M NOT LEAVING YOU!
MOM!
MOM, I CAN *HELP!*
MOM, LOOK OUT!
I CAN SAVE—
NOOO...

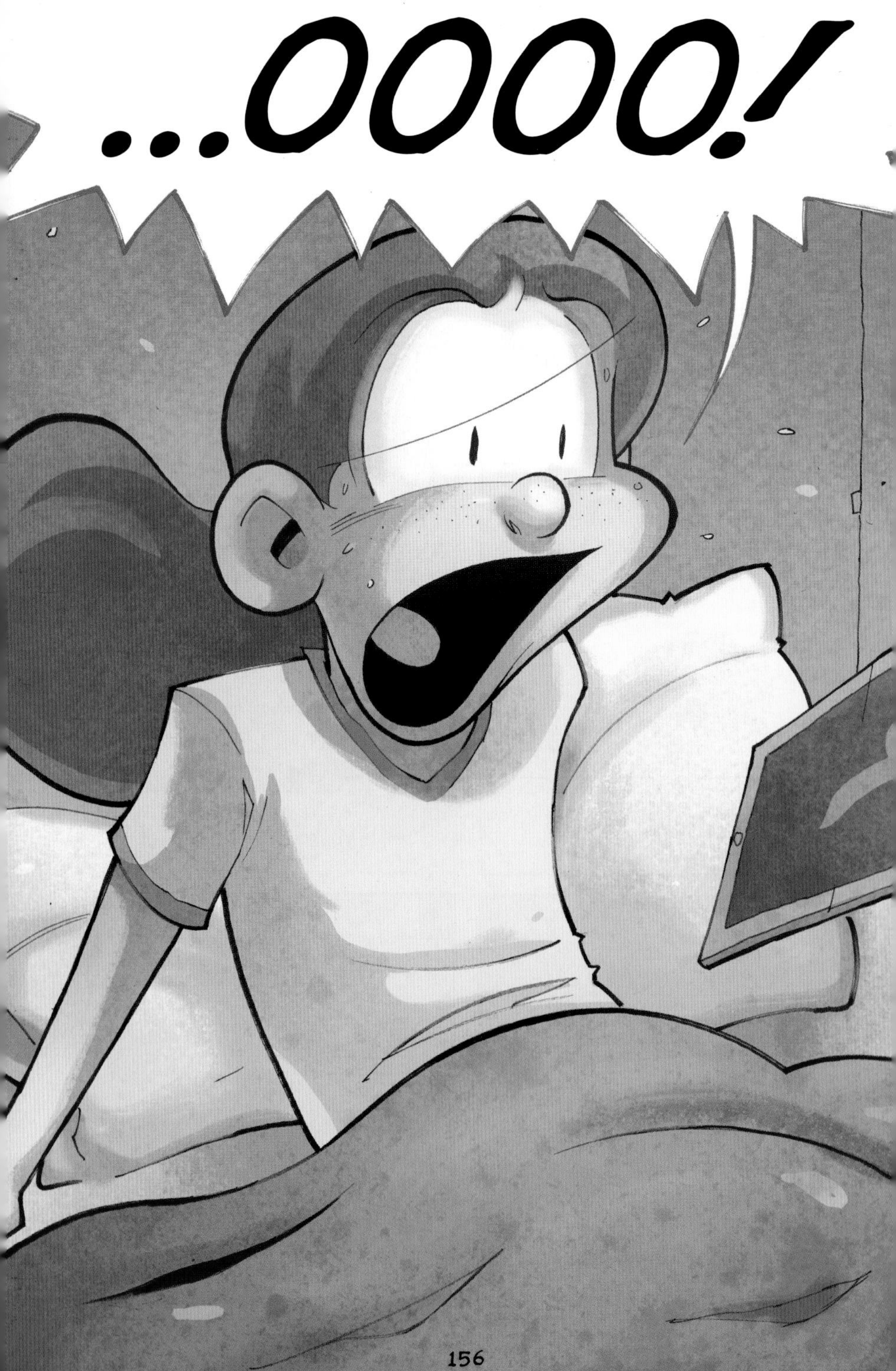
...OOOO!

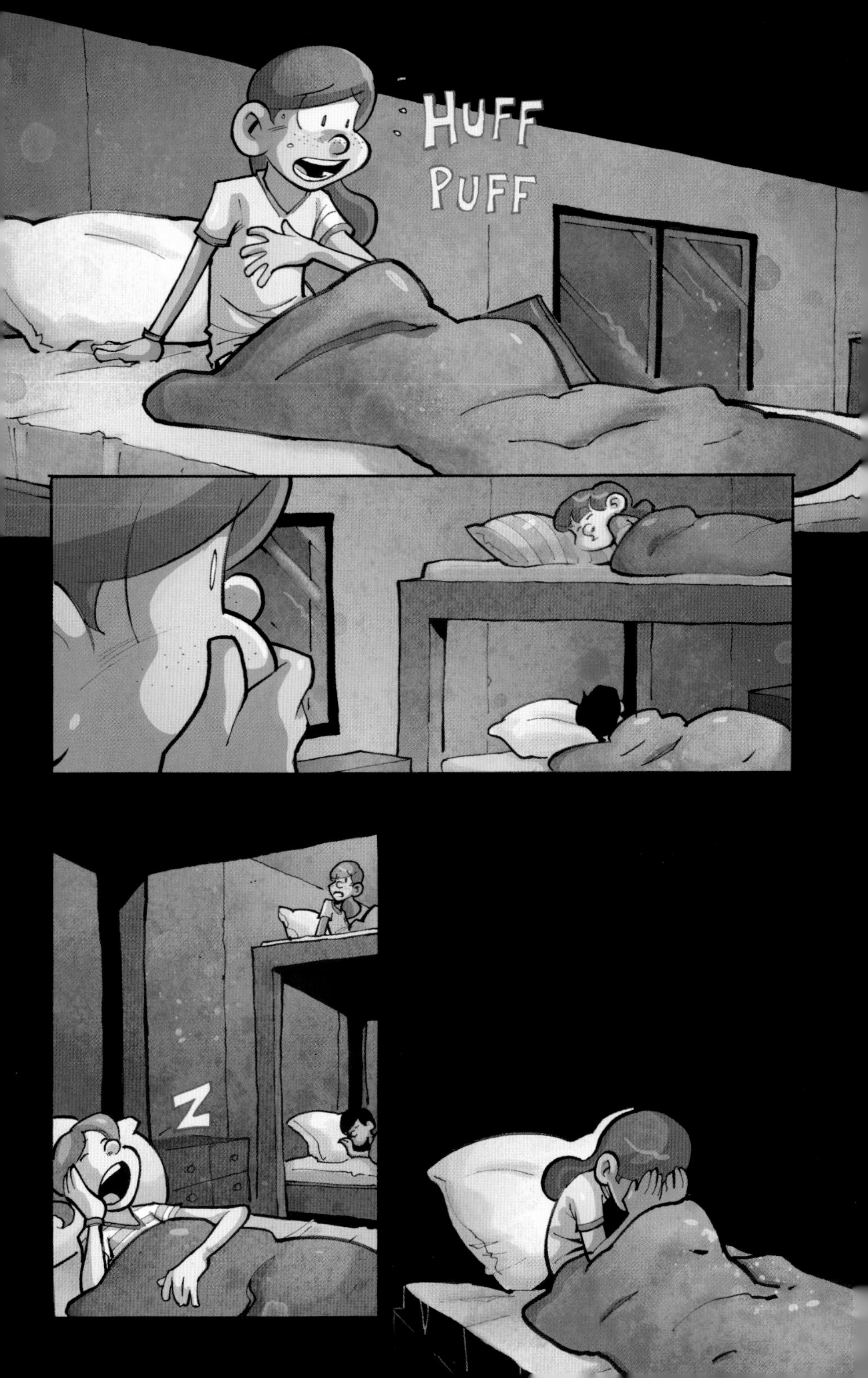
HUFF
PUFF
Z

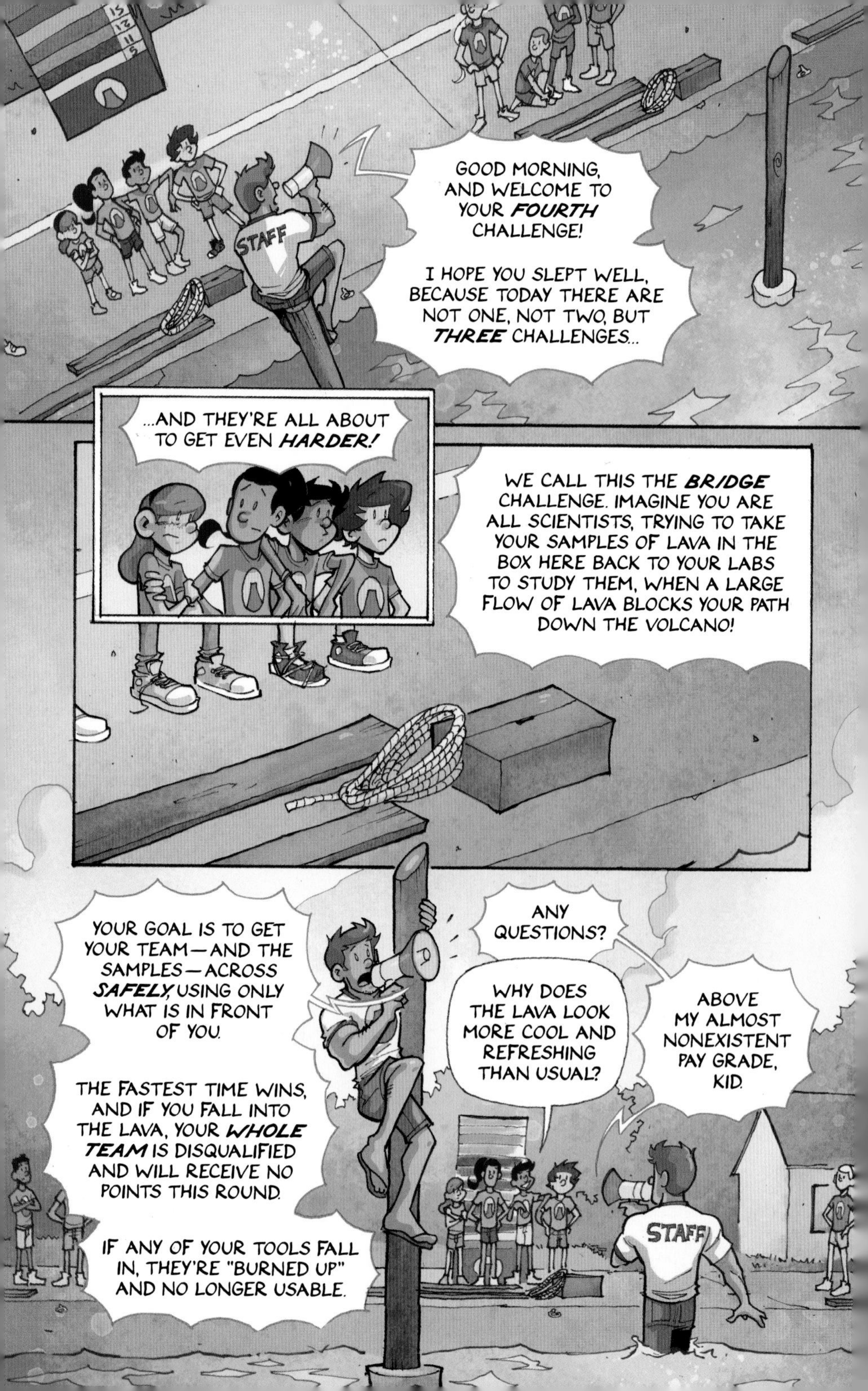
GOOD MORNING, AND WELCOME TO YOUR FOURTH CHALLENGE!
I HOPE YOU SLEPT WELL, BECAUSE TODAY THERE ARE NOT ONE, NOT TWO, BUT THREE CHALLENGES...
STAFF
...AND THEY'RE ALL ABOUT TO GET EVEN HARDER!
WE CALL THIS THE BRIDGE CHALLENGE. IMAGINE YOU ARE ALL SCIENTISTS, TRYING TO TAKE YOUR SAMPLES OF LAVA IN THE BOX HERE BACK TO YOUR LABS TO STUDY THEM, WHEN A LARGE FLOW OF LAVA BLOCKS YOUR PATH DOWN THE VOLCANO!
YOUR GOAL IS TO GET YOUR TEAM—AND THE SAMPLES—ACROSS SAFELY, USING ONLY WHAT IS IN FRONT OF YOU.
THE FASTEST TIME WINS, AND IF YOU FALL INTO THE LAVA, YOUR WHOLE TEAM IS DISQUALIFIED AND WILL RECEIVE NO POINTS THIS ROUND.
IF ANY OF YOUR TOOLS FALL IN, THEY'RE "BURNED UP" AND NO LONGER USABLE.
ANY QUESTIONS?
WHY DOES THE LAVA LOOK MORE COOL AND REFRESHING THAN USUAL?
ABOVE MY ALMOST NONEXISTENT PAY GRADE, KID.
STAFF

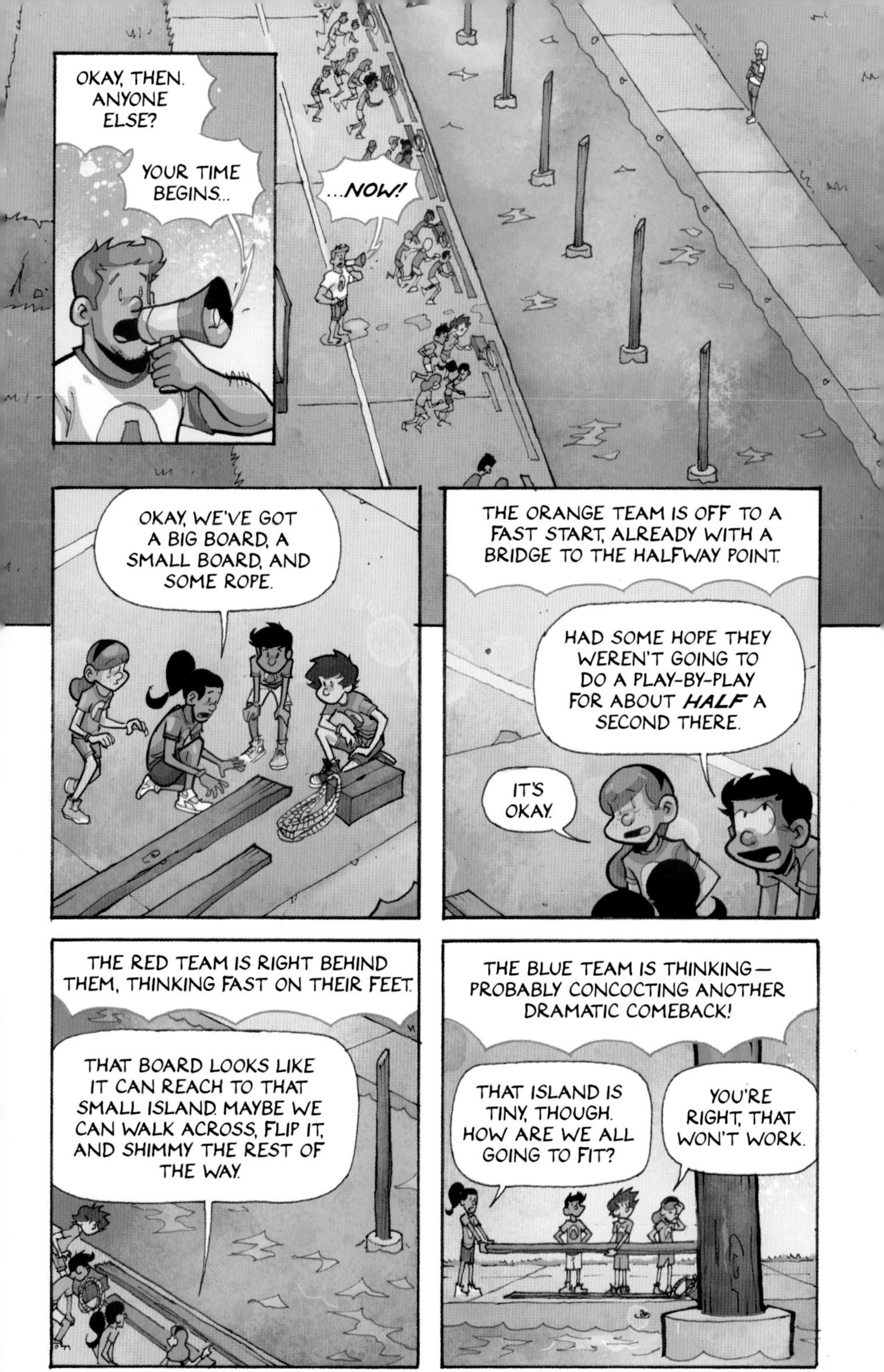
OKAY, THEN. ANYONE ELSE?
YOUR TIME BEGINS...
...NOW!
OKAY, WE'VE GOT A BIG BOARD, A SMALL BOARD, AND SOME ROPE.
THE ORANGE TEAM IS OFF TO A FAST START, ALREADY WITH A BRIDGE TO THE HALFWAY POINT.
HAD SOME HOPE THEY WEREN'T GOING TO DO A PLAY-BY-PLAY FOR ABOUT *HALF* A SECOND THERE.
IT'S OKAY.
THE RED TEAM IS RIGHT BEHIND THEM, THINKING FAST ON THEIR FEET.
THAT BOARD LOOKS LIKE IT CAN REACH TO THAT SMALL ISLAND. MAYBE WE CAN WALK ACROSS, FLIP IT, AND SHIMMY THE REST OF THE WAY.
THE BLUE TEAM IS THINKING—PROBABLY CONCOCTING ANOTHER DRAMATIC COMEBACK!
THAT ISLAND IS TINY, THOUGH. HOW ARE WE ALL GOING TO FIT?
YOU'RE RIGHT, THAT WON'T WORK.

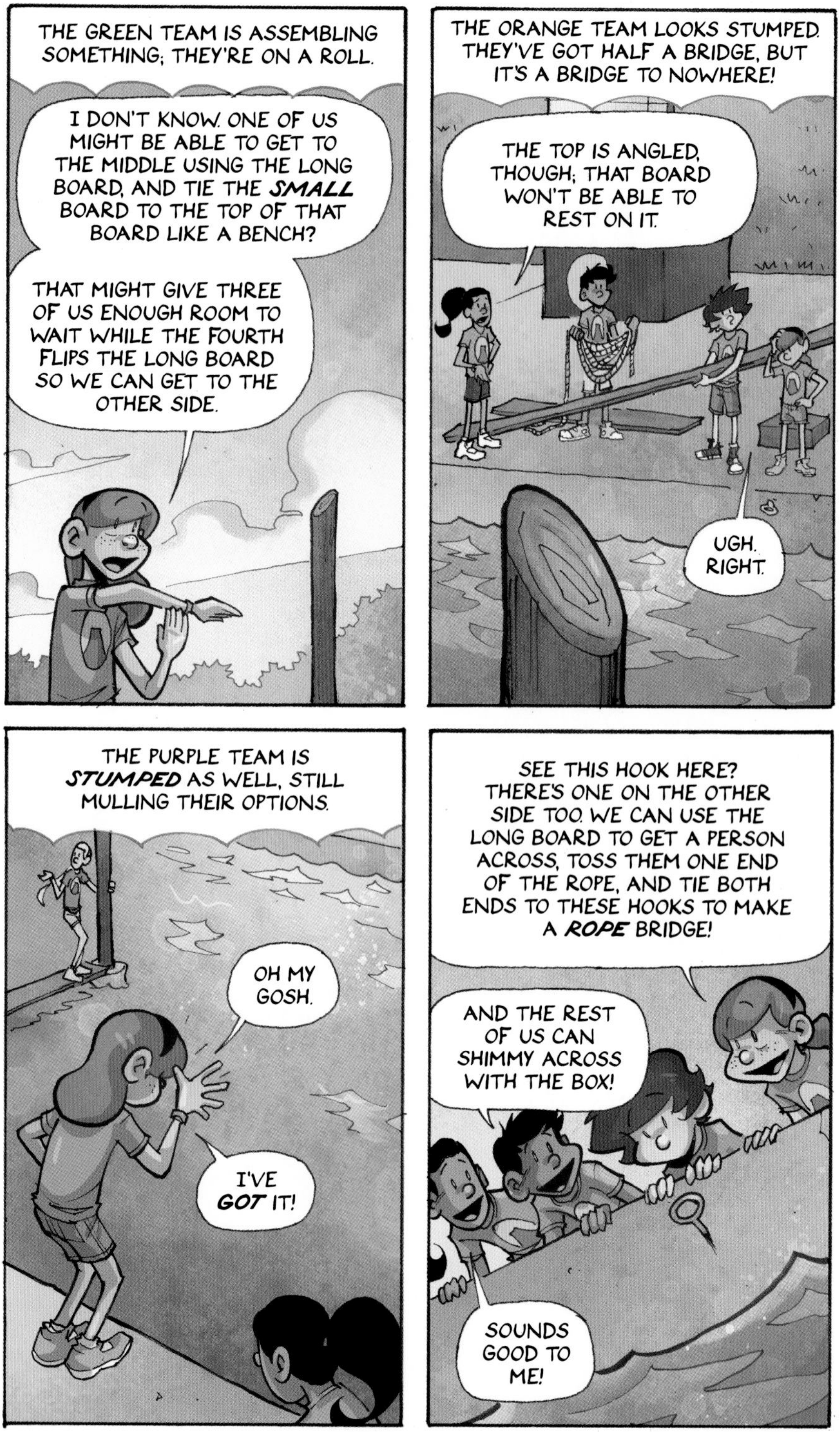
THE GREEN TEAM IS ASSEMBLING SOMETHING; THEY'RE ON A ROLL.
I DON'T KNOW. ONE OF US MIGHT BE ABLE TO GET TO THE MIDDLE USING THE LONG BOARD, AND TIE THE SMALL BOARD TO THE TOP OF THAT BOARD LIKE A BENCH?
THAT MIGHT GIVE THREE OF US ENOUGH ROOM TO WAIT WHILE THE FOURTH FLIPS THE LONG BOARD SO WE CAN GET TO THE OTHER SIDE.
THE ORANGE TEAM LOOKS STUMPED. THEY'VE GOT HALF A BRIDGE, BUT IT'S A BRIDGE TO NOWHERE!
THE TOP IS ANGLED, THOUGH; THAT BOARD WON'T BE ABLE TO REST ON IT.
UGH. RIGHT.
THE PURPLE TEAM IS STUMPED AS WELL, STILL MULLING THEIR OPTIONS.
OH MY GOSH.
I'VE GOT IT!
SEE THIS HOOK HERE? THERE'S ONE ON THE OTHER SIDE TOO. WE CAN USE THE LONG BOARD TO GET A PERSON ACROSS, TOSS THEM ONE END OF THE ROPE, AND TIE BOTH ENDS TO THESE HOOKS TO MAKE A ROPE BRIDGE!
AND THE REST OF US CAN SHIMMY ACROSS WITH THE BOX!
SOUNDS GOOD TO ME!

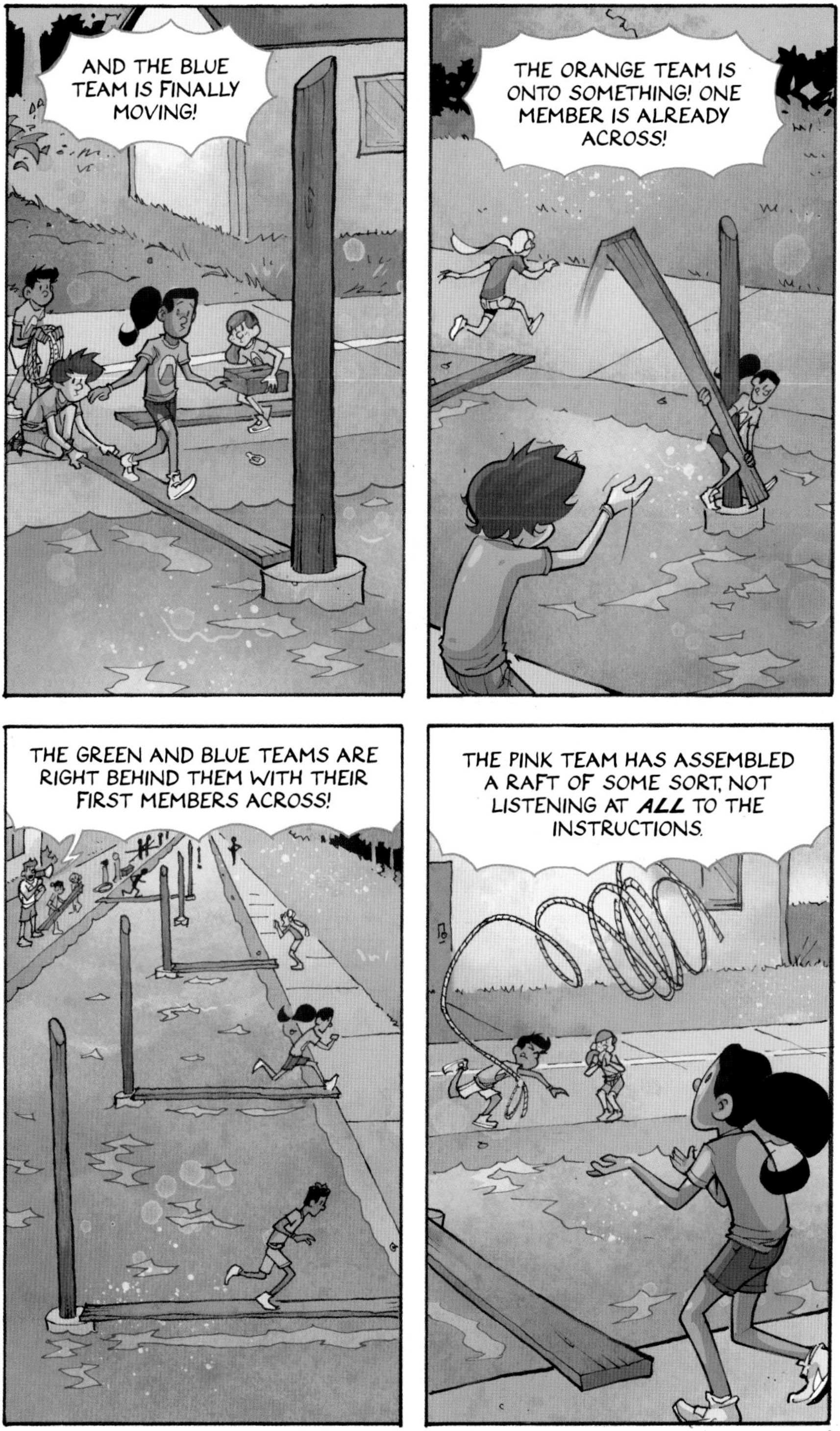
AND THE BLUE TEAM IS FINALLY MOVING!
THE ORANGE TEAM IS ONTO SOMETHING! ONE MEMBER IS ALREADY ACROSS!
THE GREEN AND BLUE TEAMS ARE RIGHT BEHIND THEM WITH THEIR FIRST MEMBERS ACROSS!
THE PINK TEAM HAS ASSEMBLED A RAFT OF SOME SORT, NOT LISTENING AT ALL TO THE INSTRUCTIONS.

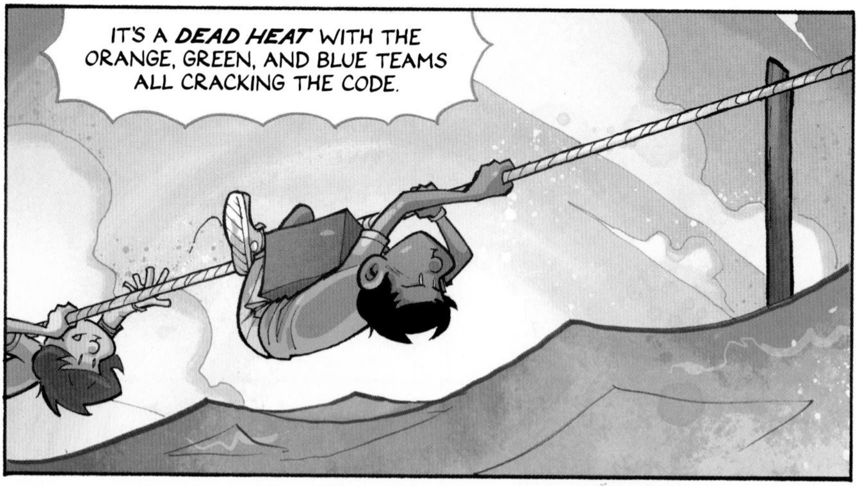
IT'S A ***DEAD HEAT*** WITH THE ORANGE, GREEN, AND BLUE TEAMS ALL CRACKING THE CODE.

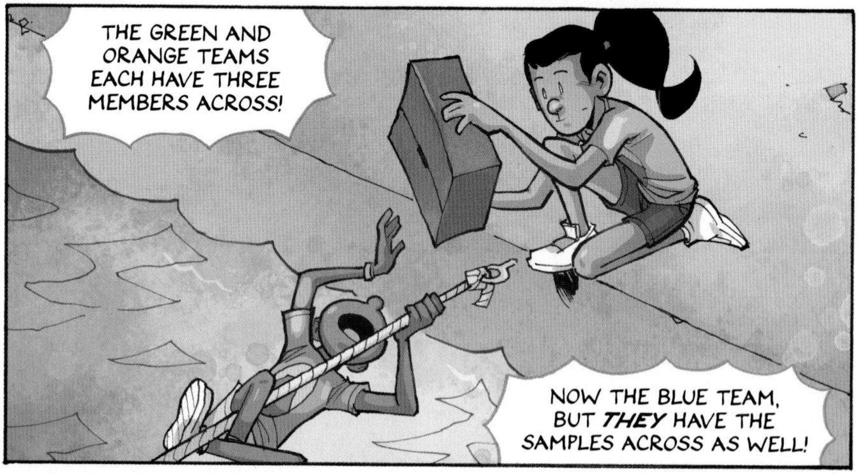
THE GREEN AND ORANGE TEAMS EACH HAVE THREE MEMBERS ACROSS!
NOW THE BLUE TEAM, BUT ***THEY*** HAVE THE SAMPLES ACROSS AS WELL!

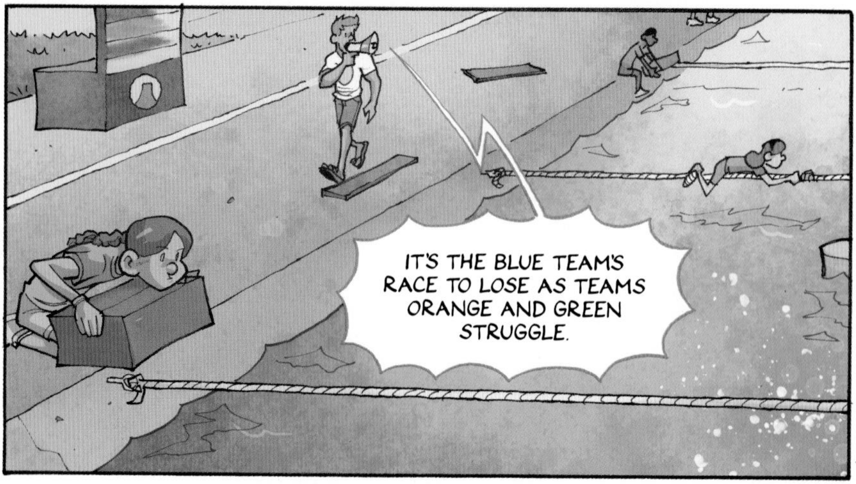
IT'S THE BLUE TEAM'S RACE TO LOSE AS TEAMS ORANGE AND GREEN STRUGGLE.

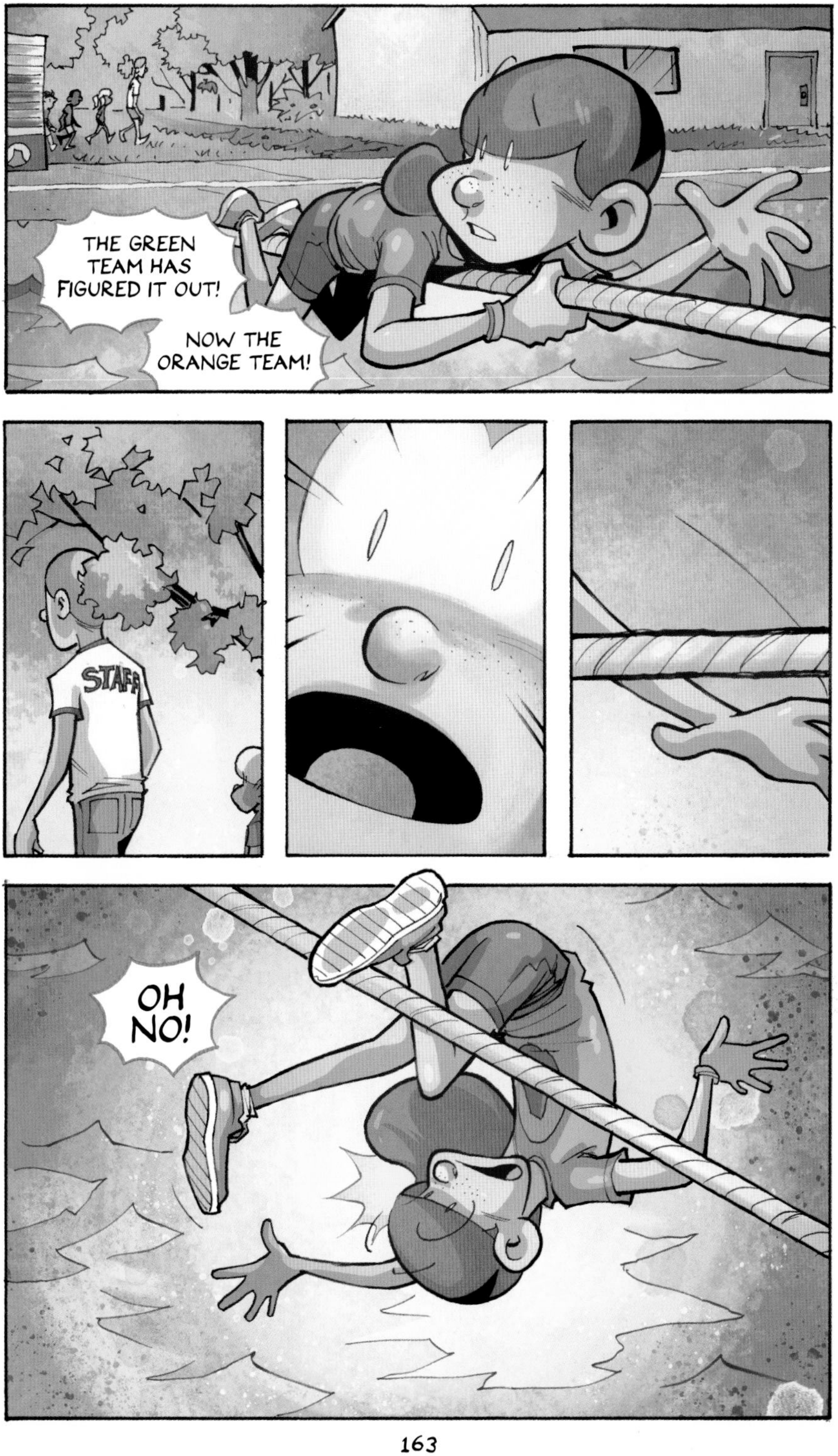
THE GREEN TEAM HAS FIGURED IT OUT!
NOW THE ORANGE TEAM!
STAFF
OH NO!

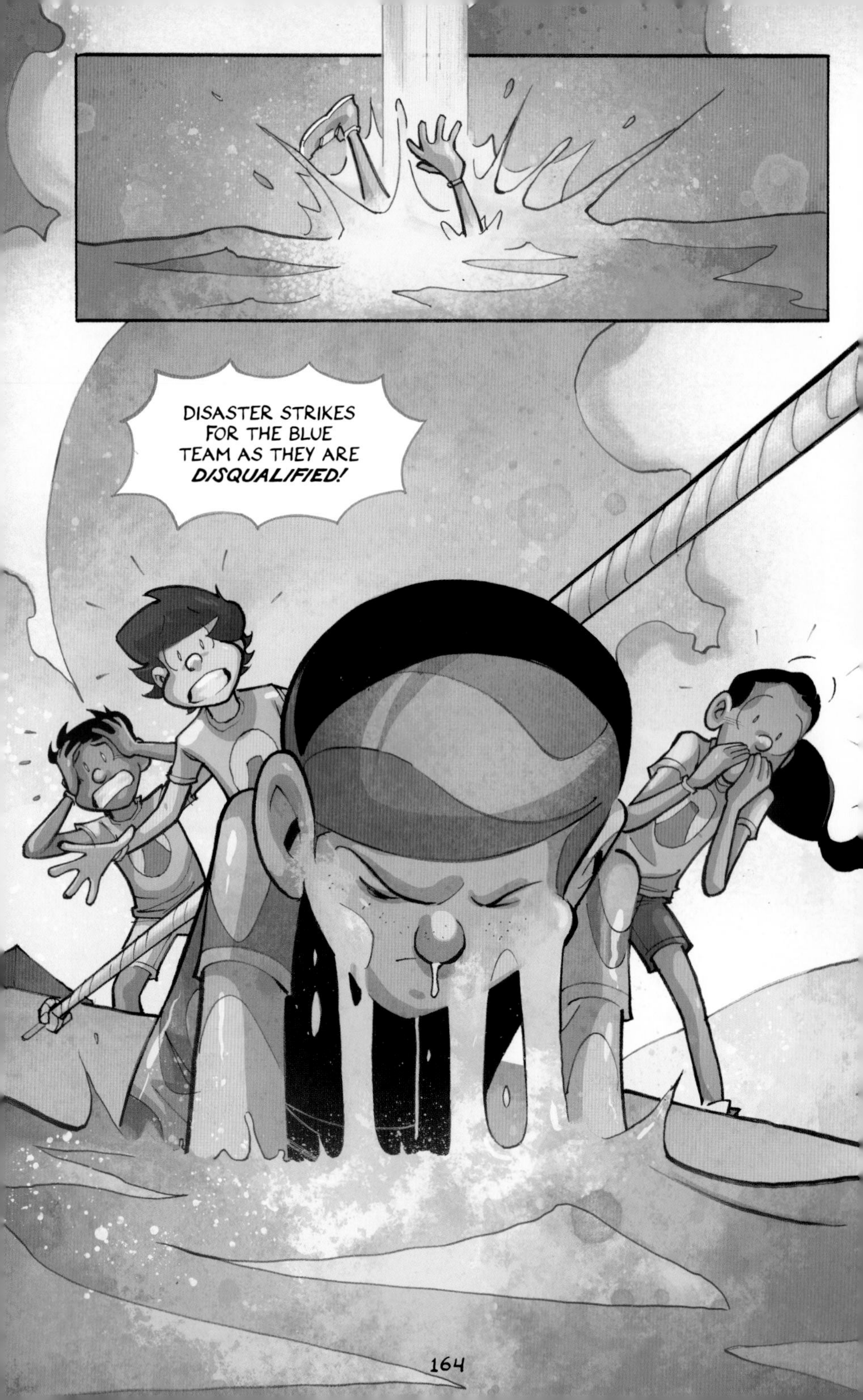
DISASTER STRIKES FOR THE BLUE TEAM AS THEY ARE DISQUALIFIED!

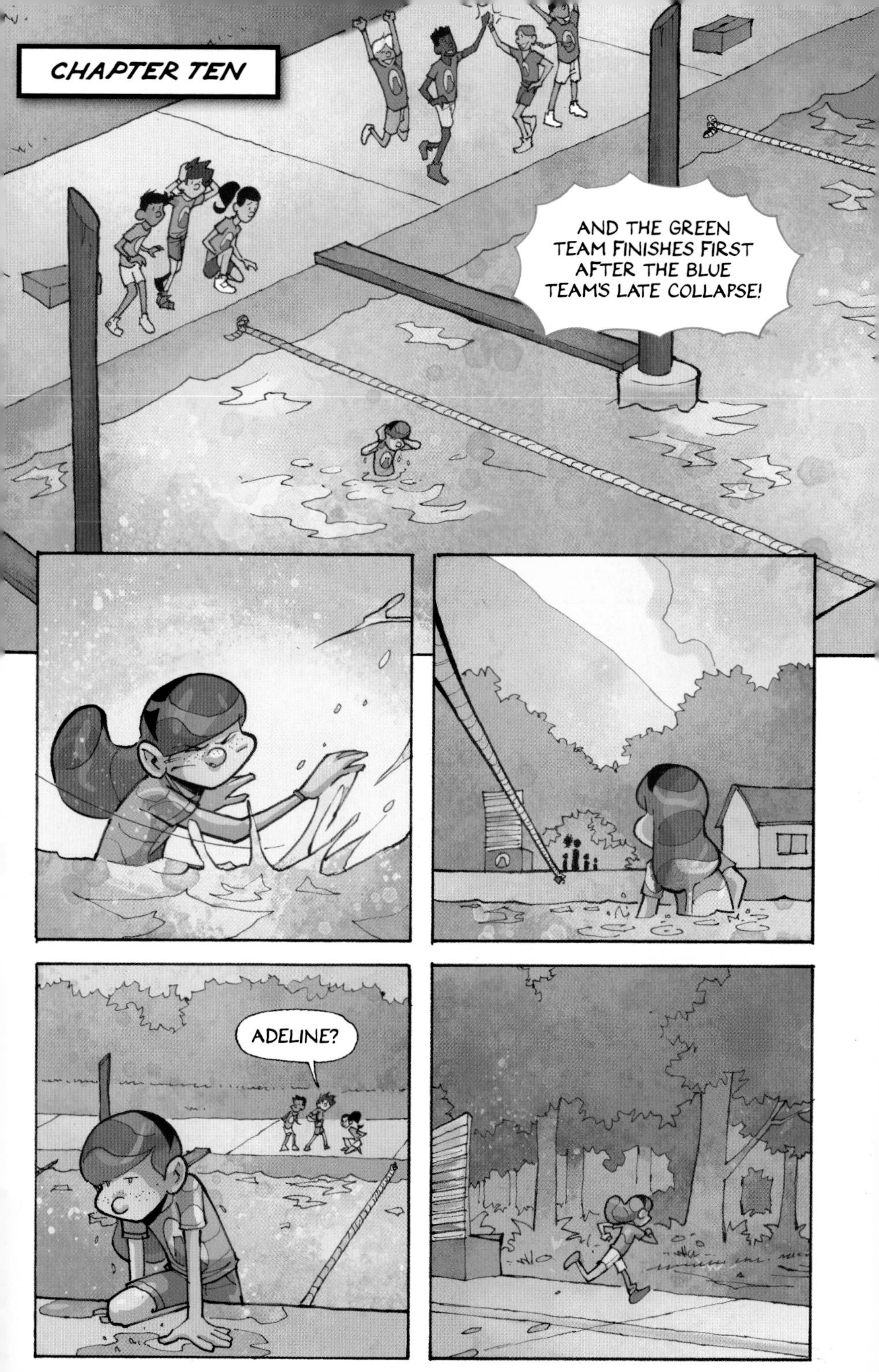
CHAPTER TEN
AND THE GREEN TEAM FINISHES FIRST AFTER THE BLUE TEAM'S LATE COLLAPSE!
ADELINE?

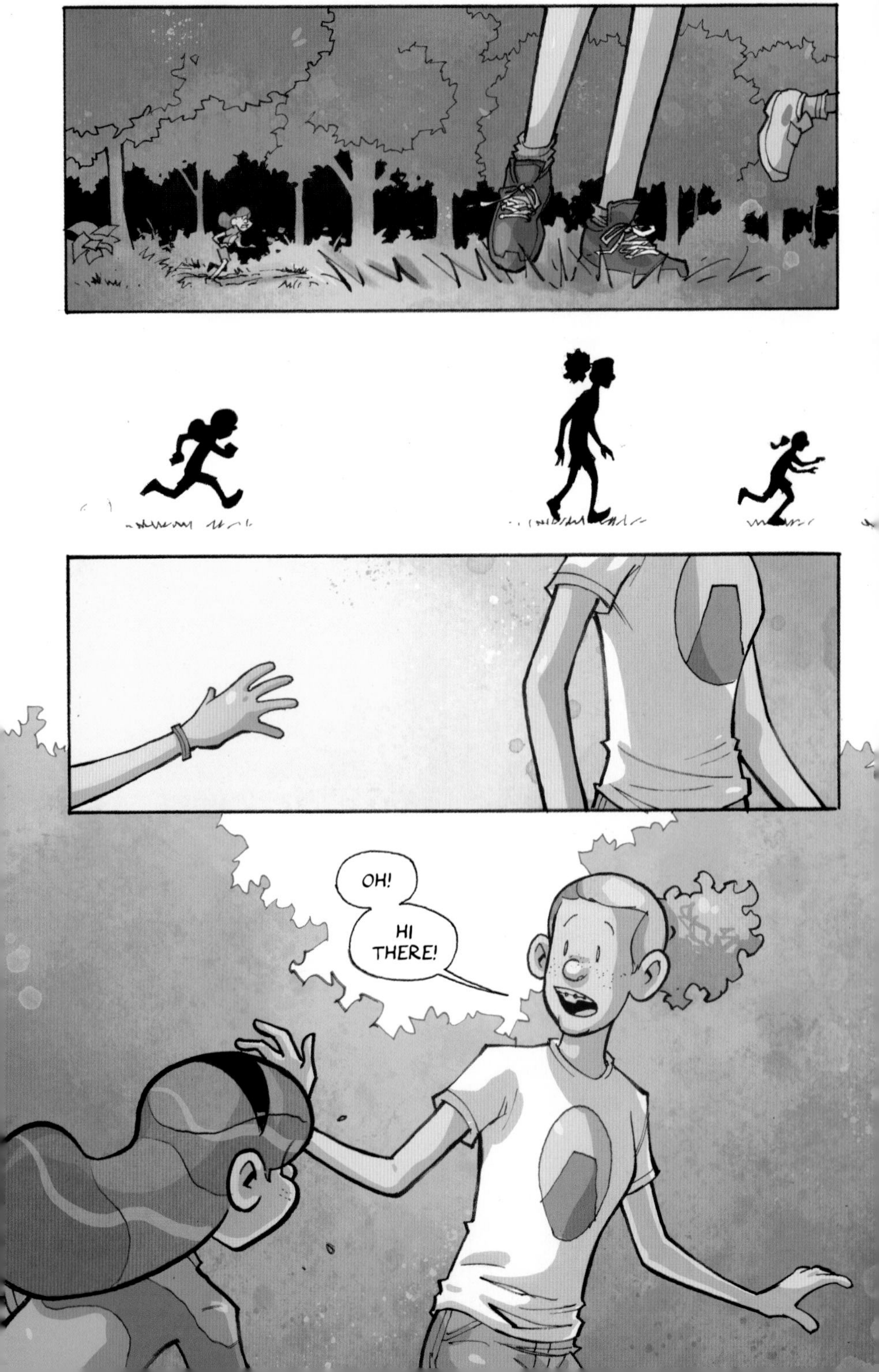
OH!
HI THERE!

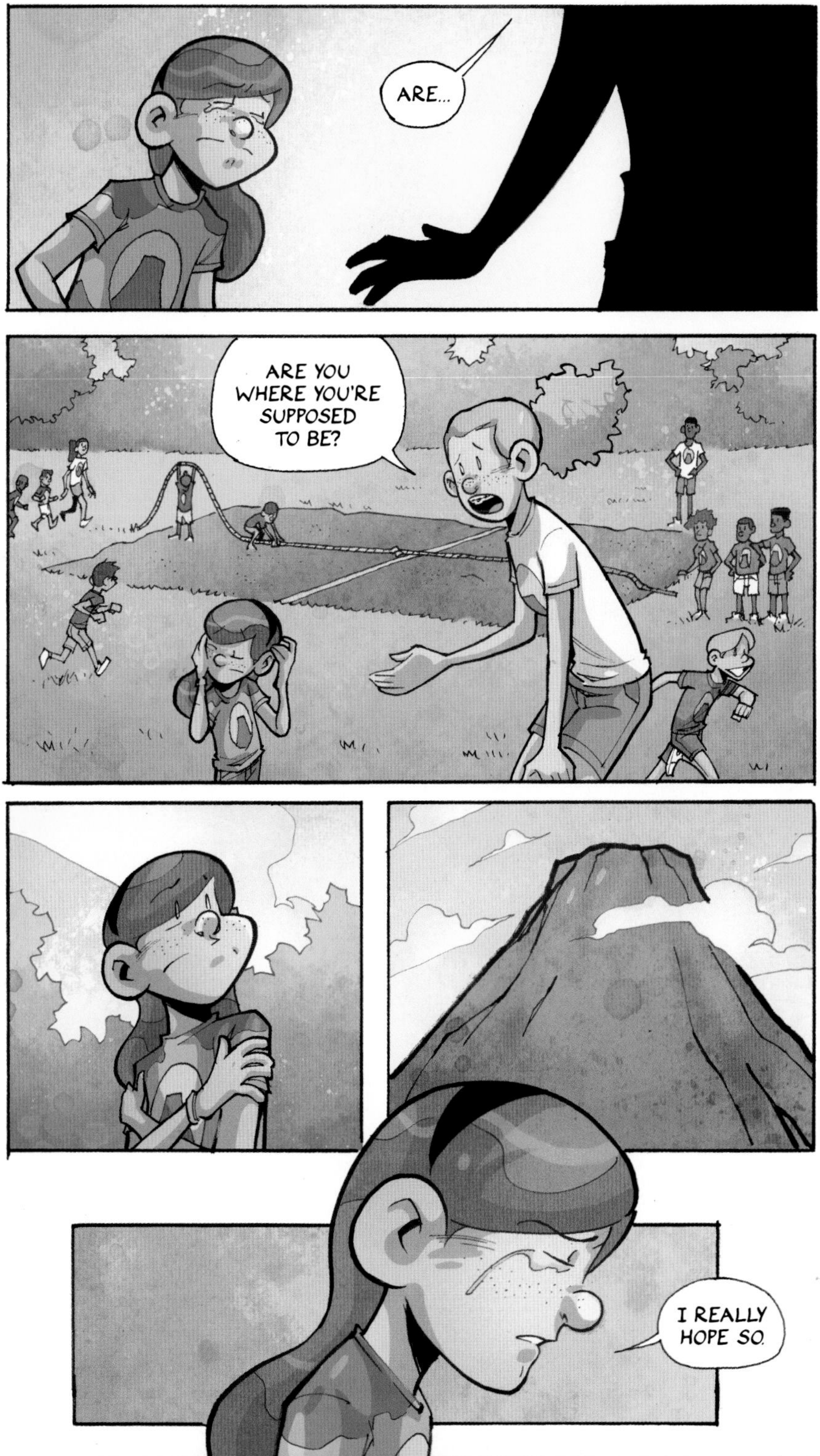
ARE...
ARE YOU WHERE YOU'RE SUPPOSED TO BE?
I REALLY HOPE SO.

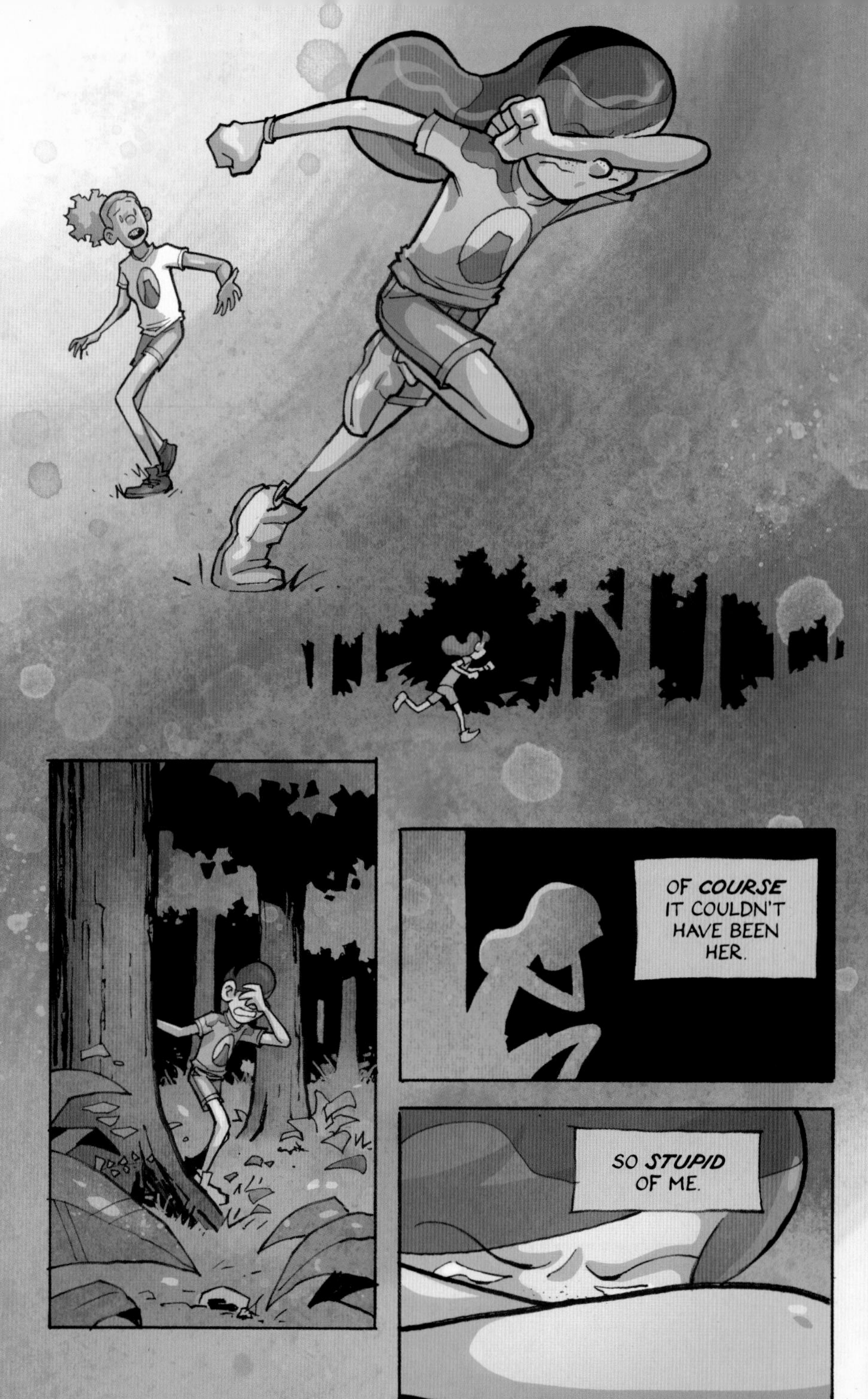
OF COURSE IT COULDN'T HAVE BEEN HER.
SO STUPID OF ME.

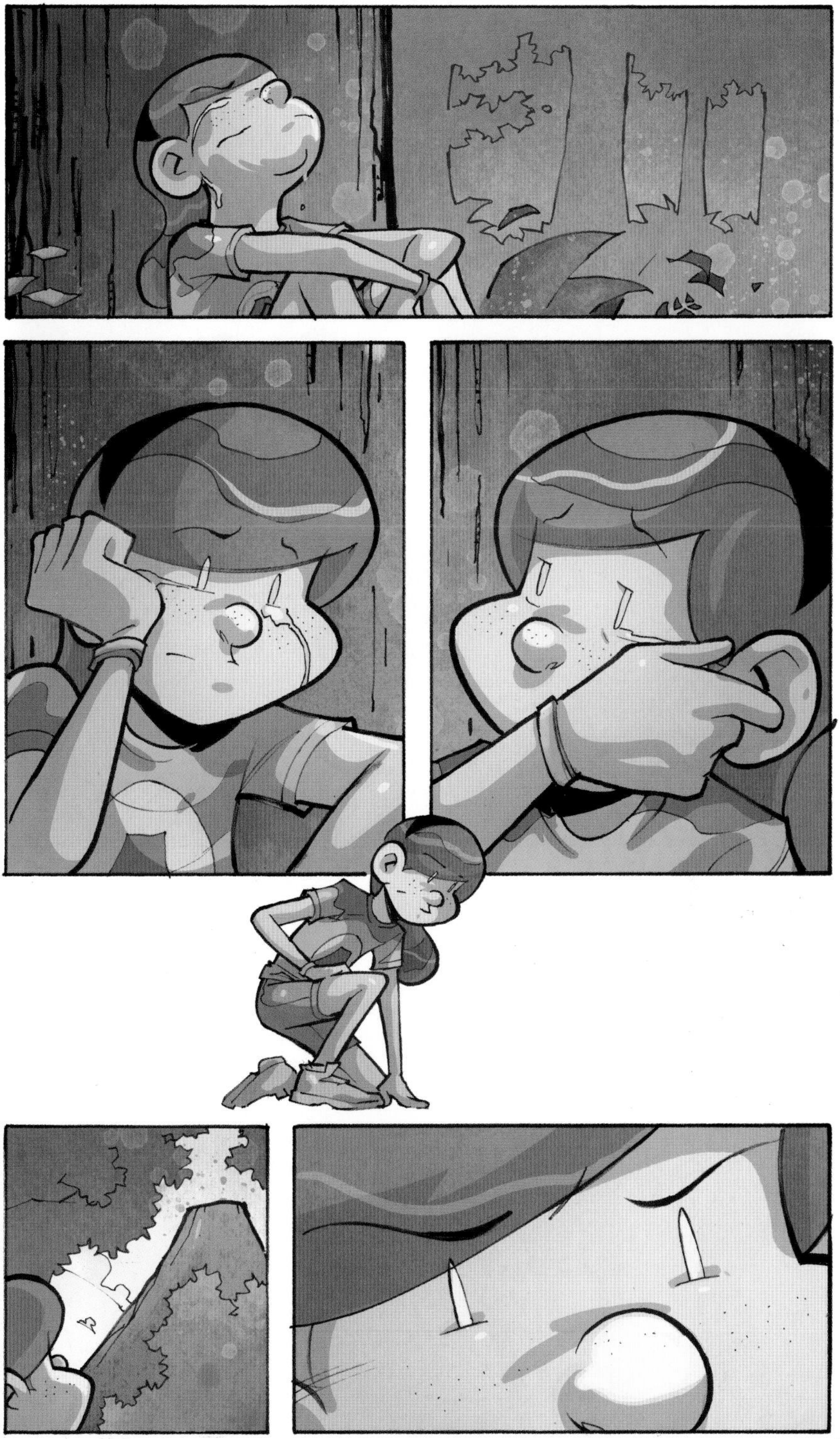

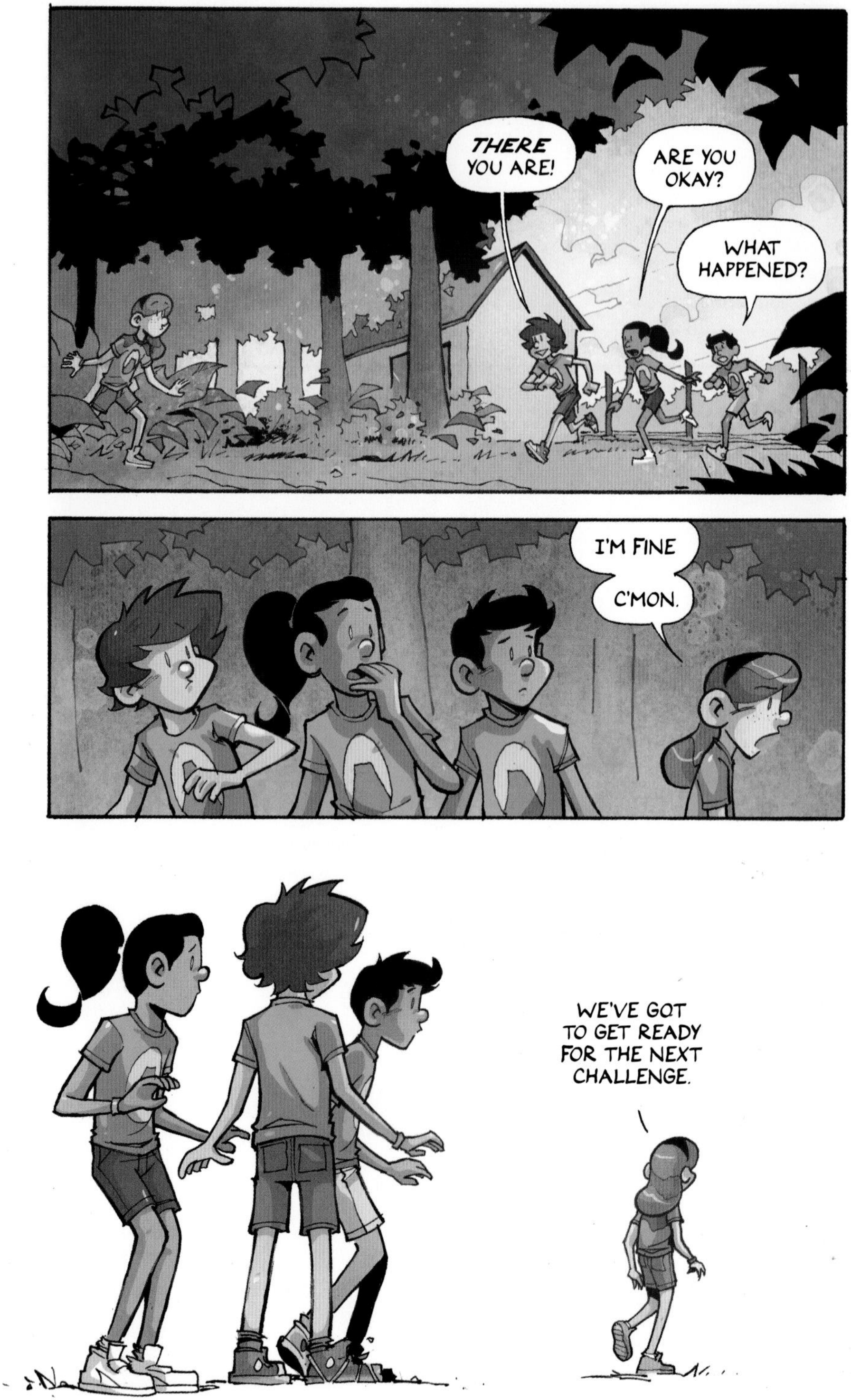
THERE YOU ARE!
ARE YOU OKAY?
WHAT HAPPENED?
I'M FINE
C'MON.
WE'VE GOT TO GET READY FOR THE NEXT CHALLENGE.

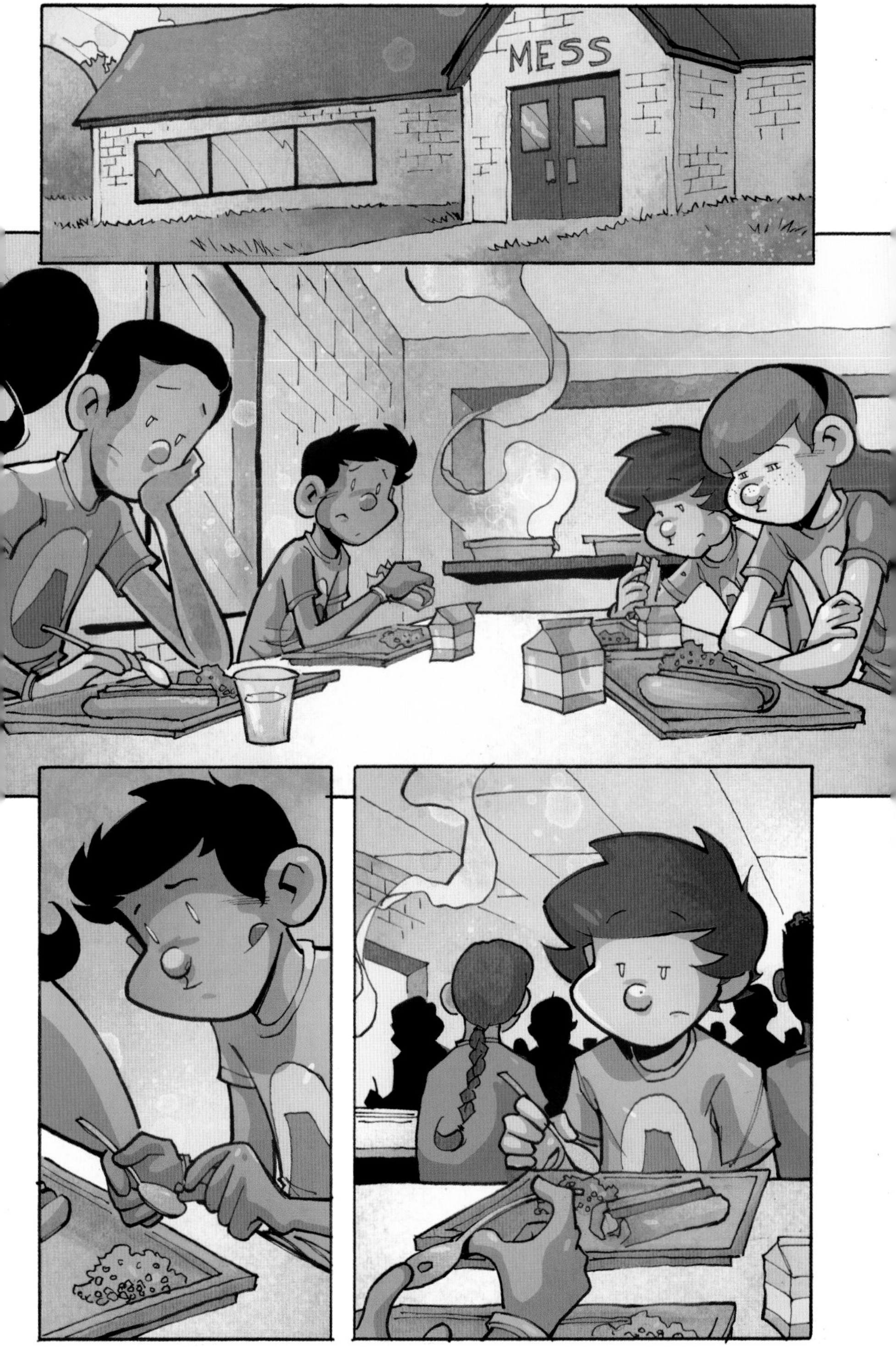
MESS

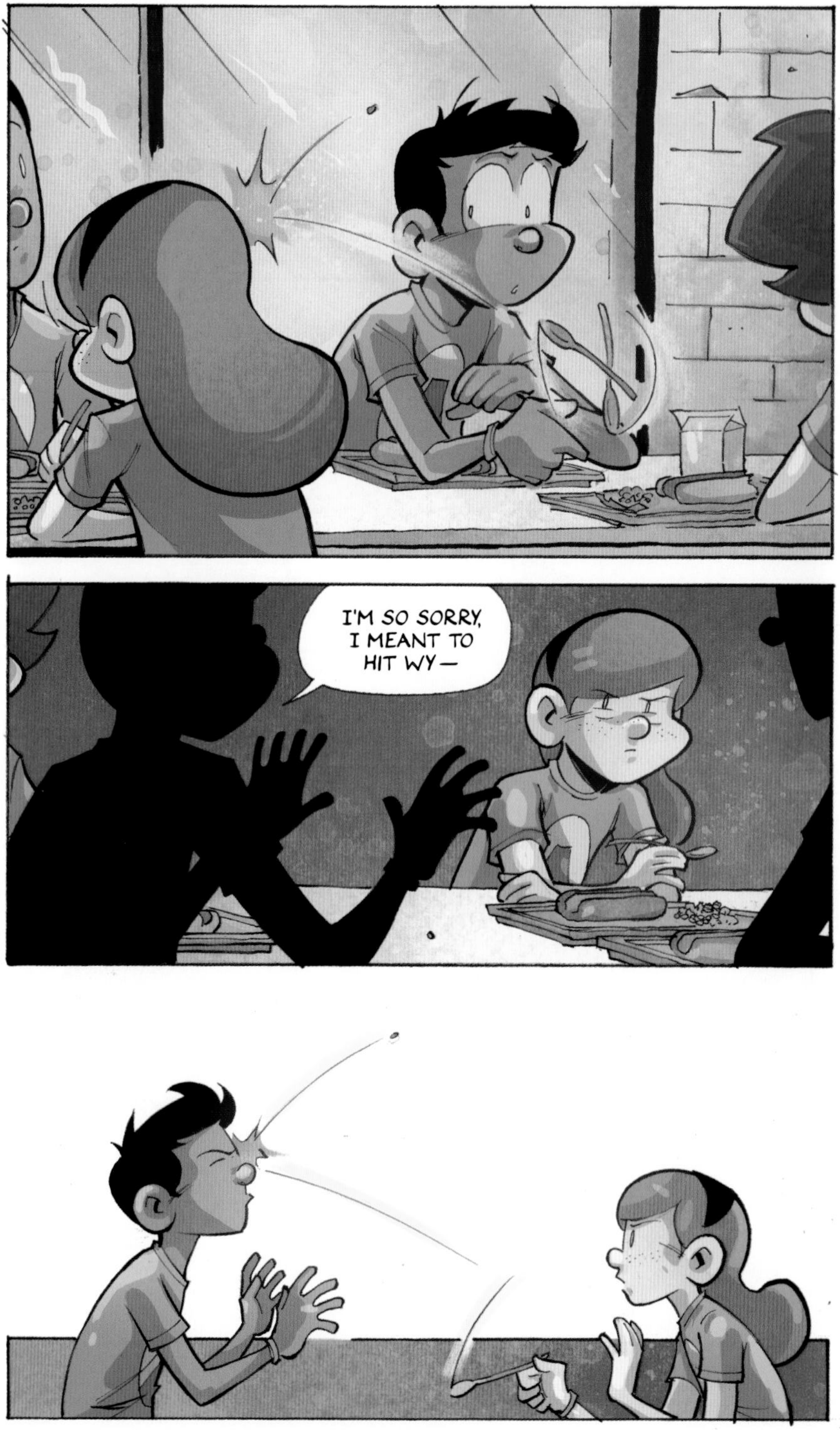
I'M SO SORRY, I MEANT TO HIT WY—

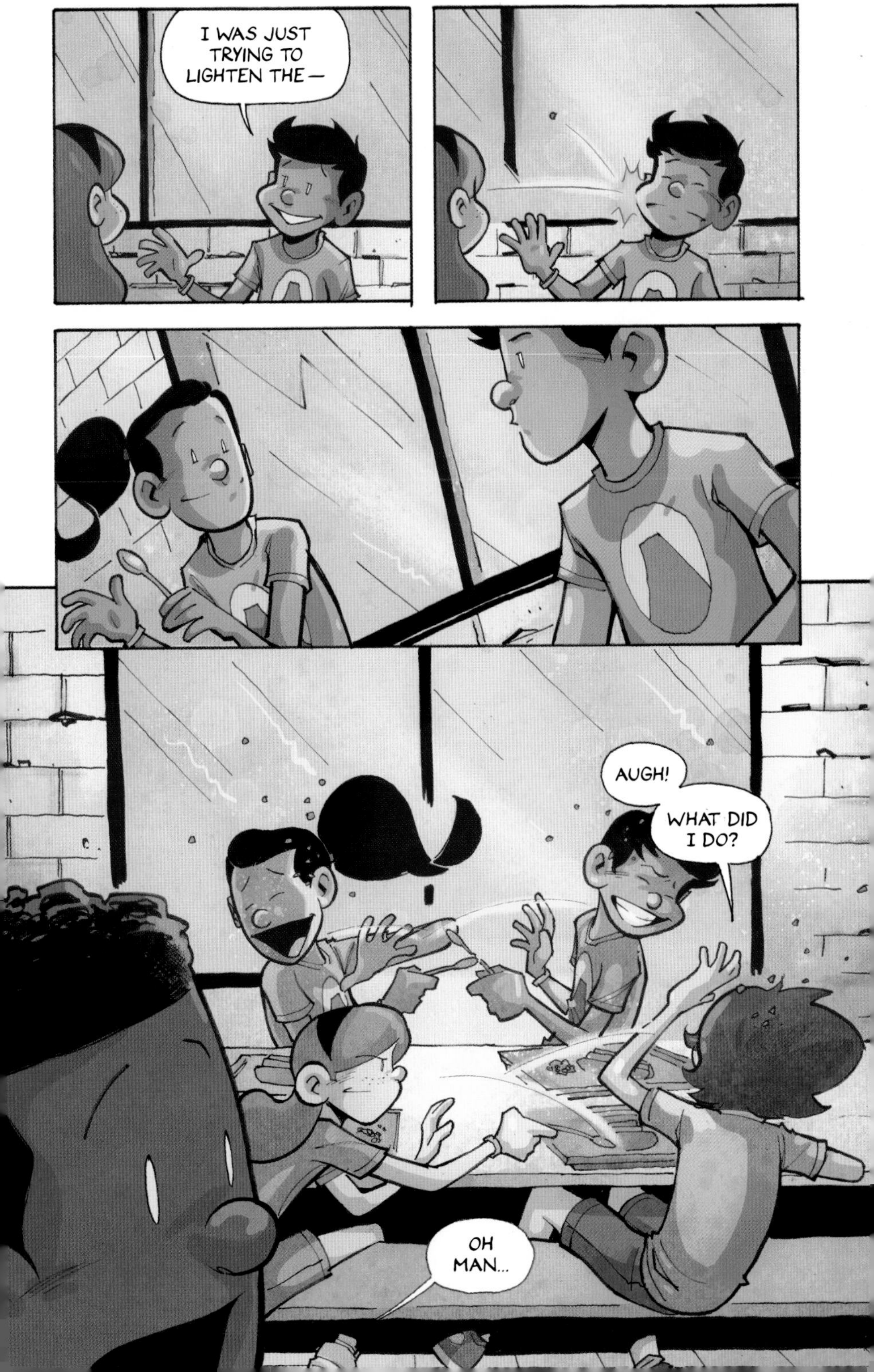
I WAS JUST TRYING TO LIGHTEN THE—
AUGH!
WHAT DID I DO?
OH MAN...

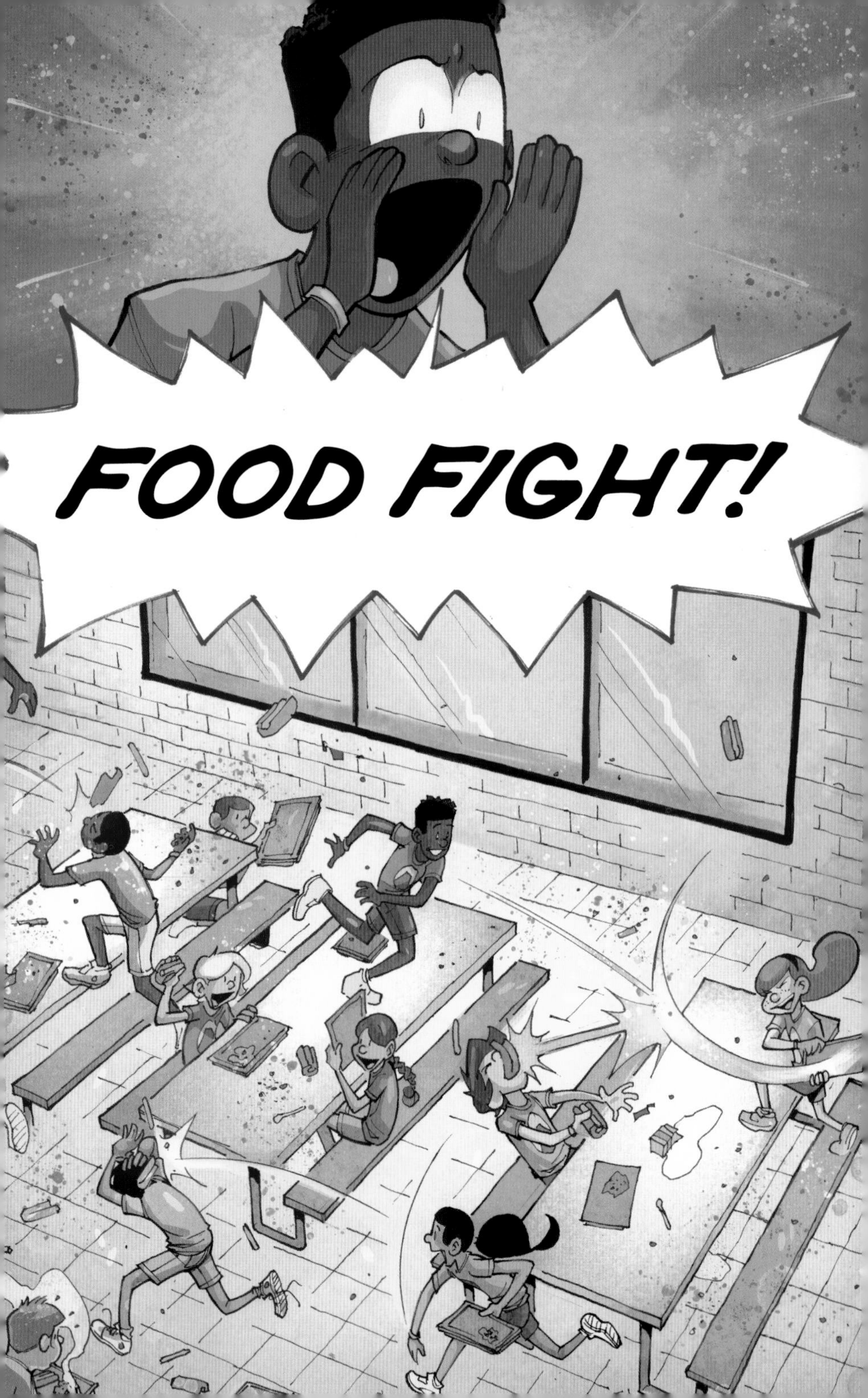
FOOD FIGHT!

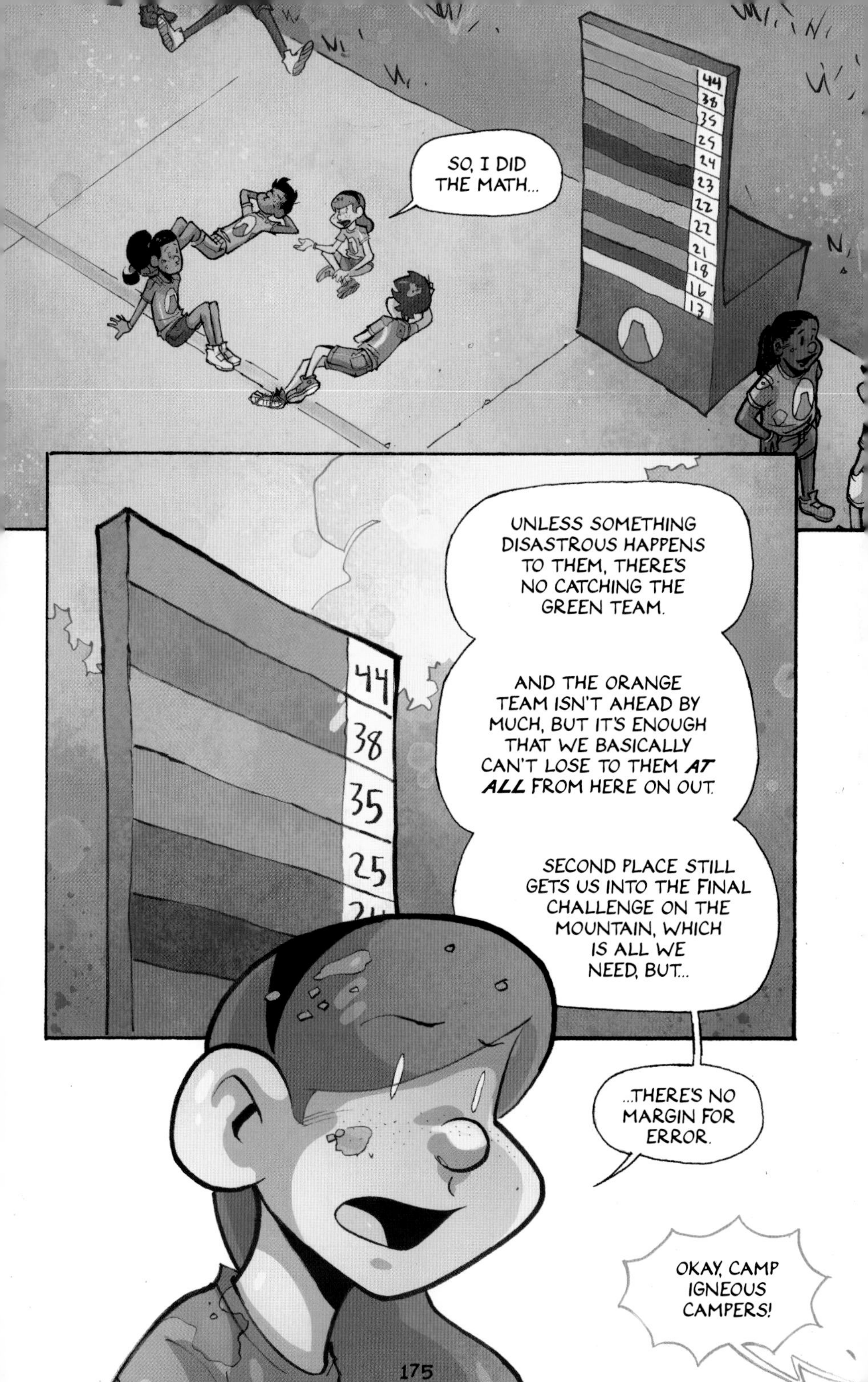
SO, I DID THE MATH...
44
38
35
25
24
23
22
22
21
18
16
13
UNLESS SOMETHING DISASTROUS HAPPENS TO THEM, THERE'S NO CATCHING THE GREEN TEAM.
AND THE ORANGE TEAM ISN'T AHEAD BY MUCH, BUT IT'S ENOUGH THAT WE BASICALLY CAN'T LOSE TO THEM ***AT ALL*** FROM HERE ON OUT.
SECOND PLACE STILL GETS US INTO THE FINAL CHALLENGE ON THE MOUNTAIN, WHICH IS ALL WE NEED, BUT...
44
38
35
25
...THERE'S NO MARGIN FOR ERROR.
OKAY, CAMP IGNEOUS CAMPERS!

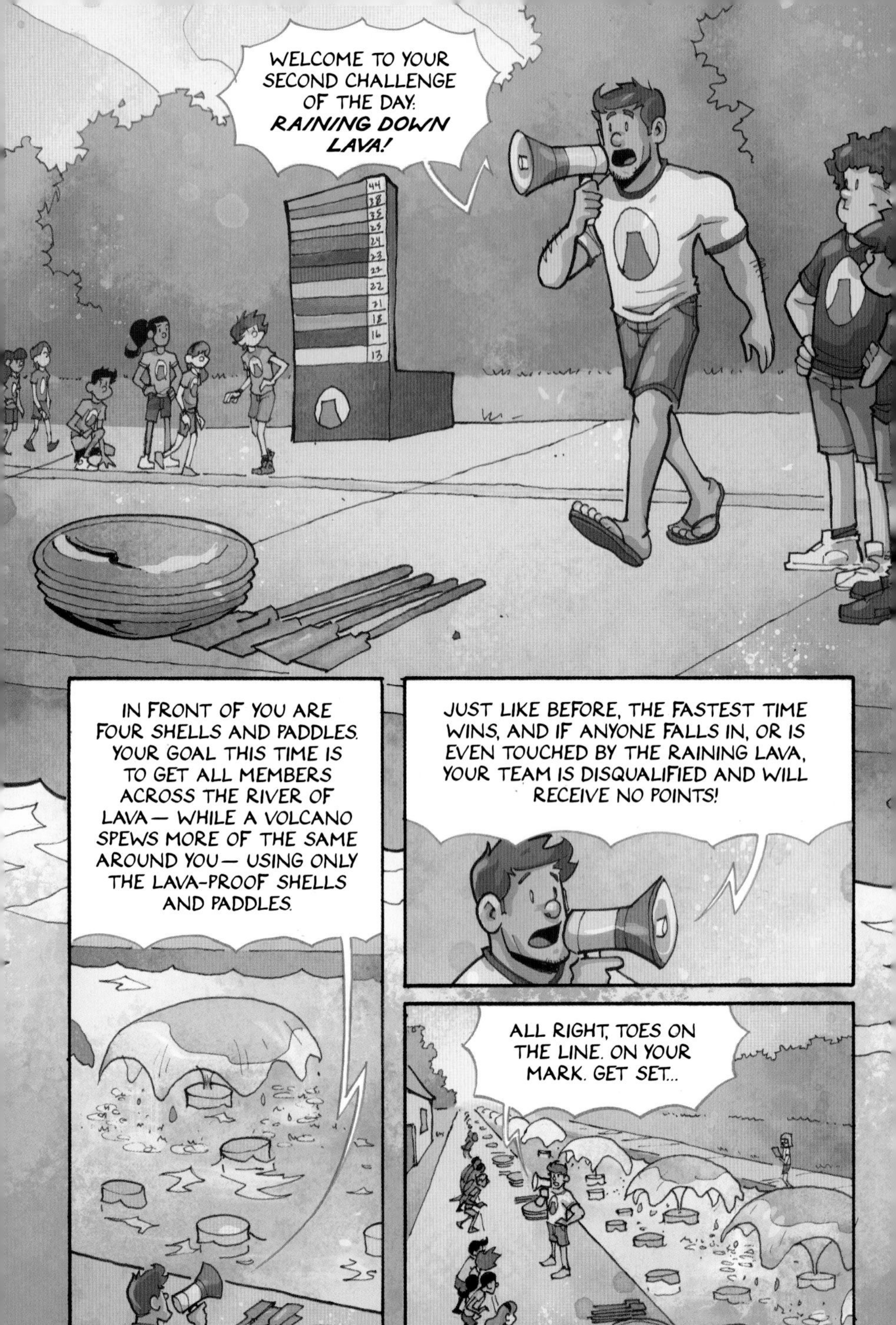
WELCOME TO YOUR SECOND CHALLENGE OF THE DAY: *RAINING DOWN LAVA!*
IN FRONT OF YOU ARE FOUR SHELLS AND PADDLES. YOUR GOAL THIS TIME IS TO GET ALL MEMBERS ACROSS THE RIVER OF LAVA— WHILE A VOLCANO SPEWS MORE OF THE SAME AROUND YOU— USING ONLY THE LAVA-PROOF SHELLS AND PADDLES.
JUST LIKE BEFORE, THE FASTEST TIME WINS, AND IF ANYONE FALLS IN, OR IS EVEN TOUCHED BY THE RAINING LAVA, YOUR TEAM IS DISQUALIFIED AND WILL RECEIVE NO POINTS!
ALL RIGHT, TOES ON THE LINE. ON YOUR MARK. GET SET...

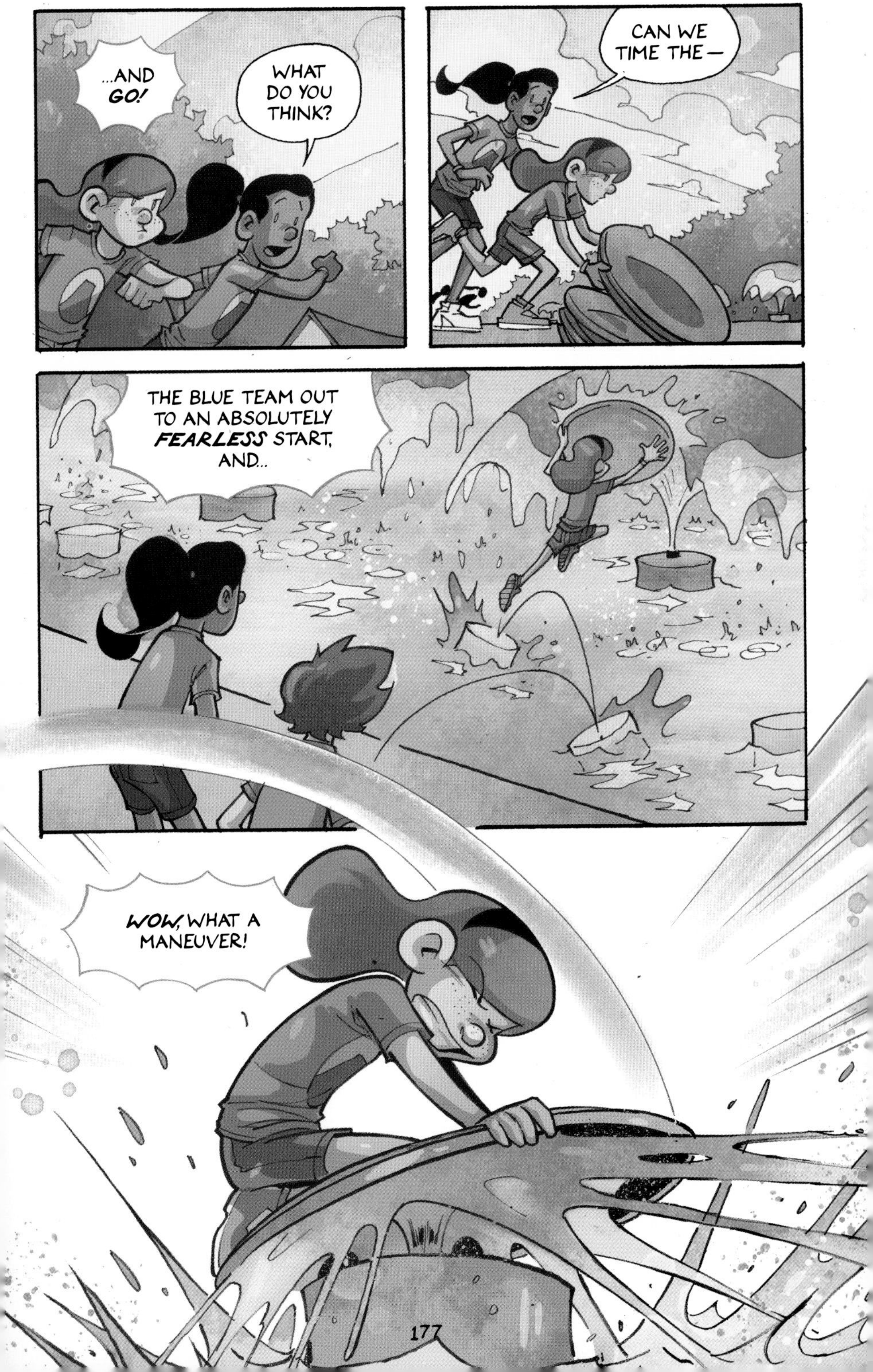
...AND GO!
WHAT DO YOU THINK?
CAN WE TIME THE—
THE BLUE TEAM OUT TO AN ABSOLUTELY FEARLESS START, AND...
WOW, WHAT A MANEUVER!

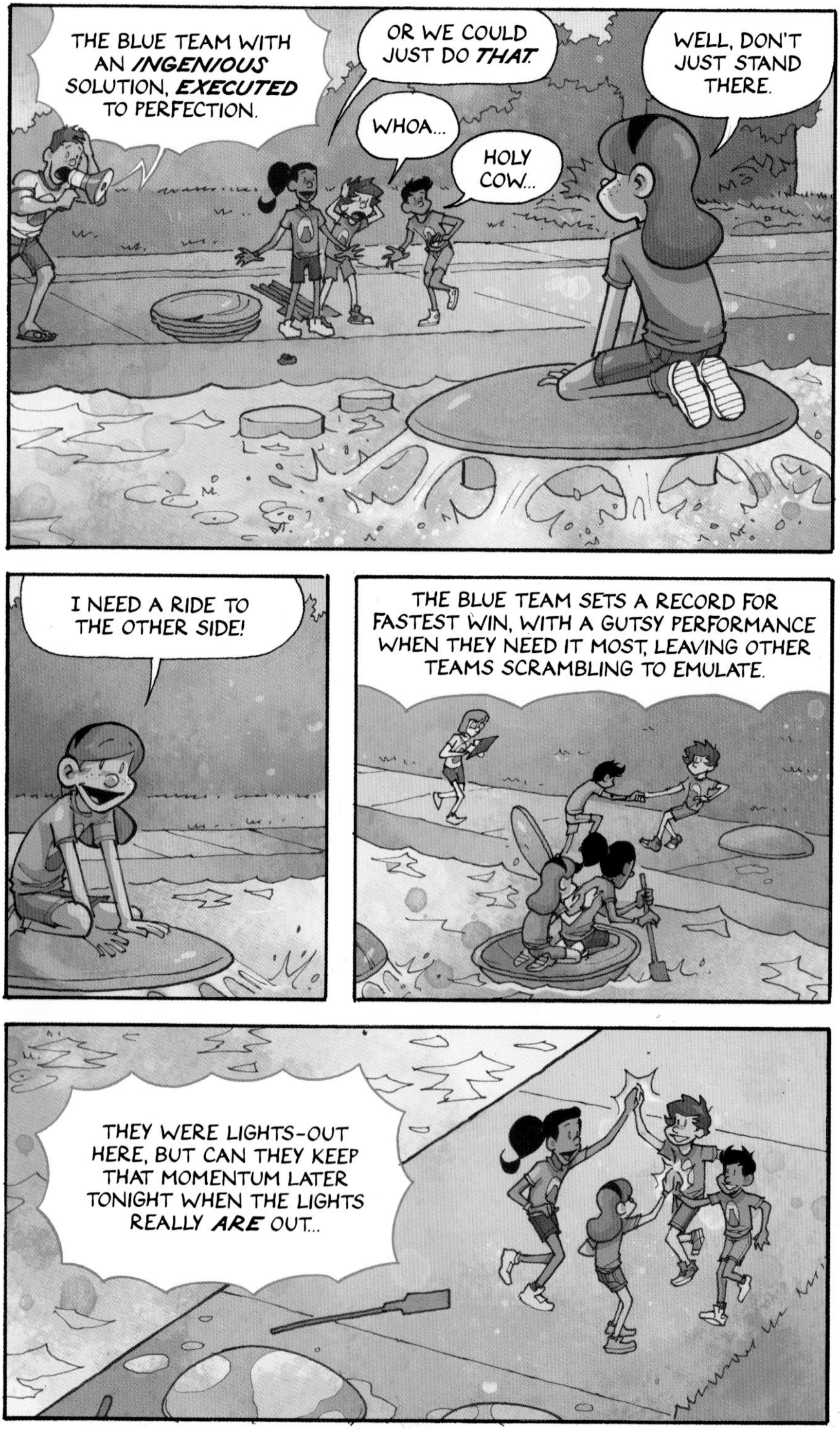
THE BLUE TEAM WITH AN INGENIOUS SOLUTION, EXECUTED TO PERFECTION.
OR WE COULD JUST DO THAT.
WHOA...
HOLY COW...
WELL, DON'T JUST STAND THERE.
I NEED A RIDE TO THE OTHER SIDE!
THE BLUE TEAM SETS A RECORD FOR FASTEST WIN, WITH A GUTSY PERFORMANCE WHEN THEY NEED IT MOST, LEAVING OTHER TEAMS SCRAMBLING TO EMULATE.
THEY WERE LIGHTS-OUT HERE, BUT CAN THEY KEEP THAT MOMENTUM LATER TONIGHT WHEN THE LIGHTS REALLY ARE OUT...

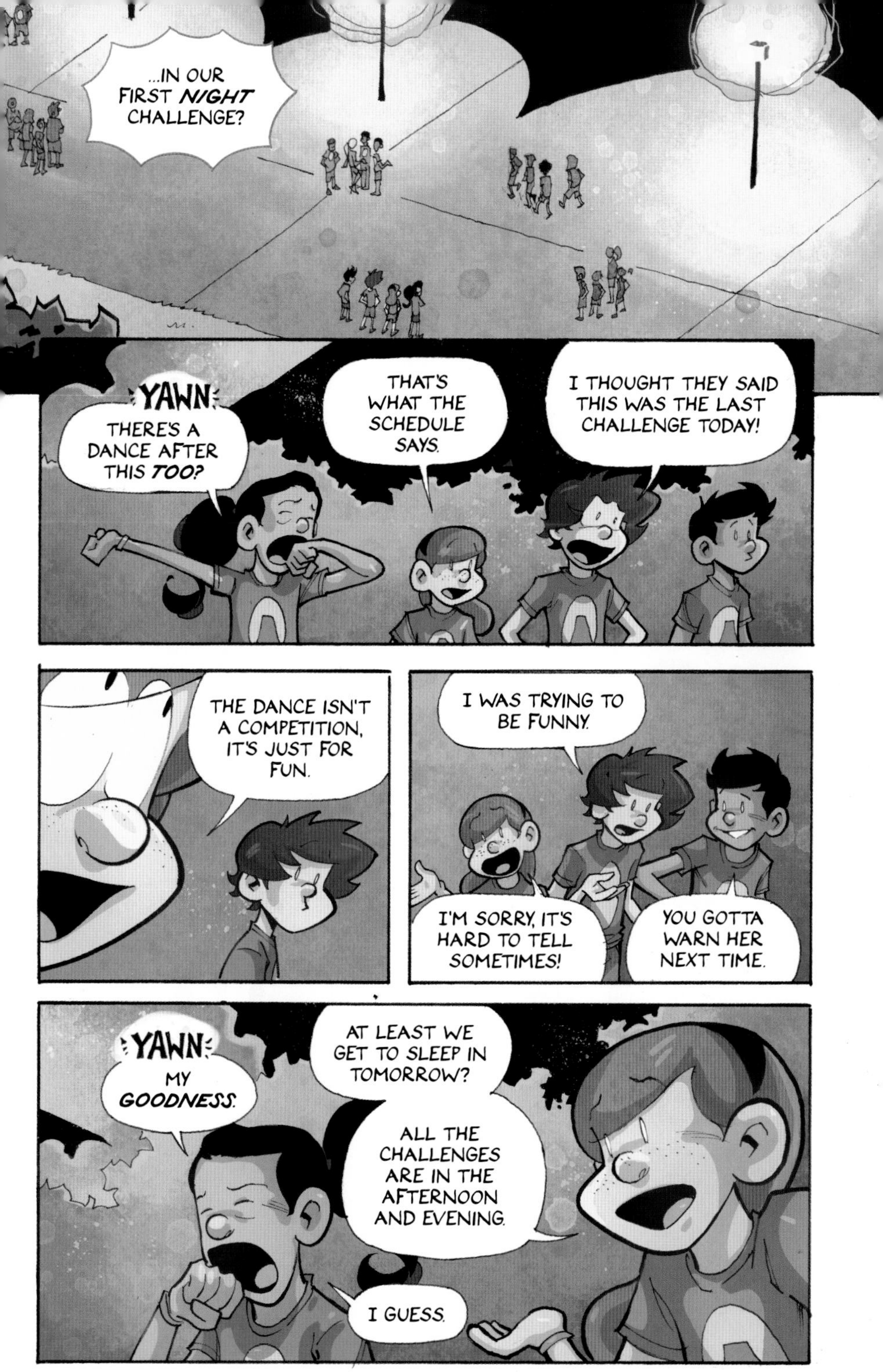
...IN OUR FIRST NIGHT CHALLENGE?
YAWN
THERE'S A DANCE AFTER THIS TOO?
THAT'S WHAT THE SCHEDULE SAYS.
I THOUGHT THEY SAID THIS WAS THE LAST CHALLENGE TODAY!
THE DANCE ISN'T A COMPETITION, IT'S JUST FOR FUN.
I WAS TRYING TO BE FUNNY.
I'M SORRY, IT'S HARD TO TELL SOMETIMES!
YOU GOTTA WARN HER NEXT TIME.
YAWN
MY GOODNESS.
AT LEAST WE GET TO SLEEP IN TOMORROW?
ALL THE CHALLENGES ARE IN THE AFTERNOON AND EVENING.
I GUESS.

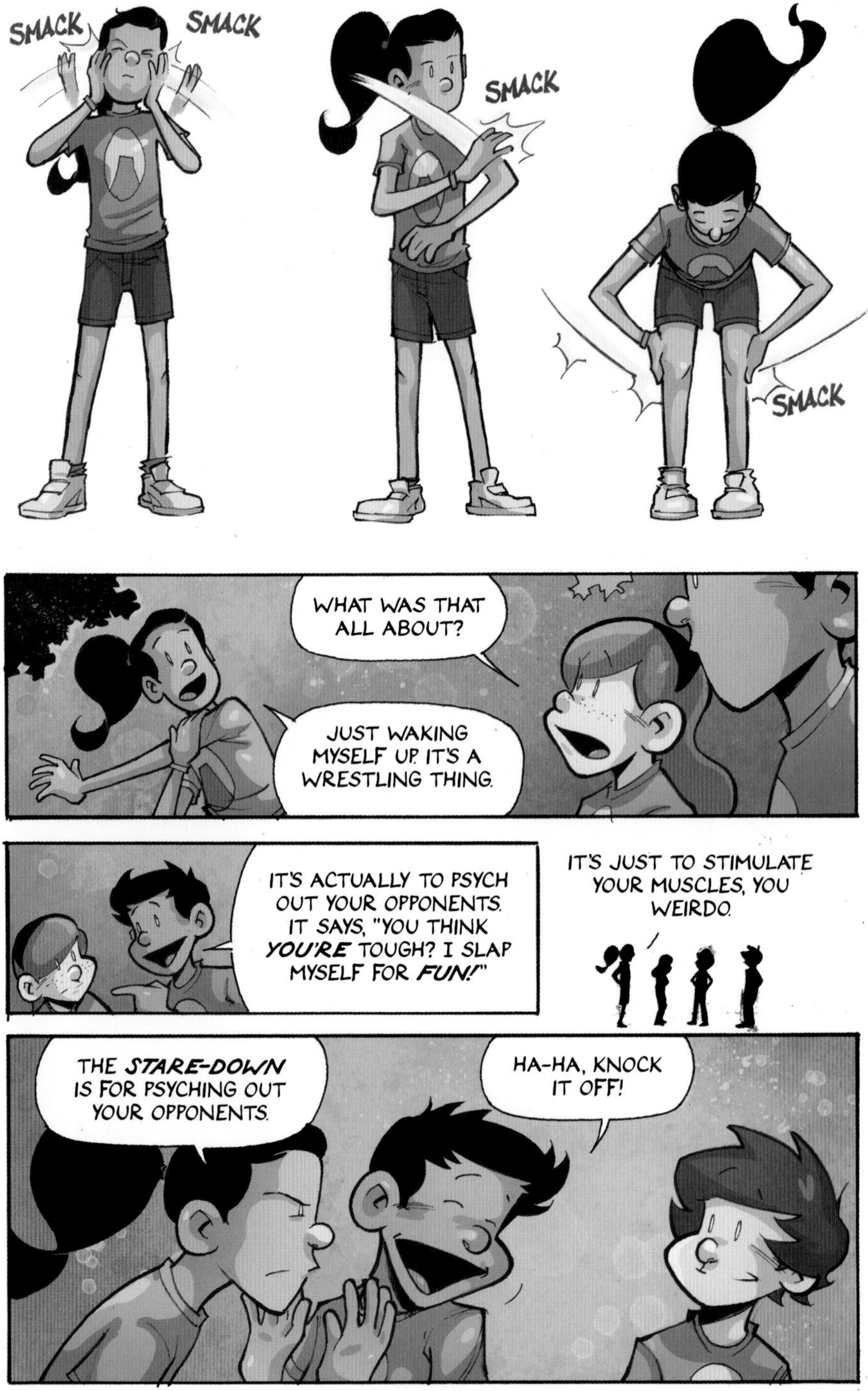
SMACK
SMACK
SMACK
SMACK
WHAT WAS THAT ALL ABOUT?
JUST WAKING MYSELF UP. IT'S A WRESTLING THING.
IT'S ACTUALLY TO PSYCH OUT YOUR OPPONENTS. IT SAYS, "YOU THINK YOU'RE TOUGH? I SLAP MYSELF FOR FUN!"
IT'S JUST TO STIMULATE YOUR MUSCLES, YOU WEIRDO.
THE STARE-DOWN IS FOR PSYCHING OUT YOUR OPPONENTS.
HA-HA, KNOCK IT OFF!

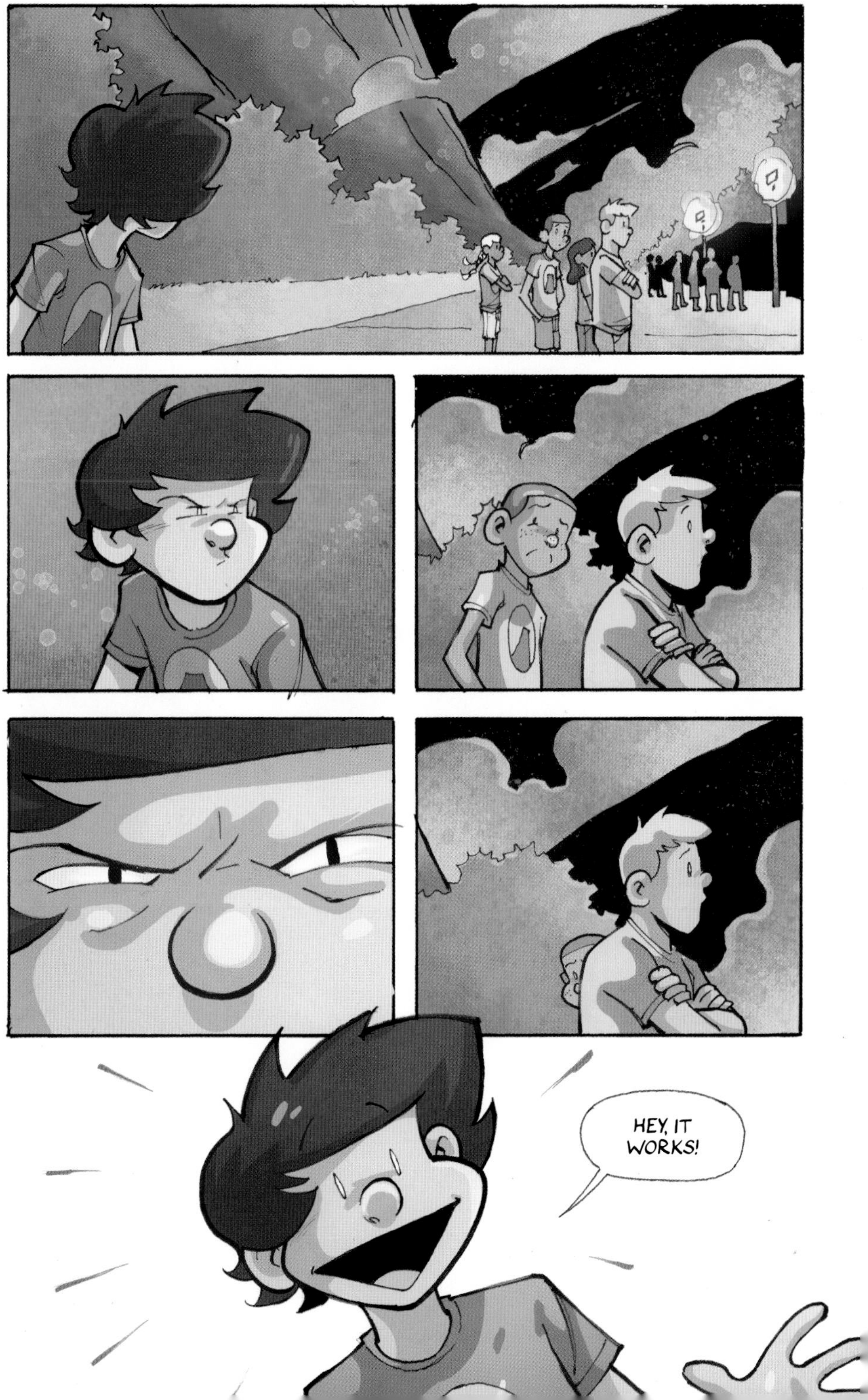
HEY, IT WORKS!

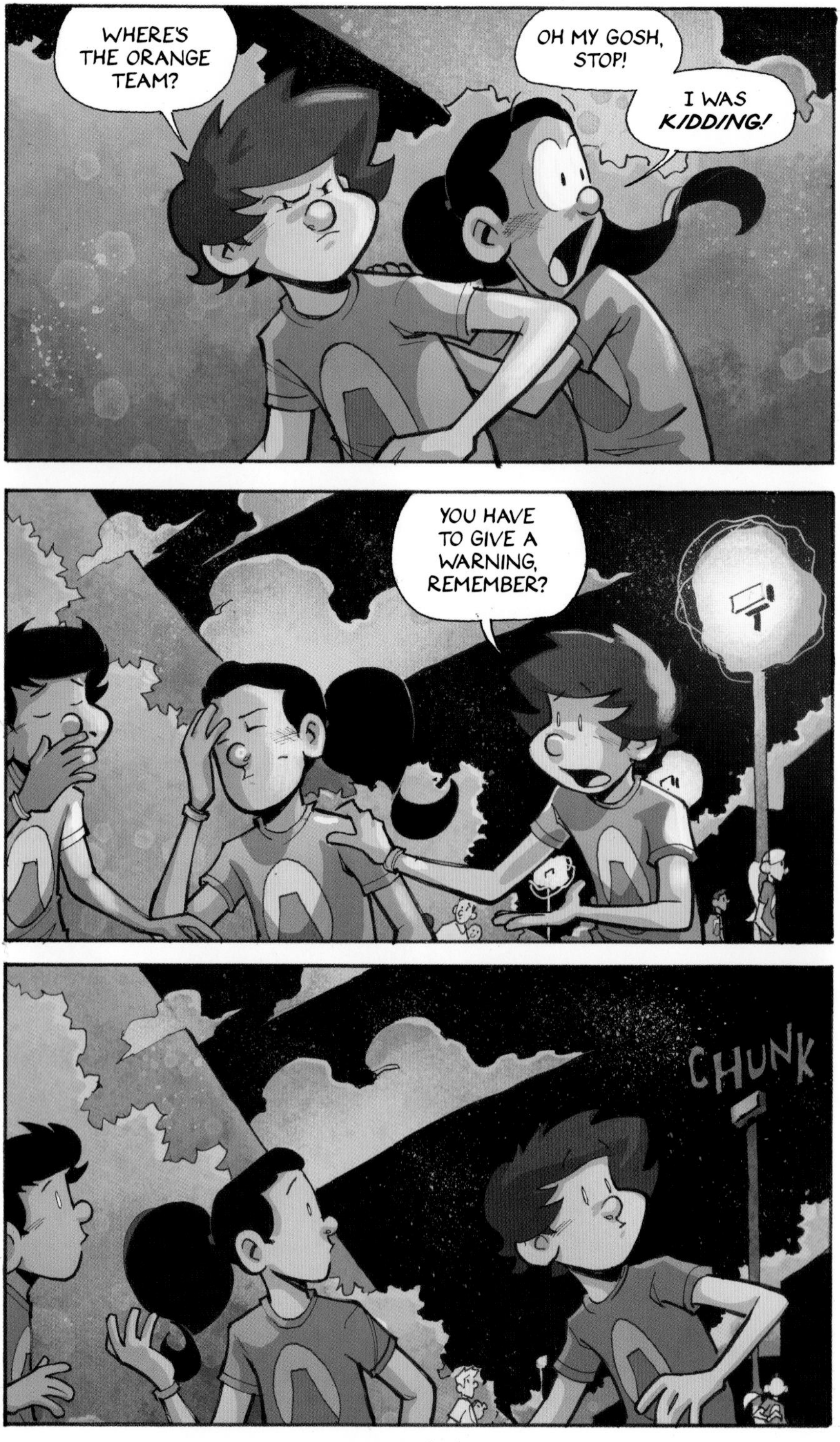
WHERE'S THE ORANGE TEAM?
OH MY GOSH, STOP!
I WAS KIDDING!
YOU HAVE TO GIVE A WARNING, REMEMBER?
CHUNK

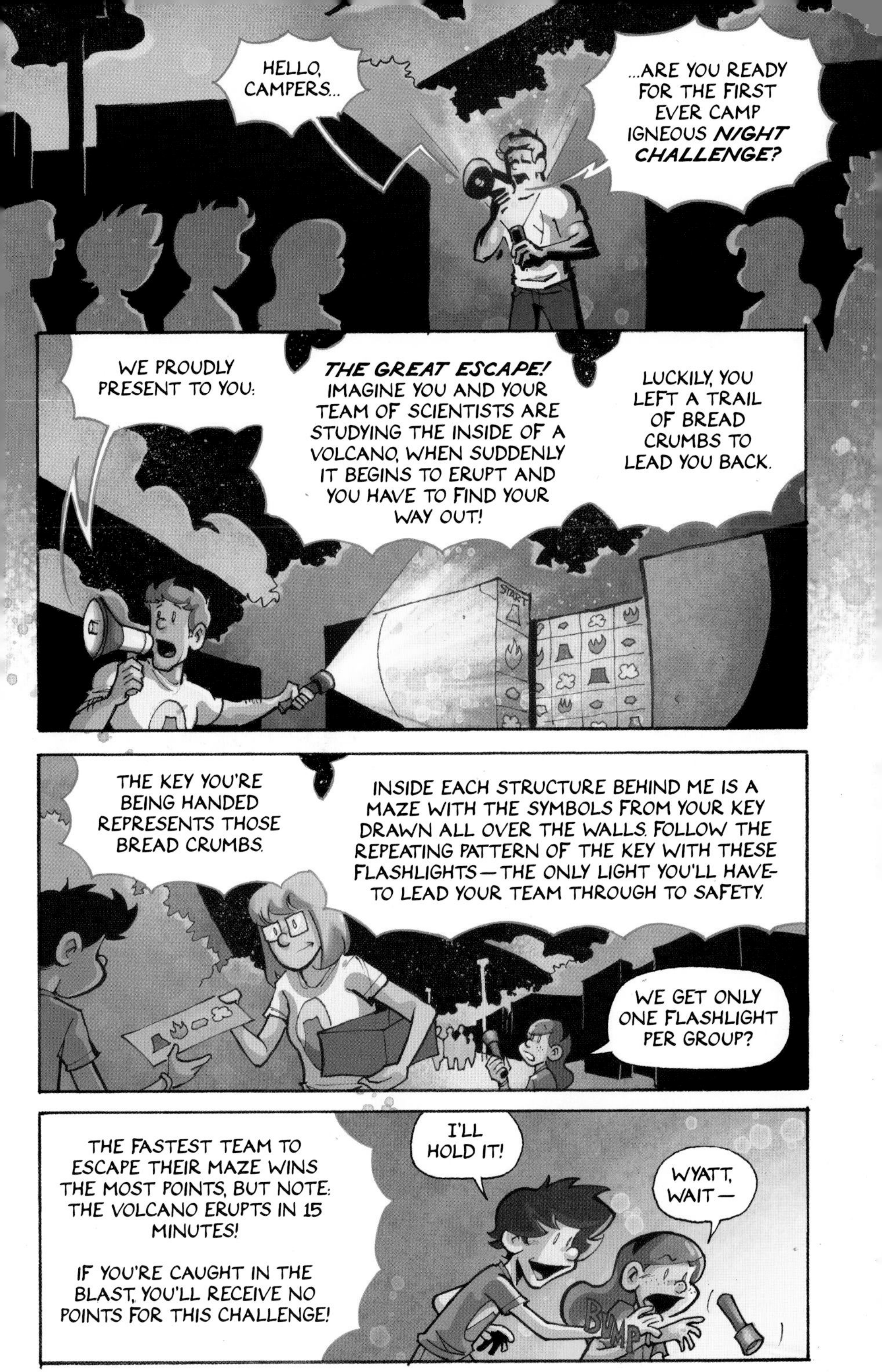

HELLO, CAMPERS...
...ARE YOU READY FOR THE FIRST EVER CAMP IGNEOUS NIGHT CHALLENGE?
WE PROUDLY PRESENT TO YOU:
THE GREAT ESCAPE! IMAGINE YOU AND YOUR TEAM OF SCIENTISTS ARE STUDYING THE INSIDE OF A VOLCANO, WHEN SUDDENLY IT BEGINS TO ERUPT AND YOU HAVE TO FIND YOUR WAY OUT!
LUCKILY, YOU LEFT A TRAIL OF BREAD CRUMBS TO LEAD YOU BACK.
START
THE KEY YOU'RE BEING HANDED REPRESENTS THOSE BREAD CRUMBS.
INSIDE EACH STRUCTURE BEHIND ME IS A MAZE WITH THE SYMBOLS FROM YOUR KEY DRAWN ALL OVER THE WALLS. FOLLOW THE REPEATING PATTERN OF THE KEY WITH THESE FLASHLIGHTS—THE ONLY LIGHT YOU'LL HAVE—TO LEAD YOUR TEAM THROUGH TO SAFETY.
WE GET ONLY ONE FLASHLIGHT PER GROUP?
THE FASTEST TEAM TO ESCAPE THEIR MAZE WINS THE MOST POINTS, BUT NOTE: THE VOLCANO ERUPTS IN 15 MINUTES!
IF YOU'RE CAUGHT IN THE BLAST, YOU'LL RECEIVE NO POINTS FOR THIS CHALLENGE!
I'LL HOLD IT!
WYATT, WAIT—
BUMP

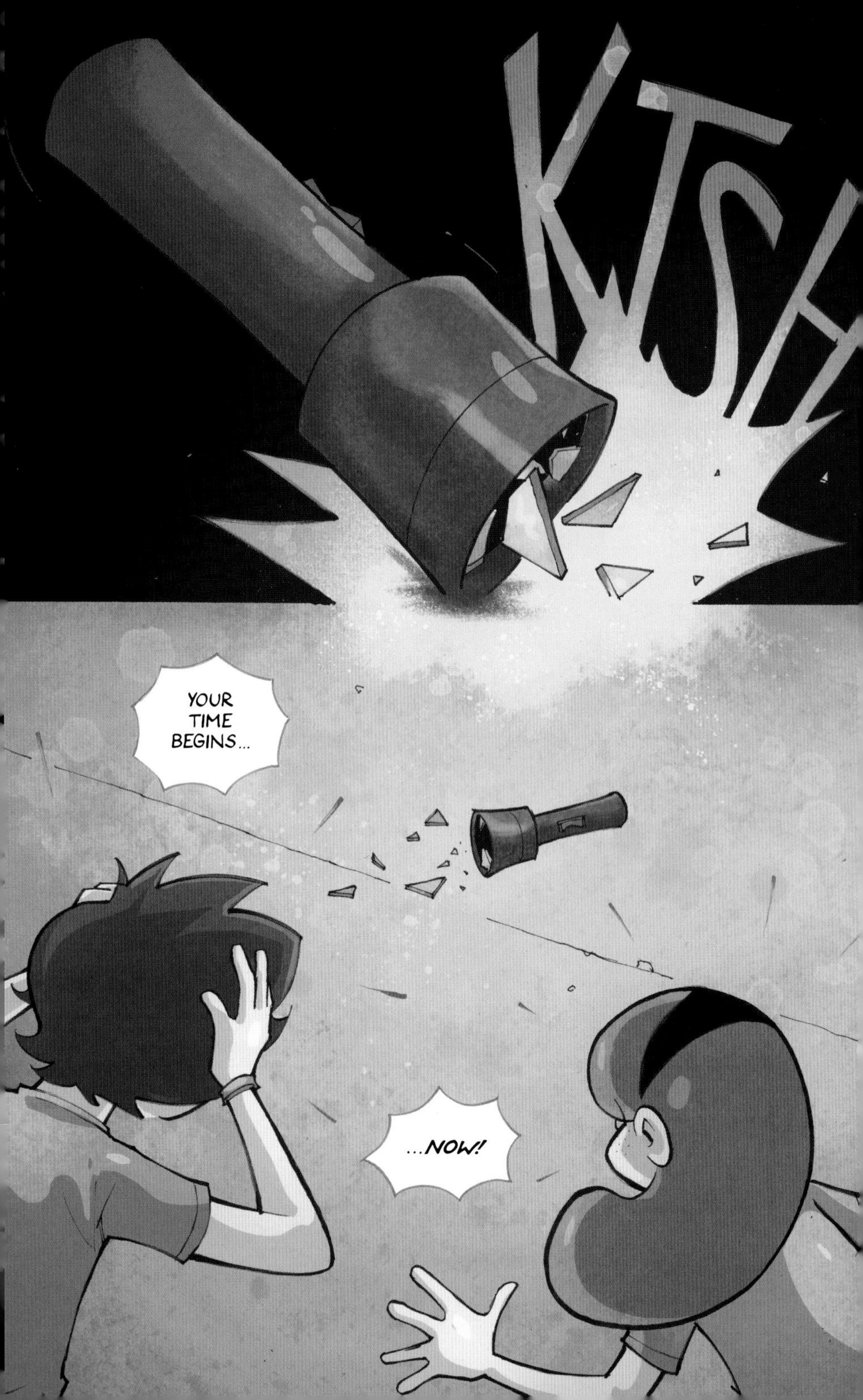
KTSH
YOUR TIME BEGINS...
...NOW!

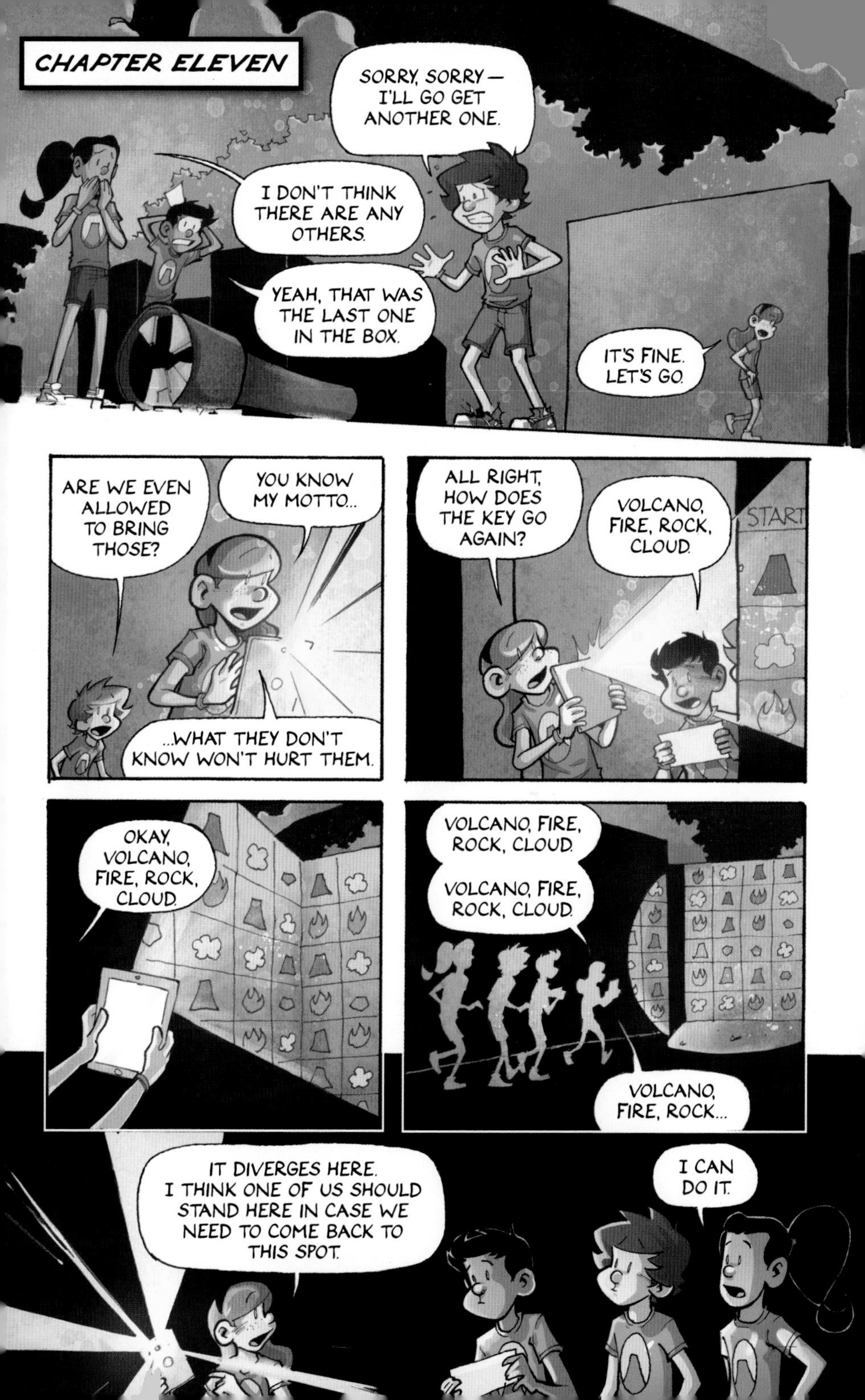
CHAPTER ELEVEN
SORRY, SORRY— I'LL GO GET ANOTHER ONE.
I DON'T THINK THERE ARE ANY OTHERS.
YEAH, THAT WAS THE LAST ONE IN THE BOX.
IT'S FINE. LET'S GO.
ARE WE EVEN ALLOWED TO BRING THOSE?
YOU KNOW MY MOTTO...
...WHAT THEY DON'T KNOW WON'T HURT THEM.
ALL RIGHT, HOW DOES THE KEY GO AGAIN?
VOLCANO, FIRE, ROCK, CLOUD.
START
OKAY, VOLCANO, FIRE, ROCK, CLOUD.
VOLCANO, FIRE, ROCK, CLOUD.
VOLCANO, FIRE, ROCK, CLOUD.
VOLCANO, FIRE, ROCK...
IT DIVERGES HERE. I THINK ONE OF US SHOULD STAND HERE IN CASE WE NEED TO COME BACK TO THIS SPOT.
I CAN DO IT.

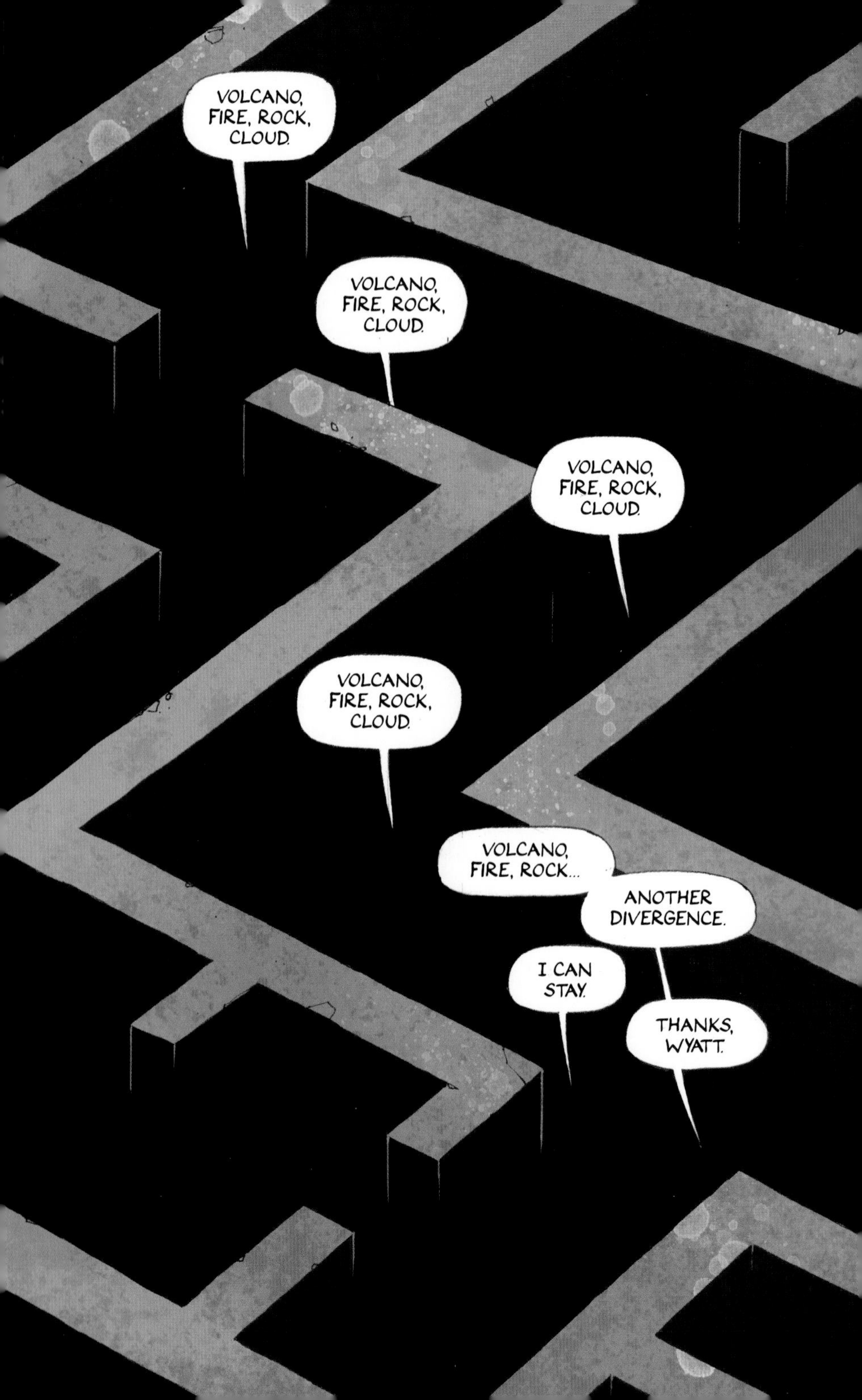
VOLCANO, FIRE, ROCK, CLOUD.
VOLCANO, FIRE, ROCK, CLOUD.
VOLCANO, FIRE, ROCK, CLOUD.
VOLCANO, FIRE, ROCK, CLOUD.
VOLCANO, FIRE, ROCK...
ANOTHER DIVERGENCE.
I CAN STAY.
THANKS, WYATT.

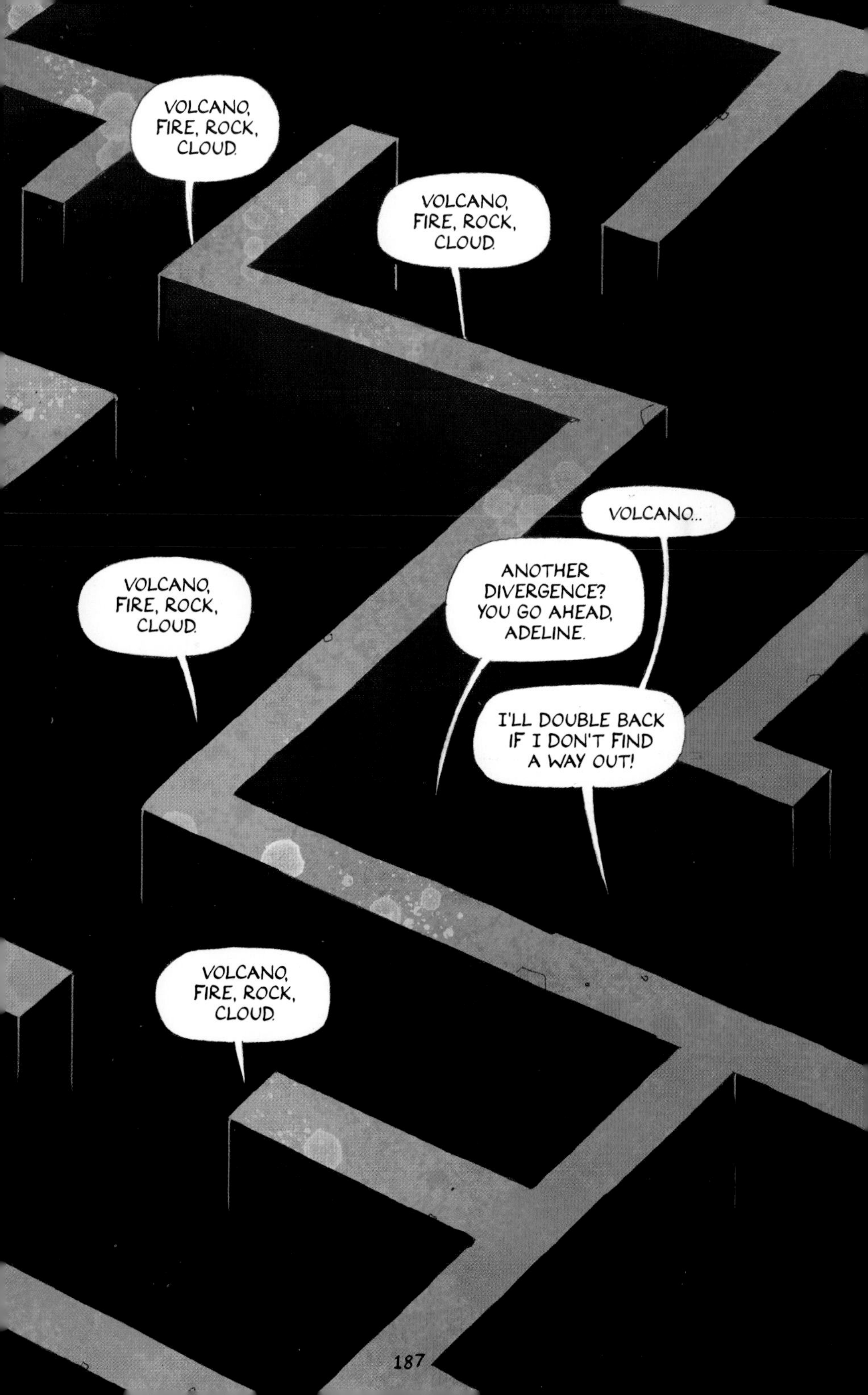
VOLCANO, FIRE, ROCK, CLOUD.
VOLCANO, FIRE, ROCK, CLOUD.
VOLCANO...
ANOTHER DIVERGENCE? YOU GO AHEAD, ADELINE.
I'LL DOUBLE BACK IF I DON'T FIND A WAY OUT!
VOLCANO, FIRE, ROCK, CLOUD.
VOLCANO, FIRE, ROCK, CLOUD.

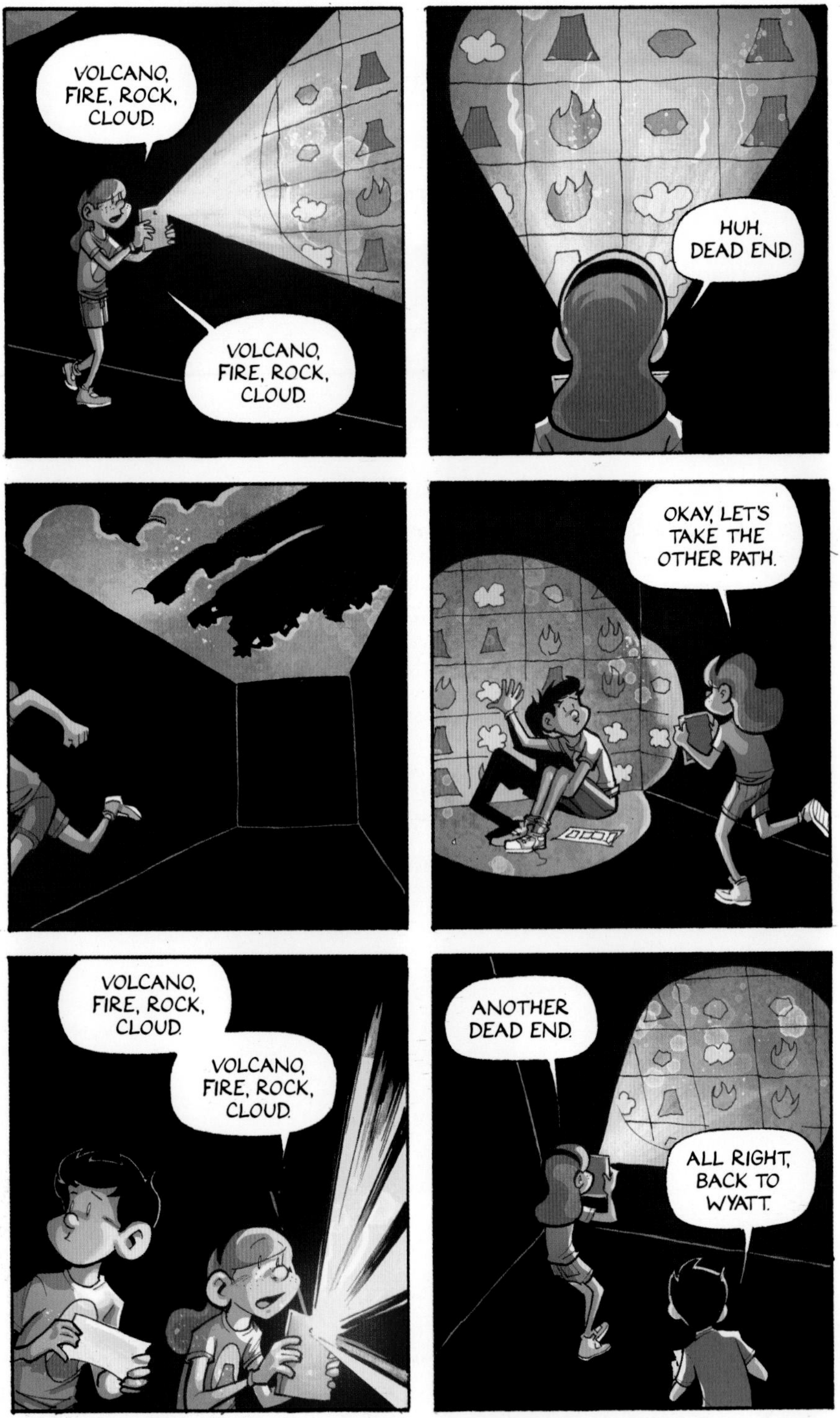
VOLCANO, FIRE, ROCK, CLOUD.
VOLCANO, FIRE, ROCK, CLOUD.
HUH. DEAD END.
OKAY, LET'S TAKE THE OTHER PATH.
VOLCANO, FIRE, ROCK, CLOUD.
VOLCANO, FIRE, ROCK, CLOUD.
ANOTHER DEAD END.
ALL RIGHT, BACK TO WYATT.

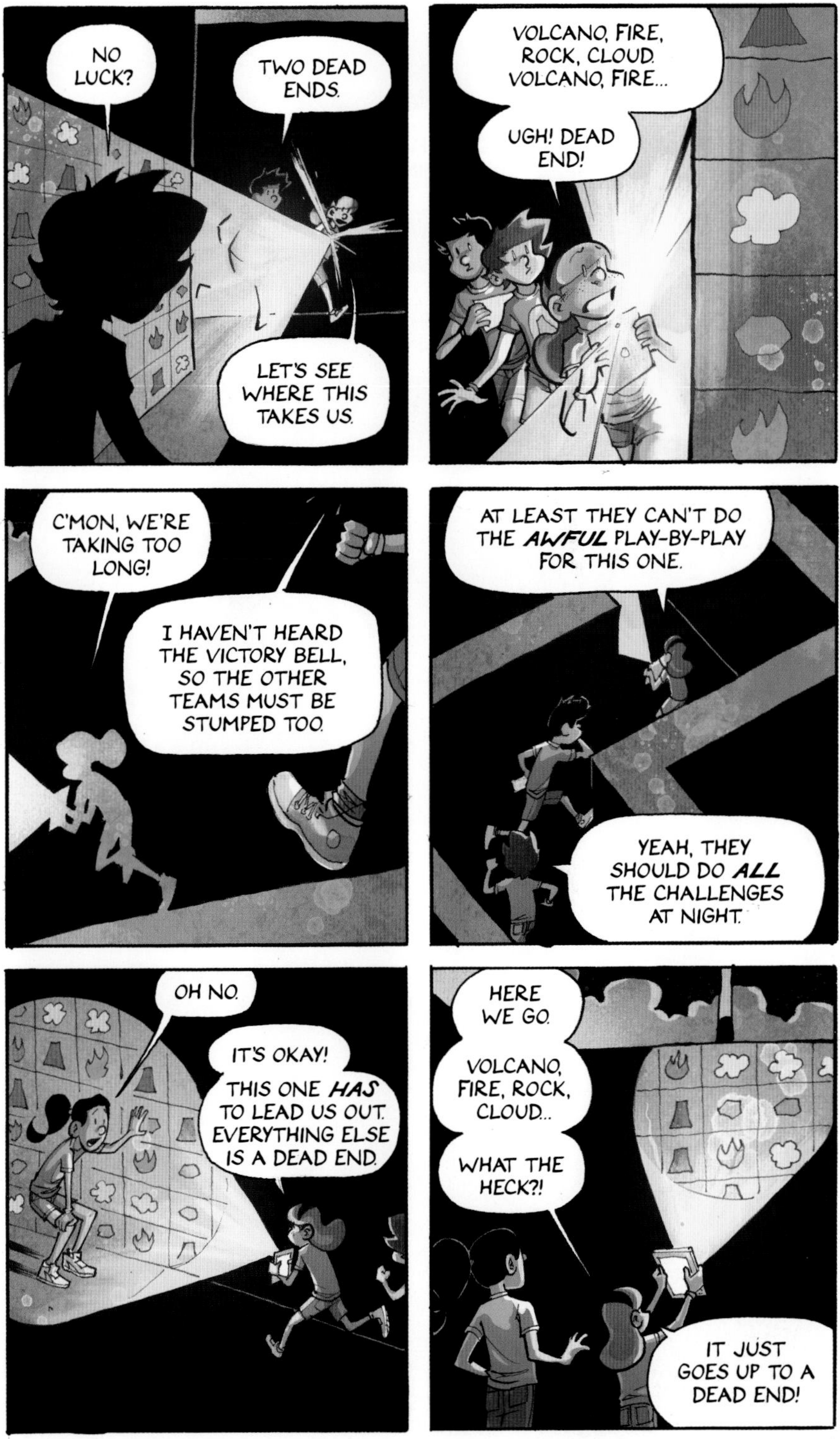
NO LUCK?
TWO DEAD ENDS.
LET'S SEE WHERE THIS TAKES US.
VOLCANO, FIRE, ROCK, CLOUD. VOLCANO, FIRE...
UGH! DEAD END!
C'MON, WE'RE TAKING TOO LONG!
I HAVEN'T HEARD THE VICTORY BELL, SO THE OTHER TEAMS MUST BE STUMPED TOO.
AT LEAST THEY CAN'T DO THE AWFUL PLAY-BY-PLAY FOR THIS ONE.
YEAH, THEY SHOULD DO ALL THE CHALLENGES AT NIGHT.
OH NO.
IT'S OKAY!
THIS ONE HAS TO LEAD US OUT. EVERYTHING ELSE IS A DEAD END.
HERE WE GO.
VOLCANO, FIRE, ROCK, CLOUD...
WHAT THE HECK?!
IT JUST GOES UP TO A DEAD END!

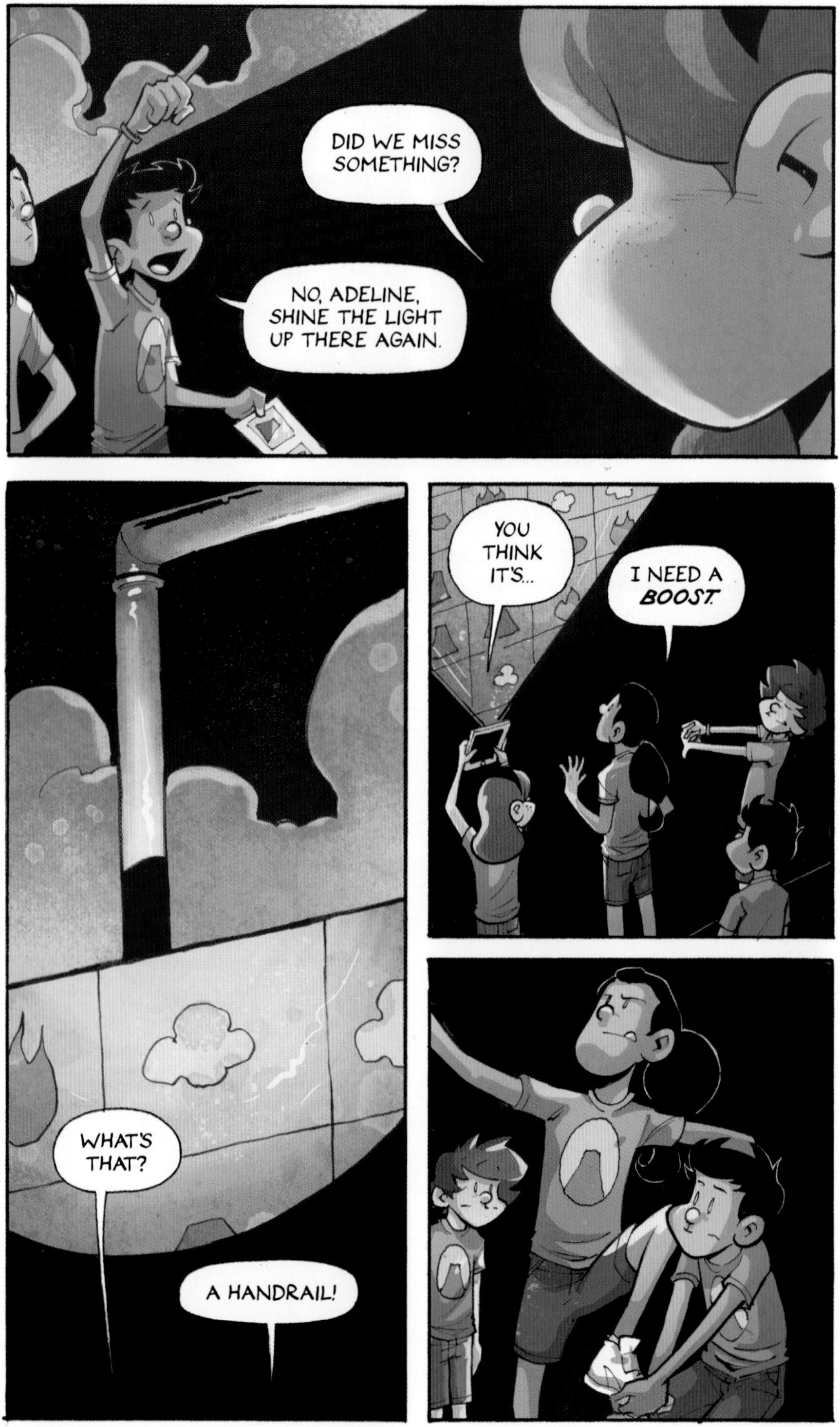
DID WE MISS SOMETHING?
NO, ADELINE, SHINE THE LIGHT UP THERE AGAIN.
WHAT'S THAT?
A HANDRAIL!
YOU THINK IT'S...
I NEED A *BOOST.*

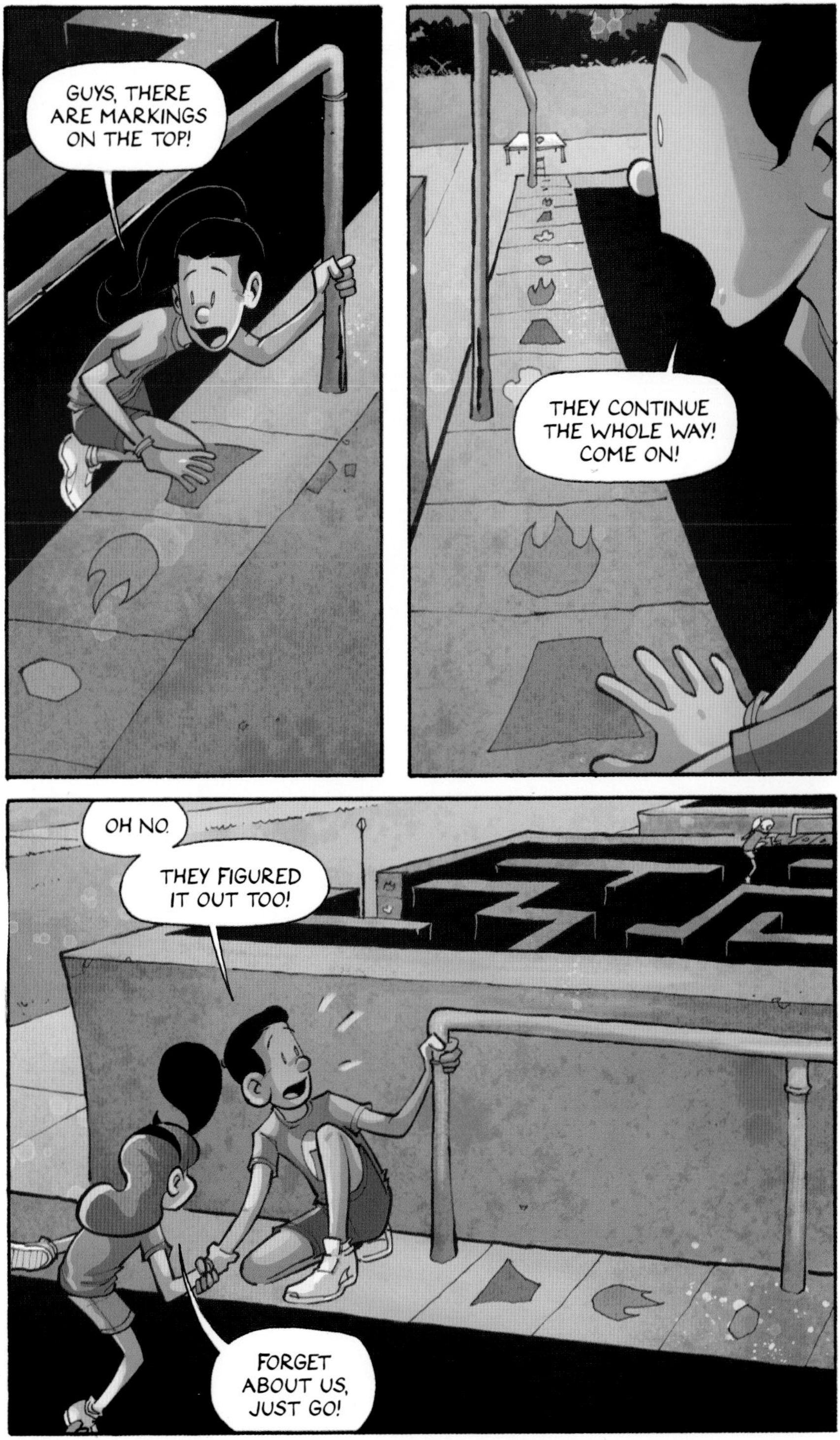
GUYS, THERE ARE MARKINGS ON THE TOP!
THEY CONTINUE THE WHOLE WAY! COME ON!
OH NO.
THEY FIGURED IT OUT TOO!
FORGET ABOUT US, JUST GO!

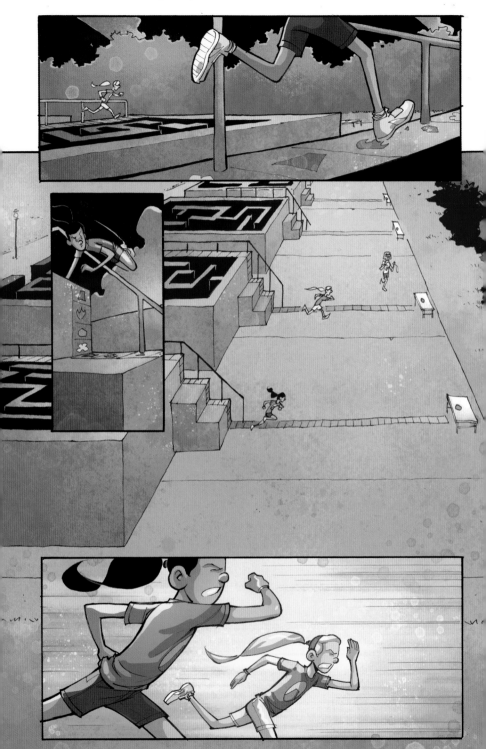

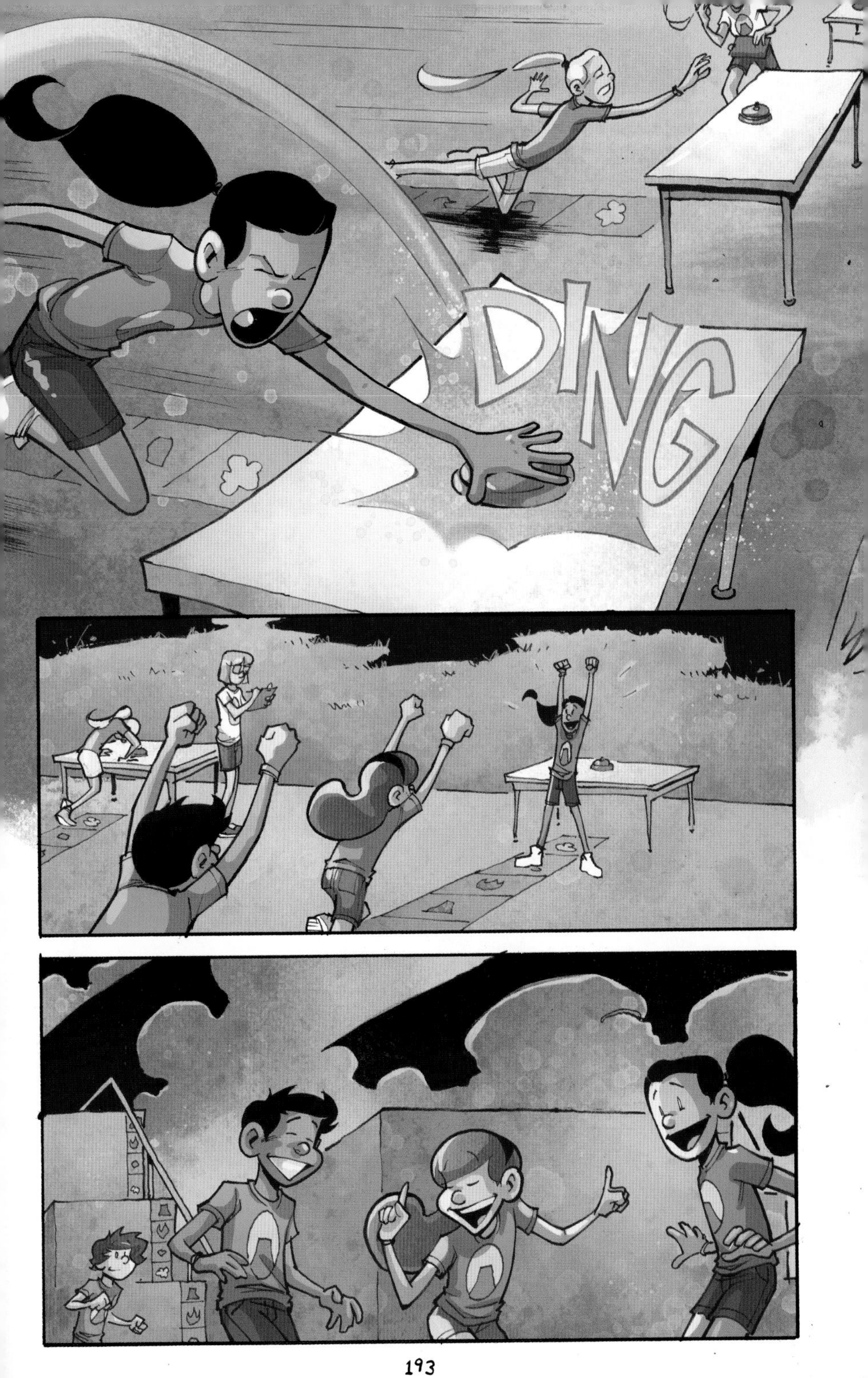
DING

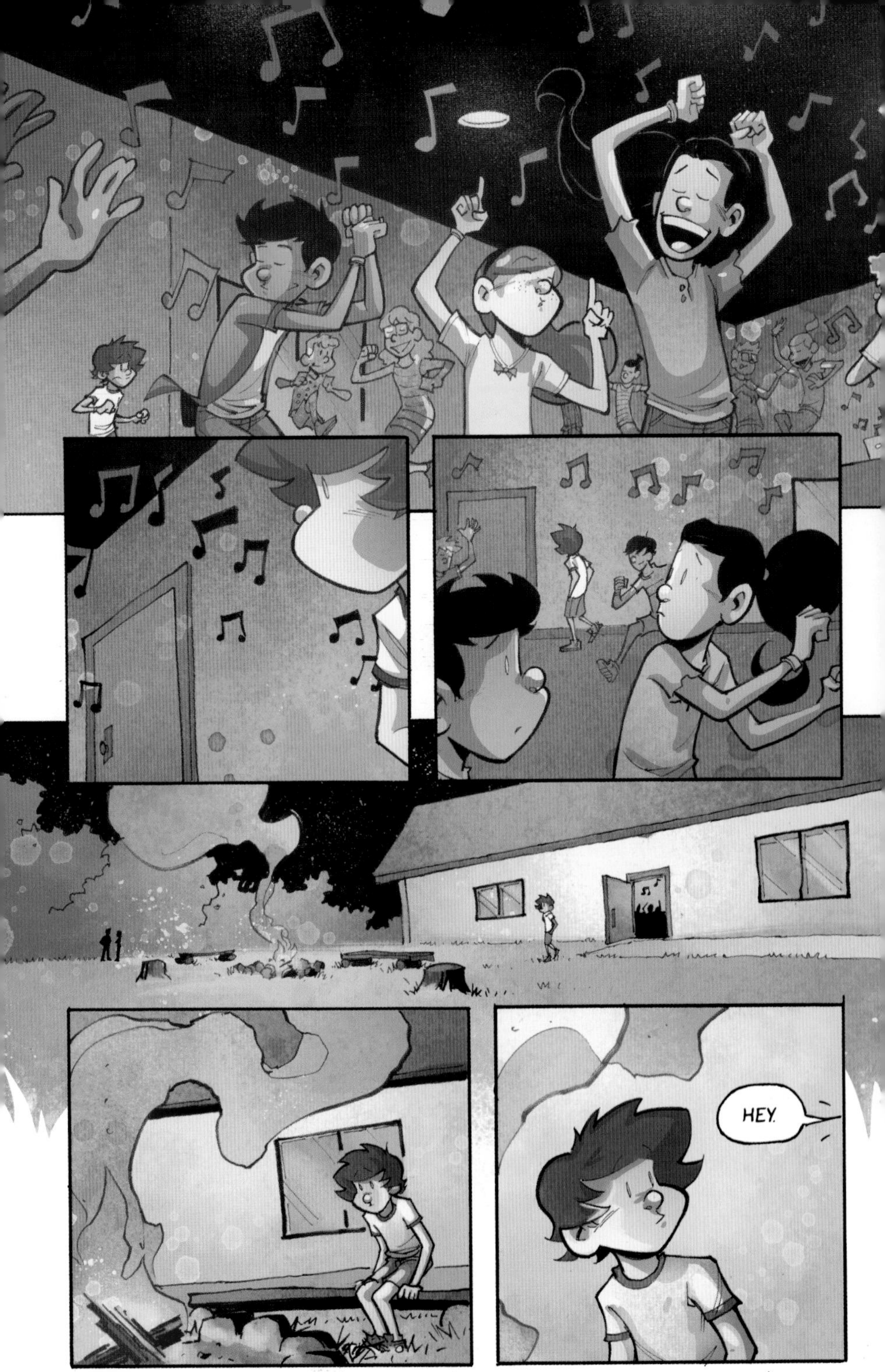
HEY.

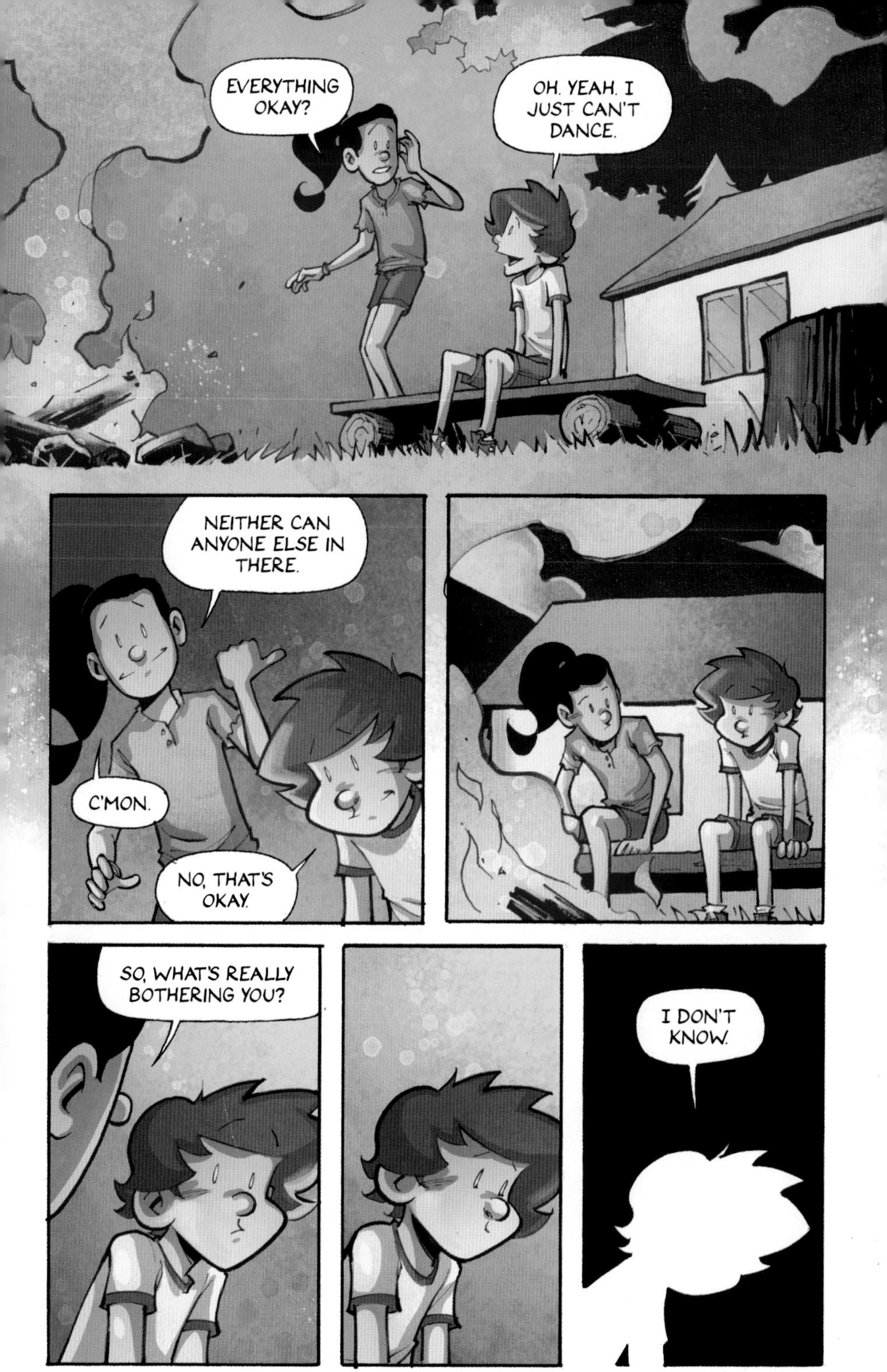
EVERYTHING OKAY?
OH. YEAH. I JUST CAN'T DANCE.
NEITHER CAN ANYONE ELSE IN THERE.
C'MON.
NO, THAT'S OKAY.
SO, WHAT'S REALLY BOTHERING YOU?
I DON'T KNOW.

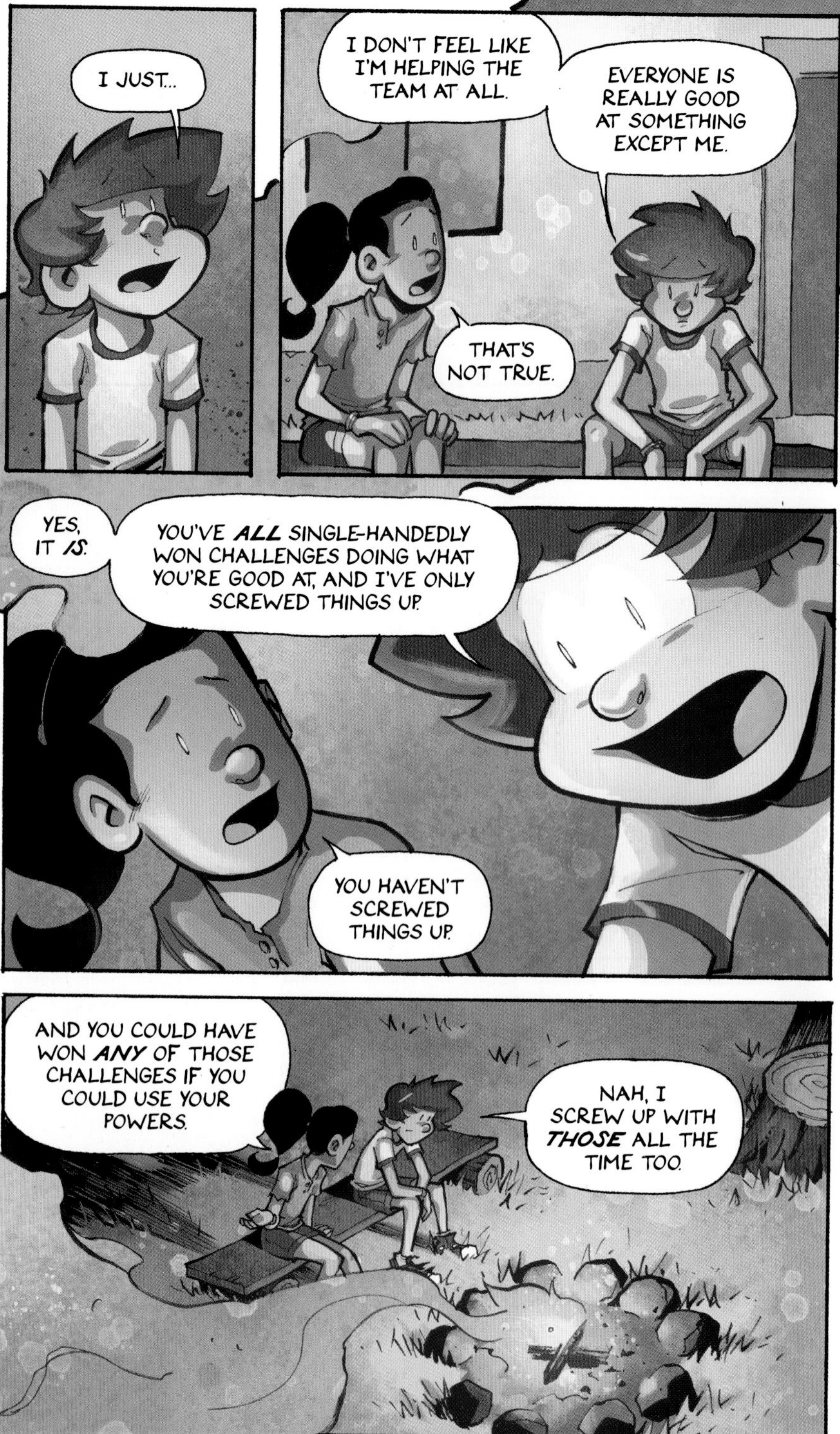
I JUST...
I DON'T FEEL LIKE I'M HELPING THE TEAM AT ALL.
EVERYONE IS REALLY GOOD AT SOMETHING EXCEPT ME.
THAT'S NOT TRUE.
YES, IT *IS*.
YOU'VE ***ALL*** SINGLE-HANDEDLY WON CHALLENGES DOING WHAT YOU'RE GOOD AT, AND I'VE ONLY SCREWED THINGS UP.
YOU HAVEN'T SCREWED THINGS UP.
AND YOU COULD HAVE WON ***ANY*** OF THOSE CHALLENGES IF YOU COULD USE YOUR POWERS.
NAH, I SCREW UP WITH ***THOSE*** ALL THE TIME TOO.

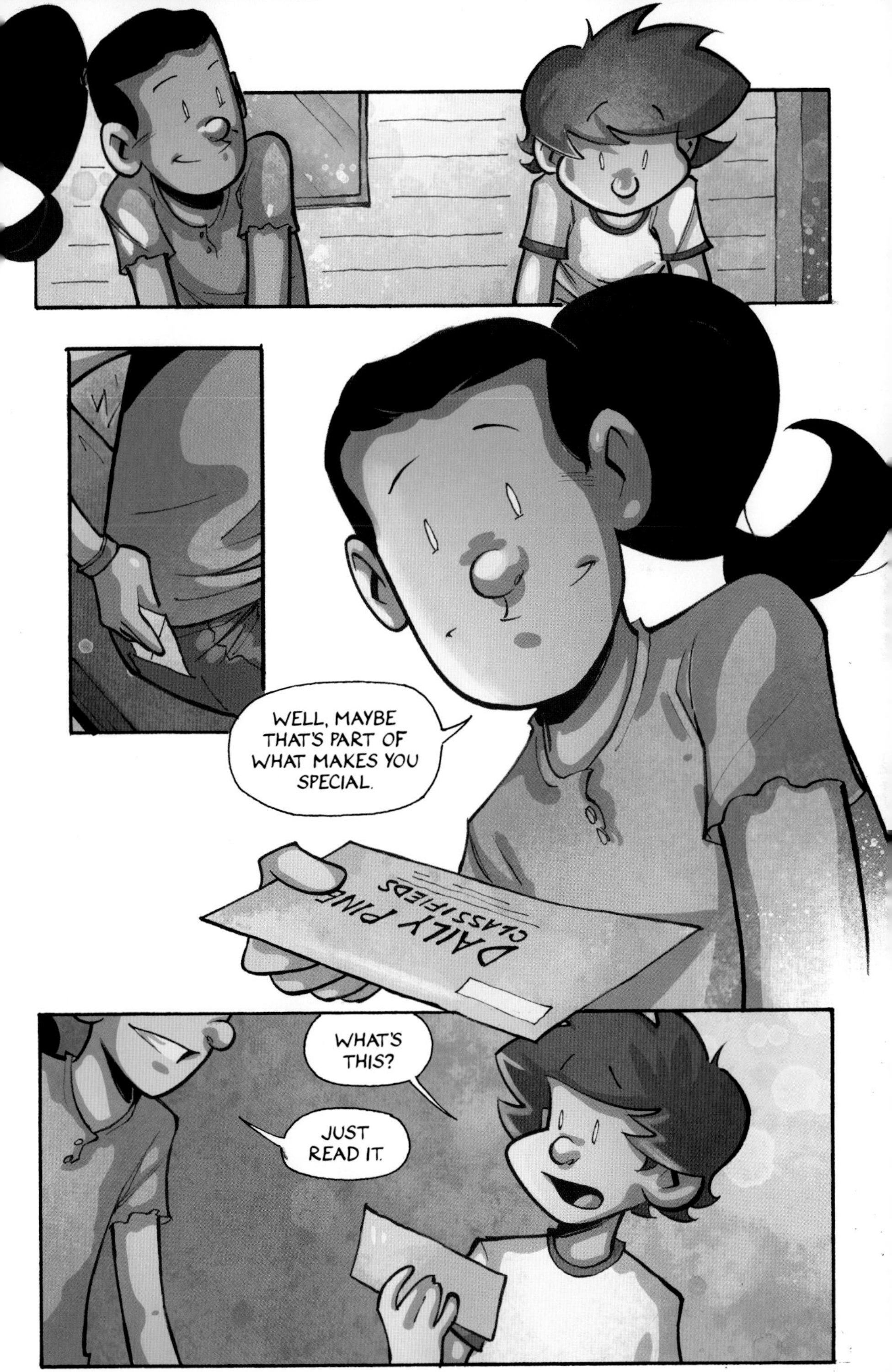
WELL, MAYBE THAT'S PART OF WHAT MAKES YOU SPECIAL.
DAILY PINE
CLASSIFIEDS
WHAT'S THIS?
JUST READ IT.

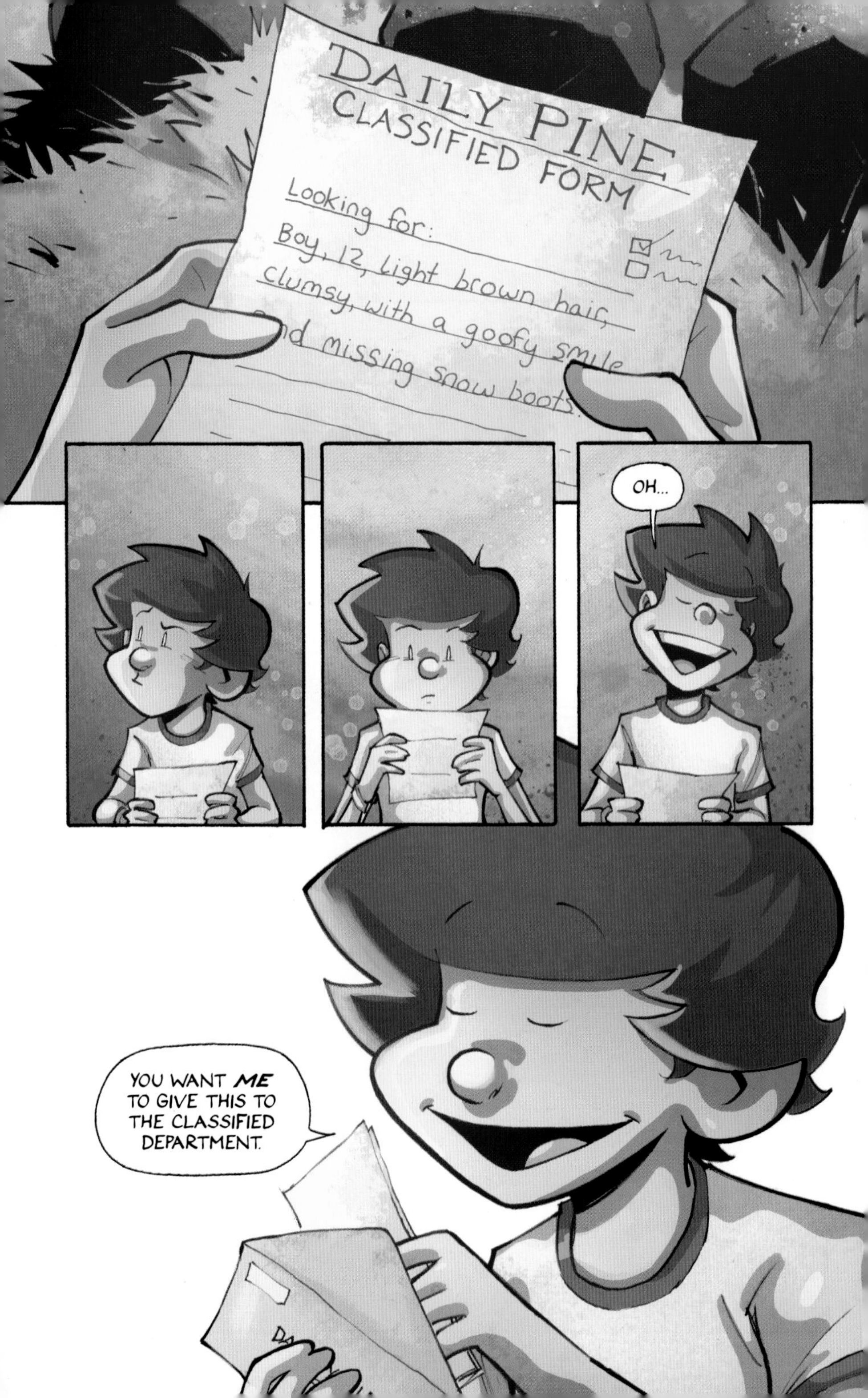
DAILY PINE
CLASSIFIED FORM
Looking for:
Boy, 12, light brown hair,
clumsy, with a goofy smile
and missing snow boots.
OH...
YOU WANT ***ME*** TO GIVE THIS TO THE CLASSIFIED DEPARTMENT.

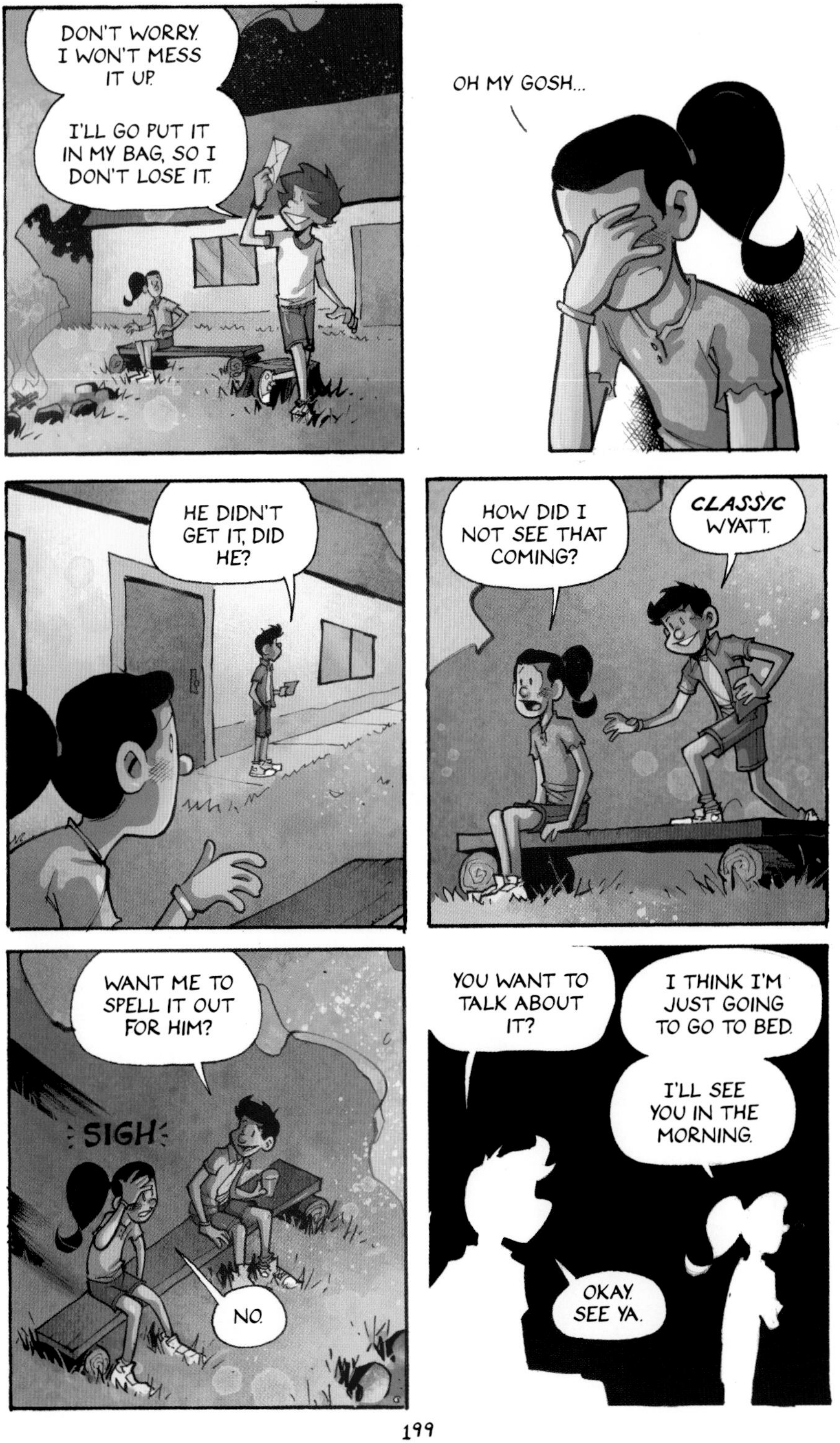
DON'T WORRY. I WON'T MESS IT UP.
I'LL GO PUT IT IN MY BAG, SO I DON'T LOSE IT.
OH MY GOSH...
HE DIDN'T GET IT, DID HE?
HOW DID I NOT SEE THAT COMING?
CLASSIC WYATT.
WANT ME TO SPELL IT OUT FOR HIM?
SIGH
NO.
YOU WANT TO TALK ABOUT IT?
I THINK I'M JUST GOING TO GO TO BED.
I'LL SEE YOU IN THE MORNING.
OKAY. SEE YA.

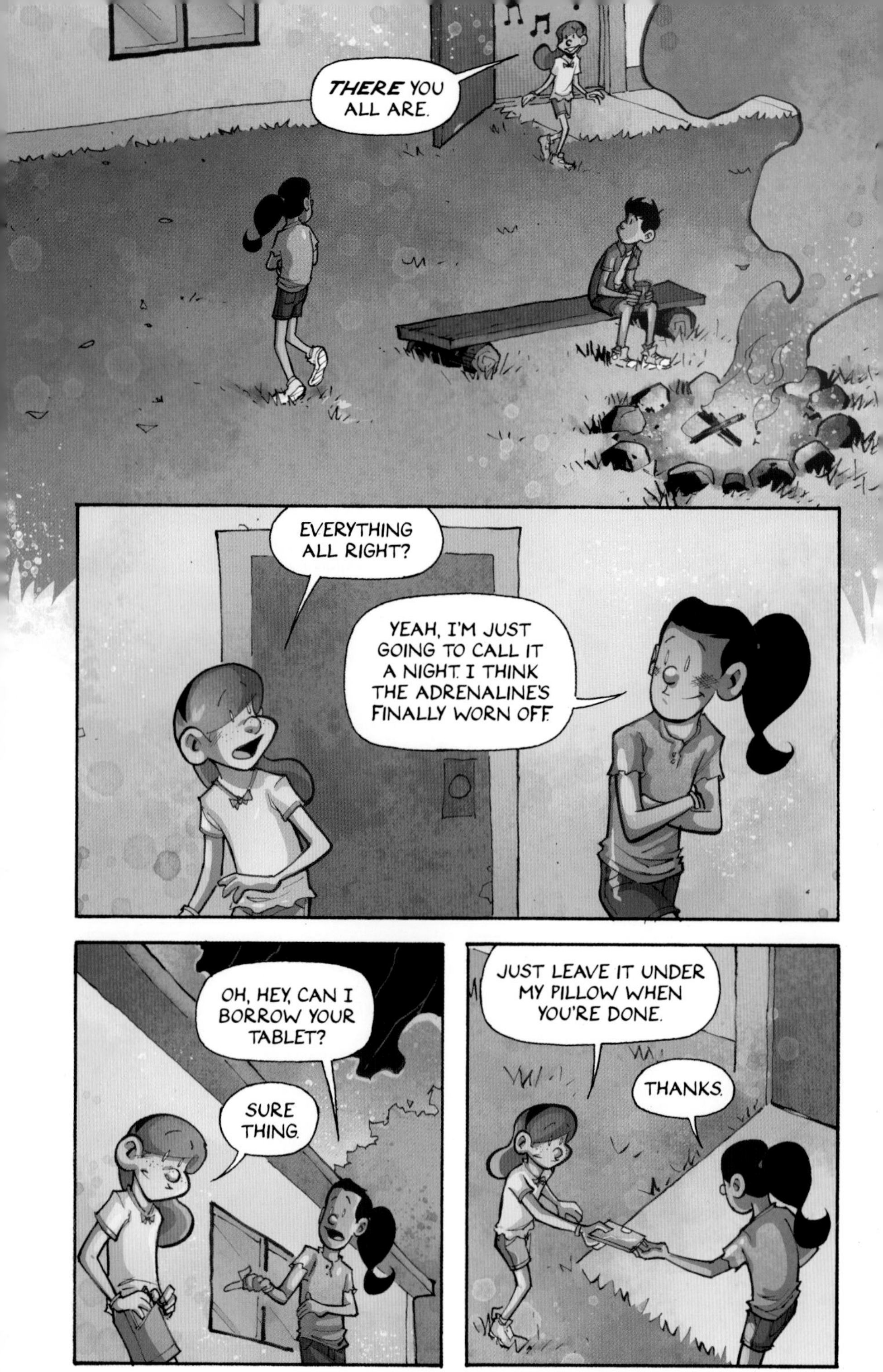

THERE YOU ALL ARE.
EVERYTHING ALL RIGHT?
YEAH, I'M JUST GOING TO CALL IT A NIGHT. I THINK THE ADRENALINE'S FINALLY WORN OFF.
OH, HEY, CAN I BORROW YOUR TABLET?
SURE THING.
JUST LEAVE IT UNDER MY PILLOW WHEN YOU'RE DONE.
THANKS.

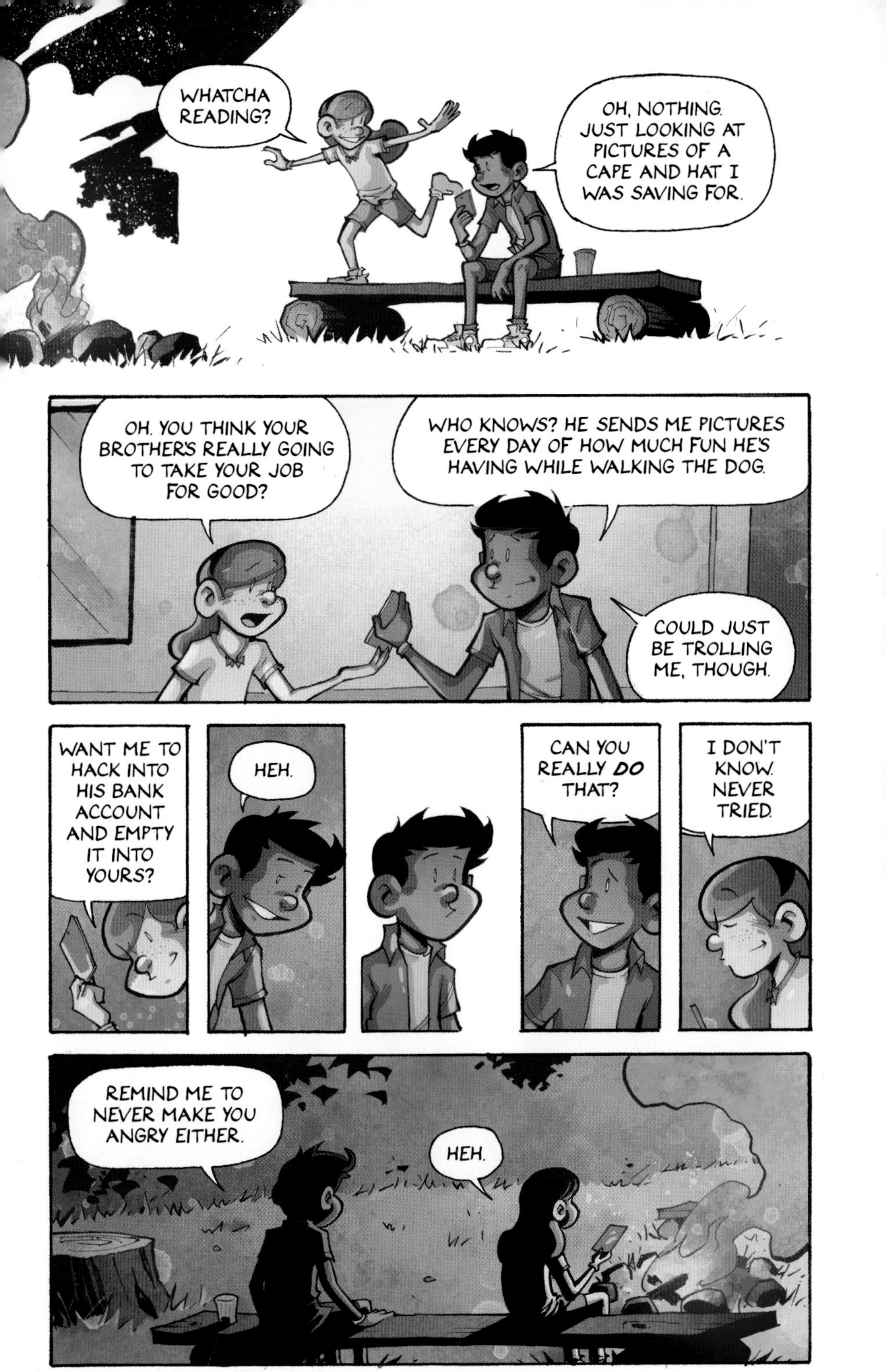
WHATCHA READING?
OH, NOTHING. JUST LOOKING AT PICTURES OF A CAPE AND HAT I WAS SAVING FOR.
OH. YOU THINK YOUR BROTHER'S REALLY GOING TO TAKE YOUR JOB FOR GOOD?
WHO KNOWS? HE SENDS ME PICTURES EVERY DAY OF HOW MUCH FUN HE'S HAVING WHILE WALKING THE DOG.
COULD JUST BE TROLLING ME, THOUGH.
WANT ME TO HACK INTO HIS BANK ACCOUNT AND EMPTY IT INTO YOURS?
HEH.
CAN YOU REALLY *DO* THAT?
I DON'T KNOW. NEVER TRIED.
REMIND ME TO NEVER MAKE YOU ANGRY EITHER.
HEH.

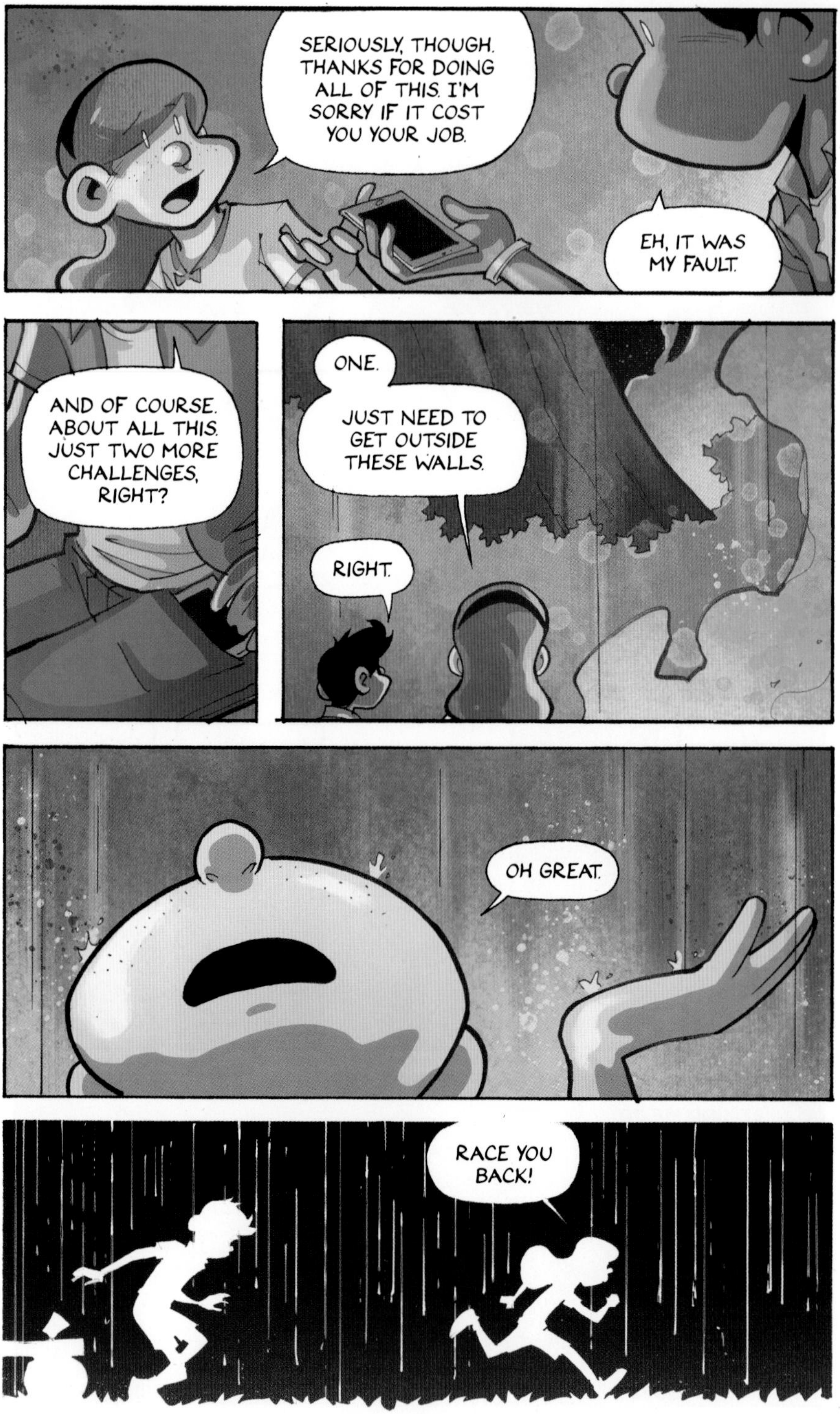
SERIOUSLY, THOUGH. THANKS FOR DOING ALL OF THIS. I'M SORRY IF IT COST YOU YOUR JOB.
EH, IT WAS MY FAULT.
AND OF COURSE. ABOUT ALL THIS. JUST TWO MORE CHALLENGES, RIGHT?
ONE.
JUST NEED TO GET OUTSIDE THESE WALLS.
RIGHT.
OH GREAT.
RACE YOU BACK!

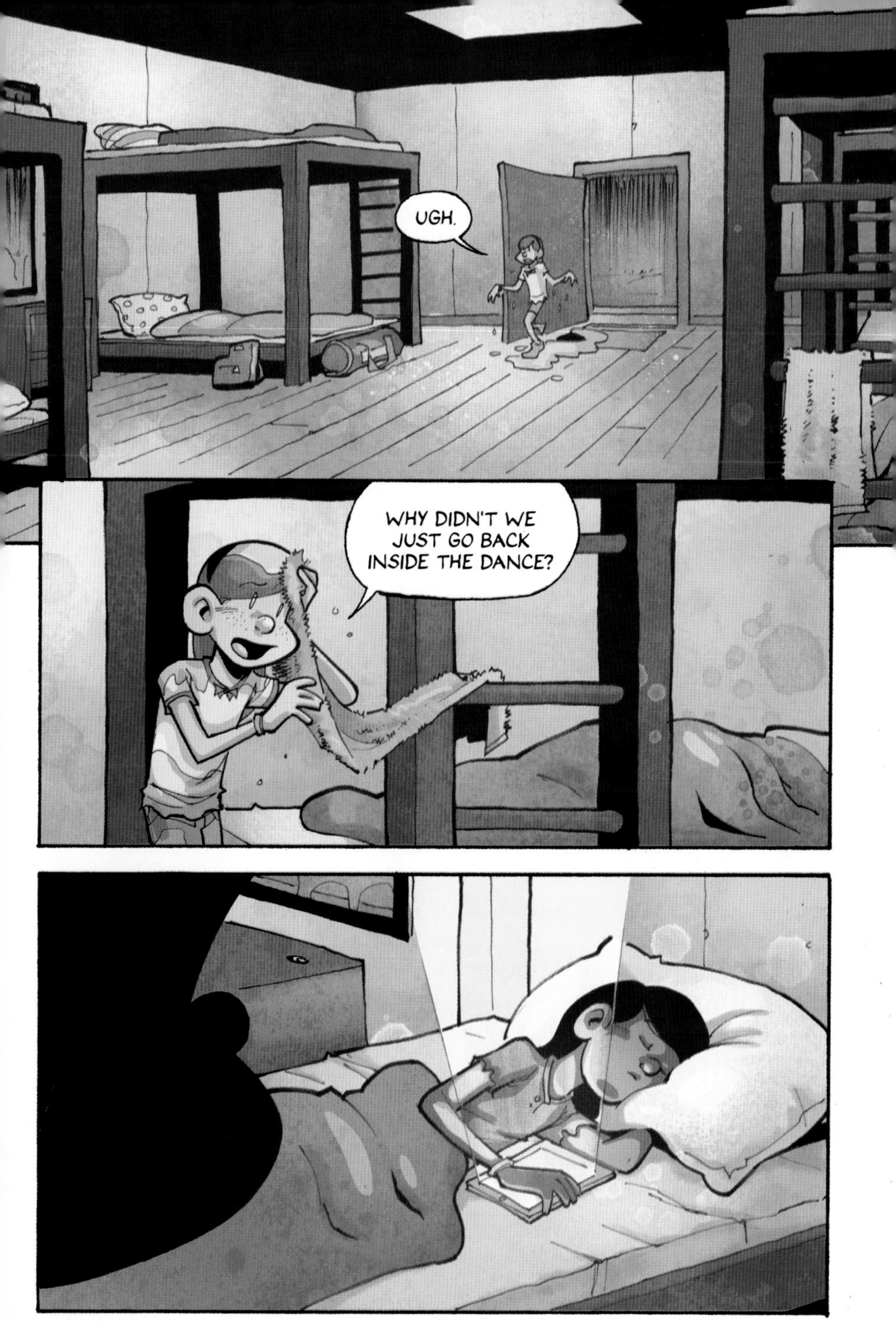
UGH.
WHY DIDN'T WE JUST GO BACK INSIDE THE DANCE?

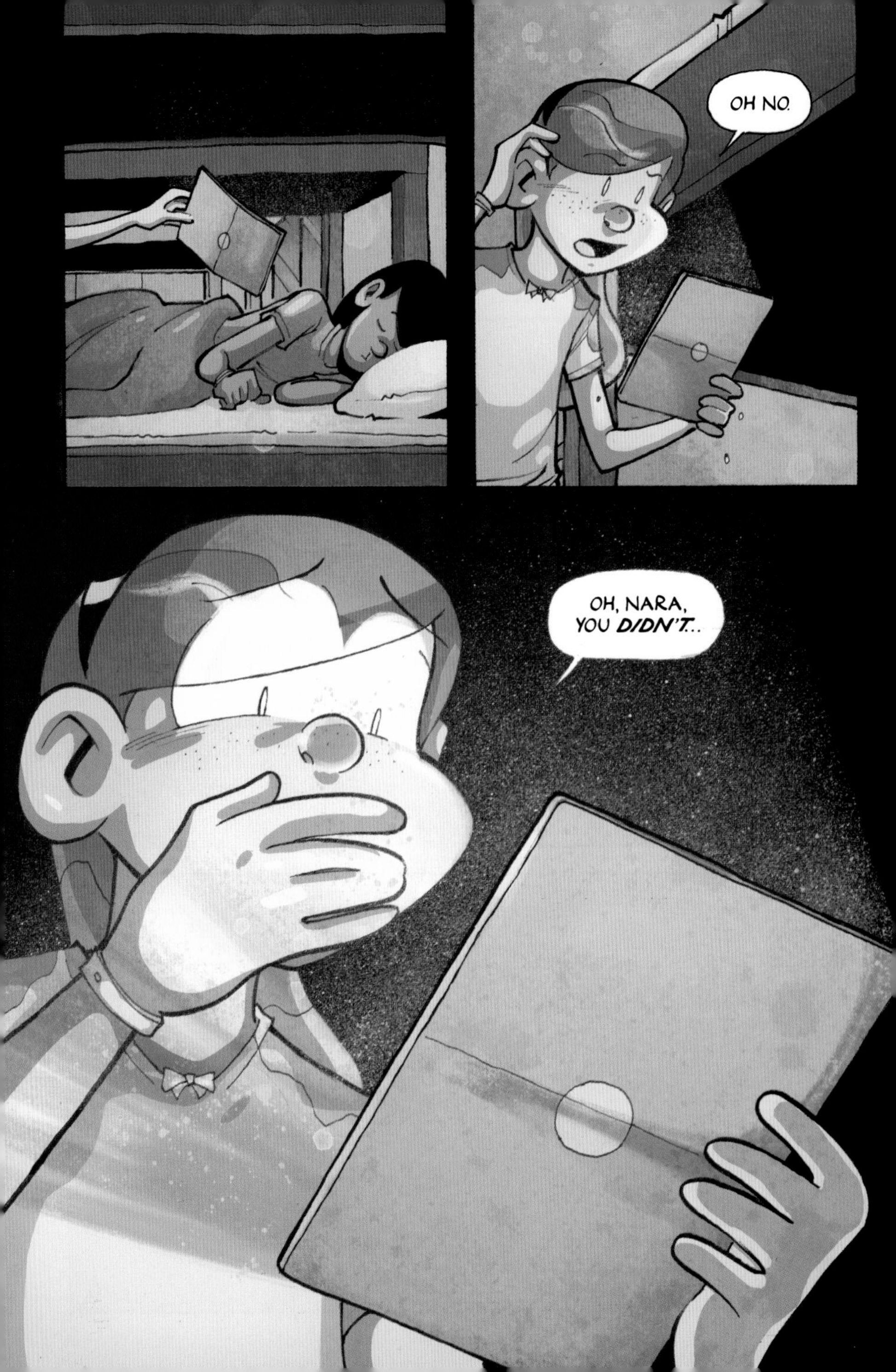
OH NO.
OH, NARA, YOU *DIDN'T*...

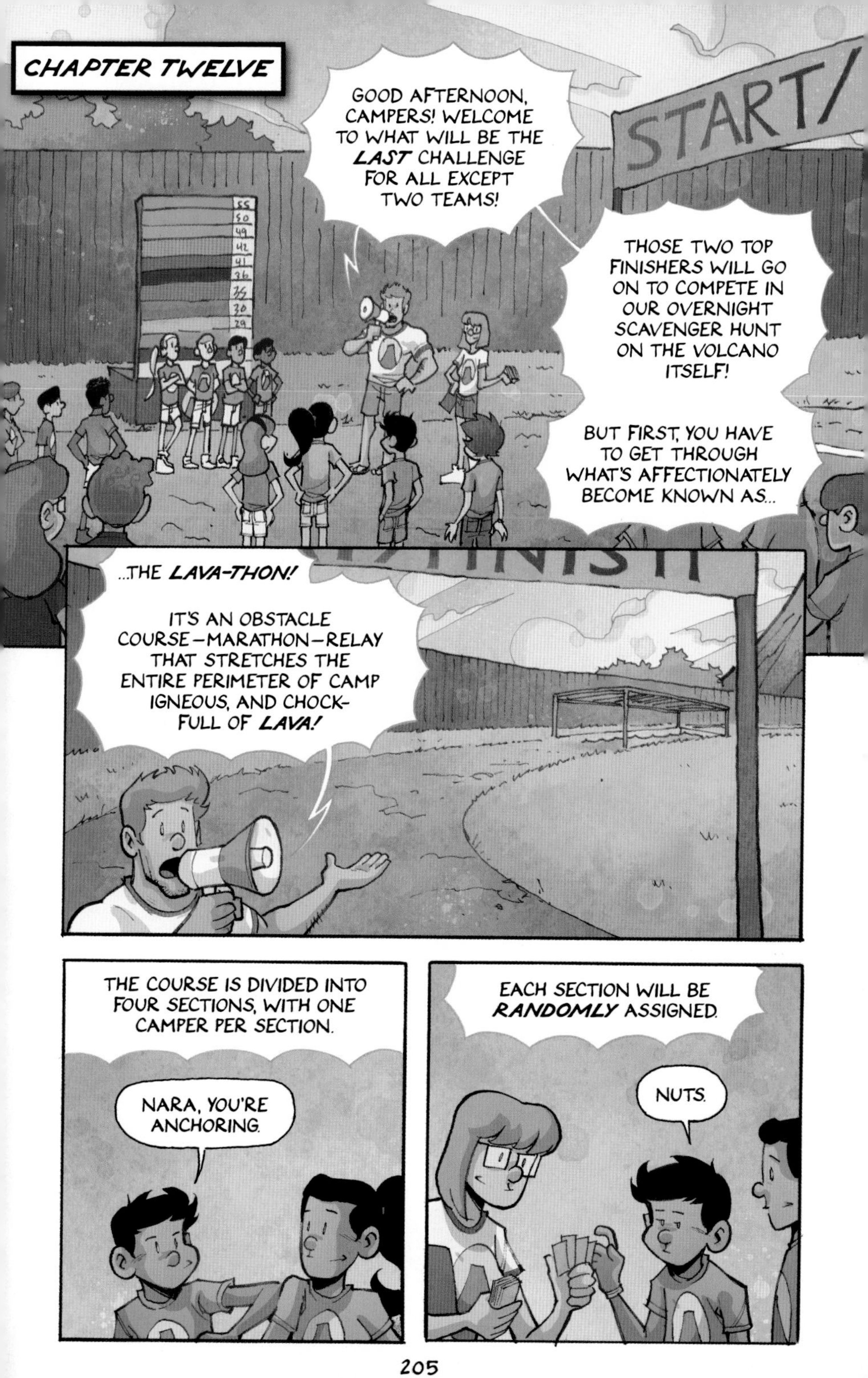
CHAPTER TWELVE
GOOD AFTERNOON, CAMPERS! WELCOME TO WHAT WILL BE THE LAST CHALLENGE FOR ALL EXCEPT TWO TEAMS!
START/
THOSE TWO TOP FINISHERS WILL GO ON TO COMPETE IN OUR OVERNIGHT SCAVENGER HUNT ON THE VOLCANO ITSELF!
BUT FIRST, YOU HAVE TO GET THROUGH WHAT'S AFFECTIONATELY BECOME KNOWN AS...
...THE LAVA-THON!
IT'S AN OBSTACLE COURSE—MARATHON—RELAY THAT STRETCHES THE ENTIRE PERIMETER OF CAMP IGNEOUS, AND CHOCK-FULL OF LAVA!
THE COURSE IS DIVIDED INTO FOUR SECTIONS, WITH ONE CAMPER PER SECTION.
NARA, YOU'RE ANCHORING.
EACH SECTION WILL BE RANDOMLY ASSIGNED.
NUTS.

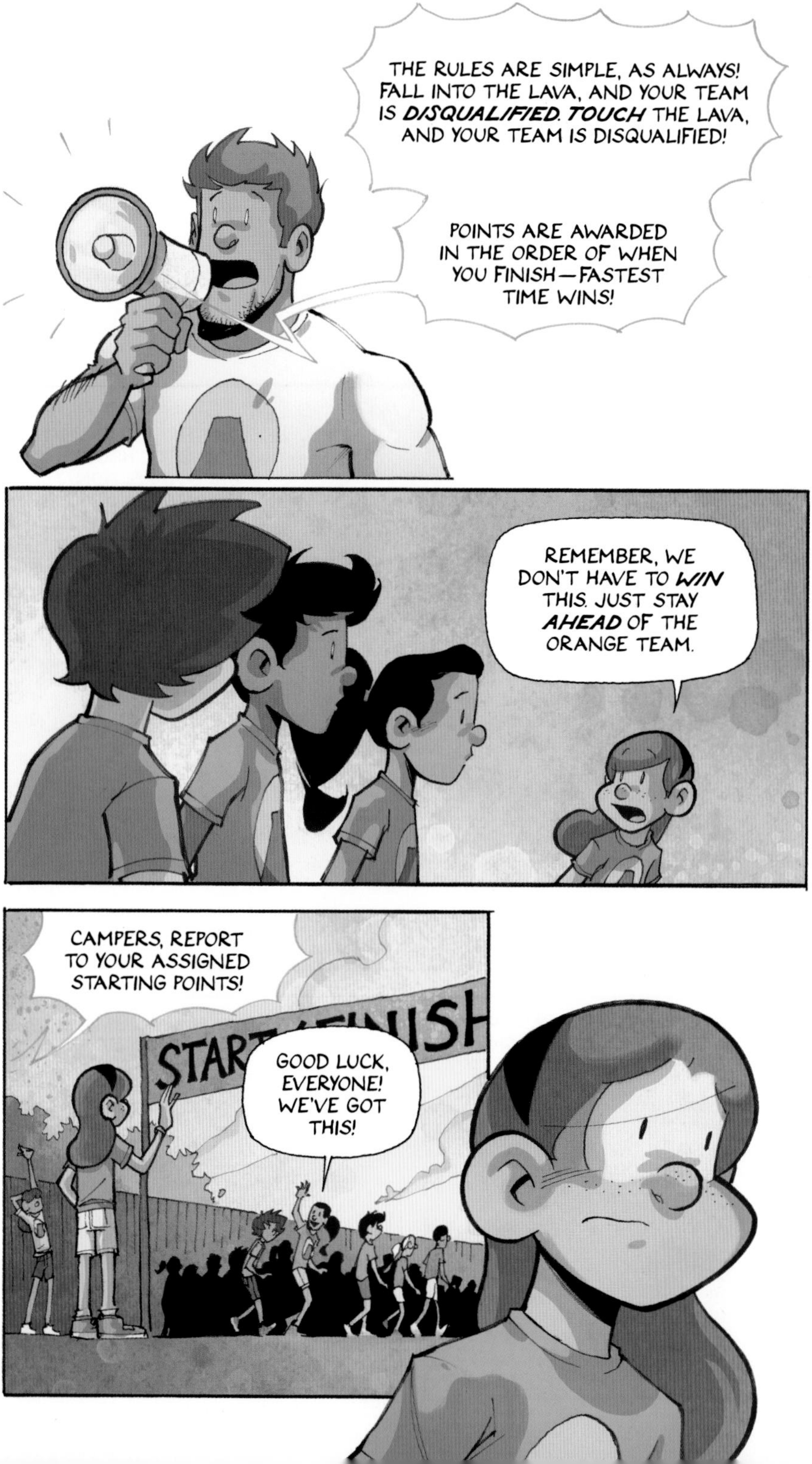
THE RULES ARE SIMPLE, AS ALWAYS! FALL INTO THE LAVA, AND YOUR TEAM IS *DISQUALIFIED. TOUCH* THE LAVA, AND YOUR TEAM IS DISQUALIFIED!
POINTS ARE AWARDED IN THE ORDER OF WHEN YOU FINISH—FASTEST TIME WINS!
REMEMBER, WE DON'T HAVE TO *WIN* THIS. JUST STAY *AHEAD* OF THE ORANGE TEAM.
CAMPERS, REPORT TO YOUR ASSIGNED STARTING POINTS!
GOOD LUCK, EVERYONE! WE'VE GOT THIS!

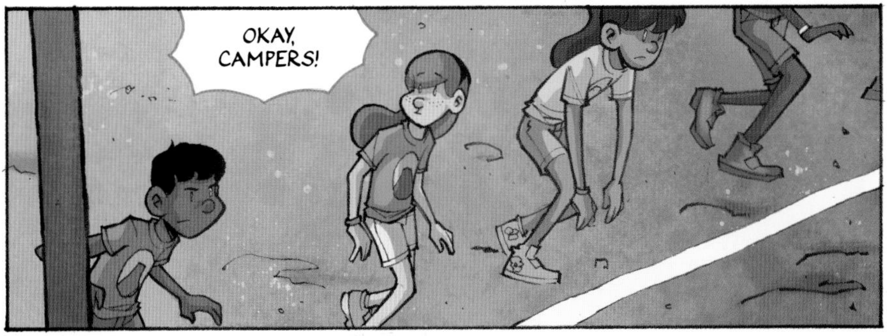
OKAY, CAMPERS!

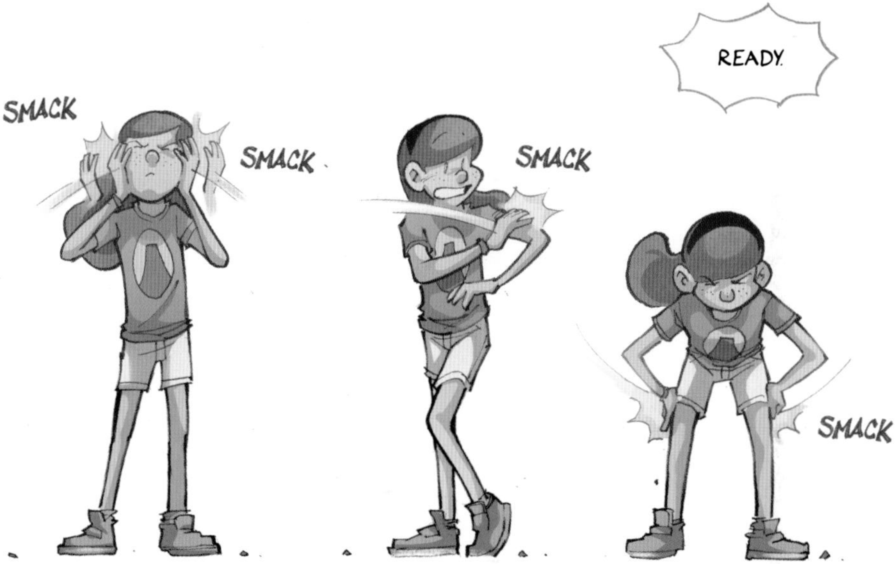
READY.
SMACK
SMACK
SMACK
SMACK

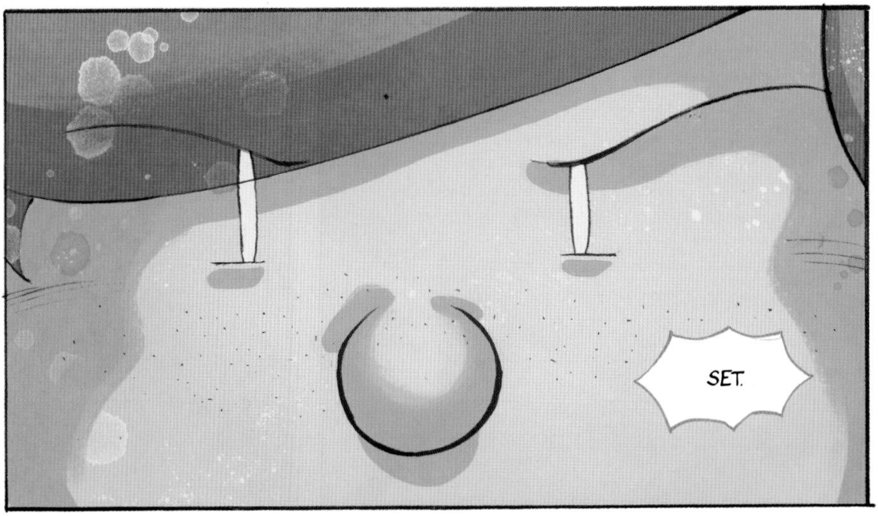
SET.

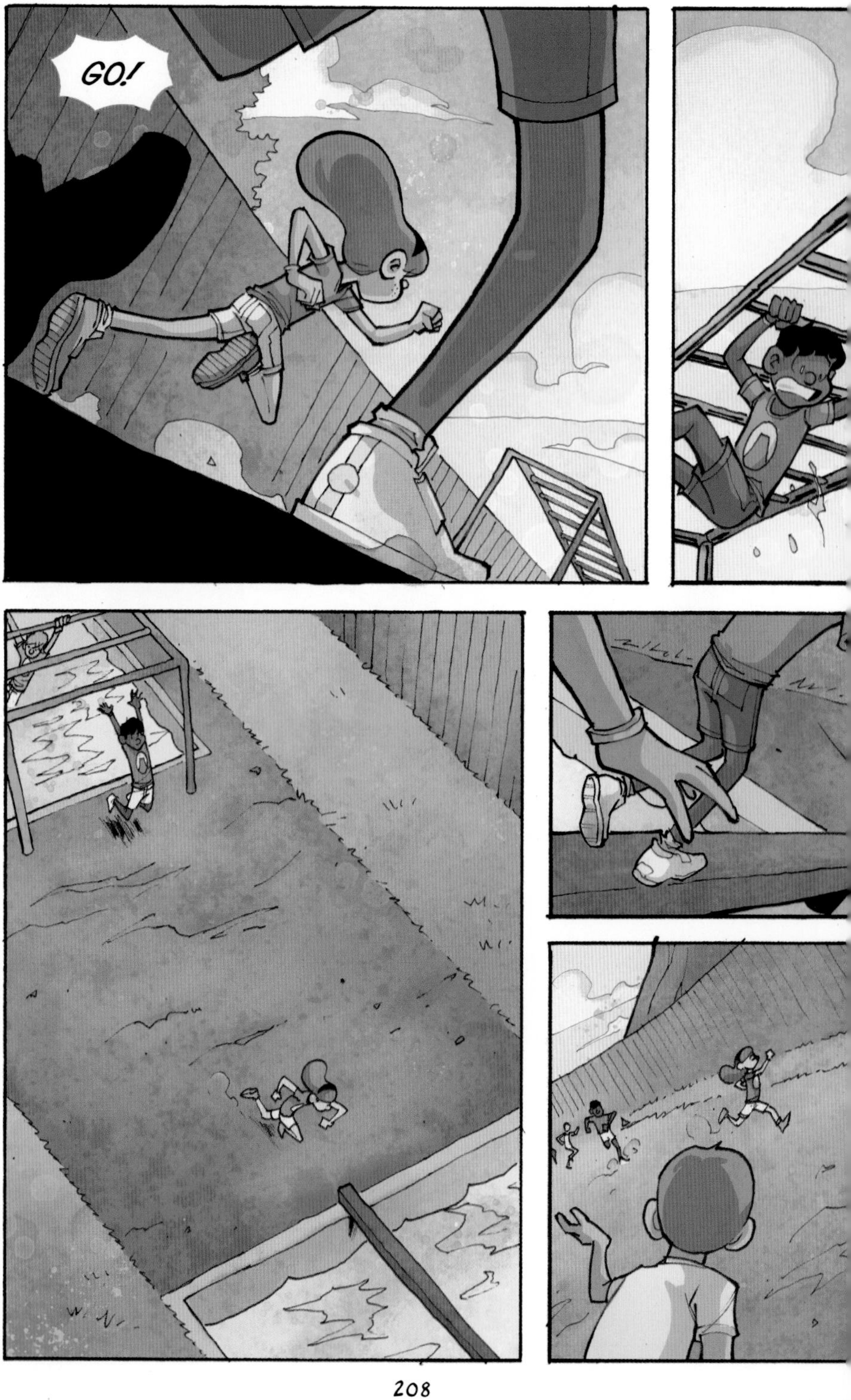
GO!

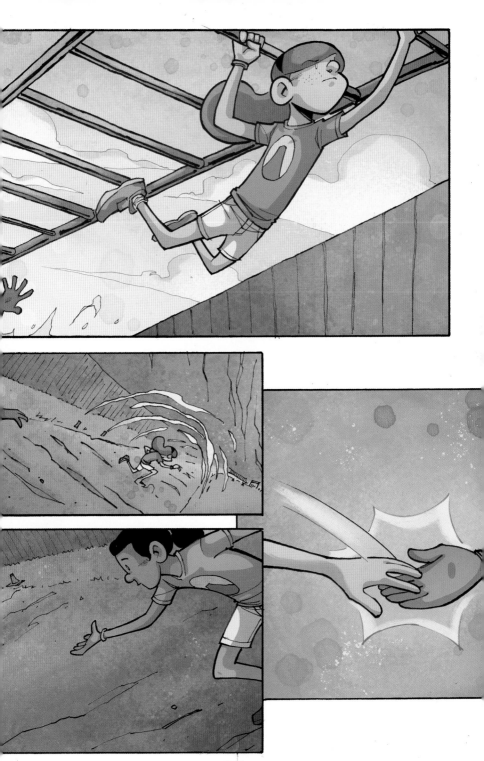

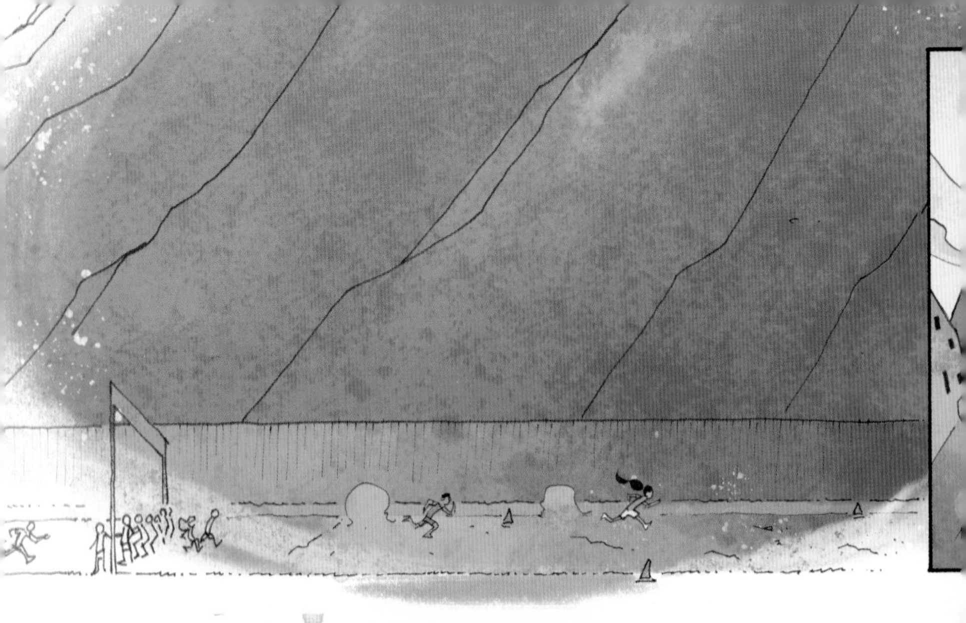
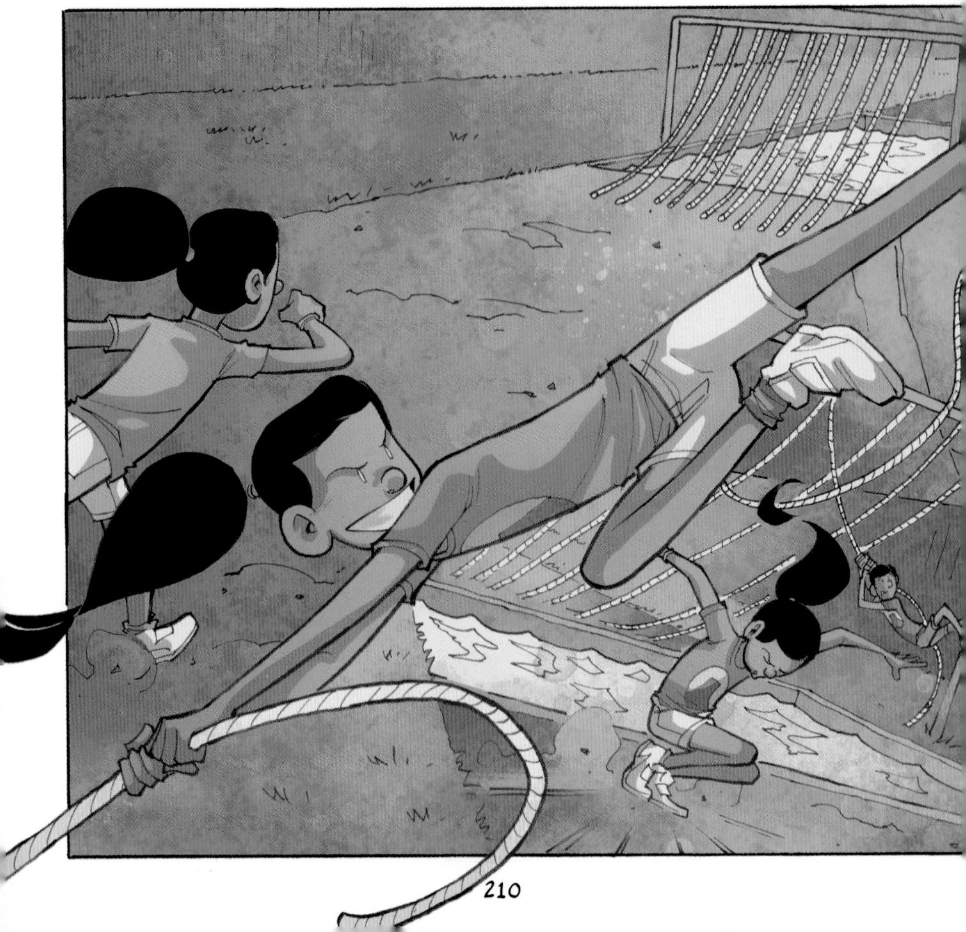

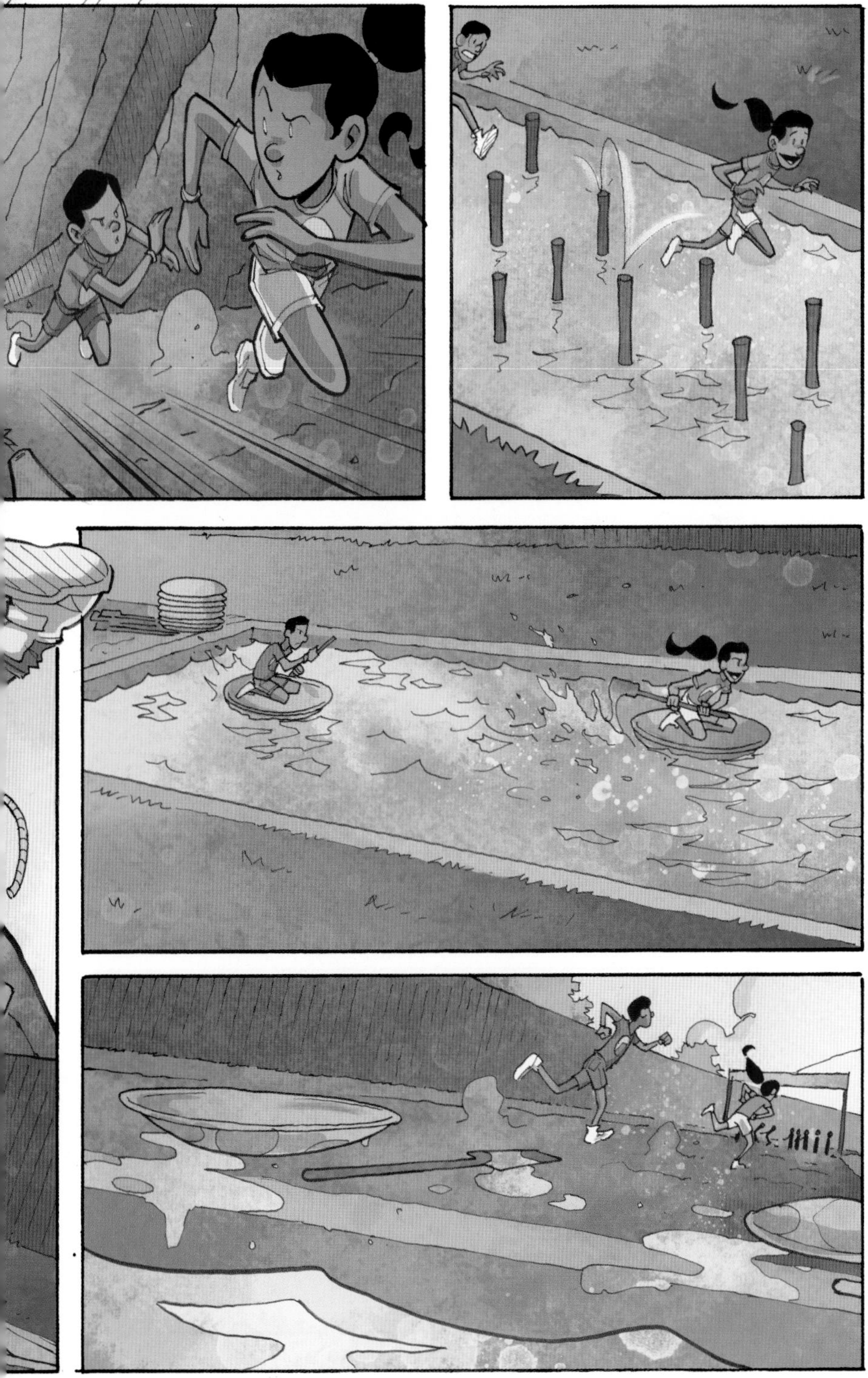

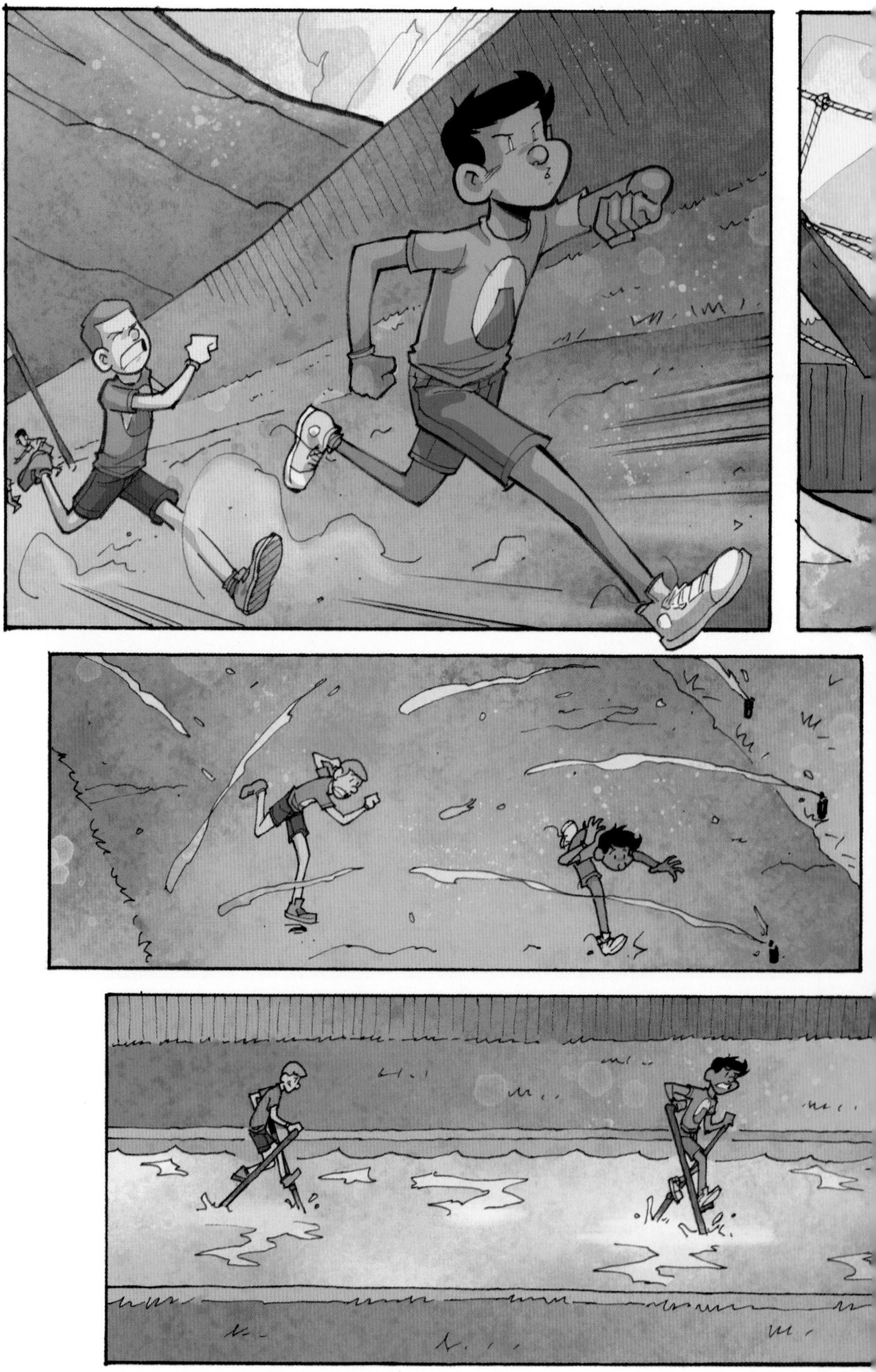

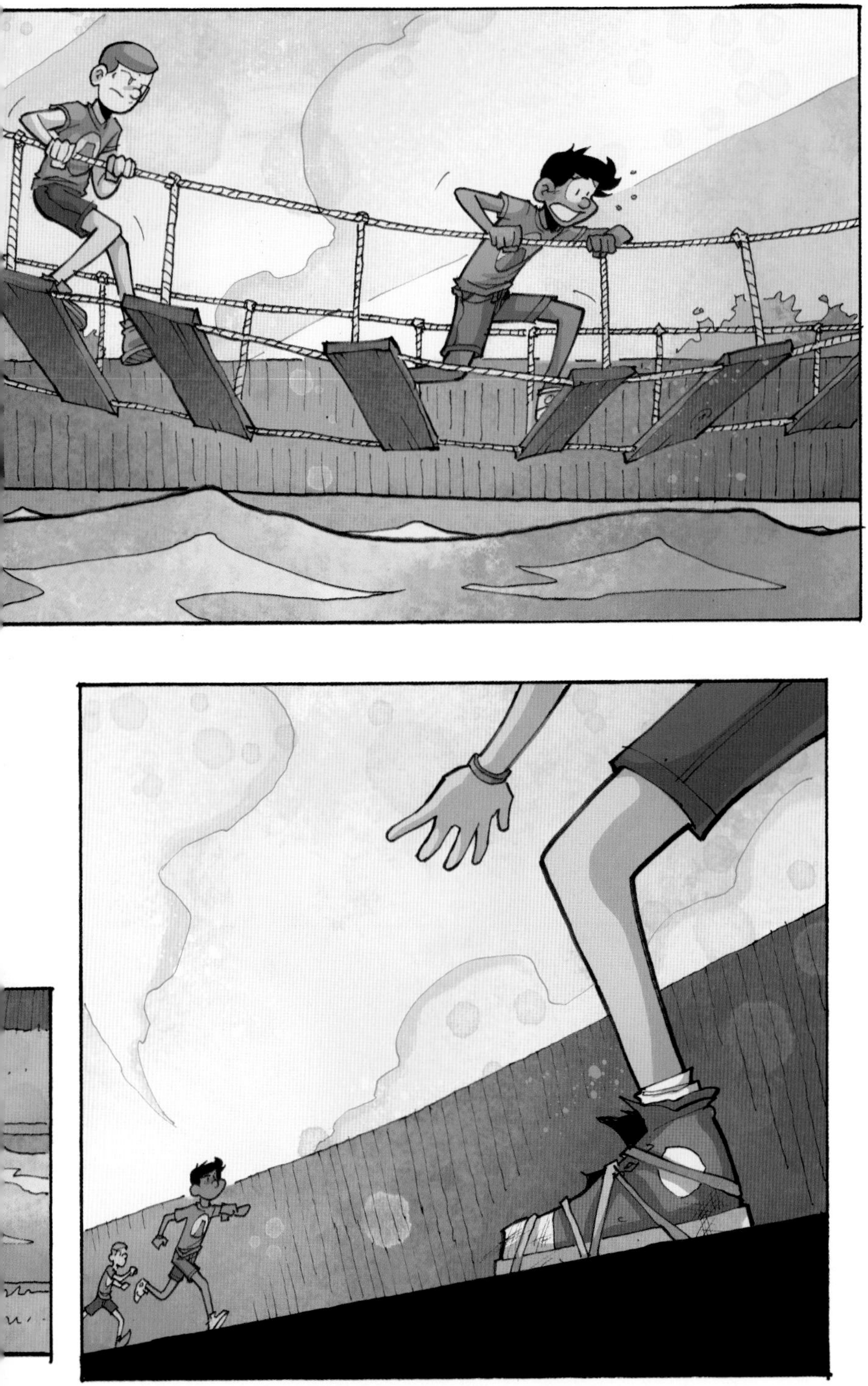

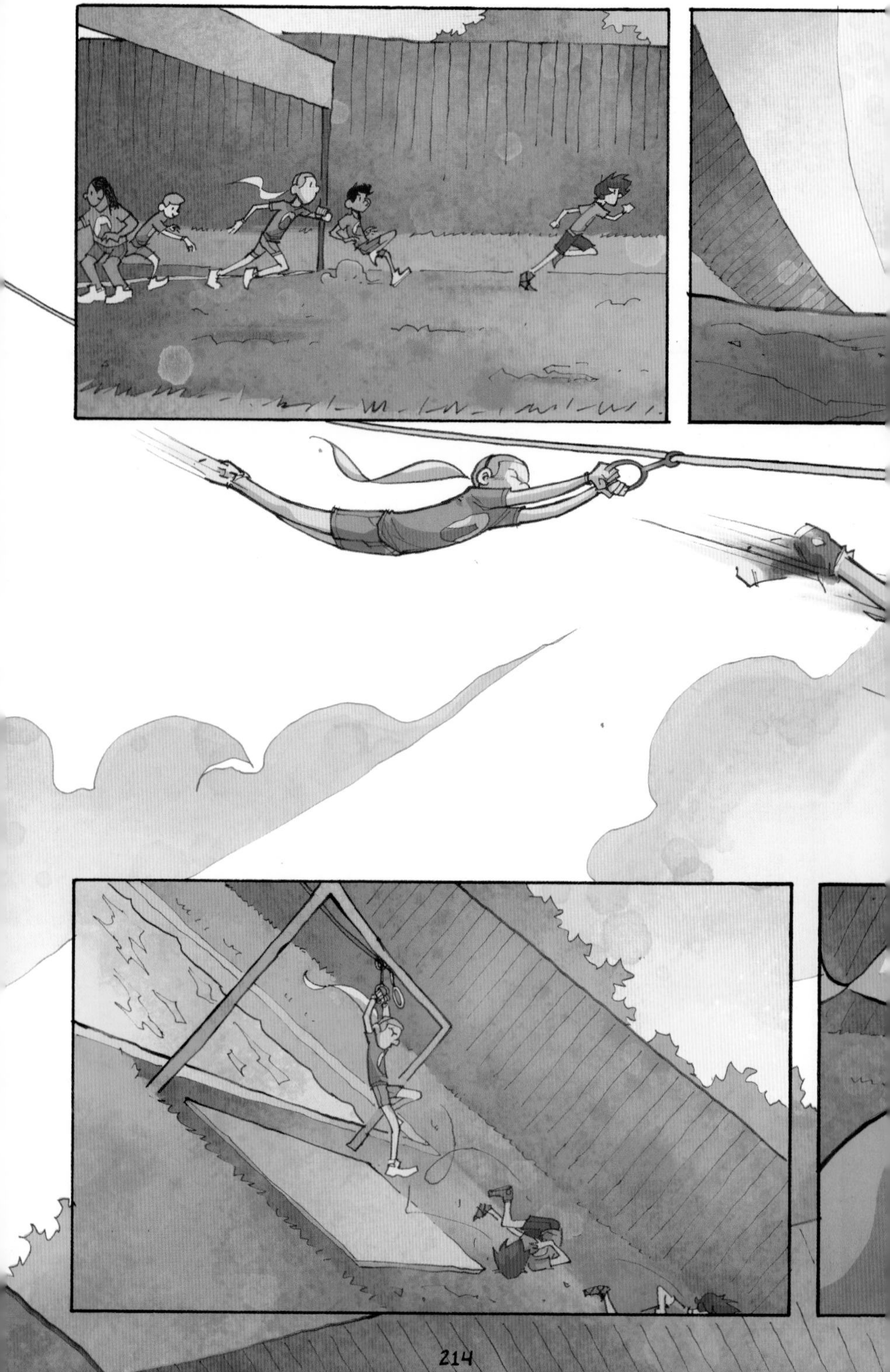

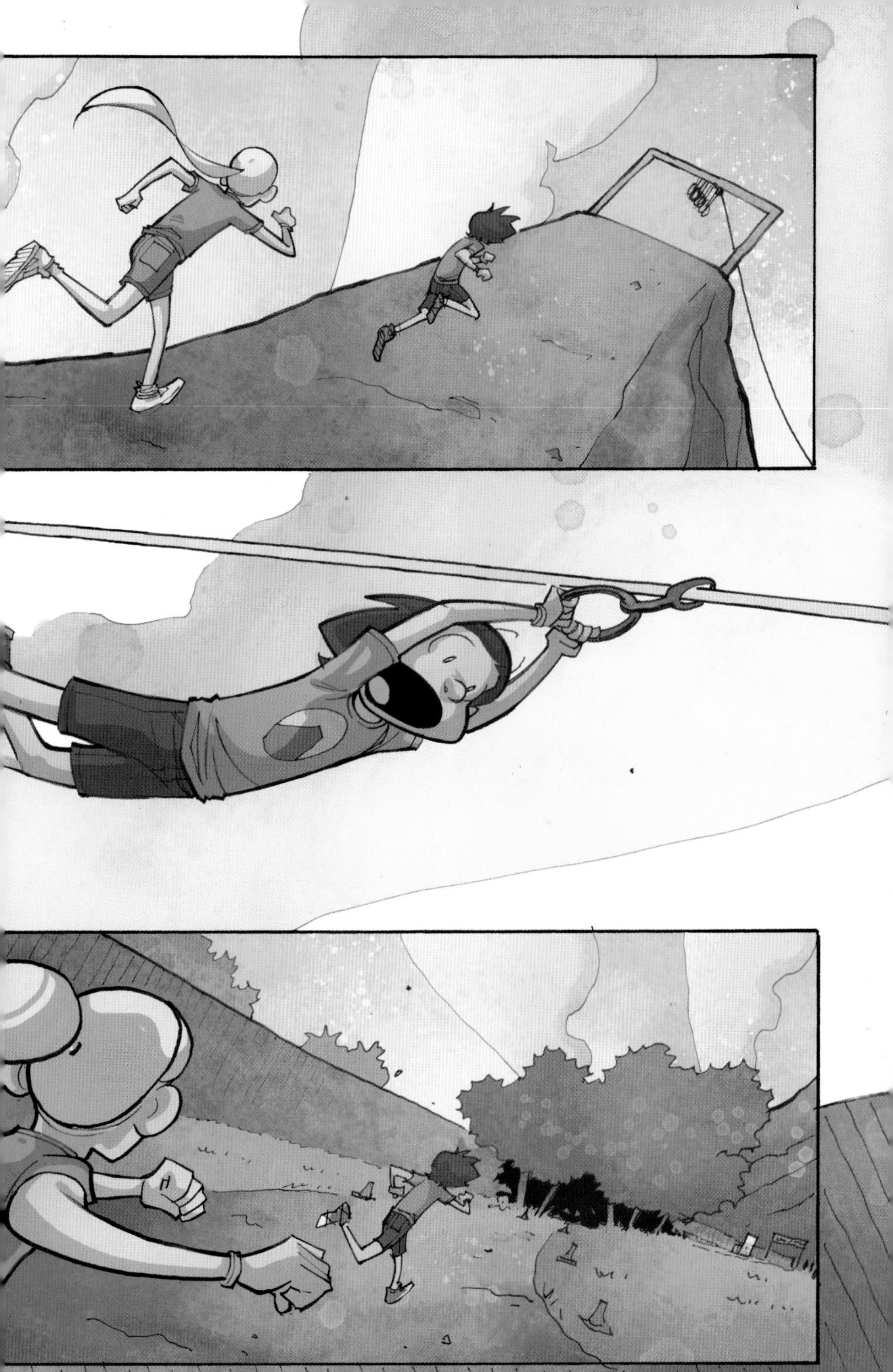

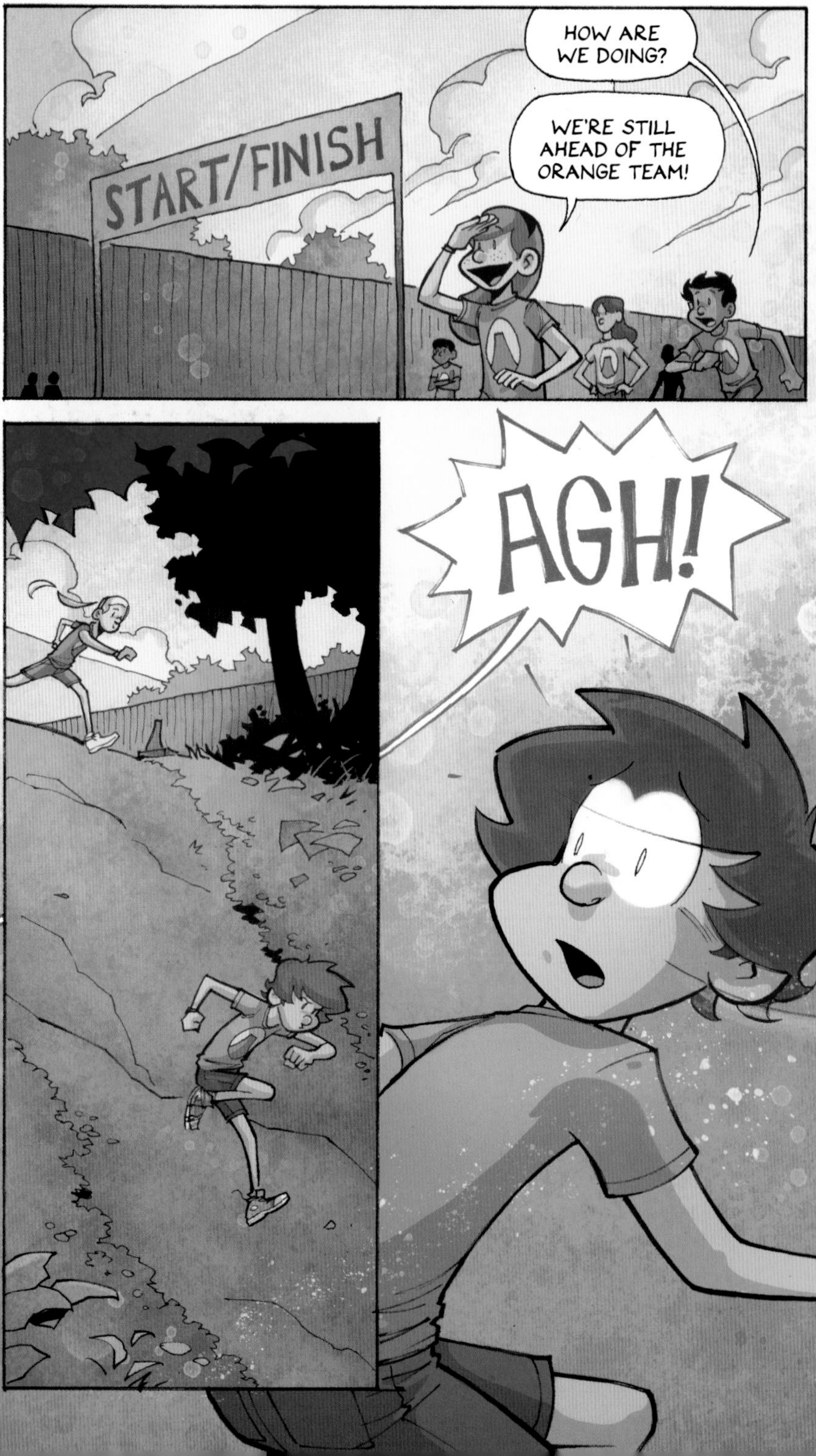
START/FINISH
HOW ARE WE DOING?
WE'RE STILL AHEAD OF THE ORANGE TEAM!
AGH!

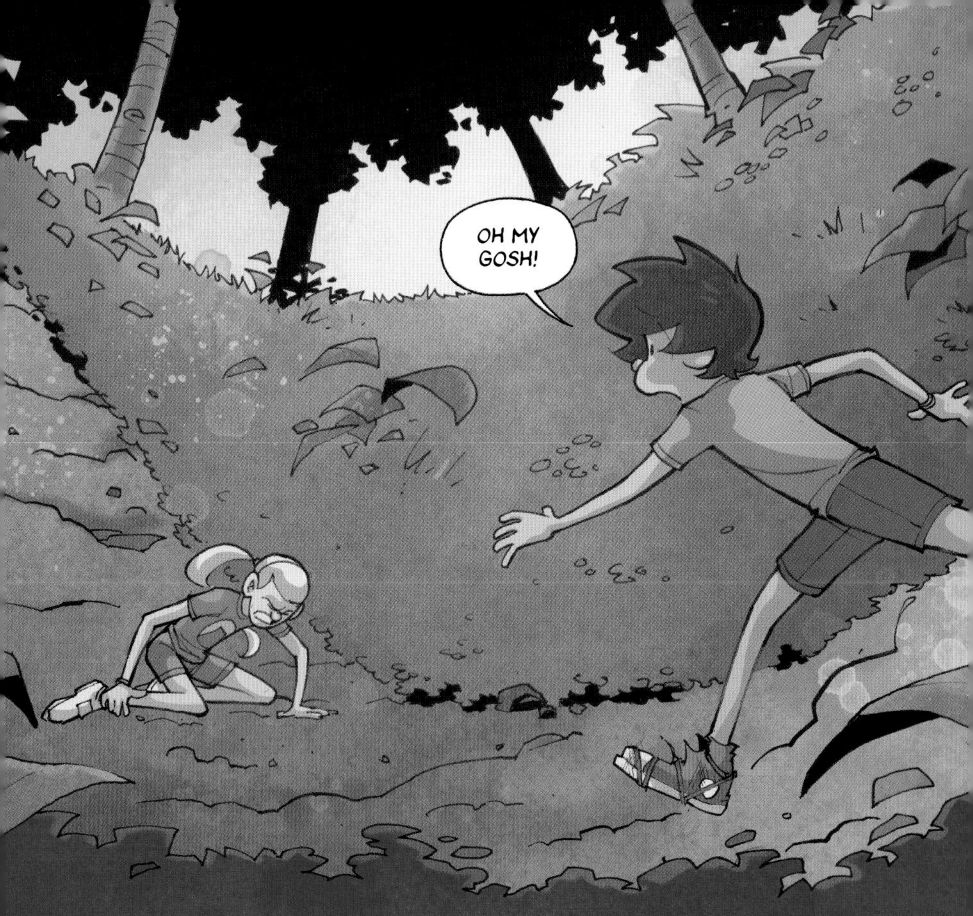
OH MY
GOSH!

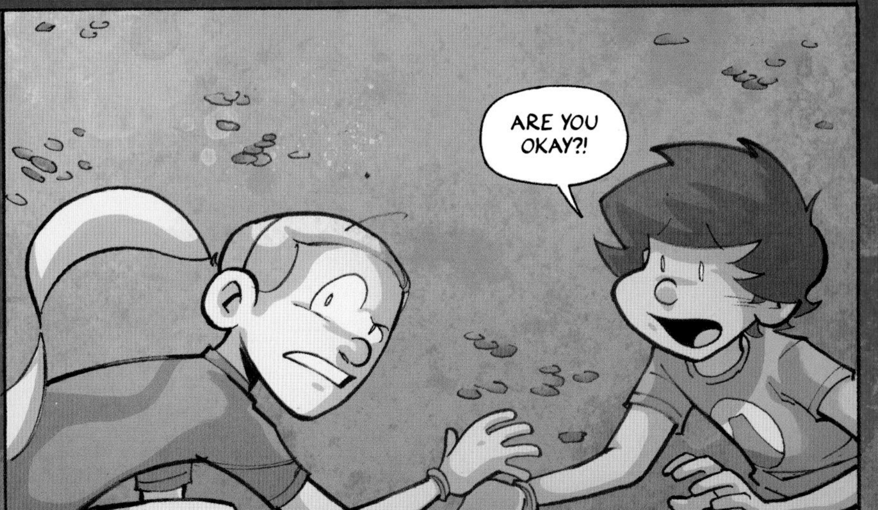
ARE YOU
OKAY?!

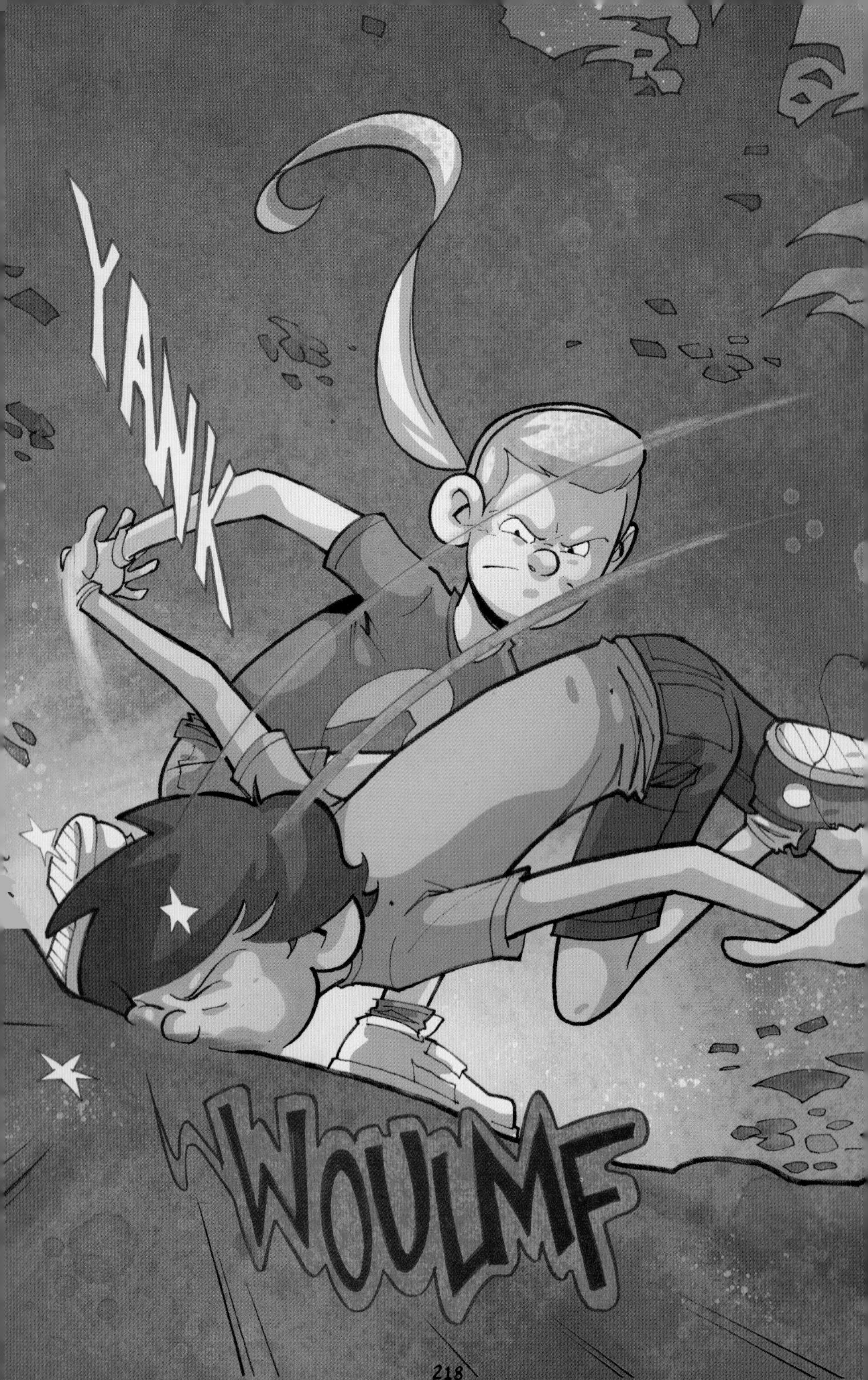
YANK
WOUMF

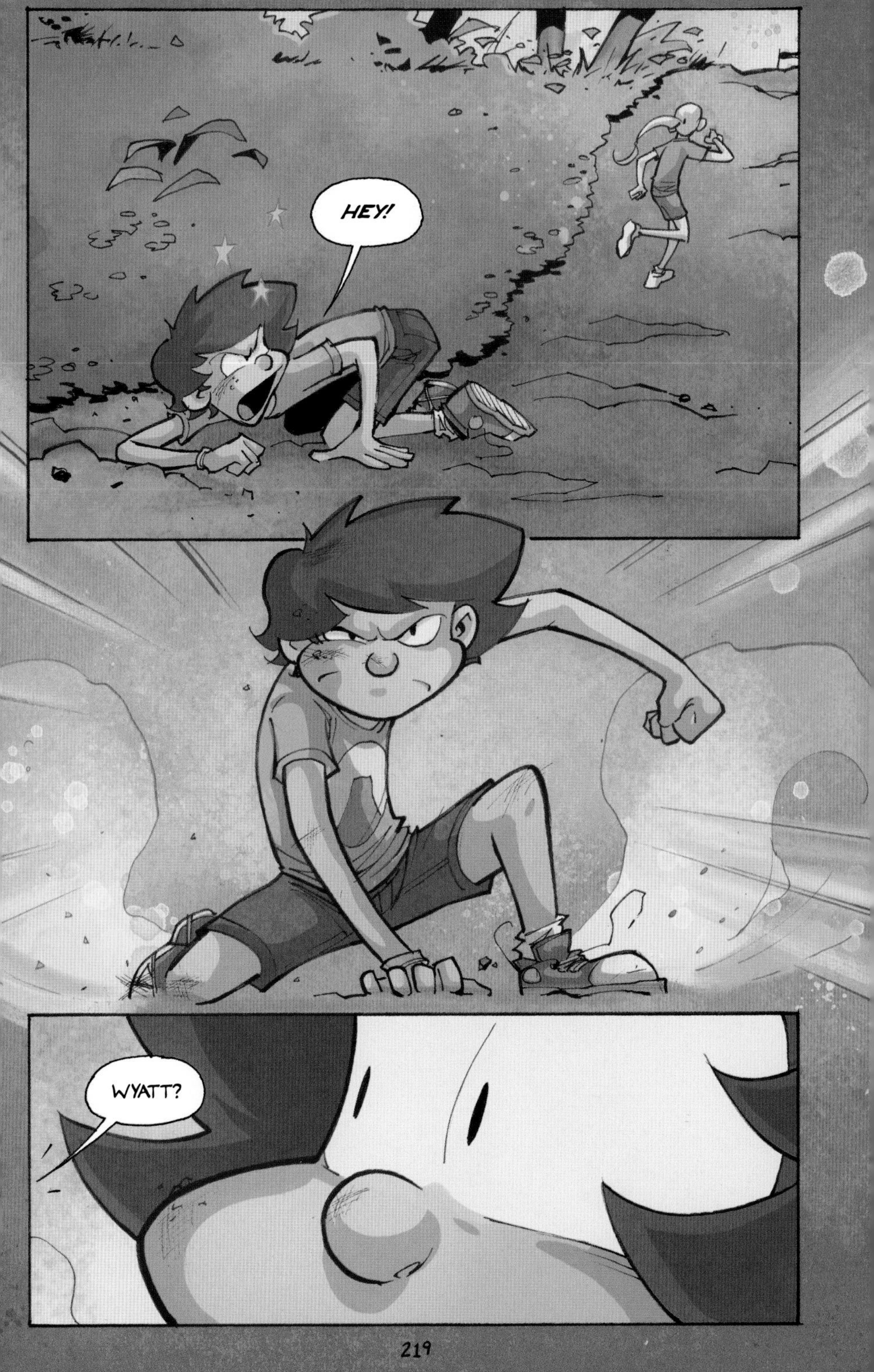
HEY!
WYATT?

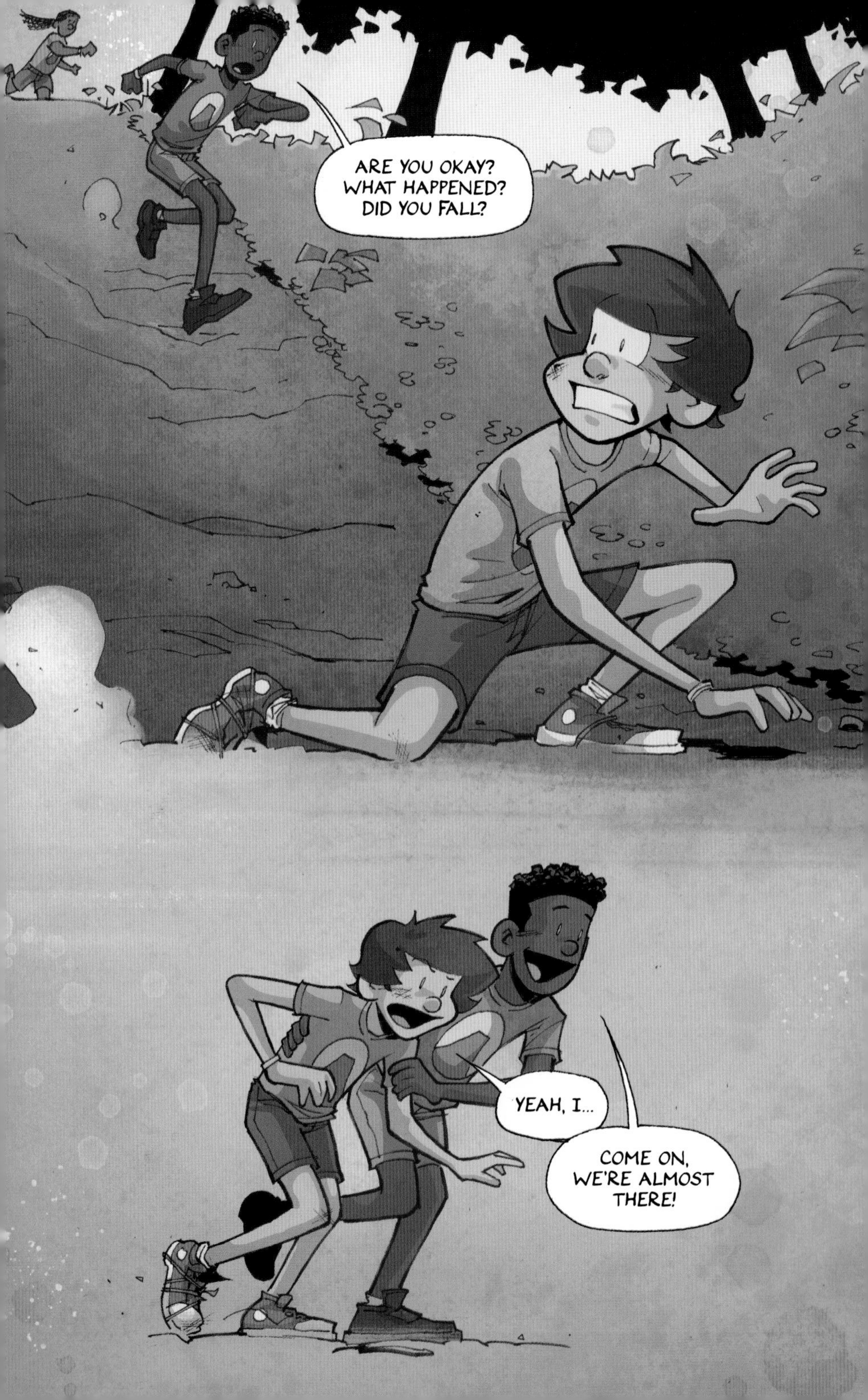
ARE YOU OKAY? WHAT HAPPENED? DID YOU FALL?
YEAH, I...
COME ON, WE'RE ALMOST THERE!

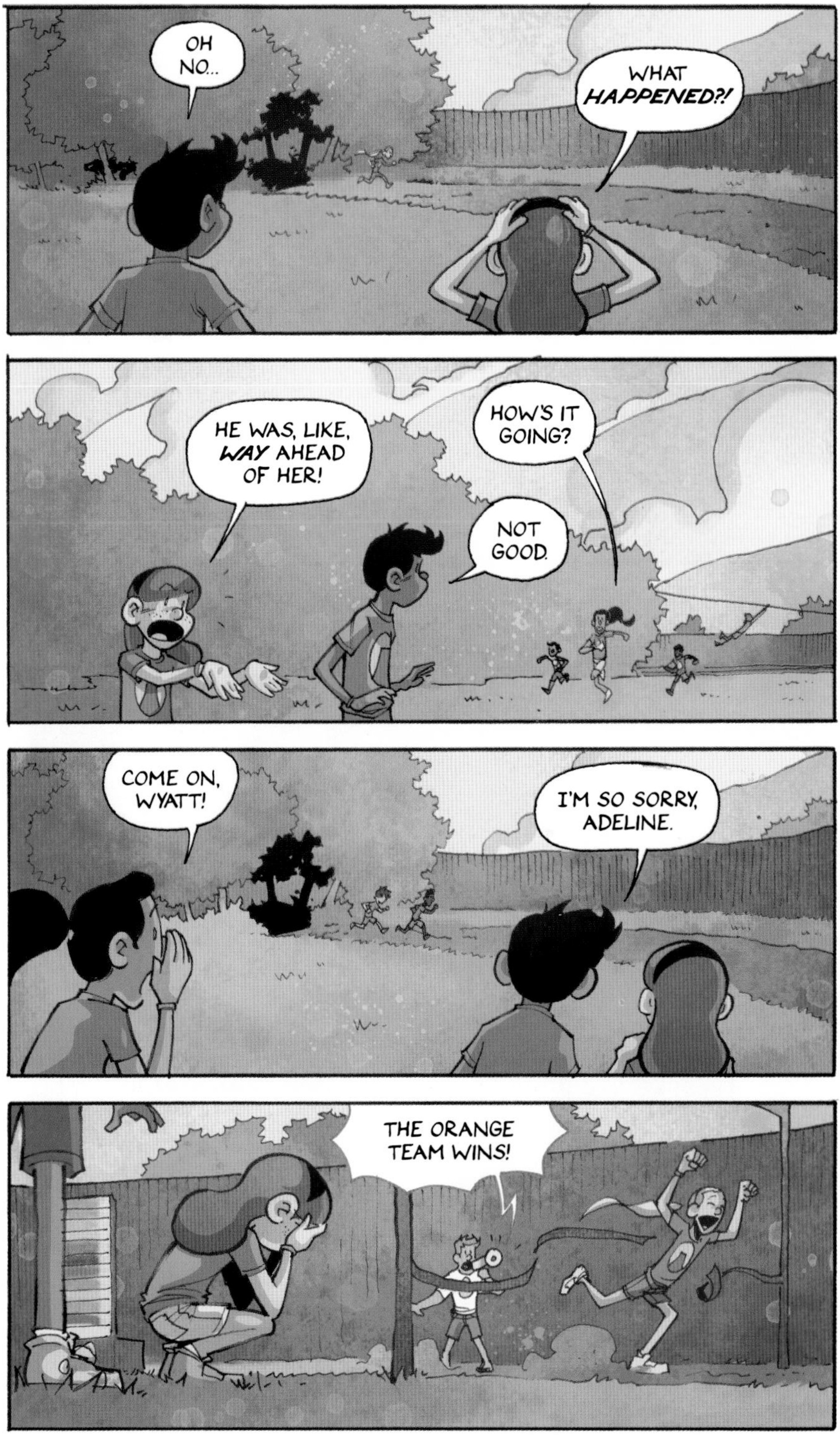
OH NO...
WHAT HAPPENED?!
HE WAS, LIKE, WAY AHEAD OF HER!
HOW'S IT GOING?
NOT GOOD.
COME ON, WYATT!
I'M SO SORRY, ADELINE.
THE ORANGE TEAM WINS!

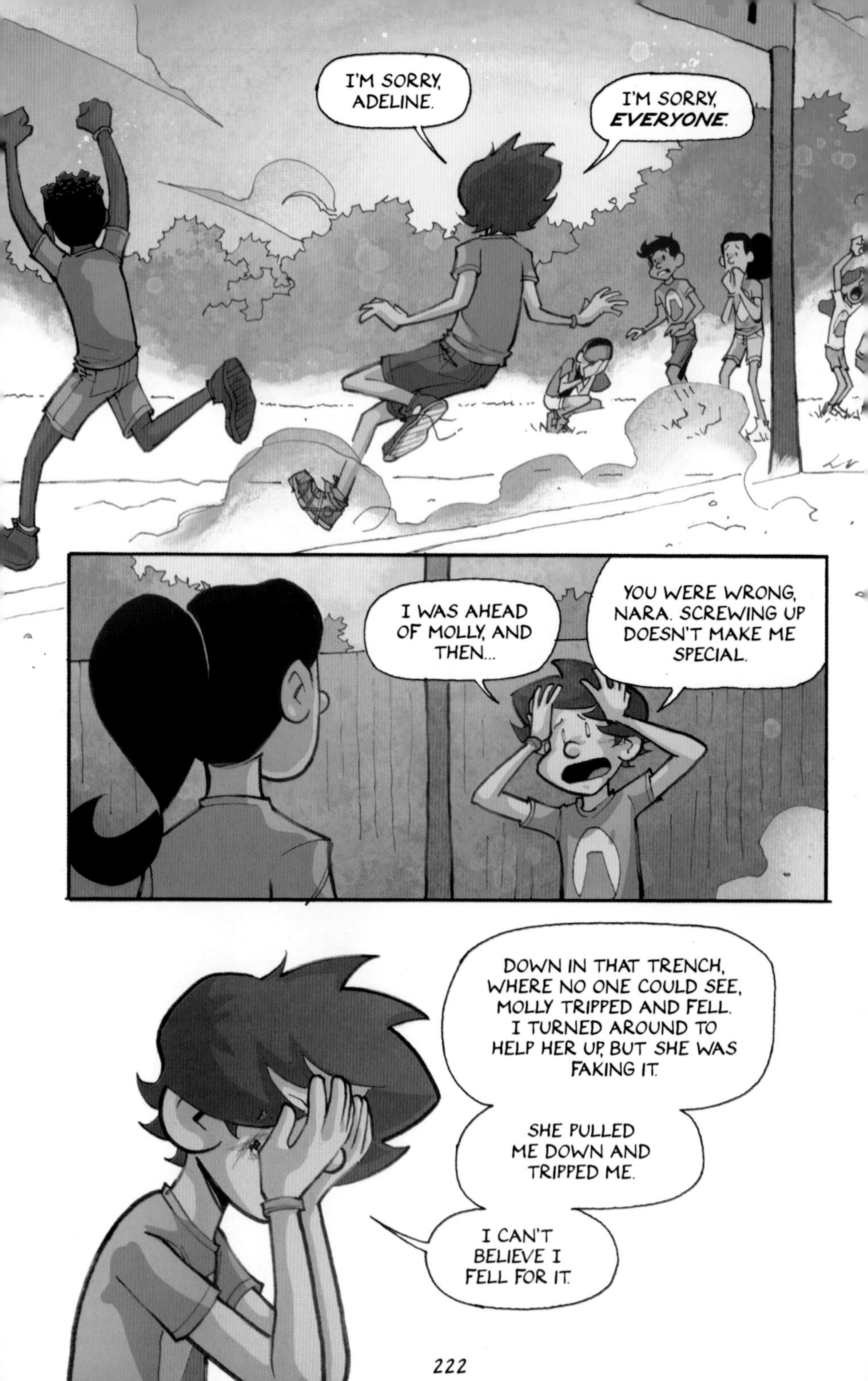
I'M SORRY, ADELINE.
I'M SORRY, EVERYONE.
I WAS AHEAD OF MOLLY, AND THEN...
YOU WERE WRONG, NARA. SCREWING UP DOESN'T MAKE ME SPECIAL.
DOWN IN THAT TRENCH, WHERE NO ONE COULD SEE, MOLLY TRIPPED AND FELL. I TURNED AROUND TO HELP HER UP, BUT SHE WAS FAKING IT.
SHE PULLED ME DOWN AND TRIPPED ME.
I CAN'T BELIEVE I FELL FOR IT.

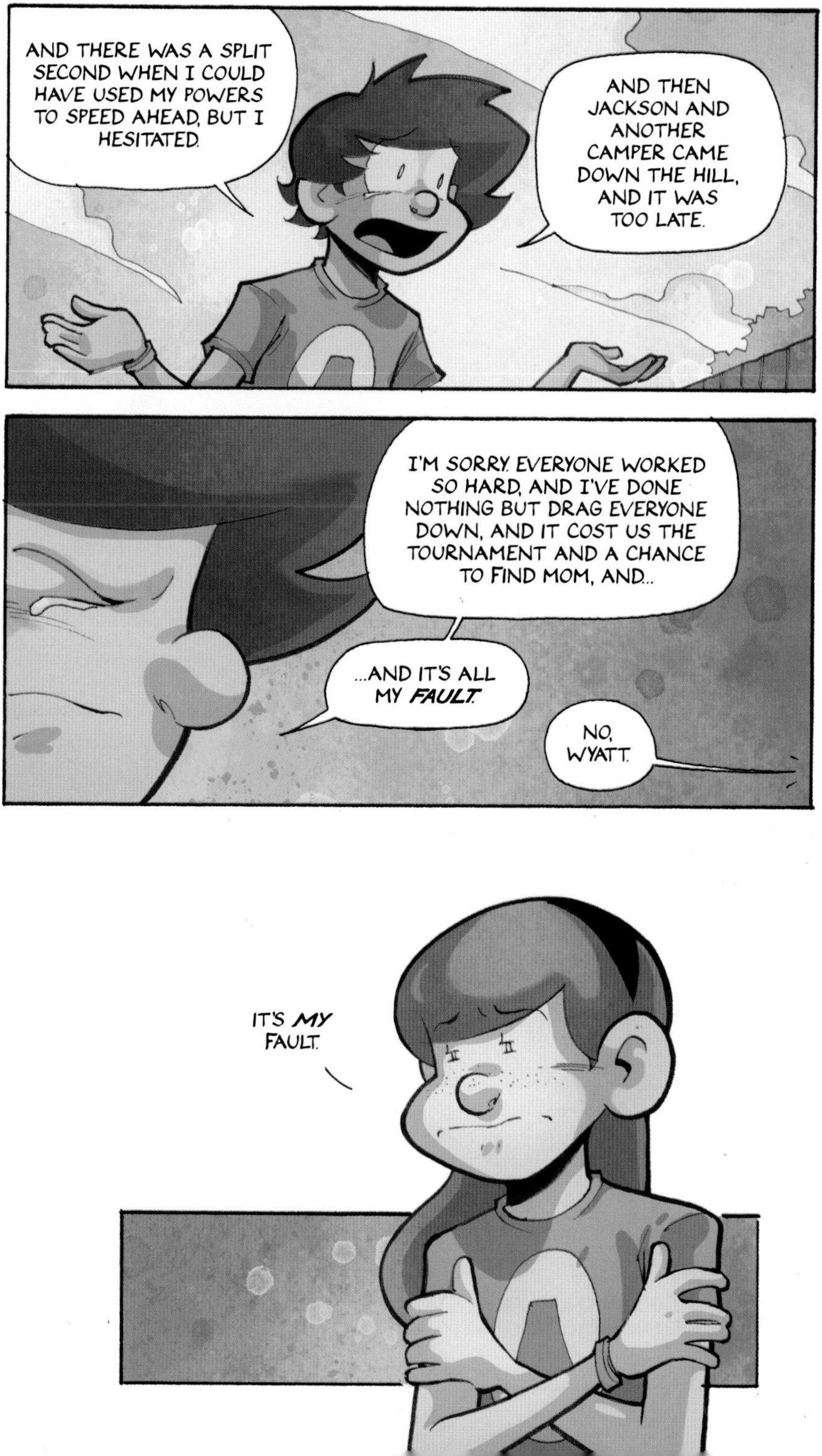
AND THERE WAS A SPLIT SECOND WHEN I COULD HAVE USED MY POWERS TO SPEED AHEAD, BUT I HESITATED.
AND THEN JACKSON AND ANOTHER CAMPER CAME DOWN THE HILL, AND IT WAS TOO LATE.
I'M SORRY. EVERYONE WORKED SO HARD, AND I'VE DONE NOTHING BUT DRAG EVERYONE DOWN, AND IT COST US THE TOURNAMENT AND A CHANCE TO FIND MOM, AND...
...AND IT'S ALL MY FAULT.
NO, WYATT.
IT'S MY FAULT.

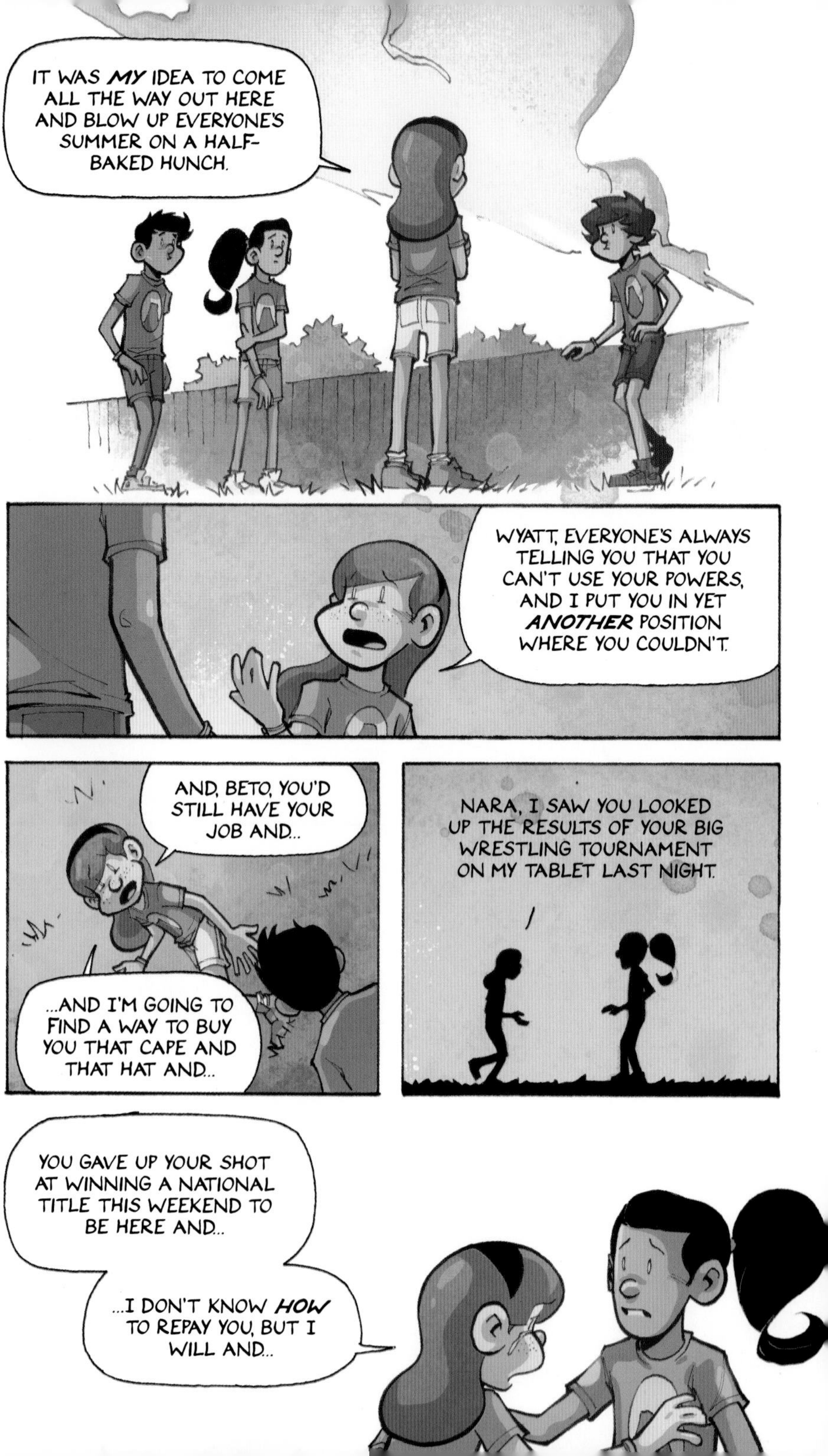
IT WAS MY IDEA TO COME ALL THE WAY OUT HERE AND BLOW UP EVERYONE'S SUMMER ON A HALF-BAKED HUNCH.
WYATT, EVERYONE'S ALWAYS TELLING YOU THAT YOU CAN'T USE YOUR POWERS, AND I PUT YOU IN YET ANOTHER POSITION WHERE YOU COULDN'T.
AND, BETO, YOU'D STILL HAVE YOUR JOB AND...
...AND I'M GOING TO FIND A WAY TO BUY YOU THAT CAPE AND THAT HAT AND...
NARA, I SAW YOU LOOKED UP THE RESULTS OF YOUR BIG WRESTLING TOURNAMENT ON MY TABLET LAST NIGHT.
YOU GAVE UP YOUR SHOT AT WINNING A NATIONAL TITLE THIS WEEKEND TO BE HERE AND...
...I DON'T KNOW HOW TO REPAY YOU, BUT I WILL AND...

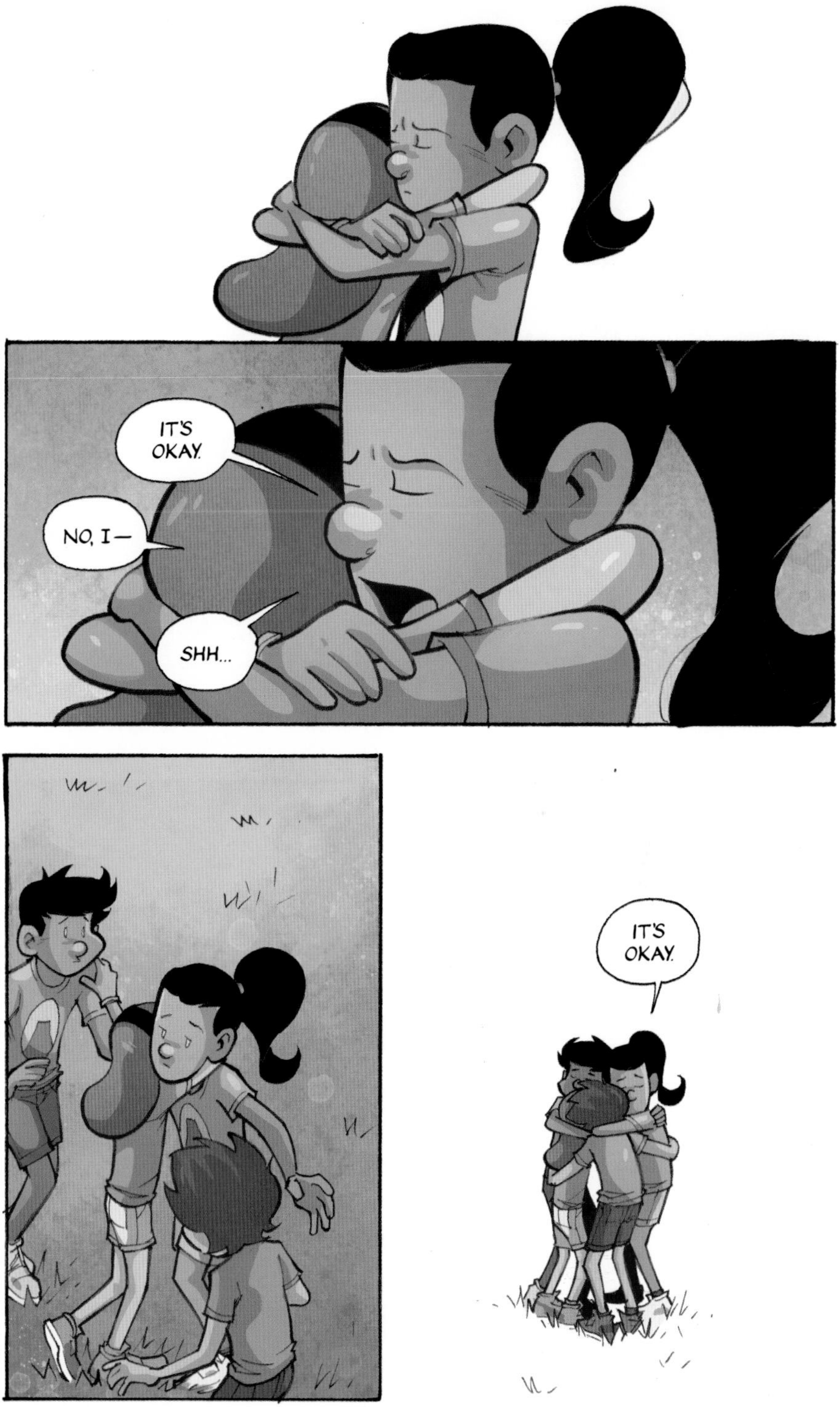
IT'S OKAY.
NO, I—
SHH...
IT'S OKAY.

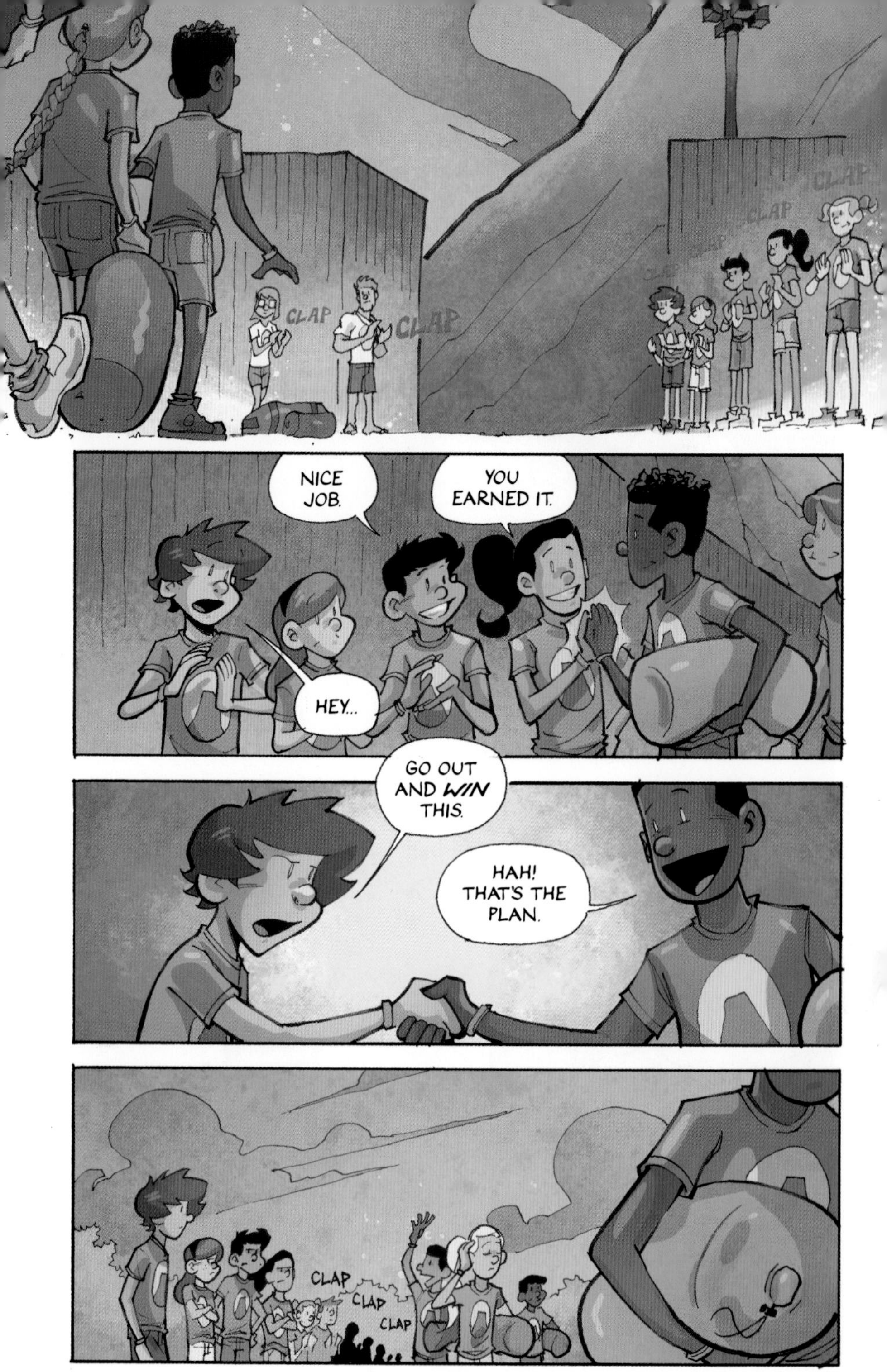
CLAP
CLAP
CLAP
CLAP
CLAP
CLAP
NICE JOB.
YOU EARNED IT.
HEY...
GO OUT AND *WIN* THIS.
HAH! THAT'S THE PLAN.
CLAP
CLAP
CLAP

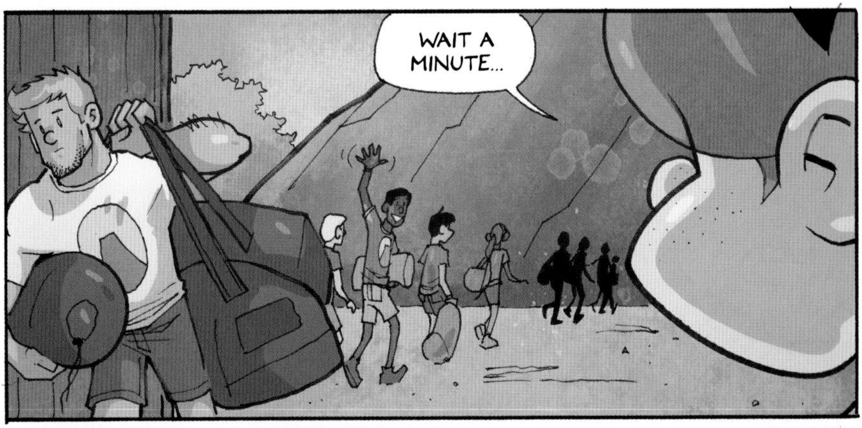
WAIT A MINUTE...

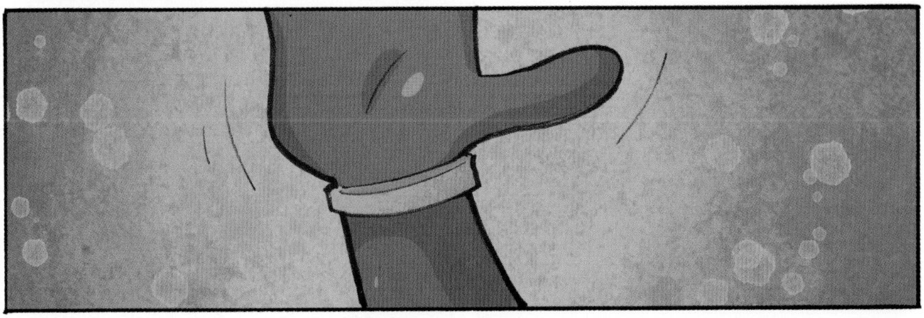

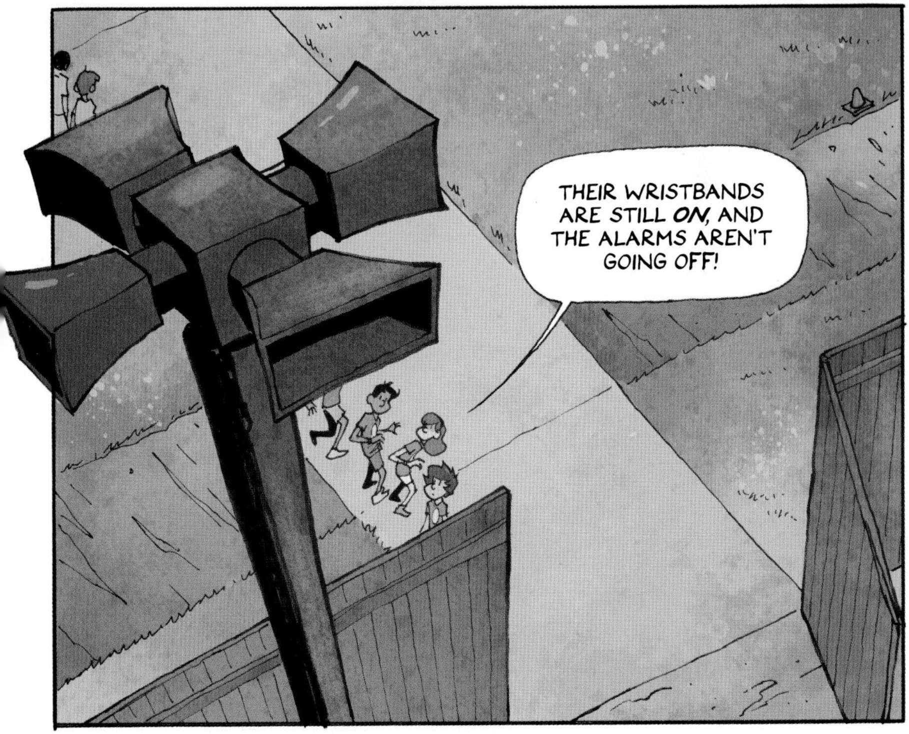
THEIR WRISTBANDS ARE STILL ON, AND THE ALARMS AREN'T GOING OFF!

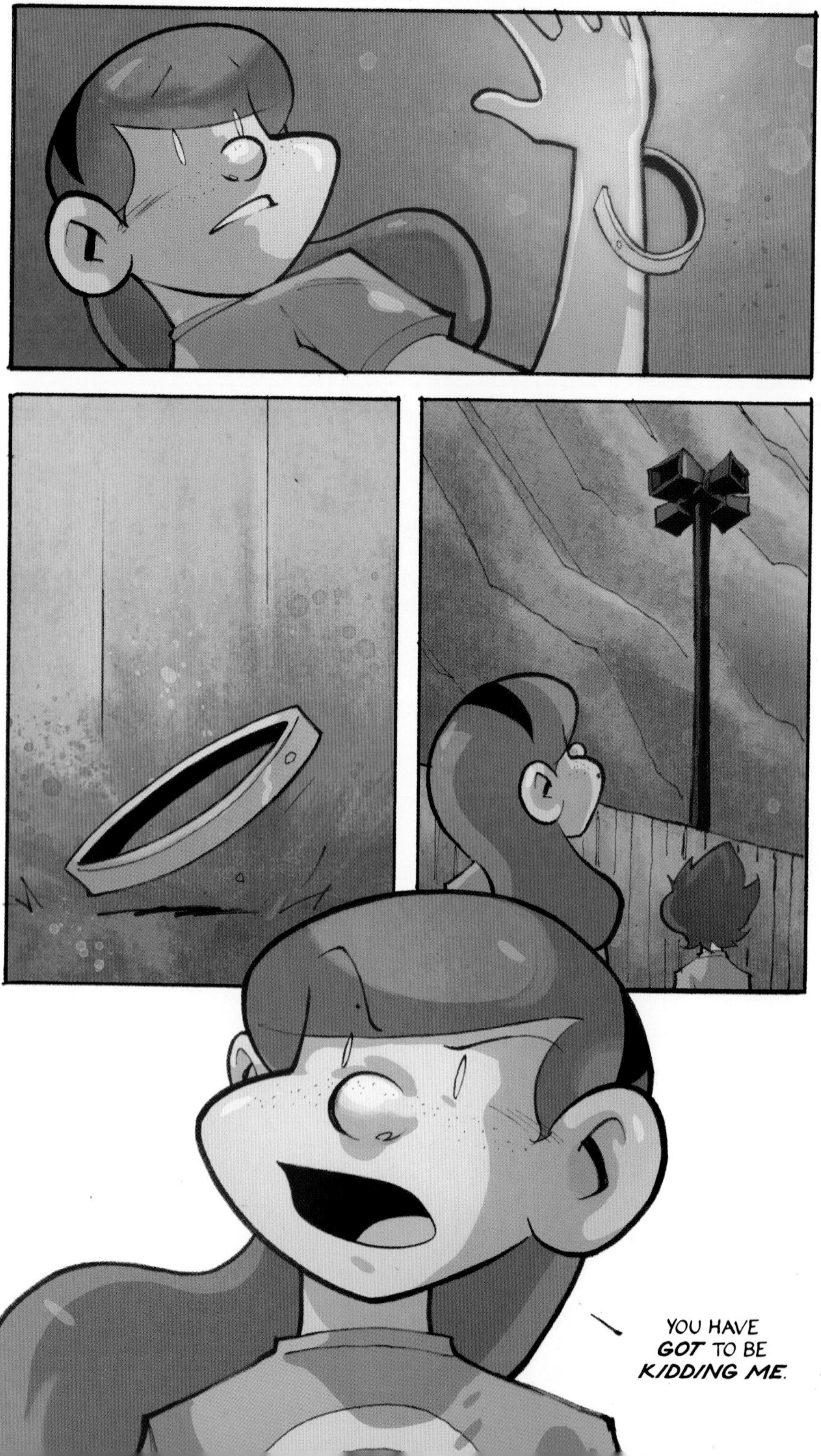
YOU HAVE **GOT** TO BE **KIDDING ME**.

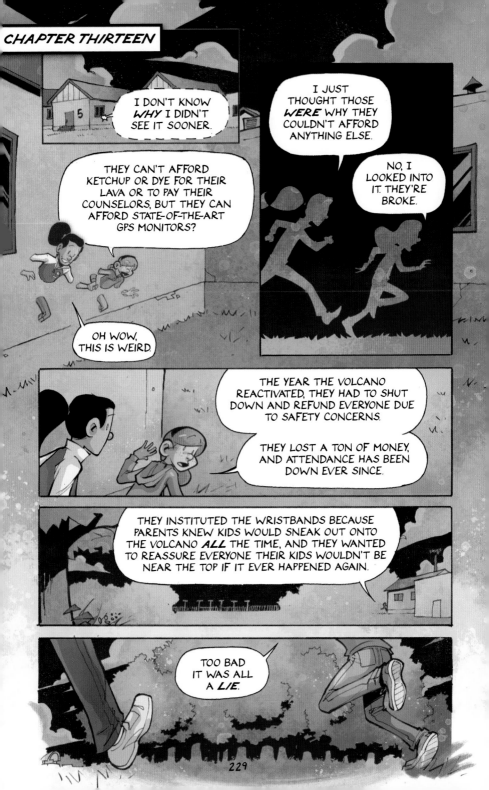

CHAPTER THIRTEEN

I DON'T KNOW *WHY* I DIDN'T SEE IT SOONER.

I JUST THOUGHT THOSE *WERE* WHY THEY COULDN'T AFFORD ANYTHING ELSE.

THEY CAN'T AFFORD KETCHUP OR DYE FOR THEIR LAVA OR TO PAY THEIR COUNSELORS, BUT THEY CAN AFFORD STATE-OF-THE-ART GPS MONITORS?

NO, I LOOKED INTO IT. THEY'RE BROKE.

OH WOW, THIS IS WEIRD.

THE YEAR THE VOLCANO REACTIVATED, THEY HAD TO SHUT DOWN AND REFUND EVERYONE DUE TO SAFETY CONCERNS.

THEY LOST A TON OF MONEY, AND ATTENDANCE HAS BEEN DOWN EVER SINCE.

THEY INSTITUTED THE WRISTBANDS BECAUSE PARENTS KNEW KIDS WOULD SNEAK OUT ONTO THE VOLCANO *ALL* THE TIME, AND THEY WANTED TO REASSURE EVERYONE THEIR KIDS WOULDN'T BE NEAR THE TOP IF IT EVER HAPPENED AGAIN.

TOO BAD IT WAS ALL A *LIE.*

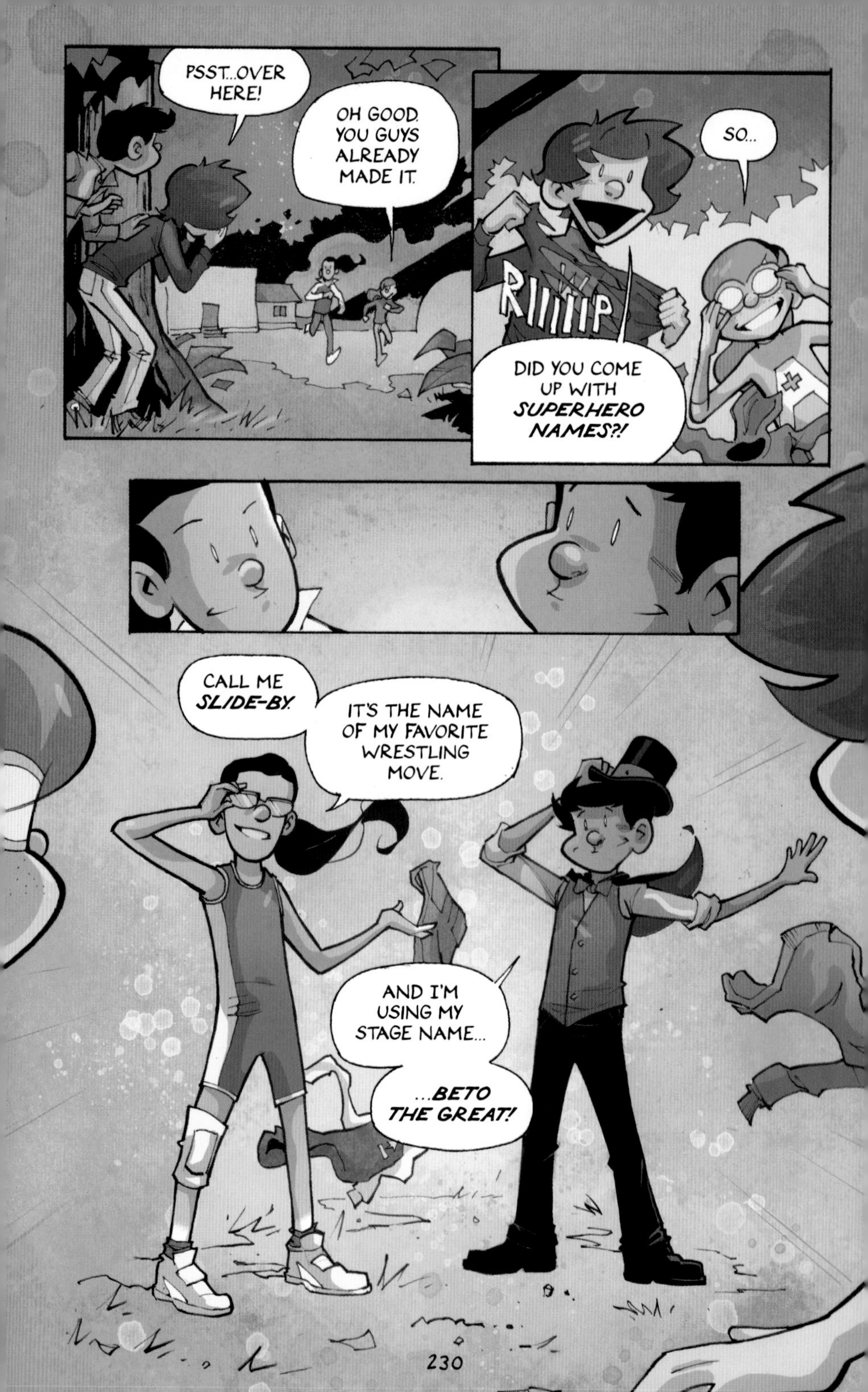
PSST...OVER HERE!
OH GOOD. YOU GUYS ALREADY MADE IT.
SO...
RIIIIP
DID YOU COME UP WITH *SUPERHERO NAMES?!*
CALL ME *SLIDE-BY.*
IT'S THE NAME OF MY FAVORITE WRESTLING MOVE.
AND I'M USING MY STAGE NAME...
...BETO THE GREAT!

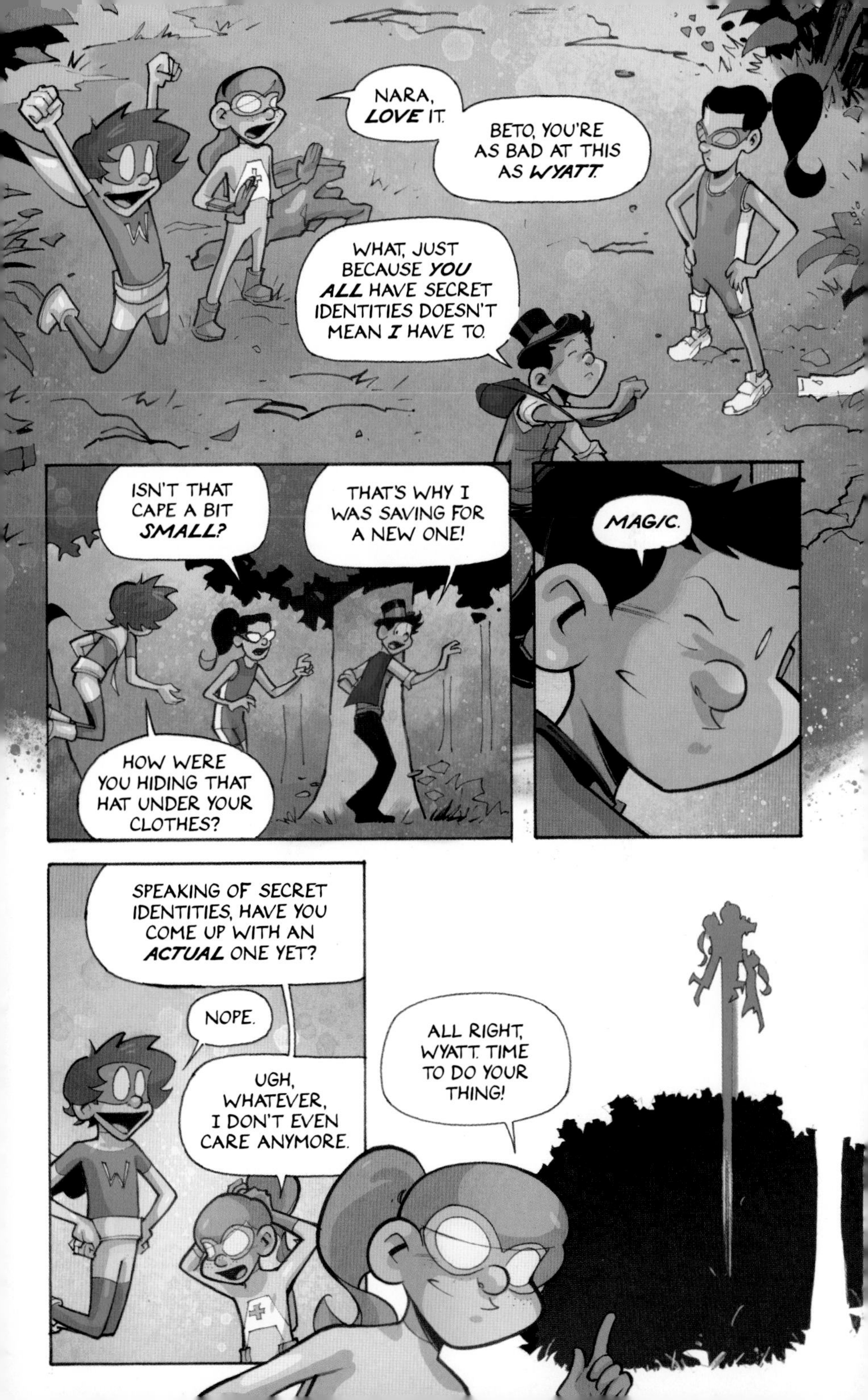
NARA, LOVE IT.
BETO, YOU'RE AS BAD AT THIS AS WYATT.
WHAT, JUST BECAUSE YOU ALL HAVE SECRET IDENTITIES DOESN'T MEAN I HAVE TO.
ISN'T THAT CAPE A BIT SMALL?
THAT'S WHY I WAS SAVING FOR A NEW ONE!
HOW WERE YOU HIDING THAT HAT UNDER YOUR CLOTHES?
MAGIC.
SPEAKING OF SECRET IDENTITIES, HAVE YOU COME UP WITH AN ACTUAL ONE YET?
NOPE.
UGH, WHATEVER, I DON'T EVEN CARE ANYMORE.
ALL RIGHT, WYATT. TIME TO DO YOUR THING!

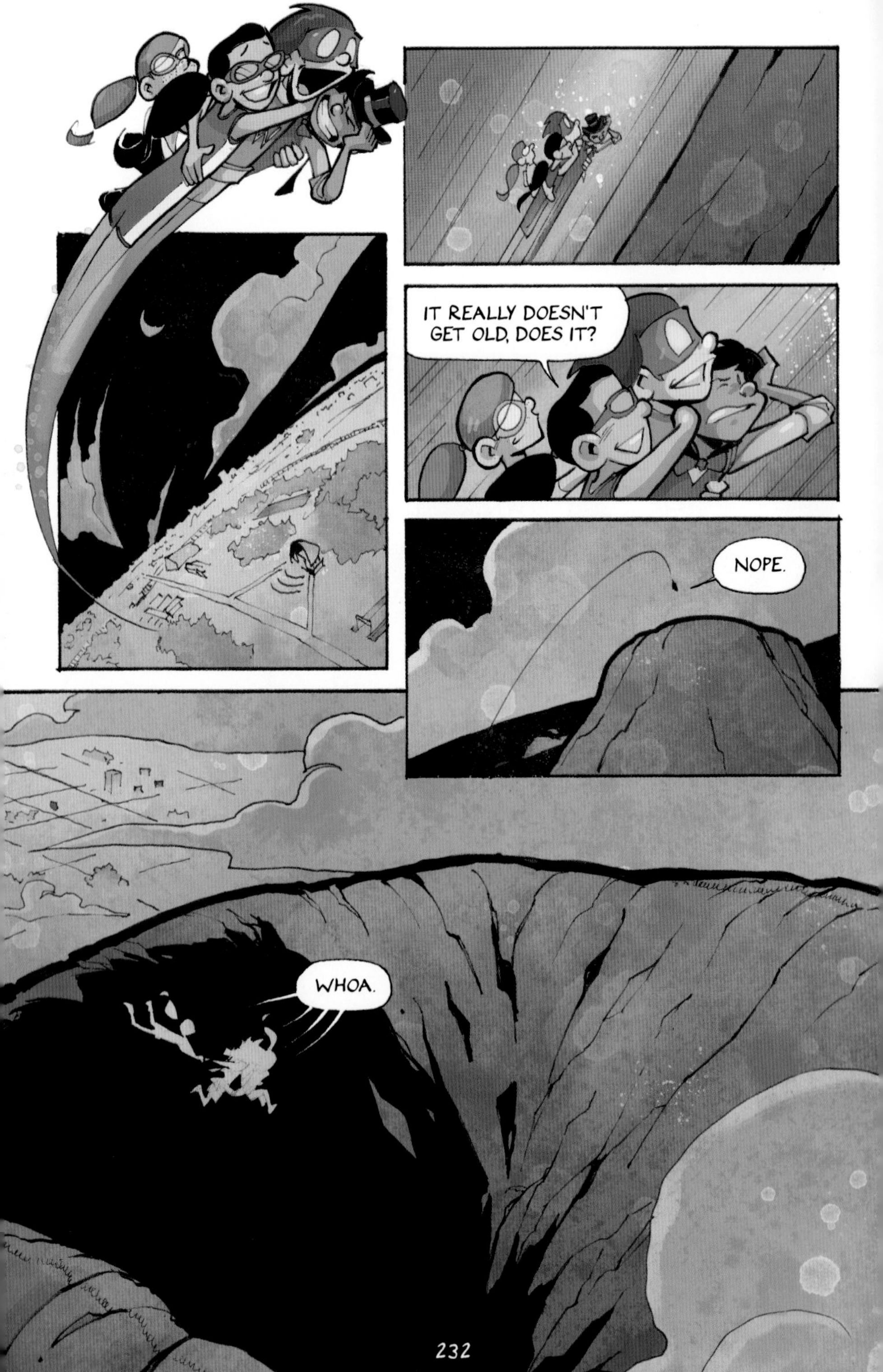
IT REALLY DOESN'T GET OLD, DOES IT?
NOPE.
WHOA.

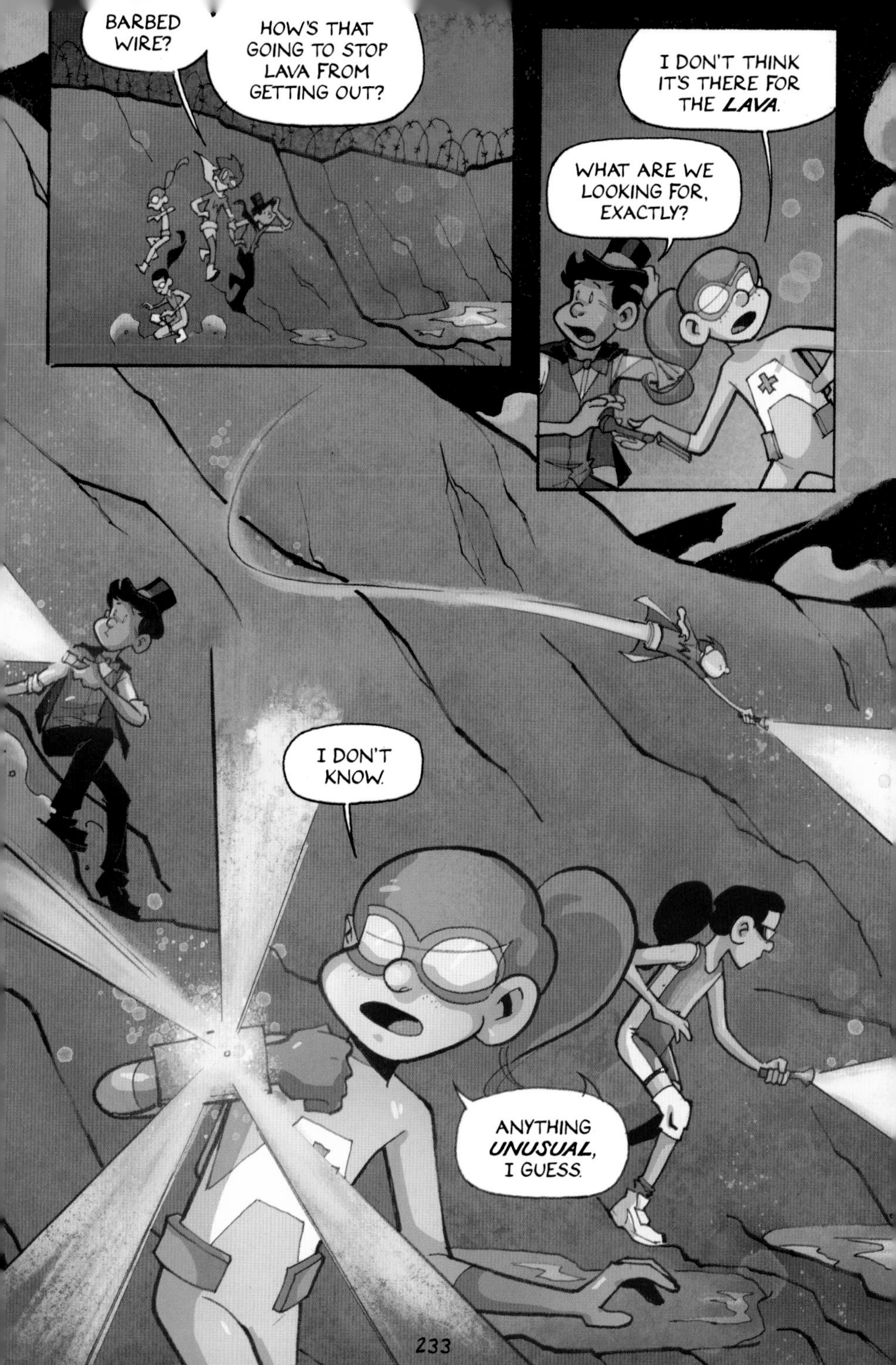
BARBED WIRE?
HOW'S THAT GOING TO STOP LAVA FROM GETTING OUT?
I DON'T THINK IT'S THERE FOR THE *LAVA*.
WHAT ARE WE LOOKING FOR, EXACTLY?
I DON'T KNOW.
ANYTHING *UNUSUAL*, I GUESS.

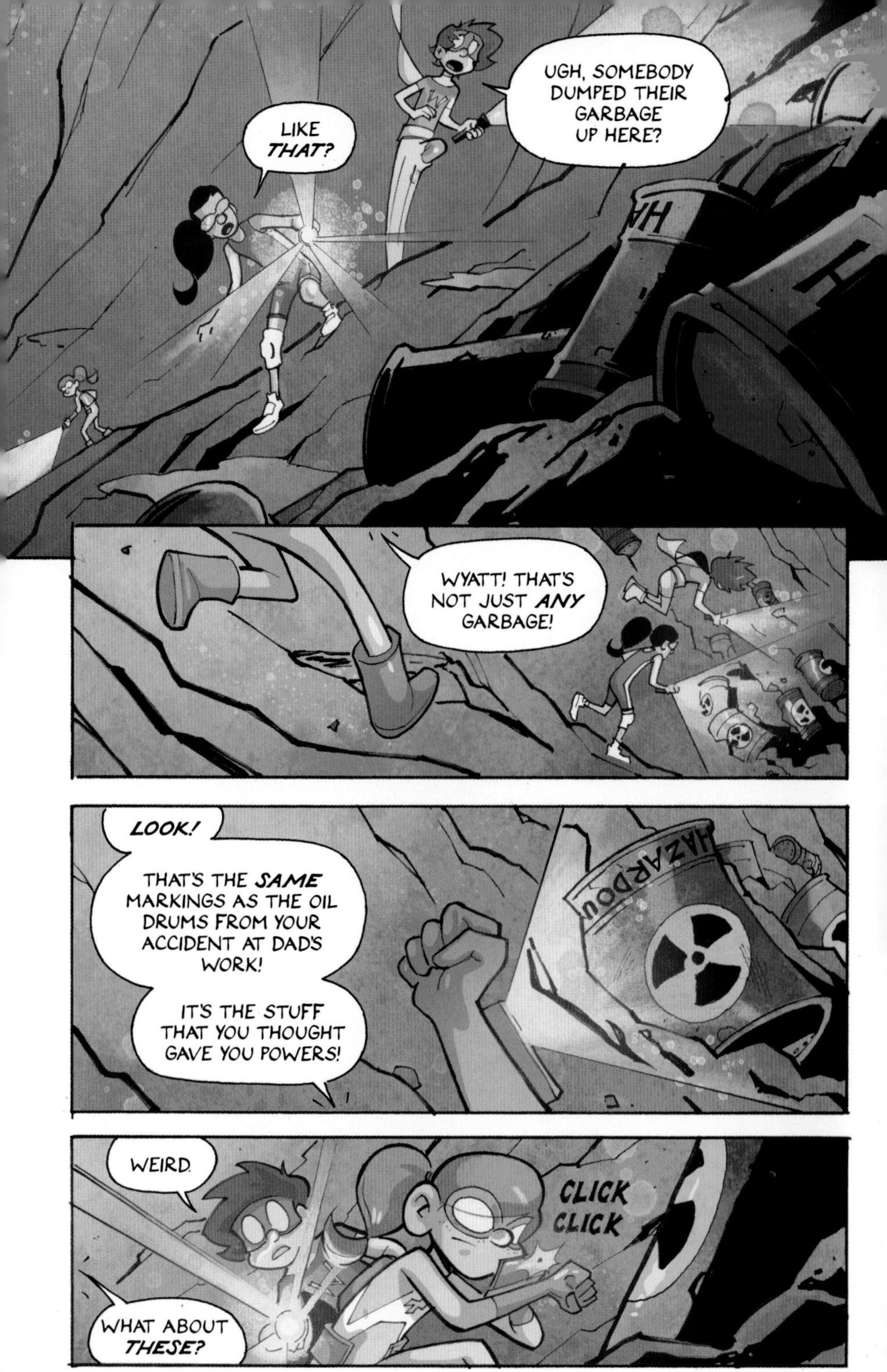
UGH, SOMEBODY DUMPED THEIR GARBAGE UP HERE?
LIKE *THAT?*
WYATT! THAT'S NOT JUST *ANY* GARBAGE!
LOOK!
THAT'S THE *SAME* MARKINGS AS THE OIL DRUMS FROM YOUR ACCIDENT AT DAD'S WORK!
IT'S THE STUFF THAT YOU THOUGHT GAVE YOU POWERS!
HAZARDOU
WEIRD.
CLICK CLICK
WHAT ABOUT *THESE?*

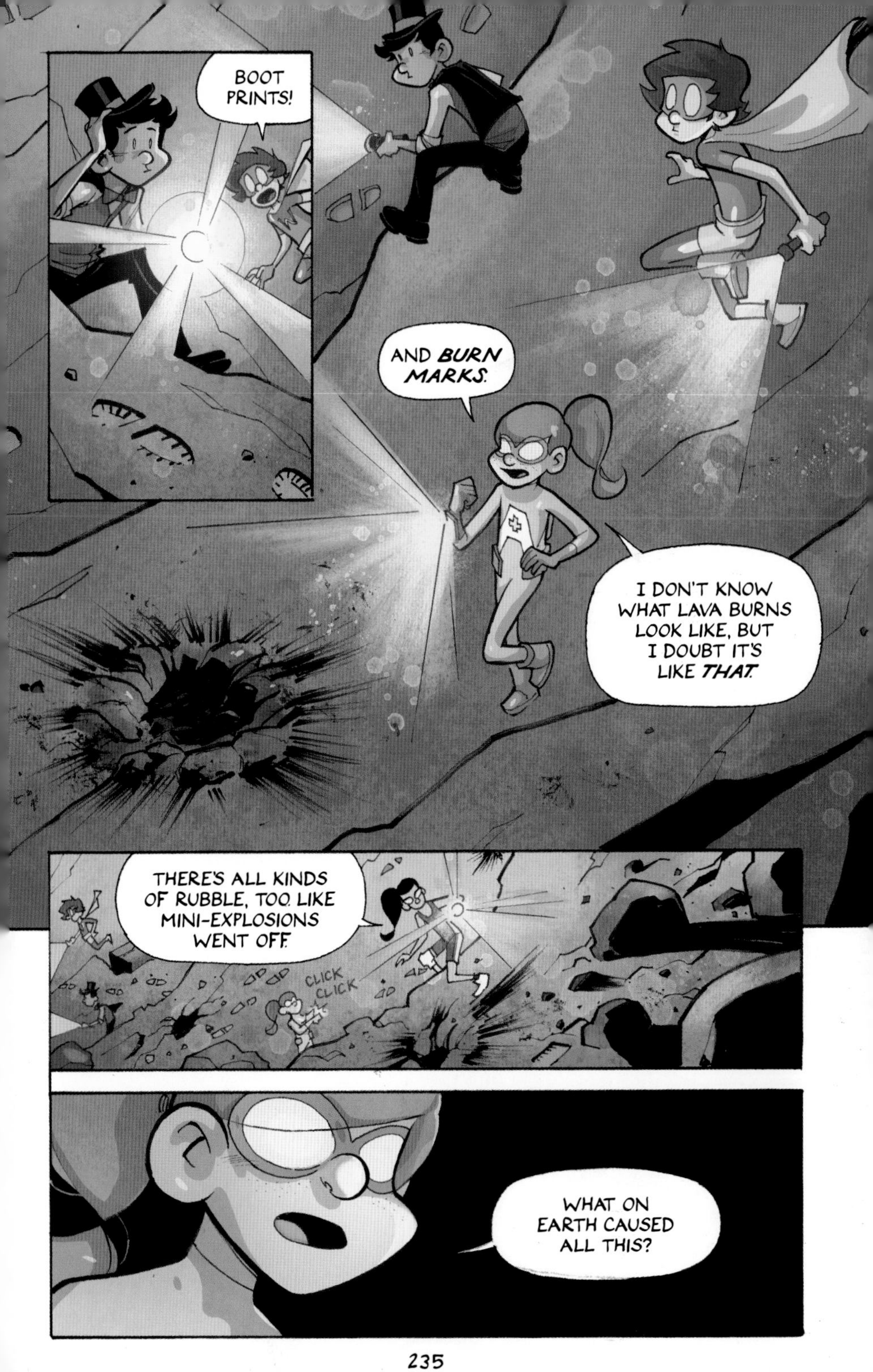
BOOT PRINTS!
AND BURN MARKS.
I DON'T KNOW WHAT LAVA BURNS LOOK LIKE, BUT I DOUBT IT'S LIKE THAT.
THERE'S ALL KINDS OF RUBBLE, TOO. LIKE MINI-EXPLOSIONS WENT OFF.
CLICK CLICK
WHAT ON EARTH CAUSED ALL THIS?

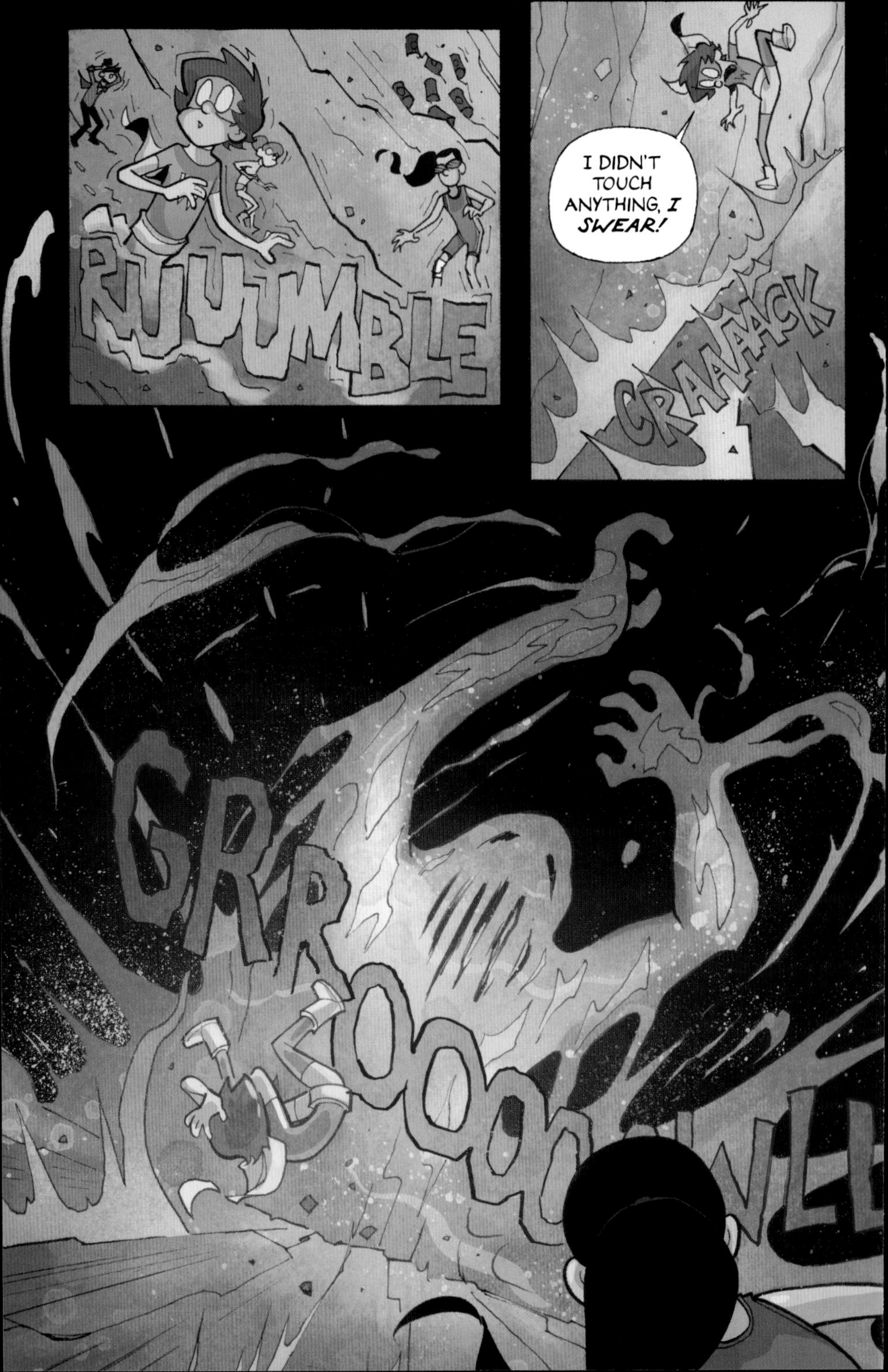
RUUUMBLE
I DIDN'T TOUCH ANYTHING, *I SWEAR!*
CRAAAACK
GRROOOOOWL

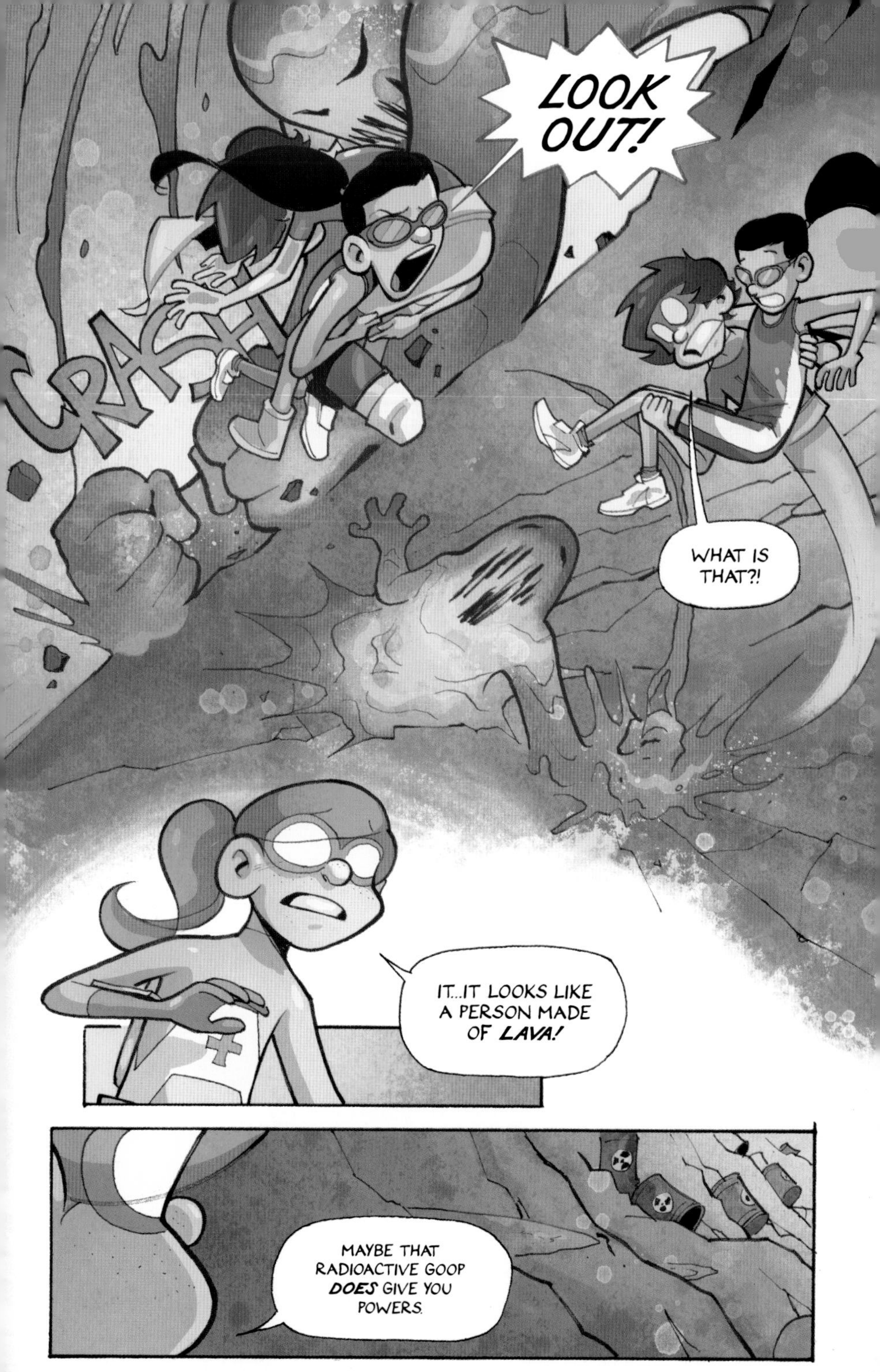
LOOK OUT!
CRASH
WHAT IS THAT?!
IT...IT LOOKS LIKE A PERSON MADE OF *LAVA!*
MAYBE THAT RADIOACTIVE GOOP *DOES* GIVE YOU POWERS.

WE'VE GOT TO GET OUT OF HERE!

I'LL DRAW IT AWAY!

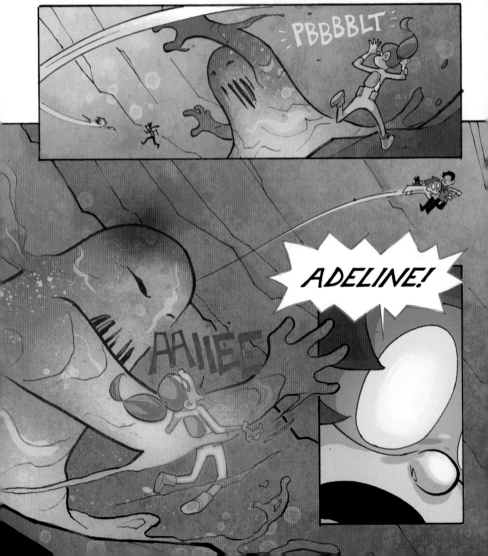

PBBBBLT

ADELINE!

AAIIEG

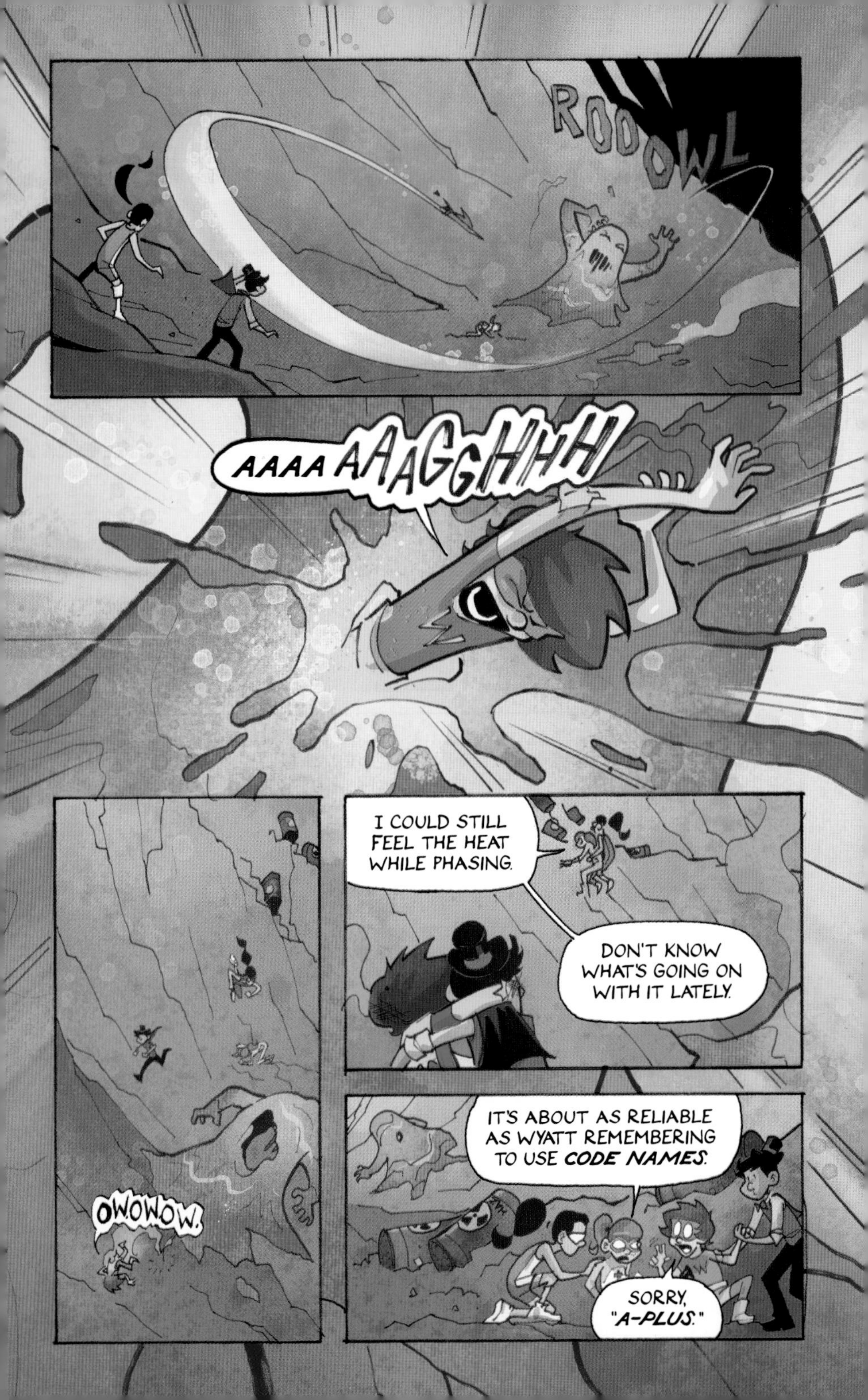
ROOOWL
AAAA AAAGGHHHH
OWOWOW.
I COULD STILL FEEL THE HEAT WHILE PHASING.
DON'T KNOW WHAT'S GOING ON WITH IT LATELY.
IT'S ABOUT AS RELIABLE AS WYATT REMEMBERING TO USE CODE NAMES.
SORRY, "A-PLUS."

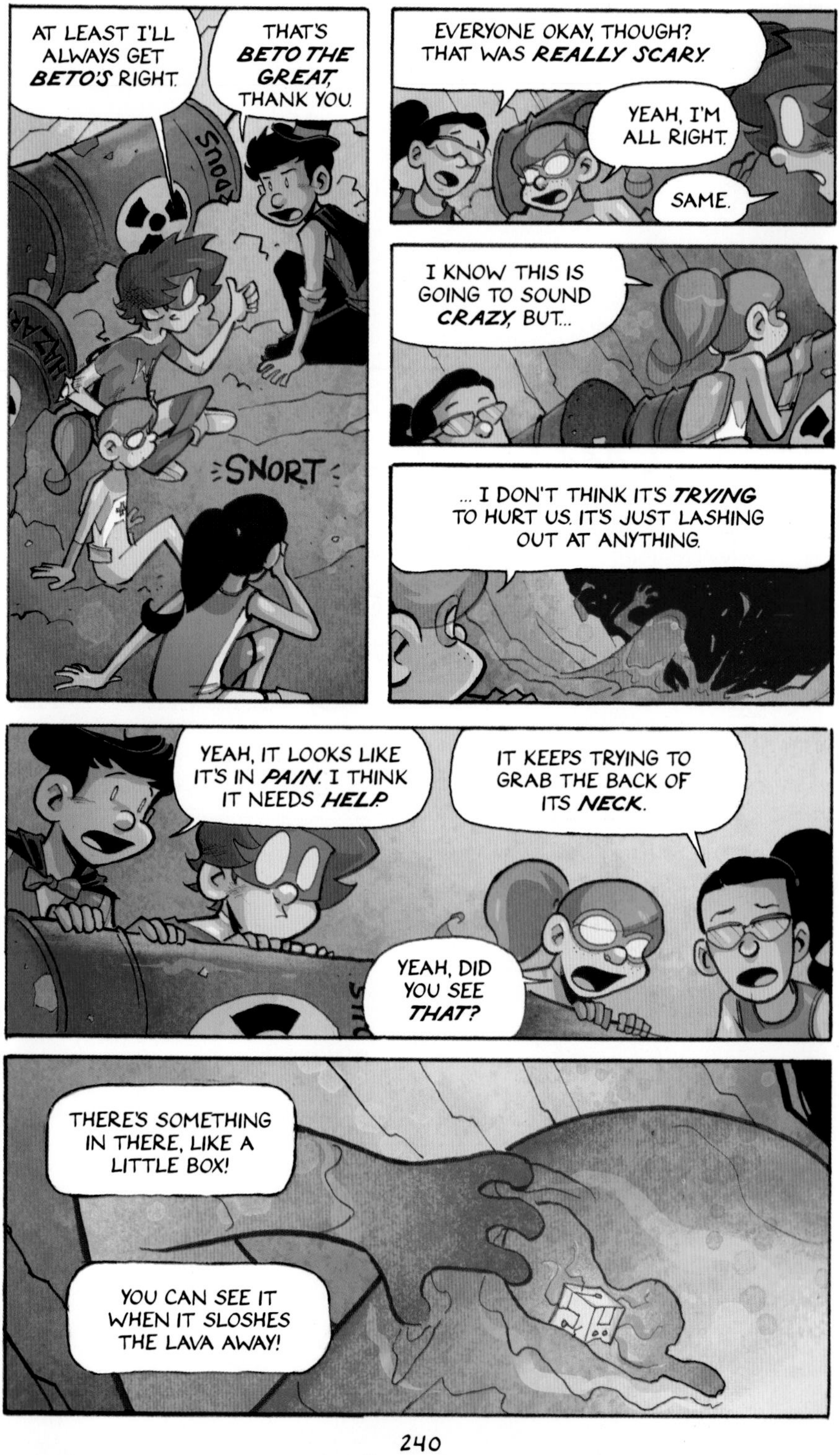
AT LEAST I'LL ALWAYS GET BETO'S RIGHT.
THAT'S BETO THE GREAT, THANK YOU.
SNOUS
SNORT
EVERYONE OKAY, THOUGH? THAT WAS REALLY SCARY.
YEAH, I'M ALL RIGHT.
SAME.
I KNOW THIS IS GOING TO SOUND CRAZY, BUT...
... I DON'T THINK IT'S TRYING TO HURT US. IT'S JUST LASHING OUT AT ANYTHING.
YEAH, IT LOOKS LIKE IT'S IN PAIN. I THINK IT NEEDS HELP.
IT KEEPS TRYING TO GRAB THE BACK OF ITS NECK.
YEAH, DID YOU SEE THAT?
THERE'S SOMETHING IN THERE, LIKE A LITTLE BOX!
YOU CAN SEE IT WHEN IT SLOSHES THE LAVA AWAY!

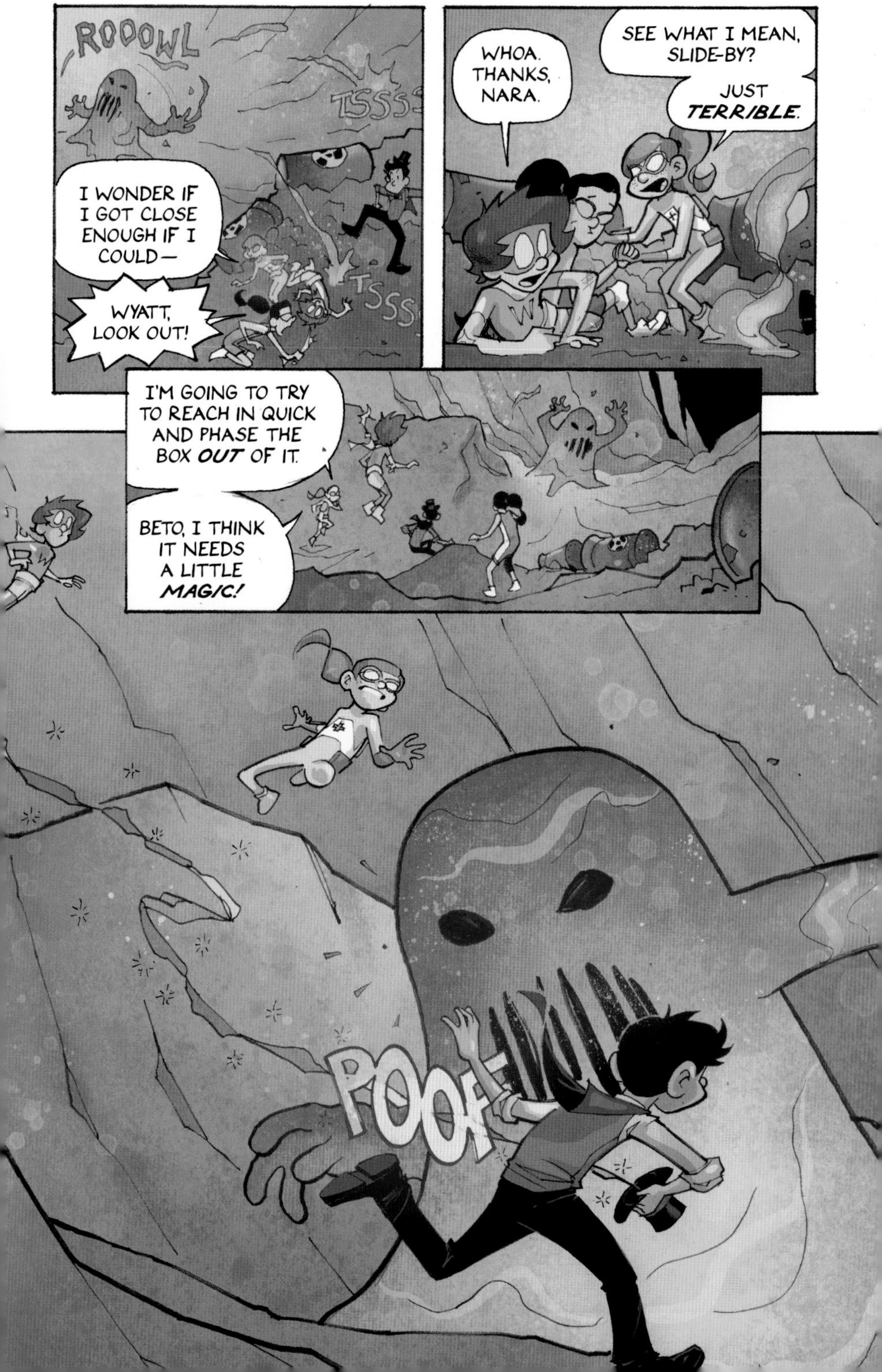

ROOOWL
TSSSS
I WONDER IF I GOT CLOSE ENOUGH IF I COULD—
WYATT, LOOK OUT!
TSSSS
WHOA. THANKS, NARA.
SEE WHAT I MEAN, SLIDE-BY?
JUST *TERRIBLE*.
I'M GOING TO TRY TO REACH IN QUICK AND PHASE THE BOX *OUT* OF IT.
BETO, I THINK IT NEEDS A LITTLE *MAGIC!*
POOF

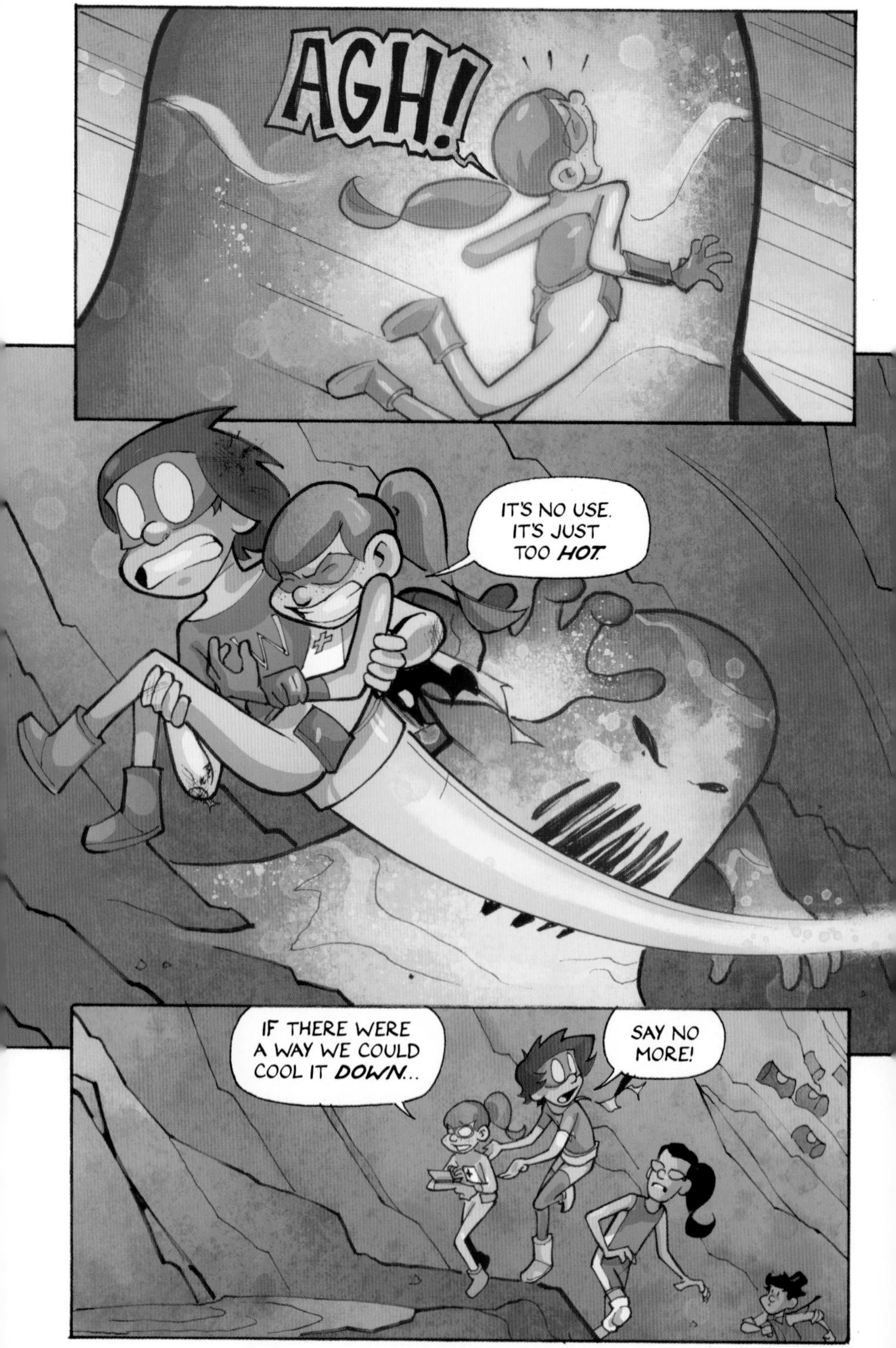
AGH!
IT'S NO USE. IT'S JUST TOO HOT.
IF THERE WERE A WAY WE COULD COOL IT DOWN...
SAY NO MORE!

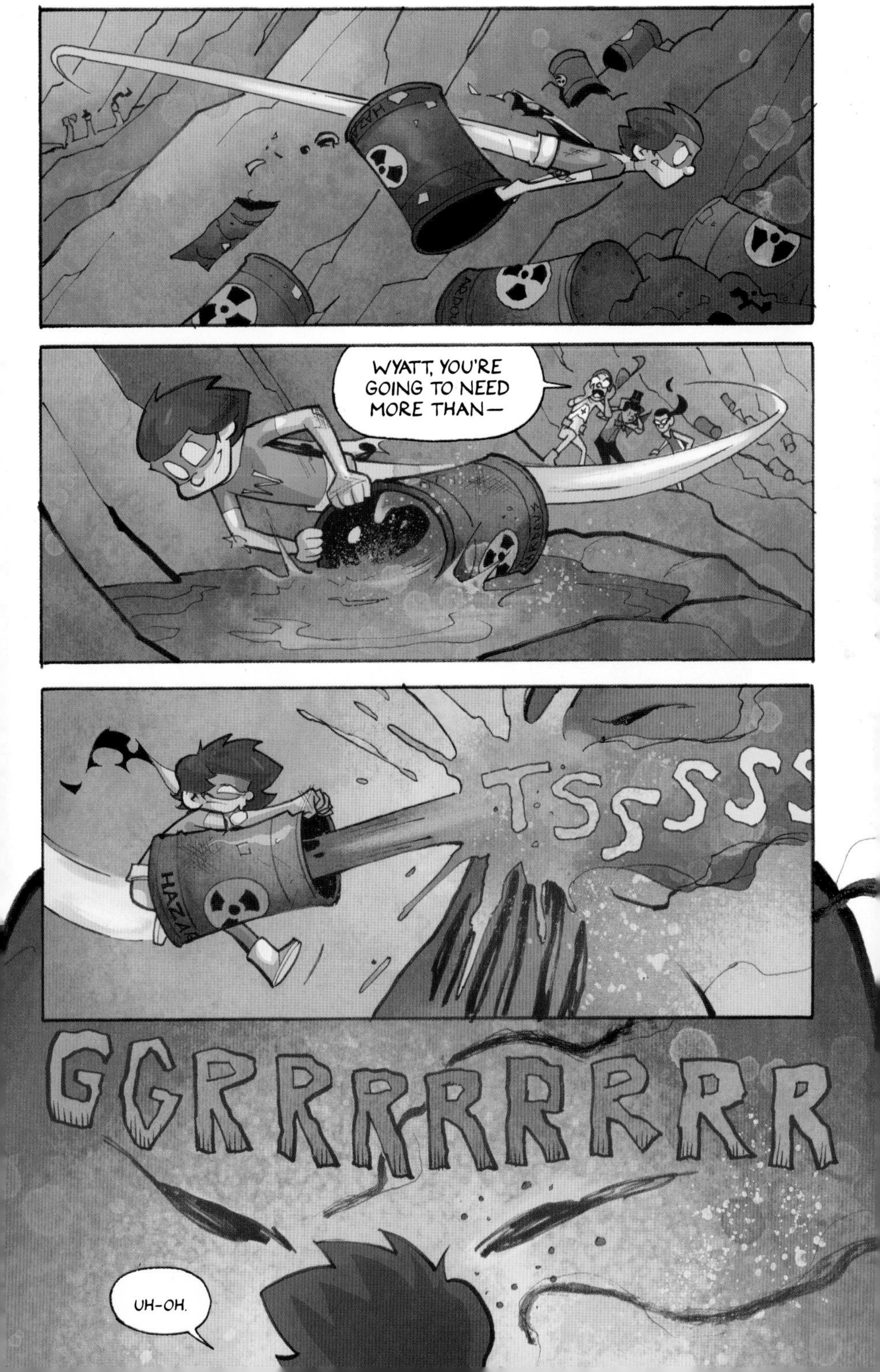
WYATT, YOU'RE GOING TO NEED MORE THAN—
TSSSS
GGRRRRRRRR
UH-OH.

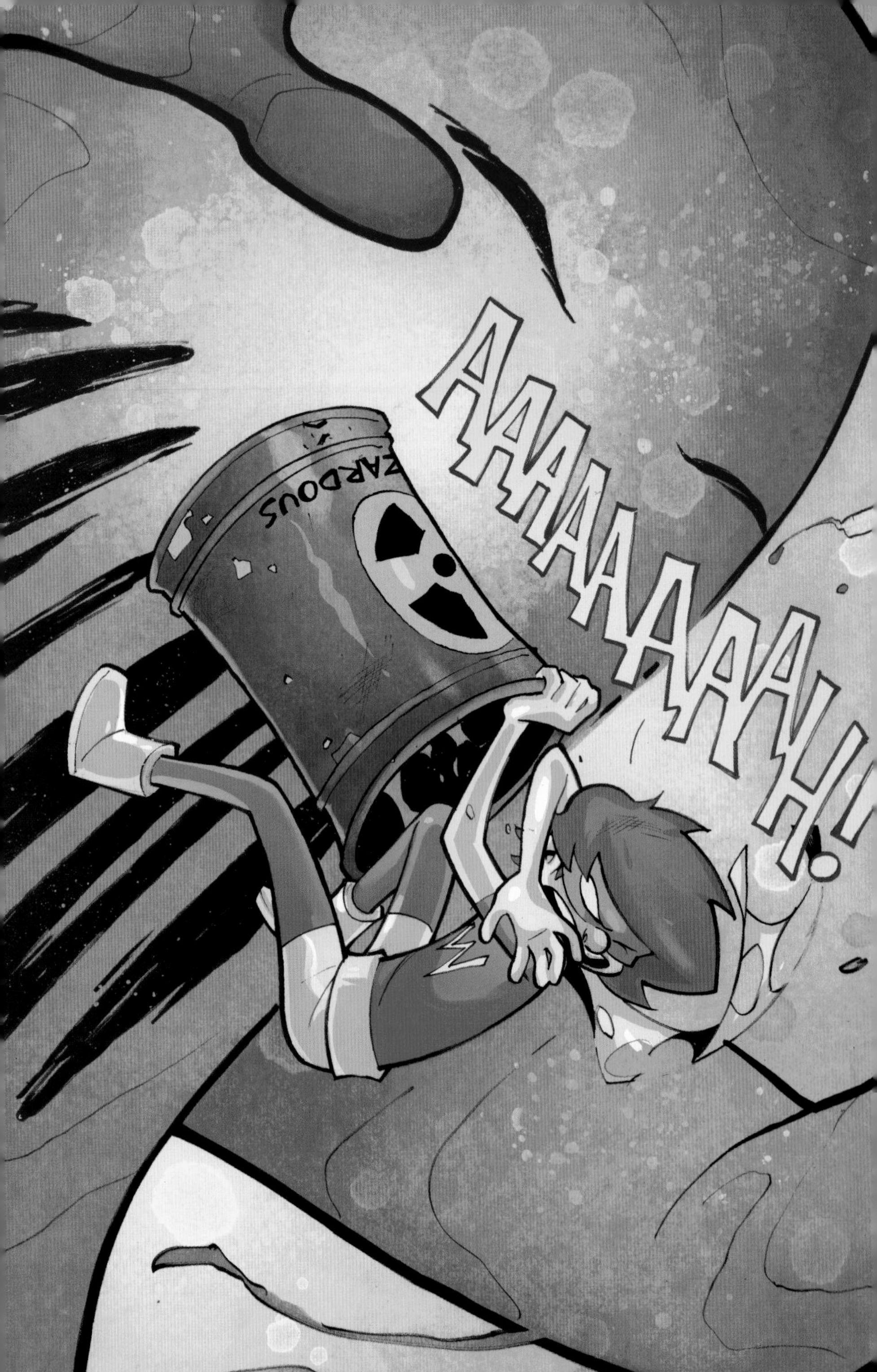
ZARDOUS
AAAAAAAAAH!!

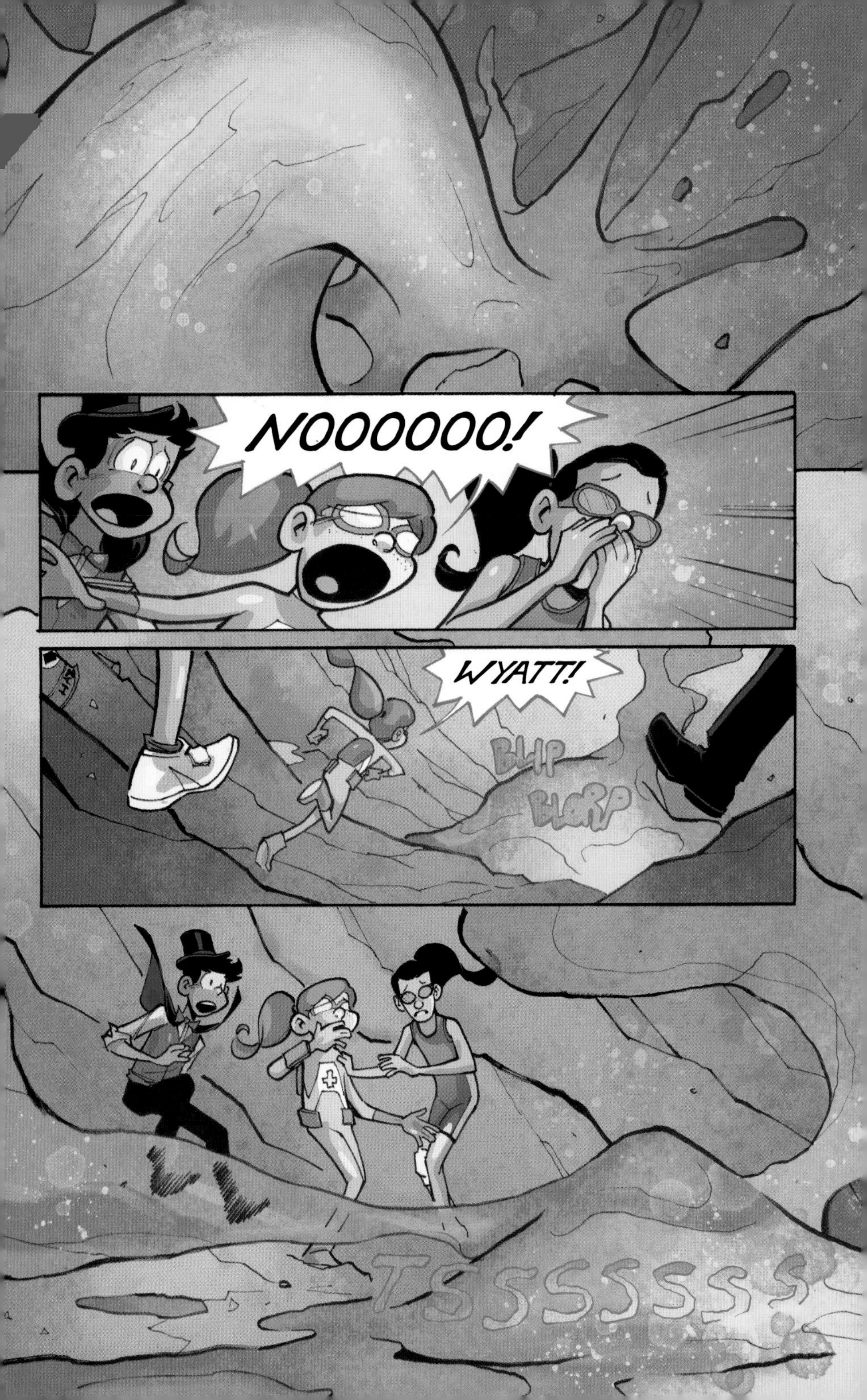
NOOOOOO!
WYATT!
BLIP
BLORP
TSSSSSSS

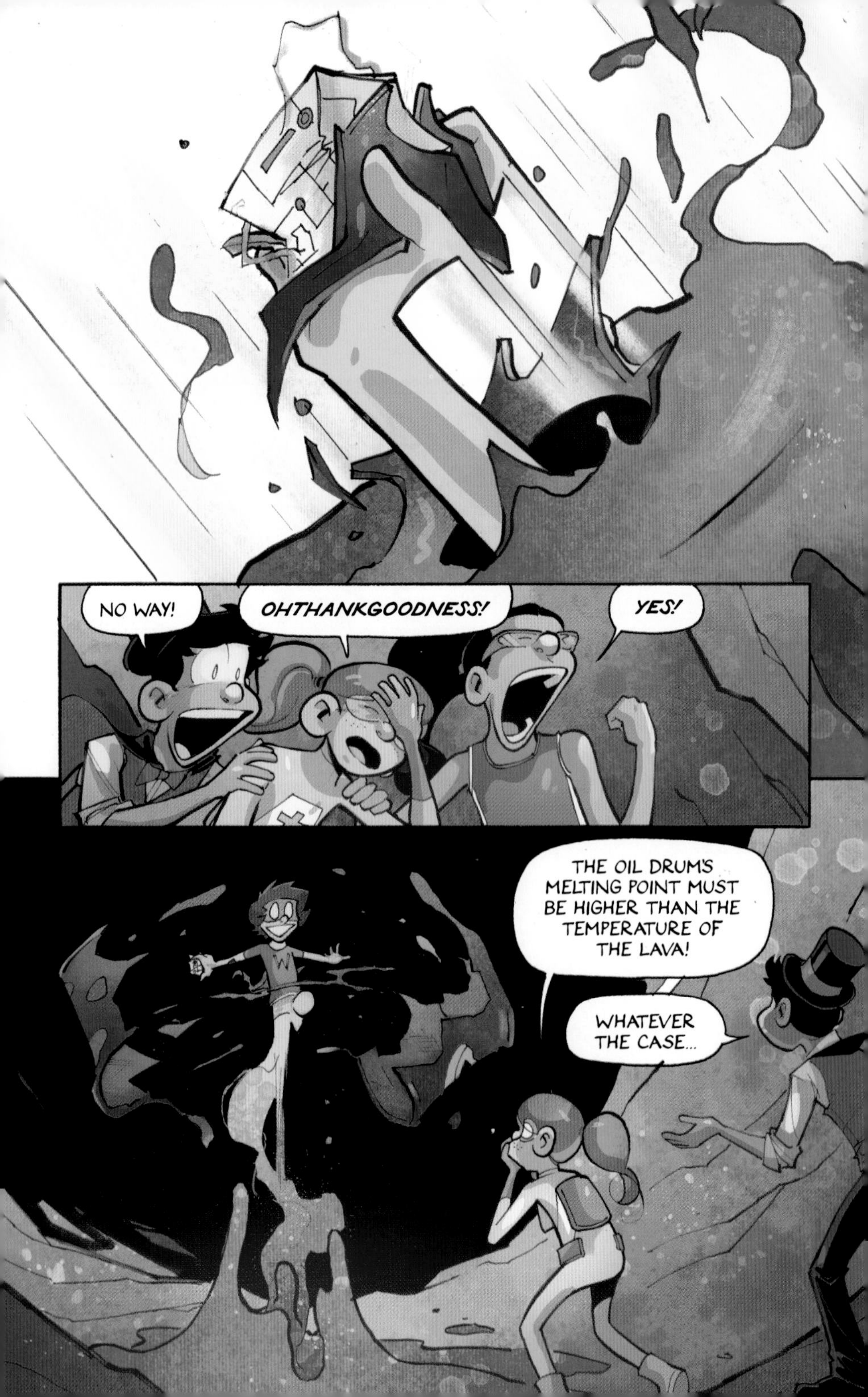
NO WAY!
OHTHANKGOODNESS!
YES!
THE OIL DRUM'S MELTING POINT MUST BE HIGHER THAN THE TEMPERATURE OF THE LAVA!
WHATEVER THE CASE...

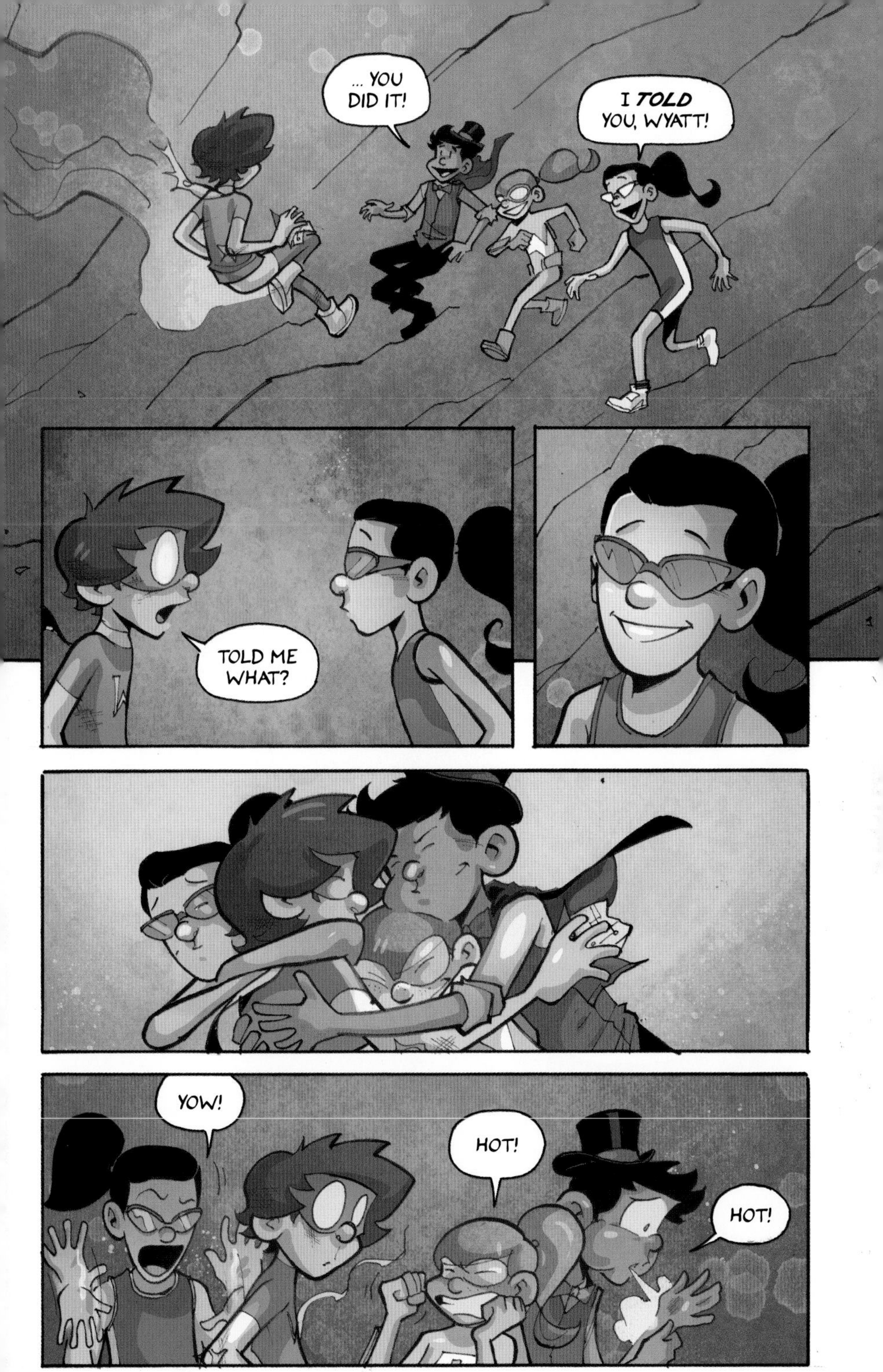
... YOU DID IT!
I *TOLD* YOU, WYATT!
TOLD ME WHAT?
YOW!
HOT!
HOT!

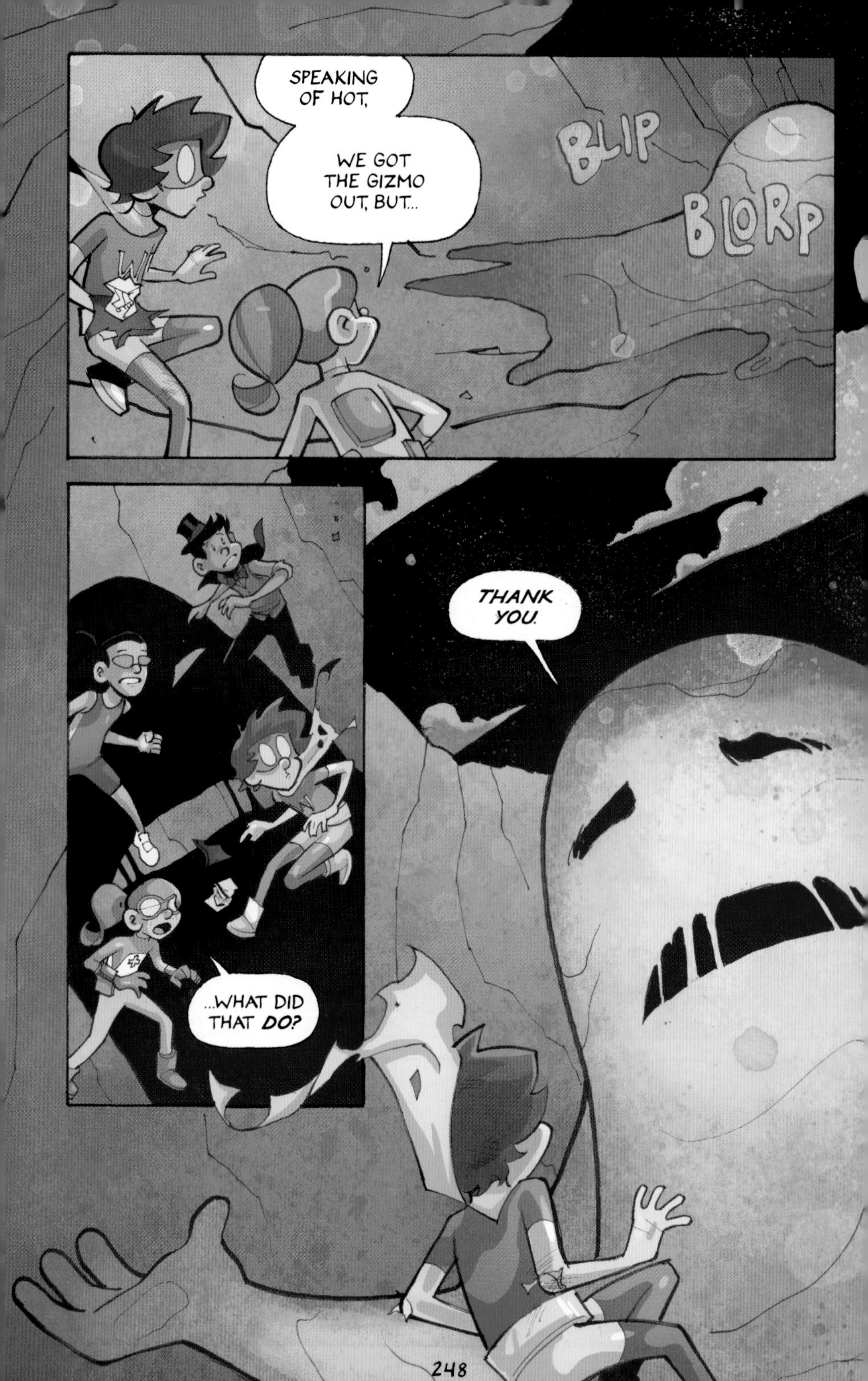
SPEAKING OF HOT,
WE GOT THE GIZMO OUT, BUT...
BLIP
BLORP
THANK YOU.
...WHAT DID THAT DO?

CHAPTER FOURTEEN

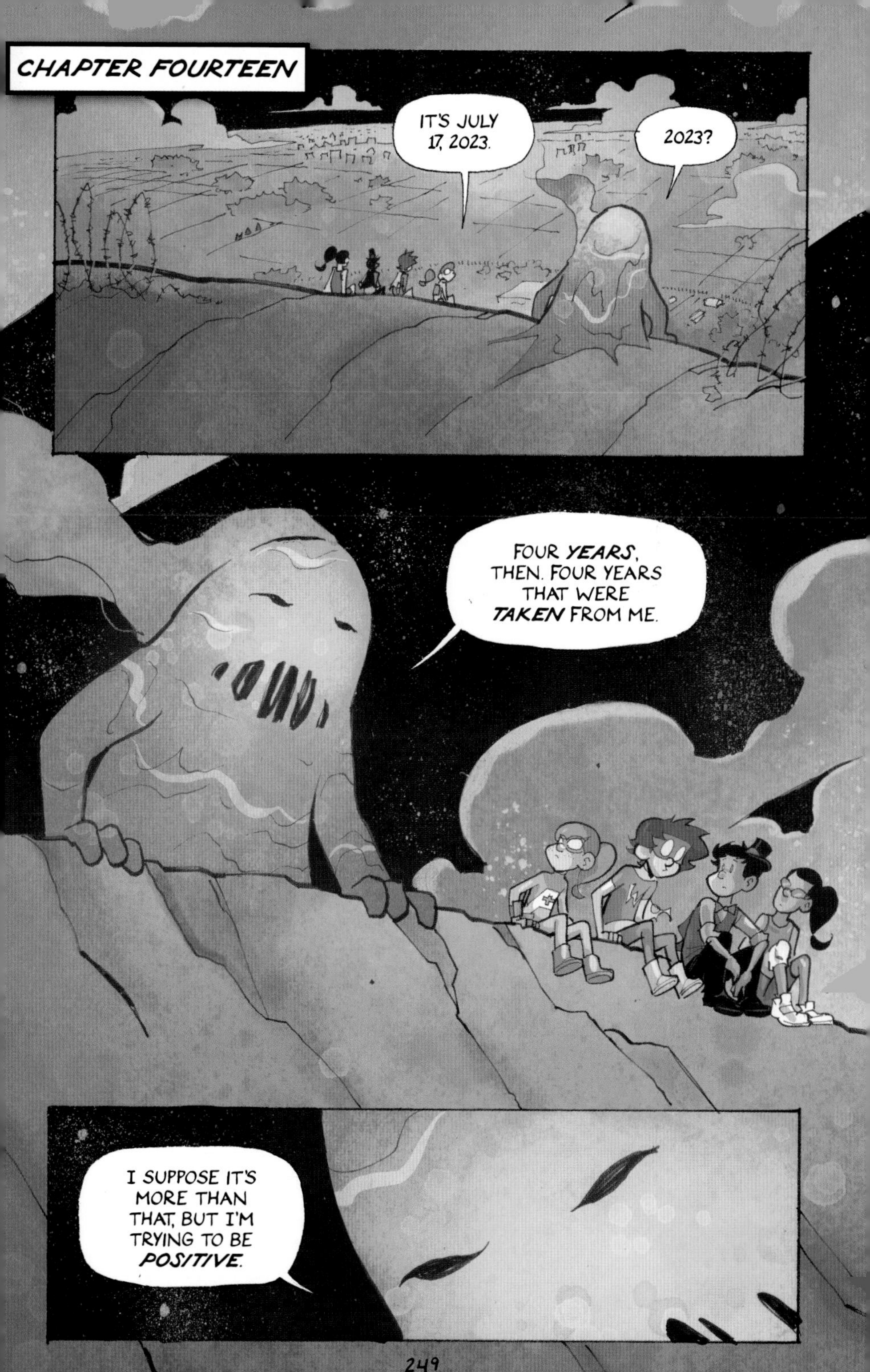
IT'S JULY 17, 2023.
2023?
FOUR *YEARS*, THEN. FOUR YEARS THAT WERE *TAKEN* FROM ME.
I SUPPOSE IT'S MORE THAN THAT, BUT I'M TRYING TO BE *POSITIVE*.

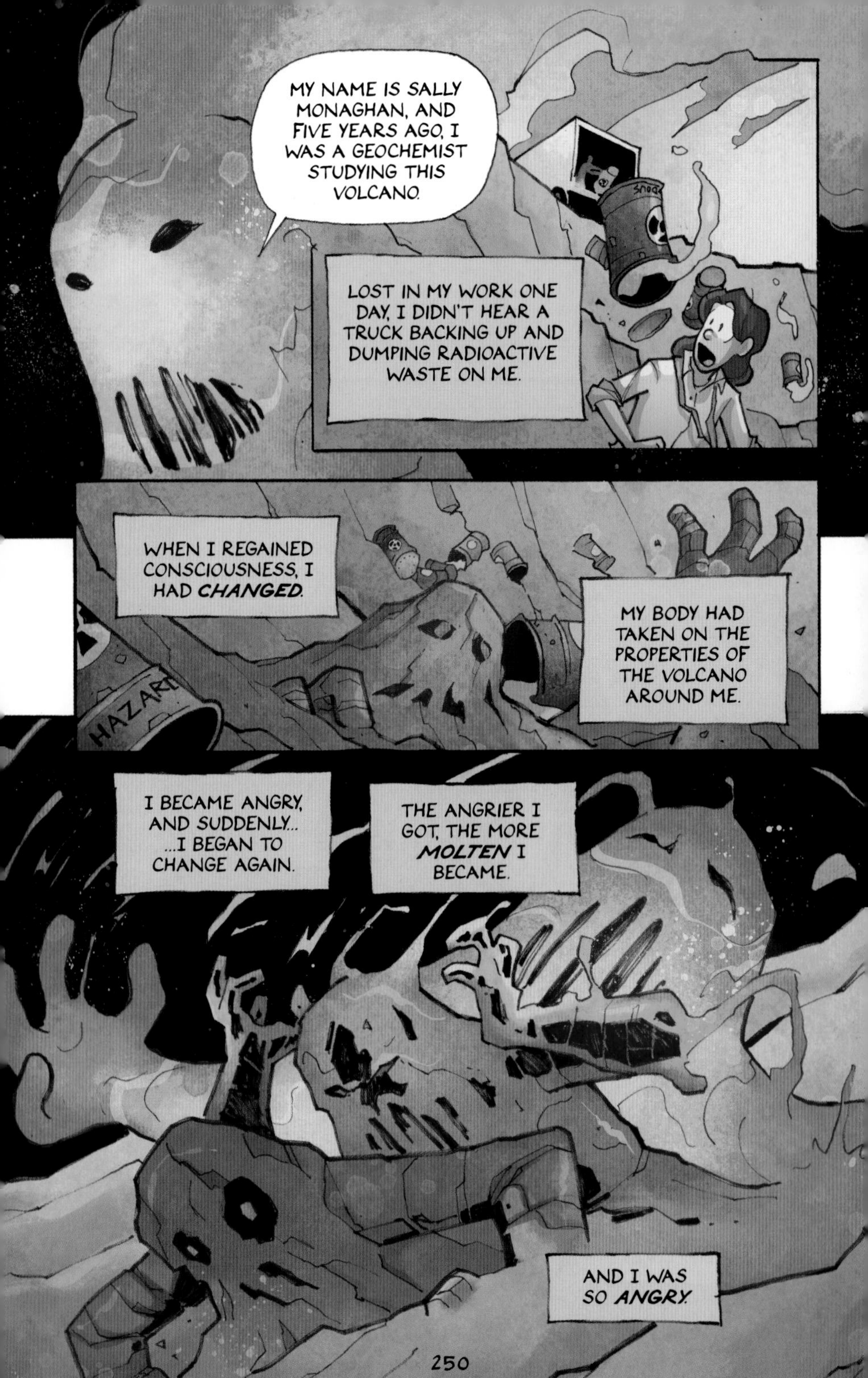
MY NAME IS SALLY MONAGHAN, AND FIVE YEARS AGO, I WAS A GEOCHEMIST STUDYING THIS VOLCANO.
LOST IN MY WORK ONE DAY, I DIDN'T HEAR A TRUCK BACKING UP AND DUMPING RADIOACTIVE WASTE ON ME.
WHEN I REGAINED CONSCIOUSNESS, I HAD *CHANGED*.
MY BODY HAD TAKEN ON THE PROPERTIES OF THE VOLCANO AROUND ME.
HAZARD
I BECAME ANGRY, AND SUDDENLY... ...I BEGAN TO CHANGE AGAIN.
THE ANGRIER I GOT, THE MORE *MOLTEN* I BECAME.
AND I WAS SO *ANGRY*.

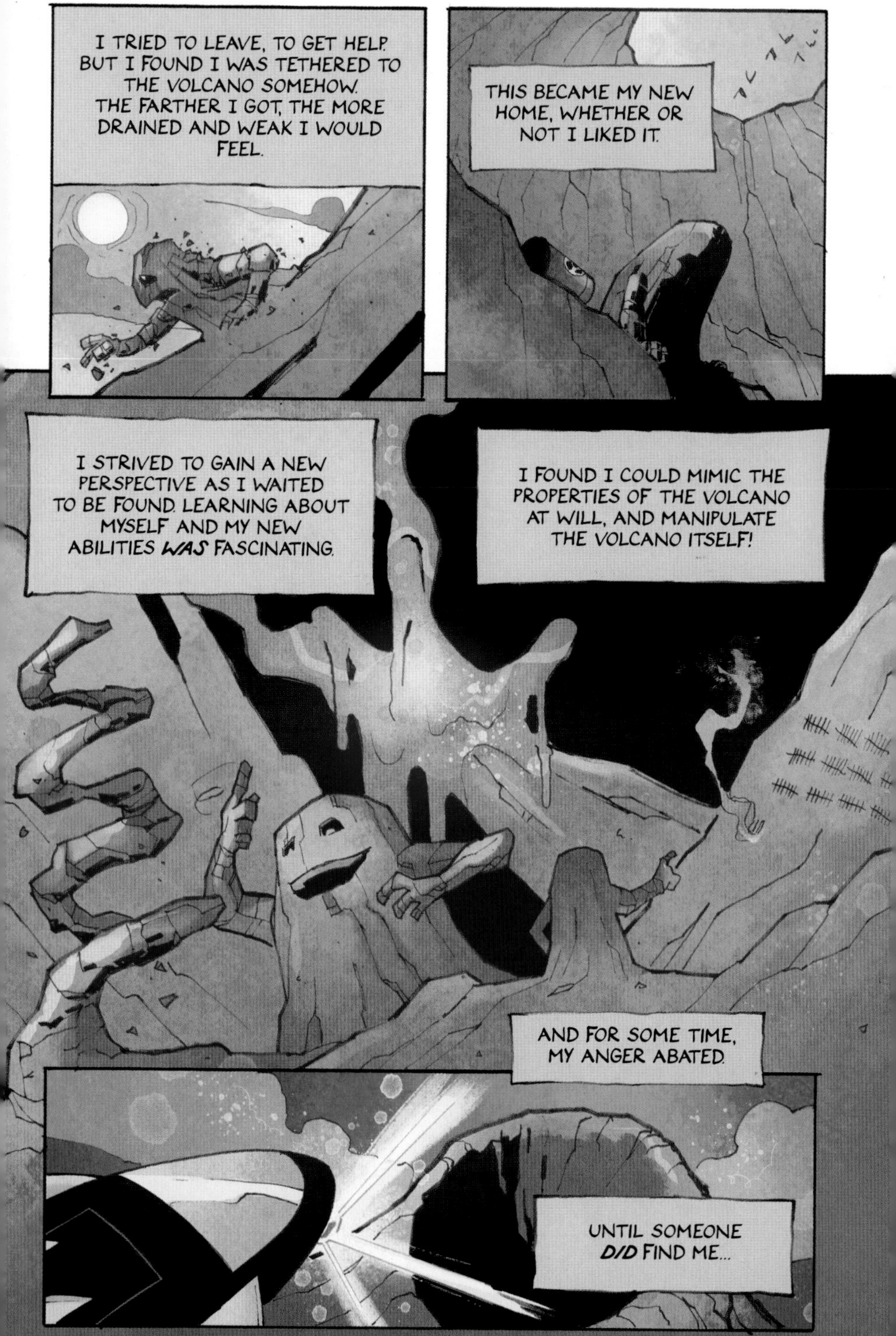
I TRIED TO LEAVE, TO GET HELP. BUT I FOUND I WAS TETHERED TO THE VOLCANO SOMEHOW. THE FARTHER I GOT, THE MORE DRAINED AND WEAK I WOULD FEEL.
THIS BECAME MY NEW HOME, WHETHER OR NOT I LIKED IT.
I STRIVED TO GAIN A NEW PERSPECTIVE AS I WAITED TO BE FOUND. LEARNING ABOUT MYSELF AND MY NEW ABILITIES *WAS* FASCINATING.
I FOUND I COULD MIMIC THE PROPERTIES OF THE VOLCANO AT WILL, AND MANIPULATE THE VOLCANO ITSELF!
AND FOR SOME TIME, MY ANGER ABATED.
UNTIL SOMEONE *DID* FIND ME...

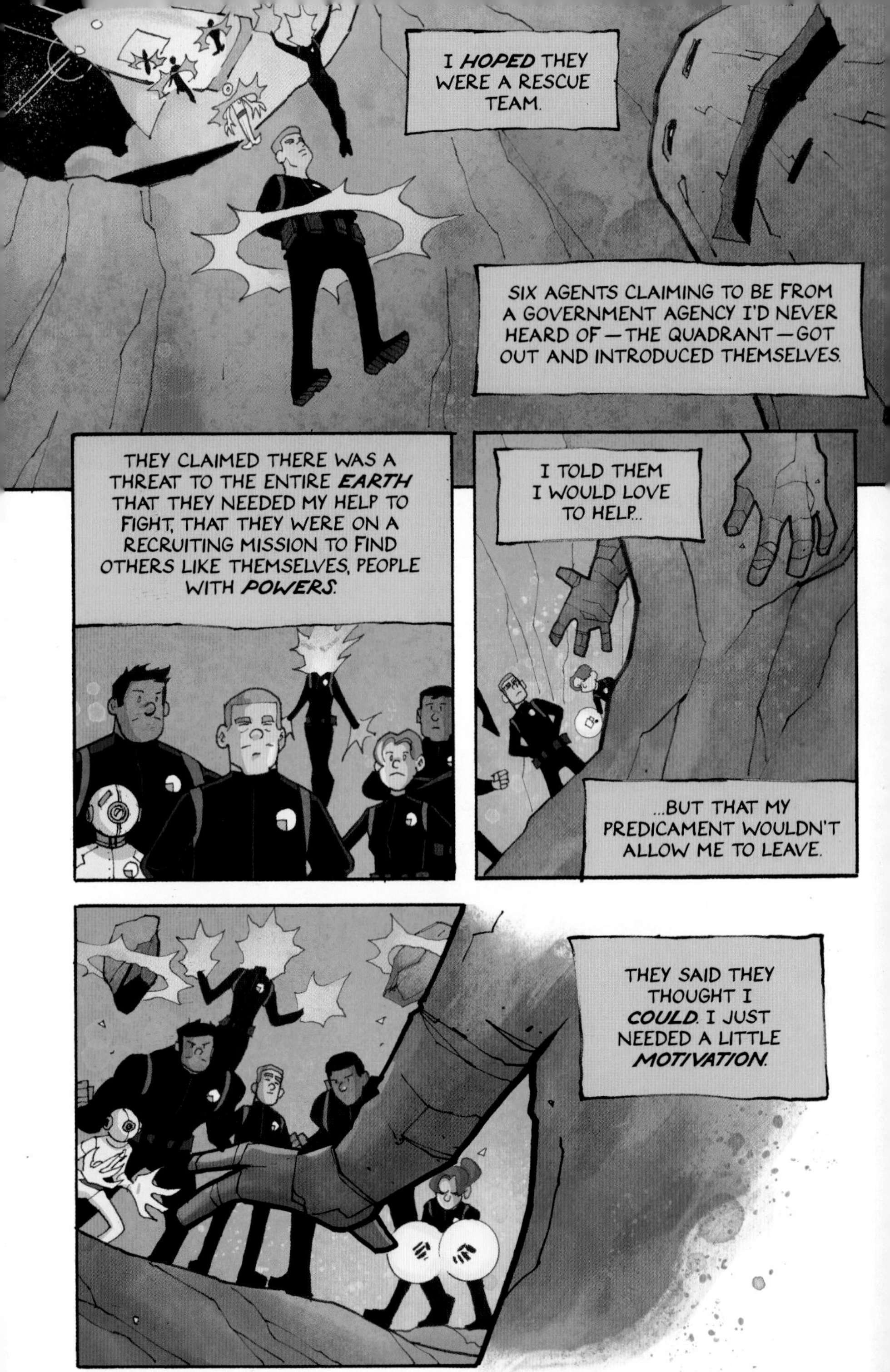
I *HOPED* THEY WERE A RESCUE TEAM.
SIX AGENTS CLAIMING TO BE FROM A GOVERNMENT AGENCY I'D NEVER HEARD OF—THE QUADRANT—GOT OUT AND INTRODUCED THEMSELVES.
THEY CLAIMED THERE WAS A THREAT TO THE ENTIRE *EARTH* THAT THEY NEEDED MY HELP TO FIGHT, THAT THEY WERE ON A RECRUITING MISSION TO FIND OTHERS LIKE THEMSELVES, PEOPLE WITH *POWERS*.
I TOLD THEM I WOULD LOVE TO HELP...
...BUT THAT MY PREDICAMENT WOULDN'T ALLOW ME TO LEAVE.
THEY SAID THEY THOUGHT I *COULD*. I JUST NEEDED A LITTLE *MOTIVATION*.

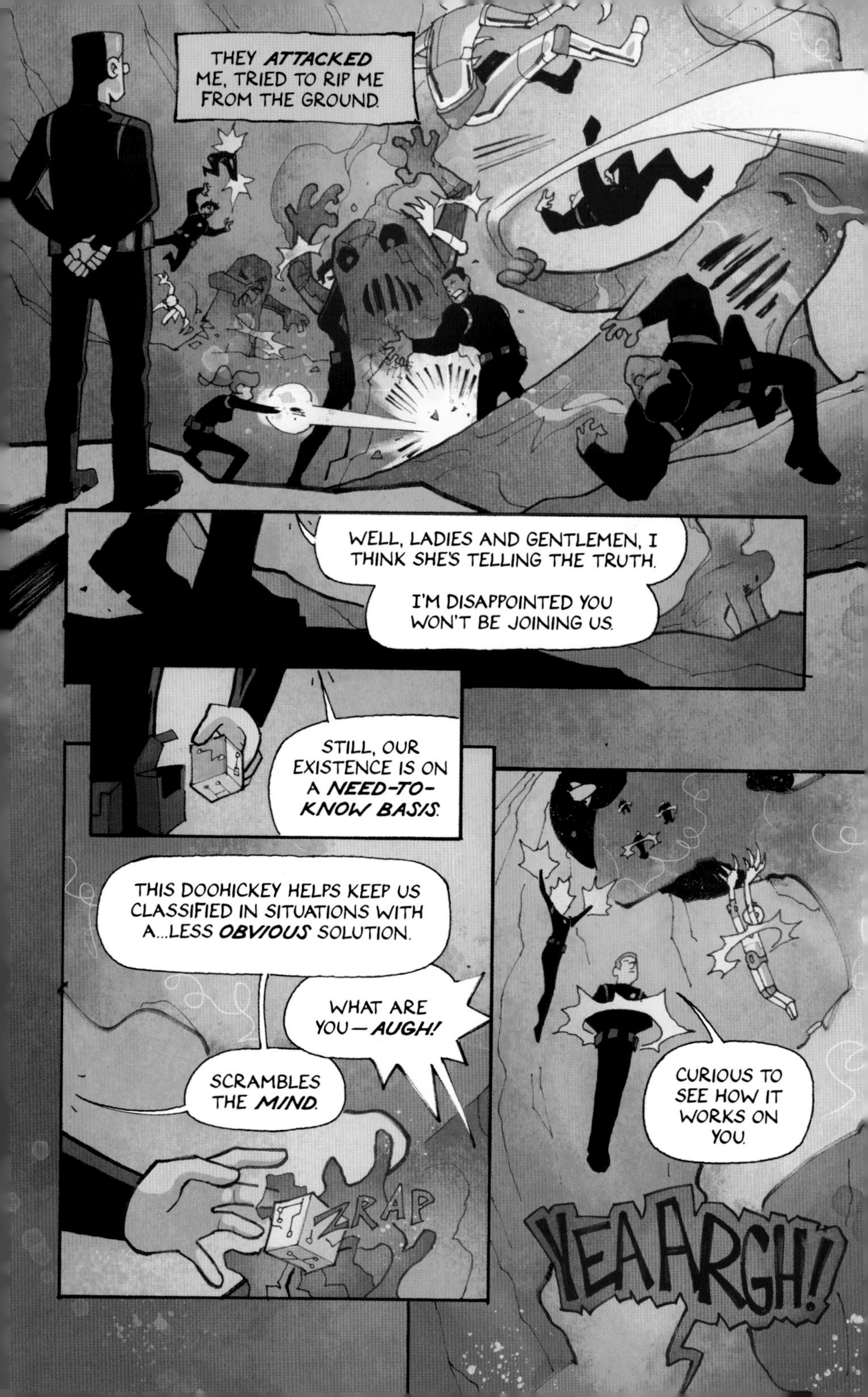
THEY ATTACKED ME, TRIED TO RIP ME FROM THE GROUND.
WELL, LADIES AND GENTLEMEN, I THINK SHE'S TELLING THE TRUTH.
I'M DISAPPOINTED YOU WON'T BE JOINING US.
STILL, OUR EXISTENCE IS ON A NEED-TO-KNOW BASIS.
THIS DOOHICKEY HELPS KEEP US CLASSIFIED IN SITUATIONS WITH A...LESS OBVIOUS SOLUTION.
WHAT ARE YOU—AUGH!
SCRAMBLES THE MIND.
ZRAP
CURIOUS TO SEE HOW IT WORKS ON YOU.
YEAARGH!

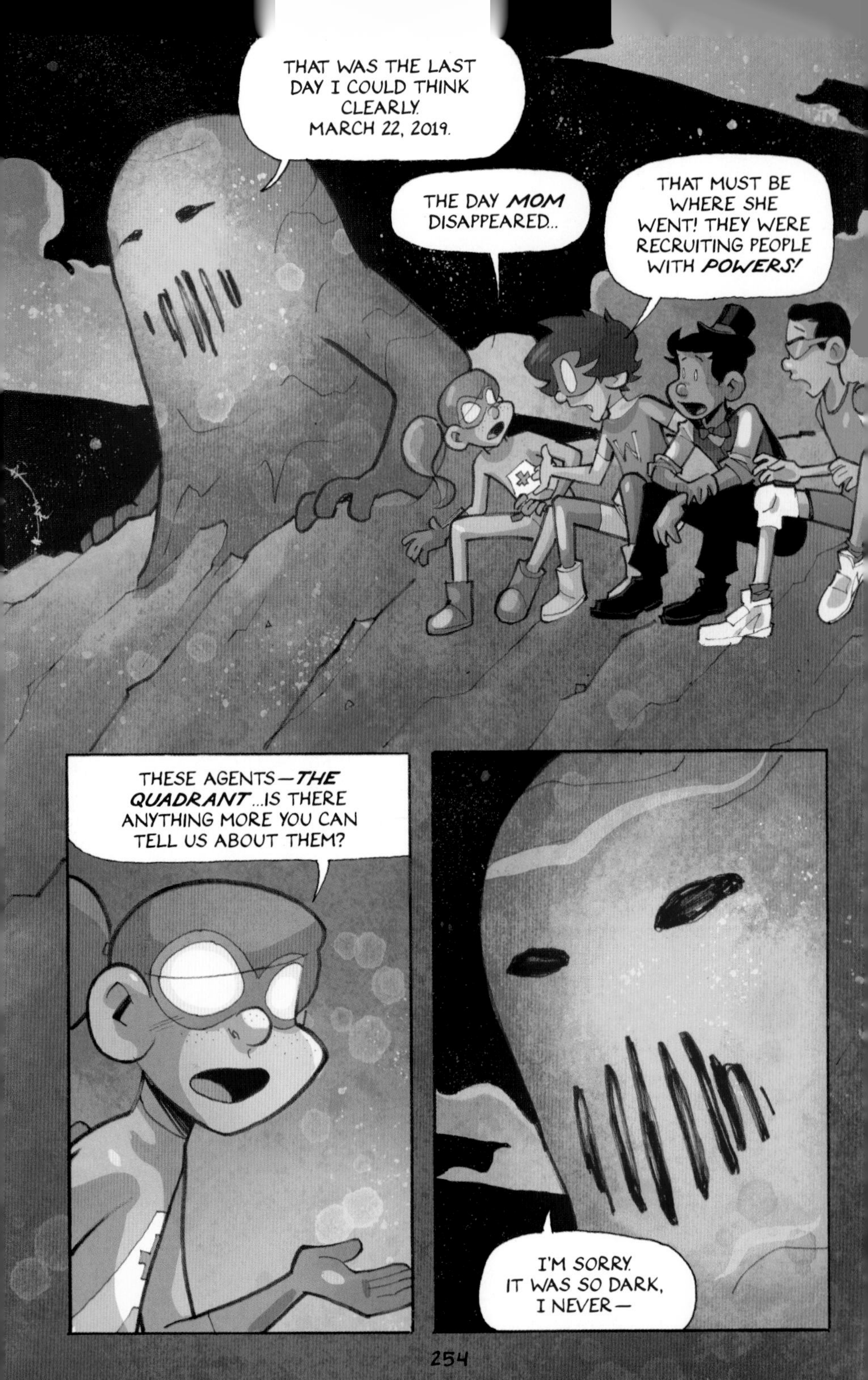
THAT WAS THE LAST DAY I COULD THINK CLEARLY. MARCH 22, 2019.
THE DAY MOM DISAPPEARED...
THAT MUST BE WHERE SHE WENT! THEY WERE RECRUITING PEOPLE WITH POWERS!
THESE AGENTS—THE QUADRANT...IS THERE ANYTHING MORE YOU CAN TELL US ABOUT THEM?
I'M SORRY. IT WAS SO DARK, I NEVER—

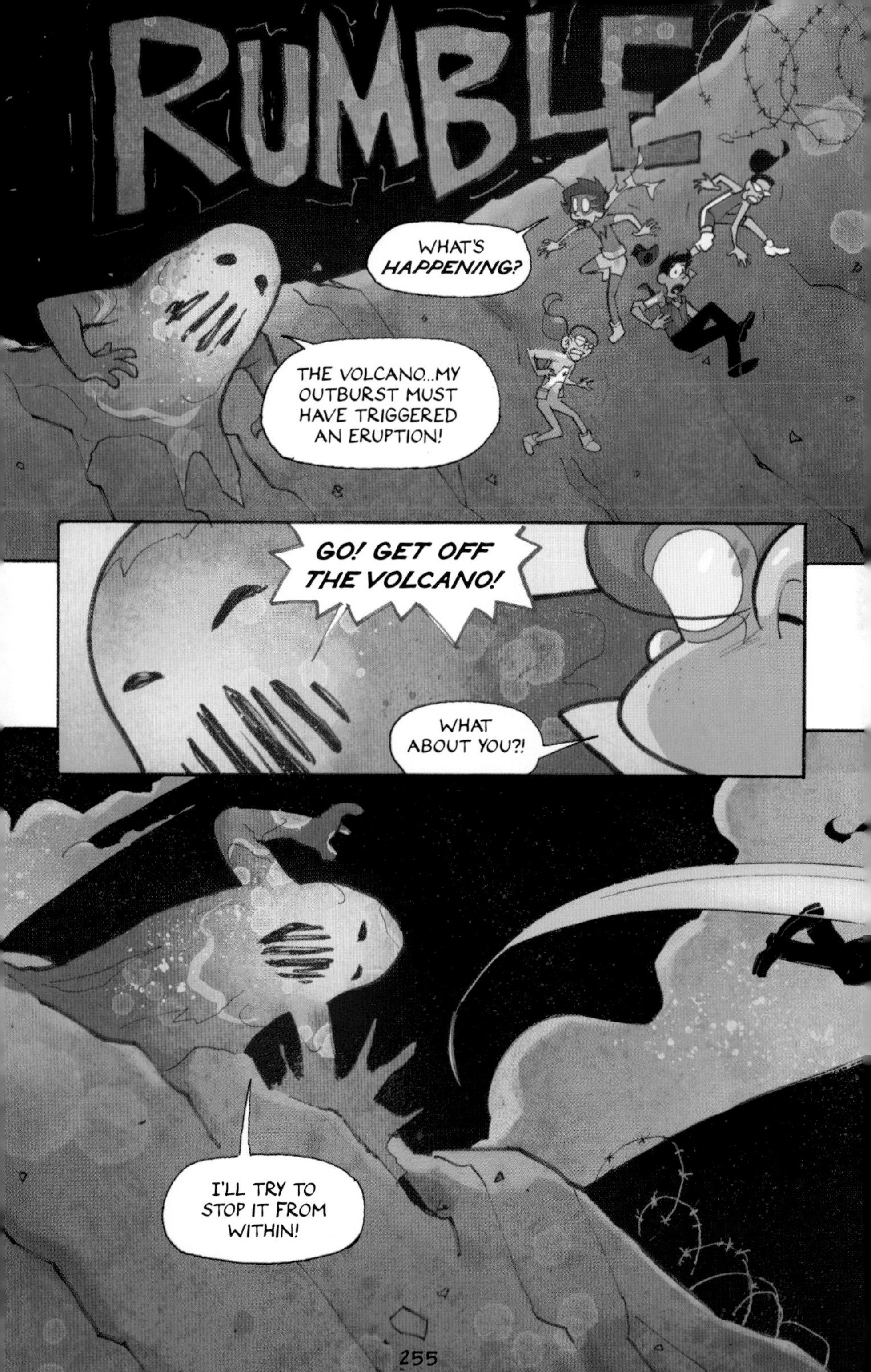
RUMBLE
WHAT'S *HAPPENING?*
THE VOLCANO...MY OUTBURST MUST HAVE TRIGGERED AN ERUPTION!
GO! GET OFF THE VOLCANO!
WHAT ABOUT YOU?!
I'LL TRY TO STOP IT FROM WITHIN!

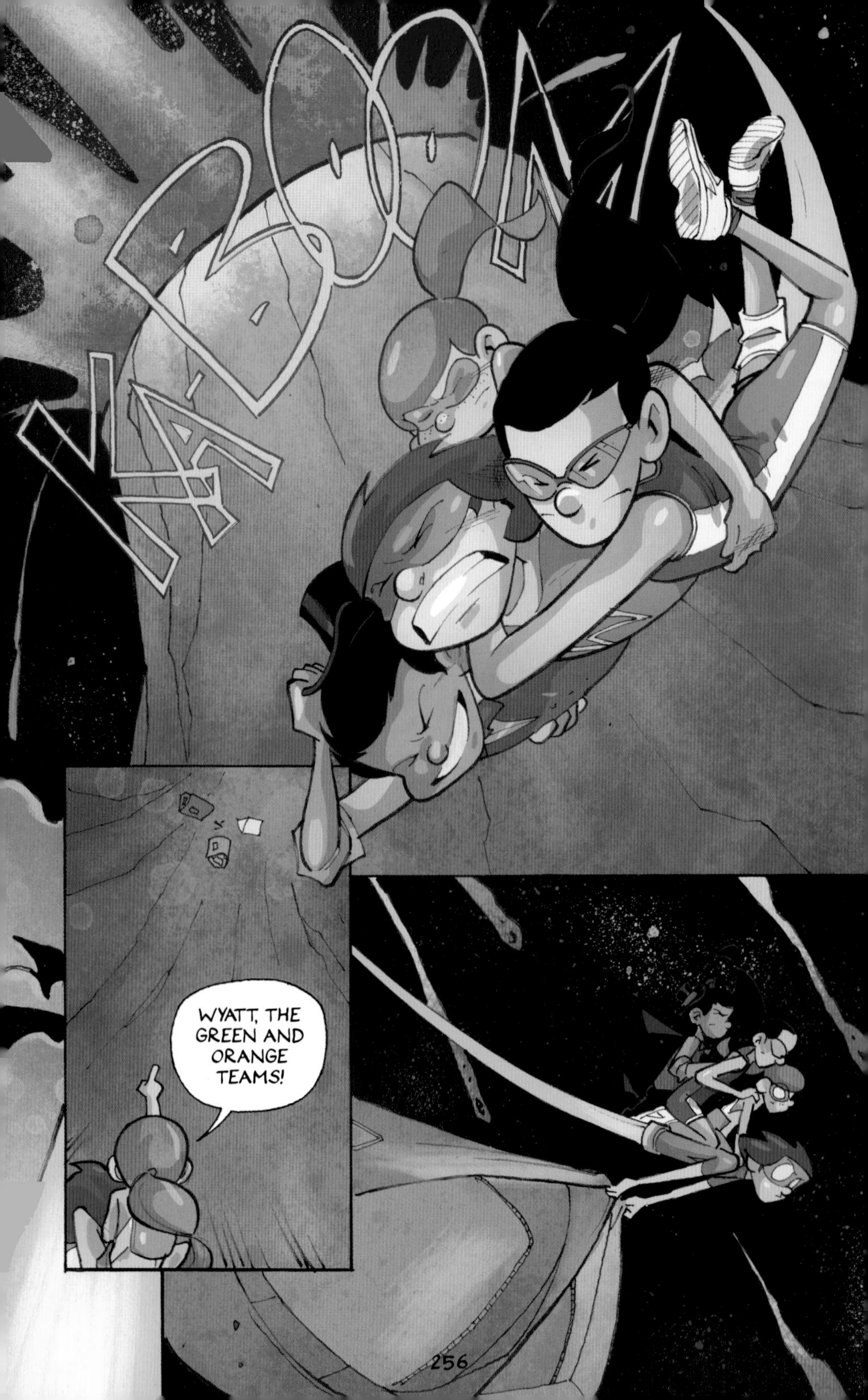
KA-ZOOM
WYATT, THE GREEN AND ORANGE TEAMS!

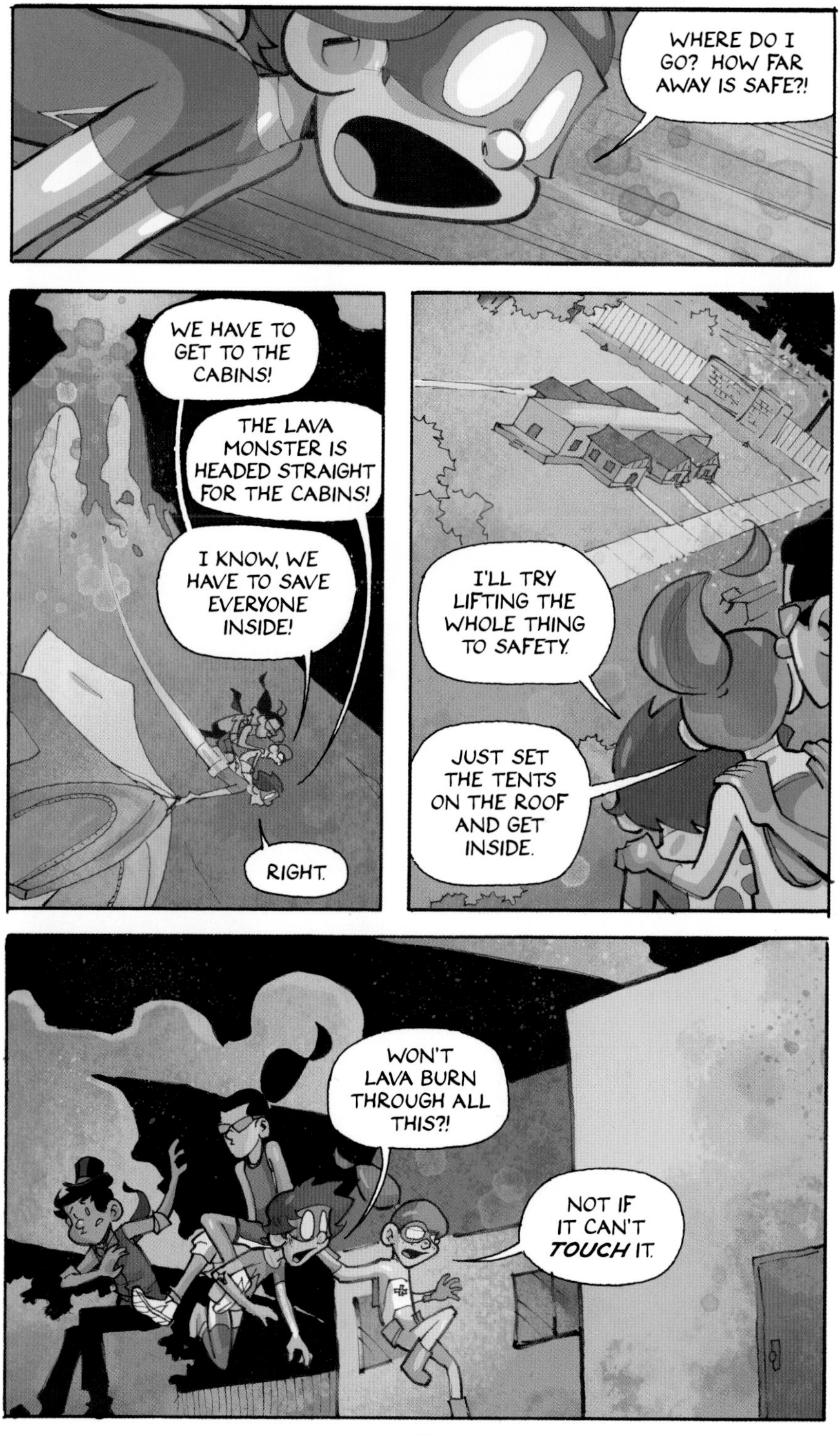
WHERE DO I GO? HOW FAR AWAY IS SAFE?!
WE HAVE TO GET TO THE CABINS!
THE LAVA MONSTER IS HEADED STRAIGHT FOR THE CABINS!
I KNOW, WE HAVE TO SAVE EVERYONE INSIDE!
RIGHT.
I'LL TRY LIFTING THE WHOLE THING TO SAFETY.
JUST SET THE TENTS ON THE ROOF AND GET INSIDE.
WON'T LAVA BURN THROUGH ALL THIS?!
NOT IF IT CAN'T *TOUCH* IT.

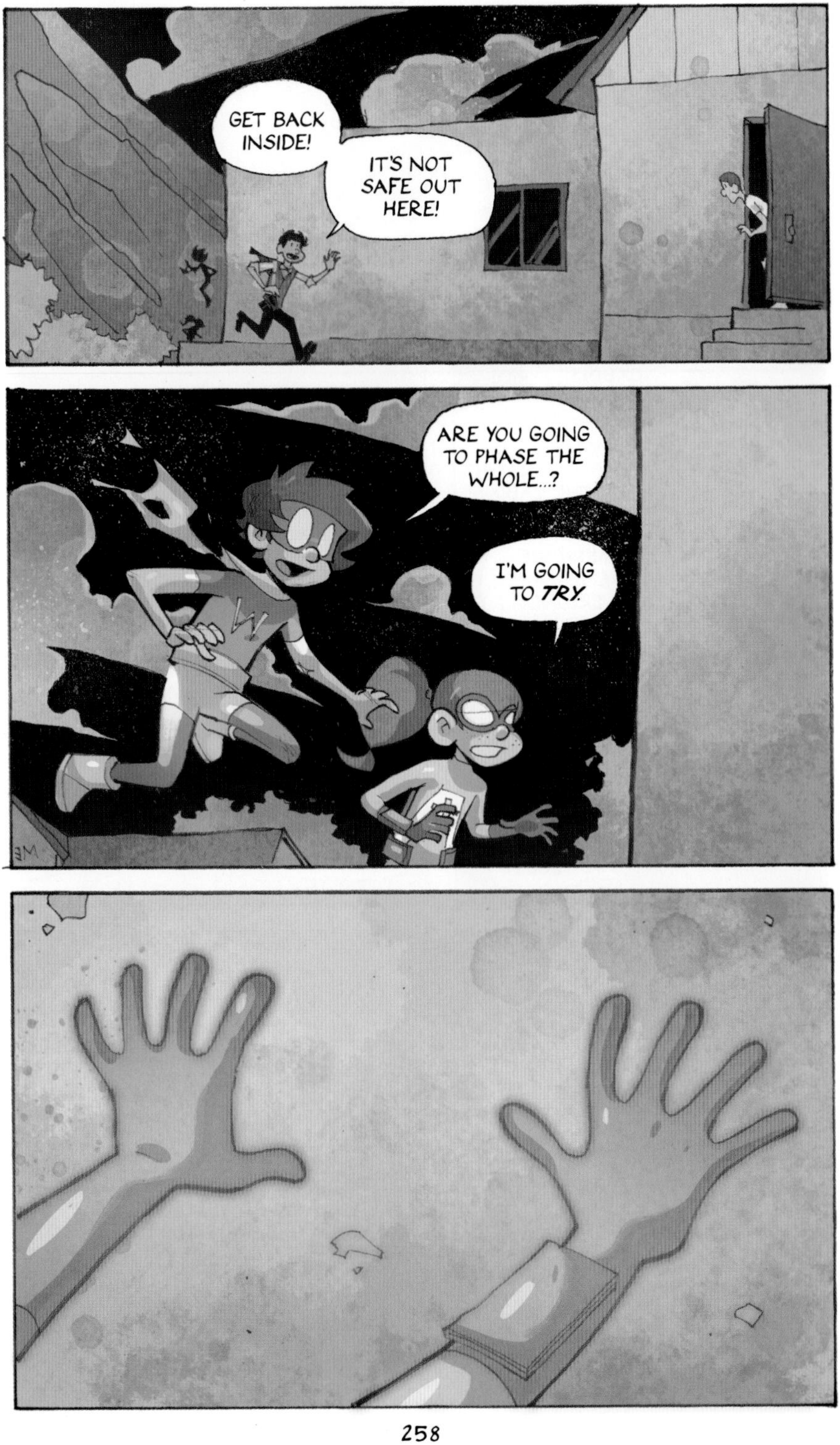
GET BACK INSIDE!
IT'S NOT SAFE OUT HERE!
ARE YOU GOING TO PHASE THE WHOLE...?
I'M GOING TO *TRY*.

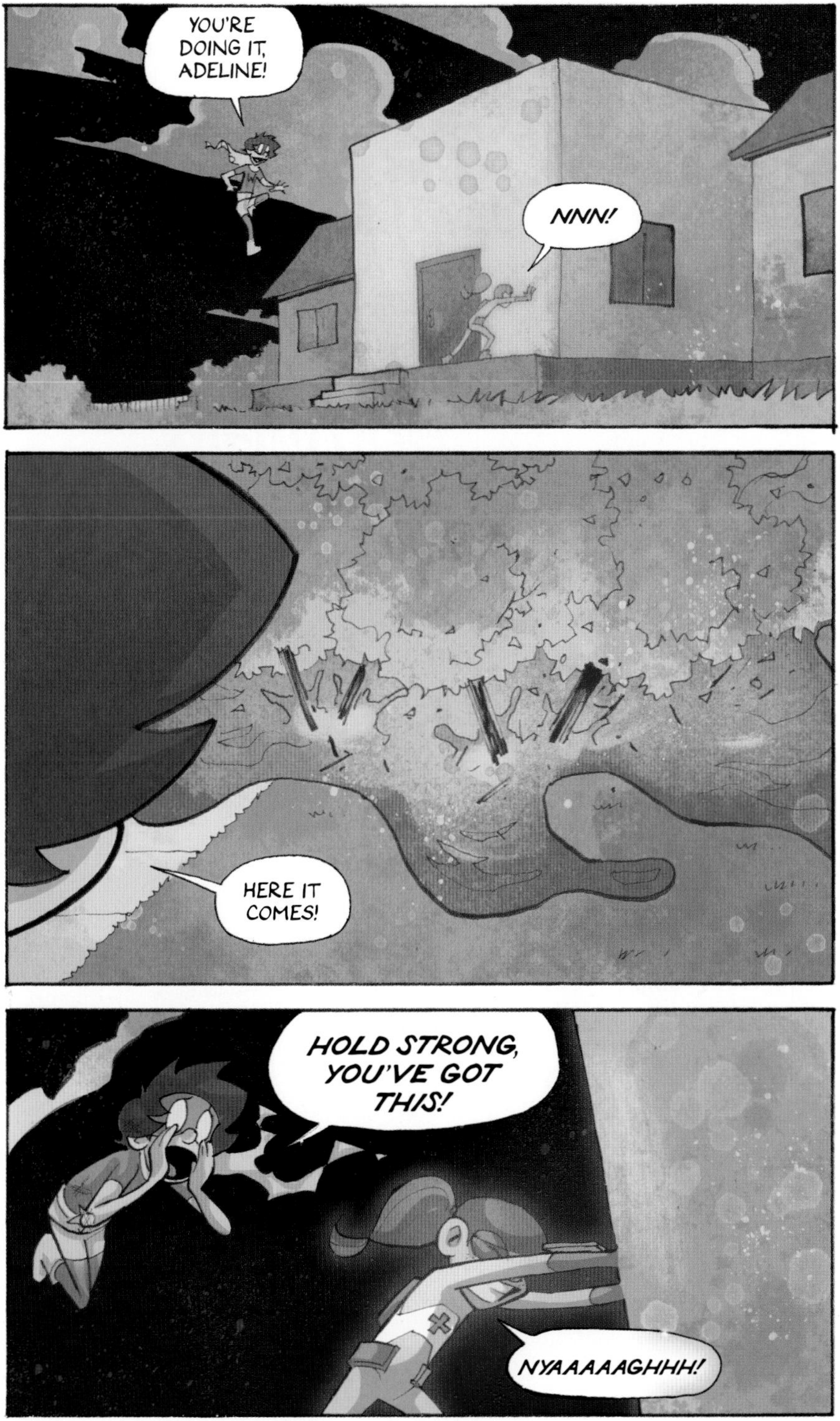
YOU'RE DOING IT, ADELINE!
NNN!
HERE IT COMES!
HOLD STRONG, YOU'VE GOT THIS!
NYAAAAAGHHH!

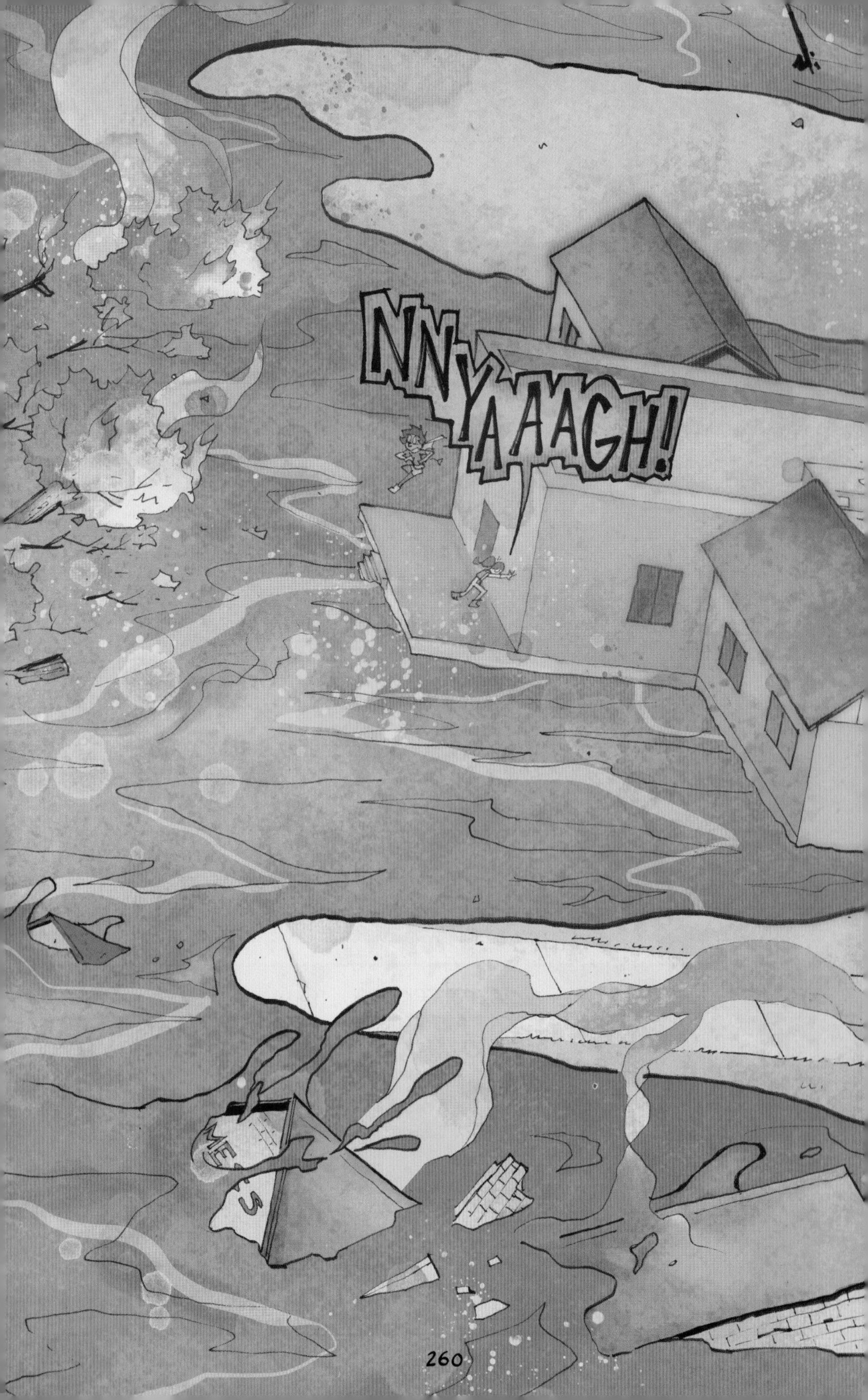
NNYAAAGH!

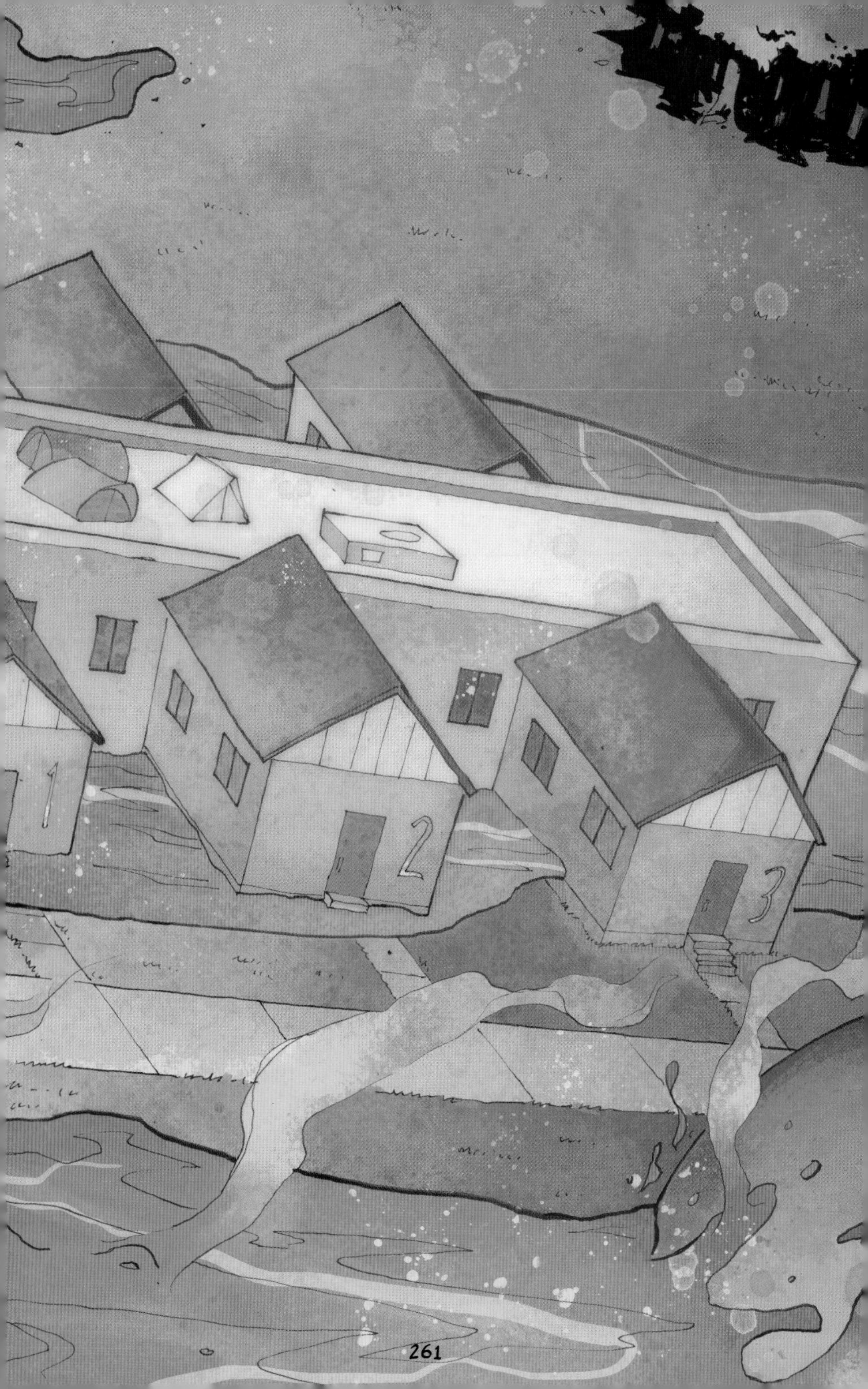
1
2
3

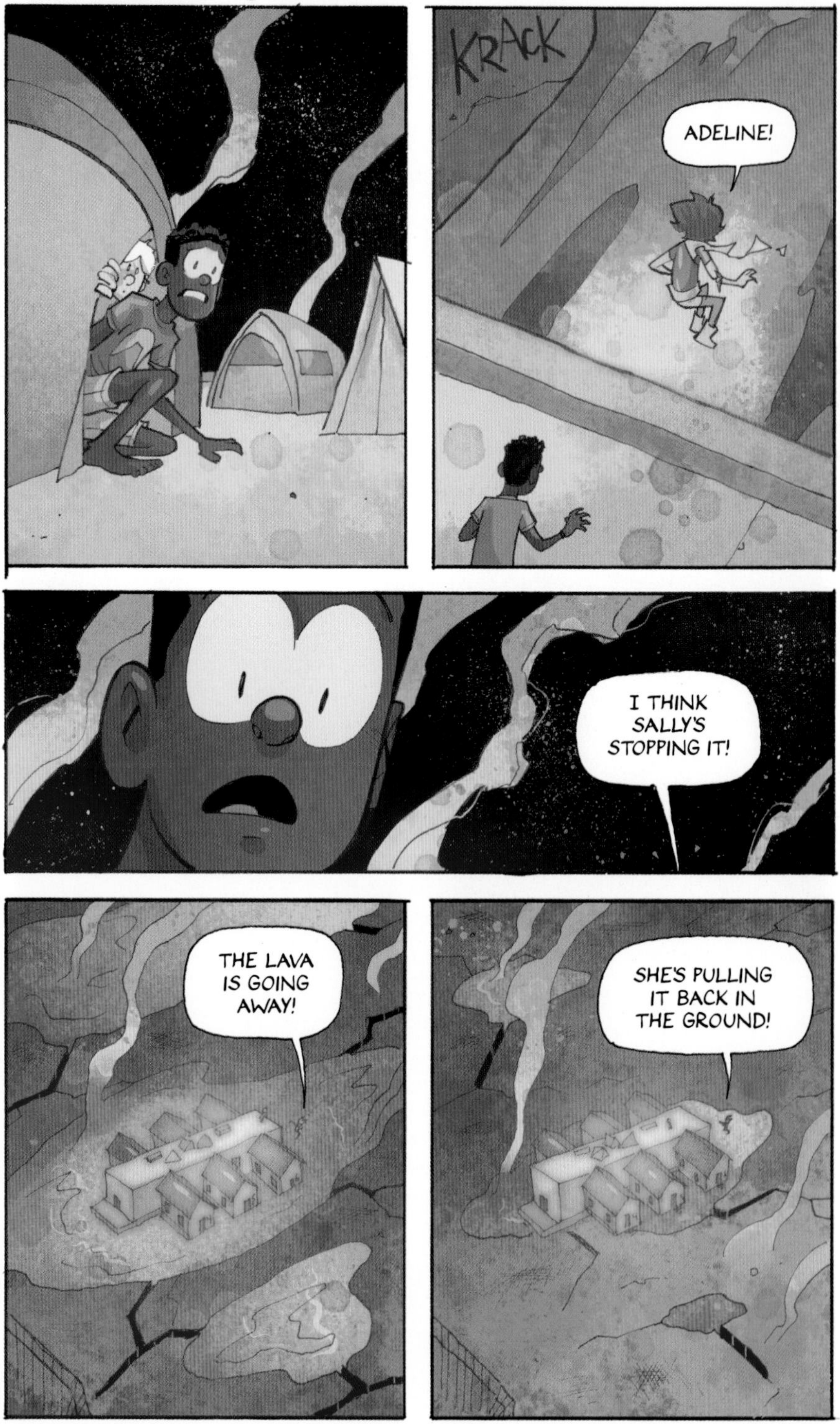
KRACK
ADELINE!
I THINK SALLY'S STOPPING IT!
THE LAVA IS GOING AWAY!
SHE'S PULLING IT BACK IN THE GROUND!

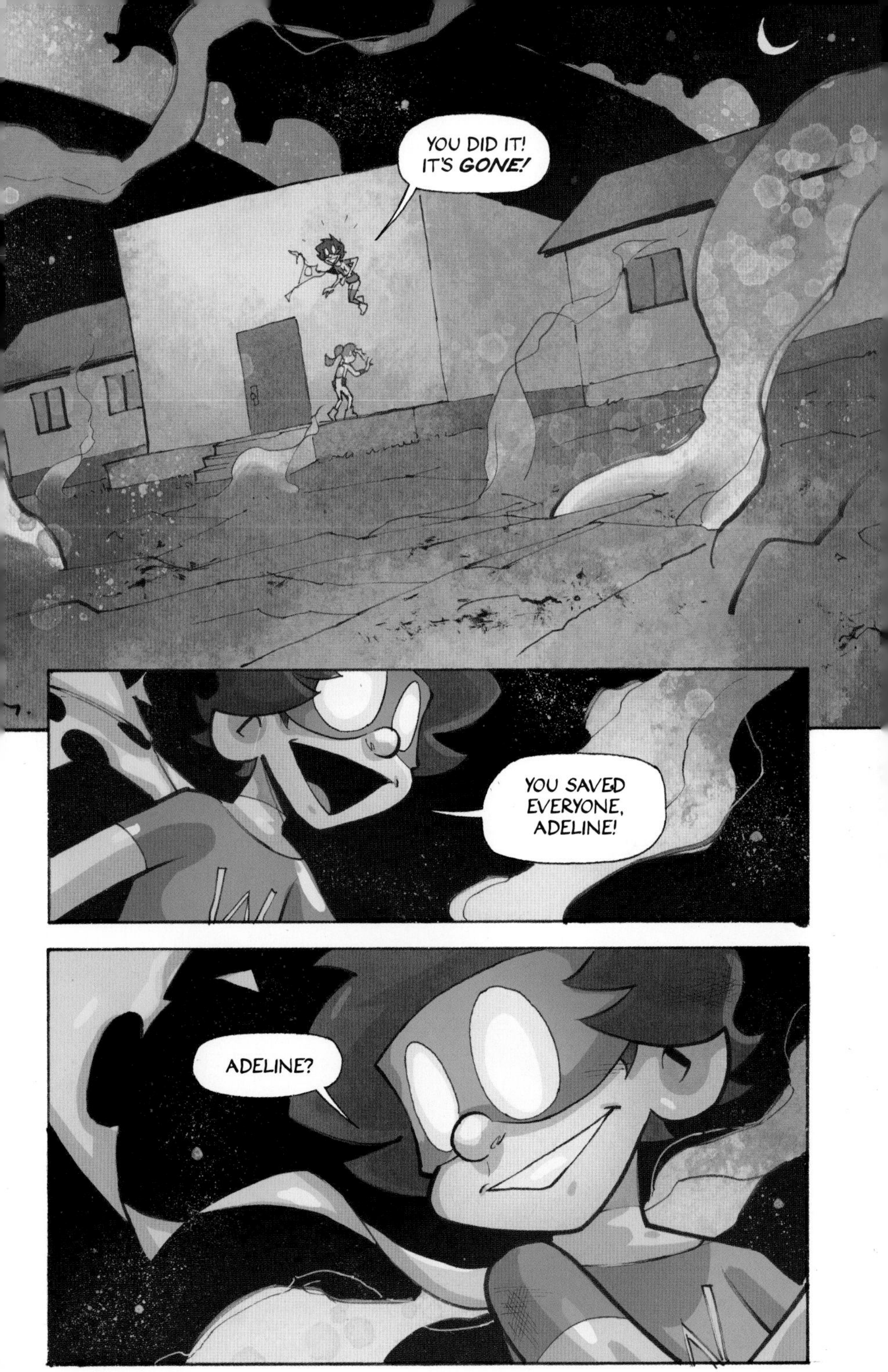
YOU DID IT! IT'S *GONE!*
YOU SAVED EVERYONE, ADELINE!
ADELINE?

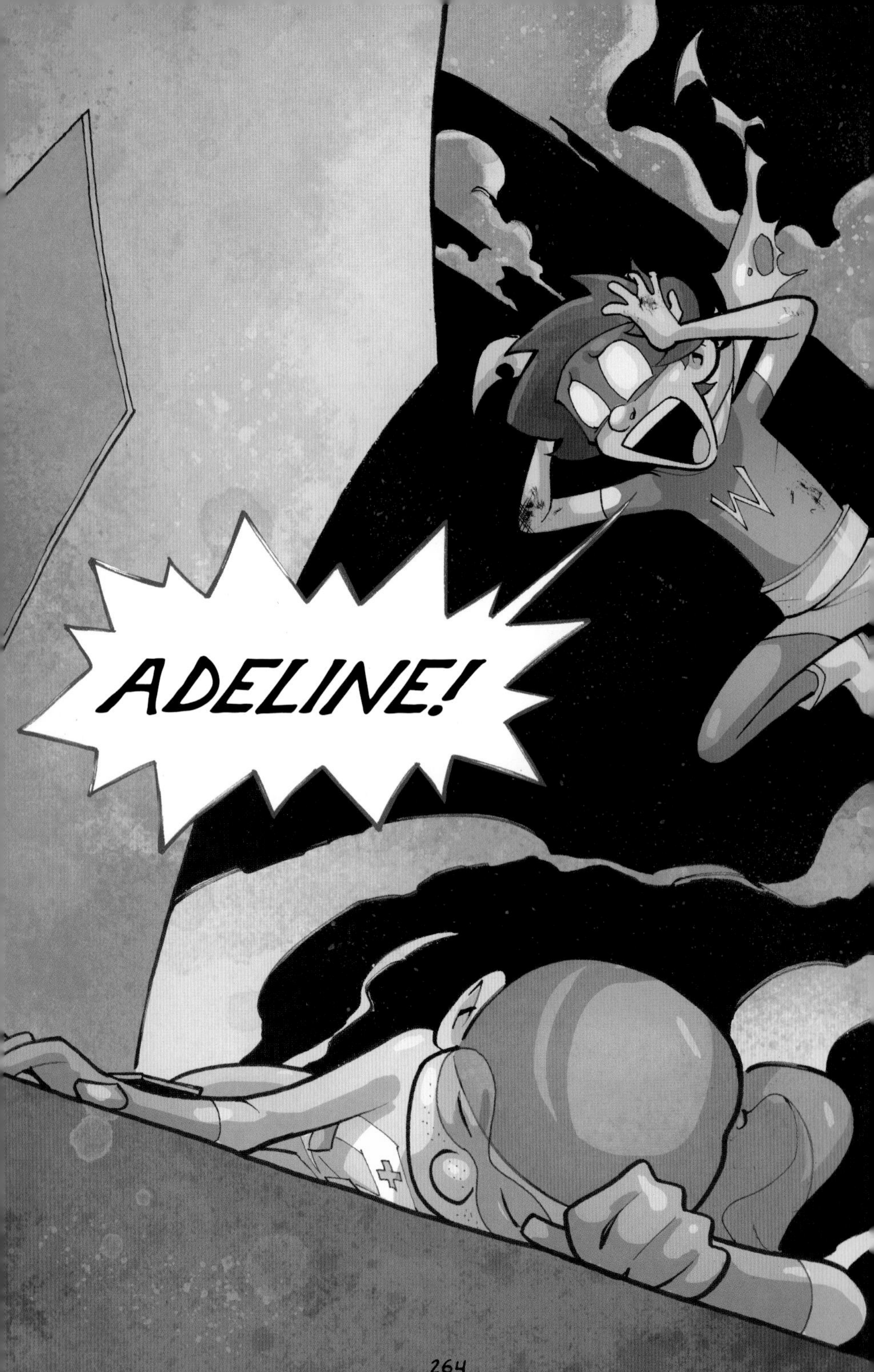
ADELINE!

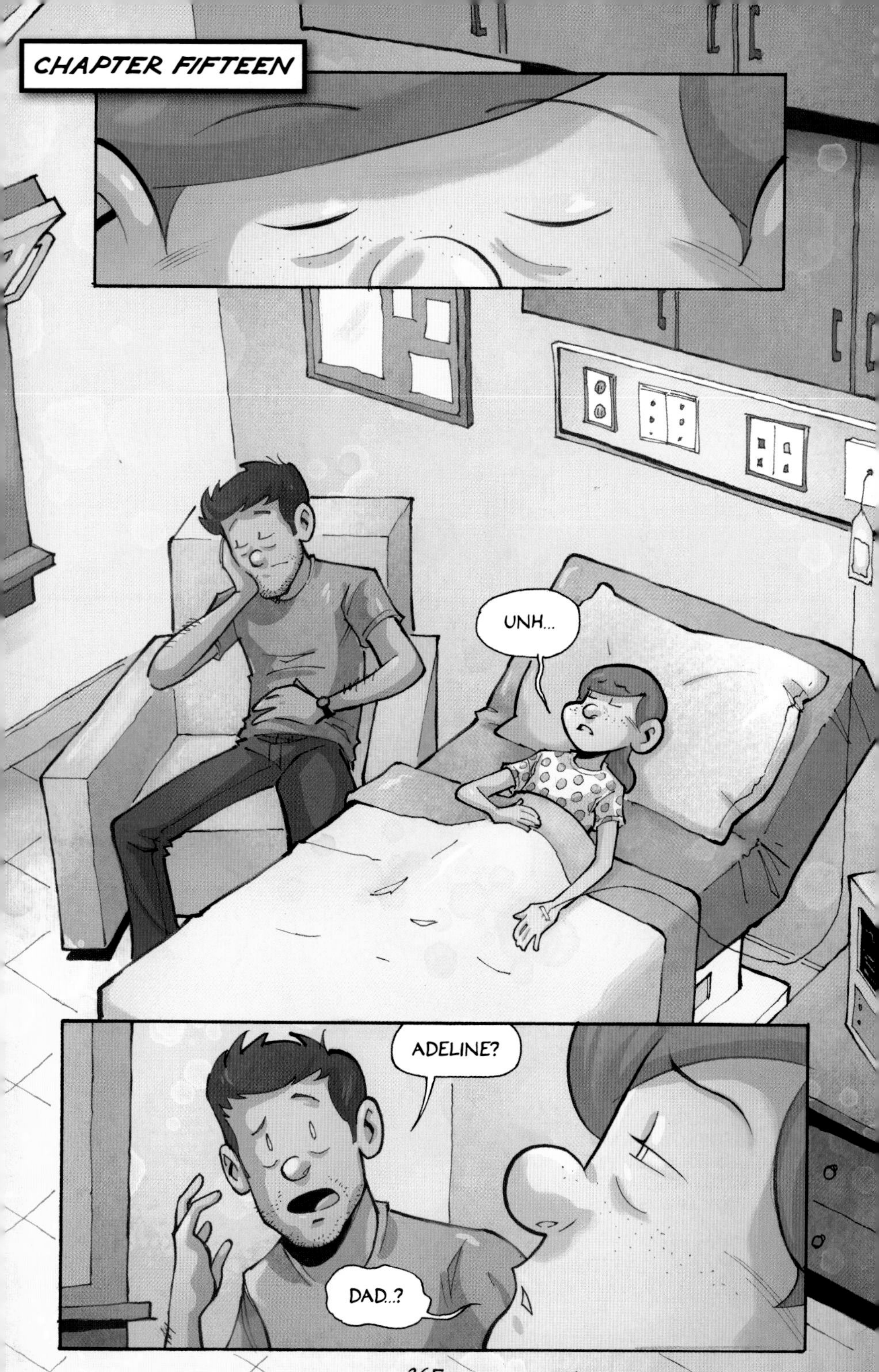
CHAPTER FIFTEEN
UNH...
ADELINE?
DAD...?

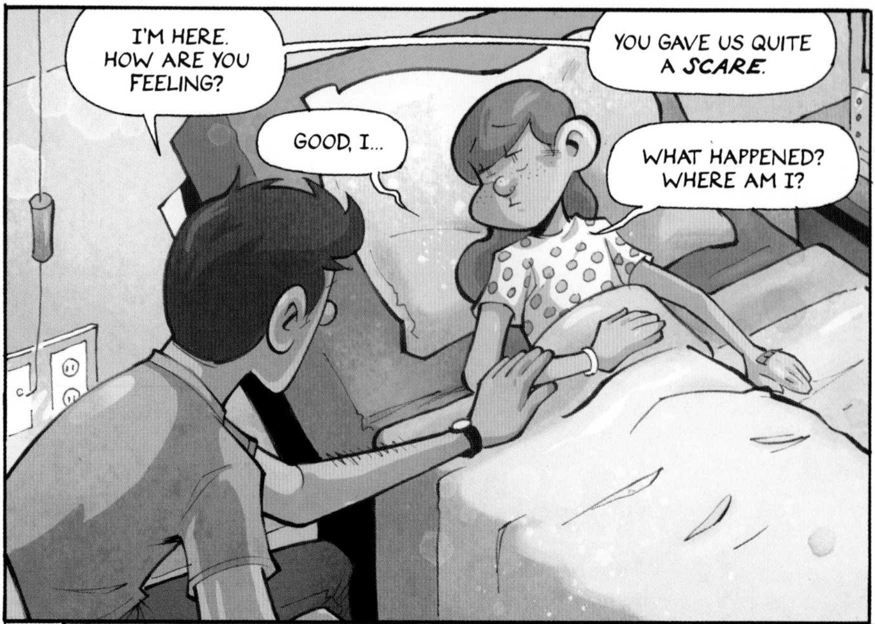
I'M HERE. HOW ARE YOU FEELING?
YOU GAVE US QUITE A ***SCARE***.
GOOD, I...
WHAT HAPPENED? WHERE AM I?

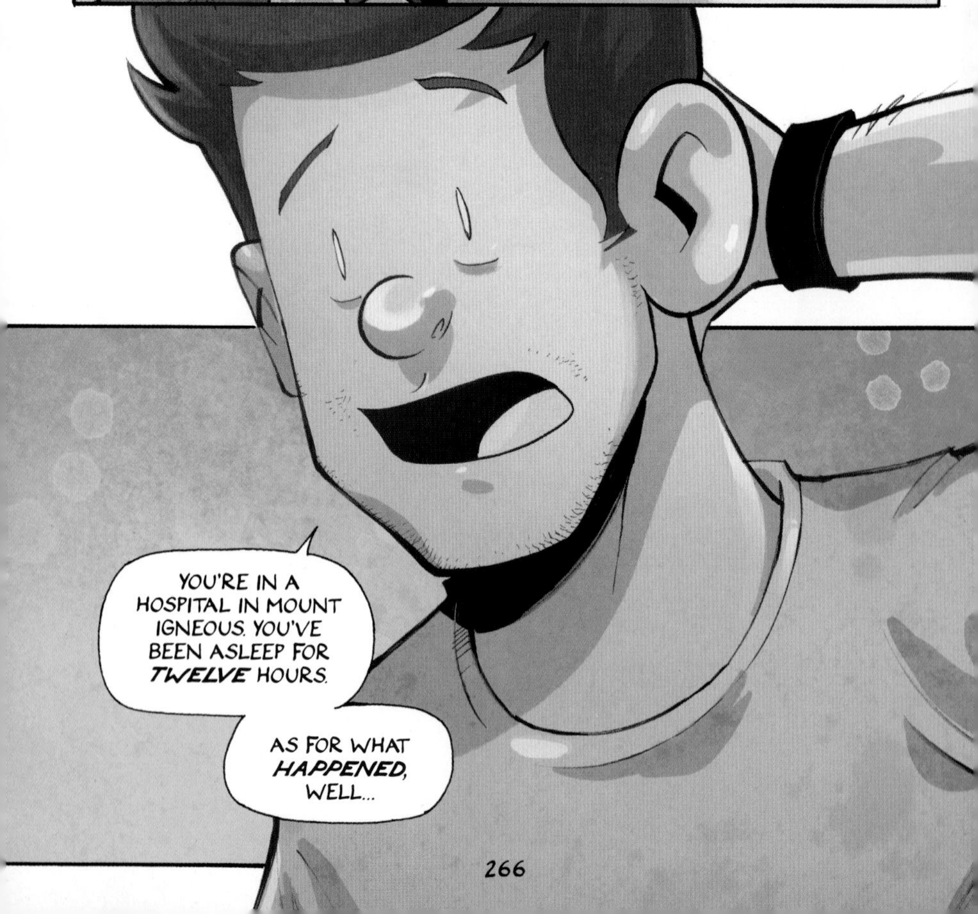
YOU'RE IN A HOSPITAL IN MOUNT IGNEOUS. YOU'VE BEEN ASLEEP FOR ***TWELVE*** HOURS.
AS FOR WHAT ***HAPPENED***, WELL...

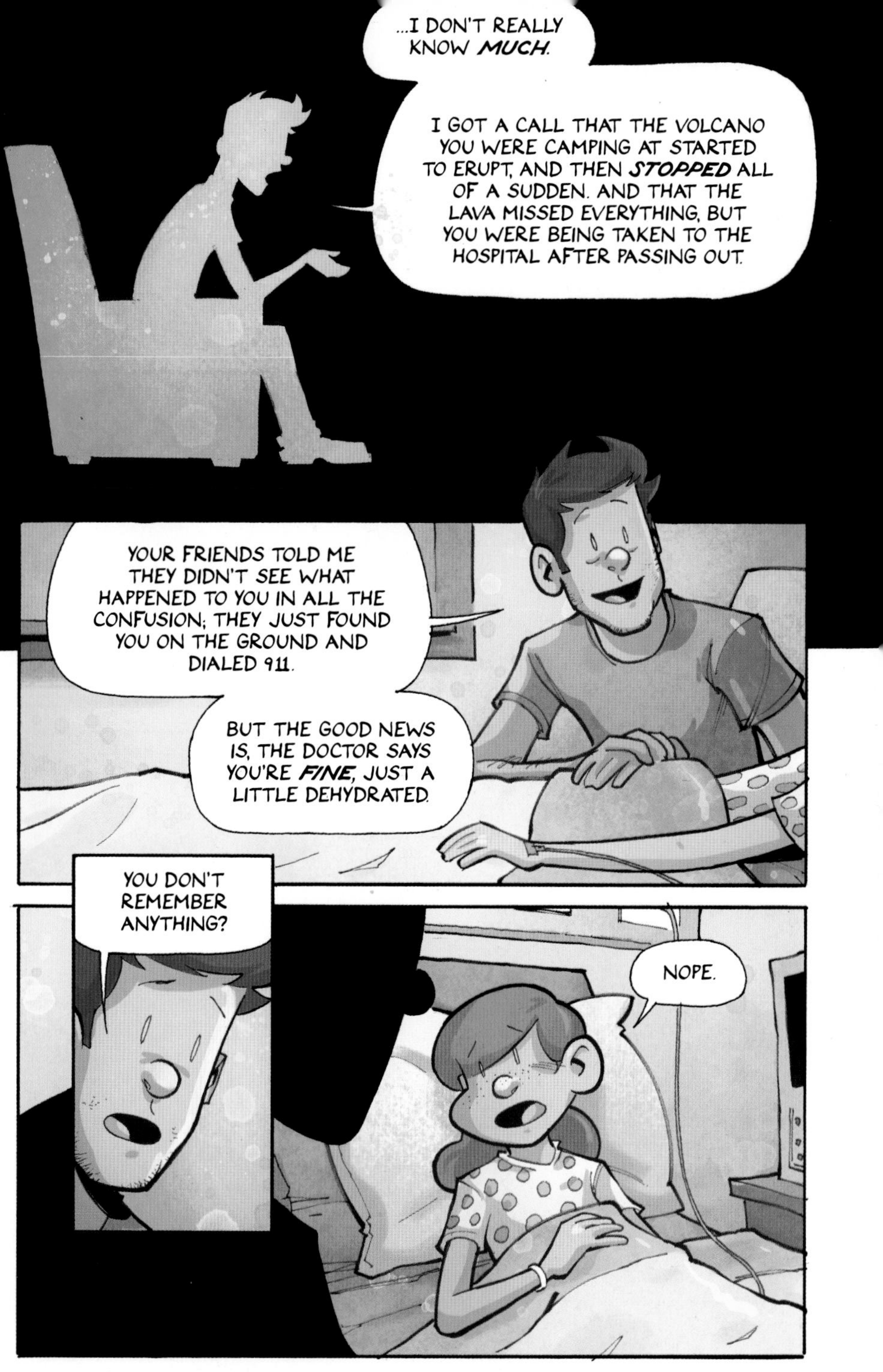
...I DON'T REALLY KNOW *MUCH*.
I GOT A CALL THAT THE VOLCANO YOU WERE CAMPING AT STARTED TO ERUPT, AND THEN *STOPPED* ALL OF A SUDDEN. AND THAT THE LAVA MISSED EVERYTHING, BUT YOU WERE BEING TAKEN TO THE HOSPITAL AFTER PASSING OUT.
YOUR FRIENDS TOLD ME THEY DIDN'T SEE WHAT HAPPENED TO YOU IN ALL THE CONFUSION; THEY JUST FOUND YOU ON THE GROUND AND DIALED 911.
BUT THE GOOD NEWS IS, THE DOCTOR SAYS YOU'RE *FINE*, JUST A LITTLE DEHYDRATED.
YOU DON'T REMEMBER ANYTHING?
NOPE.

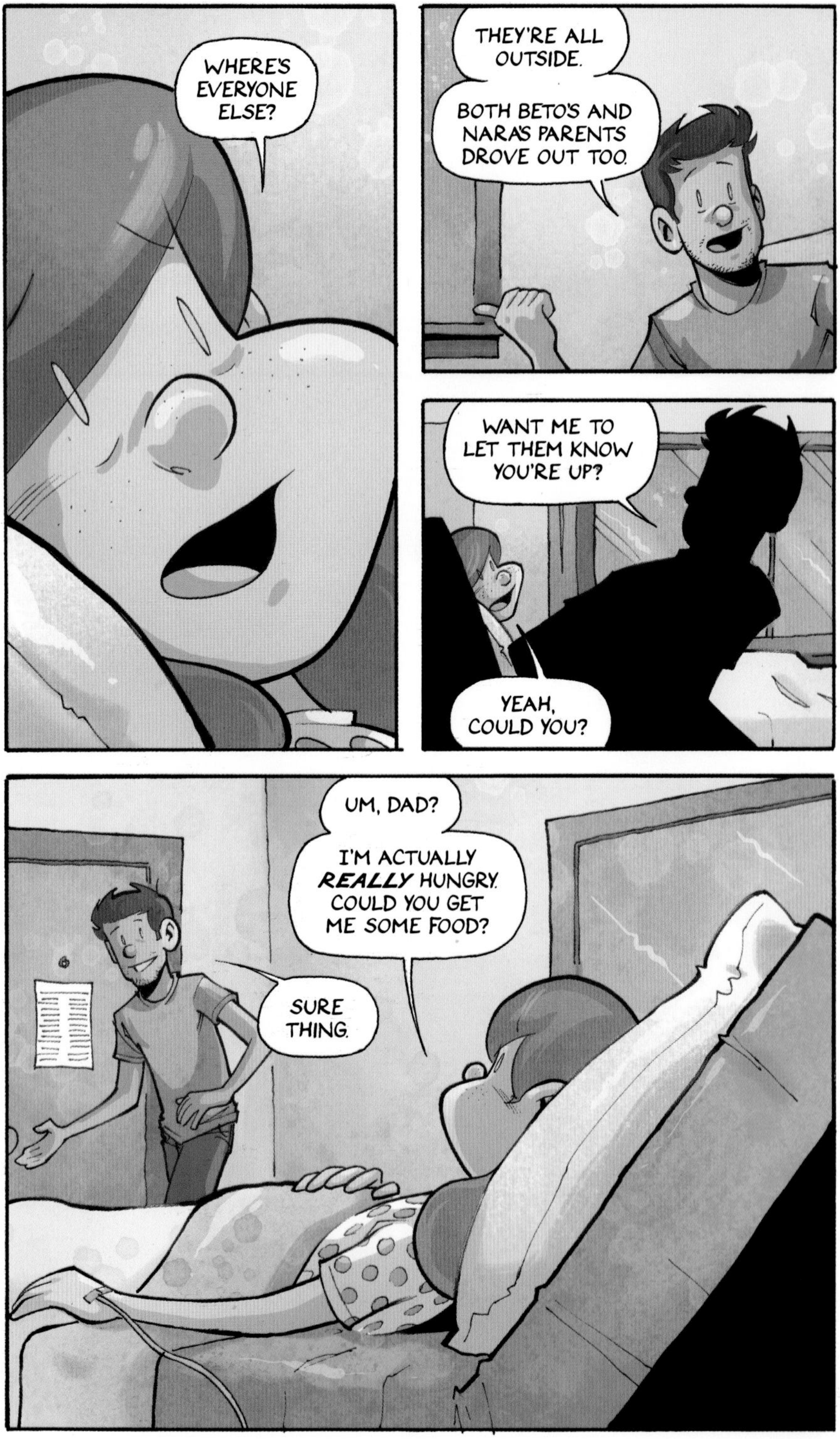
WHERE'S EVERYONE ELSE?
THEY'RE ALL OUTSIDE.
BOTH BETO'S AND NARA'S PARENTS DROVE OUT TOO.
WANT ME TO LET THEM KNOW YOU'RE UP?
YEAH, COULD YOU?
UM, DAD?
I'M ACTUALLY *REALLY* HUNGRY. COULD YOU GET ME SOME FOOD?
SURE THING.

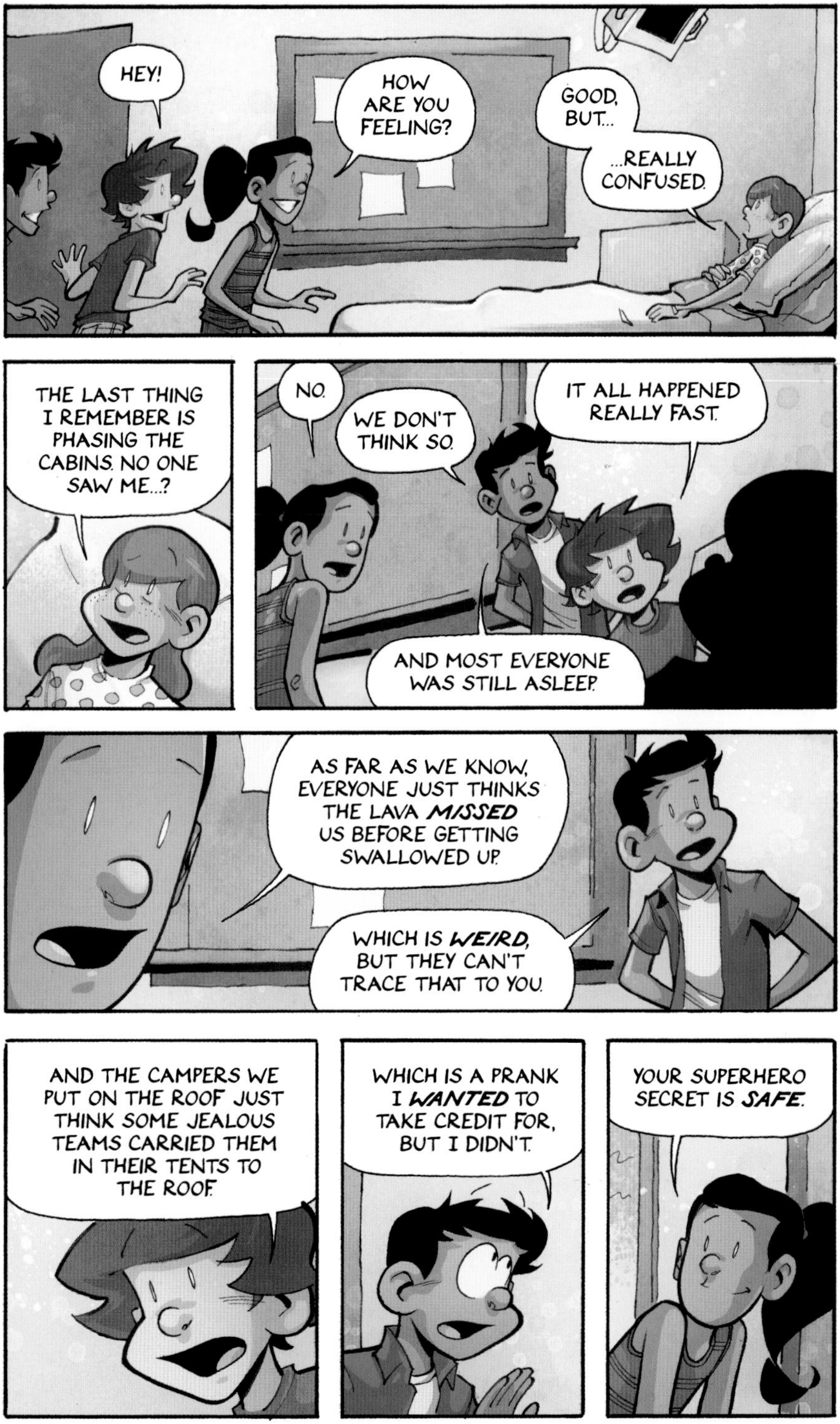
HEY!
HOW ARE YOU FEELING?
GOOD, BUT...
...REALLY CONFUSED.
THE LAST THING I REMEMBER IS PHASING THE CABINS. NO ONE SAW ME...?
NO.
WE DON'T THINK SO.
IT ALL HAPPENED REALLY FAST.
AND MOST EVERYONE WAS STILL ASLEEP.
AS FAR AS WE KNOW, EVERYONE JUST THINKS THE LAVA ***MISSED*** US BEFORE GETTING SWALLOWED UP.
WHICH IS ***WEIRD,*** BUT THEY CAN'T TRACE THAT TO YOU.
AND THE CAMPERS WE PUT ON THE ROOF JUST THINK SOME JEALOUS TEAMS CARRIED THEM IN THEIR TENTS TO THE ROOF.
WHICH IS A PRANK I ***WANTED*** TO TAKE CREDIT FOR, BUT I DIDN'T.
YOUR SUPERHERO SECRET IS ***SAFE.***

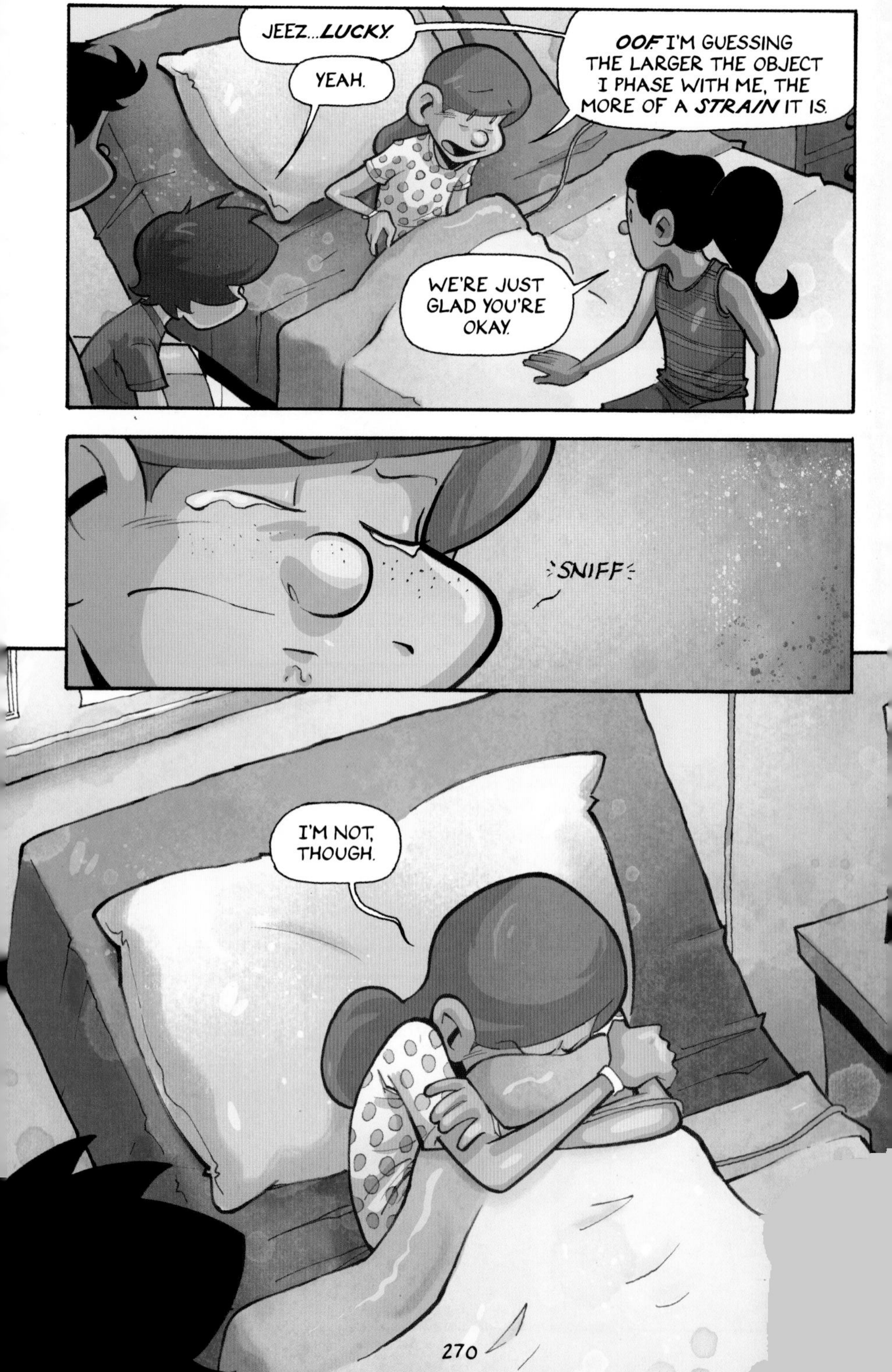

JEEZ...LUCKY.
YEAH.
OOF. I'M GUESSING THE LARGER THE OBJECT I PHASE WITH ME, THE MORE OF A STRAIN IT IS.
WE'RE JUST GLAD YOU'RE OKAY.
SNIFF
I'M NOT, THOUGH.

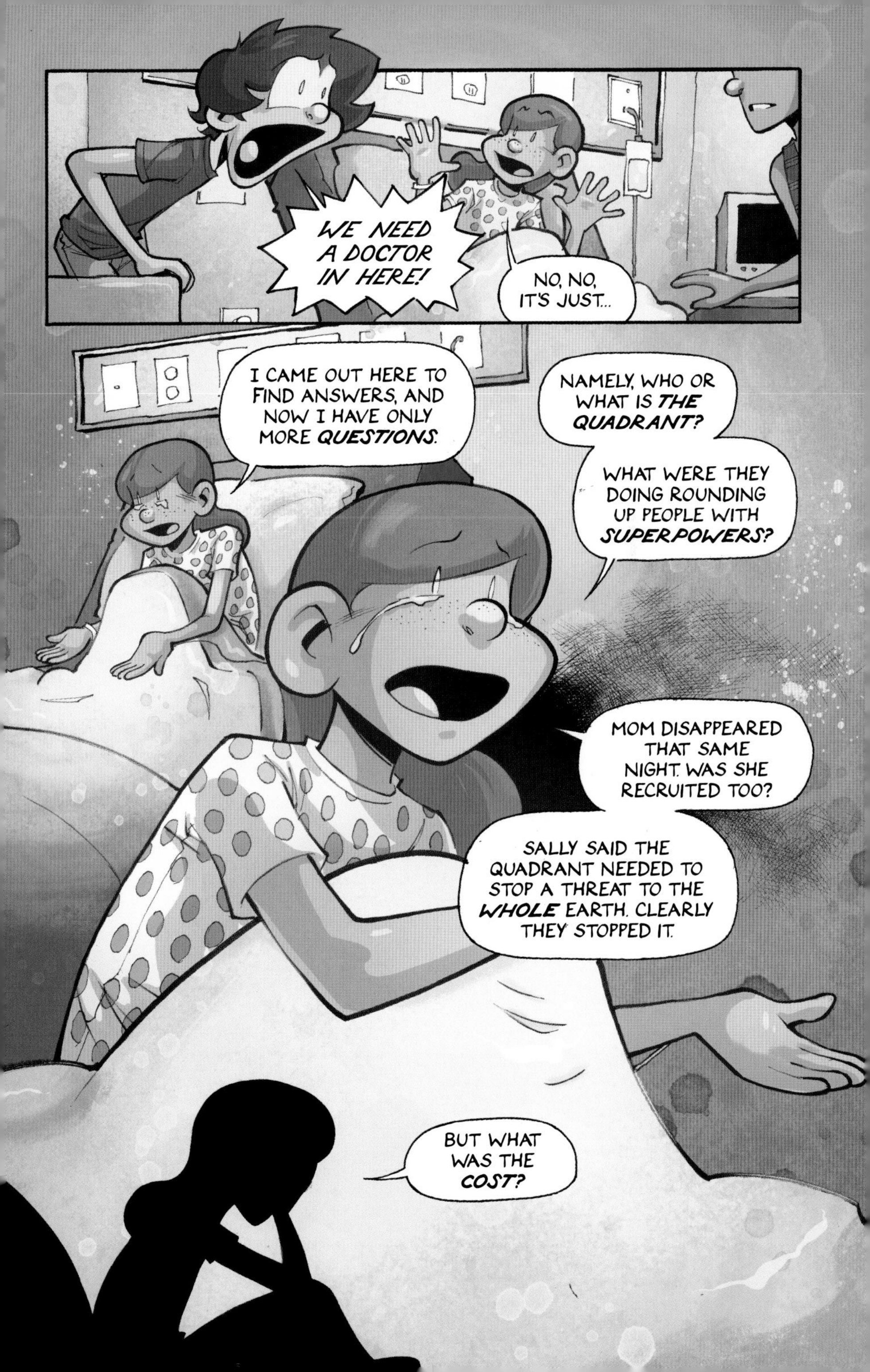
WE NEED A DOCTOR IN HERE!
NO, NO, IT'S JUST...
I CAME OUT HERE TO FIND ANSWERS, AND NOW I HAVE ONLY MORE QUESTIONS.
NAMELY, WHO OR WHAT IS THE QUADRANT?
WHAT WERE THEY DOING ROUNDING UP PEOPLE WITH SUPERPOWERS?
MOM DISAPPEARED THAT SAME NIGHT. WAS SHE RECRUITED TOO?
SALLY SAID THE QUADRANT NEEDED TO STOP A THREAT TO THE WHOLE EARTH. CLEARLY THEY STOPPED IT.
BUT WHAT WAS THE COST?

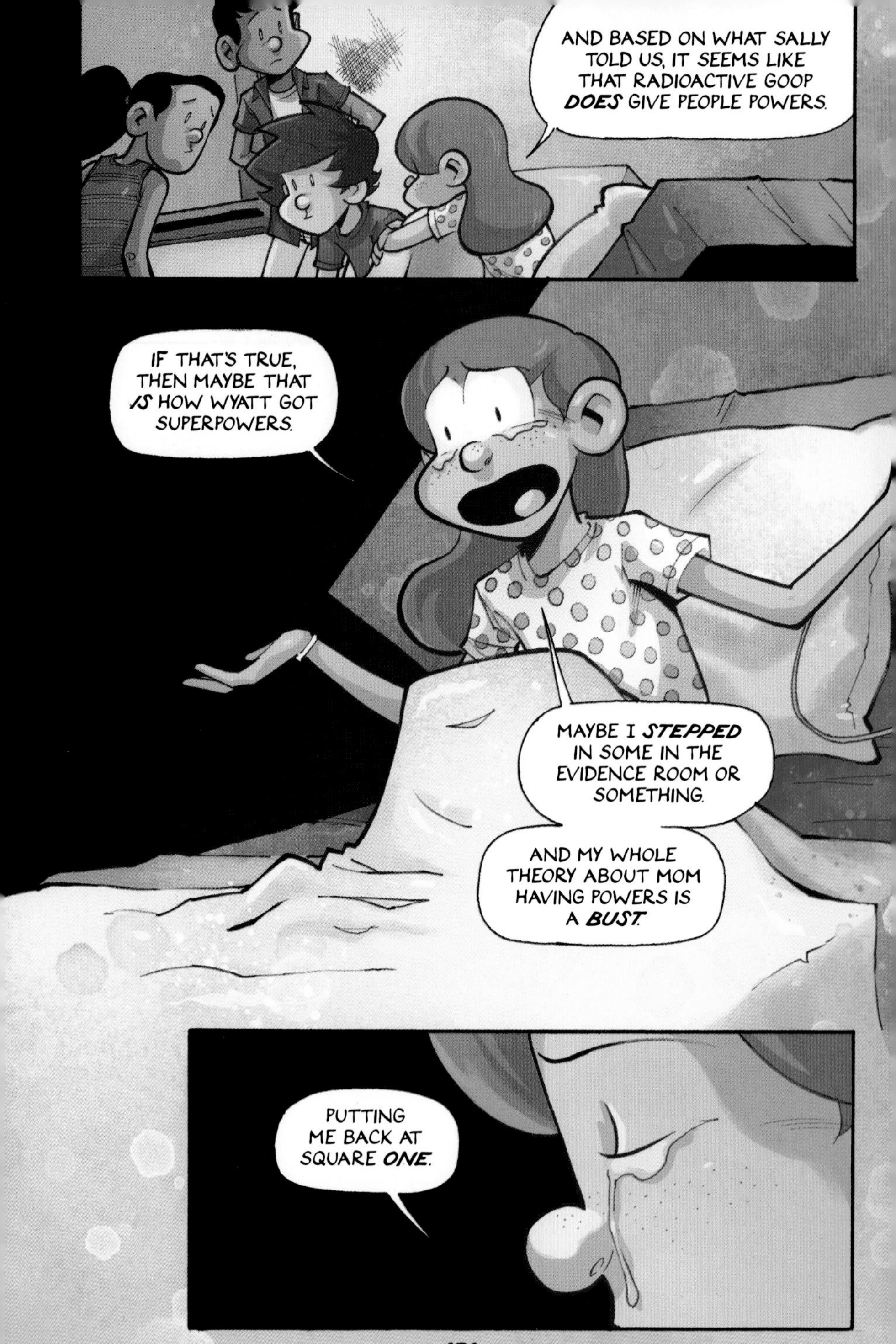
AND BASED ON WHAT SALLY TOLD US, IT SEEMS LIKE THAT RADIOACTIVE GOOP *DOES* GIVE PEOPLE POWERS.
IF THAT'S TRUE, THEN MAYBE THAT *IS* HOW WYATT GOT SUPERPOWERS.
MAYBE I *STEPPED* IN SOME IN THE EVIDENCE ROOM OR SOMETHING.
AND MY WHOLE THEORY ABOUT MOM HAVING POWERS IS A *BUST.*
PUTTING ME BACK AT SQUARE *ONE.*

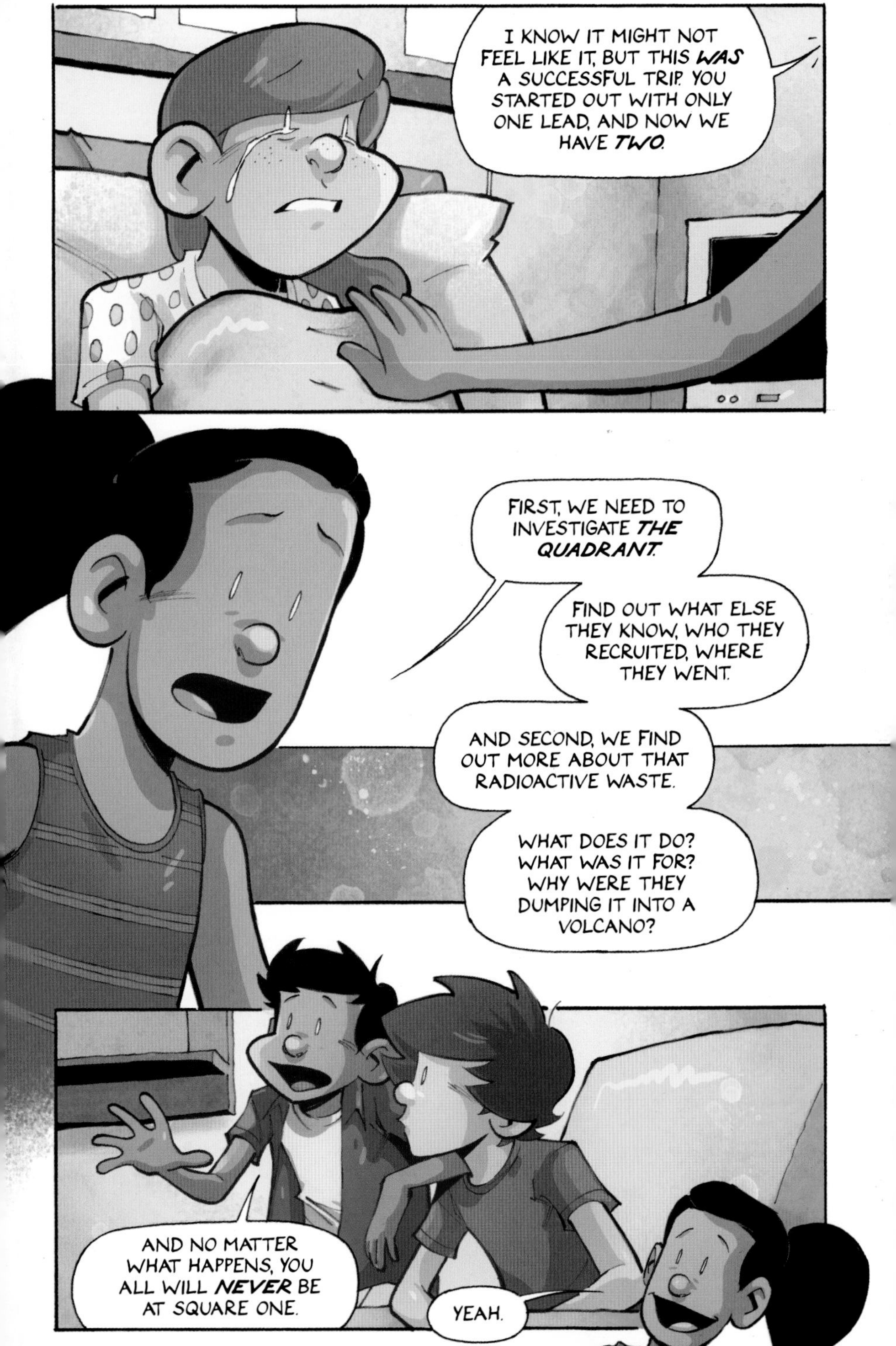
I KNOW IT MIGHT NOT FEEL LIKE IT, BUT THIS WAS A SUCCESSFUL TRIP. YOU STARTED OUT WITH ONLY ONE LEAD, AND NOW WE HAVE TWO.
FIRST, WE NEED TO INVESTIGATE THE QUADRANT.
FIND OUT WHAT ELSE THEY KNOW, WHO THEY RECRUITED, WHERE THEY WENT.
AND SECOND, WE FIND OUT MORE ABOUT THAT RADIOACTIVE WASTE.
WHAT DOES IT DO? WHAT WAS IT FOR? WHY WERE THEY DUMPING IT INTO A VOLCANO?
AND NO MATTER WHAT HAPPENS, YOU ALL WILL NEVER BE AT SQUARE ONE.
YEAH.

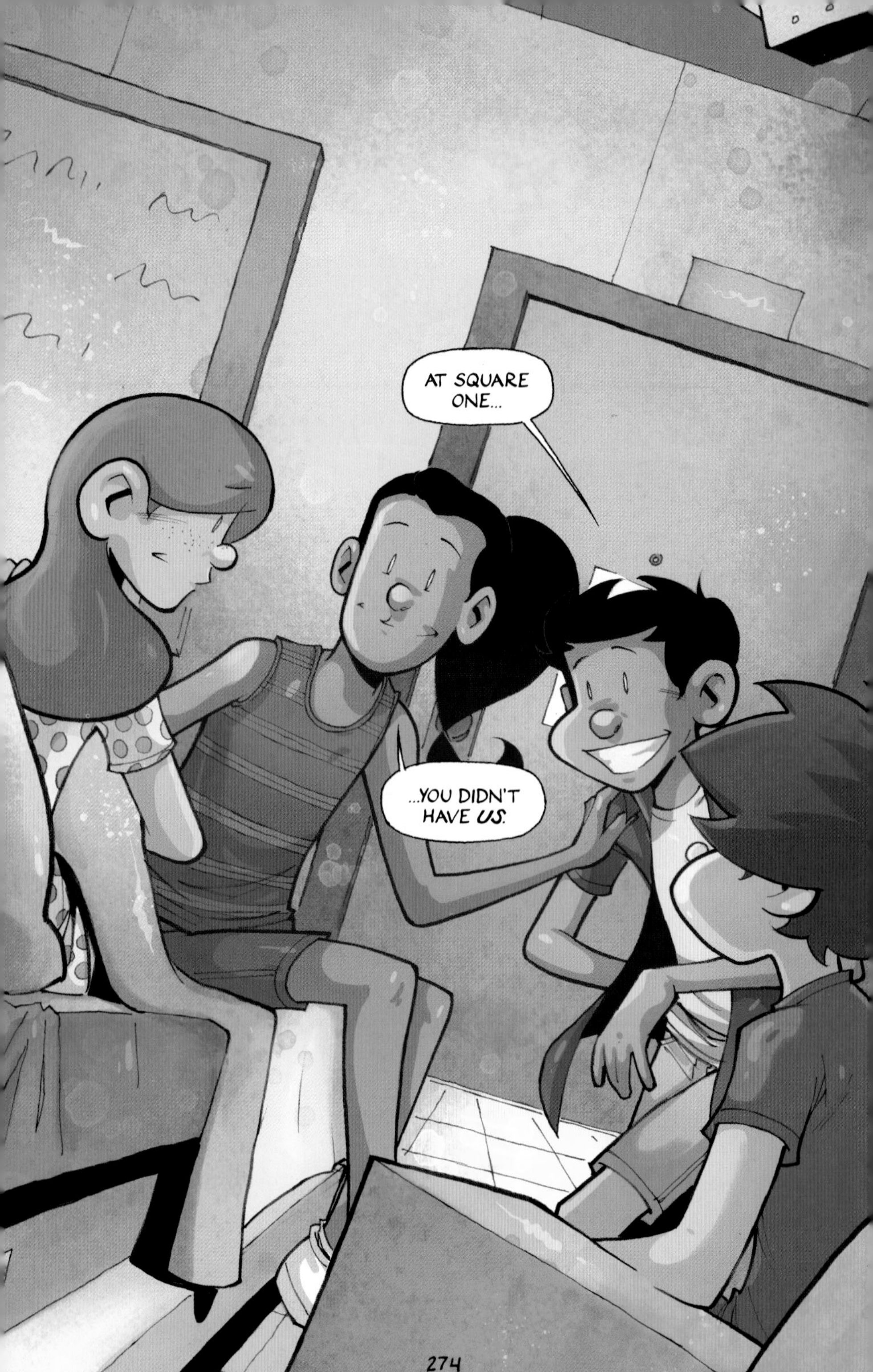
AT SQUARE ONE...
...YOU DIDN'T HAVE *US*.

EPILOGUE

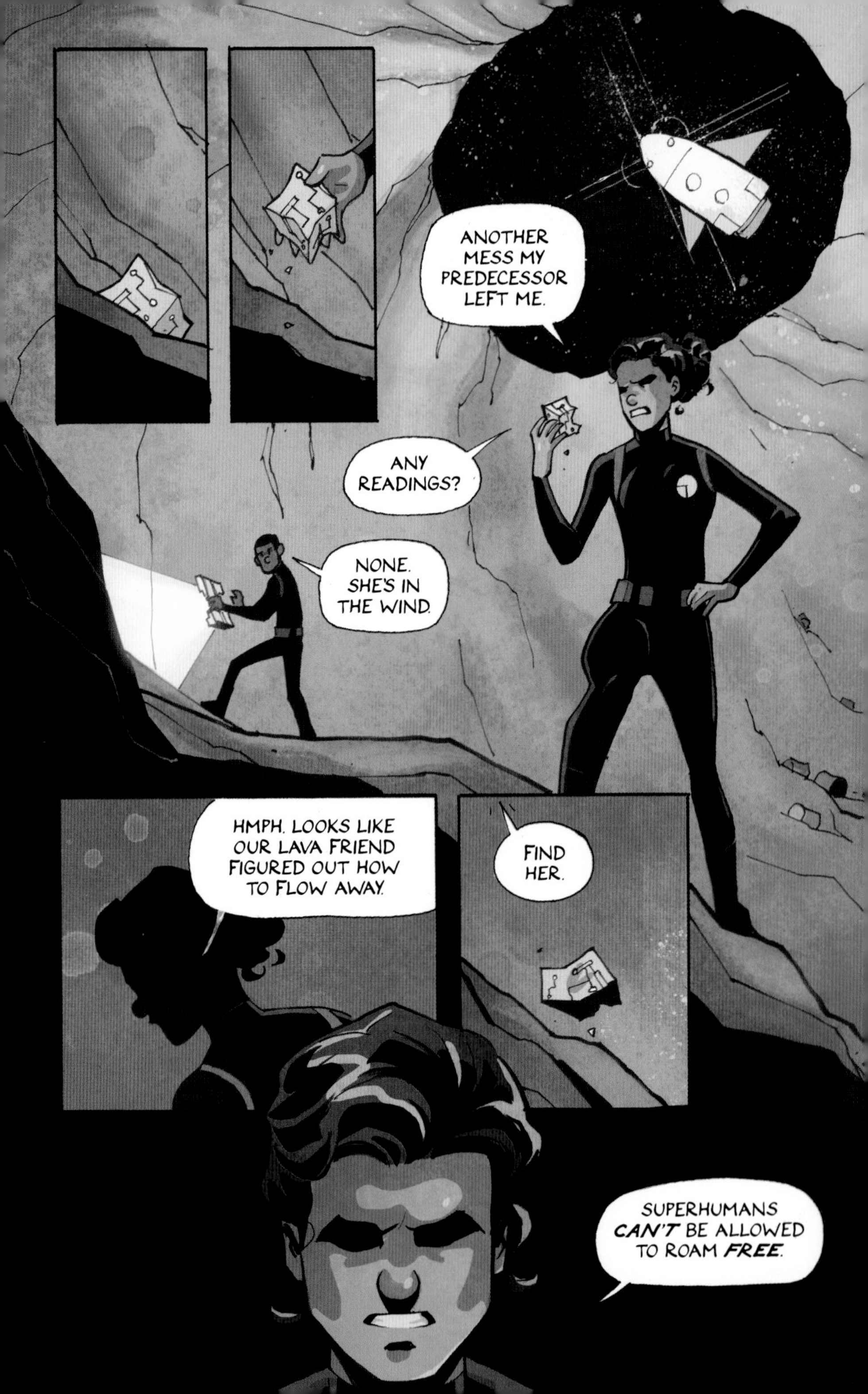
ANOTHER MESS MY PREDECESSOR LEFT ME.
ANY READINGS?
NONE. SHE'S IN THE WIND.
HMPH. LOOKS LIKE OUR LAVA FRIEND FIGURED OUT HOW TO FLOW AWAY.
FIND HER.
SUPERHUMANS *CAN'T* BE ALLOWED TO ROAM *FREE*.

FIND OUT HOW
IT ALL STARTED!

SORT OF SUPER
by Eric Gapstur

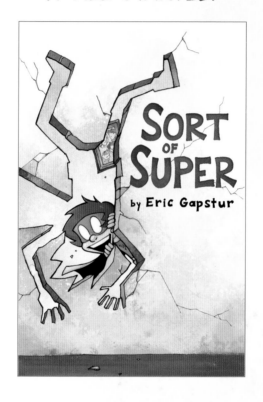